CP HARRISON

979-8-88945-168-6 paperback
979-8-88945-169-3 ebook
979-8-88945-170-9 hardback

Printed in the United States of America.

Brilliant Books Literary
137 Forest Park Lane Thomasville
North Carolina 27360 USA

NIGHT AGAIN

PLAY IT AGAIN

I would like to dedicate this book to my loving wife, Yanhua.

If it was not for her love, support, and belief in me,
I do not think I could have finished this book.

CHAPTER 1

"Company," yelled the Captain.

Each of the platoon leaders followed this command by turning their heads and yelling in unison over their right shoulder, "Platoon".

After a brief pause, the Captain said the word that everyone was waiting for, "Dismissed!"

What followed was a mad rush into the barracks with yells and screams that would have made General Lee proud of his army. Luckily, the Captain remained in charge of the company and Sergeant First Class James Mitchell stayed in his position behind the platoon. As it was, one or two soldiers bumped the Lieutenant as they went by him, with an "Excuse me, Sir" as they continued to run in to the building. Had the 1st Sergeant taken charge of the company, as was the usual case, Mitchell would have been the one in front of the platoon and his platoon certainly would have run him down. The mad rush had come because the captain had just given the entire company a weekend pass. After 3 weeks in the field, everyone was in a hurry to get cleaned up and be the first one out the gate.

Originally, the company was to have only gone out for a few days, but word was, there were things happening and the Army wanted everyone to max out the training schedule in as short a time as possible. However, the total blackout of any kind of news made facts impossible to find out and the rumor mill was going full blast. There were talks of anything from an overseas deployment to total war. The few days the company was to be in the field turned out to be more than a few weeks. The men in Sergeant Mitchell's platoon were getting a tad bit anxious, not to mention ripe. When the Captain announced the weekend pass, the entire company cheered and yelled. If the First Sargent hadn't been there to yell an "At Ease!" Nobody would go anywhere.

Before heading into the barracks and the solitude of his room, Sergeant Mitchell let things calm down a little first. Unlike everyone else in the company, Mitchell wasn't interested in heading into town so quickly, just to get drunk. All he was looking forward to was a good hot shower and just a little quality rack time. He had his own car, so he didn't have to fight to get a taxi. He could afford to wait a little while and relax a little before he headed in to get a good meal. As Mitchell stood there, he slowly looked around at the other companies in the area. It was only slightly different with those companies as was with him, but the outcome was the same. At the word dismissed, there was a mad rush for the door into the barracks.

Mitchell took a deep breath and finally went into the barracks. He could hear a bunch of loud talking as he passed by the Orderly Room. All the platoon leaders were in there and they were all having quite a discussion. Sergeant Mitchell didn't stand around listening. He was afraid he would get caught and pull into something or another. His pass was in hand; he had his own room with his own private bathroom and shower, his own car. All he had to do was get to his room before anyone saw him. The endeavor getting to his room was successful, so he quickly went in and closed the door. After sitting on his bunk, he started by taking his boots off. Throwing the boots into the corner where he would collect everything for cleaning later, he just laid back on his bunk. He thought about nothing in particular but only laid there and closed his eyes.

The pounding on his door woke him up. He didn't think he had closed his eyes for more than a couple of seconds. He had just enough time to open his eyes when the door flew open and without waiting for a response from him, Staff Sergeant Redcloud, or as most people called him, "The Chief", came strolling in.

The Chief was one of the squad leaders in Sergeant Mitchell's platoon. Redcloud was a full-blooded Sioux Indian, a black belt in Kung Foo, an expert in just about every kind of weapon there was, and this was Sergeant Mitchell's best friend. They both came into the Army at the same time and met up in basic training. After basic training, they were stationed together for just about their entire time they were in. They fought together in the middle east and when Mitchell got wounded; it was Redcloud who carried him to safety and probably saved his life. But right now, none of that mattered. Sergeant Mitchell didn't want to deal with him, knowing what he wanted. Mitchell threw his head back down on his pillow and started regretting not locking the door when he came in.

"Come on, you're not gonna just lay in that bed, are you?" Redcloud said as he stood at the foot of Mitchell's bunk with his hands on his hips. "We got a pass and there's plenty of beer in town."

Jim thought about trying to fight with him, but then came the realization that it was a wasted effort. Slowly sitting up, he just stared at Redcloud.

"What are you waiting for?" The Chief shouted at him. "We're already gonna have some serious catching up to do. You need to hurry up and get ready."

Jim took a deep breath and said, "First, I need a good hot shower. Next, I need a good steak before we drink. Last, I have a car. We can go anywhere at any time."

Redcloud looked down and thought about it for a moment and then said, "Hmm, sounds like you have a plan, and a good one at that." He turned to go out and said, "I'm gonna shower and meet you downstairs in half an hour."

Jim sighed as the Chief walked out, but then he turned back and shook his finger at him. "And don't be late. I'm thirsty, and hungry." The Chief added, and then was gone.

After Redcloud shut the door, and after a moment of just sitting there, Mitchell finally finished taking off his boots. He should have stood up right then and started getting ready, but he laid back for a minute, or what he thought was a minute. Suddenly, the next thing he remembered was the sound of the squad heading out, and it woke him up. His first thought was, "God, the Chief is going to have my ass." Quickly he took care of the 3 S's, shit, shower, and shave and then threw on some civvies. Mitchell headed down to the CQ desk where he found Redcloud standing by the Orderly Room door.

As he approached the Chief he asked, "What's up?"

Redcloud turned to his friend and, with his finger to his lips, he shushed him. After a couple of minutes, he motioned Jim away to an area where no one could hear them. "Something's up," he whispered. He motioned over his shoulder to the Orderly Room with his thumb. "The CO, Top and all the LTs are in the CO's office with the doors closed and there's a lot of heavy talking going on." He paused for a moment and looked around to make sure there was no one listening and continued, "I can't make out all that they're all talking about, but from the tones, I think it is serious."

"Well, let's get the hell out of here before the shit hits and we get stuck on post again."

Redcloud's head came up with a snap and he smiled and said, "What are we waiting for?"

With that, they both headed out to the car and even though no one drove it in almost a month, the battery was still good, and it started right up. As he pulled out of the parking lot, he could see there was a lot of traffic and looked like almost all of it headed to the gate. Not talking to the Chief directly, but more to himself, he muttered, "I guess there were a lot of weekend passes given out today."

They didn't get too far when the road turned into a parking lot. Slowly they made progress, but it took about half an hour before they got to where they could see the gate. Then suddenly the slow line stopped altogether. After a few minutes, Jim could see the cars in front of the line turning around and heading back. He looked over at the

Chief, and said, "This doesn't look promising." However, because of barriers and islands on the road, Jim had no other choice but to stay in line until he reached the gate. The barricades at the gate were up and the MP came over as Jim rolled down the window.

He leaned down and simply said, "All passes are canceled, the post is closed." After a momentary pause, he added, "Report back to your unit."

Without a word, Jim spun the car around and headed back to the company. The Chief said in a rather nasty tone, "You just had to have that long shower, didn't you?"

Jim said nothing. He was thinking more about all the likely reasons the entire post was on lockdown and all passes canceled. This was very unusual and serious.

When they got back to the Company, the CQ had a book and said they had to sign in. As Jim signed them both in, Top came around the corner and yelled, "Good!" He then pointed his finger at the two of them and said, "Both of you get into uniforms, grab your gear and report back to my office ASAP."

The two of them looked at each other and they both knew from the sound of his voice that Top was as serious as they have ever heard him. Without a word, the two NCOs nodded to each other and took off for their rooms. Mitchell's room was still a mess and after a quick look around. He found he didn't have a clean uniform to put on. His plan was to wash this weekend while the rest of the company was out on pass. However, the Chief insisted they go out instead. He grabbed the cleanest thing he could find and dressed in no time. His alert gear was still packed and ready since he had just returned from a three-week exercise. Not clean, but ready. Grabbing everything, he ran back to Top's office.

Redcloud had just gotten there, so they stacked their gear in the hall and went into The First Sargent's office. Top's office was the biggest mess Mitchell had ever seen in there. Normally, his office was squared away, but not this time. As they walked in, Top looked up from his desk. He motioned them to gather around his desk. "This is it boys, the shit has really hit the fan this time." He started out with. This got their attention right away. Top continued, "This is the real thing. At least the top brass seems to think so." Now Top sat down as the two of them continued to listen. "The word is that somehow terrorist, don't know what group yet has gotten a nuke onto American soil. Intel says they are intending on taking out a military base and whatever civilian casualties they can around that base. We don't have a timeline yet, hell for all we know it could already be in place."

Redcloud and Mitchell just looked at each other, but Top was on a roll, and they just continued to listen. "The post commander has assigned every unit on this post to a specific area of the fence. We are to stay in place and watch for any activity and call it in. We will call the local EOD team in to investigate and deal with whatever is found." Now Top stood up and pointed to an area on the map. "This is the area assigned to our company." As Top bent over the map to look closer, both junior NCOs went over with him. "It straddles the old range road. There is a gate in the fence at this point." He pointed to a spot on the old road and continued, "Our plan is to deploy to both sides as far as we can until we link up with whatever unit is assigned to either side of us."

Mitchell got down closer to the map to study it a little more. The area looked mostly like forest covered rolling hills. It won't be easy to see anything in that area, especially at night. It didn't seem like anyone had been out that way in ages. Not since the newer ranges opened a little further away.

Top started up again. "As you undoubtedly know, most of the company headed into town as soon as we dismissed them this afternoon. You two are the first senior NCOs that have reported back. I have grabbed a couple more stragglers before they got out of here. Sergeant Mitchell, this is going to be your detail."

This really didn't sound like the best of plans to Mitchell. In fact, it sounds like a plan on the fly, and he was getting stuck with it. But he just nodded to Top and let him continue.

Again, Top didn't even look at these two when he went on. "Sergeant Redcloud, you are to take two with you and go to the ammo point. You just need to give them our unit. I will have already called in your clearance."

Redcloud nodded, but then asked, "What am I getting and with what am I transporting it in?"

Top look up at him this time and appeared to be a little annoyed at the interruption. "There are 2 old duce-and-a-halves outside. One for each of you. Sergeant Mitchell, you're to take your detail to the arms room and load up the company weapons. You two will then head out to the point on the old range road where it meets the fence. There you'll set up a company command post and weapons and ammo distribution points. Mitchell, you'll also have an old hummer with a radio. That's the best I can get you right now. You'll report when you get there and when you have everything set up." Top stopped for a moment while he looked at both of them. Then he added "Questions?"

"Yeah, Top," Mitchell just blurted out. "Why are we going out ahead of the company for this? Why not get everyone armed and ready here and then set out for our point?"

Top leaned over with his knuckles on his desk and shook his head. "Time is short. Every unit on this post is going to be going through the same thing. The ammo point and the armory areas are going to be swamped. The roads are probably going to be packed. At best, this is going to be one giant cluster." Now Top sat down to continue. "We will not be doing much more than patrol and watch. Our top priority is to get bodies on the fence line as fast as we can. In the CO's opinion, and mine, this is going to get us there the fastest."

Mitchell thought for just a moment and then nodded. He could also see the Chief nodding too.

Top continued, "It is going to take us, and the other units, time to get everyone back, sober or drunk, and get them out to the assigned area. I want everything ready when we get there. If someone is still drunk, we'll assign them to latrine detail until they sober up and we can use them, but we will have bodies on the fence as fast as we can, clear!"

"You got it Top." Mitchell said, and then asked, "Where's our detail?"

"They should be ready and waiting in the day room." Top replied.

"Great, let's go." He motioned to Redcloud as he turned to leave.

"Mitchell," Top called before they got out the door. "The CO wants you to sign for his weapon and have it ready when he gets there."

"Sure thing, Top. No problem."

"Great, now get the hell out of here. I got other things to worry about now." Top said as he turned his back to them and went to his desk.

Mitchell and the Chief walked into the day room where there were 4 others waiting for them. As soon as they were through the door, all four of the waiting detail jumped to their feet and began asking questions. Mitchell held up his hand to quiet them and said, "We got some serious shit happening with no answers at the moment. Until we get the company back, you guys are it. Time is short and we've got an assignment to deal with and no time for questions right now."

Everyone shut up right away. SFC Mitchell was happy with most of the detail. First, he spotted Sergeant Wilson. She is a good soldier who had some time in a combat area and could handle herself with the others. Also, she was a member of Redcloud's martial arts class. SP4 Rodrigues and PFC Johnson were from another squad. He had seen them before, but didn't have any experience with them. He then looked at the fourth member of the detail and asked, "Who the hell are you?"

The new guy jumped to attention and said, "I'm Private Blake, Sergeant."

"At ease," Mitchell said to him and then added, "Enough of that attention, BS. This isn't basic anymore."

"Yes, Sergeant." He replied as he eased up a little.

"OK, this is what we've gotta do." Mitchell started out saying. "We're gonna split into two groups." Looking over at Redcloud, he said, "Chief, you take Rodrigues and Johnson and get the ammo. I'll take Wilson and the new guy, uh, what's your name again?"

"Private Blake, Sergeant," he replied, as he jumped to attention again.

Mitchell just shook his head and continued, "Yeah, Blake, we'll head to the arms room to draw weapons. Chief, bring your group there and draw your weapons first."

"Wilson, you'll drive the duce and take, ah Blake, with you. I'll grab the hummer and meet you there."

Everyone just nodded and stood there. "Grab your gear and get your ass in gear. Time is short, and we've got a lot to do."

With that last brief shout, everyone started at once. Redcloud and Mitchell ran back to Tops office and grabbed their gear in the hall. While he was there, Mitchell glance in to see that Top and the CO were looking over the map and in a deep discussion. The CO was talking a lot and Top was quickly taking notes. Mitchell didn't have time to stand around and watch, he just grabbed his stuff and headed for the hummer. When he went out the door, he found the hummer came with a trailer, but time was too short to mess around with it, so he didn't unhitch it, and just took it with him. As he climbed in the driver's side, he noticed this hummer still had a gun mounted on the top, but he didn't really think about it too much right now. Too many other things to worry about first.

They all met up at the arms room. The Chief and his two drew out their weapons and headed off to the ammo supply point. Mitchell got his detail loading the companies' weapons into the truck. Luckily, the armorer had a couple of guys for his detail as well. They got the trucks loaded up pretty quickly. Michell used the trailer on the hummer to load up the company ready load from the arms room and some rations and water. Not knowing how long they would be stuck out there before the company showed up, he figured he needed to be ready for a long wait and the company would probably need food when they finally got out where they were going.

Just as he was getting ready to head out, Redcloud showed back up. Mitchell yell over to him, "What's the problem? Why are you back already?"

Redcloud shouted back, "They had everything ready and loaded it up for us with a forklift. All we had to do was stand there and watch."

"Great. Let's get going, then."

Redcloud stuck his fist out the window with a thumb's up and waited for Mitchell to take the lead in the hummer and Wilson to follow with her truck. Then he pulled in right behind her, and the detail took off. The way to the assigned area was an old road that wasn't used much anymore, but Mitchell had been out this way before and knew the way. Traffic in the main post area was horrible. A few times, he had to pull over to wait while the rest of the team cleared an intersection. However, once they were clear of the main post area, the travel got smoother. Well, except for the road. It didn't look like anyone has looked at this road in forever. It was in terrible shape.

They took about an hour and a half to get to the site. As Mitchell pulled up, he could see the fence and there was a nice clearing to one side of the road near the gate. Pulling over, he signaled to Wilson to pull off the road into the clearing. Redcloud's truck didn't follower her in just now but stayed on the side of the road.

Mitchel then climbed back into the hummer and pulled up to a gate across the road. He just sat there for a moment, looking through the gate to just the other side. There he saw something that didn't look right, and he didn't like what he saw there.

Parked just outside the gate on the side of the road was the trailer to a semi-truck. There was no cab, only the trailer was there. It looked almost new and like it hadn't been there very long. Mitchell sat there looking at it for a couple of minutes when Redcloud came up and pounded on the side of the hummer.

Mitchell jumped, "What the hell, you scared the shit out of me!" Mitchell yelled at his old friend, but Redcloud only smiled back at him.

"What do you think that is?" Redcloud asked.

"Looks like a trailer to me. What do you think?"

"I think we need to check it out, don't you?" Redcloud answered back.

"You heard what Top said. We only look and report. EOD will come out and take care of it."

The hummer had the radio that Mitchell had already set up with the frequency he was to use, so he grabbed the radio mic and called the company. It took a couple of tries, but finally the company radio replied. It was Top on the other end. With Top answering his own radio, that told Mitchell that not much of the company is back, yet.

"Top, we have arrived on site." Mitchell reported.

"Great, get things set up there. We are having a bit of trouble getting everyone back. The MPs are doing a verification of everybody as they come through the gate. It is taking way too much time." Top said back with an obviously disgusted voice.

"Yeah Top, I hear ya, but we have a little problem here." he paused, but there was no response from the other end, so he continued "When we pulled up, we found a semi-trailer parked just on the other side of the gate. It appears it was put there recently. I don't have a way to notify EOD to get out here."

Top replied with a simple, "Wait one."

"Roger," Mitchell said back and looked at the Chief.

"I guess they aren't ready for anything yet." he said as Mitchell threw up his shoulders in a shrug.

Redcloud gave a little laugh and headed back to the trucks. Mitchell listened as he heard him giving some orders when the radio came back up. "OK, Mitchell. I understand your situation, but EOD is having the same problems as the rest of us. They have no one to send you. I checked with the CO. You're to investigate, but touch nothing until you report back to me. Clear?"

"Roger Top, I've got it, but how do I get outside the gate? It's chained up and we don't have any bolt cutters?"

Top was upset this time. "Use your head, Mitchell. You've got a couple of big trucks out there. They usually make very good keys, out."

Wow, he never heard the First Sergeant that upset before. Mitchell figured something else was going on back there. But he had no time to worry about that. He had orders, and it was now time to try a little lock picking.

"Sergeant Redcloud, bring your duce up here, I've got a job for you." he shouted back.

A moment later I heard the diesel startup and Redcloud was next to the hummer in no time.

"Chief, I want you to open that gate for me." Mitchell said, pointing straight at the gate.

Redcloud looked down at his friend with a smile. "You're sure?"

"Orders from the CO. We're to go out and investigate the trailer."

Redcloud leaned back inside the duce where he got this big shit-eating grin on his face. He then leaned forward, as he put it in gear and revved up the motor. A second later, he was off. The gate opened with little resistance. It pulled loose of the post on the right side and then went down where the duce ran over it.

Redcloud leaned out the window and yelled back, "Piece of cake."

Mitchell simply smiled and shook his head, then turned back and yelled for the rest of the detail to grab their weapons and get up here. He then grabbed his weapon and walked forward to the trailer.

Redcloud joined him by the trailer as Mitchell signaled the rest of the detail to form a half circle around the trailer, then he yelled back at Wilson, "Sergeant Wilson. bring the hummer up and get on the 240."

Wilson ran back and hopped into the hummer and drove it right up next to the trailer. It was pure luck that this hummer had a M240 machine gun mounted on it. Redcloud saw it was there before he went to the ammo point and scrounged a bunch of ammo for it.

Mitchell motioned Redcloud to circle around to the back while he went down the other side. The trailer looked to be new, but not brand new. There were no marking or numbers on it at all. When he got back to the rear, he could see there was no plate on it either. The only noticeable thing about it was there was a giant oversized lock on the back.

"What now?" Redcloud asked.

"My orders were to investigate, not touch and report back," he said with another shrug.

Walking over to the hummer, he grabbed the radio. Wilson came down from the 240 and asked, "What's going on, Sarge?"

Mitchell gave her a wait one signal while he reported what they found to the company. He then got another wait one.

While he waited, he thought it was good to bring everyone up to date on what was going on. Calling the detail together, SFC Mitchell laid out what they had been told. When he finished, you could have heard a pin drop. Well, there was still the noise from the forest critters, so maybe you could hear a nail drop.

It took a little while to explain everything and all the consequences, so before anyone could ask and question, which from the looks on their faces would be many, the radio came back up.

This time, it was the CO on the line. "Sergeant Mitchell, we still don't have anyone to send to you and I have taken this all the way up to post. You are to shoot open the lock and carefully open the trailer. Look around inside and touch nothing. Then report back for further instructions."

Mitchell keyed up the mic. "Understood, and I'll call back as soon as we can."

"Out." was the only response he got back.

He looked around. Everyone was still here and heard everything. Mitchell could see in their faces they all found this as highly unusual as he did. He then told everyone to form a semicircle around the back of the trailer. However, before she could move, he pointed at Wilson. "You stay there. Keep the 240 trained on the side of the truck. If anything happens, you open up and cut the damn thing in half." Before she could respond, he turned back to the rest and said, "Lock and load."

Then turning back to Wilson to give her more instructions, but saw she was already working on the 240. She quickly racked the handle back, then opened the cover and placed the first round in position and closed the cover and was quickly on the trigger.

Redcloud and Mitchell walked to the back of the trailer and, using their lights, they gave it a very careful looking over. Neither of them saw anything, so Mitchell signaled his friend to move back while he positioned the lock where he could get a shot at it without shooting into the trailer. Then he moved back a little way and pulled his own pistol. A 9mm isn't very big but should be big enough to open that lock without the over penetration he would have gotten with his rifle.

Once more, he looked around. He saw everyone was ready. Bracing himself as best he could on the front of the hummer, he took careful aim. Yelling, "Fire in the hole." he let go a single round. The lock jumped when he hit it, but didn't open.

After waiting a minute or two, he repositioned the lock and tried again. This time, the lock shattered with only the hooked bar left hanging on the door. There was no penetration of the door, and everything looked good.

The Chief walked up to the door and reached to grab the hook from the lock, but Mitchell yelled at him to wait. He wanted to have another close look around that door.

They both climbed up on the back and looked closely around the entire edge of the door. When they were finished, they both look at each other and then simply shook their heads no. Jumping back down, Mitchell carefully removed the remaining piece of the lock. Slowly, Redcloud moved the locking handle on the door. Every time it made a little squeak, he stopped and waited. Finally, he had the latch open.

"Chief, when I tell you, I want you to very slowly open the door about an inch. Hold it there." Jim said, "Don't let it move and don't open it anymore. I want to see what I can see before we open it all the way."

Looking around, SFC Mitchell signaled everyone to be ready and to stay low. He then used a thumbs up motion to Redcloud, who started opening the door. After he opened it a little, he stopped.

Looking into the crack of the door and shining his light, Mitchell couldn't really see anything. "It looks like it might be empty." he said to Redcloud.

Redcloud just dropped his head and let out a little laugh.

"Open it up, slowly," Mitchell told him.

It took a long while to get the door open and Mitchell continued to look in the door as it opened. Once it was fully open, they both stepped back to check it out.

After a moment of looking in the trailer, they both simply nodded to each other and, without a word, they climbed up into the trailer. Before going any further, Mitchell yelled back over his shoulder, "Keep an eye out and be ready."

Slowly, Redcloud made his way up the inside on one side of the trailer while Mitchell went up the other side. It was surprisingly clean inside. Soon, their light showed a box of some sort at the far end. Slowly, they made their way to the box. When they reached the box, they just stood at each end, looking at it. The whole thing looked to be about eight feet long, about 3 feet wide, and maybe 2 feet high. It appeared to be made of some kind of flat metal. It might be lead. There was nothing unusual about it except there was some type of panel or small pad on the front about halfway along the side. They walked around to the front to get a closer look. Mitchell got down on one knee to get a closer look. The only thing he could see was a very small wire coming from the bottom of the panel and running down the front of the box and disappear under it.

Mitchell tried to a look under the box, but couldn't see anything and as he went to stand, he lost his balance and went forward. He caught himself by putting a fingertip on the box.

Suddenly, the pad light up. There was a numerical touch pad and a timer on the screen. The timer was already at 14 seconds and counting down.

Redcloud and Mitchell looked at each other and, without a word, both ran to the back of the trailer. As he cleared the door with a jump to the ground, Mitchell called out to the team, "Take cover, get down".

He followed Redcloud into a ditch and got down. It was about that time Mitchell realized how foolish it was to run a few feet and take cover when this was possibly and nuclear bomb.

He was just turning to Redcloud to say something stupid when everything went white and then black.

CHAPTER 2

As Mitchell became aware of things again, all he could hear was a voice asking if he was all right. He stirred slightly and tried to open his eyes, but when the light hit him, all he could feel was a shot of sheer pain that ran from the top of his head right down to his toes. Then everything went black again.

Sometime later, again he stirred, but this time he heard Redcloud talking. He was telling Mitchell to wake up, but keep his eyes closed for now. The pain that shot through his whole body was still there, but not at the same level he had felt earlier.

"What time is it?" Mitchell asked while keeping his eyes closed.

Redcloud blow out a breath and then said, "Hell, I don't know. It is daytime. That's about all I can tell you right now."

Mitchel cracked open an eye again, only to get another shot of pain through his body. However, after working through the pain a while and squinting through that eye. He could only open the one eye right now. Looking around, he could make out was Redcloud sitting next to him. His long-time friend looked down and smiled, saying, "Glad to have you back. I was beginning to worry."

Mitchel opened the other eye and turned his head to look around. Again, more pain. Redcloud put a canteen to his mouth, saying, "Take a little drink. Only a little, though." After a pause, he added, "It helps some."

Mitchell took a sip of water and soon could feel it helping, but as Redcloud said, only a little. Again, Mitchell looked around. It was now daytime. From the position of the sun, he guessed it was somewhere around noon. He also realized it was also too cold for this time of year. Continuing to look, he could see the duce and the hummer. He could also see the trailer. Everything looked like it should. "Are the others ok?" he squeaked out.

Redcloud looked up to survey the area, "Everyone is still alive, but they are all out cold just like you were." He then paused for a moment to listen "Every now and then I'll hear one of them stir a little, but when I get there, they are still out. You're the first one, after me, to wake up."

Mitchell tried to get up on one elbow, but that was beyond his ability at the moment. All he got for the effort was another shot of searing pain.

Redcloud put his hand on the shoulder of his friend and gently pushed him back down. "Let's wait a little while longer before you try to move. It took me more than half an hour to move after I woke up." He stopped to listen again, then continued, "After I could move, I found that drinking water helps. So, if you'll just lie there a little while longer and drink, I think you'll be able to move soon."

Mitchell worked through the pain and could soon move his arm. He took the canteen from Redcloud. The Chief helped him move up a little so he could drink. The pain to do this was agonizing, but he continued to work through it and even felt a little better. Now that he was up a little, Mitchell could see things a little better. He was making out that something wasn't right, but couldn't put a finger on it right away. He looked at the woods and most of the trees, except the evergreens, were bare. "What's up with the trees?" he asked Redcloud.

"The trees are the least of your concerns, my friend." was the reply with a little laugh. "You ain't seen nothing yet!"

It took a moment, but that got the attention of Mitchell to shake some cobwebs loose. Struggling through the pain, Mitchell got into a full sitting position. He was still behind the trailer and in a small ditch that was along the side of the road. However, the ditch appeared to end just a few yards away from him. He began looking around and could see some of his people, but not all of them. Wilson was not there, and the new guy was missing. "Where's my team? Where are Wilson and the new guy?" Mitchell asked.

Pointing to the hummer, Redcloud said, "Wilson is in the hummer and the new guy is on the other side of the road in a ditch. I didn't want to move anyone, not knowing what happened and all. I thought it best to wake you first and piece together as much information as we can before they wake up."

That seemed to satisfy the immediate concerns about his team, but put Mitchell to thinking about what happened. "How long have you been awake?" Mitchell asked Redcloud.

"About 2 hours, I would guess." Was the reply, then the Chief looked at his watch. "This thing is useless. It stopped working. I checked the rest of the group, and all the digital watches were dead. Yours is an old-fashioned mechanical watch, and it looks like it stopped running last night when the bomb went off."

Mitchell suddenly thought, yeah, that's right, the bomb. "What happened with the bomb? I see the trailer is still there. It couldn't have been that bad."

Redcloud gave a little laughed again, "Like I said, you ain't seen nothing, yet." He then stood up and put out his hand to his old friend to help him up. "If you're ready, I'll help you stand up."

Mitchell held a finger up to tell his friend to wait a moment and took another swig out of the canteen. He then put it down and grabbed Redcloud's hand. That was a bad idea. Trying to stand almost caused him to black out again. However, he slowly got into a crouched standing position, with the Chief's help. While he waited to regain his balance and bearing, he surveyed the area again.

More things now stood out. The surrounding grass was green, but just a little way away, it was brown and dry. The fence was mostly all gone. Only a little left and the gate was still there under the duce. Just where the grass turned brown, the road appeared to be gone, along with the other duce. When he looked at Redcloud, his friend just smiled and motioned him to walk with him.

They first walked over to the hummer, where they could see Wilson crumpled up in the back. Her side was moving, so they could tell she was breathing. Then he looked up at the semi-trailer. It wasn't ok, like he originally thought. Most of the very front end was missing. The parking wheel stands still, propped up what remained.

Redcloud helped Mitchell over to the side of the trailer, where he could get a closer look. The side was smooth and not blown out, like it should be from a bomb. It looked like it was just cut with some tin snips. The cut was shiny and not burned, again like it should have been with a bomb. Nothing he was seeing looked right to him.

The Chief then took him to the rear of the duce. It was sitting right where he left it after he pushed through the gate. The very back corner had been cut off as cleanly as the trailer was. The truck was still OK from the looks, just the clean cut on the corner. However, when he looked down, he could see that where the road ended and there was about a 6 inch drop off. It curved away from the truck and looked like it had made a rough circle around the entire area.

Looking at the Chief, Mitchell asked, "What'd you make of this?" pointing to the ground.

Redcloud just shrugged his shoulders and shook his head. "I don't have the foggiest idea what is going on. I had hoped you might have an idea."

Mitchell decided he was still in too much of a fog and only shook his head this time. After standing there a few more minutes, he felt the cold setting in. "Why is it so cold in the middle of the summer? Something is very wrong here." Mitchell just stood there looking around a little longer, trying to take everything in all at once. Finally, he suggested, "Let's head back and get a fire going. When these guys wake up, they're going to be cold."

Redcloud nodded and helped him back. On the way, they stopped to pick up some fire-starting material and after they returned, Mitchell sent the Chief off to gather some firewood. It was easy to see there was plenty of it lying around, so he didn't think they would freeze today.

While Redcloud was away, Mitchell set up a fire pit and got the starter ready. He didn't have too much to work with and quickly finished that part. Sitting back down, he went over everything that has happened. He was still feeling the pain, so he knew some of his thinking was probably not very clear. While he sat there, all kinds of things kept bouncing around in his head. Crazy thoughts. Then he suddenly remembered the radio.

With a lot of effort, he slowly got back up and headed over to the hummer, where he grabbed the radio. Everything was dead. The radio had no power. He checked the battery in the hummer and that appeared to be fine. He then disconnected the radio from the hummer and switched it to the internal battery power. Still dead.

About this time, there was a sound from the back of the hummer. He heard Wilson stirring. He turned in the seat and reached back to put his hand on her shoulder. "Don't move right now. I'll go get you some water. That appears to help a little. Just lay still and don't move or even open your eyes. "

Now concerned more for Wilson than himself, Mitchell could walk back to the fire pit and grabbed the canteen. It was already about half empty. He quickly made a note to check the water they brought, but he wasn't really too worried. They brought some water with them, so they had enough for a little while. It should last long enough for the rest of the company to get here. When he got back to Wilson, she hadn't moved but was out again. He climbed into the back of the hummer and straighten her out a little. He was afraid she would cramp up from laying so long like that. While doing this, she made a sound. A sound that was all too familiar to him. It was the sound of pain.

Talking softly to her, Mitchell leaned close to her ear and told her to wake up. When she didn't react, he continued to say it, more slowly, repeatedly. Finally, he saw her eyes move. Quickly, he added, "Keep your eyes closed. If you open them now, there will be a lot of pain."

She must have heard him because she didn't open her eyes. Still, her head moved a little and then her face cringed in pain. He put his hand under her neck to help hold her head. Then, putting the canteen to her mouth, he told her the same thing Redcloud had told him. "Here, take a little drink and try not to move. The water will help and after a little while you'll be able to move."

She took a sip of the water and tried to say something, but all that came out was a noise that was nothing like a word. Again, he told her to just lay still. Then he laid her head back down and told her, "I'm going to go check on the others."

As Mitchell came out of the hummer, Redcloud returned with an arm full of wood and set it down next to the fire pit. "I'm going to wait to start the fire until the others wake up.", he said.

"You don't need to wait. I think Wilson is waking up now. She moved some, and I gave her a sip of water. I'm gonna check on the others now."

Redcloud went back to the duce and grabbed his gear. He took out his entrenching tool and started breaking up the smaller pieces of wood with it.

Slowly, Mitchell walked around to the rest of the group. They were all still in the same position they were in last night when everything went to hell. Rodrigues and Johnson were both on the road and easy to see. The new guy, Blake, was laying in the ditch. He must have been face down. The soft powdery dirt that was there covered his face. It is possible Redcloud moved him, or maybe he tried to move himself and passed out again from the pain. Either way, Mitchell thought they all looked okay. He stopped as he stood up to look around and gave a quiet little laugh. Thinking that by "okay" he meant everyone was still breathing. He again looked down at Blake and continued the thought about being okay. Now that he's thinking more clearly, none of them will truly be okay for a long time.

Walking back over to the fire pit, Mitchell sat down. The Chief was busy getting the fire ready. He now had a quiet moment to think. Slowly, he started laying out a plan. He softly said to Redcloud,

"The radio is down and out. No power either from the hummer or batteries. The company should have been here long ago. If we don't hear something back by later this afternoon, you and I will take the hummer back and see what we can find out."

The Chief slowly looked up and in a concerned voice said, "I've got a terrible feeling we will not like what we find back there."

True enough, Mitchell thought, "Yea, I hear you. I'm getting the same feeling."

Slowly, the others woke up. Mitchell and Redcloud became very busy with them for a while and didn't have time to think about their situation. Wilson was first to wake. They carefully got her out of the hummer and set her near the fire. Both Mitchell and Redcloud still had a little pain, but it was letting up, slowly. However, they could see Wilson was having a hard time dealing with it. Next came Rodriguez and then Johnson. It wasn't too long, and they were sitting by the fire. Blake was last and as soon as he moved; he puked. Quickly, he passed out again. The two leaders took turns watching him until he woke up again. They took it a little slower this time and even though he still puked some more; he didn't black this time. They carried him over to the fire to sit with the others.

Now the team was all awake, however, they were all still suffering from the pain and Blake remained sick. While they were all recovering, Mitchell went through the hummer and duce. He found they had enough rations to feed the company for several days, so they were good with food. They had brought two five-gallon cans of water, so they were also good with water for now. He started the hummer, and it appeared to run fine. It even still had most of a tank of fuel. When they get back to the main post area, he figured they needed to get some more. Fuel was the only thing they needed.

The sun was getting very low now. It must be late afternoon or early evening. The sky had cleared up a little, but it never got warmer. Redcloud had gathered more wood, and the fire was going nicely so they would all just stayed put to keep warm. There wasn't much talking for a long time but then Wilson started it when she asked, "What happened Sarge?"

"I don't know." Was the only reply Sergeant Mitchell could muster at the moment. He could see that it didn't sit well with anyone, however true it was. He sat there trying to think about what to tell them, but really couldn't think of anything. Nothing he thought of made any sense.

He finally decided he had to tell them something and laid out his plan of action. "Listen guys, the radio is down. I do not know what happened to us last night, but the company should have been here by now. I know something is up, but this is the spot assigned to us." He let that sink in a little and then continued, "It's now almost dark and with what happened to the road I don't want to try anything at night. We'll hold this spot until morning. If we don't hear from the company, or anyone else, Redcloud and I will head back into the company and see what happened."

Rodriguez spoke up first. "What about us? Are you going to just leave us here? "

"You'll stay on point until we return. When I was going through the duce, I found a couple of hand-held radios. They appear to be still working and we'll use them."

Wilson chimed in now, "Do you really think that kind of radio will carry all the way back to the company?"

"I don't know." Mitchell answered her, "But it is the only thing we have, and I think it will work, but it will be at the very limit of what they should be able to do."

They all sat back and thought about that for a while. No one asked any more questions, so it would appear that this settled their concerns for the moment.

Before it got dark, Redcloud got some water boiling with the canteen cups and everyone had some hot rations to eat. Even Blake was feeling a little better now and ate a little of the food.

After they ate, Mitchel asked Rodrigues how he was feeling.

"Not great Sarge, but better." He replied.

"OK, you take the first watch. I'll move the hummer to the middle here and we'll set up watch in the turret." Mitchell told him.

"Johnson," he said, turning to him, "You'll take over in 2 hours." Then to Blake, "Blake, you'll follow in another 2 hours."

Turning to Redcloud he said, "Chief, you'll follow Blake and I'll take the last watch in the morning."

"If you guys see anything, don't shoot. We don't know what happened and we don't want to shoot our guys just because they are just late getting here." That, at least, brought a little smile to everyone. "I'll be sleeping next to the hummer. Just quietly wake me and I'll figure out what we do next."

Wilson just kept looking at her leader until she couldn't hold it in any longer. Finally, she said, "What about me, Sarge?"

"You're on watch now." he said. "When Redcloud and I head back in the morning, assuming we will still need to do this, you'll be in charge. I want you to be rested because there are a lot of things I need you to do while we're gone."

She just stood up and tossed her garbage onto the fire and went over to the hummer. She grabbed the binoculars out of the front and moved up into the turret. After a quick check of the machine gun, she slowly scanned the area all around the little camp. "Looks clear for now." She reported back to Mitchell, "But we are going to lose the light soon."

Everyone else finished the food and cleaned up the area. Then they all went and grabbed their gear out of the duce and found an area to catch some sleep. Mitchel, however, moved over to the trailer to look some more at it and called Redcloud over so he could talk to him alone.

"Chief, have you been able to make heads or tails of this yet?" he asked him, while whispering.

"Not really. Everything is so strange and out of place." He whispered back.

They were almost talking in whispers. "Let take this one step at a time. First, look at this trailer. The entire front end is missing. This is roughly where the bomb set. Next," they moved back to the edge of what remained of the trailer while he continued to talk, "These edges do not bend out like they should have been and there are no burned marks like I would expect."

The Chief stepped up and carefully felt the edge of the trailer floor. "Look at this Jim." He said pointing along the edge. "The cut is not straight. It curves ever so slightly. And, the curve continues up the side and across the roof."

Mitchell hadn't noticed this before, but the Chief was right. "If I was to guess, the center of the area would have been right were we found the bomb on the truck. It looks like everything for about 5 to 10 feet from where the bomb was, just vaporized."

"How'd that happen?" Redcloud asked.

"I don't have the foggiest," was again the only reply Mitchell could muster.

"Well, if this was the nuclear bomb we were looking for," Redcloud paused for a moment, then went on, "and if it went off, I think everything would have vaporized like this."

"Yeah," Mitchell said as he thought about it, "but that doesn't explain what happened to the rest of us and everything else."

"Just an idea." Redcloud said, shrugging his shoulders.

"Yeah, well, we need something to explain everything, and that ain't it," he shot back at him.

The Chief just stood there looking down at the ground, shaking his head slowly. Mitchell glanced at the trailer again and then slapped the Chief on the shoulder and motioned to head back to camp.

Other than the normal animal noises throughout the night, things were silent. Almost too quiet. They didn't hear any noises like airplanes, trains, cars, nothing that one would think they might hear, even out here.

During his watch, Mitchell just sat through the sunrise and didn't wake anyone up. His leadership training told him it was best if he just let them sleep. He also wanted more quiet time to think about everything that had happened. He tried to put all the pieces together, but nothing was fitting into the puzzle like it should. Like how everything surrounding them was wrong. The weather was cold; plants were dead; the road had disappeared, were only a few of the things that made little sense. Then there was the problem about the bomb. If it was a nuke, then they should all be dead, but if it wasn't, then the damage shown is all wrong.

Finally, Wilson stirred and one after another, they all woke up. His quiet time was going to have to wait. While they were stirring, he stirred the fire back to life and put on a couple of canteen cups of water to boil. At least he thought they could still have powdered coffee.

After the coffee, Sargent Mitchell called Wilson over, "Listen, while Redcloud and I head back to the company, the first thing I want you to do is to take an inventory of everything we have. Look through the trucks and also get me an idea of how much fuel we still have." Sargent Wilson was back in character now. She looked around to take in of what they had left. However, before she had a chance to even think about it, Mitchell continued, "Next, send one person out to look for water. We only have a limited supply, and I don't know how long it will have to last. Also, I want you to set up and guard post that overlooks our camp but make it well hidden."

Wilson was nodding the entire time. "Last, I want to set up an ammo point. At a minimum, get all the mags we have loaded and ready to distribute." After he finished, he could see she was thinking really hard, so he added, "Do you have any questions?"

"No, not about what you want, but lots of questions about this whole damn mess." She replied.

"Yeah," he said, looking around, "I know what you mean, but dammed if I have any answers for you right now."

Wilson smiled and gave him a sarcastic, shitty little salute, then turned and went after the team. Calling Redcloud over, he climbed in behind the wheel of the hummer. When Redcloud jumped in on the passenger side, he asked, "What's the plan?"

As Mitchell started the hummer, he turned to his friend and said, "The road, mostly, was straight getting out here. Using what's left of it, I plan to head off in that direction and see if we can backtrack. It looks like a natural forest, so the driving should be slow, but I think it's doable."

As they started moving, The Chief gave Mitchell a thumbs up and then pointed in the direction they should be going. Mitchell then hit the gas. As soon as they made the little jump off the road, the ground surface wasn't too hard, but still very rough. This caused their progress to slow down so they could monitor things.

After more than a couple of hours, they came out of the woods onto a small ridge. This should have been looking over the main post area.

"I think I know where we are." Mitchell said. "This is the ridge I run up every morning and cross over to behind the motor pool and then back down to the company area." He was pointing out his usual running route as he spoke. The Chief just sat there. His head turned as his friend pointed the route out, but all the two of them could see were fields of open, grassy areas and more woods.

"This makes little sense!" Redcloud shouted, hitting his fist on the dash.

Mitchell got out of the hummer and walked out a little way to the front. Where he squatted down and picked up a hand full of dirt. As he was thinking, Redcloud just sat in the hummer.

In his mind, a strange idea was forming. So strange that he didn't think it was possible, but nothing else made any sense. He just continued to look over what should have been the main post area. Following the landscape in front of him, he could picture the building that should have been there. Some of them, down to the exact location.

While scanning what was there, he noticed something far off on the horizon. "Chief, come look at this." He shouted back to Redcloud without turning away.

Slowly Redcloud got out of the hummer and came up beside Mitchell. Mitchell then stood up and pointed to the horizon. Some miles away in the southeast, there was a column of smoke. "What do you make of that?"

Redcloud was raised on the reservation and was about the best tracker the Army had ever known. In this type of environment, he was the one and only expert.

"Could be natural, but if I had to guess, I'd say that was manmade." He said thoughtfully. He hurried back to the hummer and got the binoculars. After studying it for a while, he said, "Yeah, that's got to be manmade. Maybe a campfire or something along that line."

"This we have to check out." Mitchell said, walking back to the hummer. Grabbing the little radio, he tried to call Wilson. After the second try, he heard her come back. The signal was extremely weak, and it was difficult to make out everything she said, but the gist of it, she wanted to know if they found anything.

"We found nothing so far, but there is smoke on the horizon we're going to check out. It is probably too far for the radios, so we will be out of range for a while. We'll call back when we are on the way back." he told her. The signal was weak at best, and he needed to repeat it several times before she could copy everything.

"OK," Mitchell called to Redcloud, who was still looking at the smoke column. "Let's load up and move out."

Before they left, they gathered up some rocks and built up a little rock marker. Then Mitchell took a bearing so they could find their way back. As they came down off the ridge, the field was a little smother, but not by much. When Mitchell looked back in the mirror, he could see the tracks of the hummer through the grass. Looking over at Redcloud, he said, pointing over his shoulder, "I don't think it will be too hard to find our way back."

Redcloud followed his motions and looked back. He gave a little chuckle and said, "Yeah, we're leaving a real easy trail to follow." Then he looked at his friend and smiled while adding "Even you could follow that trail."

Even though the going was rough, Mitchell took one hand off the wheel and flipped him off, but only for a second as he had to keep both hands on the wheel because there were lots of rocks and wood all over and he didn't want to wreck the hummer right now.

After crossing the open field, they came back into a thinly wooded area. The ground was a little smother but covered with logs and fallen branches. Mostly, the hummer just when through it, but there were a couple times they had to make detours around some areas. After a while, they topped a little rise where they could see the smoke was close ahead. It looked like it was coming from behind the next hill. Mitchell backed the hummer down into a small clump of bushes and motioned for Redcloud to get out. "We'll go the rest of the way on foot until we check this out."

They both grabbed their weapons and headed up the hill to where the smoke was coming from. As they crested the top of the hill, they could see a small house or cabin next to a stream in the little valley. This was the source of the smoke.

"Looks like we found it." Mitchell said to Redcloud as he was getting the binoculars, but before he could get them out, he heard a shot and heard the bullet hit the tree just to the left of him.

Both of them immediately hit the ground. An instinctive reaction that came from more than a couple of time of being shot at. Mitchell rolled to the left and got behind the tree that was hit and the Chief rolled right to just behind a small rise in the ground. Digging out the binoculars, Mitchell moved to where he could get a good look at the cabin.

Other than looking very rustic, there didn't seem to be anything really strange about it. Maybe it was a hunting bunk. There were a couple of windows with wood shutters on this side. He figured the door must be on the other side, leading out to the stream. There was what looked like a well to the left and a small, well kept garden on this side. There was a stack of wood next to a chopping block just on this end.

As he leaned out to get a better look, another shot rang out and hit the dirt in front of him. Again, his instincts took over, and he ducked for cover. Quickly, he focused the binoculars on the cabin to see if he could tell where the shot came from.

Now, things got a little strange. There was a large cloud of white smoke in front of the window on this end of the cabin.

"Hey Chief," he softly called over to Redcloud, "Check it out. Looks like he is using black power."

Redcloud stuck his head up to look. "Must be black powered hunting season right now."

"Are you sure? It's the middle of the summer." Mitchell shot back at the Chief, who should have known better. There's no hunting going on this time of year for anything.

"Yeah, you're right, but then why is he shooting at us?"

"Good point, why don't you just wonder down there and ask him?"

Redcloud slowly backed down from the ridgeline and came across next to the leader.

"Listen, if he is shooting black power, then it will take a while for him to reload. We can work our way down the hill at him. It's not too far and we should be able to make it in a couple of jumps, maybe three at the most." Redcloud said.

Mitchell peeked from behind the tree and took a quick look around the area. There were lots of small hiding places they could get to between the runs. With the slow reloading time and a little cover, they should be able to do this easily.

"OK, you go first and I'll cover. Just on this side of the house, there is a small mound of dirt. You head for that and I'll head for the well."

Redcloud stuck his head up and took in the entire area in less than a second. After taking it all in, he looked at over and nodded.

"Before you take off, put one round of smoke from the 320 just in front of the window on this end, but be careful of the other window. I'm guessing he could move there and start firing at you."

"Why not just flatten the whole place with a couple of HE rounds?" Redcloud asked.

Mitchell just looked at him with a smirk and replied, "Because I have a few thousand questions I would like to ask before you blow him away."

The Chief just shrugged his shoulders with a smile and said, "Have it your way, ready."

Mitchell then popped up and put three rounds in the wood around that window and Redcloud laid a perfect shot just in front of the window. He took off running toward the right side while Mitchell took off to the left, where he got behind a tree just to the downhill side of the ridge and put a couple more rounds around the window. Redcloud got behind some thick brush.

He then signaled Redcloud to move first while he started putting fire around the window to keep their heads down. He didn't want to hit the guy, just wanted him to stop shooting. As he started firing, Redcloud took off running toward the house. He got to just this side of the garden and found a pit to get down in. Just before he took cover, there was another shot from the other window. It came very close to Redcloud, but he moved and gave a thumb's up.

Now it was Mitchell's turn to run. Redcloud put another round of smoke at the other window and started laying down cover fire. Mitchell took off running and made it all the way to the well. This was as good as he was going to get. He had a good close cover of the window and could now see the front door. However, while he was running, another shot came from the original window on this end. Two people, at least.

"Inside the cabin." he shouted out, "We've got you surrounded and could bring the entire cabin down on top of you." Then pausing for a moment to let that sink in.

"We mean you no harm and only wish to talk. Come out of the cabin with your hand up and move toward me at the well."

It didn't take too long to see the door open, and a middle-aged man came out with his rifle up in the air.

"Lean the rifle up against the wall and move towards me." Mitchell said in a voice that he hoped sounded official, but not too frightening.

The man did as he was told, and then shortly a young woman came out with another rifle. She did the same thing the man was told to do. They both slowly walked towards the well. When they were a couple yards from the well, Mitchell stood up and told them to stop, but kept his rifle pointed right at them.

"Anyone else in the cabin?" he asked nicely.

"No," the man said with a heavy accent. "My daughter and I are the only ones here."

"Sargent Redcloud, clear the cabin."

The man and his daughter looked at each other and he blurted out, "Sargent? I didn't know."

Mitchell put a finger to his lips to quiet him until Redcloud came back out and shouted a simple "Clear."

As Redcloud came up behind them, Mitchell said, "Check them, just to be sure."

He slung his weapon over his shoulder and patted down the man. It was easy to see he was nervous, but he let the Chief finish. But when Redcloud moved to search the girl, the man yelled, "You keep your hands off my daughter. I give you my word she is unarmed."

The chief looked at his Sargent who then waved him off but still kept an eye on the girl. He then started to question them, "Who are you and why were you shooting at us?"

"My name is Schmidt. August Schmidt. This is my home. I have never seen men dressed as you and with the Indians here not being friendly, I wasn't taking any chances."

His English was OK, but with a very heavy German accent. "What's your name?" he said to the girl.

"Katherine." was her only reply. Again, with a very heavy German accent.

"You can both put your hand down." He then told them and lowered the muzzle of his rifle a little.

They both slowly lowered their hands and, while still very nervous, they appeared to understand that no one was going to shoot them. Mitchell moved over to the front edge of the well and sat down. A moment later, the girl moved towards him. He jumped back up and pointed the rifle at her.

Immediately, she froze. After a moment, she pointed to the well and made a drinking motion with her hands. He smiled and lowered the rifle again and let her get a drink. She brought up a bucket of water and offered some to both Mitchell and to Redcloud. They both declined, and she took some back to her father.

"I hear in your speech that you are German, I think."

Mr. Schmidt looked a little puzzled and, after a moment, said, "We are from Bayern. Part of the German Confederation."

Mitchell looked over at Redcloud, who appeared not to catch this reference. Looking back at Mr. Schmidt, he said, "Yes, I know this area in southern Germany."

Again, Mr. Schmidt looked confused, but said nothing.

"Your English is very good." He continued and then, looking at his daughter, I added, "Does she also speak English?"

Schmidt thanked him for the reference to his English ability and smiled, but then turned to his daughter and said, "No, she knows a little English, but out here she has very little time to practice it."

"My friend and I are a little lost. Where are we?" he then asked.

"Sir, you are in Tejas." He said flatly.

Mitchell was taken aback. Even though he was suspecting something like this. He looked over at Redcloud and even though he showed no outward reaction to this new, Mitchell knew him well enough to see he had also realized the meaning of this.

"Tejas, you say?" he asked questionably.

Schmidt nodded back.

"And what might the date be?" he asked and then, after seeing the look on Schmidt's face, he added, "We have been away for a long time and out of touch with anyone."

"Let me see, If I figure this right, in a couple of weeks it will be the Year of our Lord Eighteen hundred and Thirty-Six."

That did it. Now the biggest question had been answered. Somehow, they have been pushed back in time for almost 200 years. He got up and walked away a little. He needed to take a few minutes of quiet to let this set in.

When he turned back around to Mr. Schmidt, he asked again, "Eighteen thirty-six, you say?"

"Ya," he replied, thinking, and then added "Next week should be the Holly days of Weihnachten, or as you call it in America, Christmas. The week after will be the beginning of the new year."

Mitchell motioned Redcloud over to him. As the Chief slowly came up beside him, he said, "It was a nuke and somehow it has sent us back in time."

"But how?"

"I don't know. But now everything is adding up. I'm no scientist, but you can see for yourself. Does this look like a normal family home from our time?"

Redcloud looked around at the cabin and the clothes that Schmidt and his daughter were wearing and then took a long, sweeping look around the entire countryside and then looked back at his old friend. "What are you going to tell the others?"

"Others?" Mr. Schmidt spoke up.

Mitchell hadn't realized they were talking loud enough for these two to hear them.

"There are more of you?" He added.

"Mr. Schmidt," Mitchell started out slowly, "this is going to be very difficult for me to explain to you. I don't even know where or how to start."

Schmidt just stood there, looking at them. Mitchell wasn't sure how much his daughter was understanding. She was only standing behind her father and now and then he would catch her and her father whispering something. This, however, was about the least of their concerns right now.

"Yes, there are others. I have a detail of four more soldiers with me. We left them at the point we should be patrolling. I am going to send the Sergeant here back to bring them up. While he is away, I am going to see if I can figure out what is happening. Once we are all together, we'll sit down and talk it out."

This stopped any more questions from him, for now.

He then looked at Redcloud and said, "Go get the rest. When you reach the marker radio, Wilson and tell her to get everything packed up." He then looked back at Schmidt and his daughter, but they didn't seem to be interested and this time he was talking a little lower, so they probably couldn't hear them. "I'm going to stay here and see if I can get some more information from these two and figure out what's going on."

"Yeah, have fun with that." Redcloud said and then added, "What do you want me to tell them?"

"Don't tell them nothing. When they get here, we'll all sit down and hash this out."

Again, he looked over at their two new friends and smiled. "Let's have a little fun with this. When you get here, it might be dark. I want you to come over the ridge with all the lights on and geared down. I want to make as much noise at possible."

Redcloud looked at the two and smiled as well. "They'll both end up shitting their pants"

Mitchell laughed a little. "I don't want to give them a heart attack, so I'll prep them a little, but yeah, there may be some shitty laundry tomorrow."

Redcloud turned and trotted back up the hill, and in a moment, was out of sight.

CHAPTER 3

Walking over to the cabin, Sargent Mitchell picked up the rifles Schmidt and his daughter had left there. They were a couple of real nice Kentucky long rifles with flint locks. He opened the pans on both and blew the powder out. He then called Mr. Schmidt over and handed both back to him.

Schmidt just walked up and nodded to him and took the rifles and put them back up on the wall inside the cabin. Mitchell followed him in, and his daughter came in a little after.

After looking around, he saw a small but clean place. There were two beds near the widows in the rear, separated by what looked to be a blanket hanging from a rope, and at the other end of the cabin there was what looked to be a kitchen in one corner. There was also a small table near the kitchen with a couple of chairs. Mr. Schmidt motioned for him to sit in one chair while he grabbed a couple of cups and came over to the table and sat in the other chair. His daughter began messing around in the kitchen area and soon brought over a small pot. He could smell what he thought must have been tea. She poured some for her father and their new guest and went to the other end of the cabin and sat on the bed.

Schmidt kept looking at Mitchell's rifle that he had leaned against the wall where he was sitting. Finally, he spoke. "What kind of gun is that? I've seen nothing like it before."

Mitchell looked over at his weapon and gave a little chuckle. "Yeah, I suppose you haven't." He took a long drink of the tea and quickly wished he hadn't. It was about the most bitter tasting tea he had ever had. He choked on it a little, but before they could do anything, he spoke again. "This is going to be very difficult to explain and I don't have all the information I need to answer all your questions." he told them and then added, "I don't know that I ever will."

Schmidt looked at his guest as he spoke. However, whenever he stopped talking, his eyes went right back to the rifle. Finally, Mitchell reached over and picked up the weapon. He dropped the mag out and cycled it to eject the round in the chamber and then handed it to Schmidt.

Slowly Schmidt took it from his hands, and quickly he got a strange look on his face. "It's so light. How can you fight with this?" he blurted out.

Mitchell laughed a little and showed him the round that had ejected out.

He took it and carefully looked at it. "This is what it shoots?" he asked.

"Not exactly," Mitchell replied. "It is a little more complicated than that. This part on the end," He pointed to the actual bullet, "Is the part that shoots."

"But it is so small!" Schmidt exclaimed.

Again, Mitchell smiled and continued to explain the construction of a modern round of ammunitions to him. He appeared to understand what was being said, as he kept nodding his head at the explanations. Mitchell would not go into the ballistics with him, he just wanted him to get the idea about a self-contained cartridge.

After looking it over for a while, Schmidt placed the round back on the table and looked at the rifle again. It then dawned on Mitchell that this was going to be a lot more difficult to explain.

"How does this work? I've seen nothing like this before." He asked

Mitchell decided that would have to wait until he understood a little more about the entire situation they were in. "Mr. Schmidt," he started, but was interrupted.

"Please, call me August." He said.

"OK, August," he continued, "That is going to take a lot of complicated explaining. There are other things you need to understand before I get into the complicated things."

He looked the rifle over again, and then carefully handed it back. Mitchell replaced the round in the magazine and put the mag back in the rifle, but didn't chamber a round this time. He then set the rifle back against the wall and looked back to August.

After a short awkward moment of silence, August spoke up. "4 more people you say."

Mitchell nodded to him while he sipped the tea.

"I think it will not be enough room in here for everyone." He went on.

Mitchel looked around and yep, August was right. This cabin was small for the two of them. Now he has brought 6 more people in.

"Don't worry about my people, we will take care of ourselves." he said.

"Not my way." August said, and then stood up. "We will all eat as a family. If you will help, we can put together a table outside where there will be room for everyone to sit."

That sounded like a good idea to Mitchell. He needed something to occupy himself with while he tried to figure out what was going on. "That sounds like a plan to me." he said to him, but all he got in response was a strange look.

August and he put together a table outside that was big enough for everyone to sit at. They found some boards that worked ok, and they cut some short timber for legs. He didn't have many nails, so they just tacked down the corners and stood a couple timbers up in the middle for support. Chairs were easy. They just cut some bigger timbers to about the right height and put them around the table.

Looking at his watch, it was mid-afternoon now, and he was guessing Redcloud should be back in the clearing by now. Knowing how he drives, he probably made a little better time than they did getting here. Now he was worrying about him breaking the Hummer. They've got no way to fix it if it gets broken. Can't even repair a flat tire. He made a mental note to talk to him about this as soon as he gets back.

While Schmidt went into the cabin, Mitchell put together a fire pit between the garden and the well. He wanted a place where they could all sit comfortably and talk. Everyone could either bring their dinner chair over to sit or sit on the ground. This would also be a suitable spot to pitch tents for the night.

After a little, August came back out with his rifle in his hands. Just then, Mitchell realized he had left his rifle in the cabin. What a stupid mistake that was. Now, he was at the mercy of his host.

August must have seen the concern on his guest's face and laughed. He looked down at his rifle and said, "I need to go hunt some meat for dinner."

Mitchell looked down at the ground with a little smile and said, "Not to worry. My Sergeant Redcloud is probably the best hunter around these parts, and we have enough food to keep us for a little while. When he gets back, I'll send him out to hunt us up enough meat."

August looked back down at his rifle and leaned it up against the wall inside the door. Then He walked around to look at the garden. Mitchel knew immediately what was on his mind.

"Yes, we may be a little light on the vegetables. December, you say. This is not the time of year to plant even cool weather crops." He said, walking over towards his host near the garden. "You have a fine garden for you and your daughter, but it will not be enough for all of us. We'll need to find something else that will work."

"My daughter takes care of the vegetable patch. I am not a good farmer, but her mother taught her well before she passed away." He said.

"How long ago did your wife pass?"

"It was about three years ago. There was a dreadful winter, and she became very sick. We lived south of here and after I buried her, I could not stay there. I moved this way with my daughter to start a new life, again."

Mitchell could see the sadness in the face of this man as he was remembering about his wife. "Three years is not a long time. It will take time for wounds like that to heal."

"Thank you." He said with a simple nod.

It was getting late in the afternoon now and Mitchell still had not had time to sit and think. He explained to August that he needed some quiet time to get his head together. After another strange look, but August appeared to understand and nodded his understanding.

This time, he didn't forget. He went back into the cabin and grabbed his rifle and made a note to himself that the next time he left it like that, he would have to kick his own ass. He then nodded to Katherine and went out the door.

Once outside, he looked around. For just a moment, he forgot about all that had happened and just took in all the beautiful landscape. Everything was so natural. However, this feeling only lasted a fleeting moment and quickly he was back in the real world. Finding a small hill not too far from the cabin, he headed to a nice tree there and sat down. Taking out his canteen, he slowly took a drink. Now he had a quiet moment to think about things and wished he knew more about all that science fiction stuff and time travel and physics, but he was just a simple soldier. However, he could put one and one together and usually get the right answer. Granted, the numbers he was thinking of now are a little bigger than one plus one, but from what he had as evidence, he could only guess his answer was right.

Somehow, they had been transported back in time to the year 1835, soon to be 36. There was something important about that, but he couldn't remember was it was right now. They all appear to be well. No radiation sickness, just a little shock and disorientation when they woke up. The entire area around the trailer where the nuke was also appears to have been transported back.

He thought about the trailer. The bomb vaporized the front of the trailer. This was about a 10 foot area. This may be normal and left it at that. Then there is a roughly circular area up to about 150 feet out from there that had also been transported back in time. Then everything outside that area appears to be normal for this time.

A really far out idea formed in his head. What if, when the nuke went off, past the initial small area that was vaporized, there was some kind of pressure or energy wave that pushed, not transported, but pushed them back in time? After a short distance, the pressure wave dissipated and outside that everything was destroyed.

A crazy theory, for sure. However, that was the only thing he could come up with that made any kind of sense. Maybe once the others find out the truth about their situation, they will have an idea, but for now, this is all he had to go with.

Having thought it out a little, he relaxed a little. Now he just sat there a while, taking in the beautiful countryside. No noise, no cell phone, only a bug or two to bother him. He thought he might just start to like this area.

It didn't take long to doze off for a while. When he opened his eyes again, it was getting dark. He stood up and stretched, and then gathered his things and headed back to the cabin. There was a little light coming from the window, and there was a small fire in the pit he had built. When he was a couple hundred yards away, he heard the distinctive sounds of the duce off in the distance. He hurried his pace and got back to the cabin just in time to see August and his daughter come out of the cabin door, rifles in hand.

"Hold on a minute," he yelled at them. "That is just my people coming back."

They both stopped and looked at him, but then the deep sound of the diesel revved up and that got their attention back. This time, they both had their rifles up to their shoulders and were ready to fight off this new monster that was coming.

Mitchel got there and slowly walked up to them. "Have you ever seen a steam engine?" he asked.

August nodded but didn't lower his rifle. His daughter just looked at her father and followed him.

"These are machines, something like a steam engine, nothing more." He told them and then added with a little more force, "Nothing more than a machine."

August looked at this strange man standing behind him and slowly lowered his rifle. Katherine again just followed her father's lead.

Mitchell slowly walked over and gently took the rifles and leaned them up against the side of the cabin. The two of them let him have the rifles, but he could see that neither one of them was thrilled about the idea of handing them over.

They could hear the duce clearly now. The best guess was it was coming up the rise on the other side of the hill. Soon, it would top the hill and be down here in a couple of seconds. Mitchell slung his rifle over his shoulder and put his arms over their shoulders and gently eased them over to the fire pit.

Just about the time they got there, the Hummer came up over the crest of the ridge. From the way it was being driven, Mitchell knew it was Redcloud driving. Another mental note: talk to him quickly about his driving.

August and his daughter backed up, but Mitchell still had his hand on their shoulders to steady them. "That is just the smaller of the two machines I have. It is being driven by Sergeant Redcloud."

"How do you know it is him?" Katherine asked.

My god, he thought. That is the most this girl has said since he met her. "I can tell by the way he drives." He answered her with a laugh.

As Redcloud came down the hill, he had the lights on high beam and the hummer was bouncing all over the place. When he got near the fire pit, he hit the horn for a quick burst, then stopped about 50 feet away.

Redcloud jumped out of the driver's side and the new guy, Blake, slowly climbed out of the passenger side. His ride with Redcloud clearly shook Blake up.

Redcloud ran over to stand next to his old friend and their new friends with a big smile. "I just had to get down here first to watch the look on their faces," he said, pointing to August and Katherine.

"Yeah, you and me need to have some words about that, real soon." he sternly said back to him.

Just then, the duce topped the hill. They had it geared down, and it was making all kinds of noise. This time, August and his daughter were terrified. Mitchell could feel Katherine shaking under his hand that was still on her shoulder and August was stiff as a board. He couldn't tell if August was going to run or just trying to hold his shit in, but he was terrified.

He let go of August and pulled Katherine close to him and held her tight. When the duce got down to where they were, it slid as whoever was driving hit the brakes, hard. Then they hit the air horn and Mitchell thought Katherine was going to hit the ground right then. August turn to run, but Redcloud was right there to grab him.

The duce shut down and again it was deathly quiet. Wilson got out of the driver's seat. Another note to have words with her as well. "Hey Sarge." she shouted with a wave and then Rodrigues got out of the passenger side along with Johnson.

"A woman?" August said out loud. Loud enough for Wilson to hear.

"Yeah, a woman. You got a problem with that?" She shouted back.

Mitchell held his hand up to stop any more. "People, we have a situation here and it is going to take some explaining and a lot of talking. Let's get some food in us first, then we can sit down and talk this out."

Redcloud let go of Schmidt and came up to stand next to his best friend. He looked at the girl who Mitchell was still holding. This caused him to drop his arm and asked, "Katherine, could you please get 2 pots of water hot? Doesn't need to boil, but good and hot."

She looked at her father who, he guessed, translated for her, then she looked back at him and with a smile she simply said, "Yes."

When she had left, Redcloud stepped closer and whispered, "Hm, you are fast."

"Yeah, right!" Was the only thing that came to his mind trying to dismiss Redcloud's remark. "That little stunt with the air horn was bad, so she's probably going to go change her clothes before she can do anything."

"Wasn't it great, though?" Redcloud shot back at him with a big shit-eating grin.

"I thought it would be, but I'm thinking now I was wrong. These people are so far out of place with us it is not fair." Mitchell said back. "I've been thinking this over. We need to be a lot more careful about what we are doing in the here and now."

"Then I guess it is as bad as I thought." The Chief replied and then continued, "Did you figure it out?"

"I have a couple of ideas, but only one makes any since and as impossible as it sounds, I think we're stuck with it."

"OK," the Chief said "But, I'm starved, so let's grab some food and then you can lay it out for all of us."

Mitchell motioned Redcloud to follow, and they headed for the table. Everyone had found a seat and August and his daughter were bringing out a couple of pots of water. Johnson and Rodrigues had run over to the duce to bring back a couple extra boxes of MREs. They put the boxes on the table and after some decisions and negotiation, everyone had a pack of food. Mitchell was sitting next to Katherine, so he was helping her get into the food and showed her how it all worked. Redcloud helped August get his. Everyone was just chatting, mostly about the trip here and the reaction the Schmidt's had when they drove up. Mitchell kept trying to steer the conversation away from the obvious things like the cabin and the lack of facilities, electricity and such. However, soon it got to where it had to be addressed.

"OK, quiet down for a moment." Mitchell said, standing up. As he walked around the table, he stopped behind August. "First off, I would like to thank Mr. Schmidt, August, and his lovely daughter Katherine," at which point Katherine turned her head down and sheepishly smiled at everyone, but he just continued, "for their wonderful hospitality. They have told me we are indeed in Texas, or as he calls it, Tejas."

It was Rodrigues who spoke up. "Tejas, they haven't used that name since the Texas Revolution."

Again, August was set back by this statement. "You are so very right, Rodrigues." Mitchell said back while shaking his finger at him. "That brings up the next point of interest. August here has informed me that next week should be Christmas and the following week will be New Year's day for Eighteen Thirty Six."

Now Mitchell just stepped back and let that sink in. It didn't take long and this time it was Johnson who spoke up. "Come on Sarge, you surely don't believe that crap, do you?"

August spoke this time, saying to Mitchell, "You let your nigger talk like that? It was bad enough to have him at our table."

This was a problem Mitchell hadn't thought about. In this time, blacks would still be slaves.

"Who are you calling a nigger?" Johnson stood up and shouted.

Mitchell quickly jumped back to stand behind August and held up his hand to quiet Johnson. "Sit back down, Johnson. We need to explain how things are from where we come from so they can understand. This will take a little doing, so don't get excited about it right now."

Johnson sat back down but made it very obvious that he was not happy.

"To tell you the truth, from what I have seen and experienced the past day, I believe I do." Was the answer to Johnson.

"You don't really expect us to believe we have traveled some two hundred years into the past?" Said Wilson.

Now came the moment he had been waiting for and dreading. August stood up and shouted, "What is this nonsense? You are telling me you are from the future?"

"Yes August, that is exactly what I am telling you." Mitchell said, looking him straight in the eyes.

August started going off in German. Mitchell knew a few words of the language, and some were not nice words, but there was no way he could keep up with him. August then turned to his daughter and quickly translated everything for her. She didn't really say much, only ask her father a couple of question, which he appeared to answer with, "I don't know." Katherine might have been in shock by now because she said nothing. She only sat there and stared at her father.

"August, August…" Mitchell repeatedly called his name to calm him down. Finally, he could quiet him, and could continue "August, I know this sounds impossible to you." August made a grunting noise with that comment, but then Mitchell continuing "It is just as impossible for us to believe it as well. I don't understand how it happened, but I have a theory." Taking a brief pause, he waited a moment but, since no one else had a comment, he continued, "August, my team was sent out to patrol an area to look for a bomb. This type of bomb is powerful. It is not something that is easy to make, and it is not something I fully understand how it works. For example, a single one of these bombs could destroy everything for a circle of about two to three miles. Anyone living within ten miles of this bomb when it went off would probably die after a short time, maybe a week or two." He stopped again because of the look on the face of their new friend. Everyone else in the group had lived with the horrors of this possibility since before they all were born, but this was the first time these two had ever heard of such a thing. August quickly translated for his daughter, at which point she quickly turn to look at Mitchell.

"I am sorry, but I don't know of any way to explain this anymore clearer to you. I know you must have lots of question and after I am done, I will sit with you and try to answer them the best I can. But, for now, let me continue with my theory of what happened."

August appeared to accept this for now and moved next to his daughter so he could translate on the fly. "Either way, you think, for now, this is what I know happened. The terrorist, bad guys," he added, looking at August and his daughter, "somehow got a hold of one of these bombs from the government and said they were going to use it against the American Army. They sent us out to look for it, and I guess we found it." Again, he paused, but all his group knew this much and had no questions so far.

Now comes the questionable part. "While checking out what we thought might be the bomb we were looking for, I accidentally touched it. I think it must have been rigged to go off if anyone touched it. This is all the facts we have. The rest of this story is my theory of what happened. When the bomb went off, everything in about a ten-foot radius got vaporized." Looking at August he explained, "Vaporized mean it just ceased to exist anymore."

Continuing, "From that point I believe that some type of pressure or energy wave or something pushed us back in time. This wave appeared to dissipate after about one hundred fifty feet. I believe we were pushed out ahead of the radiation and that is why none of us are sick right now. After that, I guess that there was the destruction that we would expect from a nuclear explosion." Mitchell stopped to let his explanation sink in a moment and then he added, "And that is my theory. If anyone has a better idea and can explain some of this to me, then please let me know. I'm simply guessing at all this from what I've seen."

Wilson was the first to speak up. "OK Sarge, if this is so, how come we haven't heard about something like this before? There have been many tests and even the two live drops on Japan in World War Two."

"Well, I guess there may be a couple of explanations. First, I don't recall ever hearing of anyone being near the explosions of the tests and the drops over Japan were air bursts. They exploded something like a thousand feet in the air. I think, if there was something that happened in the air over Japan back in the 1800s, it would not have been a big deal. As far as the test goes, there were ground, air and underground tests. The only thing that would have been sent back would have been a few scraps of metal or wood. An underground explosion might have triggered a minor earthquake as the new ground pushed the old group out of the way, but an earthquake wouldn't have set off any alarms 200 hundred years ago." Mitchell closed out his argument by adding,

"Another thing, I don't know if the power of the bomb has anything to do with how far back you go. Some of these things may have been sent back thousands of years. We just don't have the information."

After a little while of silence, the new guy, Blake got up to put his two cents in "I know you guys don't know me and I've only been with the unit, what two days, but I have been going to college and I hoped to be a teacher someday. There are theories about time travel. In one theory, some think that once you travel back from your time, you create a different timeline from the one you were on. That timeline changes the instant you are there. Your original timeline continues on to whatever destiny, only without you." Blake's last comment really sunk in on the rest of the team.

Johnson now had something to say. "So, you're telling me that because of a bunch of terrorists I might now be a slave!"

Being the only black man on the team, Mitchell hadn't even considered that point. "Johnson, you will never be a slave. I promise you that. However, this is something we'll have to deal with in the future. Right now, we have got to figure out what our immediate problems are."

Again, Blake stood up. "You heard Rodrigues say that they have not used the name Tejas since the Texas Revolution. If the dates are right, this is the Texas Revolution, and it has already started. If it hasn't happened already, it soon will. I don't know the exact dates, but Jim Bowie should have driven General Cox out of San Antonio. Now we need to decide how we are going to act."

That had been bothering Mitchell about the year. He knew there was something about that year, but he couldn't put his finger on it. The Texas Revolution started in 1835 and end later the next year. The Alamo was going to happen in about 3 months.

"Wait a minute you guy." Wilson spoke up again. "We can't just go mucking around with history. If we interfere with what is going to happen, we will change all of history. Some things might be good to change, but we might end up changing a lot of things to bad or worse. Johnson, you're worried about slavery. What if what we do here now changes the outcome of the Civil War and the South wins? Slavery will continue for God knows how long." She paused at this before continuing, "I'm just saying we have to be very careful about what we decide to do."

"Wilson's got a valid point." Mitchell commented, however, no one else wanted to speak right now. "Ok, I've laid out some facts, what happened before the bomb went off. Some theories about what might have happened to us to get here. And last, the inescapable fact of where and when we are right now."

After a moment, he added, "There is another fact that I think I need to throw out there. We don't have a snowball's chance in hell of getting back. Face it folks, we are stuck here. We have to decide what we are going to do in the here and now."

Now, there was a lot a murmuring, some of it came from August and his daughter as he translated everything trying to explain things to her. However, Redcloud was extremely quiet throughout the entire conversation. Walking over towards him, Mitchell quietly asked, "What do you think?"

"To quote a line from a pretty wonderful movie "" I think we're in a world of shit"", and we are." Was his simple reply.

Mitchell knew there was more to his silent friend's line of thinking. So, he just stood there and waited for him to continue. After a little while he said, "Wilson's point is we can't mess with history, but she is wrong. In the earlier explosions, if it sent someone back and changed history, we wouldn't even know it. Everything would look normal to us. Besides, we've already messed with history just by being here and having dinner with the Schmidt's. What if we take that, and with our knowledge of the future? We could try to steer the future of humanity to a better future than what we know will happen?"

Mitchell just stared at his friend. It amazed him he could have such a depth to him, one that he had never seen before. "That is pretty deep thinking for a simple Indian boy. Yeah, after Blake explained where, I mean when, we were or are, shit. I'm already getting confused.

I had the sudden desire to run right down to San Antonio and help them boys."

Redcloud said nothing, so after a little while Mitchell added, "Maybe that is exactly what we should do." He said, thinking. "That might be a good short-term thing to do, but what about the long-time goal? I mean, do we get messed up in the Civil War, do we go to Europe and shoot Hitler while he's still a baby? There are lots of things we can do. What we should do, is another question? I don't have a clue."

"Whatever we do, we need to decide together, as a team, and work towards the same goal." Redcloud answered back.

"Yeah, you might be right. I'm not looking to get tied up in the Civil War. That was a mess. But you're right, we need to stick together on this."

August and his daughter were both still sitting at the table, looking at Mitchell. "Chief," Mitchell said to Redcloud, "have the guys pitch the tents around the fire pit and set up camp there. It will help to keep them occupied for a while." Then, looking at their hosts, he told Redcloud, "I'm going to sit with the August and his daughter and try to explain more to them."

"Have fun with that." Redcloud said with a smile as he walked away.

Mitchell just shook his head and said, "Yea, right."

Watching his friend walk away, he thought that there is not much that can upset the Chief. He is still the same rock, no manner what year it is.

As he took a seat next to August and his daughter, he grabbed his canteen and brought out the cup. After getting some hot water, he made a quick cup of coffee and offered some to both of them. August held his hand up and shook his head and got up to go into the cabin. Shortly, he returned with a bottle and a couple of small cups. It took little to guess what was in the bottle and when he offered one cup. Mitchell nodded and took it.

He gave the coffee to Katherine and explained about the sugar and creamer for it. After she tried it with nothing, she put both sugar and creamer in and now she appeared to be alright with that. He then sat down, and August poured out something into each cup. Taking a small sip and it made him think of some of the German schnapps he had at a beer fest once. It was pretty good.

"OK, I will try to answer your questions as best I can. Remember, I don't have all the answers and I might not want you to know some things about us right now, but I will do the best I can."

August spoke right up. "Where do you come from?"

"We are all in the United States Army, stationed together right here in Texas."

August interrupted him now, "Texas, as you say, is part of the United States of America?"

"Yes. I will try to explain a brief history later. Right now, I think it is more important for you to understand who we are and where and when we come from." August just nodded and Mitchell continued, "I don't think we have moved from where we were stationed. We have only gone backwards in time. We come from the year 2025." He then stopped a moment for that to sink in.

He waited for August to translate for his daughter. Her eyes got as big is quarters when he told her the date.

"What is it you do for the Army? You have so many different people in your group. You have women, niggers, and Mexicans. Is your nigger a slave, or does he fight?" August asked, with no malice in the question.

"Let me explain something to you first. Where we come from, all people are treated the same. The word 'Nigger' is only used to insult people with dark skin, like PFC Johnson. In our time, we talked about his people as blacks or African Americans." When August said nothing, he added, "That is why Johnson jumped up, ready to fight you. The way you talked about him was terrible."

"I meant no harm or disrespect to anyone. It is very unusual to see a ni..., black man that is not a slave."

"Yes, I understand, and I will talk with Johnson about this. This may present a problem to us later and I need to deal with it quickly. In our time, we have eliminated slavery. All men, and women for that matter, are free and have the same rights as any other person." As he spoke, he looked over at where Johnson was pitching a tent.

Yes, indeed Mitchell thought, having him in the group, in this time, might be a small problem, but as he is one of his soldiers and as the leader, he can't let anything happen to him because of the color of his skin.

When he looked back August, was leaning close to his daughter and whispering into her ear. "You don't need to whisper to Katherine. I understand your need to translate things for her, and I can wait while you do that."

August nodded and continued to tell his daughter about what had happened. He took another sip of the schnapps, Apfelkorn, he thought, as he remembered what he could of that beer fest.

When August had finished translating for his daughter, she asked, "Women are treated the same as men?"

"Yes," Mitchell replied, "women may vote and drive and to hold just about any job they want. In fact, in one of our recent elections, a woman came very close to being elected as President."

"Mein Gott!" August blurted out, but his daughter just smiled a little. However, she quickly lost the smile when her father turned back to look at her.

They continued to talk for quite some time while Mitchell answered their question. He stayed away from some subjects like the Civil War, in fact all wars, especially WWI and WWII. All the more difficult things that he didn't really want to get into right now.

When they finished the schnapps August had brought out, Mitchell had figured he had too much to drink to continue, so he excused himself and went over to their little camp. The guys were sitting around the fire and talking lowly. Redcloud was back aways from the group, just watching. As Mitchell walked up, they all stopped talking and just looked up at him.

"I know you all have stuff to ask and tell me, but let's hold off until morning "Johnson, I need to have words with you, but I think it is probably best I have it with all of you." They all just looked up at him and now Redcloud had moved closer to the team. "Things are a little different in the here and now. Johnson," he said, pointing to him, "You took offence at the word nigger. We can't do that now. In this time, that word had a completely different meaning that it did on our time. In this time, it is not meant as such a bad a word as the way we used. However, it was still not meant to be nice, even in this time"

Johnson appeared to understand, and he just nodded a little and looked down at the ground, but said nothing.

"And Wilson," he said, which snapped her head up.

"But, I didn't say anything!" she complained to him.

"I know, but the women of this time were thought of only as housekeepers and baby makers. A woman in uniform who is trained to fight will be a problem to explain."

She started to say something, but he held his hand up to stop her.

"I know what you're going to say, and I would probably agree with you, but when we are in public with other people around, both of you, and you as well Rodrigues, will need to play the part, depending on the situation at hand."

After a quiet pause, he continued more softly now, "You need to remember, we are the ones out of time. If we try to step in and change everything right away, they might burn us all as witches or something."

Then he turned to Redcloud. "I almost forgot about you. Indians were mostly thought of as lower than slaves. We come from more than a century into the future and look how little some of our ideas about other people have changed."

He could see that this notion did not sit well with Redcloud, either. Redcloud just shuffled his feet around and kicked a small rock away.

"We have to stick together and watch each other's backs. That is the only way we are going to survive."

There were lots of head nodding, and Mitchell figured now was the time to lay it all out. "Folks, we've got no way of getting back to our time. So, I am going to make the last decision as the NCOIC of this group. We are no longer in the United States Army. That doesn't exist for us anymore. However, we still need to stick together and decide what to do. My decision is that each of you will have a vote for what we will do next. The rank structure for our group will stay the same. I am still the leader and Redcloud is the second. Each of you knows your place, but when it comes time to speak and to vote, we are all equal."

They each looked around at each other and slowly nodded in agreement. Then Johnson spoke, "What if one of us doesn't agree with what the group says and wants to leave?"

"For now, all decisions will be voted on and it must be a unanimous decision. If someone doesn't agree, then they can leave the group, but they leave with nothing from our time. Especially, none of the weapons and no ammo. They leave with nothing that might help to prove they are from the future. That way, if they try to tell someone about the future, people will only think of them as an idiot or a crazy man, or woman."

After a moment of thought, he asked, "Is this agreeable to everyone?"

A lot of nodding, but Mitchell wanted it to be firmer about the agreement and added, "A show of hands, all agree?'

Slowly, everyone's hand went up. Some faster than others.

"OK, so be it. My name is James. From now on everybody can call me Jim. I don't want to ever hear a Jimmy."

That got a little laugh out of them.

As he figured, Johnson spoke up, "OK, I'd like to call a vote to change the rules about people leaving the group. I think we should all be able to take away our own weapon and some of the ammo and food."

Mitchell took a step back to the center and said, "OK, we have a motion to discuss. Anyone want to speak on this matter before the vote?"

Johnson continued. He laid out his arguments, and it seemed Rodrigues might agree with him. When he had finished, Mitchell asked again if anyone wanted to speak.

"If no one has anything more, then let's vote. All in favor of Johnson's proposal to change the rules about leaving the group, raise your hands."

Only Johnson and Rodrigues put their hands up. "OK, as per the rules, this was not a unanimous agreement, so the motion fails."

Johnson quickly stood up and cussed a little as he went off to his tent.

"OK guys, I think that is enough for now, beside we don't have the entire group here now to make any more decisions tonight. I don't know about the rest of you, but I've had it. I'm going to bed."

Without a word, Redcloud pointed to Jim's tent, and Mitchell headed straight there. While he was checking it out, Redcloud came up and put his hand on his shoulder. "How long do you think it will take before someone tried to get away or they all rise to take power away from you?"

Mitchell just shrugged his shoulders and answered with as straight a face as he could, "I don't know. I guess it depends on how good you are at having my back. I assume you have my back?"

Redcloud only slapped him on the back, hard, and smiled before he walked away.

"Ouch." he shouted to Redcloud's back as he walked away. He turned back to his tent and went inside. Someone already rolled his bag out for him, and he immediately crawled in and with the help of the schnapps, he was asleep in no time.

CHAPTER 4

Mitchell woke up to a beautiful sunrise. It wasn't warm by any means, but a lot better than yesterday morning. As he laid there, he couldn't help but go back over the things that had happened yesterday. It was a lot to lie on the team, but he had no real choice. What happened affected all of them and they all had the right to know and have a say in what was happening, at least as much as they knew what was happening.

Evidently, he was not the only one up. He heard someone else stirring just outside his tent. When he opened the flap a little further, he saw August looking over the garden and saw Katherine bringing up some water from the well.

As Mitchell crawled out of the tent, August turned to him and laughingly said, "You people from the future sleep very late." He then turned back to the contemplating the garden.

Mitchell looked east and could just barely see the sun above the horizon. Laughing a little himself, he thought it must have been the schnapps. He headed for the well and brought up a bucket of water for himself and splashed some on his face. God, was it cold. That was enough to get his blood flowing.

Looking around, nothing seemed to have changed much from last night. But, then again, he wouldn't really expect it to. He headed towards the circle of tents and started rousting everyone out. When he got to Redcloud's tent, he didn't get any response to his calls, so he opened the flap. The tent was empty. He stood up and looked around, but didn't see anyone.

Slowly, the group gathered around the table. They each dragged their chairs back from around the fire pit and made themselves comfortable. Again, they brought some rations from the truck. Mitchell was thinking at this rate even the extras they had for the company will be used quickly. They are going to have to come up with an alternate plan, fast.

Just as he was fixing his coffee, Mitchell heard a shot. It was a single shot. It sounded like it came from a little way off to the west. About a half hour later, Redcloud came back into view. He had something on his shoulder, but Mitchell couldn't quite make it out.

As he got closer, Mitchell could see it was a deer. It didn't look to be very big, but it was a start for getting supplies. Even at this distance, he could see Redcloud had a big smile on his face. When Redcloud got closer, Mitchell walked over to meet him. He was right; it was not a big deer. Now he could see it was a young stag. He guessed it wouldn't even dress out at 60 pounds.

"This should last a couple of days. Maybe a week if we use it wisely." Redcloud said as he strolled past his old friend. August pointed to the side of the cabin. There was a large pole sticking out of the side with a rope on it. He helped Redcloud hang the deer as everyone gathered around to watch.

Mitchell went over and patted the Chief on the back and turned to the gang. "This is what we need to do now, folks. We must pitch in and help. For the time being during the day, we are all going to have chores to help. We need to fix a place for us to live besides the tents. We need to enlarge this garden and start looking for wild fruits and vegetables. There will be wood to gather and chop, and I am sure Mr. Schmidt here will have plenty of other things for us to help with. We are going to earn our stay."

The group slowly got the idea that they were not on a picnic here and that this was going to be a lot of work. Mitchell heard some mumbling, so he added, "In the evening, after dinner, we'll gather around the fire pit to plan our future."

That got them moving, at least a little more. "Let's grab some breakfast and then I'll assign some chores for each of us."

Breakfast was rather quiet. Only the occasional, pass me this or that. When everyone finished eating, Mitchell got up and signaled August to come up beside him. "August, I am going to need your help to get these guys to work. Is there anything that needs taken care of right away?"

He thought for a moment. "There are always repairs that are needed, but nothing that needs fixing right now. The one thing we are very short on is food," he then nodded to Redcloud, "except meat, of course. I'll butcher up the deer. Tonight, it is my turn to show you what a good meal is."

"OK, this is what I want to start with. Blake, first thing I want is a complete inventory of everything we still have. Find a pad someplace and write it down. Rodrigues and Johnson. I want you two in the garden. Clean up what is there and start expanding it. We need it to be at least twice the size it is now."

He could have sworn he heard a 'shit' come from one of those two.

"Wilson, you go with Katherine to look for things we can eat." He told her.

"Why, because I'm a woman?" She said back to him, a little angrier than he liked.

"No, because you're a sergeant. You go so Katherine can teach you what to look for and what we can eat. After you lean, you teach the others so they can do that job. But you have to learn first. Also, if I remember right your German is passable. Her English is weak, and she'll need to teach in German." he told her rather sternly and then added, "Are those good enough reasons for you, Sergeant?"

Wilson hung her head down and more politely said, "Sorry, boss, you're right. I was out of line. I know you better than that. Won't happen again."

"Forget it." he told her. "It's been a hard couple of days."

She turned to Katherine and said something in German. Mitchell guessed Katherine understood her because she went in the cabin and brought out a couple of baskets and they were off towards the woods.

"Wilson," he shouted at her, "take your weapon. I want everyone to be safe."

She ran back to her tent and came out with her rifle and slung it over her back and the two of them took off.

"Chief," he said, now turning to Redcloud, "although you have already done your share of the chores for today with that deer, it's not over yet. I want you to help August skin and butcher that deer. I know you've done it before, but you've been off the reservation for quite a while now and I just want to make sure you haven't forgotten anything. You need to make sure the skin is good. Stretch it and dry it. We may need it for trade at some point."

The chief simply drank down his coffee and went with August to start on that deer.

As for himself, he grabbed an ax and headed off to chop some wood. There was a woodpile off to the side of the cabin, and he quickly chopped some wood for the fire pit tonight. But if they were going to live here, they need a better place to live. He was going to have to go into the woods and start taking down some trees to build a cabin for his team.

It had been a long time since he had to do any work like this. He had only cut down a couple of trees when he saw Wilson and Katherine headed back to the cabin. They had a little success today, because he could see that they had something in the baskets.

While he was swinging the ax, he took his watch off, so he dug it out of his pocket. He had no way to set it, so he could only guess, but judging from the watch and the sun, he thought it must be about noon time. Also, his stomach agreed with his assessment of the time. He put the ax over his shoulder and picked up his rifle and canteen and headed back to the cabin.

August and Redcloud had the deer meat all cut up and had built a spit to cook it over the fire pit. They had a good size piece of meat over the fire and Rodrigues was slowly turning it. As he got closer and the breeze was just right, the smell was wonderful.

The guys did a fair job of cleaning up the garden, however the work to expand it had gone nowhere. "Johnson, how come you didn't expand the garden yet?" Mitchell shouted over to him.

He trotted over to where the Boss was. When he was closer, he said, "August said not to worry about that right now. He said it was not the time to plant and there were other things that needed doing first."

Mitchell just nodded at him and gave him the thumbs up sign. Johnson went back and over to Rodrigues where he took over turning the meat while Rodrigues showed him how to do it.

Mitchell just leaned the ax up against the side of the cabin and sat on one of the chairs to rest. Redcloud had been washing up at the well, but as soon as Mitchell sat, he came over to him. "Boy, that August is good with a knife. He knows what he's doing when it comes to skinning and butchering."

"Did you learn anything?"

"Yeah," he replied, "there is a trading post a couple days' ride to the east. A couple days by horse. We could make it in an afternoon with the hummer. "

"Sure, we'll just drive right up there and tell 'em to fill it up, too." Mitchell said rather sarcastically. "You saw how there two reacted to your driving. Just imagine what an entire group of them would do."

Redcloud thought about that for a couple of seconds and then started laughing. He was laughing so hard, Mitchell thought his friend might fall off his dinner log.

"No," the Boss said slowly. "If we go, we're gonna have to go by horse or foot."

Redcloud stopped laughing, mostly, and said, "August has one horse. Maybe we can catch a couple more. I can break them, but can any of these guys ride one?" With that, he started laughing again.

"Maybe there's a wagon around here." He said to Redcloud, As August was walking this way. "August, do you have a wagon around here?"

"There's a busted up old wagon over there." He said, pointing to a bunch of brush.

"Let's have a look." Mitchell said as he slowly got up. Now, he could feel the work he'd been doing.

August led the way, with both Redcloud and Mitchell following. When he got to the pile, he moved some of the old brush and other junk out of the way and they could see a small wagon. The wheels looked to be OK, but August said, "One axel might be broken."

"You think this we can fix it?" Mitchell asked Redcloud, but August spoke up.

"I only have a few tools. This would take more work than I can do by myself, but yes, I think it can be fixed."

Redcloud just looked at his former boss and shrugged his shoulders and nodded agreement.

"OK, this afternoon, we'll try to pull it out of here and take a better look at it."

With that decided, they all headed back to the cabin. The gang was gathering around the fire pit. Everyone looked like they were starving. Mitchell had to admit, it smelled really good.

"Grab your kits and let's eat." Mitchell shouted. He didn't have to repeat it this time. Everyone scattered. August picked up the big knife and poked around at the meat. After a couple of grunts, he must have decided it was ready. Everyone was back now and had their plates ready. August began slicing off pieces and put it in the plates as the line move by. After everyone had theirs, Mitchell stepped up and sliced off a piece for himself and found a little spot to eat. The meat was really tasty and tender. He didn't know what seasoning August put on this meat, but it was good.

Some were already getting up for seconds and Mitchell wasn't far behind them. When he got back to his spot, Redcloud came over and sat next to him. "We should jerk some of this meat to keep for later. I can do it, but I don't know what they have to marinade the meat with."

"Yeah, you're right. If we don't do something fast, this meat will go bad, fast." After thinking about it a little, he added, "This is stuff they do, or should do, all the time. He must have some stuff to do that with."

"Probably, but until now, it's just been him and his daughter. We're going to put a heavy burden on all the supplies they have."

After a moment to think, he said, "I think we're gonna have to make a trip to that trading post more sooner than later. After lunch, I'm gonna take Johnson and Rodrigues to work on the wagon. I may need your help as well."

Pointing back up the hill where he had been cutting trees, he said, "I want you to take the hummer up there and drag those trees back down. Then look for some small trees we can cut to make a coral. I like the idea of catching some horses. We can use them or trade them for supplies."

After letting the meal settle in his stomach a little, he felt the need to take a shit. He pulled out one of the little packs of toilet paper and headed for the outhouse. On the way, he saw Wilson coming out of it. He guessed she asked Katherine about the facilities. When he got close to Wilson, he asked, "How bad?"

She knew exactly what he was asking about and simply said, "Real bad."

That's when he noticed the outhouse was in a terrible place with relation to the well. This is something they'll need to address quickly. They still have a clean stream that is close and can get water from it. It will just be a longer walk to get a drink.

God, Wilson was right. The outhouse was about as bad and any place he had ever had to use. And he'd used some terrible ones. "We're going to have to deal with this quickly," he mumbled to himself as he sat on the hole. Damn, if it wasn't cold, too.

The afternoon went well. Redcloud brought down the trees and started looking for fencing materials. With August's help, the four of them got the wagon back to the cabin area and looked it over. The rear axle was broken. It looked like it split along the grain, but not too badly. It must have gone on the way here because it looks like they tried to hold it together with some rope. They got the wagon up on some stumps and could take the wheels off the rear. The hard part came when they tried to remove the axle. August had a few tools, but nothing to use for this type of work. Johnson came up with the idea to check out the duce and hummer to see what they had. There weren't very many tools in the trucks, but he found enough to let them work the axle free.

Once they got it out, they found it was much worse than they originally thought. It didn't look like it was repairable. They would need to cut a new one. "August, have you ever tried to make an axle before?" Mitchell asked him.

Before he could answer, Johnson spoke up, "My granddaddy was a carpenter. He didn't like to use power tools. He did everything by hand. When I was young, he tried to teach me how to do things."

Surprised, Mitchell looked at Johnson but didn't say anything for a moment. He then asked, "You think you can do this?"

"I can try it. I guess I'm about the closest thing you got to a wagon repair man right now." He said with a smile.

Mitchell had to agree to that point and just patted him on the back and said, "You're probably right. What do you need?"

He thought about it and looked around. "Those trees you cut today are no good. They're too green. I need some dry wood to work with."

August spoke now. "There are some dry logs over behind the little house." He said, pointing to the outhouse.

They could see a small pile of logs over there. Mitchell wasn't fond of the idea of spending time near that outhouse, but it looked like he didn't have a choice.

In the pile, they found a couple of logs that might work. They were long enough, but Johnson wasn't sure they were big enough.

Johnson took the logs over to an area near the garden with help from Blake. They set up a little work area and August showed them what tools he had. The tool selection wasn't much, but Johnson said it will take longer, but he thought he could get a rough example of the axle. Of course, he said it wouldn't be much, but it should function for a while.

The afternoon went by in no time and before he knew it; it was gathering time for dinner. The girls had put together a stew from the deer that Redcloud had gotten this morning, together with some vegetables they picked from the garden and some stuff they hunted up this morning. The dinner was excellent.

Mitchell stood up and raised his canteen cup, saying, "I'm not sure which one of you put together this stew, but it is delicious. I know it is not saying much, but this is probably the best meal we've had since we got here."

The rest of the group all stood up and raised their cups and joined in on the praise for the food.

Mitchell then added, "While we are discussing being here, there is much we need to talk about."

Now, everyone sat back down, and it got silent. "Let's clean up and move over to the fire pit and get comfortable. This is going to take a while."

Everyone chipped in and they had the eating area cleaned up in no time. When they got to the fire pit, everyone grabbed a place to sit, and August brought out a little keg of something. Mitchell could probably guess what it was, but said nothing as he went to each of them and poured a little into each cup.

When he had finished, he sat and poured himself a drink, and everyone raised their cup again. "To newfound friends and a long and happy future." Mitchell put that last part in just to get the conversation flowing.

Wilson was the first to speak up. "OK Sarge, now that you've so blatantly put it out there, what is our future?"

"Well, that is what we are all going to talk about and decide on." He said, looking around at his team. Then he turned to August. "August, we are going to be talking about things that you have no way of having any knowledge of. I must insist on one thing. You must agree to the rules I have set out for my team and join us, both you and your daughter, or you must leave our little discussion group whenever we have these talks."

August looked over to his daughter and they had a brief discussion in German that he couldn't follow. Mitchell looked at Wilson and she just made a motion with her hand over her head, telling him she didn't understand it either.

August and his daughter suddenly stopped talking, and he sat there thinking for a little while. Mitchell took a sip of the drink August had provided while they waited for him. He then looked up at Mitchell and said, "I don't know what we might get into, but I think I like your group and the things you have shown me already have decided for me to follow you."

"Great," he said, "does your daughter agree with you on this matter and does she fully understand what I am asking of both of you?"

August just laughed a little. "She is the one who is insisting on this."

That got a little laugh out of just about everyone. "Oh, how wise the young ones can be sometimes." Mitchell said back to him while he nodded to his daughter. He thought she understood what they were saying because even by the firelight, he could see her blush and smile as she put her head down.

"OK, guys and girls, this is my short-term plan. We get the wagon fixed and take it over to the trading post and see what supplies we can pick up. While Johnson, and his apprentice, Blake," Mitchell just threw that in there for a little laugh, "get the wagon fixed. We need to come up with some stuff we can trade when we go there."

Rodrigues put a couple of cents' worth in by saying, "We could try to make some tequila. That is always a good for trading."

Wilson threw in. "Redcloud could get some more skins and meat to trade there."

Redcloud spoke up now. "Yes, these are good things to trade, but the one thing that is going to bring in the supplies we need is horses. We need to round up some horses and herd them over to trade."

August added, "That is true. There are not enough horses for the people who live here now, and more are always needed, but they are difficult to catch. I only have the one horse and it is good to pull the wagon but can't chase other horses."

"Chief, do you have an idea on how to do this?" Mitchell asked Redcloud.

"I have a couple of ideas. Either way we go, it is going to require a lot of work. I don't know how fast we can get it all together. How soon do you plan to need them?"

"Well, that all depends on what we plan for our long-term goals." Looking around the group, Mitchell asked, "Anyone have any ideas about what we should do?"

"Sarge," Rodrigues quietly said, "We all know what's going to happen in a couple months. Are we just going to sit here and do nothing to help?"

"We talked about this before!" Wilson shouted at him. "We can't go messing around with history."

August stood up. "You say we all know. I know nothing. What is going to happen?"

Everyone shut up quickly. "August," Mitchell said, walking over to where he was. "I have told you we have somehow come back in time. In our time, this has already happened. In about 2 months. Santa Ana will bring an Army north and there will be a couple of battle where he kills all the defenders of a place in San Antonio and another place in Goliad. The ones in San Antonio will fight and lose and Santa Ana has anyone who survived, killed. In Goliad, there is a fort with over 200 soldiers who surrender to him. He has all of them shot."

August muttered, "Mein Gott!" and then he translated for Katherine.

"What my people are trying to decide is, do we help them and change our history, or do we let things happen as they should?" He said to August, but sternly looked around at his team.

Mitchell added, "There are many things we don't understand. First, we don't know what happens to our timeline after the bomb we found went off. It could get everyone together to put an end to terrorism forever. It could just as well set the world into a war were more of these weapons are used and the world, as we knew it, will is destroyed."

He let that sink in for a little and then he when on. "Now, if we decide to go down there and help those people in San Antonio, we have no way of knowing what that will do to the future. It will undoubtable change everything that we know will happen. Will it be for the better or worse? Who can say?"

"Blake, you said that there is the thought that our own timeline remains intact and will continue on without us and no matter what we do here and now, and it will not affect what we knew?"

Blake quickly answered, "That's one thought about time travel, however there and many ideas about the subject. Until now, there has been no way to prove any of this."

"Well, it is not a theory anymore. We need to decide about what to do. I can tell you this. If we decide to do nothing to help, then we are going to have to go somewhere into a wilderness area to live out the rest of our lives and die a very lonely death. We have already changed thing by involving August and Katherine." Letting that sink in, he added, "It is now not a matter of if we change things, it is a matter of how much we are going to change things."

No one said anything. They all just sat around staring into their canteen cups and occasionally taking a little sip. Having said his piece, he went back to his log and sat down. He was watching the rest of the team and could see Wilson wanted to talk, but she, like the others, just sat there.

It was Blake who finally stood up to talk. "Like Sergeant Mitchell said, we have already affected this timeline. We have to decide how far do we go. We don't know what our affect has already had on history. If we plan it carefully, we might affect the future to be better."

Wilson piped up now. "That's a pipe dream. If you think you can control things now and know how it will affect the future, you're crazy or very dumb."

"Maybe," Blake said, "But just think what might happen if we take out a few key people in history. Lee for the south. Without him, the

Civil War might be over after a few battles." He paused for a few seconds and regrouped his thoughts. "Just think of the millions of lives that could be saved if we travel to Germany and take out Hitler as a baby."

"Hitler was Austrian," Wilson said sarcastically, "are we going to kill babies now to change history?"

"To change for the better, yes." Blake shot back at her.

Mitchell could easily see where these two stood. He also thinks he knows where Rodrigues stands. Johnson and Redcloud were blank. As they haven't said anything, yet. Also, he had no way of guessing what their newest group members, August and Katherine, were thinking. They, too, are now part of this band. "I suggest we all sleep on this and talk about it tomorrow night. We still have a couple of months to plan what to do."

Redcloud was the first to get up and leave. As the rest of them drifted away, August came to the group leader with his daughter in tow. "Will you please stay a little while? There are things I must know to help me decide."

"Certainly," he replied and sat back down. "I don't know if I can answer all your questions, and I may also decide there are questions that are best left unanswered, but I will try."

"You said Santa Anna will bring an entire army into Texas and will kill many people who try to fight. What will happen after that?"

"Well, I best I can remember things from my history books. The people in San Antonio give the leader of the Texas army time to form and train his soldiers. He will run from Santa Anna until he finds the right place to fight. Santa Anna will divide his army into smaller parts. Houston…" August interrupted him.

"Sam Houston?" he asked

"Yes, Sam Houston is the leader of the Texas army. Anyway, Houston catches Santa Anna in a terrible place for him and together with Santa Anna's reduced army, he can defeat Santa Anna and capture him. Santa Anna turns out to be a coward and to save himself, he agrees to leave Texas and Texas becomes a country by itself."

Katherine asked, "What happens to this country after that?"

"You do speak English!" He said to her.

"Yes, when I need to, but not very well. My father usually tells me what is said, and I know enough to make sure he tells me right."

Mitchell had to laugh a little at that while August sheepishly smiled at his daughter. "Well, after about ten years, Texas joins the United States and becomes the largest state for many years."

"What about our Fatherland?" August asked.

"My history in Europe, for this time, is not good. Depends on where your hometown is. What we now call Germany gets involved in two major wars that all the major powers of the world will fight. Germany will fight on the losing side against America. However, it will eventually become a great power again and a powerful friend of America, but this is another seventy-five years from now."

They both just sat there thinking about what they had been told and although there was some talk between them, Mitchell got the feeling it was simply a matter of translating some things he said.

Katherine spoke next. "Who was this man they say should die to save millions of lives?"

Wow, it was strange to hear her talk, but she had a very clear mind and asked excellent questions. "His name was Hitler. After the first of the big wars, World War One we called it, Germany is blamed for causing the war and made to pay back the other countries, France, England, Russia and America, mostly. This put Germany and awful shape. The money from Germany became worthless and the German people became furious."

Mitchell was trying not to go into a great deal of detail, but it was difficult not to. "Hitler was an excellent talker and later became powerful and eventually became the leader of Germany. He blamed the Jewish people for all the problems in Germany and used his powers as the leader to gather up all the Jews, first in Germany, and later in most of Europe, and have them killed. He had over six million Jews put to death for no other reason than that they were Jewish."

He could see this had upset both of them strongly. August buried his head in his hands and just sat there shaking his head. Katherine cried and got up to leave.

"Wait," Mitchell quickly said, "as bad as this was, it led Germany into a new future. The world had learned not to put the blame so strongly on a country and the leaders of the other countries learned it was better to help Germany recover from this war and work with them to form a very strong government, like the government in America. Germany is now one of the strongest friend America has in Europe."

Katherine sniffed and wiped her eyes, but continued to head back to their cabin.

August still sat on his log and said, "Thank you Sergeant…"

"Please call me Jim. We are really no longer in the Army of America."

'Thank you, Jim. You have given me much to think about."

With that, he got up and slowly followed his daughter back to the cabin.

Mitchell just sat there, staring into the fire. He picked up a small stick and poked at it a couple of times. Then he heard someone coming up behind him. Redcloud sat on the log that August had been using. "You know I would never go against what you decide is best for the team, but I must agree with Blake. We know what is going to happen for the next almost two hundred and years. If we can change that, then I feel it is our duty to try."

"But what about messing up the timeline and all that other crap?"

"Doesn't matter," he said. "If we change our timeline, maybe it will be for the better. If this is the start of a new timeline, then all the better. We should guide it the best we can."

"Thanks, Chief." He said to Redcloud as he got up to leave.

As Redcloud walked by, he gave his friend a slap on the back and said, "I got this part covered."

This, at least, got Mitchell to smile a little. After a while, he stood up and stirred the fire until the flames were out and drank what little there was in his cup and headed off to his own tent. He, too, had much to think about.

CHAPTER 5

After the first sit-down to talk about things, nobody really talked much for a while. Mostly because by the time everyone had finished dinner, they were all dead tired. This was the hardest any of them had worked in many years, maybe longer for some others. The only one of the team that this didn't appear to bother was Redcloud. He just went about his business and said little to anyone, as usual.

Johnson and Blake were making some headway in repairing the wagon. He had a rough shape of the axle honed out, but the wagon had set so long they were having most of the problems with the metal parts. At the ends of the axle, the metal was greased, and in pretty good shape. The rest of the parts, however, were not. Johnson thought he could put it all together in another week or two. That will still give the group lots of time to get to the trading post and time to figure out what their next move would be.

Rodrigues had given up on trying to make tequila. It was a good idea, but impossible to do in the short time they had. Mitchell thought that was too bad. He felt they all could use some. It turned out the Rodrigues was a fair hunter and worked with Redcloud to help bring in some meat while checking out the horse situation.

Wilson and Katherine were continuing to work the garden and making daily runs out to look for other things the group could eat or use.

Redcloud was doing fairly well with supplying them with meat. The other day, he and Rodrigues brought in a javelin. August had a great time fixing this up for roasting. They all had a good meal that night. Still, while he had seen signs of a couple of good-sized horse herds, he had not actually seen any of the horses. What he saw were some of the local Indians. This was worrisome. Mitchell didn't want to tangle with the locals, and he didn't believe that Redcloud could talk with this bread of Indians. So far, the two of them have only seen a few and could stay out of sight. It would be best if they could just stay away from them.

Redcloud had some ideas about catching the horses by building a large corral in the woods to stay hidden from the herd as they chased them in. Mitchell and the rest didn't know the first thing about catching horses, but if the Chief thinks this has a chance, he was all for it. August and Mitchell began cutting small trees and bringing them to an area where they decided was the best place to build and hide the corral. It didn't need to be very fancy. All they were doing was stringing up the long trees between the other trees in the woods and then staking brush along it to make it look like a wall. So far, they had maybe a quarter of the circle done. There was an opening where they could chase the horses in and then close it off once they were inside. It was a long shot, but it was all they had going for them right now. While Redcloud's hunting was getting them enough food, it was not supplying enough skins to make any worthwhile trades. The horses were still the best bet.

Mitchell was determined to have another sit-down talk with the group tonight. He told the girls to have dinner ready a little early. When he thought it was time, he called a stop to the day's work while there was still plenty of light out. He made sure Redcloud and Rodrigues were back in time to join the discussion. While they were enjoying some of the stew, he announced his intentions for the talk tonight. No one seemed to object. In fact, some of them seemed to want to talk.

Like the last time, they cleaned up and headed for the fire pit. This time, however, they were going to have to do it without the generous donation of alcohol from August. It appears his supply might be getting a little low, and while he was not a stingy man, it didn't appear that he wanted to run out.

After the milling around settled and everyone got their usual seats, Mitchell started with the traditional "I think y'all know why I gathered you here tonight." He used a line from a movie. He remembered where Robert Redford was waiting for the boats he needed. He thought everyone, except August and Katherine, of course, had seen this movie and recognized what he was doing and laughed a little. "You guys have had some time to think over your positions of what you think we should do for our future." He started out.

As he spoke, he moved to the center near the fire and slowly turned so he could look at each of them. "Do we need to discuss this more, or does anyone have anything they want to add to this before we call for a vote?"

No one moved for a little while. It didn't look like any of them really wanted to start this again. It was August who finally stood up and asked, "Do I get to say anything as part of this group now?"

"Certainly August, we all may speak our minds. Go right ahead and say your piece."

August stepped up next to the fire pit and looked around. "As I understand, you say you are worried about the future of this time. I have talked much with Jim here and a couple of you as well. My daughter and I have talked a great deal about his. You are worried about your future, but this is not your future. This is the future for me and my daughter. From what I have learned, there are many wonderful things in the future. Things we cannot understand." He said, pointing to Katherine. "I don't think these wonderful things will change too much no matter what we do, but you have a chance to change some of the terrible things I have learned about. If Mr. Blake is right, it will not matter to your time. What's done is done, but it will make a great deal of difference to my time."

With his final passionate words, he slowly turned and went back to his seat. It appeared everyone was surprised at the clarity in which he spoke. Mitchell was thinking he was not the uneducated old man he had led them to believe he was.

It took Mitchell a moment to gather his thoughts to say anything, but he made his way to the center again. "Anyone else have anything to say?"

Wilson stuck her hand up, but only for a moment. She quickly pulled it back down and sat with it in her lap. It was obvious she wanted to say something, but Mitchell thought she was still very uncertain about how she feels.

"No one," he paused, "OK then. Let have a vote. I don't know how everyone wants to do this. Do we use pebbles or paper to mark our votes, or will a simple show of hands do?"

Most everyone either said hands or showed by raising their hand. "Anyone object to a show of hands?" he asked.

No one spoke up, so he put the question out there. "We all know what this vote is for. Do we go south to San Antonio and help those boys out? From there, we will decide what our next step will be."

He did a quick look around the group, and everyone nodded back to him as they understood. "OK then, all in favor of helping the Alamo raise your hands."

"Alamo?" Katherine asked.

"Sorry," he said, looking at her, "The Alamo is the place in San Antonio where the battle will be fought."

As he slowly looked at each of them, they each raised their hands to show the yes vote. He had saved Wilson for last. "I know you have concerns, but you didn't voice them. Have you made your decision?"

"I have a question. What will happen if I vote no?"

"We have to make this a unanimous decision. The only option I can think of is we decide a place that we know will not be settled for some time to come and go there and live out our lives with no outside contact."

Wilson hung her head down and he was afraid she would vote no. "I came here tonight fully intending to vote no. August's little speech gave me a point I hadn't considered before. He is right. This is not our time, this is his. If he is willing to possibly sacrifice some of the good things to correct the future, then who am I to say no?" She then slowly raised her hand.

"OK folks, the vote passes. We go to the Alamo. If August is right about the day, it will New Year's Day in about a week. We need to be there well before the end of February." H paused a moment. "Oh, and by the way, Merry Christmas to each of you. I'm sorry I don't have a gift your you, but I have had little chance to go shopping lately."

Everyone broke out in wishes of Merry Christmas, lifting the mood.

After the little impromptu party let up, Mitchell called his second over to him. "Chief, soon we're going to be going into battle. Most, if not all, these guys haven't ever been there. August and Katherine have never even touched our weapons. We need to start a training program to get everyone up to speed. Also, I'd like you to teach your martial arts to everyone."

"You want me to teach this to August and his daughter? That might be a problem. I can teach them some basic defense and maybe a couple combat move, but they are going to be far from experts."

"That will do just fine."

"As for the rest of the group, we only have a few days to get them in shape. Other than Wilson, none of them have had any kind of martial arts training. I can teach them the same as the Schmidt's."

"Fine."

"What about weapons training? We only have a finite number of rounds. Once they are gone, we are done?"

"Yes indeed, I know. Our guys don't need it other than some practice drills. Teach Katherine to load mags and teach August how to use the rifle. Let him fire a couple round. At least enough to zero the weapon."

"OK Boss, you got it." He spoke. "I'll see what I can pull together. I'll have Wilson train his daughter in fighting. Wilson is quite good, and she'll do just fine."

"Probably best if you take them for a couple hours in the morning, before we start work."

"Got it, Boss. Are you going to join us?" he asked with a smile.

"Maybe from time to time. I've got a couple of other things I'm thinking about."

Shortly, everyone had partied out and went off to bed.

It must have been only a couple minutes ago, Mitchell thought. He had just gone to sleep. The sound of Redcloud getting everyone up woken him up. A bunch of complaining and a few mumbled hard words for the Chief followed this, but no one dared to say it out loud. Not even Mitchell.

"OK, boys and girl. Today, we are going to start a training program. No more sleeping in late. We're going to start with a brief run. Everyone, grab your weapons and report next to the well in 5 minutes." Redcloud shouted at everyone.

Wow, surprise, another round of cursing, a little louder this time. Redcloud just looked away with a smile. Mitchell saw August come out of the cabin and even in this dim light, he could see he was a little confused. He put on a great big smile and walked over to where August was waiting. "Good morning." He shouted to him as he got a little closer. Even though he said it in a very pleasant voice, he didn't think August appreciated being woken up so early.

"What is happening?" August asked as Mitchell got close.

"I put Redcloud in charge of training everyone. Soon we are going to be in battle. Wilson is the only one who has even had a little combat experience. I need to get everyone up to speed before we head off to San Antonio."

"That sounds like a good idea, but does he need to make so much noise so early in the morning?"

"Well, yes." Mitchell said and then took a step closer to him and whispered, "But, don't worry about it. You'll get used to it, because I've asked him to train you and Katherine, as well."

"What?" August was taken back. "What kind of training? I've lived most of my life in this wilderness. I know how to fight."

"Yes, I know you know how to fight your way. We must teach you to fight our way, with our tactics and our weapons."

That got his attention. "You mean I am going to lean about that rifle?"

"That and a few other things. Things you never thought possible before. We might even teach you how to drive the truck."

"Truck?" He asked.

"Yeah, that thing that scared the shit out of you when my team showed up."

He shot a look of fear over at the duce. Following his gaze, Mitchell said, "No, the little one. We call it a Hummer." But before he could ask, Mitchell held his hand up to stop him. "Don't ask why it's called that. It just is."

He looked at the hummer and got a little smile on his face and rubbed his hands together. Mitchell couldn't help but to think that this might actually be fun. "Wilson is going to be teaching your daughter. Not everything that you'll be learning, but there are some things she will have to know if she is going to be with us."

August just kept looking at the hummer and nodding his head. Mitchell wasn't sure how much actually sunk in right now, but once the Chief gets a hold of him, he was sure it will all sink in real fast.

After the initial idea had worn off, August saw the team taking off on a run. He turned back to Mitchell and asked, "Where are they going?"

"Every soldier needs to stay in shape. They must have the ability to keep fighting long after the enemy is tired." August just nodded, so he continued, "One of the best ways to get in shape is to run. The Chief is taking them on about a one-mile run. Tomorrow, you'll get to go with them."

That got his attention back to me. "I'm too old to run like that."

"Yes, maybe," Mitchell answered back as they watched the group run, "but you'll still try it. Also, try to find some pants for Katherine. It will be too difficult for her to run in that dress. Maybe Wilson will have some pants she can wear."

"You are going to teach my daughter all these things, too?" He was genially shocked to think of his daughter doing these things.

"Yes, of course." He then paused a moment to gather his thought about how to tell him. "August, my friend, we may not be from this time, but I fully intend to bring in some ideas from my time. In my time, women are equal to men. I have found that, in some cases, women perform better than men. Sergeant Wilson is an outstanding soldier. She is taking special training from Redcloud to learn to fight, and she is quite good. She is an excellent shot with about all of our weapons and she is a good leader."

August just grunted a little and shuffled his feet, kicking up the dirt.

Mitchell continued, "Wilson will do most of the training for your daughter, so you don't need to worry about her. Once she starts the training for your daughter, Wilson won't allow anything to happen to her. That's how she is. Also, except for Redcloud and maybe myself, she is more than capable if whooping up on any of the others who might try something. "

"She is that good?" he asked.

He just simply nodded with a very proud "Yep."

August grunted again and asked, "Will my daughter be able to do all these things?"

Mitchell knew he needed to be careful how he answered him. He wanted to insure him that what she learns will help her survive, but it would take years to be the same level as Wilson.

"Probably not right away. It has taken Wilson a couple of years to get to where she is. Also, she came from a life that allowed women to do these things, so in her mind it was alright for her to learn these things. Your daughter will learn a lot of new things in the short time we have, but I think the biggest problem for her will be that at this time she has been told all her life that women do not do these things."

Again, Mitchell wasn't sure he understood what was being said, but August nodded, and they both quietly watched as the team ran around the hillside until they were out of sight.

After the run, they all sat down for breakfast. It wasn't much, but Mitchell still enjoyed the horrible coffee that came in the MRE packs. While sipping his coffee, he heard a little chatter about the new program, so he figured this was now as good a time as any to break it to them.

"OK guys, as you noticed this morning, we started training again." He had to wait to continue until all the bitching had died down. "You are still soldiers and we are going to be going into battle. Other than Redcloud and I, none of you have ever been close to an actual battle. We need to keep up with the training and we need to get our newest members of the group trained." He said, looking right at August and Katherine, but then added, "at least a little training."

Katherine looked at Mitchell and he knew she had some questions, but he could see she was too shy to ask. "Yes, Katherine, you have a question?"

As soon as he said that, every eye at the table turned to her and she slumped back down and looked at the ground. He could see this was going to take some time for her to get used to the idea.

"Katherine, Sergeant Wilson will do your training. She is very good, and I think you will learn a lot from her. In our time, it is not uncommon for women to do these kinds of things. Women have learned there is not much that they cannot do if allowed to do it. No, you will not have the same skills as Sergeant Wilson or even the rest of these guys, but it may give you the skills you'll need to help you survive what is coming."

She now looked a little relieved and even manages a little smile at the group. "Wilson, do you have an extra pair of pants for our new trainee?" He said with a smile.

Wilson smiled and nodded. She got up and ran over to her tent and came back with a full combat uniform. Katherine was only a little smaller than Wilson, so he figured they will fit just fine.

Katherine took the uniform from Wilson with a polite thank you and just sat there looking at it. "Well, go try it on." Mitchell said to her.

The rest of the team shouted for her also, but she didn't move. Wilson went over and stood behind her and shouted, "Knock it off!" to the group, and the shouting stopped immediately. She then took Katherine's arm and lead her back to the cabin. It took about 15 minutes before they came back out. Wilson had helped her put on the uniform and she looked just like a proper soldier. The rest of the team stood up and applauded her as they both walked up to the table.

"We only have a few pieces of clothing for now, so I only want you to wear this while you are training. The rest of the time, you can wear your normal clothes." He told her. "As for the rest of you, remember we don't have the PX here. If you tear your uniform and break something, we have no way of replacing it. I suggest you all learn how to sew."

Even Katherine laughed a little at that. "You all know your assignments, so let's get to work."

"Wilson," Mitchell called her over before she could walk away. "I want you to first teach her how to load the mags. I think that is a simple enough thing for her to do right now. Also, start teaching her some basic defensive moves so she can at least protect herself. Play it by ear and see what you can do with her."

"I've been working with her for a week now. I think she may be capable of doing a lot more than you think." Wilson said, looking over at Katherine. "Permission to adjust the training as I feel I can."

"Granted," He said, "but keep me in the loop."

"You got it, Boss," she said as she turned to walk away, but then turned back. "Oh, by the way, I've taken to calling her Kat. She said that it was OK, and I think she likes it."

"Kat, ok I'll try to remember."

Mitchell smiled at the thought of Kat as a fighting member of the Alamo. That will make a strange entry into the new history books.

He turned and headed over to Johnson to see if they needed any help. Right now, that was the most important thing for them to get fixed.

Johnson and Blake are doing just fine, so he headed out to the woods to help Redcloud build the corral for capturing the horses. He knew this needed to get done quickly as well.

It was an enjoyable stroll out to where they were working. Mitchell could look around and calm his mind for a little while. It seems like forever since he was last able to do that. Oh, but it was too short of a walk. In no time, he was there. Redcloud had been attaching the logs to the horse and dragging them to where Rodrigues was running them from tree to tree and tying them up.

They got a rhythm going and making good headway, but then August came running up. He first came up to Redcloud and was pointing back towards the cabin while he was bent over, trying to catch his breath. Mitchell grabbed his rifle and ran back to the two of them. Rodrigues saw what was going on and came running, as well.

"What's up?" He shouted as he got close enough.

Redcloud pointed back towards the cabin. "I don't know. Most of what he is saying is coming out in German and the rest I can't make out because he is so out of breath. All he can do clearly is point back over there."

So, Mitchell signaled for Rodrigues to head for the edge of the woods and the four of them started running that way. Mitchell could see Rodrigues hit the dirt just as he got to the edge of the woods. He turned back and signaled for the rest of them to get down, but to keep coming. Redcloud and Mitchell had left August in the dust and were making their way, jumping from tree to tree. He didn't know if August saw what we were doing, but he kind of copied them.

As they got near Rodrigues, he pointed to his eyes and held up four fingers, and then pointed at the hill on the other side of the stream. Mitchell slowed his pace and got close enough to see what was going on. There were four Indians on horseback, slowly riding down the hill towards the cabin.

Just then, Redcloud came up and joined his old friend, who just pointed at the Indians.

Redcloud just gave him a little sneer and said, "Yeah Boss, I can see them."

"Well, you're the Indian expert. What do you make of it?"

He brought out the binoculars and studied them for a moment. "I'd guess they are not dangerous. They don't have weapons drawn. They look to be just checking things out." He again looked at them through the binoculars and continued. "I don't know this tribe, but I don't see any signs of trouble, like war paint and such."

"Rodrigues, you and August stay here to cover us. Redcloud and I are going to walk down there and see if we can communicate with them." Mitchell said to him, and he nodded back his understanding.

"August," Mitchell then said to the old man as he came up to where we were, "You stay with Rodrigues and follow what he says."

"Are you sure?" he asked.

"No, but my expert here thinks they are not looking for trouble, but we'll be ready if they try anything."

Turning back to Redcloud, he said, "Lead on. You're one of their kind. Maybe they'll be more willing to talk with you."

"Yeah, right!" Redcloud said, rather sarcastically, looking down at his uniform. He started walking down towards their new friends and Mitchell followed right behind him.

They were carrying their rifles at port, just in case. He didn't want to start trouble, however, if there is trouble, he wanted to be ready.

The Indians had stopped short of the stream and three of them got off their horses and started walking to the stream. The other one stayed on his horse and held the other's horses. A lookout would be the guess.

Just as they got to the stream, Wilson came out of the cabin with her rifle at the shoulder. Blake and Johnson saw what she was doing and grabbed their rifles and joined her. Mitchell waved his arms to get their attention and waved for them to lower their weapons. He guessed one of them saw him and they dropped their rifles down, but kept them at the ready, however.

Mitchell figured the lookout saw him. He could hear him shout something to the others and they ran back and jumped up on their horses. They turned to and started riding slowly toward the two strange men. After a little, Redcloud and Mitchell stopped and waited for them. As they got closer, Redcloud made a sign to them, but they didn't respond. Redcloud slowly cradled his rifle across his body and just raised up one open hand. Just like they did in the movies.

This time, the Indians stopped. They all just stood their ground a short time while each side was trying to figure the other out. Mitchell was the first to make a move. He copied what Redcloud had done and slowly walked toward them. When he was about halfway there, one of them hollered something and they all turned and rode off back up the hill at high speed. Well, high speed for a horse.

Mitchell turned back to Redcloud and put his shoulders up. Redcloud just laughed a little and said, "They're probably scared of the strange white man."

Mitchell turned back and watched as they rode back over the top of the hill.

Redcloud had walked up to him and said, "My guess is they are a simple hunting party, and they weren't ready for trouble, however," he paused a moment, still watching the hill, "they could be back, and with friends and ready for a fight."

"We'll need to post guards, day and night." Mitchell, as the group leader, said to him without looking back at him. "You need to have the guys ready, so they'll know what to expect and what to look for."

"You're probably right." Was all he said in reply as he turned to return to his work.

"I'm going to head back to the cabin and talk with the others. Keep August with you to keep watch while you work."

"You got it, Boss."

While he was walking back to the cabin, Kat came out carrying one of their rifles. Mitchell then remembered when they first met, she was helping August defend their house. If she can do that, then she can also learn to fight with this group.

"What do you think they wanted?" Wilson asked as Mitchell walked up.

"My guess is they are just looking us over, right now." As Blake and Rodrigues walked up, he added, "Chief thinks they may have been a hunting party and not out here looking to cause trouble. However, this doesn't mean they can't go home and grab some friends and come back ready to fight."

Everyone just looked at each other. "From now on, I want one person on watch at all times. Kat, Sergeant Wilson said it was alright to call you Kat?"

She just nodded to him with a cute little smile.

"Kat, I want you to do most of the watching while the others' work."

That got an immediate node back.

"Wilson, tomorrow I want you to show Kat how to use one of our rifles. Teach her the basics, and after her father is up to speed, we'll take them out and let them try a couple of rounds to zero."

Wilson looked back at Kat and told her in German what Mitchell had said. Kat broke out into this great big smile and ran up and gave him a hug and then ran back to the cabin.

Embarrassed a little, Mitchell said, "I'm guessing she liked that idea."

Wilson smiled back and said, "Boss, you have no idea. She was not happy when I told her that all she was going to do was learn how to load the mags. I think she has just as much, if not more, fight in her than her father does."

"Yeah, I'm seeing that." Then he looked over at Blake and Johnson, who were just standing there with big smiles on their faces. He shouted to them, "OK, back to work. The fun time is over."

Everyone got a laugh out of that, even though he hadn't said it to be funny, and went back to whatever they were doing.

Walking back to help Redcloud some more, Mitchell had to laugh just a little, as well. His mind drifted back to the moment that Kat gave him the hug and thought how nice that felt. He couldn't help but to think that he hoped it wasn't the same type of hug she gave to her father.

About noon, everyone headed back to the cabin and sat down for some lunch. Mostly, it was MREs with a little help from the garden, but the pickings in the garden were getting slim. "Johnson," Mitchell said, looking at him, "how long before you think you'll have the wagon ready?"

He looked back over his shoulder to his work area, saying, "I think we might have it ready in a week, if everything goes just right."

"Great, our supplies are getting low, and we need to think about heading out to the trading post." He then stopped and looked at Redcloud. "How long before you think well have something to trade with?"

"Well, boss, I'd say the corral will be ready in a couple of days. The problem is we don't really know where the horses are, and we only have the one horse to catch them."

"Well, that's not entirely accurate. We have lots of horses in the hummer." He let that set in a moment. "We can also use the drone to search for them."

That brought Redcloud up. Mitchell guessed he had forgotten about the drone. "But Boss, we don't have anyone trained to fly that thing."

"Yeah, I know, but how difficult could it be to just go up, look around and come back down?"

Rodrigues spoke up now, "Sergeant Mitchell,"

Mitchell interrupted him and said, "Everyone try, Boss. That appears to be the name I'm going to be stuck with." And then shot a smile at both Redcloud and Wilson. He didn't know which of them came up with that, but he kind of liked it over Sergeant.

"Ok, Boss." He said back with a sheepish smile, "before I transferred here, I had just got a little training on drones. Not this particular model, but one that was similar."

"Great, we now have an expert."

"I wouldn't say I'm an expert."

"When you're the only person we've got that's ever tried this before, then you're our expert." He said, pointing at Rodrigues with a smile.

Rodrigues just smiled back and nodded.

They spent the rest of lunch time talking about the excitement this morning with the visit from the Indians. Mitchell broke in and said to their Indian expert, "Chief, what do you think about this visit this morning?"

Redcloud just continued to chew on his food for a moment, then slowly said, "It's hard to say. I don't know much about these locals around here. All I can do is to compare them with what I know about my people." Everyone had their eyes glued to Redcloud now. "I would expect them to be watching us. I am a little more than certain they left one to monitor us right now."

That got some head turned around to check out the countryside.

Redcloud continued, "August, have you had any trouble with the local tribes of Indians?"

"I'd say we have had a little trouble with some of them." August replied slowly while he thought about it. "Lately there's been a group of, I think they are called, Apache."

"Apache's," Redcloud responded and soon as he heard the name. "Not good Boss. The Apache's gave the settlers in the southwest quite a problem. They are not very friendly with the white man."

"August, are you sure they are Apache?" Mitchell asked August.

"That is what I think a man called them, and Mister Redcloud is right. They are not a friendly group of people."

Looking back at Redcloud, he asked, "What do you think our next move should be, then? I don't want to be surprised. We need to be proactive about our defenses."

Redcloud sat back and thought about that a little and then sat up. "I think you're right, Boss. We cannot let them catch us with our pants down."

Kat giggled a little at that one.

Redcloud continued, "If they come at us with a small war party, then we shouldn't have any problems if we're ready. However, if it's a large force, then we are going to have a fight on our hands."

Everyone remained fixed on what Redcloud was saying now.

He leaned forward to keep everyone's attention. "These are some very bad dudes. They are trained from childhood to do nothing but fight and survive. As I recall, they are masters of deception and diversion. They like to attack from behind and they are quiet and quick, but mostly they are deadly." He let this all sink in and then continued, "Your modern weapons will do you absolutely no good if you don't see them coming. "

"Thanks Chief." Mitchell stood up because he wanted everyone to realize the situation has now changed. "Until now, we have been very lucky. Even today we were lucky to have only a curious hunting party come to check us out. I don't think we can rely on luck anymore. From now on, there are some new rules. No one is to go out alone. A minimum of two people, always. Everyone is to have their weapon and at least two full mags, at all times. There will be a lookout posted, probably on top of the cabin or some other prominent place, at all times. At night, we'll use the night vision, but because of the battery situation, we'll have to use them sparingly."

Mitchell thought that just about covered everything for now, but just then, August raised his hand. "And what are my daughter and I supposed to do? We understand nothing of you have been talking about."

He really didn't have a simple answer for him right now. "August, until we can get you some training, I don't know that there is much you can do."

"We can help to lookout. We both have eyes and don't need any training how to use them."

Mitchell had to smile at that. "Yes, you can help with the lookout, but I think it may surprise you, even about that. First thing in the morning, though, you and your daughter are getting some weapons training. I think we need to move this up in priority, given the new situation."

He saw both of them smile at that, but before he could turn to look at his daughter, she turned her head and looked down to hide her smile. August just rubbed his hands together and sat back down.

"People, I suggest we all get back to work. We have lots to do and our schedule just got bumped up. I'll be around shortly to assign watches. Blake, you did the inventory. Before you go, I need you to find me two night-vision goggles and extra batteries."

"You got it Sarge, I know right where they are."

"One last thing before we all take off. Names. We need to get our names together. We are no longer in the Army. Most of you can call my Boss, however I would prefer it if some of you used Jim. I may still call each of you by your last names until I can get used to first names. If you have a nickname, we can use that. For example, Sergeant Redcloud has always been called The Chief, or just Chief. Unless he has any objections, I suggest we use that."

Redcloud just put his hands up and said, "Sounds OK to me."

"Katherine, I understand Wilson has said it is alright if we call you Kat?"

She just nodded her head and smiled

"August, I think August fits you just fine, unless you have something else you would like us to call you."

"August is my name, and it will be my name until I die. I don't see any reason to use any other name."

"Good enough," Mitchell said smiling, "As for the rest of you, I have only known you a short time and only know your last names. How would you like us to call you?"

Wilson stood up and said, "My first name is Anna. I think I would like to use that."

"Anna it is." He said and looked at Blake next.

"Johnny." He simply said.

"Johnny," Mitchell repeated back to him, "I'll try to remember."

Johnson was next. "My first name is Milton, but most people call me Stretch. I would like to use Stretch."

Given he was over 6 feet tall, everyone could see that the name was right for him. "OK, Stretch it is."

Rodrigues was that last one to say, "My name is Jose. I will just stick with that."

"Well, real names work for August, so Jose it is."

Mitchell didn't know if the others had thought much about it before. As they cleared the table and headed back to work, he could hear a couple of them talking about their names. He didn't think the part about not really being in the Army any more had sunk in. However, he thought this may help to bring this group together a little better. It feels more like a family now, to him anyway.

The rest of the afternoon went by with no problems and supper was silent. Mitchell thought everyone may be too tired to talk much. After they ate, everyone went off to bed. He took the first watch so could make sure the night vision worked fine. Redcloud relieved him in two hours, and he immediately crashed, almost before he could get in his tent.

Morning came early again. This time, there was not so much noise about getting up and working out. The Chief got everyone in formation, if you could call it that. But before he could get them turned to start off on the run, August and Kat came out. Kat was in her uniform and looked like she fit in with the group. August, however, stuck out like the sore thumb. Mitchell didn't know that there was anything they could do about that. They had nothing he thought would fit him. He was a big man, both tall and wide. Mitchell just decided he was going to have to do with what he had.

The late comers just got in line with the rest. He decided he was going to go on the run with them this morning. Not only did he need it, but he also wanted to see how each of his group was doing. The Chief gave them a right face and once August figured out which side was his right; they were off.

The run was not a tough run this morning. Mitchell thought Redcloud toned it down a little for their newcomers. However, after they got around the hill, Redcloud signaled them to stop and spread out. The group didn't do too badly. Only August and Kat didn't know what was going on. Mitchell came up to them and told them to get down and stay low. He then made his way up to Redcloud, who was looking over the ground.

"What's up, Chief?" He asked him.

He just pointed to hoofprints in the dirt. "Looks like our band of Indians from yesterday." He then looked up and pointed off the way the tracks were headed. "Looks like they headed southwest."

Mitchell followed his look, but then the Chief moved a little further away and he moved up to stay with him.

Pointing to the ground again "Here's a single set of tracks heading back to the cabin. I'll bet this is the lookout they left behind."

"No bet." Mitchell said back to him, looking toward the tracks. "You think you can follow his tracks?"

"Yeah, probably, but what do I do when I find him?"

That was a question Mitchell wasn't ready to answer. He'd never been in this kind of situation before. He didn't know if they should preemptively take him out or try to catch him. "What do you think?"

Redcloud studied the tracks for a little while and then stood up. "He doesn't want any trouble right now. He is alone and outnumbered. However, if we go after him, he will attack, and someone may get hurt. I think we should just let him be for now and wait to meet all of them on our own ground."

It sounded like good advice, but he didn't like the idea of letting him just sit there and watch them. Mitchell then said, "When we get back, we can see if we can spot him with the drone and then keep track of him.

Going back to the group, Mitchell explained what was going on. "Rodrigues," He paused, "I mean Jose, are the batteries charged with the drone?"

"I don't know, Boss. I didn't check them." If it was put away properly, it should be charged and ready for use, but I don't know what might have happened when we were sent back."

Good point. Mitchell could only hope that only the electronics that were on and running were damaged. The batteries in the hummer and duce were OK. "When we get back, I want you to run a check right away."

"Sure thing, Boss." He said, then added, "Are we expecting trouble?"

"No, but they have a lookout out here, and I just want to keep track of him."

Rodrigues just gave the Boss a thumbs up and they were soon back off and running.

Mitchell had to drop back to stay with August. At first, Kat wanted to stay with her father, but he told her he'd watch her father and to stay with the group. He didn't do too bad for an old man who had done nothing like this before, but he thought, tomorrow he is going to be hurting some.

When he and August finally got back, Rodrigues came up and said, "The batteries are just fine, and I've already found our friend. He's hiding in the brush about one hundred and fifty yards to the south."

"I didn't tell you to send it up to look for him. I don't want them to know we have that thing yet."

"No problem, Boss. I didn't send it up. Blake was holding it while I checked the batteries on the drone and the control. While it was on, I found him just sitting next to a tree and watching us."

"Good work." He said, "and sorry about jumping on you about it. I guess I'm a little jumpy. This is all new to me, as well."

Mitchell just left it at that and went to find Redcloud. He explained what Rodrigues told him. "What do you think we should do?"

"Just keep tract of him and when he goes away, we'll know his buddies have shown up. If he doesn't think we know about him and we don't spook him. It should be easy to watch him, watch us."

"That sounds like a plan. He doesn't know what we can do, so he's not hiding. This shouldn't be too difficult. I'll have the others check on him a couple times a day using the same process they used to find him."

"Yeah, that works for now. Have you decided what to do when his buddies show up?"

"Not really, I'm just making this up as I go." Mitchell said and smiled as he turned to walk away.

Lunch time came around and everyone gathered for lunch. It was a little quiet now and everyone was looking at the spot where their friend was.

"Listen guys," Mitchell started out rather abruptly, "if you keep staring at him, he is going to get the idea we're on to him and move. Don't worry about him. He will do nothing until his friends show up. All we have to do is keep an eye on him."

"What if we lose him?" Blake said.

"If we lose him, we find him. We have technology he can't even dream of. We can find him by his body heat, day or night, rain or shine." He said, trying to keep things a little light. "Come on guys, lighten up a little. I'll let you know when it is time to worry. Right now, it is only time to stay alert. Worry will come later." He said, smiling.

Some of the team smiled back, but he couldn't tell if they were real or fake smiles.

"You can do these things you say?" August asked.

"Yes, but the problem is it all runs on electricity, and we only have a limited supply of that."

"What is electricity?" Kat asked slowly, trying to pronounce the word correctly.

"You know what lightning is?" He asked.

She nodded back.

"Lightning is electricity. It is an enormous amount of electricity. We have learned to use just little bits of it to power things. We can save the electricity in things called batteries and use it to power our tools. Our problem is that once we use the electricity in a battery up, we don't have a way to get more."

Kat continued to nod as he explained. Again, he wasn't certain she understood it all.

"Do you understand?" He asked.

"Yes, I think I understand some of what you say. I don't understand how to use it."

"Maybe when we teach you some of our things, you will understand more."

"Maybe." She smiled and got up to leave the table.

"Jose, after lunch, see if you can still see our friend up there."

Redcloud handed him the binoculars, and Rodrigues quickly located the lookout. "Yep, he's still right where he was before." He handed the glasses back to Redcloud and added, "I would think he must be getting hungry about now or his friends are coming back sooner than we thought."

Mitchell looked up the hill to where he was watching them. "Hadn't thought about it that way. What do you think, Chief?"

"Not sure, but worth keeping a closer eye on him. You know you can see that area from the window in the cabin. Someone could sit in there and watch his every move."

"Good idea. After lunch, I'll show Kat how to use the binoculars and she can watch him all afternoon."

Kat had just come back and heard what he said. She lit up like a thousand-watt bulb. Then Mitchell turned. He didn't want her to think much of it, so he just smiled and nodded and went on talking about other little things until lunch was over.

After they had cleaned up and everyone headed back to work, he motioned Kat to follow him into the cabin. Once they were there, he took the binoculars out of the case and showed her how to focus and adjust the lenses. She caught on quickly and as soon as she took her first look, he couldn't get her to stop so he could explain what he wanted her to do. She kept looking all around. When she turned to look at him, he thought it scared her. He hadn't explained that looking at something close through these might be strange. She jumped back and if he hadn't been there, the binoculars might have been on the floor.

"You must be very careful with these. They can break very easily." he then stepped close to her and put the strap around her neck. This was the first time he had been that close to her since they got here, other than the quick hug she gave him. He was feeling a little strange. He thought, for a moment, maybe she was feeling the same thing because her face turned bright red, and she stepped back and put her head down. "I'm sorry. I didn't mean to upset you."

She looked him right in the eye and whispered, "You didn't upset me.", and then looked back at the floor.

Just then, August came into the cabin. "What's this?" he asked.

"I was just showing Kat how to use these and telling her to stay in the cabin and watch our friend up there on the hill."

"Oh, she gets to use your tools before me?" he said.

Mitchell wasn't sure if he was serious or playing with him. "I don't think they will notice if a woman isn't outside doing things. If you suddenly went away, I think he might notice."

August thought about that for a moment and then smiled and nodded. Mitchell quickly added, "You know, when she needs to take a break, you could come in for a short time to give her a break." That seemed to satisfy the big man and he appeared to be happy about that.

Mitchell then told her to have Wilson call him if there were any changes and he left to go help Redcloud with the corral. Before he walked out the door, he looked back to see how she was doing and found her with the binoculars in place, staring at the hill.

Mitchell went over to the hummer and grabbed two of the radios. He handed one to Wilson and put the other in his pocked. This was a little faster than August trying to run messages up the hill to where we were working.

It was late afternoon, and they had made a lot of headway on the corral. Mitchell thought by tomorrow they might have it finished.

Suddenly, the radio cracked. "This is Wilson. Can you hear me?"

"Yeah, I hear you just fine, what up?"

"Our friend now has company." Wilson was all business now.

"Copy. Heading back. Just have everyone act normally until we get there."

"No problem. Kat and I are the only ones that know right now."

"Good. Keep it that way until we get there."

"Roger, out." and she was gone.

Mitchell called Redcloud and Rodrigues over and explained to them what was happening. He told them to wait until he was about halfway to the cabin and then for them to follow him down. He didn't want to spook the Indians by having all of them come back at once.

Once he got back, Mitchell went into the cabin and Kat handed him the binoculars. He checked it out and saw there were two others with their friend up on the hill. They were keeping low, but not really trying to hide. He could now see three together, but how many of them were there in total? That was the big question.

After supper, everyone gathered around the fire pit for a little while. Mitchell had to let them know the situation now that things had changed and there was a very good chance they would be attacked. "Okay guys, things have changed." He waited a moment to continue. He wanted to make sure he had everybody's undivided attentions. "Our friend up on the hill now has his friends with him."

All at once, just about everyone turned and looked up the hill. Mitchell thought it was probably dim enough that they couldn't really see anyone at this distance, but just in case "Yeah, that's right, let everyone turn and look so they know we know." That quickly snapped everyone back around.

"Now I have a plan of action." Looking at Rodrigues, he asked, "Jose, is the drone ready?" And Jose just nodded. "Great, when we break up, I want to try it out and see if we can look at our friends up there."

"I've never flown at night. I don't know if I can do that."

"Look, there is no one else to try. Also, there is nothing to interfere with this. We will not try to get close to them. We fly high, get a location and count, and land. A very simple plan."

"I guess I can try to do that." He said, reluctantly.

"No sweat, it will be a piece of cake." Mitchell said, confident that he could do it.

Talking to the rest of the group now, "Soon I want everyone to head off to bed. Blake..."

Blake interrupted him, "Johnny."

"OK, Johnny, you grab the drone and set it in the open out in front of the cabin and head to bed. Jose, you and the Chief head for my tent with the controller."

August raised his hand and asked, "May I come to watch?"

Thinking a moment, Mitchell said, "Yeah, I suppose that would be alright. What do you think, Chief?"

Redcloud thought a moment, then said, "If the fire is low enough, they shouldn't be able to see us."

August just smiled and rubbed his hands together again.

"The rest of you are to be ready to head out. If things look favorable, we are going to head up there and take them on. Blake, after you place the drone, get everyone a set of night vision and then wait in your tent. Everyone will wait in their tents until we scope it out. I'll let you know what's happening then. Questions?"

There were the expected looks around at each other, but no one had questions.

"Kat and Anna, I want you ladies to head out now. The rest of us are going to put out the fire before we take off."

Johnson must have been a city boy. "Why is it just us putting out the fire?"

Redcloud laughed a little, and said, "Because it is very difficult for girls to pee on a fire."

Kat was the only one that didn't laugh. Mitchell thought she might be a little embarrassed to hear talk like that. Johnson just put his head down. He was also a little embarrassed.

With that, Wilson walked Kat back to the cabin and then went to her tent. The boys began putting out the fire. They didn't have enough to finish the job, but the flames we gone, with only the gentle glow on the embers left. Blake went off to do his chores and Rodrigues went to get the controller. Johnson went to his tent.

With Mitchell's tent closed up and very crowded, Rodrigues turned on the controller. The screen lit up, but there wasn't anything showing. "Switch to thermal." Mitchell told him.

Rodrigues flipped a switch, and the screen got brighter, but still not much else to see. "OK, take it up to about 200 feet and hover." He spoke.

Rodrigues played with the controls and soon they could clearly see the cabin and then the tents and the heat from all of their bodies.

August muttered something, but Mitchell's German was not good enough to understand him. Rodrigues looked up at August and said, "Oh, brother, you ain't seen nothing yet."

"OK, good." Mitchel said as it reached altitude. "Slowly rotate and move to the south, where our friends should be."

Rodrigues did as he was told. As it moved over the stream, they could see some little animal in the field beyond. He had to adjust the altitude as it got closer to the hill. Once he was over the top of the hill, they could still not see the rest of them.

"Pan around to the area and let's see if we can find them."

Rodrigues made a full circle of the area, but there was nothing in sight. "Get higher and look around again." Mitchell said to him.

Jose continued to rotate as he gained altitude. Shortly, there was a hot spot in the viewer. Mitchell just tapped him on his shoulder and when Jose looked at him, he motioned for him to move that way.

Once closer, they could see there were twelve distinct body signatures. They were all grouped together and appeared to be sleeping. Once the drone was above them, Mitchell motioned him to get higher and to rotate.

After he got a little higher and their field of view opened, they could see one more hot spot. Rodrigues moved closer to this one. Once he was close enough, they could see the body moving. Thinking he could hear the sound of the drone, Mitchell told Rodrigues to back off and come home.

"Chief, what do you think?"

Redcloud thought for a moment, then said, "We can take them out with no problems. Would someone get hurt? Maybe, but there is always that chance." He then slowly added, "Should we take them out first or wait for them to move?"

"August," Mitchell said, "What do you think they will do?"

"I believe they are going to attack us, probably first thing in the morning."

"I think you are right." Mitchell said to him and then added to the others, "We are going to have to take them out first tonight."

Looking around, he could see that everyone here agreed. "Chief, do you think you can get up there and quietly take out their watch?"

"I think I probably can, but just in case, you guys should be in place first." And then in the air he drew a picture. "If you move out to the south and then sweep around to their camp, you should be there in less than two hours. Once you are in place, I'll move in from the other way and take him out. Once he's gone, I'll join you and we'll capture the rest in one move."

"Good plan, except I don't want to capture any of them. We don't have resources to keep them under guard and I don't suspect they will just give up. We are to take them down, permanently."

Even in the dark inside of the tent, he could see Redcloud didn't like this idea. "I'm sorry, Chief, but this is not a normal situation. You said you can't talk to them, and I don't believe they will be much in the mood for talking, anyway. They are here to kill us, plain and simple."

Redcloud looked down and played with a little stick that was on the floor. Reluctantly he said, "Yeah, I know, but I don't like it."

"I don't either and if it makes you feel any better, I would do the same if I suspected that whites or Mexicans or anyone else were trying to attack us."

"I understand fully, but no, it doesn't help much."

"OK, we leave in 15 minutes. I'll get the others together and lay out the plan. Chief, you're on your own and August, I want you and your daughter to stay in the cabin and be ready, just in case something goes wrong."

Before he could leave, Mitchell added, "And August, please be careful who you're shooting. It will be dark, and it should be us returning. However, I will call your daughter by her new nickname, Kat, before we cross the stream coming back."

August smiled, knowing he was referring to their first meeting, and said, "I understand."

August quickly left the tent and Rodrigues had to cover the screen before it lit them up to their friends out there. "I'm going to have to teach him about light discipline, as well." Jose said.

"Yeah, I know, they have much to learn from us." Mitchell said.

Rodrigues shut down the drone and controller and moved them to his tent. Mitchell gathered the others, and they met at the hummer. He thought about leaving Wilson at the hummer to man the machine gun but thought she would have had a fit, and next to Redcloud and himself, she was the only other one that had any kind of combat experience. She spent most of her tour in the camp. However, she has a little combat time. Right now, that was a rare commodity with this group.

"Everyone keep low and extremely quiet. These guys are good, and we can't afford to spook them." Then to Redcloud Mitchell said, "OK Chief, give us two hours to get into place. I'll double tap the radio when we are in place. You reply the same when our watcher is gone."

Redcloud just nodded and turn away.

"The rest of you stay with me. We have limited battery life for the night vision, and I want to save them as much as we can. I'll let you know when to switch on, but for now, just be careful where you step." He looked at each of them and they looked ready, worried a little, but ready. "Going hot, weapons on safe."

There was the sound of the bolts quietly being cycled and then Mitchell said in a low voice, "Move out at 5-second intervals. Wilson, take the rear."

He didn't look back to see if she understood this was not a slap, but a very important position. As he led the group, he needed her at the back to keep an eye on these new guys. He simply turned and headed out. He could hear the others as they started out. When he got to the stream, he crouched down and waited for the other to catch up. Once they were all there, he gently scolded them about how much noise they were making. He told them they needed to be much more careful. These Indians might have already heard them coming. He knew, or at least hoped, that this was not the case, but the closer they got to them, it could very well be.

They crossed the stream. It was noisy, but not too bad. When they got to the other side, Mitchell quietly said, "move out." And they were on their way again. This time it was a little quieter, and he just hoped it was quiet enough.

When they reached the hilltop, he waited again, and once they were all together, he tapped each of their night vision goggles. They understood it was time to use them. Now, when they moved out, things were better. He heard almost no noise at all. He signaled them to form a line abreast of him and move out together. For new guys, they did well. Whoever had trained them did a fair job of it.

As they got to the tree line, Mitchell could see the bright lights from the body heat of their horses. He would guess they were less than one hundred yards from their camp. He signaled the group to stop and get low. Then he waited a little to ensure all was quiet before he gave the double tap on the radio to tell Redcloud they were in position. They were actually a little early, but he suspected Redcloud was already in position. Now they just had to wait until they had his signal that the watch was taken out.

After about thirty minutes, Mitchell got the double tap of static in his ear and knew that Redcloud had done his job and was on his way. He waved to both sides and when he got a response from everyone; he motioned for them to advance slowly and to stay even with him.

Very carefully, he stood up and moved forward. It was all going smoothly, and he could see they were about fifty yards from the camp.

He could even see some bodies of the Indians as they slept. Then he heard a horse snort, and it sounded like it was pawing at the ground. He quickly put up a fist and everyone stopped and got low. Two of the Indians immediately sat up. In the night vision, Mitchell could see them looking around. Neither of them stood up, but just sat there looking and listening. On the far side of their camp, he could see Redcloud as he moved up. Mitchell waved to the group and gave them the sign that he could see him and to hopefully not shoot at him.

After maybe ten to fifteen minutes, the two Indians laid back down. Mitchell gave them another fifteen minutes before he signaled to move on.

When they were within a few yards, something spooked the horses and quickly all the Indians were up. Mitchell aimed and let go with the first round. Before they left on this mission, he made sure everyone understood that there would be no automatic fire. However, within a matter of less than a minute, all the Indians were down. A quick check show they were all dead.

They did a quick check around the camp but found little. There was only a little food and the horses. The bad news was that in the attack, one horse got wounded. Reluctantly, Mitchell had to put that horse down. Luckily, though, that still gave them enough horses to use and even some to trade.

Blake was just standing there looking at the bodies and without thinking said, "Their scalps would bring a pretty penny at the trading post."

His mistake was he said it loud enough for Redcloud to hear. Redcloud immediately dropped his rifle and, in less time than anyone could react, he had Blake down in a choke hold. It took the combined strength of the rest of the group to pull Redcloud off him. Blake just laid there coughing. Redcloud picked up his weapon and stormed away.

"You know, that was about the dumbest thing I have ever heard anyone say." Anna said as Mitchell kneeled by Blake's side.

Blake couldn't say anything. He was still choking and trying to catch his breath.

Standing up after a while, Mitchell looked around and found Redcloud over next to the horses. He slowly walked up to him. Redcloud turned and quickly said, "I don't want to talk about it."

"I know, but he was just a dumb kid and didn't realize what he was saying."

"Yeah, just like the rest of you white men."

"Hey, don't give me any of that white man crap. You and I have been through too much together. You taught me much about your people and you know how I feel. I'm as sorry as I can be about this group of men, but we didn't really have much choice in the matter. You know what they would have done to us, and the women in our group." Mitchell waited and then continued, "I gave you all the chances I could to give me an alternative idea."

He could see his old friend put his head down and nod. He then continued, "Is that what is really bothering you? That you couldn't come up with a way not to have to do this."

He turned away and leaned on one horse with his head down.

"Look, man, I know how hard this was, especially for you. The team was new, and we didn't have any chance for them to train and get to know either of us." Mitchell stopped. He could see he wasn't getting through with this line of thinking. Changing his line of thought, he said, "Did it ever occur to you that maybe there was nothing you could have done differently, given the circumstances?"

He raised his head up and said, "That is the whole problem. As you said, I am the Indian expert. I should have been able to come up with a plan the didn't amount to the slaughter of all those men."

"Not so, my friend. You forget that this is not our time. You're still thinking in term of our time. In these times, most of the Indians and the whites are mortal enemies and there is nothing we can do in just a few short days to change that."

"Yeah, I know, but it doesn't help."

"Well, maybe after this little scrap we are about to get into, is over. We can go north and see about helping your people before it all turns bad for them."

That got his attention. He jerked up and said, "What are you saying?"

"I've been thinking, the next biggest thing will be the civil war. It will probably still happen no matter what we do here. I also think that there are too many ways we can do something wrong and mess that up. We're going to make the argument to the group that we stay out of that one and let it run its course. If it goes wrong, we can try to step in and fix things, but I feel it is best we let that one work it out by itself."

"You know Johnson will not go for that." Redcloud answered back to him.

"Maybe, we will have to see, but that is for later. Now," he continued, "after the Civil War, the Indian Wars came next. There is much we can do while the North and South are fighting to prepare the Indians. We can start with your people and try to get them together and fight on a couple of fronts."

Now he fully had Redcloud's attention. He stood back up and turned to look at Mitchell, so he continued, "I don't mean to fight them head on. That was a mistake of the past, our past. This time, we know what is going to happen and we know how to play the game. We ensure the treaties are not arbitrary, but very specific. We make sure they are ratified by the government and signed by the president." Mitchell had his full attention now. "Then on the other front we know what will happen and about when. We know about the gold in the Indian lands that the white men of this time don't yet know about. Also, we know what industries will be big. We take that gold and invest it in those industries, in the interest of the Indian people. We then use that power to influence the government to pass laws to protect the Indian's rights and their native lands. That, with the power of a whole united native American people, we can influence the future of this time."

"Yeah, it sounds reasonable, but can you get this group to agree to this?"

"That, my friend, will take a little time to work on, but I think it is doable."

That seemed to bring him out of that dark place, at least for now. They both turned and headed back to the group. As Redcloud approached, Blake stepped up, with what looked to be a brand-new back eye, and said, "Look Chief, I'm very sorry for what I said. I was just thinking about things out loud. It was a wrong though," he paused and turned towards Wilson, who was rubbing the back of her hand, and then turned back to Redcloud, "I didn't mean any disrespect to your people. I'm very sorry about all this."

Redcloud looked at him a little, then said, "These are not my people; however, they are people and to take their hair to make a couple of bucks is despicable." He then turned and headed back in the cabin's direction.

"Bury these men. Then gather up the horses and bring them back home. We'll all sit and talk about this when things cool down. Right now is not a good time." He then turned to leave, and Rodrigues started walking back to the cabin. "Where do you think you're going?" He shouted at him.

"Back to get a couple of shovels, unless you want us to use our hands." He answered back.

"No, sorry. I guess we're all a little touchy after this. Com'on, I'll walk with you."

Mitchell put his hand on the other man's shoulder and they both started walking. He didn't worry about them doing it right. He knew Wilson won't let them get away with a sloppy job.

Back at the cabin, things stayed quiet for several days. The work went on, but the group was not the happy family they used to be. Redcloud hasn't said two words to anyone since they had that fight the other night. The rest of the group just avoided him and went about their work. The only one that got anywhere with Redcloud was Rodrigues, and only because they were working together on the corral.

Most of the time, August was with them, but stayed separated to keep watch. However, sometimes he would also help with the work.

Today they all gathered for lunch and after they had started a quiet meal, Redcloud spoke up and simply said, "The corral is done." He then went right back to eating.

"Great," Mitchell shouted, "when do you think you'll be able to get some horses?"

Redcloud just looked at him and said nothing.

Slamming his fist down on the table. "Enough is enough." Mitchell shouted. This caused Kat to jump. She had seen none of them angry before. She knew something was wrong, but she, like the others, said nothing. "Yes, the other night has left a very distasteful feeling with everyone. It was not something that we liked to do, but it was something that we had to do, and we didn't do it lightly." Everyone had stopped eating and mostly just looked down. "And then when it was all done, one of our newest persons, one who had never even thought about combat before, said something that was stupid and was even more distasteful than what we did. None of this is something we can take back, and it's something we can't afford to take forward with us. Something has to be done."

Mitchell let that sink in a moment before he continued, "I don't know what we can do to get over this, but we must. This, for some of us, is not the first time we have had to kill," He said, looking right at Redcloud, "but I can almost certainly guarantee one thing. This will not be the last time we must kill. We won't always be able to choose who we must kill. Sometimes, like the other night, we just have to take our fights as they come."

To Mitchell's surprise, Blake stood up and walked over to Redcloud. He just stood there for what seemed like forever. Everyone could see he was shaking slightly. Slowly he said, "Chief, I was wrong to say what I said. In a moment of weakness, I was speaking from the ignorance of what I had learned in school. You have shown me my error and all I can do is say I am truly sorry and ask for your forgiveness."

He then put out his hand out to Redcloud. Redcloud had turned to listen to him, but when his hand came out, he turned back to the table and just sat there for a moment. He then leaned forward and put his two enormous fists on the table and used them to stand. Blake took a step back, but then stood his ground with his hand still out.

Redcloud looked at each member of the group as they sat around the table. Some just looked back at him, while others nodded their agreement with what Blake had said. He then turned to Blake and looked down at his hand. In a swift and strong motion, Redcloud reached out and grabbed his hand, and pulled Blake to him. Redcloud then put his arms around Blake and held him in a hug.

Wilson was the next one. She ran over and held both of them in a hug. Kat was the next to follow. Before anyone could say anything, everyone was in the giant circle hug. Mitchell was the last to join.

Their little group was a family again. The hug went on for several minutes, but slowly broke up. Everyone went back to their seats. Slowly the chatting about the daily happening started up again.

After lunch was over, Mitchell again asked Redcloud about the possibility of going after the horses.

The Chief replied, "After lunch, I plan to have Rodrigues take the drone up and see if we can see any sign of a herd."

"Just how do you look for sighs with a drone?" Asked August.

"Good question," replied Redcloud. "I'm hoping to see some dust clouds and then fly in that direction to see what I can see."

It sounded like as good a plan as anyone could think of. If anyone knew anything about horses, Mitchell was sure it was Redcloud. He told him, "Sound like a plan. Let's hope you can see something quickly. We don't have too much of a change left on the drone to fool around with."

"Boss," Rodrigues spoke up, "We can charge this new model drone from the battery in the hummer or even the duce. We have all the recharge time in the world. I also found the adapters to charge all the other batteries."

"OK, keep me posted, but do nothing without letting me know first."

"You got it, Boss"

"Johnson, how are you and Blake coming along with the wagon?"

Both of them stood up, and then Blake sat back down. Johnson looked at Blake as he started talking. "I think we may have it by tomorrow or the next day. This afternoon, we should get the remaining hardware ready and attach the axle to the wagon. If everything goes right, we can try to mount the wheels tomorrow. We'll probably need some help to get it in place." He finished, but kept standing.

"Good. Is there anything else?"

"Well yeah, Boss," he said, "what are we going to use to pull it? I'm afraid that unless we carry a very light and useless load, the one old horse that August has won't be able to handle it. Another thing. Even if you get more horses, I don't know if we have enough harness to handle more horses."

Mitchell turned to look at August. He spoke right up. "We had the harness for a two-horse team. The other horse died from a snake bite shortly after we got here. I haven't used the harness since then. I can try to find it."

"Well yes, man. We are going to need that and if it needs repair, we have to take care of it before we need it."

August nodded and got up to leave.

"Don't worry about the other horses. We have the horses from the other night. We should be able to use them. I think they are younger and stronger. They should be able to pull the wagon just fine."

He wasn't really sure about that, so he looked at Redcloud. Redcloud just shrugged and gave him a quick nod. Everyone seemed happy with the plans, so they finished eating and went back to work.

That afternoon, they got the axle attached to the wagon, and the wheels back on. When they put the wagon back on the ground, it looked right, but what did any of them really know about this old antique? August wasn't there to check their work. He was off looking for the harness. So, Mitchell got everyone together, and they just pushed it around a little. Everything seemed to work like it should.

A little later, August came back. He found the harness in the attic, if you could call it that, and carried it out to where they were working. He just dropped it on the ground and began checking out the wagon. "This looks a little rough, but I think it will work." He said as he continued to look it over. When he finished, he stood up and looked over at the pile of harness he dropped earlier. "This will be another problem. It is all there, but some of it is old and broken."

Mitchell looked over at the pile of leather that he had brought out. He had to admit he didn't know the first thing about this contraption. "How bad is it and can we repair it?" he asked while looking at it.

August walked over to the pile and sorted things out. "Most of the important parts are still good, but the leather has dried up and I can't say how long it will last." He said as he separated the pieces. He put the pieces that looked to be damaged in a separate pile. When he finished, the damaged pile was small. Mitchell said, "We are very lucky. Only some straps need to be repaired. I think, for a quick fix, we can use some of those deer hides that Mr. Redcloud has supplied us. Maybe we can get some good leather at the trading post."

"You only need to call him Redcloud." Mitchell said to him, smiling.

August looked back at him with a very serious face and said, "I have seen Mr. Redcloud angry, and I have seen how big he is. I will call him Mister if that is alright."

Mitchell looked away to keep from laughing and said, "Yes, that is fine."

With the help of August and Kat, as well as Redcloud, they had the harness repaired and ready for the horses two days later. The horses, however, were not ready to be hitched to a wagon. It was going to take a couple more days to get them used to their new jobs. They were no longer the free running ponies of the Indians, but a heavy work horse for this group. They trained two pairs to pull the wagon. That left them with eight horses to trade. Mitchell didn't want to approach August about his horse. They could still use it as a saddle horse.

Redcloud finally found a small herd of horses, maybe a dozen, about five miles northwest of them. They planned the next day to head that way with August's horse and the hummer and use the drone to see if they could get them into their trap.

"Tonight, we get to bed early. We have a long day tomorrow." Mitchell said as they all gathered around the fire pit. "We have about a month to get to San Antonio and set ourselves up. When we get the horses in the trap, we are going to head out immediately to the trading post." Everyone looked around and appeared to be happy about this. Then he added, "I don't think we will come back here."

Kat looked the most upset about this. Her English had improved since they first got here, and she now could understand most of the things that were said. She stood up and ran to the cabin. August stood to follow her, but Mitchell motioned him to just stay. He got up and walked down to follow her.

When he walked in the door, he found her trying to think about what to take. "Kat," he said, but she didn't turn to look at him. "We are a family and families work together. It is late tonight, and we can worry about what to take in the morning."

As he talked, he stepped closer to her. Suddenly, she turned and threw her arms around him. She was crying softly.

After a moment, he grabbed her by her arms and held her away. "What's the matter?" he asked.

She turned away and motioned around the cabin. "This is my home. I don't want to leave here."

"I know this place is important to you, but you have moved before. This is no different." He said, trying to calm her.

"I am older now. I wanted to make this a proper house and live here for the rest of my life."

"You know about us, and you knew things were going to have to change. You and your father agree with all the things we were planning."

"Yes, but I didn't think it would be so soon." She said as she cried again.

Mitchell turned her back around to face him and held her close. At first, she just stood there crying, but then she slowly wrapped her arms around him. It felt so good. He put his hand behind her head and gently put her head on his shoulder. He swayed a little and just let her cry it out. After a while, she stopped crying and lifted her head up to look him in the eyes. He leaned forward and closed his eyes. He expected they would kiss, but she suddenly pulled away and turned away from him. Mitchell slowly lowered his arms, and she went to the other side of the cabin and stood there with her back to him.

"I'm sorry." He whispered. "I was caught up in the moment and holding you made me feel like I haven't felt in a long time."

She didn't look around but through the sniffles she said, "That is alright, but I think you should go now. I will be alright, now. We can gather the things to take in the morning."

He turned around and headed for the door, but before he got there, she turned and said, "I do thank you, though. The way you held me gave me great comfort."

He looked back at her and showed her a big, toothy smile, and nodded while tipping his hat. He then turned back to the door and was gone.

Kat waited a moment to be sure he was gone and then sat down on her bed. Slowly, a little smile came out on her face.

The next morning came early, as usual, however this time they didn't line up for a run. Instead, they gathered at the table for some quick breakfast. Mitchell looked around the table and focused on Redcloud. "Chief, how many do you need to herd the horses?"

"Well, I'll need someone to drive the hummer. I'll need Rodrigues in the hummer to run the drone. I'll be on August's horse, trying the guide the herd. We'll need the rest of you to close off the corral after the herd gets in there."

"Wilson can drive. She's the best driver after you and me." He said and then threw in, "Well, me, at least." He half expecting Redcloud to say something, but that never came.

"You can take Kat with you. I think she'll get a thrill out of that." He added talking to Wilson and watched the big smile on Kat›s face appear as she realized what he said. He continued to lie out the plans for today. "I don't want to use the duce on this. It is too big., too noisy, and too slow and uses too much fuel. In fact, we are going to bury the duce and use the fuel for the hummer."

"Is that going to give us enough space to take everything when we leave?" asked Johnson. "There are a lot of tools I think we should bring with us for the wagon."

"Yes, with the trailer and the back of the hummer, I think there will be enough room for the important things. We're not going to take everything with us. What we don't take, we can bury with the duce or trade off at the trading post." After saying it, Mitchell could see everyone was thinking about the future. So, he went on. "After we finish with this mission in San Antonio, I think we can come back here and plan our future involvement in this timeline."

No one said anything, but he could see on their faces there was a lot of thinking. This kind of thinking right now was going to distract them from what needed to be done today and lead to someone getting hurt. He quickly got them focused back on today's tasks. "Johnson and Blake, you guys head up to the corral and get ready to close it off. I'll radio you when we are on our way. August will be in charge in that area."

"You want us to take orders from a civilian?" Blake asked.

"No, we are no longer in the real Army, remember? I want you to take orders from the eldest, and most experienced in this mixed-up family." he answered him with a smile.

It was easy to see August swell up with what Mitchell said, but it was true. In the job they had to do today, other than Redcloud, no one else had any experience handling horses. Mitchell needed him there to make sure they didn't scare that herd away before they get into the corral. "You guy will need to be ready, but out of sight. If the horses see you, you just might scare them off before we get them in the corral."

"Don't worry, ah…Boss," August stuttered over what to call him and Mitchell had to smile at that, "I will make sure we are ready, and we will get those horses." He then added as he turned away, "If you get them to us."

August turned to head off in the corral's direction and motioned for Johnson and Blake to follow, which they did. Mitchell then got his crew together, and they headed off to the hummer. Last night they siphoned out fuel from the duce and fueled up the hummer. Everyone had their weapons and enough mags to keep them safe. He made sure they all understood not to fire them because of the shortage of ammo, though. Only use them if they had to.

As they all piled into the hummer, Redcloud had already mounted and was riding off. He had a radio, so they could keep in touch, so he headed toward the last known location of the herd and turned to wave as he crossed the stream.

Now comes the fun part, explaining things as simply as he could to Kat. Mitchell didn't want her to be overwhelmed with all the new things, but he wanted her to understand what was happening. Her English had improved since he met her. He guessed practice makes perfect. After he opened the door for her, she slowly looked around the cab, but they were in a bit of a hurry, so he couldn't wait too long. He tapped her on the shoulder and pointed to the set. She understood. Slowly and carefully, she climbed into the seat, still looking all around. Once she had settled, he closed the door and went to the other side and climbed in. Wilson and Rodrigues climbed into the front seats. "Wait," he said before Wilson started the hummer. Mitchell leaned over to Kat and said to her, "This is going to make a lot of noise. That is alright, it is supposed to. This is a powerful machine. Also, things are going to happen fast, so I won't always be able to answer your questions. If there is time, I will try to tell you about things before they happen, but I can't think of everything, and I am going to be a little busy once we find that herd. So, the most important thing is to remember to hang on when we get moving."

He could see she was nervous, but she gave him a polite smile and simply said, "I understand."

Now, he turned to Wilson and said, "Start her up and let's get going."

Wilson smile and just before she started it, she turned to look at Kat. As she started it, there was the normal grinding of the starter turning the motor over, but when it caught and the hummer came to life, Kat jumped and brought her hands up to cover her mouth. Wilson wasn't sure if she was trying to stifle a scream or what, but Mitchell put his hand on her shoulder. When she finally looked over at him, he simply smiled at her.

He turned to Wilson and said, "Follow Redcloud, but keep your distance. I don't want to spook his horse. Also, I don't want to break the hummer. I have plans for this in the future."

Wilson looked puzzled by that comment but nodded and threw the hummer in gear. They started off at a slow pace and when they got to the stream, they just went right on through. It was a little rough and Kat looked scared, but she held on and didn't say anything. After crossing the stream, it was a little smother going. Right now, they were going slow enough that the hummer just climbed over rocks and sticks in the way. Kat just sat there, looking out the window.

Later, Kat had become very interested in everything that was in the hummer. She closely watched Wilson driving. Then she focused all her attention on Rodrigues when he opened up the controller case. Mitchell, of course, was watching her. More often than not, he had to smile as he watched her curiosity about everything that was so new to her. When she leaned forward to see what Rodrigues was doing, Mitchell leaned forward also, so she could hear. "The machine in the back, behind you," she spun around to look, but he continued, "can fly. It has a way of taking a picture that we can see it on this device. It will allow us to find the herd and keep watching it while we chase them."

Shaking her head a little, she leaned back and nodded to him. He thought she understood what he was saying, but not having anything to compare it to, she didn't understand exactly what she would see. Kat continued to study everything that was happening closely.

They traveled for about an hour, but then Redcloud stopped on a ridge ahead of them. As they got closer to him, Mitchell could see his horse was getting a little nervous. He told Wilson to stop, and he got out to walk up to Redcloud.

When he got next to him, Redcloud pointed to a dust cloud about two ridges northwest of them. "I think that is probably going to be the herd. I need Rodrigues to send up the drone and check it out. We'll need to see what they are doing. If everything is quiet, we'll circle around and start the chase from the other side. I don't want to start a stampede, but just a gentle nudge to get them going in the direction we want."

Mitchell turned and signaled for Rodrigues to send up the drone. He could see him, and Wilson jump out of the hummer and head around back. Kat slowly got out. He thought it might have taken her a little time to figure out the door handle. In just a couple of minutes, he saw the drone head up and Rodrigues started walking towards Mitchell and Redcloud's way. Kat was following and only taking her eyes off the control unit long enough to watch her step.

Mitchell pointed off in the dust cloud's direction, but it wasn't really visible anymore. Rodrigues replied with a thumbs up, and he could see the drone fly right over their heads and in the direction he had showed. When Rodrigues finally got to them, the drone was out of sight. He put the control unit on the ground and laid down behind the controls. Kat was right over his shoulder. Mitchell had to tap her in the shoulder so he could get in to see what was happening.

It wasn't more than a few seconds when they picked up the horses on the screen. "There they are!" Kat shouted. She was so excited. Everyone smiled at her, which embarrassed her immediately, and she sat back.

"Hey, Boss," Redcloud said, studying the screen. "I don't think this is the same herd we saw the other day. There looks to be more horses than what we saw before."

Rodrigues leaned forward to study the screen. "Yeah, Boss.", was all he said.

Mitchell looked over at Redcloud, but he was busy studying the terrain. The Chief pointed to the left and said, "If we can get them to move into that valley, it will act like a funnel almost all the way back to the corral."

Mitchell stood up and followed the valley he was looking at. He was right. It followed the way they wanted to go. The problem would be keeping the horses in the valley. "How do you plan to keep them in that valley all the way back and then turn them at the right spot?"

"Well, I think keeping them in the valley will be the simplest part of this trip. Once they are there, they should tend to follow it, along as long as we don't push them too hard. I can ride one side to keep them in the groove. You can run the other side and as long as they only hear you, you shouldn't scare them too much. When we get close to the turning point, you can circle ahead, and everyone spread out to make them turn."

"You really think it is going to be that easy?"

He didn't even look at Mitchell when he said, "Hell, I don't know. I've herded horses before, but that was with modern tools. I've never done anything like this. In theory, it should be that simple. If we get moving, we should get back before dark." Redcloud said, looking up at the sky to check the sun.

Mitchell instinctively looked at his watch, but quickly put his arm down before anyone saw. "Alright people let's get moving." he said.

Redcloud turned to Rodrigues and said, "Before we leave, I want to try something. Move to the right of the herd and then come down some and slowly move in towards them. I want to see if the drone will be enough to get them moving."

Rodrigues looked up at the chief. "I got ya.", he said.

Quickly, he had the drone in position and slowly started moving towards the herd. As the drone got closer, some horses started moving away. None of them seemed to be spooked. They just started moving slowly and stopping now and then to graze. "That's good," said Redcloud, "Don't get too close. Just keep your distance and let them move away from you." Redcloud then looked at his boss. "I'm gonna head to the other side and stay low. After the herd passes, we'll start trailing them."

"I ain't got enough juice to chase them all the way back." Rodrigues spoke up.

"Once we get behind them, you can recover it before it falls out of the sky." As he got up on his horse, he continued, "Swap out the batteries and get that one charged. We may need it down the road."

"Got ya, Chief." Rodrigues replied. With that acknowledgement, Redcloud turned and was off at a run. It looked like something out of an old western movie.

Mitchell turned to the hummer and signaled Wilson to come up to get them.

In just a couple second, the hummer was right here. Kat was still unsure of this machine and took a couple of steps back. He saw this and said, "Don't worry, you'll soon get used to this, just like the rest of us."

Again, she just gave him a simple little smile and nodded. He wasn't sure that she believed him.

It wasn't long before they could see the herd go by. For the most part, they stayed in the valley. Some strays came up the hill a little, but only to stop and graze a little, and then ran back to the rest. After they were past, the team recovered the drone and piled in the hummer. Mitchell told Wilson to wait before she started it. After the last of the herd was out of sight, he told her to start it up and to take it very slowly.

Every now and then, they would catch sight of Redcloud. Mitchell didn't know how he knew, but every time he stopped and waved at them.

Carefully, he let Kat climb up into the turret. They had removed the gun this morning because he didn't think they would need it. He told her she was their eyes. She had the binoculars and every time they stopped; she was right on the job. They found that by letting the herd get out of sight and then hurrying to the next ridge; they could keep the herd in sight without spooking them. Twice, they stopped and appear to be content with grazing. For these times, Mitchell had Rodrigues deploy the drone, and just like before, they would move again.

After a couple of hours, the horses came to a little stream. They stopped to graze and drink. Redcloud called Mitchell on the radio. "Let them rest a while. We can eat a little as well. Have Rodrigues send up the drone and look ahead to see what is there. I'm going to the top of this hill and see if I can get the corral on the radio."

"Plan.", was the simple one-word reply. Rodrigues had heard, so he and Wilson were already out and getting the drone ready. Kat watched from inside the hummer until they moved it where she couldn't see. She quickly jumped out to watch this thing fly. Mitchell thought she would never get enough of watching it fly.

Everything was moving along fine. They got the herd moving again after eating and pressed on. After a couple more hours, they could raise the corral gang. After letting them know they were close, Redcloud had the hummer team move to a point near the corral and set up a line. Wilson was on the left flank with the hummer. Kat was next. Rodrigues followed, and lastly Mitchell. They were spread out about 100 yards apart. He told them that only Wilson could fire her weapon to get the herd to turn. Once they started, the rest of them should be able to wave and shout enough to keep them going.

This was the most dangerous part of the entire project. Once Wilson started firing her rifle, the herd would undoubtedly start running. Mitchell warned everyone to watch out. Running scared, these horses wouldn't stop for anything.

While the team was gone, August and his team had been working hard. They had done the best they could to create a large funnel at the opening to the corral. It was good thinking, and he only hoped this all worked.

As the horses got close, Redcloud called to let everyone know. Mitchell stood up and waved to signal to everyone and each of them signaled back that they were ready.

As the herd came into sight. They slowed. Mitchell was afraid they would all turn around and they would lose them. Before they got scared of the people, he heard a couple of shots fired. That got them running. They were headed right at Wilson. Watching her, Wilson jumped into the hummer and moved it further out. From that point, she should be able to turn them better. He could hear her laying on the horn from where he was, and that worked just as good as a rifle shot.

The herd turned just as they had planned. Kat began waving and shouting. Now Mitchell could see Redcloud. He had crossed over to this side and was keeping the herd from making a U-turn. This was turning out to be a classic maneuver. The horses went straight into the corral. The coral gang began closing it up and the rest of the team came running up to help. As near as he could tell, they had almost 2 dozen horses in there.

Everyone was celebrating. Going around and slapping each other on the back, shaking hands and great big hugs. After a little while, the horses settled down and so did the people. They walked around and checked the perimeter of the corral. Everything was solid, so they headed back to the cabin. It was still early enough, so Kat fixed supper. Someone started a fire, and everyone gathered around the fire pit. August brought out the last of his personal stock and started handing out drinks. This was going to turn into a party, whether Mitchell liked it or not.

He quietly slipped away and went back to the cabin. The door was open, and he quietly stood there watching Kat as she fixed the dinner. She turned to pick something up and saw him. She was a little startled and jumped a little. Mitchell shyly said, "I came to see if you could use some help. You are always in here taking care of feeding us. I think maybe it is time one of us helps you."

"This is what a woman does for the men in her life.", she said back shyly.

"Maybe. In my time, however, men and women work together to do things. We have found that by doing things together, a man and a woman become closer in life." He said as he moved closer to her.

She stopped fixing the food and turned to his saying, "Oh, is this what you want? You want to be closer to me?"

She was a clever woman and not so simple that she couldn't see right through him and now, he was the one on the spot, "I..a", he stuttered, "I wouldn't mind getting to know you better."

Mitchell couldn't believe what was happening. He was always so confident with other women. Now he didn't know how to handle this situation. What was acceptable between a man and a woman in his time might just get him shot. She saw right through him, and he could see a devilish little smile on her face. After watching him a little, she finally said, "Yes, I think I can see you would."

"Shit," He muttered under his breath. Now he was not sure what to do. He decided he can't just turn and leave. Finally, he tried to change the subject and said out loud, "Would you like some help or not?"

Kat smile again and turned away from him, but he could hear in her voice that she knew what he was thinking and that he was scared. She said over her shoulder, smiling, "If you can do it without getting blood in it, you can chop up these vegetables for me."

He didn't know what to say back to her. This is a side of her he had never seen before and didn't expect. He just moved over to the cutting board and picked up the knife, and started quietly chopping the vegetables.

"Not too small, it will cook too fast.", she said.

"I know how to chop food and cook." He said sarcastically.

"Oh, really. I would not have known.", she said back, even more sarcastic.

He just kept chopping and also kept his mouth shut.

To his relief, Blake stuck his head in the door and said, "Hey Boss, August is looking for you."

"I'll be right there." He said and Blake ducked back out. Then to Kat he said, "I'm sorry, but I need to go see what your father wants."

She shot back at him "I know what he wants. He does not want me to be alone with you."

Before Mitchell could answer her, she walked over and planted a big kiss right on his lips. He was so shocked and almost fell as he stepped back and made a quick dash for the door.

Walking back to the fire pit, Mitchell's head was in a spin. Kat had caught him by surprise, and he had acted like a little schoolboy. Thank God Redcloud didn't see that. He'd be hearing about it for the rest of his life.

"Where have you been?" August shouted at him as Mitchell got to the pit. He was about six sheets to the wind already. "I have been looking for you."

When he stopped short, August came over to him and threw his arm over his shoulder. "I was seeing if Kat needed any help. She had a very busy day, and I just wanted to give her some help."

August began shaking his finger at Mitchell long before he could get the words out of his mouth. "I know what a soldier wants. She is my daughter and if you want to talk to her, you do it where I can see you. None of this going behind my back."

"Yes, sir, I have no intention of going behind your back. I truly only wished to help her."

"Maybe, but I have already noticed she has an eye for you." He said while Mitchell tried to hold him from falling.

He didn't answer back, but he saw Redcloud sitting close by. He could see the big shit-eating grin on his friend's face. "Come on, August. Let's find you a placed to sit down before you fall down." He then tried to steer him to the seat where he and Kat usually sat together. August turned and tried to sit, but missed the log and fell on his butt. He then just laid down and passed out.

Mitchell picked up the jug, and to his surprise there was still a sip left in it. Not for long, though. He tipped the jug up and finished it. Unfortunately, it was not enough to help. Redcloud was waiting like a vulture. As soon as August was down, he got up and headed towards his old friend.

"So," he started out, "You got something going with Kat?" he said with a big smile.

After thinking it over for a moment, he replied, "To tell you the truth, I'm not really sure."

"Not sure?" Redcloud said. "I've been watching both of you. So has everyone else. I think you're the only one that isn't sure."

"What are you talking about?"

"Kat has had eyes for you since just about the first day we met them."

"You're crazy. We hardly talk. Today was the first time I've been with her for more than a couple of minutes."

"Maybe, but it's been the talk of the entire group for a week or two."

Redcloud was just eating this up. He was having way too much fun at the expense of his old friend. Mitchell looked around and as soon as he did, everyone looked away. They were also watching the two of them talk. Now that Mitchell had seen them, he could hear a little giggle, but couldn't tell where it was coming from.

He just stood up and said, "You're all full if it.", and headed off towards the corral. I need some time to think about this.

He forgot the radio was still on. It cracked to life, and it was Redcloud. "I was told to tell you that dinner is ready," he paused and then added, "Honey!"

"Knock it off." he shouted back into the radio and turned it off.

By the time he got to the table, most had finished eating and just sitting around talking. August was gone. "Where is your father?" he asked Kat as he walked by.

"Sit here.", she said, pointing at her father's seat. "He was not in any condition to eat. We put him to bed. He will sleep through the night."

Mitchell stopped and looked around and then his stare settling on Redcloud. He looked at him and smiled. He then looked away.

Mitchell politely said, "Thank you." and sat down next to her. She got up and fixed him a plate of food. As she put it down in front of him, she brushed up against him. He didn't move and had to admit it felt real nice. "Thank you." he said again. He was simply at a loss for words.

He again looked up at Redcloud. He was just sitting there with one leg crossed over the other and smiling back at him.

"When are we leaving for the trading post?" Redcloud finally asked.

"Just as soon as we can bury the duce and pack up." He quickly said back, grateful for a change in subjects.

"Why bury the duce? We can use it."

"I want to leave a stash of supplies here and the duce will use too much fuel. We can bury it in a hillside where it will be easy to dig out after we finish in San Antonio."

"Okay, but you plan to take the hummer with us?"

"Yeah," he answered and slowly continued, "the hummer is multi-fuel, while the duce is strictly diesel." He let that sink in a minute. "If we get the duce to the Alamo, we won't have enough fuel to bring it back and I don't want to leave it there when we leave." Mitchell continued to eat while Redcloud thought about it for a minute.

After a couple bites, he continued, "The hummer will carry enough supplies. We can hitch the wagon to the trailer and pull both. The horses can be tied to the wagon as well. I figure that after draining the duce, we'll have enough fuel to get us there and some of the way back. We can run it on kerosene or even booze if we have to."

He could see Redcloud thinking this all over. "How much ammo do you plan to take with us?"

"I think about half should do the job there. Remember, we won't be the only ones shooting. I plan to hold our fire until absolutely needed. We will lull Santa Anna into thinking it will be a pushover and then wipe him out."

Kat was taken back "You can do this?"

Mitchell forgot she was sitting there and that her English had improved enough to understand what they were talking about. "Yes, I believe we can do this. It will not be easy and there will still be people who will get hurt and even killed."

"But if you have all this power, why do you not use it and destroy the Mexican army?"

She was understanding what they can do, but to her they might seem to be all powerful. Mitchell had to get this idea out of her head. "Yes, we can do many things, but we have our limitations. We have a limited amount of ammunition. This can't be replaced now. Once it is used, it is gone. I have to decide what will work and use only this for now." She looked him right in the eyes as he tried to explain to her. He could see he was not getting fully through to her, so he continued "We have knowledge of what will happen in the future and while I can't tell you everything right now, you have to trust me when I say we will need to save some things for the future."

She took him by the arm and said, "I do not understand everything, but I do trust you."

He put his hand on hers and said, "It will be enough. Don't worry, if everything works out, there will be far less killing on both sides, but it will still be a bloody mess."

She squeezed his arm and then turn back to the table. When Mitchell turned back, Redcloud was again smiling at him. Mitchell just hung his head and started shaking it back and forth.

After finishing dinner, Mitchell said good night to Kat, and she gave him a brief hug and turned and ran back to the cabin.

Redcloud and Mitchell walk over to the fire pit and sat down. Everyone else had gone to bed. Mitchell sat on his usual stump and said, "Okay Chief, you may be right. What do I do now?"

His long time and oldest friend didn't reply for a moment. He stirred the fire back to life and sat down next to Mitchell. "You know I know nothing about women, but I know something about men. Especially fathers. If you intend to continue on this road with Kat, you will need to explain your intentions to August and ask his permission."

"Permission?" He asked.

"Yes, in this time it is important to get the father's permission to court his daughter. If you don't and he saw what I saw sitting at the table tonight, it would be grounds to kill you outright."

Wow, Mitchel knew the Chief was right, but he hadn't even thought that far out yet. He got up and took his turn at stirring the fire. He didn't have the skills of the Chief and lost the last of the flames.

Redcloud stood up and said, "Good night, Boss. I'll leave you to think it over, but consider this. Whether or not you like it, she is moving fast. If you don't want to piss off August, you better talk to him soon, like the first thing in the morning."

"Thanks Chief." He slowly said, while he was thinking. After Redcloud left, he sat for a long time at the fire. He wouldn't mind being with Kat. She is nice looking and quite the lady. When she needs to, she can fight. Also, she is very open-minded. She would have little trouble fitting into his world. He just didn't know if he could fit into her world, and no mistaking it, this is her world, not his. He looked over at the cabin. Even though the lights were out, he could see her clearly laying on her bed, in his mind.

Finally, Mitchell walked to his tent. Even with all the activity of today, sleep didn't come easy. He ended up tossing and turning all night.

Mitchell guessed he finally dozed off because the next thing he knew, Redcloud was yelling at everyone to get up. Today, he was going to use the lack of sleep as an excuse not to go on the run. He slowly came out of his tent and as he walked over to the group, Redcloud spoke up, "You OK, boss? You look like shit."

"I feel like shit." he replied.

Redcloud came over and gave him a wink, then said out loud, "You'd better sit this one out. I don't want you to get sick now."

Mitchell smiled up at him and nodded a thanks.

Kat came out of the cabin in her uniform and came over to where he was sitting. "Are you alright, Jim?" she asked as she put an arm over his shoulder.

He said "Yeah, just didn't get much sleep last night. Too much to think about right now."

Redcloud called "Fall in." and Kat looked over. "I have to go now. I will check on you when we get back."

"I'll be here. Where is your father?"

She turned as she was walking away. "He'll be out in a moment.", she said and then added with a smile, "He also isn't feeling well this morning."

Mitchell smiled and waved at her as she turned to fall in. In a couple of minutes, they we at the stream and crossing over.

August slowly came out of the cabin. He looked worse than Mitchell felt. He carefully worked his way to the table and sat down. "How about a cup of coffee?" he asked him.

He looked up at Mitchell with very blood-shot eyes and simply nodded.

He got the fire going and put on a pot of water to get hot. Then he sat next to August at the table and slowly said, "I need to talk with you this morning before the others get back."

August didn't look up, but simply said "I need another drink."

"I'm sorry, my friend, but I think you finished it all last night."

He made a sound and Mitchell thought he might puck all over the table, but then spoke "I was afraid of that. It was the last of anything I had left to drink."

'Well, don't worry about it. We'll see what we can get at the trading post when we get there."

"You said you wanted to talk to me?" he asked.

Mitchell had no idea where or how to do this. "Yes, I need to talk to you about Katherine."

He sat up with a bolt. "Yes, what about her?" He said with as stern a voice as Mitchell had ever heard from him.

"Ah, Sir" He started out. He had practiced this all night, but now that the time was here, the words just stuck in his throat. "I think Kat, ah, Katherine, may have feelings for me. Until yesterday, I was unaware of this."

He could see August was getting a little red in the face, but he just sat there staring at him. He continued. "I also have begun to have feelings for her. Yesterday, I discovered her feeling, and I felt so warm in my heart. The way and man and woman court in my time differ greatly from now. I wish to respect both you and her and do the right thing for this time. I would like to ask your permission to court your daughter."

August sat there for a moment, then he slowly got up to a standing position. His face was beet red, and Mitchell wasn't sure what he did wrong, but he was ready to get up and run. Suddenly, August reached out and grabbed him by the shoulder. He was a big man and had no problems lifting him up off the stump where he was sitting. He held Mitchell up for what seemed like an eternity. To his surprise, August finally broke out into a great laugh and pulled him into one giant bear hug.

When he finally let Mitchell down and shouted out "Mien Gott, boy. It is about time you finally saw what the rest of us have seen for weeks."

Mitchell just stood there in a dumbfounded state. He didn't know what to say. August continued, "I have been waiting to have this talk with you. My daughter was thinking you didn't like her."

"What are you saying? I only found these feeling yesterday when she kissed me." Oops, he wasn't supposed to say anything about that, but August just looked at him with a smile.

"Yes, she told me this morning. She had to do something to get your attention. You were acting like a stupid little boy. She told me she had to kiss you to get you to notice her."

Mitchel just dropped back down on his stump. He couldn't think. How could he be so blind that he couldn't see all of this happening when everyone else could?

After a while, he came to his senses and finished making the coffee. He handed August his and slowly sipped his own. He was still in a daze when the team came back from the run.

As everyone gathered at the table, August stood up and said, "I have given this fine young man permission to court my daughter."

Everyone stood up and cheered and applauded. There were lots of slaps on the shoulder and comments of it's about time, and so on.

When the congratulations stopped, Kat came over and took his arm and put her head on his shoulder. He was thinking about how nice it was to be in heaven, but then he saw Redcloud and August off to the side and laughing. Finally, they shook hand and parted. It was at this point he realized that he had been set up. He didn't know if it was just a few or all of them working together, but he had definitely been set up. But, who cares. He thought they may have set him up, but he was getting the better end of the deal.

When things finally settled down, they all finished breakfast. Mitchell stood up. "First, thank you for your well-wishing for Kat and I." Kat took his arm, and everyone let out another cheer. He had to hold his hand up to get them to stop so he could continue. "Today, we'll prepare to leave. First thing I want to do is dig out a spot on the ridge over there," He said, pointing back over his shoulder, "so we can bury the duce. It will not help us with what we have to do, and it will hold a stash of supplies for when we come back here."

Everyone was quiet. He wasn't sure if they agreed with him or what, so he just continued, "August, take Jose and go up and check on the horses. We may have to get them some food. We'll get to that first if we need to. The rest of us get ready to dig. Kat, I want you to go through the cabin and gather all the things into three piles. First, what we want to take with us. Remember, we have limited space. Two, what we can leave here for our return. Last, what we can trade at the trading post."

She smiled up at him and nodded. "Anna, I want you to do the same with the stuff we have."

Wilson again didn't look happy about her assignment, but this time she didn't ask him about it. "Let's move. I would like to leave tomorrow. The day after tomorrow at the latest."

The work went well. By the end of the day, they had a good hole dug out for the duce to back into. Kat and Anna did their part and with only a brief discussion about a few things they had settled what to do with everything.

August and Jose took care of the horses. They hauled water up to the horse. There was enough grazing material for them for the day or two that they would be there. They were quite calm now as the water was poured into a couple of big tubs.

Mitchell had to talk to Redcloud. "How much trouble do you think we will have taking the horses to the trading post?"

"Well, we shouldn't have too much trouble. It's not a long drive and if we take it slow and easy, the horses should be fine. Although, I expect we might lose four or five on the trip. I need to get a couple of the guys trained to ride the Indian ponies. If we use the hummer to herd them, we will probably lose most of them. I think the guys should be able to handle the ponies as long as the horses behave."

"Yeah, you're probably right. I'll have Wilson follow some ways back with the hummer. Kat and August will drive the wagon. Will that give you enough to handle the herd?"

"Well, that depends." He said.

"Depends on what?" Mitchell asked him.

"Depends on what you plan to do. Are you gonna pussy out and ride the hummer or are you gonna help us on horseback?"

He was afraid this was going to come up, eventually. The Chief and him went back a long way, and he knows Mitchell had a bad time with a horse in the past. It is just another one of those things he wouldn't let his old friend live down. "I guess I'm gonna be on horseback with you guys."

Redcloud laughed, "Tell you what, Boss. I even give you August's old saddle to help you stay on this time."

Mitchell just sneered at him and walked away. He could hear Redcloud laughing as he did. When he passed Wilson on her way to the diggings, she asked, "What was the Chief laughing so hard at?"

Mitchell simply replied, "Old memories about nothing."

She stopped and looked at him as he passed, but didn't dare say anything more.

They spent the rest of the day getting everything packed into the right vehicle. By supper time, most everything was packed. And everyone was completely drained, so there was little talking. What little talking there was, dealt with particular items and where to pack them. As soon as they had finished eating, everyone headed off to get some sleep. Tomorrow was going to be their last day here, and this might be the last chance they would get to catch a good night's sleep for a little while.

Mitchell was the last to leave the table. Kat had already gone to the cabin, and he just wanted to sit in the quiet and think. He got little time for thinking. Shortly, he heard the cabin door open and close. It was too dark to see who it was, but he was hoping it was Kat.

Tonight, he was in luck. It was her, but she hadn't seen him and was headed up the hill towards his tent. He watched her for a little. She was making her way slowly and being very quiet. "Hello." He whispered.

She jumped and turned to look his way. Quickly, she saw him and turned to come to him. When she got close to the table, he stood up and held out his hand for her. She took it and the warmth of her hand in his was such a pleasant feeling. Reaching out with his other hand, he pulled her to him. He didn't kiss her right away. He just wanted to see into her eyes. She just fell into his arms and returned the stare as she looked deep into his soul.

Shortly he softly said, "Out for a stroll on this pleasant evening." And then smiled.

He didn't know if she could see him smiling, but there was no mistaking the big, shy smile on her face. "I was just going to talk to you."

"Yes, I think we need to talk." He said, while keeping his voice very low.

She turned and took his hand and walked towards the stream. Of course, he followed. They slowly walked until they reached the edge of the stream, where she stopped. He came up beside her and put his arm around her waist. He could feel her tense up a little, so He dropped his arm and just held her hand. Slowly, she moved his hand back around her waist and said, "I think I like this better."

This time, though, he held her a little tighter and leaned over to kiss her, but she quickly turned away. And said "No, not yet."

He didn't say anything, but continued to hold her close to him.

They were quiet and just stood there listening to the water as it went over a couple of rocks close by. Then, very quietly, she started talking. "I know I understand little of what you talk about when you talk with your people. I understand you are from our future, but I don't understand how you came to be here. You have told us things about your powerful machines and the people of your time. Anna has told me a little about the women of your time and I can see by the way she is, what your women are like.", she said thoughtfully. "I don't know that I can be like these women, and I don't know that you would be happy with me."

Mitchell turned her to look at him. Even then, he still had to put his finger under her chin to make her look up into his eyes. "Kat, since we have been here, I found you to be a very smart and caring person. You learn things quickly and are curious to learn more." He paused as she looked down. He stooped down to keep her eyes looking into his and continued, "You handle yourself well when there is trouble, and you don't run and hide. And, most importantly, your mind and your heart are open. You're not afraid of new things. You want to lean. Also, to my eyes, you are quite beautiful."

Now she dropped her head and turned away. He took her firmly by both shoulders and turned her back to face him. "Look, you say you don't understand things. I'm telling you now that you are not alone. We don't understand how we got here, either. We don't understand how to live and survive in this time. Without you and your father, we might not have survived this long. Yes, we have powerful machines and weapons, but they can't help with simple things to live that we don't know about. You have taught us much about this new time that we must learn in order to live now. We cannot change this time to be like ours was. We must learn and change to live in this time."

Slowly, she lifted her head back up and said, "Do you think you could live with me?"

Now, he pulled her to him and held her. "Yes, my dear. I believe we will have a great life together in this future, whatever it might bring us." He whispered into her ear. She put her arms around him, and they just stood there, holding each other for what seemed like a long time.

Slowly, he broke the hug, but still held her with one arm as they turned back towards the stream. "Do you understand what we are going to be doing?"

"Yes," she replied quickly, but then added, "I think. You are going to help the soldier fight the Mexican Army in San Antonio."

"Yes," He said, "but do you understand why?"

She just shook her head.

"In our time, people made a great many mistakes, and some bad people did some very terrible things. We know when these things will happen, and we know who these people are. We plan to fix as many of these mistakes as we can and guide our future to be better."

"How do you know this will make things better?", she asked.

"We don't know for sure." He said. She had asked the right question. She had quickly picked up on the problems and he didn't know how to answer her. "Let me give you an example. I told you a little before, but there is more. In about one hundred years, a man will come to power in Germany. He will start a war. It will involve the entire world. While the world is fighting this war, this man will murder more than six million people. Men, women and even children, simply because they are Jewish."

"This is true?" she asked, quite surprised.

"Yes, this is true. Now think about it. What if we can kill this man before he takes power? Not only would we save the lives of those six million people, but all the others. I'm talking about the soldiers and innocent people who died just because they were in the way during the fighting." He paused to see if that was settling in.

"Yes, I understand, I think.", she said. After a moment, she added, "But, how do you know that killing this one man will make things better?"

"That, my Dear is our biggest problem," He answered her, "We don't. We could make things worse. Let me explain."

He stopped and sat down. She sat next to him. "Oh, the ground is cold.", she said.

"Would you like to go back?"

"No, I am fine."

He continued, "Soon, there will be a war in America. Brothers will fight brother and families will fight families. It will be mostly the northern states fighting the southern states."

Kat interrupted him, "Slavery?", she asked.

What a beautiful mind she had. Surprised, he said "Yes, how did you know?"

"We have heard some talk about this already. Some people are against it, while others cannot live without it. Also, I see the way you work with your negro."

"Yes, slavery will be one issue, but the war will start over who has the power to make the rules. The state or the federal government. Slavery is just one thing and will not become an official reason to fight until about two years into the war." He stopped to see if she understood.

She said nothing, but just kept looking at him, so he continued, "I have talked with the Chief and we both agree not to get involved in this."

"Why?" she said, surprised. "You could stop this war and save many lives."

"Maybe, this war will probably happen no matter what we do and there is no one person or a single act we could do to change it. The war was what, as bad is it was, changed things in America. Black people, that is what we call them now. To call them Negros in our time is considered a terrible insult." He paused again to let that sink in, but she said nothing, so he continued. "Black people will become free and as you can see with Stretch, they are equal to every other person. They will be able to vote and live anywhere they want to. They will become educated, and some will have major ideas that will change the lives of everyone. One, after a long time, will even become President of the United States."

"This is true?" she said again. He thought she was so amazed and overwhelmed by what he was telling her she cannot believe that these things could be true.

"Yes, it is true. Now, because this war is probably going to happen no matter what we do, there are too many things we can do wrong and cause the outcome of the war to change. If the South catches one of us and forces us to talk, they would have a knowledge of the war that could change things. We can't allow this to happen."

"Yes, I understand. You could change things to be worse."

She had grasped the problems that they will be facing. He thought, now it will be this easy to get the vote from the rest of the team to stay out of this one.

Kat continued, "You could do more damage to the future by anything you do. How will you know what to do?"

"I made a rule that whatever we decide to do, we must all agree to do it, or we do nothing and let the future take care of itself."

"That seems very wise.", she said after a little thought.

"You and your father are now part of this group and have the right to vote on what we will do, and just like before, we must all agree."

She smiled up at him and said, "I will support my man."

"No," he said. "That is not how it works for us. You are a person on your own and must decide to do what you feel is the right thing in your heart. You don't have to support me and anyone if you don't feel it is the right thing to do. We will all sit around and discuss the ideas. It may take many days or even weeks of discussion. Everyone will be able to say whatever they want."

Kat looked concerned. "But what if I don't agree with you or the others?"

"That is your right. You don't have to agree if you feel strong enough." He could see the direction her thoughts were going. "Don't worry about us. I will still care about you, even if you vote against me. In fact, I will probably respect you more for standing for you what you believe."

Watching the look on her face as it sunk in, he added, with a smile "Of course, depending on the mood of the discussion, I might be upset a little," he paused a moment, "but I will get over it. Never think that we can't argue about something. These kinds of argument can help to make our lives together even stronger."

She looked up at him with a strange look. He thought she understood, but this was a new idea for her, and it will take some getting used to.

He added, with a smile, "And besides, if we argue, the best part is making up after." And he gave her a little nudge with his elbow.

He believed she got what he was saying because she immediately looked down and away.

They sat there for a little while longer, but the night was getting cold. After a while, he could feel her shiver. "Come, it is getting cold. You need to get inside." He said.

She looked at him and nodded. He stood up and helped her to her feet. When she stood, her face was very close to his. He couldn't resist. He just closed his eyes and leaned forward. To his surprise, she also leaned into him, and they kissed. This was the first joint kiss they had. It was not too intense, but it was quite wonderful and did last a long time. After a little while, she pulled away and looked down.

He pulled her close to him and just held her. In a moment, he felt her shiver again. He turned back to the cabin and began walking with her very close to him. At the cabin door, he leaned in and gave her a little kiss on the cheek. "Good night, my Darling. Sleep tight."

"Good night, my love.", she replied and quickly turned and went inside.

He turned and walked up the hill to his tent. Before he could get inside, he heard a soft, "Very touching kiss."

This time, it was Mitchell's turn to jump. He turned to see Redcloud sitting just outside his tent. "Were you sitting there the whole time?"

"Ah, yep.", was all he said.

As he opened his tent, he said over my shoulder at him, "Mind your own business!", and went inside.

As he closed up the tent, all he heard outside was a soft laugh.

The next morning came early, as usual. After their morning run, minus August, they had their breakfast. When it had ended, everyone looked at the Boss for their assignments for the day. "Guys, let just get the rest of the stuff packed today. Tomorrow morning, we'll take off for the trading post."

August stood up and said, "We have a lot of meat. Tonight, we will have a feast."

"I will gather the vegetables we have left in the garden." Kat said.

"I'll help you." Spoke up Wilson.

"Sounds like we're gonna have a party tonight." Mitchell said and stood up.

Looking at the young men at the table, he said, "You guys haul up some wood and we'll get a good fire going for our last night."

"Ah, after we finish the packing." He quickly added.

Most of the group laughed, or at least smiled, as they got up from the table.

Before lunch, they had everything either packed or stored. They then began burying the duce. They had already buried most of it, and all they had to do was fill in the back, where they had their supplies under a tarp. After lunch, they finished up the burial duty and Redcloud supervised the camouflage of it.

When Mitchell came back to get them for dinner, they had completed the work. Now they were just playing around. The duce had totally disappeared and wouldn't have known it was there if he didn't already know it was there. Everything looked so natural he would not have even seen it. He saw a few rocks piled up in front of it. "What's this?" He asked, pointing to the pile.

Johnson was closest to him and came over. "Chief says we may not recognize the area when we come back to collect our stash. We put a marker out so we can find it."

"Good idea, nice job."

Johnson turned and shot a thumbs up to the rest of the gang. Mitchell just shouted out, "Anyone hungry?"

"Yeah." Came from just about every mouth. They all headed back to the table area, where August had been roasting something over the fire. Pig, Mitchell thought.

August brought a large cut of meat over to the table and set it down in front of them. It smelled wonderful. The girls came out of the cabin with a couple of pots. One was full of carrots and the other had a few potatoes. There was what looked to be a mixed salad already on the table.

Mitchell stood up as everyone else sat down. He said, "People, this is truly a feast. August, you have outdone yourself with this. And ladies, you have done wonders with what remained in the garden."

Everyone was sitting up and in a party mood. "It's a shame we have nothing left to drink." He said, looking right at August.

All eyes turned to look at him. He just stood there and shrugged his shoulders and put up his hands. "I could tell you how good it was, if that will help.", he said to everyone.

Everyone started laughing and those close to him patted him on the back. This was going to be a great last night, even without the booze.

The meal was fantastic and as the night closed in, they all headed over to the fire pit. There was a huge pile of wood there. Most of it was dry, but some that really weren't ready to be burned yet. What the hell, who cares? They got the fire going and everyone was laughing and joking. Anna started singing some song from our time. It was a light-hearted song and had a little beat to it. The guys clapped to the beat. Quickly, those who knew the song joined in, and even August and Kat were clapping along. The song was one of the younger people's songs, so Mitchell didn't sing along. Redcloud, as was normal for him, just sat there smiling at everything."

After the song and a short round of applause, August stood up and sang. Even though he was singing in German, Mitchell kind of recognized the song. It was something he thought he heard at a beer fest or two that he had gone to. Only Kat joined him in the singing, but that didn't detour him in the least. He danced around the fire, clapping his hands and getting everyone to follow along with the clap.

Johnson was the next one to jump in. It was some kind of rap song. Mitchell had to cough a little to let him know some words were not acceptable, but it turned out to be alright. His dancing was something else. August watched with great interest. He even tried to copy some of the moves, but mostly, he was too old and too fat to keep up.

They all had a good laugh. Even Kat was laughing at her father. For the first time, she had moved to sit next to Mitchell. Mitchell had noticed, but didn't know who else did. He was sure Redcloud noticed because he kept looking Mitchell's way and smiling.

After a while, August stood up and asked Redcloud, "Chief, how do your people celebrate something like this?"

Mitchell was sure August had caught Redcloud off guard. He sat up straight and looked around at everyone, while they all looked back at him, waiting for an answer.

"Well," he thought about it a moment, "we celebrate very much like this. We have a big feast. Usually deer or even buffalo."

"What is buffalo?" Kat asked.

"Buffalo is a plains animal." Redcloud answered, "The herds are so large that if you stand on one side, you can't see the other side. They are known to the native Americans as the thunder beast because when the herd is on the move the ground shakes and it sounds like thunder."

Redcloud had now stepped out into the center near the fire. He grabbed a couple more logs and threw them onto the fire. Walking around, he said, "After the food, we would all sit around and tell grand stories of the hunt or a fight. Of course, the stories would grow in greatness the more it was told and depending on who was telling."

"Just like we do.", said Wilson.

"Exactly, just like the white man." Redcloud stopped to let that set in. Continuing, "After the story telling dies out and the little ones fall asleep, we sing the songs of our ancestors that tell the history of our people. We will dance to honor and ask our gods for blessings."

Redcloud just stayed by the fire and watched the group as they followed his story. August finally spoke up. "Your people do the same things we do. Has this always been this way or do your people copy what the white man does?"

"No, my people have always been doing this. It just goes to show you that the white man and natives are not that much different, deep down."

Kat raised her hand and asked, "Would you please sing us one of the songs from your people and show us a dance?"

"I don't sing.", he answered her flat out.

"Please," she said, "the others have shown us, and I saw you sing to Anna's song a little."

"Ah….", everyone joined in and shouted at Redcloud. They were all laughing and poking fun at him. Redcloud tried to move back to his seat, but Mitchell stepped up to stop him. He knew he might take his life in his own hands, but he grabbed his arm and tried to lead him back to the fireside.

Redcloud just stood there. Finally, he held up his hands and everyone slowly quieted down. "Alright, I show you a dance. This dance is called the Grass Dance. After consulting with the medicine man, a young disabled boy went out on his own and was given this dance in a vision. It represents the swaying of the plains grass. Everyone needs to gather around the fire."

They all gathered in a circle around the fire. Redcloud ran through the movements. He then went through is slower and they all tried to follow along. Everyone was laughing and having a good time. Redcloud was getting a little frustrated.

"Listen people." He shouted out. "You asked me to show you this. The natives considered dance to be a way to honor their god. It is a serious and not used to clown around."

Kat looked at her new boyfriend when Redcloud said "clown around". He just held his hand up and said, "Later."

Redcloud continued to show the dance. It wasn't complicated, but it took a little practice to get the movements down. After a while, they were looking pretty good. However, after doing this for about an hour, they were all ready to sit down.

"Thank you, Chief." Kat said before he sat down. He turned and gave her a very polite bow.

"Tomorrow, we leave.", Mitchell started out, "We have a long way to go. Things will not be as easy as some of you might think. We will have several river crossings that will make it even more difficult with the hummer. Just the weight of it alone will be problems. I want to keep as low a profile as possible. If I thought we could do it, we would only travel at night. However, we are not familiar with this country, and I think there is too much danger of trouble sneaking up on us at night." He waited for this to set in on everyone's minds before he continued. There didn't appear to be any questions, so he went on. "First, we will hit the trading post for supplies. We will leave the hummer away from the trading post and only take the wagon and a couple of people. I don't want too many of us in there together. Johnson, aw Stretch, you'll stay with the hummer along with Jose. I do this, and I'm ashamed to say it, because of your race. And in this time and this place, I don't want to start anything that will slow us or cause any trouble."

"Don't worry, Boss, I understand," said Rodrigues.

He then looked over at Johnson. He could see Stretch wasn't happy with the decision, but he nodded his understanding.

"When we get to San Antonio, you two as well at Anna, are going to have a difficult time of it because of the way people see you now." again he waited for a comment or complaint, but there was none. "This, however, is something we will deal with together, as a team."

He looked around at the group, and even August was nodding his agreement. "Let get to bed, you horse wranglers will have the hardest day tomorrow and I think you'll need a good night's sleep."

There was a little sadness in the mumbling as the party broke up. Mitchell thought they would have liked to keep it going a while longer, but no one really said anything. They all knew he was right. The group slowly broke up and everyone headed off to their beds. He took Kat by the arm and walked her back to her cabin. As he leaned in to give her a goodnight kiss, August came around the corner. He made a little cough and went around the two lovers to the door. As he went in, he turned and gave them a sweet smile and then closed the door. Looking into her eyes, with only the light of the moon, made this an irresistible romantic setting. What he had intended to be a quick peck on the cheek to say good night turned into a deep and passionate kiss. When they finally stopped, Kat looked down in her shy way. He took his finger and put it under her chin and lifted her head and said, "There is no one around, and this is between you and me. You don't need to be shy or ashamed. It is a natural thing between two people who are in love."

This put a smile on her face. She quickly put her arms around his neck and gave him a very warm hug, and then turned and went into the cabin. He stood there a moment, holding on to the last sight he had of her. It took a while to tear himself away, and he strolled up to his tent. When he got there, he looked over at Redcloud's tent, half expecting to see him sitting there with that stupid smile on his face, but it looked like he, too, had gone to bed.

CHAPTER 6

As normal, Redcloud was up and rousting everyone else out of the sack. Mitchell could never understand how he could wake up so early without an alarm clock. This morning, however, there was no exercise formation. They quickly had some cold MREs and went right to work. They broke camp and threw the tents and last-minute items into the hummer, trailer and wagon, depending on what it was. Redcloud had been working with the guys to teach them how to ride a horse. Rodrigues was the only one who had ever ridden outside a carnival pony ride, but he had never ridden bareback before. Mitchell had never done this either and from what he understood, it took a distinct set of skills over a saddle broke horse. The guys quickly caught on and by now were actually not too bad. He had seen none of them fall off their horse in a day. They practiced herding the horses around the corral. It was a small area and not ideal, but it was what it was, and all that they had.

Redcloud took his gang up to the corral and in a short time, Mitchell got a call on the radio saying they were on their way and that everything was looking good. He had Wilson take off with the hummer and take point. She, with Kat and him, would jump quickly ahead from ridge to ridge. This kept the hummer away from the horses and let them have some eyes out in front. With no maps, it was also good to let them scout out the best route. August followed in the wagon. Mitchell wanted him to stay ahead of the herd and behind the hummer. However, if there was even the slightest problem with the wagon, he would fall off to the side and let the horses pass and then make the best time he could. They all had their rifles and August had both his and Kat's. Mitchell told everyone if there was a problem, or they could not raise the others on the radio to fire two shot. He told August to fire both his and Kat's off, one right after the other, and the others would come back to help. Redcloud could also let him know with the radio if there was a problem.

His primary concern at this point of the trip was not to stir up the horses. If they ran, he didn't think they had the men or skills to stop them and their trip to the trading post would be in jeopardy. The morning, however, went smoothly, and they only had a couple of quick pauses near water to let the animals rest and drink. They made what he thought was good time, however that night, when they made camp, Wilson told him they had only gone about eleven miles.

He laughed to himself, thinking about what he had said the night before when he told them it was going to be a long trip. As they set up camp, Redcloud stopped the herd a little way behind them in a small clearing. He had two guys riding around the horses to watch them. They were their most precious item right now. Getting them to trade would either make the group or break them.

As August pulled the wagon into camp, Mitchell asked, "How long do you think it will take us to get to the trading post?" After he climbed down, he turned to him, stretching out his back. He stood back up and looked off in the direction they were going and slowly said, "I would say three, maybe four days." He then took time to stretch some more and rub his butt. "If we make as good a time as we did today. But I think there may be a stretch or two where we will get slowed down some."

"Further than I had hopped, but I think we will still be Okay, as long as we don't have any problems." Mitchell casually answered him, repeating back his concerns.

August slowly walked away with a little stiffness and still rubbing his butt. Mitchell could only imagine what he was going through. He thought tomorrow that he will ride with him, to keep him company and maybe even learn how to drive this thing, as he looked over this junk pile of wood.

Dinner tonight was quick and quiet. It was not only August who was stiff with a sore butt. The horse wranglers also were feeling sore in places they didn't know existed before. It is a shame the Army put nothing more than aspirin in the basic first aid kits. Mitchell handed them out to everyone that needed them but told them that tomorrow they were just going to deal with it because they didn't have that much left.

As usual, Redcloud didn't appear to be bothered by any of this. He just set up his tent and ate his dinner in total silence. Before dark, he had gathered up a couple more of the guys to stand watch over the horses. This time, it was Mitchell's turn. He took one of the Indian ponies they had captured and rode out to watch the herd. When they got there, he pulled up alongside of Redcloud and asked, "Do you think we lost any today?"

"No," was his simple reply. Then Blake and Rodrigues rode up and said that everything was quiet. Redcloud then looked at Mitchell and said, "We were lucky today. The herd stayed together and behaved nicely. We will be extremely lucky if the entire trip goes this way."

Mitchell looked over the clearing and saw the horses gently grazing. Realizing it probably wouldn't take much for them to lose the entire herd.

While he was thinking, Redcloud turned and rode back with Blake and Rodrigues. He shouted over his shoulder, "See ya in a couple of hours."

With the others gone and darkness settling in, Mitchell found it a silent evening. Johnson rode off to the left side, and he rode around the right. The horses didn't appear to worry about them much. As they neared, they would raise their heads and look around for a minute, and then go back to grazing. He thought they were just about as tired as he was, because they didn't really move more than a few steps at a time while they grazed. Johnson and he kept riding in circles around the herd. Two times in each circle, they would stop and chat when they passed. Other than that, it was quiet.

A few hours later, Redcloud came riding up with Wilson. It turns out that even she was going to take part in the rotation. She rode fairly well. Probably as good as the rest of them. It must have been near midnight. He didn't have his watch on. Recently, he had taken to not wearing it. It seemed a useless idea to keep tract of time. Here and now, you worked when it was light. Your stomach told you when it was time to eat, and you went to bed when it was dark. Why keep the watch?

They rode up to meet the new night riders as they came into the clearing. "Everything is quiet, so far." Mitchell said as they all came to a stop. "Anna, good to see you can ride." he told her with a smile.

"I could ride, almost before I could walk. I was raised on a farm, and we had lots of horses." She said and then adjusted her butt on the horse and added, "Ouch, of course I haven't ridden anything with four legs in many years."

Even Redcloud laughed at that. "What time you want relieved?" he asked him.

"You can wake the guys about three and send them back out." Redcloud replied. "Then I'll come back at six o'clock and we'll head the herd out."

"Not much sleep for you or your guys." He said.

"About the same as everyone else, I suppose." Redcloud said, and then added, "There'll be plenty of time to sleep while you're trading these nags."

He then quickly rode off, with Wilson following him.

As Johnson and he rode back, he was thinking about what Redcloud said. He hadn't thought about it before, but now that he was thinking about it. Going in there with a black man, they could pass off as my slave. Mitchell was sure that Stretch wouldn't like it much. A Mexican in their group probably wouldn't cause much problems either. But, given the trouble with the natives in this area, there would undoubtable be trouble if they rode in with an Indian in their group.

When they got back to camp and quickly settled the horses down, he went straight to bed. However, as he crawled into his sack, he found a lump in there. When he reached in, he found a little wind-up alarm clock. So, that's how he did it all these years. Mitchell thought he was just good, and now he could see that he was good. Good at cheating. He smiled as he set the clock for three hours and quickly went to sleep.

When the clock went off, it was a low sound, but enough to wake him, even as tired as he was. Johnson had pointed to the others tent before he went to bed, so he first woke them and tossed each an MRE and reminded them it was not a good idea to keep Redcloud waiting. That helped to get them moving, and they quickly got their horses and were heading out of camp.

"Don't get lost on the way." he laughingly shouted at them as they were leaving. They just turned and waved, but he could see them checking to make sure they were heading in the right direction.

He went back to bed and reset the alarm for another three hours. When the alarm went off this time, it was a little more difficult getting up. He slowly dragged himself out and woke the others. After a quick breakfast, they broke camp. Redcloud rode in and grabbed some food. He then grabbed some for Blake and Rodrigues and mounted back up, but then leaned in towards Mitchell. "I left the guys there and told them to slowly start the herd in this direction. I suggest you get Wilson in the hummer and get her out of here fast. By the time August gets the wagon hitched up, we should be here."

"I plan to ride with August today. He had to handle that team all by himself all day yesterday. I going to lend a hand with the wagon."

Redcloud sat back up and laughed, saying "I hope you can drive that thing better than you drive the hummer."

But, before Mitchell could think of a quick reply, Redcloud turned and was gone. He just stood there a moment, shaking his head. He turned to the camp to get these guys moving. In no time, Wilson and Kat took off with the hummer. Johnson went with them. August was hitching up the team and when Mitchell asked him how this all went together. August gladly showed him how to hitch up the team.

Learning to hitch the team wasn't difficult, but he could see it would take doing it more than a few times to get as good as August was. They climbed up on the wagon. Turning, they could see the herd off in the distance, but they weren't close enough to hear yet.

August set a pace for the wagon that moved them a little further out in front of the herd and then let the team slow down a little.

After they had traveled along for a while, August let Mitchell take the reins and steer the wagon. It wasn't difficult. The biggest problem he had was learning to use the brake as they went downhill. He thought a couple of times that he might lose it. Looking over at August's face, he figured he thought so as well. But they were all learning new skills and kept moving right along.

Kat learned to use the radio and Wilson was also teaching her things about the stuff from their time. Including men, it would seem. Everyone was learning to handle horses, both riding them and herding them. It was difficult to get used to how slowly they were moving, but after a while Mitchell started looking around at the country. Maybe this was the way to do it. In his time, they moved at such a fast pace they never took the time to look around at everything. He could see some wild animals now and then. Mostly they ran away from them, but after a couple of time the animals just stood there and watched as they went by.

They were into a routine now, and the days just went by as they continued to move. Soon, Kat came up on the radio. She said they had reached what she thought was the Brazos River. She seemed to think they could not cross it with the wagon or the hummer.

"What do you think?" Mitchell asked August.

"It sounds like we are right where I thought we were." He said, sitting up and looking around. "Tell them to wait there for us. Until I can see, I don't know which way to go."

"Kat, you guys just wait there. We'll figure out which way to go when August can check it out."

He guessed Wilson had to translate for her because her reply took a long time. "Roger." She said, as Wilson had taught her. "We are taking cover in some brush near here. Anna doesn't want anyone to see us."

"Good idea, out." He said back, knowing Wilson would explain the radio talk to her.

"Chief, did you get all that?" I radioed back to Redcloud.

"Yeah, I heard. We are going to slow down the herd as much as we can while you check it out but, be quick about it. We are not too far behind you."

"Roger." he said into the radio and then to August, "Let's pick up the pace a little. We need to decide what is what before Redcloud can get there with the herd."

August nodded and then added with a smile, "Roger, Boss". He gave the two horses a snap of the reins and they jerked ahead sharply.

Mitchell couldn't tell if we were really moving any faster or not. Although, after about a half hour, they came over a ridge and he could see the river. He could also see it was too deep for them to cross. The wagon might cross, but the hummer would flood out before they got too far. He now wished that thing had come with a snorkel on it.

As they came down to the river, Kat and Wilson came out from the tree line on the left. They met them and climbed up on the wagon. "Where's Johnson?" Mitchell asked.

"I left him guarding the hummer." Wilson said.

"Why?"

"Two reasons," she replied rather sharply. "First, I want to find an excellent camp before we drive so we don't burn a lot of gas driving all over."

After she paused too long, he asked, "And the other reason?"

She said in no uncertain terms, "And, before you men show up and start running all over, us ladies would like a little privacy to bathe."

Mitchell looked over at August, who was trying to hold back a laugh. "I see!" He started to say, but was cut off by Kat.

She said, "No, that is the problem. We don't want you to see."

Now August couldn't hold it back. He roared out a laugh but said nothing. Mitchell smiled and said to Kat, "No, when we say 'I see', like this, it means I understand."

"Oh," she shyly said back and looked down again.

This time, he put his finger under her chin and sharply raised her head. "There is no reason for you to be like this. You never have to put your head down." Then, more gently, he added, "If you say something wrong, it is probably not." August looked over at him and gave him a nod of approval.

As they approached the river, August stopped the wagon and looked up and down the river. He then pointed south to the right and said, "if I remember correctly, there is a crossing down south of here." He then sat back down and turned the wagon to parallel the river.

About a mile downriver, sure enough, there was a crossing next to a small waterfall.

"Here we can cross with no problems." August said as he stopped the wagon.

Mitchell looked around where August had stopped them and thought that was right where he would have also stopped to make camp.

"Redcloud, are you still there?"

"Yeah, you haven't lost me yet." Came the reply.

"When you get to the river, turn right."

"Yeah, I just did and I'm following your trail." Redcloud said back in a rather arrogant tone.

Mitchell had forgotten how good a tracker he was. He didn't don't know if Redcloud was playing with him or if he genuinely felt hurt. "Yeah, sorry about that." He answered back. "We found a crossing about a mile downriver." After a moment he added, "but take your time. The ladies want some private time before you guys show up."

"What?" came back the reply.

"They say they both need a bath."

"Don't we all, but now?" he said.

"I guess they want to clean up before we go shopping." He replied.

"Jeeze," came back the reply, "Okay, we'll slow down. Call me when we're clear to come in."

Mitchell thought he was playing it up, but he could never tell with Redcloud. "Roger, and grab Johnson on your way."

"Yeah, I found him. He's going to follow up with the hummer."

"Roger, out," he said back and put the radio down.

"Alright. We are going to set up camp here. You go wash up in the river or do whatever it is you need to do."

Kat fumbled around in the back of the wagon and grabbed a little box and what looked to be a couple of towels. She and Wilson jumped down and headed over to the waterfall. Quickly, they were around behind the brush and out of sight. August and he set up the camp. August gathered a little wood and started a fire. As he set up a cook area, Mitchell only had his tent and one for August, so he quickly set them up.

After about 30 minutes, Mitchell heard Kat scream. he grabbed his rifle and rain to the river where they were washing. He found a pile of their clothes and Wilson's rifle along the bank. As he came up, he saw three men on horses just standing in the middle of the river watching the girls. The girls were staying down in the water to keep themselves covered. The men on the horses didn't seem to see him, or they just didn't care. Mitchell thought they were fixated on the half-naked women in the water to think about anything else.

As August finally came up beside him with his old flintlock, the men finally noticed them. Mitchell leveled off with his rifle and yelled, "Ain't nothing you need to be seeing here. Just keep on riding."

August brought his rifle up and stood off to Mitchell's side. "Move on." He shouted at them.

None of these men had any of their weapons out, so they were not in any hurry to do anything. Slowly, they turned their horses and continued to cross the river. As they got to this side, they held up and took one more look at the women.

"If you want to live, I suggest you get that though right out of your head." Mitchell said to them.

They looked back at him and then at each other. He couldn't hear what they were saying, but they just spurred their horses and rode off, away from the river.

"You ladies okay?" He shouted over to Kat and Wilson.

Wilson shouted back, "We will be as soon as you leave so we can get out of the water."

With a very polite bow, he turned around and left. August was right behind him. However, as he passed by their things, he bent down and picked up Wilson's rifle. He then turned back to tell her he was taking it just as they stood up.

It wasn't intentional, but got an eye full. Wilson was still in her modern-day underwear, while Kat was in what looked to be a slip. They both saw him and dropped back into the water. Kat said something in German. He believed it was a good thing he didn't understand her.

"I'm just letting you know I'm taking your weapon back, so you don't worry about it."

"Yeah, okay," Wilson shouted at him. "Now get out of here and quite peeking."

He turned away and muttered to himself, "I wasn't peeking," then thought about it and added, "but, boy did I see."

Kat and Wilson soon came back into camp. They both looked refreshed, but Mitchell could see they were angry. Wilson first came over to him and grabbed her rifle. "I'm sorry," he said, "I wasn't peeking. I didn't think you would be up and, on the move, when I turned to tell you."

"Yeah, I figured that. Don't worry about me, but Kat was not happy that you saw her. Even though she was still more dressed than most women of our time, she was still very embarrassed." Wilson said.

"Yeah, I'll talk to her shortly. I think it is best we keep an eye out for your newfound admirers. I have a sneaking suspicion that they may be back." He then said and as she turned to leave, he got on the radio "Chief, you can come in now, but keep the hummer out of sight. We just had a run in with three of the locals here and I don't think they have completely left us."

"Copy. We'll keep an eye out for them. Which way did they right off?" he asked.

"They headed out of here about southwest. They didn't leave on the best of terms but at gunpoint."

Redcloud replied, "Roger. I'm going to take Rodrigues and swing wide around to see if I can catch them. I have night vision and may not come in until after dark." Mitchell was just about to reply when he came back on and said, "So don't shoot me."

"Tempting, but Wilco." he said back with a smile.

A few minutes later, they heard the hummer coming up. Mitchell went to meet it and showed Johnson where to park it in the trees just behind the camp. He couldn't tell if maybe it could have been seen driving up from the direction the three men went in, but he had to take the chance.

After dinner, which was again a silent meal, Mitchell took Kat off to the side and they walked along the river. "I'm very sorry for what happened today. I didn't mean to peek at you or to embarrass you. It's just I had to tell Anna that I didn't want to leave her rifle lying around, just in case someone else came by. It was totally an accident that I turned to see you."

"I understand, I think. Anna tried to explain to me about men and women of your time. I can't understand that something like this is common in your time.", she said openly.

"No, I don't think you understand fully. This is still not a common thing or a proper thing for my time. Men and women still try to maintain their privacy. But, in my time the clothing that women wear does not cover the body like women wear now. Women can show their legs and even more. There are still laws, in most places, that say what men and women can and cannot show in public, but it is not nearly as restrictive as the rules of this time. When I saw you, you were still more covered than most of the women of my time."

She smiled at him. "I understand what you are saying, but it is not possible for me to change the way I think."

"Yes, I know. I just want you to understand that I was not trying to see you or embarrass you."

"I understand." She smiled back at him again.

He leaned very close to her and whispered, "I was not trying to see you yet. Soon, maybe.'

She whispered back, "Not until after we are married." And gave him a gentle kiss that seemed to last for eternity, but in reality, it lasted only a few seconds.

It was just after dark when Redcloud and Rodrigues came riding in. Mitchell had warned the group to be careful. With that and night vision, he figured Redcloud would be safe.

Mitchell came up to Redcloud as he got off his horse and said, "Well?"

"You were right. If it's the same three guys, they are running a cold camp about a half mile that way." He said, pointing off the way those men had ridden off.

"I couldn't get close enough to see if they were just camping there for the night or if they intend to pay you another visit." He added to his report.

"Doesn't matter. We're gonna need to double up tonight. Not only are we going to need riders for the herd, but also keep a watch on the camp." He said to him.

"There is another option." He suggested.

Mitchell thought he knew where Redcloud was going with this, and he wanted to head it off before he got to his point.

"In the other case, it was clear they were going to attack us. It was us or them." He said, looking him straight in the eyes. "In this case, however, it is not so clear. If it was, I would have no problems taking them out."

Mitchell turned back to the rest of the group that had been gathering around and listening. "We're gonna let those three make the first move. It is only three. They think there are only the four of us they saw." He turned back to Redcloud. "It is a small enough group, and we have the technology. I am not as concerned about them as I was with the other band."

Mitchell walked away when Redcloud grabbed his shoulder. He was expecting a fight, but Redcloud simply said, "I hear something." He reached up and took the night vision out of the bag on his horse and put them on. Within a few seconds, he found what he had heard. "I guess they're making the first move. What now Boss."

Quickly, Mitchell laid out a plan. "The four of us that these men know about will stay in camp. The rest would hit the woods and cover us. If they come in here, we take them. If they just try to sit outside the camp, we can sneak up and take them one at a time. Try to do it without shooting, but if you have to shoot, remember, no automatic fire, single shot only. Any questions?"

Redcloud asked, "Who is going to decide when to shoot?"

"Well, Chief, I'm gonna be here in camp. You're the one with the night sight, you're gonna have to make the call. I know you, and I know you can make the right call when the time comes."

"Blake," Mitchell called on the radio. He was still on watch for the herd. Quickly, he laid out the situation and the plan. "Keep the horses calm. If they want to move away from the noise, let them, but try to keep them together. Whatever you do, don't spook them more."

"Roger." was the single reply.

Before Blake could sign off, he asked back, "Do you have night vision?"

"Negative." was the reply from Blake.

"Okay, just do the best you can, out."

August, Kat, Wilson, and Mitchell moved over to the fire. August had brought up some water, and they had it hanging over the fire. He felt everyone deserved a hot meal tonight. They still had plenty of MREs to last for a while and tomorrow, they should be able to pick up some supplies.

The four of them just sat around the fire, bait for the wolves. Shortly, Mitchell heard a double tap on the radio. Redcloud signaled their friends were on their way. It didn't take long before he heard them. It surprised him that men of this time were so noisy. He heard them long before they got close.

The group was just chatting like a normal camp when their three friends came out to where they could see them. Mitchell had switched out his rifle for the one Kat used against him. He didn't want these three to get a close look at his.

"Everyone remain still." Said one of the three. "Don't even think about grabin' for that rifle!" he added.

He and his friends had their rifles up to their shoulders and were ready for fire. Michell just raised his hands, as did the others, and slowly stood up. "You got no call to shoot anyone." Mitchell said as he turned to look at them. He assumed the one talking was standing about two feet in front of the others, and they were all separated by about ten feet. He could barely make out the two in the back, and then suddenly one of them was gone.

The leader of the group didn't notice at first. Whoever had taken his friend out was very quiet about it. Mitchell could only guess it was Redcloud. After a little, the leader stepped forward and turned to check on the other two. He saw the one on his right, but when he turned to his left, he quickly saw his friend was missing. "Moss, where are you?" he yelled out, but there was no answer.

He spun back to the group and raised his rifle up again. "Where'd Moss go?" he said to them.

"How would I know?" Mitchell answered back to him. "You've had us in your sights the whole time."

The remaining two then looked around. There was no moon to speak of, so it was very dark. They were very nervous. A minute later, the other man was gone, without a sound. When the leader saw this, he yelled out, "Who's out there?"

There was no reply. This made him even more nervous. Then a soft, but stern, voice came from the dark. "There are four rifles aimed at you. If you don't put down your rifle, I will order them to shoot. You have ten seconds to decide."

The man looked around and swing his rifle erratically in all directions. The voice, they recognized as Redcloud, said "five seconds."

The man backed away, but still kept his rifle up. Suddenly, all hell broke loose. There was a single shot the kicked up the dirt at the man's feet. This caused him to fire his rifle. Now he was empty. Next came about a dozen shots. Not automatic fire, but single shots, well aimed, all around the man's feet. He turned to run, but only got a few steps when Redcloud stood up and cloth-lined him with a rifle butt.

As the man laid there gasping for air, Redcloud reached down and recovered the man's rifle, while Rodriguez and Johnson turned him over and began to tie him up.

Mitchell walked up to Redcloud and grabbed his shoulder. "Nicely played." He said with a great big smile.

"Well, we used more ammo than you would have liked. It would have saved ammo if I had just shot him. But I figured you would prefer I didn't." Redcloud softly said back to him and then added, "As much as I would have liked to."

"Yeah, right! I hear ya." Mitchell replied, fully understanding his meaning. "You guys bring them into camp and make sure they're tied up nice and tight."

The guys had packed some of the zip ties they had from their patrol and used it to secure the hands and feet of the newfound friends. August would have liked to have a turn at them, but Mitchell stopped him. "We'll take these three into the trading post. This will help to tell us what kind of people we are going to be dealing with." He said to him and then added, "It would be better to bring them in, alive and in one piece."

August was not happy with his thinking, but he let it stand.

Mitchell had other problems to think about. Now, they have to act like people of this time. The hummer had to remain hidden. No more MRE's. And as much as possible, they had to keep their modern weapons out of sight. They now had enough rifles from this time to watch these guys. With what they had from the Indians and these three, they were building quiet an arsenal for this time period. He had to do everything he could to hide the fact that they didn't belong.

Suddenly, the radio squawked to life, "Hey, is everything over there? Is everyone OK?" It was Blake. Mitchell had forgotten about him. Quickly, he moved to the far side of the wagon to answer him. "Blake, stay off the air. Everyone one is fine. We have prisoners. Out!" he sternly replied. He then turned the radio off.

When He came back around, Redcloud was standing over the leader with a big knife out. Mitchell could see he was ready to scalp these men. He ran back over there and Redcloud looked at him with a slight wink, stooped down and grabbed the leader by the hair.

"Redcloud!" He shouted. And Redcloud looked up and him and slowly stood up, bringing the leader's head with him. When he was fully standing, he let the hair go. The man dropped back to the ground with a thud that even Mitchell could hear at this distance. "A word, if you please."

Redcloud threw the knife into the ground right next to the head of one of the other me and walked over to him.

"What the hell do you think you're doing? We talked about this, and it was you who said even this was disgusting." Mitchell said in a low but stern voice.

Redcloud just stood there with his hands on his hips and turn back to look at the three tied on the ground and then turned back to him and laughed. "I guess if I fooled you, I must have fooled them as well."

Mitchell was dumbfounded. Redcloud must have seen the stupid look on his face and continued. "When you got the radio call, I had to come up with something quickly to distract them. I never thought my acting ability was that good, but I guess it must have worked. If you believed I was ready to scalp them, they must have believed it, too."

It took a second for Mitchell to catch on. Once he did, he couldn't help but to laugh at himself. Redcloud was acting, and doing a splendid job of it, while he was dead serious. He could only imagine what was going through the minds of their prisoners.

"Sorry Chief, you really had me scared." He said, while still laughing a little. "I truly thought you were ready to scalp them."

Kat had come up to the wagon but stayed around the corner. At this point she came around the corner and said to Redcloud, "You truly would not kill those men?"

Redcloud turned to her. "My sweet young girl." He started out, "We don't do such things where…ah…when we come from. Jim here forgot to turn off his radio, which would have caused a problem when we take these me to the law. I needed to cover for him. These men don't know about us, but they know that the Indians of this time would do such a thing. It did not take much to make them think this was going to happen while Jim did what he had to do on the radio."

Kat looked back at those men on the ground and whispered something in German.

Redcloud softly added, "No, I would never do something like this to anyone, alive or dead." He then walked around her and back to the camp.

Kat came over to Mitchell and put her arms around him. He reached around and held her close to him. "You are truly good people," she said softly.

He didn't have the words to reply. He just held her more tightly and laid his head on top of her head.

Morning came early, as usual. Redcloud was up, rousting people out of the sack. As soon as Mitchell came out of his tent, he went to check on their prisoners. Johnson was on guard and as he walked up, Stretch stood and kicked them to wake up.

As they stirred to life, Mitchell squatted down next to the leader. "Today, we are going to take you back to the trading post. With any luck, by evening you may hang in a tree." he said to him, but loud enough for all to hear.

One of the other men spoke up, saying, "This was all his idea. He said he just had to have that young girl. He said we could share the other one."

"Thank you," Mitchell said over his shoulder, "but I already figured out what was going on. It doesn't matter. All of you took part and all of you will suffer the same punishment."

He let that sink in for a little while. He got up and went over to grab some food. When he came back, he had a nice plate of stew. Well, nice for MREs, but these men didn't know this. As he ate, he asked questions about the trading post and about these me. The leader wasn't very responsive, but his friends were. He learned who was running the post and about the others. Since August had been there, the trading post had grown into a tiny town. There were a few houses and a small stage stop. There was a coral at this end of town where they could put the horses and the two men both seemed to agree the man running the trading post was a hard trader, but more or less honest.

When he got what he could out of them, he told Johnson to cut the hands of the two that helped and sent him for food. He let the two men sit up, but kept their feet bound.

"What about me?" cried their leader. "I need food too."

"Well, you didn't supply me with any information I needed, so I don't supply you with food. Maybe, when we get you to town, they will feed you before they hang you." Mitchell said as he stood back up.

"They'll never hang me. Them's my friends and I will come after you, kill you and still take that nice young thing to play with." He gloated at him.

"Well," He started and then added sarcastically, "my friend." He then squatted back down next to him, "In that case, I wouldn't worry much about you coming after me to hurt that lady, or anyone else. If they don't hang you, I will surely castrate you."

He stood back up, but before he left, he added, "Either way, you'll never hurt a woman again."

As he turned and walked away, there was so much foul language coming from him, Mitchell quickly turned and kicked him in the head. He was quiet after that.

They hitched the wagon. Redcloud and Rodriguez headed off for the horses. Johnson sacked out and the rest of them headed into town with their fiends tied to the wagon and trailing behind it. Blake was following up.

They had to give Blake a quick lesson on how to handle a flintlock rifle, but that didn't take too long. Mitchell had his 9 mil in his belt, but out of sight. They had most all the weapons they had captured in the wagon, along with their own. August and Mitchell carried his and Kat's rifle. The intent was to trade what we could for food and other supplies.

After they crossed the river, Redcloud and Rodriquez drove the horses over and they all went the short distance to the town. When they reached the town, August stopped the wagon as a block in the road and Mitchell opened the coral gate. Blake and Mitchell could turn the herd into the coral and secure it. They did a quick count and there were only nineteen horses left. They had lost more than he had hoped, but still had more than he originally planned, so he guessed they were still ahead of the game.

He told Rodrigues and Redcloud to head back to camp and they would follow directly. The two waved and quickly rode off down the road.

August headed the wagon up the road to what looked to be the trading post and pulled up in front. Mitchell had arranged for him to do most of the talking and trading because, one, they knew him, and two, he knew better how to deal with them than he did.

While August was inside dealing, Mitchell told the girls, "I want you two to buy a couple nice dresses." And before Wilson could speak, he added, "We need to pass you off as a person of this time. Yes, I know what you are going to say, but this will, hopefully, avoid problems down the road."

She said something, and he threw in, "Please, just do it for me without an argument."

Wilson stopped and quietly said, "OK, boss, but only for you. However, if I get one comment for the others, you had better buy some medical supplies while you're in there."

"Understood. I'll warn the others." He smiled back at her.

Wilson just turned away and folded her arm in front of her. He could see she was obviously not happy with the idea.

August and the shopkeeper came out to check out the other stuff they had for trade. He quickly saw the men tied to the back of the wagon. "What is this?" he said.

Before August could answer, Mitchell said, "These three tried to raid our camp last night. They were going to have their way with our womenfolk."

"Johnny, is this true? What this man says?" The shopkeeper asked, but before Johnny, Mitchell guessed was the leader, could answer, he turned back to him and said, "I have known these men for several years. I cannot believe they would do such a thing."

The one the man called Johnny yelled, "These people are lying to you! You know me. You know I would never do such a thing."

Mitchell signaled Blake with a pre-planned signal. He quickly got down from his horse and rifle butted Johnny in the belly. Then he took out a rag and gagged him. After that was done, he cut the other ones loose from the line and brought them up to Mitchell.

Mitchell led one of the men into the store with August and the shop keeper following. He stood him in front of the counter and said, "If you want to live, you'll tell these men." he motioned to the others that were in the store, "what happened."

It was Moss, Mitchell thought, that was first up. He started out softly, "Mr. Perkins, we"

Mitchell nudged him and put his hand on the knife he now had, and said "Louder, so all can hear."

Moss started over again. "Mr. Perkins, Johnny and us saw these two girls washing in the river. When we stopped to watch these two men," He raised his hands and pointed at August and Mitchell. "came from the brush and held rifles on us. We meant no harm, we was just lookin'." He stopped.

"Go on, out with the rest of it."

Moss slowly continued. "They told us to ride on and we did, but Johnny wanted that young girl."

August broke in, "My daughter!"

Mitchell turned and put his hand on August's shoulder, and he settled down. He turned back to Moss.

"We rode on for a while and Johnny made us stop. He told us we were going to go back to get them girls. He told Bill and me we could have the other girl, but he wanted the young one for himself. Bill and I didn't want to, but Johnny didn't give us much choice. Mr. Perkins, you know how Johnny can get sometimes." He said to the shopkeeper. Continuing, Moss said, "We came back later that night and tried to sneak up on them. We didn't know there was more of them. They got the drop on us one at a time and now they brought us back here."

The shop keeper had kept quiet the whole time Moss was talking. He turned and looked at the other men in the store. Then to Mitchell, "How do we know you didn't force Moss to say these things."

"Blake," Mitchell yelled out the door, "Bring in the other one."

Shortly. Blake brought in the other man that now they knew as Bill. "Ok, Mr. Perkins, is it?" and the shopkeeper nodded, "you question this one without me. I separated the two when we came in here, so you could hear the story from both of them."

Mr. Perkins looked around the room at the other men, and they all appeared to nod. After Mr. Perkins and a couple of the other men that were there question Bill and then talked to Moss again, it was done.

In these times, a trial was quick and final. The men from the store gathered together and discussed it on the other side of the room. After a short time, they came back and Mr. Perkins spoke for them. "We have decided that your account of the story is true. We will take care of Johnny, don't worry." Mr. Perkins stopped and looked down at the floor. Slowly he continued, "I too have a daughter that will soon be of the age to marry. I don't want scum like that around to destroy her future."

August looked him in the eye. "This man is truly filth and should be destroyed."

Mr. Perkins looked right back at him "If you're still here this afternoon," he paused "You'll see them hang."

Mitchell spoke up now. "Mr. Perkins, this is not my town and I don't want to overstep your decision, but Moss and the other man, Bill, were not the ones who started this. They seem like good men who were led astray by an evil man. I don't believe they deserve to hang with scum like him."

"I don't know you, Mister, but I know these men." Mr. Perkins said. "They have been friends since they were children. I know Johnny is the leader and the other two are follower. They share as much in the guilt as Johnny."

Mitchell stepped back and held his head down and nodded his understanding.

Mr. Perkins turned to a couple of men and instructed them to tie the three of them up to a tree in the middle of town and to stand guard on them. He then turned to August and said, "You have come here to trade. Let's get on with that."

Kat and Anna both came into the store. Anna got some looks because she was still wearing her man pants and shirt. Mitchell quickly explained there was an accident, and this was all the clothes they could find for her to wear. Mr. Perkins called for his wife and the three of them went to the back room to try on some other clothes. In the meantime, the men also picked out some pants and shirts for this time and they got enough for the other three.

Mr. Perkins was indeed a good trader. His prices were fair, Mitchell guessed. He also seemed to give them a good price on the horses and rifles they had to trade. After they got enough supplies to last a while, He planned for a couple kegs of refreshments to end up hidden in the wagon. Mitchell knew August had forgotten about the drinks, but he hadn't.

After they had concluded their business, they headed out of town. A small group had gathered in the middle of the street. They stopped to watch, with the others, as the three men were put up on horses and ropes put around their necks. They could see Moss and Bill were crying, but Johnny only starred at him. Just before the horses were chased off, Mitchell gave Johnny a brief salute, and he tried to get off the horse, but that only left him to hang slowly.

Kat turned her head as the men swung, but Wilson starred right at them. Kat said, "That is horrible."

Wilson turned to her and said, rather sharply, "Not as horrible as the things they would have done to you and to me after they had killed your father and the rest."

Mitchell started to say something to Wilson, but then he saw the realization in Kat's eyes that she fully understood where Anna was coming from. She also turned and watched as the three men died.

Kat was indeed a strong woman.

With that, August slapped the rains, and they were on their way.

Back at camp, they had a fine meal and after the meal, Mitchell broke out the drinks. He waited until August excused himself to take care of his business and, while he was away, he quietly got one keg out from hiding. When August came back, they all had a drink, except for him. Mitchell didn't know if he could smell it or just figured out something was not right, but they had fun letting him try to search for the drink. Finally, Kat got the keg out and poured him a big drink and they all laughed as he sat to enjoy it. And, yes, he enjoyed it.

"Now that everyone is in a good mood, I have other news I picked up at the store." Mitchell said and after they all quieted down a bit he continued, "It appears we are right on schedule. The revolution has started. Jim Bowie ran General Cos out of San Antonio. However, they have not really started fortifying the Alamo, yet."

He paused and took another sip of his drink before he continued. "I also talked with a man who drew me a simple map showing some good trails to get there. There will be some streams and rivers to cross, but he said that this time of year the water levels are low and we shouldn't have any trouble finding a ford if there isn't a bridge."

The news was not as well accepted as he hoped. He thought mostly everyone was more interested in the drinks. However, he continued, "Tomorrow morning, we leave for San Antonio. If everything goes well and we don't run into any trouble, we should be there in about a week. Maybe a little longer, because we need to be careful with the wagon and take it slow. So, it's getting late. Let's drink up and get some sleep. I still want to post a watch. I'll take the first shift tonight, since most of you are in no condition to handle that right now."

That brought them down a notch or two. He let the reality sink in as they finished their drink and slowly headed off to bed. Redcloud had already turned in and August was just about ready to pass out, anyway. He helped Kat get him to his bed, and he was snoring in no time. She didn't have much to drink, so she sat up with her man for a while and they just sat quietly by the fire for a long time. After a while, she pulled away and turned to him. "I can't get the sight of those three men hanging from the tree out of my mind."

"I know," he said, trying to console her, "it is not an easy thing to do, watch men die. It is, however, sometime necessary for the good of the rest of the people."

"Do the people of your time still believe in the Bible?" she asked.

He was taken aback a bit. This was not a subject he considered discussing with her before now, but thinking about it, it was a subject that was probably going to come up at some time. "Yes, the people of my time still believe in the Bible." He paused, not knowing how much he should reveal to her right now. He thought he should at least prove to her the belief was still there. "In a way." he continued, "it is how we came to be here. In my time, there is another fight going on between some followers of the Muslim religion and others, mostly Christians and Jews, throughout the world. It was a group of Muslims that got that bomb I told you about that sent us back here. The power of this bomb is beyond belief. Even the scientist of my time did not know about these properties of the bomb."

"Do you think you are going to be able to fix this problem for your time in our time?" she asked.

How did he answer that? He simply said, "I don't know if we can fix that one."

Now she let out a big yawn. "I think it is time for you to go to bed, my dear."

She tilted her head up and looked at him with a smiled "Yes, it's been a long day."

He stood up and lifted her, and they kissed a little. He then walked her to the tent that she was sharing with Wilson. J

He unzipped it for her, and she went in and turned to give him another kiss. Before their lips could touch, though, Wilson made a grunting sound and Kat just ducked in and was out of sight. He zipped it back closed and walked back to the fire.

After stoking the fire a little, he grabbed the night vision and strolled over to the river to relieve himself. Then he turned on the night vision and took a long look around. The night was quiet. He saw a few animals scurrying around, but that was about it. He walked all around the camp and didn't see anything. Just the way he liked it, nice and quiet.

About two hours later, Redcloud came out to relieve him and take the watch. He hit the sack and had the best night's sleep he'd had in many weeks. Too bad it was so short.

CHAPTER 7

Morning already? My God, Mitchell thought. He had just gone to bed. It was Rodriguez this time that woke him up. He figured maybe even Redcloud might need to sleep late occasionally. As He crawled out of his tent, he was quickly reminded how wrong he could be. He saw Redcloud was just running down the road, returning from his morning run.

"Hey, sleepyhead." He said as he ran by him. Mitchell thought he couldn't wait to see how long Redcloud could keep this up when they start out on the trail to San Antonio.

Mitchell walked over to the back of the wagon where the food supplies and just grabbed a packet of coffee mix. He put it in his canteen cup and poured some hot water in to mix it. He was lucky that most of the others didn't care for the coffee, so he had a good supply built up already.

Looking around, even in the dim light of the pre-sunrise morning, he could see people packing up and getting everything ready to head out. He went back to his tent and got his act together as well. While he was packing his kit, Kat came over. "Could you use a little help?" she shyly said.

"I suppose an extra hand or two would be helpful." He said as she smiled back at him, but then, trying to be cute, he added, "Do you know where I might find a couple of free hands?" He said with a little laugh.

Wrong answer, stupid. He was feeling so comfortable around her he forgot she was not from his time and didn't fully understand some of the sarcasm they might use. Instantly, she got an angry look on her face and turned and stomped away. He just fell back on his butt and called out to her, "Wait, please, I was only joking." She, however, just kept going.

Mitchell heard the footsteps behind him, and even before he heard the voice, he knew who was there. Redcloud must be constantly watching him. All he said as he passed by was "Smooth move, Slick."

Mitchell didn't respond to him. What could he say? He was right. He was going to have to work this out with Kat later. Right now, he needed to get packed.

It was a little after sunrise when they were finally all packed and ready to head out. Redcloud and Jose stayed on horseback. Blake and Johnson went with August. Mitchell felt it would be good for them to get some time learning to drive the wagon. That left Wilson, Kat and him in the hummer.

While Kat and Wilson headed off to the hummer, he got together with August and Redcloud to layout the plan. "We'll stay on this path for a while and then take an almost due south trail. This will hook up with a main road that should take us right into San Antonio."

August spoke up. "I know this trail. We used it when I first came down here."

"Great. After we get there maybe, I'll put you in the hummer to lead the way."

August liked that idea. They broke up the meeting and he headed for the hummer. He figured he was in more trouble that he thought. When he got there, Wilson was in the driver's seat, but instead of being in the back seat, Kat was in the other front seat. It was plain to see that he was about to get the whole back seat to himself.

He played like this was a good thing. Walking up to the passenger door. The window was open, and he just leaned in. "Good, you had the same idea that I had." He said and then just turned and went to the back door and climbed in."

Wilson turned around and said, "What do ya mean, same idea."

"I wanted Kat to sit up front so she could watch you and learn to drive." He said with a very polite smile.

He didn't know if Wilson had figured out what he was doing, but she just looked over at Kat and smiled. Kat, on the other hand, was even more difficult to read. He couldn't tell if she was excited about the news or upset that he had turned her show of anger into something else.

"If you're ready, let's head out." He said in a happy-go-lucky way. "We'll head on down the road a mile or two and shut down and wait for the others to come up." Wilson was listening to him, but he couldn't tell if Kat was just interested in how this thing ran or thinking of clubbing him the first chance she got. He continued, "Going like this should quickly get us some eyes out front and let us conserve as much fuel as possible."

"Got it, Boss." Wilson said and then went to start the hummer. Quickly, she changed the pace and called for Kat's attention. She slowly went through the steps to start it and then went through it again for real. Kat was all eyes. Following everything Anna did. As Wilson moved, she described what she was doing with her feet while still looking at the road. Kat tried to keep up and was trying to watch the road and Wilson's feet at the same time.

Mitchell just sat back and watched. His plan was working. He was going to use this as best he could to get her mind off his stupid rambling until he could sit down and talk to her about it. They slowly got out on the trail and before she took off, Anna checked the mirrors to see if the rest of the group was following. Satisfied, she hit the gas. Kat let out a little gasp as they shot off down the trail. This was the first time they had a, more or less, smooth surface to run on and Wilson was having a little fun with it. As for Kat, it looked like the first time a kid rode on a big roller coaster. He could see it terrified her, but still determined not to show it. A strong woman, indeed.

It only took us a few minutes to find a place a couple miles down the road where they could pull off and wait for the rest. Wilson backed them in out of sight, just in case. Mitchell climbed up in the gun turret and scanned around with the binoculars. Everything was clear, so he climbed down and got out. He quickly made the excuse that he had some private business to attend to and walked away. When he was safely out of sight, he cut around and headed back to where he could watch.

He found a nice place to hide, but he quickly realized how stupid this was. First, if they caught him, he would be in bigger trouble than he was in now. Second, he didn't need to do it. From what he could see, Anna got busy teaching Kat how to drive. Kat was in the driver's seat and Anna was showing her all the gages and dial and explaining things to her. After a little spying, he just went off to finish taking care of his business and decided it was best not to do any more spy work.

About an hour later, the rest of the gang showed up. A quick check in with Redcloud and he headed back to the hummer to repeating the same maneuver. When he returned to the hummer, Kat was still sitting in the driver's seat. He said, "Not yet. You still have much to learn before I let you take us down the road."

Kat hung her head down and slowly got out and went to the back door. Mitchell said, "No, I said you still have much to learn. You're not going to learn much by looking at the back of Anna's head. You're still in the front seat."

This appeared to delight her. She quickly went around to the other side and climbed in. "Anna," he called her over to him, "The next time we stop see if you can find a good flat clearing. While we wait for the others, you can give her a little time behind the wheel." She quickly glanced back at Kat, and he added, "This is between you and me, for now. She is not ready to be on the road yet. Maybe later. But it will not hurt to let her try it out while we wait."

Wilson gave a thumbs up and said, "Gotch ya', Boss."

"Let's hit it then." He said, and Wilson went through the whole drill again with Kat, just like the first time. Kat was still following everything Wilson did. Quickly, they were off again.

The next stop was a little further than the couple of miles they had planned, but Wilson was looking for the right place to stop. When she pulled over, Mitchell just stayed in the back. Wilson got out and motioned Kat around to the driver's seat. When Wilson told her to get in, Kat shot a look back at him. He said "Wilson's the teacher. I'm just watching. You should do as she says, when she says."

Kat quickly got in and waited for Wilson to go through the drill again. She wasn't prepared for what came next. Wilson said "Ok, show me if you remember how to start it."

Kat went through the drill and explaining what she should be doing. Wilson said "No, I mean start it up."

Kat looked back at Mitchell. Again, he simply said, "She's the teacher. Better get used to listening to her."

Kat quickly turned and just sat there for a moment. Slowly went through all the right steps and started the hummer up. When the hummer caught, she quickly sat back and bounced a little in the seat. Mitchell gave a little applause. She turned, and it had to be the biggest smile he had seen on her yet.

Wilson shut the door and came around to the passenger side and climbed in. Again, Kat got a worried look on her face. Wilson just smiled at her and said, "You're doing just fine. We will not do more than just go in a couple of circles." Wilson then just sat back and calmly told her, "Ok, like I showed you, foot on the brake then move this lever into drive." She then quickly added before Kat could move. "Oh yeah, both hands on the steering wheel."

Mitchell had to stifle a little laugh.

Kat did just as she was told. He felt the hummer pop into gear. Wilson then told her to slowly let off on the brake pedal. When Kat had her foot completely off the pedal, she got a little worried look on her face. "It's not moving." She said in a worried voice.

"Yes, this is normal. We are on a little uphill slope and on soft ground. You are going to have to use the gas pedal now."

Kat looked down at the pedal and moved her foot over to the gas pedal. "Ok, now just put your foot down slowly until you feel the pedal." Wilson said.

Kat did and Mitchell could hear the motor rev, just slightly. Still, the hummer didn't move.

"Ok, now just push a very little on that pedal until it moves."

Kat looked down again, even though her foot had not moved off the pedal. Mitchell quietly said, "You'll need to learn to do this without looking down at the pedals."

Kat smiled, but didn't turn to look at him. The motor revved a little more. Suddenly they were moving, but it was a jump and it scared Kat. She let off the gas and the hummer soon stopped.

"That was great. Now you need to do it a little smoother and once you move, you can let up a little on the gas pedal, but not all the way. That way, we will keep moving. Once we start, I want you to only go a little way and then put your foot on the other pedal again to stop us." Wilson said with a calm voice. She was an excellent teacher.

Kat did it again, and this time it was just a little smoother. She went about 20 yards and stopped. However, Mitchell then realized Wilson didn't tell her to do it gently. He just about slid out of the back seat.

Kat quickly turned and said, "Are you alright?" She was genuinely worried about him. Maybe he was out of trouble.

"I'm just fine, but I think that will work for the first time driving. You did very good. Next time we'll working on turning." Kat was excited to hear that, but then he added, with a smile, "And gentle stopping."

Wilson laughed. Mitchell thought if she hadn't, he would again be in trouble. He figured he may never learn to shut up while he was ahead.

Wilson switched seats and turned them around and parked in the bushes again. It was about an hour and a half when the crew caught up. When they got there, Kat jumped out and ran over to her father.

The conversation was in German, but he bet he could tell exactly what she was telling him.

August climbed down and came directly to Mitchell. "You let my daughter use this thing." He couldn't tell if he was angry or excited. "You told me I could learn. When do I learn?"

Mitchell held up his hands and said, "Wow, my friend. You'll get your turn to learn. First, I need to have a good crew ready to drive the wagon. Right now, you are the only one that can drive that thing."

August stepped back, thinking about what he'd said. He slowly nodded. "Yes, I can see what you say. When?"

Mitchell assured him it would be soon. He first needed to make sure the rest of his crew could drive the wagon. "Tonight, in camp, we are going to train both of you to use our weapons."

Now, he got excited again. He rubbed his hands together again. Mitchell stopped him when he said, "You're not going to shoot them for a while. Not until you can do the same things I expect from any new soldier."

August looked at him with a big question mark on his face. 'First you'll need to understand how it works." He said and then quickly went on, "Next you'll need to take it apart and put it back together again. Once you can do that, you'll need to do it blindfolded." He paused when he thought about all that. "Then, and only then, will I let you shoot it."

The excitement was now gone. His shoulder slumped, and he slowly turned to go back to his wagon.

"August," He called to him. August stopped and turned. "I assure you, it's not that difficult and won't take long. Maybe a few days."

August looked up now and he could see the excitement back in his eyes, but then his stupidity stepped in again and he told him, "Redcloud's an excellent teacher."

"Redcloud!" he said. Mitchell again couldn't tell for sure, but he thought it was fear in his voice this time. He turned back and continued on to his wagon.

"Chief." Mitchell called to Redcloud.

He turned on a dime and came at Mitchell on a run. He stopped on a dime and could give nine cents change. Mitchell thought "God, was he good on that animal."

"What's up, boss?" he asked.

He could see Redcloud was now totally in his element. "Tonight, I want to start training Kat and August with our rifles. Start with theory and simple operation. This is going to be worse than teaching at basic training. You're gonna have to teach them about cartridges and modern bullets and such before you can even think about handing them a weapon."

"Yeah, I thought you might stick me with this." He said, leaning on the saddle.

"You're the best I have, and I think this may take the best. You can keep two guys with you to help. I think Kat will probably be alright with it, but August may be too excited to focus and learn. Use your best judgment, but I have to warn you. He is already totally afraid of you."

"I'll be on my best behavior with them, don't worry. You'll have expert shots in a couple of days, Boss," he said and then kick the sides of his horse and was off again.

"Now, I'm worried," Mitchell mumbled to himself as Redcloud rode away.

He turned to head back to the hummer, and he heard a call from Kat, "Wait."

He stopped and waited. When she got to him, she reached out and grabbed his hand. She started talking before he had a chance to say anything. "I just wanted to say I am sorry for the way I was this morning. Anna explained to me about what you said. I didn't understand your meaning, and that you said in fun."

This time, Mitchell put his head down. "I have found you to be such a clever girl. I sometime forget we are new to you. You would truly fit in well with my time." She smiled, and he continued, "Beside it gave me an excuse to let you learn to drive." He said with a smile.

This time, he thought she understood he was fooling with her. She smiled back and leaned over and gave him a kiss. The kiss was a little too long and Anna honked the horn. That got their attention and as they separated, they both laughed.

When they got back in the hummer, Wilson leaned back and quietly whispered, "Out of trouble, I see."

He smiled back and said, "Yeah, and thanks for the help."

She turned back around and started the hummer, but before she took off, she looked over at Kat and then back to him and said, "Gotta keep the Boss happy."

But, before he could say anything, she gunned the hummer, and they were off with a jump.

The next stop was right on two miles. Kat and Anna went for a brief drive while Mitchell scanned the area. To the southeast, he could see some smoke. It appeared to be fire, maybe several camp fires. He'll need to have Redcloud check it out when he gets here. This stop looks like a good place for lunch.

The team made good time this round. When they came into sight, it was Johnson driving the wagon. When he got there, he pulled it off the trail and parked it just like a pro.

"Nice job, Stretch. You look like you've been doing this all your life."

"Never touched anything like this in my life. It is kind of fun though." But after he tied off the reins and climbed down, he added, "But we gotta get something to sit on. My ass is killing me."

August heard him and started laughing. "You just got to get more padding on that butt, like me. I don't have a problem." Then he turned and walked back, but they both could see by the way he walked he was lying to them. Stretch pointed, and they both had a good laugh.

"Ok, let's break out some lunch." Mitchell yelled.

They had picked up some tortillas at the store and August sliced some meat for a kind of wrap sandwich.

Mitchell walked around to see how everyone was doing. Mostly stiff backs and sore butts, but everyone was in good spirits.

"Chief, did you see the smoke about southeast of us?" He asked when he got around to Redcloud.

"Yeah, I saw it. Without getting closer, I can't tell you much." He said while continuing to eat.

"You want to take off and check it out?" He asked as the Chief turned to look that way.

"No, I don't think we need to bother. If I was to guess, I say it is a village or camp. White or native, can't tell you." He said as he took a bite of his wrap.

Mitchell just continued to look that way. Redcloud continued with his advice, "If I go and it's native, then we may have the same trouble we had before. If they're white and see me, we'll still have the same trouble as before. Best thing to do is just continue our path and let them stay on theirs." He took another bite but continued to talk with a mouth full of food. "If we meet up with them later, we can worry about it then."

Mitchell had to admit it was sound advice, and he didn't have any better ideas. "Plan." He simply said and walked back to get himself some food.

Kat already had a plate ready for him. He felt he could get used to this real fast. He always had to worry about everyone else. It was sure nice to have someone worry about him for a change. They sat and just chatted about the area and ate.

After lunch, they headed back out. As they pulled onto the trail, Mitchell saw Blake take the reins of the wagon. He guessed August was going to make sure he got his chance behind the wheel of the hummer as soon as he could.

The rest of the day went on without and problems. There were a couple of small streams to cross. They waited with the hummer at each of the crossing, on the off chance the wagon broke down or there was some other trouble.

When it finally came time to camp for the night, Wilson found a good spot near a stream and plenty of cover to hide the hummer. She pulled up, and they unloaded the hummer. Wilson then parked it out of sight.

Blake was getting the hang of driving the wagon, but not as good as Johnson was. He got it into the clearing without too much trouble. Now the two of them needed to learn how to unhook the horse and hobble them, so they still had them in the morning.

Redcloud wasn't with the group when they pulled in. As Rodrigues rode up, Mitchell asked, "Did you lose the Chief on the way?"

"No, boss, he wanted to circle the area to check it out. He said he'd be back here before dinner," Jose replied, and then added, "Oh Yeah, he said not to shoot him when he comes in."

As he laughed, Mitchell just waved him away. He rode over to take care of his horse. Good thing they got the horses, saddle and kits from those three that tried to mess with them. They offered the other horses they had, and Mr. Perkins took the offer. He had Rodrigues take three more of the wild stock to Mr. Perkins in return. All they ended up keeping were only four of the Indian ponies to pull the wagon.

After about an hour, Redcloud rode into camp and put up his horse. When he finished, he came over and stood near the fire. Mitchell didn't think anyone else caught on, but He thought Redcloud was having a little trouble sitting. The words saddle sore came into mind, but he wasn't the one who was going to voice them out loud.

He casually walked over to Redcloud and asked, "So, how are we doing?"

He straightened up, rather stiffly. He took a drink and said, "Things look quiet, but we shouldn't stay here long. There is a footpath along the stream and signs that it might be well used. Probably natives and I don't have any way of know who."

"Sounds like good advice. We'll move out first thing in the morning." Mitchell said out loud and then leaned in closer and whispered, "Are you alright?"

Redcloud looked around to make sure no one was near and replied, "Just a little stiff. It's been more than a few years since I've had so much saddle time."

"I hear ya," Mitchell said, "You want to ride in the hummer tomorrow?" He added.

"Na, I'll be fine, beside we are all going to go through this, eventually. I'd just prefer it to be sooner, for me."

Mitchell hadn't given it much thought, but Redcloud was right. The hummer can only last so long. They are all going to need to adapt to what is available at this time. He decided he would start acclimating to this time after the Alamo was over.

"Do you think we need to post a watch tonight?" He asked Redcloud.

"It probably wouldn't hurt to post watches from now on. We can always hope it remains quiet, but best to be safe."

"I'll have Wilson run up a watch schedule for everyone, including and newest family members." He knew who Mitchell was referring to. "Besides, I think she is feeling left out of things lately. I really need to keep her focused on the mission at hand, and this will help."

Redcloud threw the little of water he still had into the fire, where it puffed a little steam. He turned and walked away, saying, "I'm going to set up my tent and rack out a little.".

Mitchell said back, "I'll call you for dinner."

Without looking, he said, "Fine, just don't call me late for dinner."

He smiled a little. It was an old joke, but it fit in perfectly here. Mitchell continued to just stand there, looking at the fire, when Kat walked up. "Anything wrong? You look worried."

"No, not really. The Chief said there were signs that someone might use this stream, so I'm going to have to set up watches for the night."

"Oh," she replied and then added, "does that include me and my father?"

"Yes, but for now, until we get you trained, you'll have to use your own rifles."

He could see that didn't go over well with her, but she acted like she understood. He added, "Maybe a couple days and we'll see."

She smiled at that and put her arm into his and her other arm around his chest. It felt so nice just standing there together.

"We'd better get dinner going before it gets too dark. You need to start your training tonight if you ever expect to use our toys."

She knew exactly what he was talking about as she broke away and headed straight for the wagon to gather the food. She had taken over being the camp cook. Sometimes Anna would help, but mostly it was her. She had learned to mix a little of the MREs into whatever it was she was making, and, by God, it was good. They never knew what it was she was going to make each night. It was just a truly pot luck supper.

While Kat fixed dinner, Mitchell went to find Wilson. He thought she had just come out of the bushes and was doing up her pants. "Anna," He called to her, and she became immediately embarrassed. "Chief says he saw signs the stream is being used regularly. I need you to set up a watch list to run every night from now on."

She recovered quickly and said "OK, Boss," and then added, "You want everyone on this detail."

"Yes. We need to get everyone trained; however Kat and August will use their own weapons until we get them training with ours."

"Fair enough." She said and started thinking about it. "I'll tell the crew after dinner tonight."

"Also," He threw at her, "Redcloud is going to start the weapons training tonight. I'd like you to work with Kat, because there may be some things will need to be translated. We are moving past the conversational talk to more complex ideas and technologies." He then added with a smile, "I don't think it would help for Redcloud to use the only other language he knows. No one would understand him."

"Got it," Anna said with her own big smile.

There was the normal dinner chatter talking about the trail and thing they saw and did. Kat went on more than Mitchell had ever heard her before about driving the hummer. The team was all smiles to listen to her talk about how exciting it was. August, however, sat there quietly steaming.

The meal was good and as soon as the mess was cleaned up, Redcloud called Kat and August over near the fire where they could see better. He gathered up three rifles. He gave one to each of his students and kept his rifle for himself.

Kat. Didn't really do much with hers, but August was looking over his rifle closely.

"I didn't tell you to mess with it yet." Redcloud spoke sternly. August put his rifle down right away. Mitchell thought he was still intimidated by Redcloud. Kat just sat there, patiently waiting.

"These weapons," Redcloud started out, "Are a lot more dangerous than anything you are used to seeing. They are also much more complicated." Now he started pacing back and forth in front of his student to keep their attention on him and not the guns.

"The first thing we are going to go over tonight is how to handle them safely." He said to them, but then he took his rifle, slapped a mag into it, rack the charging handle and put the rifle up to his shoulder. "However, before we start, I need you to understand exactly why we are doing this training this way." He said, looking over at the two. Then he leaned a little into the rifle and fired off a round. He then turned back to his students. "At this point with your rifles, you are done until you reload." He then turned back and fired off 4 more quick shots.

"Mein Gott," August said as he slowly looked over the rifle that was just in his hands.

Kat just sat there silently. Again, Mitchell couldn't tell if she was afraid or curious.

"Now, see some more." Redcloud then flipped the selector lever to full auto. He aimed into the stream. When he let go, there were only 10 rounds left in the mag. A spray of water erupted in the stream where he aimed. August stood up and just stared at the spot in the stream. Kat just sat there, motionless.

Slowly, Redcloud turned back to his student. He then dropped the magazine out and check the weapon. Next, he sat on a stump that was set up in the teacher's position in his classroom. He started talking slowly in a low tone of voice, "Now, do you understand why we have been so careful about letting you handle these weapons?"

There were slow looks around the group and then at the rifles in front of them and then nods back to Redcloud. Once he got the response he was looking for, he continued. "Folks, by the time we compete with your training with these weapons, you'll be able to handle them like experts. Your marksmanship may take a little longer because we have limited ammunition and you'll have to wait to get your practice when the time comes to fight."

"So, we are not to shoot these guns?" August seemed a little angry.

"Yes, you will get to shoot. These guns are very accurate, and you will each need to adjust the sights for the way you shoot. But we need to save all the ammo we can for the fights to come." Answered Redcloud.

This appeared to calm August, for now. Redcloud continued. "Ok, grab your weapons and come up to the back of the wagon. We will need the light from the lanterns to work now."

Kat and August picked up the rifles that were given to them. August was a lot more careful with his weapon this time. Kat just cradled hers in her arms the way they did their old Kentucky's. Redcloud had them lay them out on the tailgate of the wagon. He started going over the different parts. First, he showed them how to clear and check the rifle to make sure it was not loaded.

Next, he went into the ability of the rifle. "You people will use the M16A4 rifle. This rifle can fire a single shot or a three-shot burst, similar to what I did."

Kat raised her hand and asked, "But Chief, you shot over 3 bullets."

"Yes, very observant. You will also notice my rifle is a little different from yours. I can fire as many bullets as the magazine can hold. Also, through this bigger barrel underneath, I can shoot smoke or explosive bullets."

"Like you did when we first met?"

"Yes. That is correct. One or two of the explosive round would have brought your entire cabin down, and we would not be talking now." When Kat didn't say anything more, Redcloud continued. "I think that is a good enough lesson for the first night. You two continue to examine your rifles. Your coaches can help you. Do you have any questions?"

August shyly spoke up, "How far can you shoot with these?"

Redcloud responded, "Accurately, you can shoot out to five hundred fifty meters. However, just trying to shoot into an area and hope to hit someone or to keep them under cover it is good to about eight hundred meters. However, it can still kill out to over three thousand meters, but only by pure luck that you might hit something out that far."

August again took a long look at this marvelous thing in his hands. Mitchell again didn't know if he really understood the implications of what Redcloud was telling him or not. "Any more questions?" Redcloud asked.

This time no one said anything, so Redcloud added, "Then coaches take over." In a military manner, these two new recruits hadn't yet seen. He did an about face at marched off.

Wilson and Mitchell kind of smiled at each other. She took Kat off to the side with one lantern and he stayed at the wagon with August.

August looked a little surprised. "He can talk to you like that. You are the boss."

He looked away to smile so he wouldn't see. "Yes, I am the Boss and I assigned the Chief to be the teacher to teach you about our weapons. When he is the teacher, he is the boss and in effect has become the boss during the classes. This is the military way."

"I see." August answered. "These rifles are amazing. Is everything he said about them true?"

"Yes, everything. We have even more amazing weapons, but for now, we are only going to teach you this one. This is the basic weapon for a soldier of my time. The other weapons take unique skills to use, and we may not have time for you to learn them, for now."

"More amazing, you say?" he asked.

He simply nodded because he didn't want to continue this line right now. "Did you understand what Redcloud was saying about this rifle?"

"I believe so." He answered.

"OK, show me how you would clear the rifle to make it safe." Mitchell said.

August picked up the rifle and as he swung it around, he pointed it right at Mitchell's head. Mitchell grabbed the rifle out of August's hands and held it back away from him. "You haven't learned yet about how dangerous these are. You just pointed this thing right at my head and you haven't even checked to see if it is loaded."

Wilson and Kat stopped what they were doing when they heard him yelling at August. Mitchell stepped back and looked back and forth between Kat and August. "Safety is the first and most important rule when handling these or any of our weapons. We have a saying in our time. More people are killed by unloaded weapons than by loaded ones." He then paused a couple seconds and then continued, "Do you understand what that means?"

They both shook their heads. "It means that people accidentally shoot others, including their friends, family, lovers and children, because they thought the gun was empty and were not being careful. You always treat a gun as if it were loaded and never point it at anyone unless you intend to shoot them. And if you intend to shoot them, then be ready to shoot to kill."

He let his little speech set in for a moment. "It is simple to follow these rules, and it is something you must always have in your mind. Clear?"

They both slowly nodded at him. He turned back to August and handed him his rifle back. Slowly he took it and appeared maybe just a little angry. "I sorry, August, if I was a little strong with that last bit, but it is very important you two understand just how dangerous these weapons from our time can be."

"Yes," he said, "I believe I am understanding."

The rest of the night, they continued to go over the different parts of the rifle. "Tomorrow I think Redcloud might teach you how to take it apart for cleaning. Because this weapon is built to very tight specification, its weakness is dirt. They must be kept clean at all times. I will bet that the Chief is in his tent cleaning his rifle as we are talking."

He let August keep his weapon and continue to look it over and to get the feel. He walked over to Kat and Wilson. It appeared they, too, were breaking up. "How did it go tonight?"

"I can't believe you were so rough with my father tonight." Kat said angrily to him.

"Kat, my dear," He started out to calm her, "You are young and easy to teach new things. Your father is older and more set in his ways. He was not paying attention to how serous this matter is. I had to get his attention before he went any farther." He looked back and August was being much more careful while handling his rifle. "See, he is much more careful now. I think what I did was good. I think he also understood what and why I did it. He and I are good." He then gave her his best smile.

Wilson just walked away, but Kat returned his smile and he thought he was good with her, for now.

"What do you think about this rifle? Today is the first time you have picked it up, I think."

She answered back, and in a kind of shy voice said, "No, the first day you came to our cabin when you were not looking, I picked it up, but only for a moment."

"It's a good thing you didn't play with it. You could have hurt yourself, or someone else, badly." He playfully scolded her.

Seriously, she answered back, "Yes, I know this now."

"Wait until we let you shoot it. You'll be surprised at how easy it is to shoot, compared to your old rifles. This rifle has almost no kick and the sights are much easier to use, one you get used to them."

"I can wait. I don't really think I will need to do much shooting with it, but it is good to know how." She said, looking down into her lap.

Mitchell thoughtfully told her, "We don't know what the future will have for us. I'll bet two months ago, you didn't know you would head south with men from the future to save Texas, either. Did you?"

That got a little smile on her face, and she looked up into his eyes and simply said a long "Nooo."

"See, so you may yet play an important role in this fight that is to come." He said as he poked her with his finger.

Now she laughed, and it sounded so good to hear her do that.

"But I want you to promise me one thing right here and now." He said as seriously as he could. And when she turned to listen to him, he took her by her shoulders, "When we go into the fight, I want you to stay right next to me, but if I tell you to turn and run, you turn and run as fast as you can, and don't look back for me."

"I cannot promise you this thing." She said, "You may know some things about your future, but this is my future and now you don't know what will happen. I can promise you nothing, except my love."

He slumped back down. God, what a perceptive girl she was. Not even he had thought this clearly about it. He had been thinking they will go to the Alamo, and everything will happen exactly as it did in his past. She was right. This is her timeline and from the first day they were here, things have changed. Those three that hung. If they had never met his group, they might have made their way into Houston's Army and played a major role of some sort. How they fight at the Alamo will change the future of Texas in ways that they could not even imagine. She was right. They cannot promise anything about this future. They can try to guide, but there are so many ways they could mess it up.

He must have been sitting there thinking so deeply she got worried. She put her hand on his arm and said, "Are you alright? Did I say something wrong?"

Mitchell looked up at her and said, "No, you didn't say anything wrong. In fact, you said something very right, and it made me think if we are doing the right thing."

She leaned closer, and this time put her other hand under his arm and leaned over to put her head on his shoulder. "The way I understand it, those things that were, don't matter now and everything that will be, will be different now. You are going to make the will be things different and better than before."

"Yes, this is true, but being so complicated, I am afraid we can mess thing up for the future."

She sat quietly for a moment and then said, "You cannot mess things up that are already messed up. If you do good, you fix things. If you don't do good, you only mess thing up a little differently."

He thought about it for a moment, and he realized how simple and easy her line of thinking was. She was, in a simple line of thought, correct.

He took his arm back and put it around her, and pulled her close to him. He also snuck a little kiss and a big hug. But it was getting late, so he walked her back to the tent she shared with Wilson. and handed her rifle to her. Right away, she correctly cleared it. Wilson had taught her well. He gave her a quick kiss, and she ducked into her tent.

Mitchell walked back to his own tent and just laid there for a long time before he finally dozed off.

Later, he got up to pull his watch, and everything was quiet. The next morning, they were back on the trail again.

After a day and a half of this same routine, they found what Mitchell thought was the trail they should take to the south. This trail would hook up with the main road, if you will, to San Antonio. From the little hand-drawn map the man at the trading post gave him, it looked right. When the rest got there with the hummer, it was about mid to late afternoon. He decided this was a good place to camp for the night. Redcloud's two students had been doing very well with their training. He thought they might camp early today and before dinner, they would try to get them to zero their weapon. It was good they had 5 extra rifle that were in the second duce. They lost all the other weapon in the second duce when the bomb went off. He assigned two of the spares to the new teammates so they would have their own. Today, they would finally get to shoot them. He will have to be very careful with August, knowing he would be too excited to listen. He just hoped he wouldn't have to put him down in front of the others again.

When Redcloud and the rest got there, Mitchell informed him of his plans. Redcloud nodded to show he was ok with it. He then turned to ride off. Mitchell asked, "Where are you going?

He turned back and said with a smile, "I just don't want to be anywhere near this crew when they cut loose." He said with a laugh, then seriously said, "I just want to ride around to clear the area."

Mitchell just waved him away and turned his attention back to the camp. "Ok everyone, we're gonna take this trail to the south to hook up to the main road to San Antonio. We'll camp here for the night. Wilson, I need to see you."

She ran over and said, "What's up, Boss."

"Say nothing to the others for now, but I want you to find something suitable to use for targets."

"You're serious," she said. "You're gonna let them shoot today."

"Yeah," He answered, "I think they are ready. I cleared it with the Chief and he agrees."

"This is going to make their day. When are you going to do this?"

He looked up at the sky and around and said, "As soon as we eat and the Chief gives me the all clear, but remember, keep it quiet until I announce it."

"You got it, Boss. I'll find something we can set up, even if it's a couple of rocks."

Even Wilson was excited to hear this. He couldn't wait until Kat and August find out.

After a while, Redcloud rode into camp. The stew was ready, and they all ate, and it was just the normal talk at lunch. Kat was talking about her driving lessons. August would get quiet when she did. Then he would go on about how good Blake and Johnson were the driving the wagon, as a hint to Mitchell that he was ready to drive.

After they cleaned up from lunch, he told Kat and August to get their weapons. It was time for a little test. He ran each of them through the drills of safety, loading, clearing, jams, and functions of the rifle. Kat passed with flying color. August, also, passed, but he was a little slower and more unsure as he performed each task.

"Ok, you guys are looking good." He said to them. He then turned around and saw Blake. "Johnny," He shouted to him. "Grab me four mags and two boxes of rounds."

Before Mitchell could turn back around, he guessed both of them knew what was coming. "Ok, I think you're both ready to try it. We are going to do this one at a time. Kat, ladies first."

She jumped up with her rifle and was ready. "Just wait a minute, young lady. You're not ready to shoot, just yet." He said. "You still need to learn to load a magazine and Wilson needs to set up some targets. Also, you need to go over some good shooting positions."

She just dropped back down and sulked for a moment or two. When Blake returned with the mags and ammo, Mitchell gave one mag to Kat and two to August. He kept the last mag so he could demonstrate. First, he opened a box of ammo and took out one round. "This is one round of ammunition. Inside, this is a primer, to ignite the powder, the powder itself, and the bullet on top to hold it all in." As he went over each part, they both came in close to look. "In the back is the primer. This ignites the power when hit. Remember when we disassembled the rifle, and we took out the firing pin? That is the part that will hit the primer to make it shoot."

They both watched attentively and appeared to understand. Pointing to the bullet's end, he said, "This is the bullet. This is the only part the goes out the barrel when you shoot. When you load the round into the magazine, you must make sure you load it with the bullet to the front."

Kat spoke up, looking at the magazine in her hand. "How do I tell which way is front?"

"I will show you in just a moment." He said with a sarcastic tone. "First, I want you to lock the bolt to the rear." Which they both did smoothly.

"Next, I want you to hold the magazine like this." He said as he showed then and with a little help they both got it. "Now slam the magazine up into the rifle. Not too hard, but with just a little force."

They both followed the directions and after a little fumbling around, they got the mags in.

"Now reach up with your left hand and slap the release button like we did in practice."

Quickly, he heard the bold slam forward on two M16s.

"Great," Mitchell said, "now if you had had bullets in the magazine, you would be ready to fight."

"Now I just want you to pull back on the charging handle."

Then both did, but unlike before, the bolt stayed back. "Why isn't it working right?" August asked.

"That is because as far as the rifle is concerned, you're out of ammunition. When the mag is empty, the bolt will stay back so you can quickly put another one in, slap the release and you're ready to go again." Mitchell explained and then added "See in the heat of battle you may not notice you fired the last round and instead of getting messed up the rifle is designed to help you know it is time to reload. Remember, these mags will hold twenty or thirty rounds. That is a lot to try to keep track of while other people are shooting back at you."

After a few drills with the empty mags, he had them both load ten rounds into each mag. Wilson had set up a small jug or something about twenty-five yards away. He didn't go into why they zero at twenty-five yards and they didn't ask. He didn't really want to go into the ballistic of the round.

He had Wilson work with Kat to get into a good prone position and run over the breathing. Now he ran through the drills just as if they were back on the range at Hood.

Kat followed each of the instructions, and he gave her a chance to calm down a little. He then told her to put the selector on single fire and pay attention to her sight alignment and to squeeze off one round when she was ready.

It took a moment for her to get comfortable. After a moment, she fired one round. Mitchell watched down range and saw the dust kick up just low at about seven o'clock.

Then he looked at Kat. She was laughing. "It's so easy to shoot." She almost laughed out.

He knelt down next to her and reminded her of the dangers of not paying attention. This quickly brought her back to the task at hand.

After he explained he wanted her to use the same sight picture, she had the first time; she fired two more times. All three rounds hit about the same place.

He had her place the rifle on safe and then took her rifle and made the sight adjustments and gave it back to her and told her to fire three more rounds, just like before. This she did just as smoothly and anyone else in the group.

They went through the same procedures. This time, she hit the jug with the first shot.

Everyone was standing around and watching. When the jug shattered, there was a big cheer from everyone, even August.

Mitchell turned to August and said, "You taught her well. My friend, very well." He could see August's chest come out a little with the pride in his daughter. He let her fire off the remaining rounds. As he told her, the bolt remained locked to the rear when the mag was empty. He was counting the round and knew she was empty, and he expected her to continue to try. She, however, quickly picked up that something wasn't right and looked at the rifle. When she saw the bolt back, she looked up at him. He simply said, "Reload and continue to fire."

Kat dropped the mag like a pro and, with a little fumbling, got the second mag in and let the bolt go. Before she fired, he knelt next to her and said, "OK, I want you to pick out some targets out there. Rocks, a branch, anything. Then tell me what you're shooting at and then try to hit it."

She began with a couple of rocks that were still close to them. After hitting them, he suggested she find something a little further out. She was a pretty excellent marksman on her own, but when he suggested a branch that was sticking up, probably out one hundred and twenty-five yards, she turned and looked at him and said, "Are you serious?"

"Yes, the rifle can shoot just fine that far away. Can you?" He said with a challenge.

She turned back to the challenge and took up her position. "Remember your breathing and sight alignment." He whispered to her. Then, just before she was ready to shoot, he added, "Squeeze the trigger."

She stopped and turned to look at her man. "Are you though?" She asked.

Mitchell just threw up his hands in a surrendered.

She turned back to her task. The first shot missed, He thought, but the second shot was dead on. Another big cheer came from the group.

"OK, now I am going to let you try something that I don't want to see done after today, unless I tell you to." He said as he kneeled beside her. "We are going to try a three-round burst."

"When you're ready to shoot, you just keep holding the trigger back. The rifle will automatically fire three rounds and then stop. Then you release the trigger and do it again until you are empty."

Kat just hunkered down in a good shooting position, and he told her to put the weapon on auto.

He then heard the selector click one more time, "Fire at will."

He just rocked back onto his butt and watched her. She was very intent on what she was aiming at, but this time she didn't tell him, so he had to guess what she was shooting at.

She let go with a three-round burst. Mitchell could see a short line of dust strikes in the dirt.

When he looked back at her, he thought he heard a little giggle. However, she fired another burst and then another. The last burst only had two rounds left. She stopped and looked back at him.

He said "You're empty. See, the bold is now locked to the rear. Now take the mag out and close the bolt to keep the dirt out."

She did exactly as he told her. When she stood up, he said, "Have the Chief clear you and wait back there."

"August, your turn now. Are you ready?"

"Oh yes. Boss. I have been ready." He said as he came up.

When Mitchell got him settled, they went through the same drills that he did with Kat. His rifle was a little further out, and it took three tries before they got him zeroed. He had to assure him it wasn't his shooting, but whoever had the gun before him had it set to his liking, and they just had to change it to match him.

Once he had zeroed, his marksmanship was excellent. His eyes weren't as good as Kats for the distant targets, but he surely was deadly up close."

When he got to shoot the burst shots, Mitchell thought he might wet himself. He was so excited. But when he was all done, they all headed back to the camp.

Redcloud then took over and showed them how to clean the rifles. After a couple hours and a re-cleaning or two, Redcloud was satisfied and let them off the hook.

Now that the shooting was over, Mitchell let August break out a keg and they all sat around the fire with a drink and talked about the excitement today.

It was a very lively talk that night. He thought August was the most talkative. He couldn't say enough about how light the rifle was and how it was like shooting nothing. After a while, Kat got up and left the party to cook dinner. Mitchell went over to help her but ended up mostly just watching and chatting a little.

After dinner, they took a little stroll away from camp. She was shocked when he scolded her for not bringing her rifle with her. "That is your weapon now. It should be with you at all times, especially when you are not in camp."

She ran back to where she had left it next to the wagon and came running back. He helped her adjust the sling so she could wear it across her back. When he helped put it around her, he accidentally brushed her breast with his hand. She didn't move away, but stepped in closer. "I'm sorry. I didn't mean to touch you like that."

"I know, and I'm not sorry. Soon, someday we may be together, and I will wait. Will you?" She said so softly.

"Yes, I can wait until the time is right for both of us." He answered and put his arms around her and held her close.

They continued to quietly walk a little further down the new road. They were maybe two hundred yards when Mitchell heard a noise. He stopped and pulled her down into a crouch. He held his finger up to her lips to signal her to be quiet.

They stayed there for a few minutes, but he didn't hear anything else. Maybe a small animal. Maybe more. He motioned her to follow him, and they quickly returned to the camp.

He got Redcloud and some night vision and we went out to check it. Sure enough, there were a few shapes out in the field where they had been shooting. He couldn't make out if they were native or white, or what. It didn't matter. They were trying to sneak up on them.

He motioned Redcloud to monitor them while he went back to get the group ready.

By the time he got back into camp, Kat had alerted everyone. Wilson had handed out two mags to each, except Kat and August. She had everyone set up in defensive positions.

Mitchell went to each position and reminded them to hold their fire. "Redcloud is still out there and if you shoot at him, God help you."

This bit of humor was to help lighten the mood; however, He didn't want them to lose focus. August came over and quietly asked, "What about me? I can shoot."

"Yes, my friend, I know you can shoot and shoot very well, however you don't yet know how to fight as a team with this group. We still have much training to go over on how we use these weapons to the best advantage and a few other things about our tactics."

He just squatted next to Mitchell and remained silent. Mitchell took a moment to glance over at him. August was thinking he could see. He didn't know what he was thinking about, but he was deep into it. "Don't worry, my friend. There will be plenty of chances for you to fight with us. We have, sometimes, spent years working together, so we know what to do and when to do it. Just give it time."

Mitchell thought he understood, but it was still obvious August was not happy about it. However, right now, he had to focus on the problem out there. He switched on his night vision and could quickly pick out 5 people that were out in the open. They were obviously trying to sneak in on them. They were still quite some distance out. He could make out some were carrying rifles, but not all. This could mean they were the local natives.

After watching them make their way closer, He made out what could only be the Chief, circling around behind the group. He slowly made his way up behind one shape and, not sooner than they became one, that person was taken out and he shortly made his way to the next. Then it was a repeat of the first. He continued until he had four of them down. As he made his way to the last shape, he must have made a noise. Mitchell could see the last figure was alerted by something and dropped. Redcloud also dropped.

He continued to watch the area where they both were out of sight. After about ten minutes, he got a glimpse of one figure. He couldn't make out if it was Redcloud or not. It was only up for a second and then disappeared again. This continued on for almost an hour. Now and then, he would get a glimpse of a figure and then it would disappear. From what he could gather, they appeared to be circling each other. Mitchell kept the others informed as he quietly went to each position. Everyone was getting a little nervous, and he didn't want anyone to get trigger-happy. He was the only one using the night vision right now, so he was the only one who could make out what was happening.

Suddenly, one figure stood up and turned to run. Mitchell's guess was it was the last of the natives because quickly the second figure got up and began chasing the first one. He was sure the second was Redcloud. The native had the jump on him and on the other side of the field by now. The first figure, as best he could tell, went over a ridge and was out of sight. Shortly, he made out a rider on horseback, getting away at full speed. When what he guessed to be Redcloud got to the ridge, he just stopped and watched as the rider got away. He turned and raised his hand with the rifle over his head to signal it was all clear.

Mitchell got up but stayed in a somewhat crouched position and turned to the group. "On" was the only thing he said to let them know it was time to turn on their equipment. One by one, each of them came up on the radio and checked in. When he had everyone accounted for, he went back to the wagon to get Kat and August.

"OK, we are going to move out. I want you to pay attention to how we work together for this." He said to them. He wanted to use this for training them as much as for training his team, being that mostly, they had never worked together. He turned to walk away and said over his shoulder, "Stay close to me."

When they got back up to the front, he went down on one knee and signaled a wave to each side. When he could see that each member of the team was ready, He pointed toward where Redcloud had been working. Redcloud was already on his way back to join up with them. When he was near, Mitchell whispered in the mic, "Halt." Everyone stopped where they were and went down. He turned and signaled to Kat and August to get down as well.

Kat saw him, but it was a little too dark and August continued to stand. "Get down." Mitchell sternly said to him in a whisper.

August immediately dropped to one knee. He was worrying about August. He was a good frontiersman for his time, but he needed him to get in line with their style of fighting.

As Redcloud came near Mitchell, he handed him his radio set. As he quickly put it on and informed him about the attackers. "White men," he blurted. "They were tied up over the hill and one got away. The others are toast."

"Yeah, I saw. You're sure they were white? From what I was seeing, I was figuring natives."

"Yeah, they were white, maybe Mexican. Hard to tell in this light. We can check them in the morning."

"Wilson." Mitchell said into the mic.

"Copy." Came back a quick response.

"You should be able to still pick out the body heat of the dead. Should be four bodies out there. Take the rest of the team, find the bodies, get whatever weapons they have, and see if there are any papers or other information on them."

"Roger," Wilson responded.

"Take Kat and August with you. They don't have a radio or night sight. You'll need to come pick them up."

Before he could fully explain to them and leave, Wilson was there to get the new trainees. He quickly told Kat and August to go with Wilson and watch what they did and how they worked together.

Wilson was off with both of them. The Chief and he headed back to the camp. "You think there are more of them?"

"Nah, I think it was a small group. Probably heard the shooting this afternoon and came to check it out and see what they could steal from us."

"Could be," Mitchell said slowly as he thought about it. "we're going to have to be much more careful in the future. I think as we get closer to San Antonio, we may see more and more people."

They were almost at the camp when he heard a shot, and the radio came up with Wilson's voice. "Coyote, it was close, but everyone is alright."

"Roger," Mitchell responded and then added, "they rarely travel alone. Keep a watch and be careful."

Wilson responded with a simple "Roger."

Redcloud gave a little chuckle and said with a whisper, "She is good, you know."

He smiled back at his friend and said, "Yeah, we were lucky to get her on this detail."

The Chief stopped by the water barrel and got cleaned up. Mitchell climbed up in the wagon seat and watched the team for a little while. They slowly went from one site to the next. Stopping only long enough to pick up a few weapons and check thing out. Kat and August were near the back of the group. They wondered about trying to see what the team was doing, but he was sure it was too dark to make out much of anything. When they found the last of the bodies, he turned off the night vision to save batteries and just watched out in the dark.

After a short time, the radio came up and Wilson said, "Coming in. Clear?"

Mitchell responded with "Copy, it's clear, come on in." He didn't even wait for a response, he just shut off the radio.

The team came in and, after a quick wash of hands, they all gathered around the fire. Rodrigues spoke up first. "I think, by the way they are dressed, they might have been Mexicans. Maybe even Comancheros."

"Comancheros?" Asked August.

Before anyone else could answer, Rodrigues said, "Comancheros are Mexicans that traded with the Indians in this area. I'm not a historian, but I think they were active at this time."

Before the discussion went on, Mitchell spoke. "Yeah, maybe, but we'll see tomorrow. As for now," He said with the force necessary to get everyone's attention, "We need to be a lot more careful. The little marksmanship training this afternoon is probable what brought them down on us. We need to keep our eyes open and keep out of sight of others until we get to San Antonio."

He knew it put a little damper on the mood tonight, but it was important that they have no more encounters like this one.

No one said anything. They just sat around the fire looking at the things they got off the bodies. As Mitchell walked over, Johnson was looking over the very nice knife they found. "Boss," he said, looking up at him when he approached. "What are we going to do with these things? We didn't find much on them. Just a couple of rifles and one pistol. Also, some real nice knives." He said, holding up the knife he was looking at.

"Well, I guess it is yours now." Mitchell told him and then looked around at the others. "Does anyone have any problem with this?"

Blake asked, "What if someone else wants something?"

After thinking a moment, "I guess if there is an argument about something, then we'll have to set up a raffle to see who gets to keep it."

Blake just nodded and said, "That sounds fair enough." And no one else said anything, so he guessed it was now law within the group.

The next morning, they were all up early, as was normal on this trip. Everyone wanted to look, so they all took a trip out to the sight of the bodies. They could find three of the four easily. According to Redcloud, it looked like the fourth body might have been drug off by the coyotes.

Rodrigues said it appeared these men were Mexicans. However, it was difficult to say, and they didn't stay around to investigate. After a quick check to make sure they had missed nothing important, they packed up and were on the road quickly.

Today Mitchell let Kat drive the hummer. August was understandably upset, but calmed down when he told him his turn would come when we got to the main road. It would be there that he needed August's experience with the road to make sure they were on the right path.

Kat had learned well. Wilson sat in the passenger seat while Kat drove all day. She only had a little trouble when they crossed a small stream and later when she had to back into the brush to hide the hummer. Backing into a specific spot with a trailer attached was difficult for even an experienced driver, so she did well.

When they made their last stop for the day, it was within sight of what Mitchell thought might be the main road. He had scanned the area, and it appeared to be clear, so they set up camp and wait for the others. "You know," He said to her, "tomorrow you're on the wagon and your father will have time to lean to drive this."

She didn't say anything, but continued working on what she was doing, but it was obvious she was not happy.

About two hours later, the rest of the crew came in and after taking care of the horses and getting supper ready, Redcloud said, "There are others on the road down there."

When he looked, Mitchell saw a wagon on the road with some people walking alongside. They were heading east, though. When they got to the spot where the road they were on met the main road, that group must have seen their camp. They were, more or less, out in the open and they weren't trying to hide, except the hummer. He was sure they couldn't see the hummer from where they were.

"Come on, August," He said as he just stood there watching, "let's go down and say hello."

August just looked over at him and then at his plate. "Is it alright if I finish eating first?" He said with a smile.

"Yeah, finish eating. We're not in a hurry." Mitchell said, answering him. Then he grabbed the binoculars and checked out the people down the road. They, too, were setting up camp. It appeared there might be four or five adults and a couple of young children. He just watched them for a while. A couple times one man pointed their way, but the woman he was talking to said something and he just turned away and he just went about his business.

When August finished eating, they both grabbed the Kentucky rifles and strolled down the road to the new neighbor's camp. As they came into the camp, one man got up to come and meet them. The other two went behind their wagon and Mitchell could see them peeking out around the corners with rifles in hand.

"Evening," He shouted into the camp and then added, "May we come in?"

The man that got up to come meet him said, "Come on in, but I warn you we have you covered."

"Fair enough," Mitchell responded, "but we mean you no harm. Just come down to say hello and to find out where we are."

"Lost, er, you?" the man said as they step up to him. The man put out my hand, and both Mitchell and August did the same.

After a quick shaking of hands, Mitchell said, "Not really lost, but I just need to make sure where we are. My name is Jim, and this is my friend August."

The man smiled back nicely. He appeared to be young. Maybe early twenties. Mitchell guessed that the rest of his group must be family. "Hum, not sure where you are, but not lost, you say." The man said with a little laugh. "Sounds like a good definition of being lost to me."

"Well, it sounds better the way I say it." he said back to the man, laughing just a little.

He just gave a little laugh and said, "Come on in and have a seat. Would you like something to eat?'

Mitchell looked at the pot on his fire and it didn't appear there was much in it. "No, thank you," He responded, "We just had dinner before we came down to say hello."

They took a seat on a log that had they pulled up and then set the rifles against the log. The man looked relieved when they did this and raised his hand, just enough for his friends behind the wagon to see. They then came out from hiding, but still held onto their rifles.

"Like I said, my name is Jim, and this is my friend August." He said, as a way of introductions to the two new men. "We came down from a little way up north and heading to San Antonio."

The man looked a little surprised when Mitchell told him where we were going. "San Antonio," he said with a little surprise. "You sure that's where you want to go right now?"

"Yeah," Mitchell said and then quickly added, "I know there is trouble brewing down there. Me and my people are going down to see if we can help."

The man thought about that for a while and then said, "Well, this is the right road. Got maybe two or three days ahead of you. Maybe more, depending on the river crossing."

Mitchell looked at August and nodded. "You were right. This is the road."

They then sat there quietly for a moment. The man started talking. "My name is Frank Smith, and this is my family. My brothers over there," he said, pointing to the two men standing off to our side, still holding their rifles, "My wife Sarah, and two kids Frank junior and Mary."

"Pleased to meet you," both August and Mitchell said.

"We lived just north of San Antonio and I took my family and get out before the real trouble begins."

"Real trouble?" Mitchell asked. "What news do you have?"

"Well, rumor has it there is a Mexican Army heading this way. Some men are trying to make a fort out of an old mission in San Antonio and fight." He stopped to take the plate of food his wife brought to him.

They said nothing, and Frank continued. "They are talking about rebellion against Mexico and there are some men trying to form some kind of government somewhere up this way."

"You probably made a good decision to get your family out of here." Mitchell said to help him feel better. It's difficult for some men to run away from trouble, and he could see it bothered this man some.

He continued on with his story. "The Mexicans probably won't be here until later in the spring, maybe summer, so we aren't in any hurry."

He wanted to tell Frank so bad, that he should move a little faster and that the war will start soon, but he just listened to him and asked, "You wouldn't by any chance know what day it is, would you?"

He thought a moment and hollered over his shoulder, "Mary, what day is it today?"

Mary came over to where they were talking and said, "I'm not sure of the exact day, but I believe it is about the middle of February."

"Thank you," he said to his wife and then to Frank. "You said something about the river crossings ahead?"

Well, when we crossed two days ago, it was just a little on the deep side." He said and then pointed off to the west. "I saw signs of maybe rain to the west. The river might be higher now."

Michell just nodded as Frank told them. Watching the weather was not something he had thought about before now. He was sure Redcloud had been keeping an eye on it. He now figured this was something to think about more closely.

"I thank you very much for the information." Mitchell said to him as he stood up. "What you have told me is of great help."

Frank also stood up, and this time he put out his hand first. Mitchell took his hand and pulled the man close to him and whispered to him, "You might want to hurry your movement a little. We had a little trouble yesterday, north up this road. Comancheros, we think. We've also had some coyote troubles."

Frank looked back up the road and nodded, saying, "Thanks for the warning. We'll be pulling out before daylight."

After a round of shaking everyone's hands, they carefully picked up their rifles and headed back up the road to their camp.

As they came into the camp, Mitchell called Wilson over. "Anna, I want you to adjust the watch schedule to give me the last watch in the morning."

"You got it, Boss." She said happily. "How did everything go down there?" she asked, pointing down the road.

They continued to walk to the fire and when they got there, he answered her, "We are on the right road. The man down there is getting away from the trouble. He said we got three, maybe four, days to get there. The one problem he said we might have is possible high water at a major river crossing."

Everyone was very intent on what the Boss was saying, but for a change, it was Redcloud that spoke up. "I don't think the storm over there," he said, pointing to the west, "is that big a storm. At, lease rain wise."

"Thanks Chief," He said to him. "I was wondering if you were keeping track of it."

"Someone has to keep an eye on things around here." Redcloud said back as he turned away.

He heard a couple of snickers from the group, but couldn't make out who they were from, so he continued to pass on the information that Frank had told them. When he finished, he warned everyone, "While you're on watch tonight, watch our neighbors. One for any trouble that might try to sneak up on them, and two for any movement from them in our direction. I don't think they will give us a problem, but keep an eye out, anyway."

Everyone just nodded. The normal end of day chatter started and shortly they all broke up to hit the sack.

When morning came, it was Mitchell on watch. He watched their neighbors as they got moving. They quickly broke camp and just as the sun was coming up, they headed on down the road. Shortly after, he woke his tired group, and they did the same.

He thought Kat might tell her father that it was his turn to learn to drive, but he found she didn't. August hitched up the wagon. Mitchell walked over to him and rather sternly said, "What do you think you're doing?"

He turned and looked around with a puzzled look, "I'm getting the wagon ready, just like I always do."

"Why aren't my two other guys doing this? They should be able to do it by now."

He answered with a little more surety now, "They can do this. I am just used to doing it."

Mitchell turned and shouted, "Blake and Johnson, front and center!" And they both came running up to him. Johnson just stopped, but Blake ran up and jumped into attention. "OK, Blake, remember we aren't in the army anymore."

Blake turned a little red and both of them laughed a little. "Why aren't' guys getting the wagon ready?"

Johnson answered, "Because August always does it. We sometime help."

"Well, not anymore." He said, "From now on, the wagon is the responsibility of you two."

They just looked at each other and Johnson said, "OK Boss, you got it."

He added, "Starting today, you two are on your own. August will learn to drive the hummer."

He wasn't looking at August when he said it, but a heard a little gasp come behind him. "Kat will ride in the wagon with you, just in case you have any trouble."

He then turned back to August, who was just standing there with a smile that was touching both of his ears. "What are you waiting for? Report to Anna and she'll get you started."

He didn't think he had ever seen that old man move so fast. As he ran to the hummer, the entire camp laughed.

Redcloud came by on his horse and said, "Good luck with that today, Boss."

"Yeah, thanks. I might need it." Mitchell said back to him as he kicked his horse down the road.

After eating, they broke camp and headed out. Everything was going smoothly. August was in the passenger seat and Anna was showing him everything, just as she had done with Kat. Mitchell thought maybe Kat paid more attention to the little things, but August clearly was more enthusiastic to learn.

The day went on, just as all the others had. By the end of the day, Anna let August get behind the wheel and try to drive a little. After a jerky start, he calmed down, and the lessons went better than Mitchell had expected.

The next day, they came to the river. It was higher than he would have liked, and it was late, so they made camp. The next day they unloaded the wagon and made several trips with the supplies in the hummer. Lastly, they hooked the wagon to the hummer and pulled it across. The wagon was light and wanted to float, but they kept it right and got it across.

After loading the supplies back up, it was too late in the day to start out again. They made camp close to the river and called it an early day.

The next day it was August's turn to solo drive. He did pretty well. Maybe not as well as his daughter, but Mitchell still thought it may have been better than Redcloud's driving.

It was the next day that Mitchell sent Redcloud ahead to scout the area. It wasn't too long before he was back. "San Antonio is just a few miles further down this road." He reported.

He signaled for everyone to gather. "Ok, this is what we're going to do. First, we are going to get off this road. I mean far off. It's going to be a cold camp tonight. I don't want anyone stumbling on to us until I talk with, uh Colonel Travis and Bowie."

The gathering broke up and they moved about a half mile off the road. There was a little stream, and a nicely covered camp. After they set the camp up, he called them all together again. "Tomorrow, August, Kat, and I are going to head into the Alamo. Once there, I'll make arrangements with Travis. Once he agrees, the rest of you will come in."

Redcloud was now interested. "What arrangements?"

"I plan to offer our help, but I need to remain in command of my team. We have things they could never dream of and do not know how to use. If Travis agrees, then there is no problem."

"And if he doesn't agree?" To his surprise, it was Kat that spoke now.

"Well," He stopped to think, "I guess I'll just need to convince him I need to command my people."

This seemed to answer most of the questions, so he continued with one of his biggest concerns. "Now comes another problem. The reason I am leaving you out of the initial contact is, and I hate to say it, because of your race or sex."

He paused and looked around at the group. He had expected an argument with them, especially Johnson, but everyone just nodded in agreement.

He continued, "Let there be no mistake. When you do come in, we are going to have our hands full of prejudices that the people of this time have. Johnson," He said, turning to him, "I think it may be hardest for you. For me to arm a black man could be ground for me to go to jail and you to be hung."

He stopped to let this sink in a little. These prejudices are a serious issue right now and he didn't believe they have really considered the consequences that could happen.

Turning to Wilson, he said, "Anna, women of this time don't dress like men and don't fight like men, and so on. You are going to be laughed at and maybe even worse. Chief," he said, turning now to Redcloud, "you might have a very difficult time, as well. I'm not really sure how they will deal with you, but one thing I do know is you must control your temper." Again, he paused and then turned back and added, "For now, anyway."

This little joke got a little laugh from everyone. "Rodrigues," He said turning to him, "Being this is Mexico right now and you are Mexican, by decent, I think you will have the least amount to trouble, but you will need to remember that the," He slowed down to choose his words carefully, "the white men, even here, consider Mexicans to be second-rate people."

Everyone was considering what he had said. No one really said anything and there was a lot of shuffling around, so he continued, "I think the best thing we can do is to hit them with a little of shock and awe of our own."

Most head snapped up at this and he now had everyone's attention. "This is my plan. I am going to give Travis a little example of what we can do. When he agrees, I want you guy to come in, lights on, but not so much noise this time." He looked over at August, who vigorously nodded in agreement. "Once you come in, I want full military control. Everyone in uniform, armed, and looking sharp."

He couldn't tell if they were agreeing with him or not, so he just continued, "Redcloud, you'll be in command. When you drive in." He paused and thought for a second and then changed that. "When Wilson drives in, I'll point a place to park it. Then I want everyone to fall out and line up beside the hummer at attention. I'll bring Travis over to inspect the group and we'll play it by ear from there on."

After a moment of silence, He added, "Anyone have any comments or ideas?"

He could see everyone running this through their heads, but no one said anything, so he just let it go for now and said, "We'll run over it again after supper just in case one of you thinks of something."

They broke up the meeting, and everyone went about their business. Some by themselves and some together.

After dinner, they gathered as usual, however this time they had no fire. Everyone had wrapped up with some blankets or their sleeping bag, but still they all came together. Mitchell was very proud of the gang and thought that they were now a family.

"Did everyone consider what I said earlier?" He asked.

Everyone either mumbled a response or nodded. "Any concerns or ideas?"

Wilson spoke up first. "What do we do if the people down there turn against us?"

This got nods and agreements from the others. Mitchell had to think about it for a moment and then slowly responded to her, "If things turn bad, we have the firepower to overwhelm them and protect ourselves, but this is a worst-case scenario."

They all smiled at the idea of their fire power letting go on the people there, but then quickly came back to reality. "Any way it goes. We're all going to need to watch each other's backs." He said.

He then turned to Redcloud, "Chief, how goes the self-defense training?" He asked.

"Not too bad." was all he responded with, but when Mitchell kept looking at him, he continued. "Wilson has been working with our guys and they are coming along just fine. Kat and August are way behind, but coming along."

"I don't know that they will have much trouble once we get in there, but our guys will need to stick together."

Redcloud nodding his agreement. The others just exchanged looks. He couldn't tell what was on their minds, but he could sense that they were nervous. The rest of the evening went along with just a little small talk and nervous joking around. Mitchell judged they were in good spirits, considering what they were looking at tomorrow.

CHAPTER 8

When morning came, they were not in any hurry to break camp like they had been for the last couple of weeks. They took their time with breakfast and getting everything ready. By late morning, Kat and August were in the wagon and Mitchell was riding on a horse.

"You know," Redcloud said, smiling as he walked over to him, "it would really be very embarrassing if you fell off that horse when you rode in."

"Funny," he said back to him as he adjusted his butt in the saddle.

"Not too bad," Redcloud continued, making fun of him, "now just try to stay there."

He turned his back to Mitchell and walk away before he could answer him. So, Mitchell could only watch him walking away and laughing. He gave a little kick to the horse and walked over to the wagon. August was sitting next to Kat, and the wagon was ready.

"OK, let's move out." He said as he motioned for them to move. August picked up the rains and gave them a slap at the horses. They moved out to the road and headed for the Alamo.

The ride down to the Alamo was uneventful. They got back on the road and just headed into town. Coming from the north, they followed the small trail that led off to the west just outside the Alamo. As they got close to the wall, several men with rifles came up on the wall and some even manned the cannon that was covering this gate. Mitchell waved at the men as they rode up. Some waved back while the others just watched.

Mitchell had been to the Alamo when he took some leave and went to visit some friends in San Antonio. Just going through it on the tour was amazing, but that was nothing compared to the feelings he was having right now. Not only was he going into what was probably the most sacred places in Texas, but he was actually going to meet the men who died there, making it so sacred.

When they got to the gate that was open, a man stepped out and waved them to stop. August stopped a little way away from him and as he walked up to where he could look them over. When he got to the wagon, he first looked into the back. He paid particular attention to the rifles they had stacked on one side of the wagon. August spoke up and said, "We thought maybe you could use a few more."

Good man, August, Mitchell thought to himself. The man looking at the wagon snorted a little and waved for them to go in. However, even after they were inside, there were still men watching them. The man at the gate pointed for them to go to the left and then told them to stop. Mitchell rode up to the wagon and got off his horse and tied it to the back of the wagon. After, he walked around and took his rifle, which was in a skin bag that Redcloud had made for him. When he pulled the gun bag out, the man obviously became a little watchful of him. It wasn't until he went forward and set the bag down to help Kat down from the wagon that the man relaxed.

Mitchell turned back to the man and said, "I need to speak with your commanding officer."

"What do you want to talk to him about?" the man asked.

"Are you the commanding officer?" He asked and when he said nothing Mitchell added, "Well that is between him and me."

"Well, if you want to see him, I need to know about what." the man responded rather sarcastically.

Mitchell turned away from him and started walking away while yelling as loud as he could, "Sargent of the Guard. I need to see the Sargent of the Guard."

The man ran up to him and grabbed Mitchell by the arm. At this point He grabbed his arm, just above the wrist and spun around. This put a locking twist on the man's arm. He let out a yell and went face down into the dirt. At just that moment, another man came running around the corner of the building. Mitchell thought that this man might have seen what he did and yelled, "What's going on here?"

While still applying pressure to the man's arm, Mitchell said, "I requested to speak to the commanding officer, and he refused to direct me to him. When he grabbed my arm, I took him down."

"You can let him go now." The new man said. "I'm Colonel Bowie. What can I do for you?"

He dropped the man's arm and the man let out a little yelp as he released the pressure. Mitchell walked up to Bowie, stood at attention and gave him a salute, saying, "I'm Sargent Mitchel of the United States Army. I have a small group that is here to assist you."

Bowie looked him up and down for a moment and returned a salute. At least he thought it was a salute. "OK Sargent, let's go see if we can find Travis and you can report to him."

Mitchell just nodded, and Bowie turned and headed towards some buildings. They went into one building and a man; he recognized from pictures, was Travis, sat behind a small desk making notes.

As they walked in, Travis turned, and Mitchell again saluted and reported his intentions. Travis returned a more proper salute and said, "At ease. Mister."

He walked over and put out his hand, and Mitchell shook it. It was probably one of the greatest honors he has ever had. Travis then poured himself a drink of water and offered some to Bowie and him. Mitchell properly thanked him and said, "Before we get into this, there are a few things you need to know about me and my people and two very important conditions to getting our help."

Travis set his glass down on the table and said, "I'm intrigued. Go ahead."

"Before I continue, I would like to request you to send for Colonel Crocket. He will also need to agree to these conditions."

Travis stood up and called, "Captain Baugh."

When a man who Mitchell guessed to be the captain came in, he said "Sir."

Travis quickly said, "Find Colonel Crocket and ask him to report to my quarters."

The captain simply replied, "Sir." and turned and move back out the door.

"Please drink while we wait." Travis offered.

He raised his glass to him and to Bowie and took a sip. The water had a strange taste, but a good taste to it. All he could think about at this moment was how August would rather have something a little stronger than this to drink.

Shortly, Crockett came into the office. Mitchell easily recognized him from pictures he had seen. Colonel Travis made the introductions, and he again felt a surge of pride go through his body when he shook Crockett's hand.

"OK Sargent, we are all here. What's on your mind." Travis said as he sat back down at his little desk.

"Well Sir," He said as he walked over towards a small window. "I have five additional soldiers under my command. We have all agreed to come down here and join your group to defend this post. There is also another man, a civilian we picked up on the way, and his daughter." He then paused, not for them, but for him. This next part was going to be a little sticky. "The only problem is I need to have my people stay under my command. I will answer to you, the three of you, as the senior ranking people here, but for reasons you would not believe I need to command my people."

Travis sat back in his chair and thought about it a little. Crockett and Bowie both looked at him, waiting for his response. Finally, Travis said, "This is highly unusual. Can you give me a reason I should allow this?"

"Yes Sir, I could, but truly, I don't think you would believe me and would probably have me locked up as a crazy."

Crockett gave a little cough, Mitchel thought to stifle a laugh and shuffled around a little. Travis glanced over at him but didn't say anything. After a long pause, Travis slowly said, "I don't know that I can honor this request without some kind of explanation."

"We Sir," Mitchell took a step forward, "I have an idea about that. I might not be able to tell you the reason, but I might just be able to show you."

"OK, how do you plan to do that?" Travis asked.

"Before I continue, there is one other condition I must insist on."

"Go ahead, what is it this time?" Travis said.

"Well Sir, I must insist that there be no record what so ever of my people in the rolls or reports." He said to him and looked around at the others, "Also, as the three commanders of the forces here at the Alamo, all three of you must agree to these terms."

"That is a tall request." Said Bowie, stepping forward.

"Yes Sir, but after I have shown you my reasons, and when I think you will believe what I will tell you, I believe you will understand the reason for these requests."

"Can you give us a moment, Sargent?" Travis asked.

"Certainly, Sir." Mitchell said and headed for the door. "I'll wait outside."

After he left the office, he walked over to check on August and Kat. They were chatting with some men and a couple of women. As he walked up, August asked, "Have they agreed?"

"Not yet," He said, "but I'm still working on it." But before he could ask another question, Mitchell told him he needed to get back. He picked up his rifle bag and walked back over the Travis's office and waited outside.

While he was waiting outside, about ten minutes, he was just watching the men around the post. Things appeared to be much calmer that he thought they would be. Of course, he didn't have any idea where they were in the chain of events, as he knew them. Also, because this was not his timeline, he did not know if the chain of events would be the same. Also, as he remembered his history, they didn't expect the Mexican Army to be here before spring.

He heard the door open, and Colonel Bowie came out and motioned him back in. He grabbed his rifle bag and went back into the office.

Everyone was still in the same place and once he was in there, Colonel Travis said, "We have all agreed that if you can convince us of the need for your requests, we will agree."

"Fair enough, Sirs." He said looking around at each of them.

"Just how do you intend on convincing us?" Crockett asked.

"Funny it is you that asks, Sir." He said to him. "Your fame with your Kentucky is well known. I would like to challenge you to a match. Five bottles each. First one to break all five wins. If I win, you will agree to my terms."

"And if I win?" Crockett asked.

"If you win, then me and my people belong to this command fully." He said in a dead serious way, but added in a lighter tone, "But, I see very little chance of that."

Bowie jumped in and said, "Now that sounds like a proper challenge, Crockett."

Mitchell turned back to Travis to wait for him to approve this challenge. After a very long time, he thoughtfully said, "Agreed, if Colonel Crockett accepts the challenge."

Crockett stood up straight and bent over at the waist and, with a lot of flourishes, bowed and said, "Accepted."

"Very good. When would you like to do this?" Mitchell asked.

"I'm ready whenever you are." Crockett replied.

"Then, let's do it. What distance would you like to shoot at?" he asked him.

"Well, we don't have much space inside the walls, so let's say fifty paces." Crockett replied.

"That sounds perfect." Mitchell said to him and then turned to Travis, "Colonel Travis, could you have a couple of your men set up two benches at about fifty paces with five bottles on each bench."

Travis called the captain in again and gave him the instructions. The captain then turned and left the office. Mitchell could now hear a lot of talking outside and as the news spread, the talking got louder.

News traveled fast, even now. By the time the four of them came out of the office, the men were all lined up and down each side of the fort. The benches were set up just as he had requested, and a line drawn in the dirt, that Mitchell guessed was their firing line.

Crockett and Mitchell walked up to the line. He turned to Crockett and asked, "First one to break all five bottles wins, correct?"

"That is the way it was said." Answered Crockett.

He then turned to Travis and asked, "Colonel, would you kindly give us the go?"

Travis just stepped up behind us and said, "Get ready."

Crockett checked his rifle and got into position. Mitchell opened the bag he had, but didn't take it out just yet.

Travis asked, "Sargent, are you ready?"

He just turned to look at Crocket and said, "Ready."

Travis shrugged his shoulders and said, "Aim,"

Crockett put his rifle up to his shoulder and took aim. Mitchell just stood there and watched. It was such an honor to watch one of the greatest marksmen in American history.

Travis then shouted, "Fire!"

No sooner than the words had left the mouth of Travis, then Crockett fired his first round. It was a dead hit. The bottle, or he thought maybe a jug, blew apart. Crockett lowered his rifle and reloaded. He looked over at Mitchell and asked, "Do you intend to shoot or not?"

"Don't worry about me." He answered him. "I'll shoot when I'm ready."

Crockett didn't respond, but continued to load and fired another round. It was another hit. Each time he hit the target, the men all around the Alamo let out a yell.

Crocket was loading for his third shot when Mitchell pulled his rifle out of the bag. Everything in the Alamo went silent immediately. There was already a mag in it, so he just pulled back on the charging handle to chamber a round. He looked over at Crocket, who was intently watching him now. He said, "I'm ready now."

He looked down range and brought his rifle up. There was no wind, so this should be a simple shot. He took aim and squeezed off the first round. This time it was his jug that broke, but there were no cheers for him. He aimed at the second bottle and squeezed off another, and then another and in rapid succession, He popped each of the jugs on his bench.

He brought down his rifle and looked over at Crockett. He was just standing there and looking at him. Mitchell then said, "Now watch this." he again shouldered his rifle and took aim. This time, he pressed the selector switch for a three-round burst. He took aim at the remaining jugs on Crockett's bench and in a manner of a couple of second the bench was clear.

He now lowered his rifle. Dropped the mag and cleared the rifle. He packed up his stuff and left Crocket at the firing line as he walked up to Travis. Travis just looked him up and down and then to Crockett he said, "My quarters now." He then turned to Bowie and said, "You too, Colonel."

As he turned to walk away, he said over his shoulder, "Sargent please come with me."

Mitchell followed Travis back to his office or quarters or whatever that room was. All the way there, the whole place was silent. When they reached his quarters, Travis held the door for him and waited for both Bowie and Crockett to get in before he closed it. He walked right up to Mitchell and said, "What the hell was that?"

He took a slight step back and brought his rifle out of the bag. "Sir, this and other things I have at my command are the reasons I need to stay in charge of my people." He then handed him the rifle.

Travis took the rifle carefully and looked it all over. He bounced it in his hand to check the weight of it. As he turned to look down the barrel, Mitchell coughed and he stopped.

After a long look, he handed it to Crockett, and when he finished with it, it got pasted to Bowie. When they all had a good look at it,

Bowie then handed it back to this stranger in their midst. This time, he took out a fresh mag and rammed it in. He pulled the charging handle to the rear and let it go. He turned to Travis and said, "Sir, now it is loaded with thirty rounds and ready to fire."

Travis looked at the other two in the office and then back at Mitchell. "Alright Sargent, I think you have our attention now and we are ready to believe what you say."

He stepped closer to him and whispered. Bowie and Crockett pulled up chairs close enough for them to hear. "Sir, this can't get out, at least not now. Where and when I come from, this is the standard rifle for the United States Army. It will give you all the firepower you need to defend this post."

It just dawned on Crockett what Mitchell said. "What do you mean by where and when?" he asked.

"Without going into great detail, mainly because I couldn't explain how as I, himself, don't fully understand the how of it. My people come from almost two hundred years in your future."

He stopped to let that sink in. Mitchell could see the questions coming up, but what answers he had would make even less since to them. He just held up his hands. "I know you have many questions. Unfortunately, I have very few answers, and the answers I have are mostly guesses, anyway."

"We have some other weapons that I can use, if it gets realty bad, but my one major problem is a limited supply of ammunition."

"Now, before I continue," he said, looking at each one of them. "I must know if you will agree to my terms?"

Travis looked at each of the other Colonels and each of them nodded their agreement. "Yes, we agree on your terms. Further, to simplify things, we are not going to call you by rank, but you will have a rank of captain, so I can justify to the rest of the men why you are in command of your men."

"Well, Sir, that is another reason I need to stay in command of my people. In my time, not all the soldiers are men. Women of my time have all the same rights and responsibilities as men do. I have one woman in my command. She also is a sergeant, but a lesser sergeant."

"Is that all?" asked Bowie.

"No Sir, there is more. In my time, all men are equal. There is no difference where you come from, what color your skin is, or what you call God. I have on black soldier, one Mexican Soldier, and one Native American Soldier. What you would call an Indian."

"My God, you give your niggers guns?" asked Bowie.

"If I remember my history, both you and Colonel Travis are slaveholders." They both nodded. "Well, in just a few years, there will be a great war in the United States to end slavery. This war will go on for almost five years. In a one-day battle on both sides, more than sixth five thousand men will die or become wounded." He now let that set. "It will come to be known as the bloodiest day in American history, even in my time."

Bowie just looked down and said nothing. "Yes, blacks, as we call them now in my time, are equal in all ways to white men, red men, and men from all over the world who come to America to live, and fight, and die to protect America and our way of life. I would appreciate it if you would never use the word nigger in my presence again, Sir."

He didn't see any response from Bowie, but that is something to deal with on another day.

Travis had more urgent questions in his mind. "You say you come from our future? You say you have come to help us here in the Alamo?"

"Yes Sir," Mitchell responded each time.

"Then you must know how this will turn out for us.?" He asked.

"Yes, Sir. I know in the timeline that was my time, I know what happened at the Alamo. What I don't know is what changes might have come from me and my people because we are here, now. Some things, major things, have already happened that probably didn't happen in my timeline."

"What do you me 'timeline?'." Asked Crockett.

"Sir, may I use a piece of paper?" He asked Travis and was handed the paper. He took out his pen and drew the same picture they used to explain this to August. As he drew it, he explained how they were now on a different timeline and not everything will happen the same. However, he also told them he thought because they were still very close to where the timeline split, the changes right now would be minor.

Mitchell thought that they all, more or less, understood, because they let him go on without more questions. "Sir, in my timeline, and I believe it will still happen in this timeline. If we don't help, all the defenders of the Alamo will be killed. The history books differ on how the actual battle went, but all the men will die. Some reports say those that were captured were shot in front of a firing squad."

"What about the women and children?" Asked Crocket.

"As far as I know, all the women and children, slaves and other non-combatants were escorted north and let go. All accounts say they all survived safe."

This looked to calm some of their fears. "This is not the only failure that occurred. Part of the Mexican army will travel to the east, near the coast. Fannin will surrender his command after hearing about the massacre at the Alamo. About five hundred will surrender and then be marched out of Goliad and all shot."

"Then what good are we doing here? We need to get out of this place and fight him on the move." Said Bowie.

Mitchell was trying not to get too far into the future with what he was telling them. "I can tell you this. These men you have here held Santa Anna for thirteen days. This allows Houston to gather men and time to form an army. You gave him this time. The sacrifice of the men of the Alamo is what gave the army time to form and train. Later they will defeat Santa Anna and it is due to you and your command."

Travis was thinking hard about what he had been telling them. Crockett and Bowie were also thinking, but the burden of command was on Travis. "What is it you think you can do that will change what should happen?" he finally asked.

"After dark tonight, I will bring in the rest of my team. You are going to see things that will astonish you. Some things may even scare you a little. I have a machine that could go out and destroy Santa Anna and his entire Army. The problem is this will not win the war for you and only delay the outcome. It may even change the outcome." He explained to this group of leaders.

"In just a moment, I will let my team know to come into the fort here. I have it set that they will arrive just after dark. I'll meet them at the gate and bring them in. When they get here, I need to have a place that is secure because there are things, I bring that are very dangerous and complicated. I don't want anyone getting hurt or killed because they touched the wrong thing."

Travis seemed to understand the importance of what Mitchell was telling him. He got up and went to the door, where he called that captain again. After talking to him a while, he came back in and said, "Captain Baugh will make all the arrangements. When we are finished here, you can check with him to make sure everything is to your satisfaction."

"Excellent." Mitchell said. "Now I will call my team."

He pulled the radio out of his pocket and turned it on. There was a little burst of static but cleared away quickly. "Redcloud, you there?" He said into the radio. The three colonels were all watching in amazement.

After a minute, the radio came to life with Redcloud's voice. "Roger, we're still here. I heard the shooting. How did it go?"

"Everything is a go. All agreements have been made and we are prepping for your arrival." Mitchell replied to him.

Now all three colonels were standing right next to him, looking at the little radio in his hand. After a moment Redcloud answered and Mitchell thought all three of them jumped a little. "Roger, I figure it will get dark in about an hour. We will pull out shortly before then to find the road and be there shortly after."

"Copy sounds like a plan. Call me when you get on the road. Out." He said, closing out the conversation with his team.

When he looked up, he could see the question on the faces that were staring back at him. "Gentlemen, this device allows me to talk with my people up to about twelve miles away." he explained to them.

"How does it work?" spoke up Crockett.

Mitchell didn't know why, but it was a surprise to hear this question from him. He didn't want to go into any detail with them. This might change more of the future than he planned. "We have found a way to use electricity." He held up his hand and added, "Before you ask, electricity is the power you see in lightning. This device uses very little of that type of power and can send out a signal that another device, like this one, can pick up." He could see this was not really answering their questions, so he decided this was not the time for a lesson in basic electronics. "This is far too complicated to explain right here and now. My team will be here in about an hour, and I need to prepare for them."

After a few moments of thought, Travis turned to Crockett and asked, "David, as you just arrived with your group and you also are in command of your group, please assist Captain Mitchell in settling his group."

"Certainly," Crockett said, standing up. He then slapped Mitchell on the shoulder and asked him, "What do you need before they get here?"

He turned to Travis and gave him a proper salute and said, "Thank you, Sir. We will speak again about things."

Travis returned his salute and said with a laugh, "You can bet on that, Sir. I have many questions."

"I'll bet you do, but I don't know if I can answer all your questions." Mitchell said as he turned to leave.

Crockett opened the door for him and then followed him out. Once they were back out into the light, all work stopped, and the men turned to look at him. He could see a lot of whispering back and forth as Crockett and he walked to the wagon. As they approached the wagon, August and Kat walk up to meet them. "August, may I introduce you to David Crockett? He is the third colonel in command around here."

August held out his hand and said, "A pleasure to meet you."

"Colonel Crockett, may I introduce you to August Schmidt and his daughter Katherine." He said to complete the introductions.

Crockett continued to shake August's hand and nodded to Kat. "It is a pleasure to meet both of you." He said to them and then to Mitchell. He asked, "Are they part of your group?"

"They are now. They were the first people we met when we got here, and they are fully aware of who we are." he answered him.

Crockett looked at the two of them with what, Mitchell thought, might be a suspicious eye, but then turned to him and said, "What can I do to help you?"

Mitchell looked around and from what he could remember from his limited knowledge of the Alamo, it looked like most of the defenses were complete. He needed a place to park, not only the wagon, but the hummer as well. They needed a place that they could control to keep the curious away. He also needed a place for his people to sleep. He figured putting an Indian, a black man, and a woman together with these men would be asking for trouble.

As they walked around looking over the compound, he turned to Crockett and asked him, "What day is it today?"

He stopped and thought about it a moment and said, "I don't rightly know. I think it may be around the 15th of February."

"OK," He said, trying to remember how things went. "That means we should have about a week before Santa Anna gets here."

Crockett laugh a little and said, "No, he won't be here before spring."

"No, that was some of the incorrect information they had in this time." Mitchell casually said as he was looking around, "If I remember right he will arrive in San Antonio before the end of February."

Crockett stopped and glanced around the compound. More thinking out loud than actually talking to Mitchell, he said, "We're nowhere near ready." Then to the Captain, he said, "I have to go tell Travis."

Crockett turned to go back to talk to Travis. Mitchell called to him, "We will have time. Right now, I need you to help me find a suitable place for my people. I need a place with a low wall or a gun emplacement that can support a very heavy gun that weighs about two tons."

Crockett stopped, and after looking back at him, he said. "There are only a couple of places that could support that kind of weight. The center platform and maybe in the church. There is also a solid platform on the north wall."

"The north wall would be the best place I believe." Mitchell said to him as he turned that way.

They both headed towards the north wall. He could see the platform was not big, but he thought it might work. They would have to drive up and angle it in. They could then block the wheels and it should remain solid. If he remembers right, this is where a large part of the action was during the last attack. There was a small building to the right side and an open area between the platform in the center and the platform in the northwest corner. The northwest corner would be the best place, but he wasn't sure that it could hold the weight of the hummer.

"This area might be an excellent spot." He told Crockett as they walked up the ramp on the center platform. "Do you think the northwest corner platform could hold the weight I'm talking about?"

He walked to that side and looked at it. "I can't say. You can get up there. The ramp is strong enough, but I don't know what is supporting under the platform."

Mitchell looked over at the building. The ramp was a little narrow. He didn't think the hummer could get up there. However, even if they only put it on the ramp high enough to shoot over the top of the wall, that would be good.

"I'll need to wait until my people get here to make the final decision. There are problems with both positions, but this is the best place." He said as he looked over the entire setup. "The next problem is a gate to bring it all in. The wagon I'll bring in is a little bigger than the wagon I came with. I need some place a little wider to get in here."

"Well, there's a problem with that." Crocket said, but continued, "We only have two gates, and the main gate is now blocked with a gun platform."

This could be a problem. If he can't get the hummer in here, then his plans are going to be all messed up. As he looked around, he said to Crockett, "Alright then, we'll need to see what happens when they get here." He walked back down the ramp, heading towards the side gate. "So, the gate we came in is the only gate I can use, then?"

"Yep." was the only response from Crockett.

They walked over to the gate, and he looked it over. It was possible they might get it in here, but it was a sure bet they were going to scratch the paint doing it.

After looking things over, they headed back to Travis' quarters. Mitchell stopped short of the door and Crockett stopped and turned towards him. Slowly he said to Crockett, "When my people get here there is going to be a lot of noise and the men here are going to see things that might scare them. I need to make sure no one is going to shoot at them."

"Well, how to handle that will be up to Travis." Crockett said and added with a little laugh, "He's a good talker and he should be able to talk to the men to calm them down."

They started walking again and Mitchell said, "Yes, if I remember right, he was a lawyer, or as we call them in my time, a bottom feeder."

Crockett laughed and slapped him on the back. He obviously caught Mitchell's meaning. He then said, "I'm really beginning to like you."

They went back to talk to Travis, and he could see the commander was upset when Crockett told him what Mitchell said about Santa Anna. He immediately grabbed his hat and hurried outside. Crockett and Mitchell followed him. He headed to the main gate area and quickly Mitchell could see what he was looking for, Bowie.

"Colonel Bowie," he yelled when we got closer, "a word with you."

Reluctantly, Bowie ended what he was doing and walked over to Travis. He stopped and looked directly at Mitchell. "What do you want, Travis?"

Everyone realized Travis was trying to keep a military appearance in his stance, actions and wording, but with as many years as Mitchell had, even though it was from a different time, he could see it was an act. Travis said to Bowie but looking at Mitchell, "The Captain here says Santa Anna will be here within the week."

This got Bowie's attention, and he stood up straight, and just like the others, he surveyed the compound. "That's not enough time to complete the fortifications here." He said as he continued to look around.

Travis turned to Mitchell and asked, "Captain, what is it you think you can do for us?"

Now it was his turn to step back and look around. "I don't know that the gun platforms will support the weight of my big gun. I'm going to need to rethink my plan. Right now, I think setting one soldier on each corner of the compound and a couple to float around to wherever they are needed the most would be my best plan."

Bowie brought his hands up and yelled, "That's the best you can do?"

"No, there is more, but right now, I don't have time to explain everything to you. My main weapon needs a place before they get here, and that is my number one concern at the moment. After we get some food and our camp set and I have time to check the situation out, I'll be glad to sit down and give you a complete plan and explanation of what I can do, then." He answered Bowie's concern.

"Gentlemen," Travis started, "I suggest we work on getting the Captain and his men…uh people settled and in the morning we'll meet to discuss our options."

Crockett, who had just been listening, finally spoke, "I think that sound fair to me. This man just got here and needs some time to take it all in. Also, we need to take a breath to think about what to do. The difference of deciding now and waiting till morning won't make that much difference, time wise, but might make all the difference in our ability to plan properly."

Now Mitchell spoke up, "Gentlemen, I am not worried about our ability to defend this place. I am most concerned about the number of people we will lose doing it. I want to use my stuff the best way I can, with what I know, to minimize the casualties of your people and mine."

"Alright," said Bowie. "I'll wait until morning, but I suggest we keep this to ourselves for now. You go telling people this kind of news and we won't have a soul left by morning."

Travis said, "Agreed, we keep this to ourselves and meet in the morning." After a pause, he turned to Mitchell and said, "Will this give you enough time to come up with your plans?"

After another quick look around, he said, 'Yes Sir."Then he thought it might be time to get them used to his team. "Once my team is here, I'll get my second to check it out and see what he thinks. Sergeant Redcloud is one of the best strategists I have ever worked with. When planning for a battle, he is the best."

Again, the prejudice of this time showed. Bowie said, "You let an Indian plan the battle?"

This was getting a little old, but Mitchell wasn't about to start trouble, at least not now. He simply responded with, "He is the best."

Bowie just threw up his hands and turned away.

Travis simply said, "Then we meet in the morning." He then turned again to Mitchell and asked, "Are you all set with where to put your people?"

After a sigh, he answered him, "I thought I was, but now I'm not so sure. I was planning along the north wall, but now I don't think that will work."

"Have you looked over there?" Travis said, pointing to the chapel and the little wall for the open space.

Crockett answered him, "We haven't gotten over there yet. I'll take him over there right now."

"Carry on." Was the only thing Travis said before he turned to walk away.

"Come with me, Captain," Crockett said, and added, "What's your given name, anyway?"

Mitchell smiled a little and told him, "James, or Jim."

"Alright, Jim it is. Come on and I'll show you my area." Crockett said as he started walking in the direction Travis had pointed.

He turned and walked over towards the familiar building Mitchell knew as the chapel. As they got closer, he could see around the corner where the low wall was. He remembered they called it the palisades. He now remembered this was where Crocket and his men defended. As they got closer, he was thinking that this would be a very good place for the hummer. There was a small wall they could knockdown to get the hummer in here. If they back it in, it could be a good spot to cover the area here and could also be quickly pulled out into the main courtyard if needed.

When he and Crockett got there, he looked around the area. It was a small area and with the hummer covering it, nothing could survive for long. He turned to Crockett and said, "This might be just the perfect place to put my main gun. It could easily cover this area. My only concern is I have very little ammunition for this gun. Using it here would be overkill, but would be a great backup, just in case."

Crocket looked around at what his men had already done to get this area ready. Mitchell explained that the canon placements might need to be adjusted a little because it was going to be tight in this little area. He then took him over to the little wall and explained how the gun could be quickly moved to cover anywhere in the courtyard. After thinking and running the idea through his head a couple times, he said, "This might work, but will it be enough?"

Mitchell gave a little laugh as he thought about his question. Then he explained to Crockett, "The gun from this is powerful. This gun can fire faster and for a much longer time than the gun I just used with you."

Crockett looked from one wall of the courtyard to the other and then let out a whoosh sound as he imagined this.

He then told him a little more, "The person, probably Sergeant Wilson, will have her basic rifle as well. You saw what we can do with that." Mitchell watched as he nodded to him and then he continued, "I also have some things we call a Claymore. It shoots about seven hundred balls at a time. The range is short and not very accurate. It is used to take out an area. We have a couple of rocket launchers that can destroy any building here. We have a grenade launcher that can accurately shoot out to one hundred fifty yards and maximum range out to four hundred yards."

He just rattled through all these things. His intent was to just overwhelm Crockett without going into any great detail. He could see he had a little success, because Crockett didn't know what to say. He just stood there and didn't say a thing. Then suddenly, his eyes got wide and Mitchell expected some question about the weapons he told him about. He was not prepared for Crockett's question. "This Wilson is the woman? You're going to put the woman with my men?" He asked.

Mitchell didn't really know how to answer him. All he could say was, "Yes."

He thought for a moment and then said, "I don't know how my men will take it. I can't guarantee that she would be safe."

"I can guarantee you one thing." Mitchell said to him as serious as he could, "if anything happens to Sergeant Wilson, those men will wake up in the morning missing some very vital body parts. If they live through it. I will guarantee you they will never hurt another woman and will never father more children."

This got Crockett's attention. He turned back to look at him and he added, "My Sergeant Redcloud is very good. He has taught my people really well. Any of them will gladly take care of this problem and the victim will never even know it is coming. You can tell your men that they are personally responsible for her safety while she is here to support them." He stopped and let that sink in and then added, "I wouldn't worry too much, though. She can take care of herself, anyway.

When she gets here, I'll talk to her about trying not to hurt them too bad. We're going to need everyone in this fight to come."

Mitchell turned to walk away, but then turned back and added, "uh, this goes the same for any of the members of my team. Back, white, red or Mexican. It doesn't matter." Now he continued to walk away.

By the time he got to the short wall, he got a call on the radio. "Alamo Station, this is Rover. How copy?" He could tell it was Redcloud calling.

"Very funny," He gave a brief pause then said "Rover."

"Reporting we are on the road." He replied.

"Roger. Wait fifteen so I can prepare the people here. Then come in slowly. When you reach the Alamo, turn north and come in on the little path along the east wall. The main entrance on the south side is blocked."

"Copy." He replied and then added, "See you soon. Out."

Mitchell turned around to call Crockett, but he was standing right behind him. He smiled and said, "Your people aren't the only ones that can get around without a sound."

Mitchell just nodded to him and smiled back. He walked to the east gate and when Crockett didn't move; he motioned for him to come with him, which he did. When he was beside him, Mitchell told him, "My people will be here shortly. We need to be there to make sure the people in here don't shoot at them. It is going to be noisy, and they are going to see things they won't believe."

"What things?" Crockett asked.

How does he answer that? "First off, the wagon they will use does not have any horses. It moves by itself." He said, but then had to think about what else to tell him. "It will have bright lights on the front to see in the dark. Also, it can move very fast. Faster than any horse here." He then decided that was enough for now.

"After seeing you shoot and hearing about your other weapons, I am not a bit surprised to hear all this." Crockett said rather nonchalantly.

When they got to the gate, both Crockett and Mitchell climbed up the ramp at that corner and waited on top of the wall. Crockett yelled to the men on watch and said, "We have a, uh, wagon coming in. It is going to be making a lot of noise. Don't worry and don't shoot at it."

Mitchell was glad he added that last part. It wasn't long before they could see the lights from the hummer in the distance. By the way it was driving, he was guessing Redcloud was driving. He needs to speak with him because there was a reason, he wanted to let Wilson drive. He could hear the men on the wall talking louder and pointing at it the first time it came over a ridge and they could see the headlights. Even Crockett appeared to be a little nervous.

"Easy now," He said to Crockett and the men close to them, "This is my team coming in. There is nothing to be afraid of. This is what Colonel Crockett was telling you about." Some men were getting their rifles ready and he touched Crockett's shoulder and pointed this out.

Crockett yelled at them again, "Keep your rifles down and stay calm."

Mitchell got on the radio and called Redcloud, "Slow it down a little. The people here are getting a little nervous."

Wilson's voice was now on the other end, confirming his suspicions that Redcloud was driving, "I'll try Boss, but you know how he drives."

He could hear Redcloud laugh at that, but the hummer slowed a little. He could hear the motor pitch change telling him the Redcloud listened for a change.

"Roger, when you get here, don't come through the gate. It is going to be very close and may not fit." He radioed back.

"Copy." Wilson replied.

The hummer continued to come in. When it got closer, he could see Redcloud turn onto the small trail leading to the east gate. He patted Crockett on the should and said, "Let's go down and meet them outside the gate."

Crockett turned and followed him down and out of the gate. As the hummer got closer, Crockett stepped back and to the side. Mitchell gave a little smile, but it was already dark enough that he couldn't see it. When Redcloud was close enough to see him in the headlights, Mitchell raised his hand and motioned him to stop. Redcloud pulled the hummer to within a couple of feet of him before he stopped. Crockett had taken another step or two away, but he didn't run.

As he walked up to the driver's side window. He motioned for Redcloud to cut the engine, which he did. Once it was off, Mitchell motioned to Crockett to come over. He reluctantly did and as he got close, Mitchell said to him, "Colonel Crockett, I'd like to introduce you to my second, Sergeant Redcloud." Then, turning to Redcloud, he said, "Chief, I'd like you to meet Colonel David Crockett."

Crocket took Redcloud's hand and shook it. Redcloud got a big smile on his face and said, "It is a great honor to meet you, sir."

"The honor is mine." Replied Crockett. Mitchell forgot he was a politician and could probably hide his feeling very well, when he wanted to.

The others in the hummer were all trying to get a look at Crockett, but Mitchell said, "I'll introduce the rest of my team once we get inside. Right now, we need to move slowly to see if this thing is going to fit through the gate."

He walked around in front of the hummer, with Crockett following him. He looked at it and then at the gate. "I think it will get in, but like I said before, it's gonna be close." He motioned for Redcloud to start it up, which he did and as Mitchell walked backwards, the Chief followed his hand motions to guide it in. He was a little slow at indicating Redcloud should move to the right a little and he scraped the wall, but was quick to turn and slowly they got the hummer in. It was indeed a tight fit, but most all the paint remained on the hummer and not on the walls.

Once inside, he motioned the Chief to turn left and to follow him. By this time, Travis and Bowie were both watching as he guided the hummer in. He then motioned to stop and kill the engine, which Redcloud did. He walked around to the side and yelled, "Fall out, and fall in right here." indicating a line beside the hummer. His people quickly got out of the hummer with their rifles and in full uniform, or close to it with what they had left. He then turned and stood at attention, and waited for Travis to walk over. He and Bowie came over to him, but he didn't come to stand in front of him, so Mitchell turned and saluted, saying, "My team awaits your inspections."

Travis returned his salute and said, "Please proceed."

He did a very snappy about face and lead them over to the team. Mitchell said in a loud and professional manner, "People, this is Colonel Travis. He is the commander of this post and of the regular Army forces here." Travis nodded, and he continued. "This," He said, pointing at Bowie, "is Colonel Bowie. He is second in command and leader of the militia forces here." Then he indicating Crockett, saying, "You already met Colonel Crocket at the gate. He is commander of a small force of Volunteers."

He then turned to Travis and introduced his group. "Sir, this is Sergeant Redcloud. He is my second in command and is also an excellent scout and is my trainer for hand-to-hand fighting. He is an expert with all the weapons we have."

Travis came over to Redcloud and, after a moment, shook his hand. He then moved to Wilson. "Sir, this is Sergeant Wilson. She is also an expert on all weapons and hand to hand fighting. She is also my primary driver and my other trainer."

Travis didn't shake her hand as much as he held it in both of his hands and bowed, saying, "Mama, it's a pleasure."

Wilson quickly pulled her hand back and returned to attention. He moved on to Rodrigues. "This is Corporal Rodrigues. He is a rifleman, and also my Spanish translator."

Next came the introduction I was dreading. "Sir, this is Private Johnson. He is a rifleman and my carpenter for repairs."

Johnson put his hand out, but Travis didn't take it. He just stood there looking at Johnson with a little disdain on his face. Johnson looked down and slowly lowered his hand.

This was something Mitchell was going to have to work on, but he already knew it was not going to be easy for him. As they moved on,

Crockett came up and grabbed Johnson's hand and shook it. The look of surprise on Johnson's face was priceless. However, he just continued. "Last, Sir, this is Private Blake. He also is a rifleman, but was only recently assigned to me and has had very little in the way of training or experience."

Travis shook Blake's hand and turned around to the team. He started with, "I would like to thank all of you for coming here to join us. You are about the strangest group of soldiers I have ever seen, but today has been a day for strange things. The Captain here," he said, pointing to Mitchell, "has said many wonderful things about you and I hope that with your help, we will be victorious."

Turning to Crockett, Travis asked, "Did you find a place for this thing and his me…people?"

Crocket replied in a calm and carefree way, that Mitchell would expect from what He'd heard about him, "Yeah. We're going to put this," pointing to the hummer, "with my men on the palisade. As for quarters, we hadn't gotten that far."

Mitchell spoke up saying "Don't worry about quarter. I'll take care of that."

Travis turned to him and said, "Well, then carry on and I'll see you first thing in the morning." He then just turned and walked away.

As Crockett and Bowie came up to him, Mitchell yelled to his team, "At Ease." And then, after thinking a moment, he added "Rest."

Bowie turned to the hummer, and Mitchell could see he and Crockett were full of questions. "Gentlemen, this thing is way too complicated to explain right now. What I will tell you is simply, it is capable, given the ammunition, of cutting the post to the ground in a very short time. Also, I don't believe that any of the rifle you have would be capable of stopping it. Maybe, one of you bigger cannons."

They both just turned to look at it. He walked back to his team. As he passed Johnson, he stopped to say, "I'm really sorry about that, but we talked about the feeling here. We are going to have to just work through it. The best thing you can do is to remain professional." As he walked away, he turned back and added, "And watch your back. We all watch each other's backs."

He heard a comment from one man that had gathered to watch this whole thing, "I'd like to watch her back, move!" And then there was a little laughter from those who had gathered.

Before Mitchell could say anything, Redcloud spoke up. In a rather loud voice he said, "I'll cut the nuts off anyone who touches any of my people."

Mitchell added, "If he doesn't, I will."

The group wondered away and as the last few stayed; he walked over and gave them a good looking over. "Just want to remember you fellows, for sure."

Now, even the last few walked away. Mitchell could hear some muttering, but he didn't listen. He just walked back to his group and as he approached, Bowie said, "I'll take care of my men. There shouldn't be any trouble."

Mitchell just nodded to Bowie and said to everyone, "Let's get the hummer set and set up our camp." To Wilson he said, "Follow me and I'll show you where we plan to park this thing."

"You got it, Boss." She said as she moved to get in. As he started walking toward the area where they were going to park it, Redcloud came up to walk beside him. "Captain?" he asked with a smile.

"Yeah, I'm not fond of the idea, but it is the only way I could stay in command of my group." He said and then with a smile he added, "You will not let me live this down, will you?"

"Not on your life." was the response he got back.

Bowie and Crockett both overheard him, and they both gave a little laugh. He was sure at this point he must have turned a little red. Good thing it was night, so no one could see.

When they got to the short wall, he motioned Wilson to make a sharp right turn. Then, moving to the back, he unhooked the trailer. "You guys push this back up against that wall." he said to his men, pointing to the wall on the other side of the area opposite the palisades.

They all pushed it back. Redcloud was on the tongue and guiding it back.

Once they had cleared the opening in the wall, Mitchell went to the driver's window. He told Wilson what he wanted her to do. "Anna, I want you to back this thing in with the back up against the wooden wall. This way, if things go south, we will can move it out in a hurry to cover the rest of the compound."

"No problem, if the opening is wide enough." She said, looking in the mirror.

"If it doesn't fit, make it fit. The wall in not important." He said and backed away.

Wilson got a big smile on her face. Just about the same smile he'd seen on Redcloud's face when he told him to drive the duce through the fence. This time, however, she didn't rev the engine or do anything crazy. She backed up slowly, watching both the mirrors. By now they parked trailer and Redcloud stood in the opening and was guiding her back. When she was about a foot away, it became obvious it would not fit, as is.

Mitchell walked up to the window and said, "Just see if you can push through it."

Wilson again looked at both mirrors, and slowly back until she was up against the wall. She started giving at gas, but the wall wouldn't give.

Mitchell waved his hand to signal her to stop. This time at the window he said, "Pull forward a little and back, try smashing through."

Anna pulled the hummer about a foot forward. She then yelled out the window, "Clear?"

"Clear!" He responded once he checked to make sure everyone was out of the way.

She gave it the gas and slammed into the wall. The upper part went down, but now there was still the lower part. Wilson shifted into four-wheel drive and began giving it gas. Slowly she muscled the hummer over what remained of the wall. Mitchell climbed over and guided her back to where he wanted to park it. Once it was in position, Wilson shut it down and climbed out. He was still checking out the placement when Crockett and Bowie walked up to her. She saluted both of them. Bowie said to her, "We don't go in for much of that saluting stuff. Oh, Travis likes to play Army, but the rest of us are not the real army kind."

Wilson dropped her salute and didn't really say anything. She just kept staring at the two of them. Mitchell thought she might have been a bit star-struck. It's not every day you get to meet and talk to heroes from the past.

Mitchell came back around front once it satisfied with the placement. Bowie said to him, "She sure knows how to handle this thing."

"I told you she was good. Only the Chief and I are better, although, who is the best depends on who you ask." He replied to him. By now most of the men, he figured, must have been Crockett's, had gathered around. Some of them laugh at the comment, but most of them looked worried.

Just now, Kat and August came strolling in. Each of them carrying their Kentucky's. Kat came over to Mitchell and gave him a big hug. Mitchell guessed he must have turned a bright red because everyone that was near to him laughed. He spun away and said to his team, "Set up camp next to the trailer by the wall. This is where we'll stay."

Turning to August, he asked, "Can you bring the wagon in here and find a place for the horses?"

"You Got it, Boss." He replied with a smile. He couldn't tell if August was serious or making fun of the way the other talked to him.

Looking over the placement, Bowie nodded, saying, "That might be the best idea." All while looking at Johnson.

Johnson didn't say anything. His training was good, but Mitchell couldn't say the same about Redcloud. He approached Bowie and asked, "What do you mean by that?"

Bowie flatly said, "You might be alright with giving guns to niggers and ind…" He stopped looking at Redcloud, who stood almost a foot taller than Bowie, "But, my men won't live with them."

Before anyone could move, Redcloud drew his knife and had it against Bowie's throat. His left hand was behind Bowie's head, pushing it into the blade. The whole move was so quick that no one could react to it. Bowie didn't resist. From what Mitchell heard, Bowie was quite the knife fighter and probably knew he was not in a good position. At once, everyone froze in pure shock. Redcloud leaned forward and whispered into Bowie's ear. A second later, Bowie slowly nodded. Redcloud first released the back of his head and then lowered the knife and stepped back. But being his oldest friend, Mitchell knew his moves. He was still at the ready. Bowie slowly turned to face Redcloud. He thought there was going to be a major knife fight right in front of them. However, Bowie looked around, simply nodded to Redcloud, and hurried away. When he took his focus off those two, he saw both Johnson and Blake with their rifles at the ready. Bowie had seen what he could do with those rifles and was aware that he had two more pointed at him. He may have been a fighter and a hothead, but he knew how to control himself when things were not to his advantage. He certainly was a cool one.

When Bowie was out of sight, Crockett turned back to Mitchell and he saw Crockett gently let the hammer of his Kentucky back down. He also was a cool character in a critical situation. Crockett let out a forced laugh and said, "That was close." He then turned to Redcloud and asked, "What did you whisper to him?"

Redcloud simply shrugged his shoulders and said, "I told him if he ever calls one of my people a nigger again, I will cut his head off."

"You know, I truly believe you would." Said Crockett. "I've never seen anyone move that fast before. You'll have to teach me that one day." Then, looking back, the way Bowie had gone, he added, "I am afraid, though, you may not have made any friends with him or some of his men. You'll need to watch yourself."

Again, Redcloud shrugged his shoulders and turned to walk away. Mitchell called after him, "Come see me after you set up the camp. I need to talk to you."

Redcloud didn't stop or turn, but just continued to walk away. However, he raised his hand and waved back at him, so he knew he had heard. Mitchell then turned back to Crockett. "Could we talk about some plans?"

"Yeah, I've been waiting to hear what you are planning."

"Let's sit inside the hummer where we can have a little privacy and quiet."

This got Crockett's attention. He looked over at the hummer and Mitchell could see the excitement on his face. Mitchell walked around the hummer, and Crockett was right behind him. He went to the passenger's side and showed him how to open the door. Before he climbed in, he just stood there, looking all around. "Have a seat." Mitchell told him and then walked around to the other side and climbed in.

They sat in there for about half an hour as he laid out his plan. Of course, he had to keep stopping to explain what he meant or about the specific weapon he was referring to. During all this, he also laid out how the battle went in his timeline, as best he could remember it. When they were all done, He was suddenly hungry and couldn't remember when he ate last. He saw there was a small fire going where they set up camp. August had moved the wagon to just outside the wall. There was a pot of what I guess was, water over the fire. Looks like they were going to have MREs again tonight.

"How would you like to try some food from the future?" He asked Crockett as they started walking towards the fire.

He had to think about that for a second, but then said, "I would be delighted to join you."

When they got to the camp, Mitchell showed him the different packages they had. After a bit of explaining what each one was, he chose the chili with beans. He thought it was the fact that it had corn bread with it that drew Crockett to choose this one. After Mitchell picked his, he showed him how to heat it up and told him about all the things that came in the package. As he went through what was in the accessory pack, Crockett was especially interested in the toilet tissue.

They both just sat on the ground near the fire. "This is the standard meals for the military while we are in the field." Mitchell told him. He just continued to eat and look around at all the other things they had. The tents and sleeping bags he liked. It took a while to explain some things like the flash lights. It was Remarkable, how much he understood. "You are quite different from what I expected." He told Crockett after they had talked for a long time.

"How is that?" he asked.

"Yes, I know you were a congressman, but your real fame comes from your fighting skills and your knowledge of frontier living." Mitchell said as he leaned closer to him, "but, I have found you to be a very intelligent man and curious about everything. You also appear to me to be a peacemaker and not a fighter."

Crockett just started laughing. After a little, he leaned closer and whispered, "Don't tell other people this. If word got out, I think all my men would head back to Tennessee and leave me here."

They just continued to chat about small things while he continued to sip the drink mix that came with his meal package and then he asked, "How about you tell me a little about the future of our country? I'd really like to know if everything we are doing now is going to be worth all the trouble."

"Well, Colonel…" Mitchell started, but then he interrupted him.

"Just call me David, or Crockett, if you like. We seem to have too many colonels around here."

"OK, David, I really don't want to get into the future too much. If I tell you the things I know, it could change the future."

He thought a moment and then proposed, "It seems to me, from what you have already said, that the future has already changed. Besides, your little drawing says we are on a completely different, what did you call it, timeline."

He was right. It didn't matter now. If the theory is correct, and they have started a new timeline, then everything he knew has changed. If the theory is wrong and they are contaminating his own timeline, everything has already changed. This simple country man had a natural wisdom that could take the abstract ideas and turn them into practical thoughts.

"Your right," Mitchell said slowly. However, he still had some reservations about what to tell him. This could be a very slippery slope, and he wasn't so sure he wanted to go down. He needed to be very careful about what he tells him, in any case. Continuing, he started by just telling him about the near future. "I can tell you that after all the soldiers at the Alamo and Goliad are murdered, Santa Anna will split his forces and try to hunt down the army that Houston is putting together. That will be his mistake. Santa Anna will have only a small force, but still bigger than Houston's Army, but he will make a tactical mistake that will give Houston the advantage he needs. The Texas Army will destroy this small force and capture Santa Anna. Instead of killing him, as his men wanted, Houston let's Santa Anna go, but not before he signs paper to give up Mexico's claim to Texas."

Crockett thought about that for a little while, still sipping at his drink mix. Mitchell could see the deep thinking that was going on within him. After a long time, he finally asked Mitchell didn't want to answer. He asked, "What is it you and your people think you are going to do to help?"

He knew what he wants to say to answer Crockett, but that differed from what he believed he should tell him. He took a long moment before answering him. "I'm not totally sure what I am doing. I have no genuine doubt that we can defeat Santa Anna here and now. However, there are many things that can go wrong. What if we kill him and he never signs the surrender documents to free Texas? An important sacrifice that rallies the people of Texas like nothing else. This will not happen. A few years down the road, Texas will become a state, a slave state. This will lead to the death of hundreds of thousands of Americans in a war that will split America in half." He stopped there. He didn't believe it was wise right now to go too far into the future.

Crockett didn't respond. He just sat there looking into the fire and obviously thinking. He took another sip and said, "This drink surely needs some help. It's a shame we don't have anything to give it a little kick." He then looked at Mitchell with a look that was certainly asking if he had anything else to drink.

Mitchell just smiled and yelled over his shoulder, "August, could you please break out that keg you've been keeping safe for us?"

August turned when he called him and when he asked him about the keg, August hung his head down and moved rather slowly. He went to the wagon and dug around a little, and then finally lifted the little keg out. Carefully, he tucked it under his arm as he climbed down from the wagon and carried it over to Mitchell. As he handed it to him, Mitchell could immediately tell it was considerably lighter than he remembered from the last time they shared a drink.

"It seems to have gotten a little lighter since the last time we had a drink. I think you had better check the keg. I believe it might have a leak in it. Maybe Johnson can fix this for you." He said as August sat down to share a drink with them.

August just smiled and said, "Yes, it must be a leak." He then held out his cup.

Crocket and Mitchell just looked at each other and they both smiled. He pulled the plug on the keg and gave it a little swirl. It was indeed light. He poured some into Crockett's drink mix and just a little into August's cup before he gave himself a little to sip from it.

August considered his cup and frowned at him. He didn't say anything, however, Mitchell could see he was not happy about the portion poured for him. Mitchell plugged the keg and set it on the ground close to him. Then picking up his cup and raised it for a toast. "To the survival of these men here and Texas."

Both men raised their cups and almost in unison they repeated, "To Texas."

August tuned his cup up while Crockett and Mitchell just took a little sip. Crockett was now a little happier and commented while looking into his cup, "Now that is a lot better." He then looked up at August and Mitchell with a smile.

August held out his cup for more, but Mitchell just ignored him and continued his chat with Crockett. Eventually, he set his cup on the ground and just quietly sat there, listening to them.

After chatting with Crockett for a while, Redcloud came over and sat next to Crockett. He looked at his old friend and said, "You wanted to talk with me?"

Before Mitchell could answer him, Crockett stood up and said, "Gentlemen, it has been a pleasure talking with you, but I need to check with my men and then get some sleep." He handed Mitchell his cup and stepped past him, but before he left, he turned and said, "Besides, I believe you have much to talk about."

As Crocket turned and walked away, Mitchell said to Redcloud, "Are you calmed down now?"

"Me!" exclaimed Redcloud, "I'm always calm. It's Bowie who has the problem."

"Yeah, maybe." He responded while looking in his cup. "That little stunt, however, did not win us any friends here."

Redcloud just shrugged his shoulders and slowly responded by saying, "I was always taught, when you come into a new place, you find the biggest, meanest person there and take him down. The others may not give you any more respect, but they will sure think about giving you any grief."

Mitchell could probably argue the point with him, but he could see his reasoning. He just hoped it will not blow up into some bigger problem down the road. "That's not what I wanted to talk to you about, anyway." He said to him and before Redcloud could ask, he just continued, "I wanted to see what you think about the defenses here and how we could support them."

Now, Redcloud did the same thing that everyone had done. He looked around like he was going to see everything, even though from where he was sitting he could actually see very little of the compound, even if it was still daylight. Mitchell just kind of smiled to himself and let it go.

Kat came up behind him and sat down by his side while Redcloud was thinking. She just took a hold of his arm and laid her head on his shoulder. He turned his head to look at her and said, "Good evening, my darling."

She lifted her head and with a surprised look on her face, she replied, "Oh, you remember who I am?"

"I'm sorry my dear," He said with his head hung down, "It has been a very busy day and I have been trying to get us settled in here."

She just smiled at him and put her head back on his shoulder and then whispered, "I'll forgive you." Then she lifted her head a moment to add, "This time."

He just smiled back at her. Redcloud had now finished his considerations about what they were talking about. He asked as he started drawing a rectangle in the dirt, "How much do you remember about the battle details?"

While Mitchell answered, he continued to draw what was becoming obviously the compound here. "I don't have a great storehouse and we can't just Google it now, can we? However, if I remember rightly the initial days of the battle, there we a few attempts to attack from different directions, and all failed with no damage to the people here. It wasn't until the thirteenth day they made the last attack from all directions. The main push came against the north wall. Once they breached there, the Mexicans could swarm in, and the Alamo quickly fell."

"What about the rest of this place?" Redcloud asked.

He had to think about it. Mitchell continued to describe what he remembered. "There was a large force sent against the west wall and the main gate. The palisades area also had a large force attacking here. I'm not sure about the east wall. I don't remember hearing much about that side."

When he had finished, he saw a small group, of who he guessed were Crockett's men, had gathered around. He wasn't too sure how much they had heard. He was keeping his voice low. After looking around, he turned to Kat and said, "Dear, would you like to join us for a walk?"

She almost jumped at the thought. "August and Chief, please join us." He said as he helped Kat to her feet. Both August and Redcloud got up, and they strolled out into the main courtyard area. When they were clear of people, he turned to August. "I need you to stay here. As a person from this time, you will be less obvious as one of my people. I need you to snoop around and see what the men here are thinking about us."

At first August appeared to be hurt when Mitchell said he needed to stay here, but then as he explained what his mission was, August chest puffed up a little and, as he intended for him, he felt he had a very important job to do. He tipped his hat to Mitchell and quickly headed back to the camp area. Redcloud, Kat, and he continued to stroll around the compound. He had forgotten about the keg he just left there.

Redcloud was checking out the positions they had. When they got near the gate, Mitchell suggested they go outside. As they walked through the gate, the chatter of the men that were there suddenly went quiet. They watched them as they walked out. No one challenged them, or even spoke a single word to them. Mitchell believed they were very much afraid of them.

Once away from the compound, they turned left and walked around to the north wall. "This is where the worst of the battle will be. I'm not sure of the details, but I believe Santa Anna's forces will attack mostly from this direction. They will focus on the repaired area of the wall. Some will try to attack from the east side and from the west side, but this is where the wall is first breached and then, as defenders adjust to the battle, the south wall will fall. The palisades and the chapel are the last places to fall." He said, but then added, "If my memory serves me right."

Redcloud just looked at the wall and turned to take in the entire battle ground. "I'd really like to see this layout in the daylight. I think the claymores would work fine here. However, before I lock into a plan, I want to go completely around the grounds in the daylight. I want to see where the town is and where the likely places for Santa Anna to set up his artillery."

Mitchell stepped up beside him and quietly said, "We have to brief Travis and the others first thing in the morning."

Redcloud just looked at the ground and gave a big sigh. After a moment, he turned to him and said, "Well then, I suggest we all make a tour of the grounds around this place in the morning, and I can better lay out my plans as we go."

"Yeah, you might be right. We have a lot of things to consider before we can come up with a proper plan." He replied while he was thinking about how he would deal with this come morning.

Redcloud just made a huffing noise and turned to head back to the gate. Kate, still on his arm, pulled Mitchell in the opposite direction. "I'd like to continue our walk for a little while." She said and then added, "After all, you have paid no attention to me all day."

He bowed his head and put his hand on hers where she had his arm and just started a slow walk. They hadn't gone very far when she stopped and looked at him and asked, "How bad is it going to get when Santa Anna gets here?"

"I wished I knew," he said to answer her question.

She thought a moment, then with surprise in her voice she asked again, "But you're from the future. Why can't you tell me?"

He turned to look her straight in the eyes. "I can't tell you because what I know is going to change. Hell, it may have already changed from what I know. I can tell you what happened in my time, but I'm not an expert on this and my memory is missing many things about the battle. Blake had some higher education than I did and might know a little more, but that still doesn't change the fact that everything that happened is probably not going to happen this time."

She stepped back and looked up at the outside of the north wall. Slowly, she said, "I think I understand. You have already said enough about what happened. Enough, so I am afraid for you and my father. Can you at least tell me he will be safe?"

Now he understood where these questions were coming from. He gently grabbed her by her shoulders and bent down until she looked at him. Then, standing up, he said, "I cannot tell you that nothing will happen to your father. In battle, there are just too many things that are out of my control. I can tell you, however, that I will do everything I can to put him where I remember things were not too bad. Also, if things go very wrong, we will all climb into the hummer and drive out of here. I know the Mexican Army does not have a rifle that can penetrate the armor of that thing. But, between the first shot and the door of the hummer closing, there are just too many things that can happen."

"Where will you put him that he can be safe?" she asked.

He hadn't given thought to assignments yet, so thinking fast, he ran through what he remembered. He turned around to look at the wall. This was not the place for him. After studying things a moment, he told her, "If I remember right, the chapel was the last place to fall. He will be relatively safe there. He can fight from where the cannons are on top, and when the fighting gets bad, I'll try to get him to go inside to protect the women and children."

She looked at her man and flatly said, "He will not run like that."

"I know," Mitchell said as he smiled, "that is why I will make it sound like such an important job. I will make sure he understands it is an honor for him to protect them. He will go, because that is where I am going to tell you to go, if things get that bad."

She smiled back, saying, "Yes, I think he would do that. He is a father, and he will also care about the other children, too."

He added, "Besides, that will also put him near the hummer, so if we have to leave, he won't have to run so far."

He thought the image he painted of her father trying to run got to her and she let out a little laugh. With that, he took her hand and placed it again on his arm as they slowly headed back to the gate. Once they were back inside, he took her to the tent she shared with Wilson, and she gave him a very passionate kiss before she ducked inside.

"Everything all right, boss?" came the snide, brief comment from the shadows. Again, Redcloud was hiding and just watching everything.

He couldn't see him, so he just flipped a bird toward his voice and went to his tent. As he walked, he could hear a low laugh from the shadows.

CHAPTER 9

While morning came early, it was not nearly as early as they were used to. Mitchell crawled out of his tent and stretched. He could see Redcloud was already up and on top of the gun platform on top of the chapel. As he walked by the fire, he grabbed a cup of, what was, the hot water. It had now cooled and actually tasted pretty good.

As he climbed up the ramp to the platform, Redcloud turned and waved and shouted, "Top of the morning to you, Captain." It was an obvious attempt to sound Irish, but Mitchell thought it failed miserably.

"Shut up." He said as he got closer to him.

When they were together, Redcloud added, "A wee bit grumpy this morning, are we, Sir?"

"All right, enough is enough," He said with a little anger in his voice, "What do you see?"

Redcloud at first smiled when he could tell he had touched a nerve. He then told him, "Well, boss, there is not much from here. If you don't remember much about what happened on this side, I'm going to assume, for my planning, that not much happened here. I think one person here would work. He can fire from any of the three sides, depending on where the worst of the fighting is coming from."

Probably a good plan. Thinking out loud, Mitchell said, "True, I don't remember what happened on this side, but that doesn't mean that nothing happened. I think I'll put August up here. He is an excellent shot and if everything goes south, he won't have far to run to get to our rally point."

"Rally point?" Redcloud asked, looking at him.

"Yes, a rally point." He said, "If everything goes south, I want everyone to rally at the hummer. We'll pile in and just drive out of here."

"Well, let's hope it doesn't come to that." He said as he turned to go back down the ramp.

When they got back down to the camp area, there was a man talking to Wilson. As Mitchell came up, Wilson turned to Mitchell, saying, "They want us to supply people for guard duty. This sergeant needs a list of our people so he can add them to the watch roster."

"Thanks Anna." He said to her and then turned to the sergeant and told him, "I'm going to meet with Colonel in just a little while. I'll discuss the assignment of my people with him."

The sergeant just dropped his arms to his side and politely said, "As you wish, Captain." He then quickly turned and walked away.

After he was out of hearing range, he turned to Wilson and told her, "Prepare a watch list. We may have to support the guard watches, but I don't want it on any of their rosters."

"Got it Boss," she said and then smiled, adding "Sir."

He just gave her a quick shot and said, "You can knock it off, too." He then looked around and added, "You can tell all of them that the next one who rubs it in will regret it."

Wilson just gave him a sweet smile and turned and walked away.

"You knew this was coming." Redcloud whispered as he stepped up beside him.

Before he could say anything back to Redcloud, Crockett came up and said, "You ready? I can't wait to hear your plans."

"Yeah, I'm ready, but in order to get a better idea and help explain things, we're gonna have to take a little walk around the outside." He said to Crockett as they walked to meet with Travis.

Crockett just turned and smiled, saying, "A good stretch of the legs in the morning would do us all some good."

Mitchell liked his attitude. When they got to Travis' quarters, as he called them, Crockett held the door open for Redcloud and him. When they got inside, he could see Bowie was already there, leaning up against a window. As soon as he saw Redcloud, he stood up straight and, pointing to Redcloud, he said, "What the hell is he doing here?"

Travis just looked at Mitchell and said in a questioning tone, "Captain?"

He wasn't sure, but he thought Bowie had already relayed their incident yesterday to Travis. This was going to be a very touchy morning meeting. Choosing his words carefully. "This is Sergeant Redcloud. If you remember, I told you he was my second in command. He is the best at planning a battle. It would be wise to listen to him."

Bowie spoke up before anyone else could say anything. "Why should we listen to a … him?"

Mitchell could hear it in his voice. He was mad, mad as hell, but still enough sense to fear Redcloud. He turned to Bowie and look him in the eye as he slowly said, "Simply, because he is the best."

Crockett took a turn at trying to settle this, saying, "Gentlemen, I suggest we let this go for now. We have a much more serious issue at hand, and we need to get working on it now."

Everyone looked at Travis. He sat there for a couple of minutes, trying to figure out how best to move on. When he didn't speak up, Mitchell suggested, "Gentlemen, my sergeant and I have only just arrived here, and we didn't have time to look at this place in the daylight to even think about a solid plan. I would like to suggest we take a walk outside the compound and see what is there. I can tell you what I have and what would work the best and you can ask questions and together we can come up with a solid plan to work for everyone."

Travis nodded his head, but it was Crockett that spoke. "I think this is an excellent idea. Gentlemen, should we step outside?"

Bowie looked to Travis, and Travis nodded his agreement with the idea. Mitchell was pretty sure that Bowie was not happy about it. He believed Bowie would have rather stayed inside, where he could argue with him and Redcloud, but he strolled out the door.

Once outside, Bowie was acting more like a commander than a spoiled kid who didn't get his way. Suddenly, he was all military in his thinking. They walked across the compound to the east gate and went outside. The same route Mitchell took last night with Redcloud and Kat, but this time it was not near as pleasant.

When they reached an area outside the northeast corner, Mitchell stopped. Turning to the group, he said, "Now remember this, my memory of what happened is limited and I cannot speak to a lot of details. I remember that there were cannons place to the northeast that were slowly moved closer. Also, Santa Anna will place several more cannons inside the town, just across the river."

He gave everyone a chance to picture this in their minds. As he described the placements for the guns, he pointed, and everyone's head turned to look where he was pointing. It was a little funny, because there was nothing there for them to see now.

They continued around the wall to the north side. Again, he stopped and pointed to the wall. "This." He said, "Is going to be where the worst of the fighting happens. The Mexicans will send the largest force against this wall. They will pound it ahead of time with artillery and weaken it. As I remember, the attack actually comes from the northwest, north and northeast. However, because of the fire from your men, they will bunch together, so the attack is basically from the north." As he talked, he was pointing all over and trying to impress upon each of them how bad this got. Continuing, "This was probably the best thing for them because they actually concentrated their attack on one specific point and could breach the wall and get in. Up to this point, your men did an excellent job of defending this place."

Travis stepped a little closer and asked, "What can you do to help stop that from happening?"

Mitchell turned to Redcloud. "Chief, do you have any ideas yet?"

Redcloud walk around from the back where he had been lying low. Stepping to the front, he laid out a preliminary plan. "The first thing I would do is set up about a half dozen claymore mines out here." He stopped and held up his hand and added, "Before you ask, I'll explain what each of these things is in a moment. Let me finish with the plan first. I would set one of my people at each of the corners and I would take the middle place where the gun platform is located. There, I can use my 203 to support the cannons. I can also swing over to the northwest corner if need be."

Mitchell now turned to the group to explain what the weapons were that Redcloud had referred to, "Gentlemen," He said as he walk up to stand in front of Redcloud, "a Claymore mine is a small amount of explosive material with about seven hundred small metal balls in front of the explosive. When this mine set off, it can kill or wound everything in front of it out to almost one hundred yards." He saw the reaction of the three colonels, and it was what he expected to see. They all just gave a quick look at the area as if they were imagining rows of attacking soldiers cut down in mid-stride. Mitchell then threw in something that they might understand, comparing it to, "Yes, it is quite devastating and effective. One of these would be about the same as maybe fifty cannons firing a double canister shot all at the same time." Again, he saw what he wanted in their reaction.

Next, Redcloud stepped forward and took his weapon off his shoulder and showed it to the group of colonels. "Gentlemen, this is the M203. First, it is the same rifle that Sergeant ... ah, Captain Mitchell used in his demonstration yesterday. You will also notice there is a slight difference between this rifle and his. The large barrel below the main barrel fires a forty-millimeter explosive round, accurately, out to almost two hundred yards. With some guess work it can reach out to over four hundred yards. There are many types of rounds it can fire, but I won't go into each type right now. The main round I would use in this would have a kill zone of about five meters and can wound people out to over one hundred feet. I estimate it has the killing power of one of your smaller cannons, but I can fire up to about seven rounds a minute with a lot more accuracy than your cannons." Redcloud pause, but there were no questions.

Mitchell suspected these men were a little overwhelmed right now, as no one said anything and the looks on their faces were almost a blank stare. So, he suggested they move on to the west side and continue our inspection.

As they moved around to the west side, he could see some men working on the defenses there. As they rounded the corner, most work stopped to watch them. When they were about a third of the way down the wall, Mitchell stopped and turned to Redcloud. He stepped up and looked at the wall and then the grounds between the wall and the river. Redcloud shortly turned back to the wall and stepped back to look up and down the wall. Then, turning back to the group, he said as he turned to the wall and pointed, "This side is where I believe Santa Anna will place the remaining cannons he has. If I recall, they kept them on the other side if the river. However, this is still enough to keep heads down over here. I would place one of our people on each corner and a third in the middle with the SAW." He spun to the group and said, "You remember yesterday when the Captain fire several rounds quickly?" The group could mumble an agreement and lots of nodding. "Well, the SAW can do the same thing. These rifles have a three-round burst like you saw yesterday. The SAW, however, can continue to fire until it runs out of ammo or the barrel melts."

"What about those Claymore mines?" asked Bowie, and then added, "it seems like this would be a good place for them, also."

This time Mitchell stepped up to answer before Redcloud had a chance. "The claymores would work fine here, if we had a lot more of them. Like I explained before, we had a limited amount of ammo. I am concerned that the last attack we are making planes for might not be the final. We need to hold some in reserve, just in case this goes on longer than the original battle."

Bowie thought it over for a moment, then reluctantly said, "I suppose you might be right. Are you sure three men will be enough?"

He simply replied, "No." He then turned away, but quickly turned back and added, "That's why you and your men are going to be up there with them."

Crockett got a little giggle over that one, but Mitchel could see Bowie didn't see the humor in it.

All this time, Travis was being silent and reserved. Mitchell could see he was very interested, but he still said nothing and didn't ask questions. Crockett also said very little, but he could also see his mind was working. Bowie, however, did ask questions. Mostly negative questions. Mitchell thought that his thought line was a bit on the pessimistic side.

They continued to walk around the compound. Walking down the west wall, there were only slight comments about where the others had placed their people and ideas about what might happen during the battle. When they got to the south-west corner, he saw several small buildings. Mostly just shacks, as near as he could tell. He remembered from his trip to the Alamo, the Mexican army initially used these buildings to get close. "Gentlemen," He said when they stopped next to them, "these building will present a problem when Santa Anna tries to occupy them with troops."

"Shouldn't we destroy them now, before he gets here?" Bowie asked.

Mitchell looked back at the building's and studied them for a moment. More thinking out loud than actually answering Bowie's question, he said, "Actually, this might work to our favor if we booby trap them."

"What do you mean?" Travis asked this time.

He walked over to look at one window. The inside appeared to be a single room. If all of them were the same, this would be easy. He replied while continuing to look inside the window. "If all these building are the same, we could set some explosives and hide them and then set them off when the buildings get occupied."

"What would you use?" asked Crocket.

He turned back to him and said, "There are several things we could do. Claymores, grenades, rockets and so on." He walked back to the group to stress the next point. "Here and now, if you run out of ammunition, you can probably find some on down the road. If we run out of ammunition or any other of our supplies, they are simply gone, and I cannot replace them." He looked into each of their faces and added, "I won't know exactly what I am going to do until I see if this timeline is the same as I remember or if it has changed or I didn't remember correctly. What I don't want to do is run out of our supplies in the middle of a battle, simply because I didn't think it through correctly."

This answer seemed to quiet all further questions. So, he turned back to the wall and said, "Here I'll place another person on the south wall, probably over the gate."

Before anyone could ask, he just started walking along the south wall. When they got to the palisades, he just simply pointed to the hummer, that was now just above the wall with the machine gun ready to fire. He flatly said, "Sergeant Wilson will be on the gun here and that should be plenty."

Again, no one said anything. This time, they didn't move. He just simply pointed to the top of the chapel and said, "I'll post my last man up top there. He can go to whichever side is having the biggest problem."

Again, it was Bowie that spoke up, "Yesterday, when you pulled in, I counted six of you. So far I count you have placed eight positions."

Mitchell bowed his head and looked at the ground, because he knew this answer will not set well with any of them, "This is true," He said, but then went on, "however, August and his daughter were trained on our weapons and some of our tactics. They will be near to one of my people at all times to head off any problems."

Bowie just threw up his arms and turned to walk away, but quickly turned back. He came right up to Mitchell's face and pointed at him, saying, "It's bad enough we have to fight with your mixed group of people, but now you want to have women fight on the wall with us?"

"They have all agreed to this, and they are trained." He replied to him.

He stomped away again, but before he had taken only three steps, he turned back and again pointed his finger at Mitchell and said, "Yesterday, you tried to prove your point with your little shooting competition." He paused and looked at Crockett and Travis, and then back to Mitchell. "How about we have another little competition? Your woman, fighting one of my men."

Redcloud stepped up, but Mitchell held up his hand before he could say anything. "That sounds fair to me. How do you want to do this? Weapons or fists?" He said to him.

Bowie could see he was trying to get him to agree to his terms. He didn't fall for it. He replied with a smile, "Just some plan old dirt fighting."

"If there is no objection from Colonel Travis, I agree, with one point." He replied to him.

He responded, "What's your point."

"No one gets seriously hurt. We are going to need all bodies on the wall when Santa Anna gets here. I wouldn't want any of our resources to be laid up because of this little…ah, competition."

"Agreed." Bowie said with his hand out.

Mitchell looked over at Travis, who just simply nodded at him, so he took Bowie's hand and shook it.

Bowie turned away and started walking back to the south gate. Mitchell yelled as to walk off, "When would you like to do this?"

Bowie stopped and turned. He placed his hands on his hips and said, "I was thinking right now."

Mitchell thought for a second and responded with, "Let's make it this afternoon. We still have much to plan and I need to get my people online with the plans. I believe that to be a more important issue."

Now Travis stepping into this and said, "I think this afternoon would be the better option. The Captain is right. Our defenses come first."

Bowie just waved his hand over his head as he turned to go and yelled, "Fine, then. This afternoon." And then continued to stomp away.

Mitchell tuned to Redcloud and said, "I'll finish this briefing. You tell Wilson to get ready." Redcloud just turned to walk away, but before he could, Mitchell added, "Make sure she understands she is not to permanently hurt whoever they send out to fight her."

When Redcloud turned to respond, He just gave him a big smile. Mitchell knew he would catch the meaning of what he said. After a moment, he smiled back, saying, "I'll make sure she knows not to hurt him too bad." And he turned and trotted off.

When He turned back to Travis and Crockett, they were just looking at each other. He asked, "Would you like to return to your office to continue this planning session?"

Travis walked over to him and said, "Yes. We'll meet there in half an hour." He then turned to Crockett and said, "Could you please insure Colonel Bowie is there."

Crockett replied, "I'll see what I can do."

This was obviously not the response that Travis expected or wanted, but he said nothing and just tuned to the south gate and walked away. Crockett came over to Mitchell and leaned on his Kentucky and asked, "Did you really mean what you said about your girl not hurting anyone?"

"Oh yes," He replied and added, "She can break bones and kill if need be."

Crockett looked down, then shook his head as he picked up his rifle and said, "This is going to be interesting, I think."

"Probably not too interesting, because it will probably be quick." He said with a smile.

Crockett just smiled back and motioned him to follow Travis to the gate. When they got inside, Mitchell excused himself, saying he needed to attend to some personal matters, showing he needed to pee. He then headed to their camp. Redcloud was already talking to Wilson. When he walked up, she approached him. He could easily see she was not happy. "Are you serious? You want to show off by having me fight one of those men? I can't even stand to be near them because they smell is so bad. Now I've got to fight one."

"Hold on a minute," He said to her, "let's get one thing straight right now. This is not for showing off. Right now, they have no respect for you. To be honest, I don't think they have much respect for most of this group. These men all know each other and most of them have already fought one thing or another together. We are the new guys on the block. Before they will trust us, we need to prove to them we have what it takes. More importantly, it will prove to them that women can fight and maintain themselves, even in this man's world, that we are currently in."

He glanced over to Redcloud. He was obviously enjoying this. As Wilson spoke, his attention was fully back on her. "Boss, I don't want to fight anyone. Yes, I have the training, but I'm afraid I'll hurt whoever it is and put him out of action. Right now, we are going to need everyone on the wall."

He took her by the shoulders and forced her to look up at him. "I know you and I know what you can do. This, however, is a risk we will need to take. It is of the utmost importance that these men trust us. It is also of the utmost importance that you, mostly for the sake of Johnson and Kat, take on this fight."

Wilson backed away and slightly turned to look at the rest of the group. They were all watching to see what the decision was going to be. Finally, she saw Kat watching. Lowering her head, she quietly said, "OK, Boss, I'll fight your fight, but I can't guarantee that I won't hurt the son of a bitch they send against me."

He stepped closer to her and placed his arm on her shoulder and leaned close to whisper to her, "I know you'll do what needs to be done, and I don't expect you to let them hurt you, either. Right now, you need to find a quiet place to get with Redcloud to warm up and maybe pick up a couple of fine points from him."

She just turned her head to look at Mitchell and nodded. As she walked away, he signaled Redcloud to go with her. He knew Redcloud must have been way ahead of him, because he was already moving that way, before Mitchell motioned to him.

The rest of the group just kind of huddled together, and Kat came over to him. She wrapped her arm around his and held him close to her. "Do you think she is going to get hurt in this fight?" she asked him as she watched Anna walk away with Redcloud.

Mitchell slightly laughed, partly to relieve some of the tension, but also because, to him, it was a funny question. He leaned to give her a kiss and said, "No, not really. I am more concerned that she might hurt the man that we will need in a few days."

Kat stepped back and turned away from his face to follow Wilson as she warmed up and was talking with Redcloud.

Figuring he would not get that kiss, he said to her, "Darling, I need to go talk with Travis and the others to firm up our plans.

As he turned away, she leaned over and gave him the kiss he had been waiting for. This, he suddenly thought, might actually turn out to be a good day.

He met with Travis, Bowie and Crocket. Bowie was uncommonly quiet as they discussed the plans for defense. There was a really brief discussion. They showed him their plans, and what he showed was his suggestion for his people fit right in. Other than training them when to duck because we were going to set off an explosion or something, He was thinking things would go smoothly. As they broke up the meeting, Bowie stepped up to block Mitchell's exit. He just looked at Bowie and said, "Is there something else I can do for you, Colonel?"

He took a step towards him and said, "Where's your Indian?"

Mitchell looked at him and flatly replied, "If you're referring to Sargent Redcloud," He said with emphasis on the "Sergeant," "He is back at our camp getting things ready."

Bowie took another step towards Mitchell, but he didn't budge. They were standing almost nose to nose. "I just want to ensure this fight is going to be fair." He said with a bit of sarcasm mixed in with the anger.

Again, he didn't let Bowie bug him and flatly said, "Oh, I can assure you it will be fair, from my side anyway. You'll have to speak for your own men for assurance from your side."

The reference to his men, maybe not being fair about the fight, really didn't sit well with him. While he was still steaming, Mitchell threw a little gas on the fire and added, "Which one of your thugs are you going to throw into this fight?"

Bowie smiled, like he had just stepped into his trap. This time he took a step back and with a little too much pride, he announced, "I believe it will be me doing the fighting."

Mitchell hadn't counted on this. Bowie had quite the reputation as a fighter, but that was mostly as a knife fighter, but couldn't remember hearing much about his street fighting ability. However, he didn't know how well he covered his surprise at this news. He just nodded and said, "Oh." But, as he sidestepped to go around Bowie, he added as he passed, "I will make sure I tell her not to hurt you too much." Mitchell then headed for the door before he could say any more.

He hadn't taken but a couple of steps when Crockett followed him out. He quickened his pace to catch up with Mitchell and when he was beside him, he whispered, "Are you sure you want to go through with this? Your woman might just get killed in there."

To his surprise, this time Mitchell thoughtfully said, "Oh, it will be alright. I'm not so much worried about him hurting her as I am about what he will do when he loses."

Crockett stopped dead in his tracks. When Mitchell also stopped, he leaned over and, while still whispering, said in a rather startled voice, "Are you serious? Bowie is a known killer. He'll take her down in no time."

Mitchell just bowed his head and smiled. "He is a killer with a knife. There are no knives in this fight. I believe I remember hearing that he is a good street fighter, but I'll bet he has seen nothing like what will happen today."

Crockett stood up tall and with a smile said, "I think I would like to take you up on that bet."

Mitchell hadn't meant it as a literal bet, but what the hell. He figured, let's have a little fun. He smiled back and said, "What do you propose?"

Crockett didn't even take a second to think about it. He just came right out and said, "How about my rifle for one of yours?"

While the offer was tempting, Mitchell thought about having the rifle of the famous Davy Crockett would be something. He couldn't take the chance of him getting his hands on one of his weapons. "Sorry David, I can't take the chance on that. What I will do is bet five of our meals against that famous coonskin cap of yours."

Crockett's disappointment wasn't too obvious, but it was there. He quickly recovered and simply said, "Done."

They shook hands and turn to go their separate ways. Mitchell went back to his camp and could see Anna practicing with Redcloud. The rest of the team were all standing around watching, along with many of the defenders. Some, he thought, were Bowie's men. He quickly went over to Redcloud and Wilson. Quietly he said, "You are attracting quite the crowd. Some of these men belong to Bowie. It wouldn't be good for you to be showing them too much of your style."

Redcloud and Wilson both took a quick look around and Redcloud said, "You've got a point." And then to Wilson he said, "One of your primary advantages is they have seen nothing like this kind of fighting. Try not to show them any more than you have to before the fight.

Before they turned away, he said, "Now I have some bad news for you."

Wilson just turned back to look at him. Redcloud stopped and turned as he simply said, "Bowie."

Mitchell nodded, knowing what he meant. Wilson looked between them and then threw up her hands and yelled, "What?"

Redcloud went to her and put a hand on her shoulder, saying, "Bowie has decided he will be the one to fight you."

"Oh great," she yelled. She stomped around for a moment, then said, "I don't want to fight him. He is a killer."

"Not to worry, grasshopper," Redcloud said, recalling a line from a movie, adding, "Bowie is a great knife fighter, but this is not a knife fight. He is pretty good at grappling, but we have worked on this type of fighting, too. He is not much bigger than you and way older. You have the advantage in all areas."

Wilson just stood there, looking at the ground. She kicked the dirt a little, and the slowly said, "Yeah, maybe, but I don't like it." She then turned to walk away and added, "Not one bit."

The afternoon came, and it was time for the main event. The word was all over the compound. When they walked out of their area, there was a clearing near the middle of the compound. It took them a little pushing and shoving to get Wilson to that area. On the other side was Bowie. He had removed his coat and was just had a shirt on. When they came to the edge, he slowly started walking to the middle. As he did, the men standing around the circle started the cheer and call his name.

Wilson was still in her full uniform. She wanted to remove the shirt, but Mitchell suggested she keep it on to help absorb any punches she took. She started walking to the middle as well. When they met Bowie, he still had his famous knife on his belt. Mitchell said, as he pointed to the knife, "I thought we agreed this was going to be a no weapons fight?"

Bowie looked down at the knife as if he had forgotten to take it off. He pulled it out and held it back behind him. One of his men ran up and took the knife and held it up high as he trotted back to the edge of the circle. Most of the men cheered as he did this.

"Are you happy now?" he said, looking right into Mitchell's eyes.

With no contempt in his voice, he simply replied, "Yes, this is fine." Mitchell then motioned for Travis and Crockett to come to the center of the circle. When they both got there, he said, "I just want it understood right here and now that this is not a fight to the death. This will be more of a friendly competition and once a quarter is asked for, it will be given, immediately."

There was no response from either Wilson or Bowie, so he added, "Do you both agree to these terms."

Wilson replied, while staring down Bowie, "Agreed."

Bowie acted as if he paid no attention to Wilson and sarcastically said, "Agreed."

"Colonel Travis, would you be so kind as to start the fight?" He asked, being as polite as he could.

Travis nodded, and the non-fighters turned to leave the two fighters alone in the middle. Mitchell walked back to where his people were all standing, except Blake. He still had guard duty. He was not happy with the detail, but Mitchell felt it was something they had to do.

Travis reached his side and turned. Yelling loud enough for all to hear, he said, "Fighters, prepare yourselves."

Anna immediately took up a defensive stance, while Bowie was obviously going to be the aggressor. Travis then simply yelled, "Fight!"

As soon as the word left Travis' mouth, Bowie attacked. He ran full force at Wilson. His strategy was simple. He wanted to get in close and control the fight on the ground. Mitchell had to say that Redcloud had prepared Wilson well. She was no fool and saw this coming right away. When he was just a step away from her, she quickly pivoted to the left and brought her knee straight up into Bowie's abdomen.

Even from where he was, Mitchell could hear the air coming out of Bowie as he went down to the ground. He didn't stay there long, but now was a little more cautious. He quickly got up and turned towards Wilson. She again was in a solid defensive stance. This time Bowie slowly moved in. It looked like now he wanted to get in close for a couple of punches to soften her up. Anna was ready. Just as if she was in the sparing ring, each time Bowie threw a punch, she simply deflected it away.

After going on at this for a while, Bowie had only landed a couple of minor blows. Mostly to her arms. There was one pretty good punch that landed on her jaw, that threw her off balance for a moment, but she quickly recovered. Wilson, however, got a couple of good solid blows to Bowie's abdomen, to follow up with the knee she gave him in the start.

Now, however, it was Anna's turn to move in as the aggressor. She threw several good punches at Bowie. Nothing really landed good, but it backed him away a little. Once he was where she wanted, she pivoted using her left leg and brought her right leg up in a back roundhouse. It landed precisely where she wanted, just above the hip bone on Bowie's side.

Again, everyone could hear the air coming out of Bowie's lungs. He went down on his side. This time, however, he did not get back up so fast. Mitchell thought his age was now showing. He was getting tired. So far, the fight had been going on for about fifteen minutes and both of them were tired, but it was showing more on Bowie.

Bowie got back to his feet and again took an aggressive stance. After feinting to one side and then the other, he finally made a lung at Wilson. This time, she was not ready, and he worked his way behind her. Once he had her in a bear hug, he took both his hands and grabbed her boobs, and laughed.

Mitchell thought to himself, that was probably the biggest mistake he could have made.

Wilson looked down at the way he was holding her, and the anger was instantly all over her face. Bowie had her in a good grip, but he was not tall enough to get her off the ground. Wilson brought her right leg up and slammed her heavy army boot heel right into the top of Bowie's foot. Mitchell was sure she probably broke his foot. Bowie immediately let go of her and grabbed his leg. As he hopped around, Wilson stepped away and turned. Bowie stopped hopping and turned to her, trying not to put any weight on his foot. She let go with a front kick that caught him square in the balls.

Mitchell hadn't noticed it before, but there was a lot of cheering going on. Especially when Bowie got her by the boobs. But as soon as her kick landed and Bowie went down, there was almost immediate silence in the entire compound.

Bowie dropped to his knees, but Wilson wasn't quite through with him yet. While still in her attack stance, she yelled at him, "Two can play at that game. How's it feel to be on the receiving end now?"

Bowie tried to stand up again. Just as he leaned forward to put his hand on the ground to stand, Wilson moved forward and brought a front kick right into Bowie's face. Now, not only did he probably have a broken foot, but Mitchell also bet his nose was now broken.

Bowie went down. This time for good. He was out cold. Everyone was silent. Mitchell walked towards Wilson. Travis also came out to where they were. He looked down at Bowie, who was still out. He came over to Wilson and politely said, "I believe this makes you the winner."

Now Mitchell's team was all cheering, and they ran out to congratulate her. Even some locals were now joining in on the celebration. They came by and patted her on the shoulders and back. It was turning out to be quite the party. He couldn't help himself. When he finally got to say a word to her, he couldn't speak. He just held out both his arms and they both met in a great big hug.

When he finally let go of her, he turned to move away, but Crockett was standing there. He slowly held out his hand. That most famous of trademarks for him was in that hand. Mitchell slowly and reverently reached out and took the hat from him. "I thank you, sir. You are a gentleman."

They both traded bows and laughs. Wilson came up behind him. Before she could say anything, Crockett spoke first, "My dear lady. That was the most spectacular fight I have ever witnessed. You were remarkable."

Wilson turned a little red. Then she looked at Mitchell with Crockett's hat in his hand. "Did you bet on this fight?" She asked.

"Just a little wager, that's all." He sheepishly replied.

She reached over and grabbed the hat before he could do anything. She looked him in the eye as she placed it on her head and said, "Then I recon this rightly belongs to me." Saying that, she just turned and walked away.

Both of the men just stood there like idiots. Mitchell could only imagine the looks on their faces. They both watched her walk away with the hat and then looked at each other. There was nothing they could say, so they both just raised their shoulders in a shrug and let it go at that.

Bowie was coming around now. His men were all gathered around him. Some appeared to be worried about him, while others appeared to be poking fun at him. Something just stuck in Mitchell's mind about how dangerous it was to poke at a wounded animal. Not telling how it would turn. Crockett walked over to Bowie. He motioned for Mitchell to follow. As they approached, most of his men moved away.

Crockett squatted down and looked him over. "How are you feeling?" he asked.

Bowie just rubbed a few of the places she hit or kicked him. Looking at Crockett and then at Mitchell, but to their surprise he laughed and said, "Like a damned old fool." He then painfully rolled onto his hands and knees. Crockett took one arm and tried to help him up. Mitchell figured, not being a doctor, that he was pretty sure that Bowie's right foot was broken. Possibly a couple of ribs, as well.

He didn't help. He wasn't sure how he stood with Bowie at the moment. But Bowie looked at him and smiled, saying, "You trained her well. I won't say that was the worst fight of my life, but I can't recall when I hurt more after a simple street fight."

Trying to, more or less, console him, Mitchell replied, "You need to remember she has been training for a fight just like this for almost ten years now."

He laughed again and again jerked with pain while grabbing his side. He tried to walk but couldn't put any weight on the foot. Mitchell came around to the other side and Bowie threw his arms over Crockett and him. They began walking to the south end where his quarters were. When he got near, he looked over and could see their camp. "Take me over there." He insisted.

They turned, and when they came into the camp, all the talk stopped. Initially, Wilson had her back to him, but with the talking stopped, she turned to see what everyone was looking at. When she saw Bowie standing there, with help, she looked around like she wanted a place to run.

Bowie took a couple more steps towards her and when he was close, he dropped his arms off their shoulders and stuck out one hand towards her.

It took a moment for Anna to realize what was happening. She slowly stepped up and took his hand. "One hell of a fight, young lady." Bowie said to her.

It took her aback, and didn't know what to say. Slowly she said, "I'm sorry if I went too far and hurt you." She said. Bowie held up his hand.

He looked right at her. "It was my fault. I did something I shouldn't have, and you set me straight. You did what I would expect, but coming from a woman caught me by surprise." He laughed, but the pain was just a little too much and he went into a coughing spell.

They set him on the wall to let him catch his breath. It then just dawned on Mitchell. He said to both Crockett and Bowie, "You know I just remembered that during the original battle, Colonel Bowie was ill and laid up in his quarter for most of the entire battle." He stopped to gather how to say the next part, but then continued, "I'm pretty sure things didn't happen this way in my time, but it looks like history tries to correct itself."

He couldn't tell if either of them understood what he was saying. Hell, he wasn't even sure he understood what he was trying to say. He was just going to let this one go for now. Crockett and he got Bowie to his quarters and put him on his bed. Once his boot was off, it was easy to see the bruise already forming and Mitchell was sure Wilson broke it. "Do we have a doctor in this group?" He asked.

"Yeah, I'll go get him." Volunteered Crockett. He quickly left the room.

Bowie was now laying on his bunk. He looked at Mitchell as asked, "Are you sure this is how it is going to end for me?"

"No, not really." He answered him, sitting back. "We don't really know what happened to each man here. All we know is that everyone died. The women and children survived, and the slaves were also let to live. There were different reports from them and what was in documents they found and in the personal journals of some of the Mexican officers. The most popular belief is that you died here in your bed, but you took some of them with you before they killed you."

"What about the others?" he asked.

Mitchell leaned forward so he could look him in the eye to insure he understood and believed him. "I don't have any specific information on anyone. All we have is some tales and guesses. Some may be accurate, but we don't know about the others. Travis got shot in the head at the outset of the battle on the north wall. Crockett, there are several ideas about him. Some accounts say he was one of the last defenders and died trying to protect the women and children in the chapel. Other accounts say he survived the battle but executed right away. Others say the Mexicans to him back to Mexico City as a trophy and later executed him. There is no proof of any of these stories."

Bowie just laid back on his bed. "I truly hope you and your people will make a difference this time." He mumbled, more to himself than anyone else.

Just as he finished talking, Crockett came back in, followed by another man. This man carried the traditional black bag that is associated with doctors from this time. First, he looked at Bowie's foot. It didn't take long when he mumbled, "Broken." He then moved up and poked at Bowie's belly. As he pressed, Bowie winced in pain. Again, the doc mumbled, "At least two broken." Next, the doc looked at his face and almost laughed out, "The nose, also broken. This however, I can fix quickly." Just as Mitchell had seen in movies and TV shows, the doc put his hands on each side of Bowie's nose. He gave a quick twist and Bowie let out a howl. The doc then stood up and said to Crockett, "Not much I can do about the rest. I might try to set the foot a little later, but the ribs will just need time to heal."

The doc turned to leave. Before he opened the door, he turned back to Bowie and said, "Stay off the foot and try to find a bottle. When I return, I'll try to set your foot, but it is going to hurt like hell."

"Thanks, Doc." Bowie said as the doc went out the door.

Mitchell also stood and headed for the door. "I need to go talk with my people. We have plans to complete."

Crockett just slapped him on the shoulder as he stepped by, and Bowie only waved his hand at him as he left. When he shut the door, Mitchell took a deep breath. The fight, other than Bowie getting hurt, turned out better than he had hoped. He could see his group was still partying some. He headed over to them.

"Anna," He called as he approached, and as she got closer, he said, "Nice fight. I think you may have turned quite a few opinions to our favor. I ….."

Before he could say more, she forced her questions, "How is Colonel Bowie? Will he be OK?"

Mitchell held up his hands before she could ask for more information. He didn't want to scare her, but he thought it was important that he tell her the truth. By now, the rest of the group had gathered around. He carefully said, "Well, I think you know you broke his nose, but the doc has already fixed that. He is still as ugly as ever." That got a little smile from her and most of the people that had gathered. He continued, "He also appears to have a couple of cracked ribs. However, the worst of it is you broke his foot, but I think you already knew that."

She nodded. "Yeah, I figured that. I didn't mean to, but…"

He stopped her and said, "Oh yes, you meant to, and rightfully so. He stepped over the line, and you stomped on his foot when he did. However, don't feel the least bit bad about it. Even Bowie admitted he crossed the line and got what he deserved."

"But, that is going to put him out of the fight." Anna said, getting upset.

"Hey," He said as he stepped closer to her and took her by the arm, "That is the strangest part about this whole thing. In the original battle, Bowie was laid up and bed ridden. History is trying, in some way way, to correct itself. Bowie was never in the fight, and the records have him killed in his bed."

Wilson thought about it for a moment and then asked, "But how, we weren't' there before?"

Shaking his head, he said, "I don't know how. All I know is that history is repeating itself. Maybe not the original way it happened in our time, but the end results are the same."

Blake stepped forward and proposed a question that he hadn't thought of yet. "Boss, does this mean that the Alamo will still fall with all these people dying?"

He thought about that one for a little while before he answered, "I don't know, Johnny, maybe." After thinking a little more, he suggested that "Maybe this is all a coincidence. I don't see how we lose this battle, but we'll need to be ready if things go south."

He looked at everyone and could see some second thoughts coming around. He needed to come up with something quick. "Don't worry. I have a backup plan for us if things go south." Looking around, he could see in their eyes that most of them didn't believe him, so he added. "We will do the best we can, and when the time comes, I'll let you know the plans. I am going to be honest with you. We are in for one hell of a fight. I can't guarantee that no one will get hurt. There is always that chance. We do, however, have some things that will put the advantage in our court. You just need to stay ready and cover each other's butts."

There we slow nods and he thought, that while not buying the entire story, they agreed that they have a good fighting chance.

The party broke up and everyone went back to their normal routine. Before she walked away, he called Wilson back. Trying to act like they were back to normal, he said, "I talked with Travis. We will join the guard routine and will stand watch in the chapel along with whoever they have for gun crews up there. We'll stand in pairs. Put August with Jose or Stretch, put…"

But before he could finish, she said, "I'll put Kat with me."

He was going to say to put Kat with him, but then he realized she was right. As a captain now, he didn't pull guard duty. He just said "That's fine. Have each pair stand a four-hour shift during the night. Make sure Kat understands all the aspects of guard and keep a watch out. I don't fully trust some of these men."

"Got it Boss, I totally agree with you." She said before she turned away.

CHAPTER 10

The next day, they firmed up their plans for the help in the defense for the Alamo. Bowie was mostly out of it, so Mitchell spent most of his time working with Crockett. He had a wonderfully simple way of looking at everything. He was also quite cunning when it came down to a fight. They decided that Mitchell's people would mostly be on hold until the last day. Mitchell had explained, as he could remember being told, there were very few injuries and, as he recalled, they killed no one until the last days. Their plan is to let Santa Anna think this would be a simple siege and to let the battle continue, much as it had from his timeline.

Crockett's mind was also quite calm when we talked about things like timelines and such. Mitchell was not aware of any science fiction writings from this time, but he had no trouble understanding the ideas and even had intelligent questions as far as the technical things Mitchell had to tell him. It was like he just took everything the Capitan said as Gospel and went with it.

Other than blowing the buildings on the southwest corner, they planned to not use any of the more advance defenses until the last day of the battle. During any attack, they would limit his people to two mags and no machine guns. Their rate of fire would also be very slow so as not to alert Santa Anna that something might be up with them. They both agreed to take out some cannons that Santa Anna has in the beginning. That would be the biggest problem in their defenses.

They decided the best way was by using Redcloud with his grenade launcher. He figured that should do the trick.

With the plans in place, he turned to Redcloud to get things prepared. Over the next week, he and the rest of the team prepared spots for the claymores. They also set up sandbagged places for their machine guns and a claymore control spot. He didn't think a few sandbags would look too out of place. In fact, they were barely visible from the grounds outside the walls.

Now the biggest problem was the waiting. The original defenders started accepting Redcloud. He even started a small class on the martial arts fighting. Mostly, the younger men seemed interested. Even some women appeared to be interested. After watching the fight Anna had with Bowie, however, none of them were willing to step up to take the lessons, but they sure hung around watching intently.

Kat and Mitchell had some time to get a few moments to themselves. They were becoming very close. They took a couple of walks into the town. He tried to tell her about the San Antonio that he knew. When they crossed the river, he told her about the little motorboats that went up and down the river serving meals to tourists. They strolled down along the river where he described the River Walk area and how beautiful it was. He enthralled her with everything he was telling her. Late one evening they ate in the town and as they walked back to the Alamo and just as they crossed over the river, he got down on his knee. This was something he never thought he would ever do, but he asked. She pretended to be surprised and just a little coy, but quickly smiled and said yes. They stood there in a long embrace for quite some time. He guessed others had noticed as they walked by because he was conscious of some comments as people walked by, mostly in Spanish. He slowly parted from her, but not too far away and still held on to her, and they continued their slow walk back.

When they got back inside, most of the crew was already in bed. He took Kat to her tent and said good night. There was a long slow kiss and then she ducked into her tent. He had just turned to walk back to the fire, and he realized. He stopped and took a careful look around. Sure enough, Redcloud was leaning up against a wall, not too far away, and was smiling at him.

Mitchell went to the fire and sat on one of the rocks they used for seats. Redcloud came up and sat down as well. "Well," he said.

Mitchell just looked at him with a puzzled look and asked, "Well, what?"

He laughed at his friend and said, "Don't play that game with me. I've known you long enough. You asked her? Didn't you?"

Mitchell knew what he was talking about from the start. "Yeah, I asked, and she said yes." He said.

Redcloud stood up and slapped him on my back. He walked away, but Mitchell called him back. "I would like you to be my Best Man, if you don't have any other plans in the near future." He said politely and formally.

Redcloud stopped and turned. He had another of his big shit-eating grin on his face. Just as politely, he replied, "Certainly, I am honored to stand with you." Then he turned and as he walked away, he added with a laugh, "Just as soon as you get permission from her father."

Oh shit, he had forgotten about that part of it. In this time period, it was not a nicety to ask; it is required. After thinking about it for a while, he decided to wait until morning. If he knew August, he was probably off having a few drinks with some of the local boys.

Having made up his mind, he took a walk up the ramp to the chapel gun platform. Johnson was on guard. Wasn't much happening, so he was just looking out over the wall into nothing. As he walked up to him, He figured he must have startled him just a little. He jumped as he turned. "Jesus, Boss. You scared the crap out of me." He said and then added. "This is my third time on guard up here and you're the only one that has come up here to check on us."

As he talked, Blake, who was on the other side, came walking up. Mitchell nodded to him and then to Johnson. "How is it going? Any problems?"

First it was Blake that spoke up, "Not a thing, Boos. It's been real quiet. After being raised in the city with all that noise, it is hard to get used to such quiet."

"Yeah, I hear ya. I still have some problems sleeping at night." He replied, in just general conversation. Then he turned to Johnson and asked, "What about you, Stretch? Any problems?"

At first it was as if he didn't hear him, but then he finally worked up the nerve to say, "Yeah, boss, I'm still getting treated like shit. Outside of our group, except for a couple of people, no one will even talk to me. Even when they have to, they talk down to me or order me to do some stupid thing that they could do themselves easy enough. When you're around it's not a problem, but if you or the Chief aren't near, it's like a different world."

Mitchell stepped to the wall and sat on the edge, just to give himself a moment to think. He knew this was going to be a problem, right from the beginning, and he still didn't have an answer for him. After a while of trying to think of something to say that would make him feel better, all he could say was, "I understand what you are saying. You and I come from a different life and different culture. These people don't have the blood behind them to show them what the cost of this kind of thinking will be. You and I have it in our minds. You, as a black man with slavery in your heritage and me with people from my family fighting with the north to end the slavery. These people don't have that yet. For them, this is the way life is here and now, and here we come in and try to change it. Even in our time, we had people who still felt this way, even in the Army. But when it comes down to it, the man that is with you in that foxhole is colorless. I have never heard of anyone thinking about what color his skin is when the bullets are flying overhead."

He let that sink in for a moment. Then as he got up to head back, he added, "It may or may not happen here, but I would put a wager on it, when that battle starts, they won't even think about what color you are, especially when they see how you can fight."

Johnson said nothing directly to him, but more just thinking out loud he said, "I sure hope you're right, however I think I might just take you up on that bet."

Mitchell slowly went back down to find his tent and crash. Again, he had a little trouble getting to sleep. He also was hoping he was right about this thing with Johnson. After tossing around for a long time, he finally fell asleep.

When he woke up, there was already the noise of life around. He must have slept a little late. Everyone else was busy doing things. Redcloud had a little group going through some movement exercises. He figured that breakfast was over. The water was still hot enough so he could make something that passed as a cup of coffee. While he was drinking it, he tried to figure what day it was. He had set his watch, so the date should be right. If it was, today is the twenty-third and should be the day they get the first sight of the Mexican Army.

He walked over to the southwest corner and went up to the gun platform there. It was already later in the morning than when he usually got up, but already he could see an abnormal amount of people running around in town. Some were even heading out of town.

While he was there, Crockett and Travis came up beside him. Travis took out a long telescope and started looking at the town. Mitchell had his binoculars around his neck and as he started to use them, Travis stopped looking at the town and started watching him. As he explained how to use them, Crockett also came over to watch. He then handed the binoculars to Travis. The power of these binoculars was much stronger than that of the telescope he was using, and the view must be a thousand times better.

Travis took the binoculars down away from his eyes and started looking over them. He gently took them and handed them to Crockett, who just whistled as he looked through them. Then, the two men passed the glasses back and forth for a while, but seeing nothing, Travis finally handed them back to Mitchell. As He slipped them into the case, Travis said, "We should get someone up in the church's top as a lookout with these things."

"Sir," Mitchell said to him, "I would rather not be handing these things out to just anyone. Your lookout is a good idea, but he can do just as well with your glass."

Travis looked a little disappointed, but accepted it. "Sergeant-major," he shouted to a man who also got up along the wall to watch.

"Sir," the man shouted back with and half salute.

Travis returned a little better salute and continued, "Get a man up in the church in town and tell him to keep a watch, especially to the south and southeast. Give him my glass to watch with and tell him to ring the bell if he sees anything."

The man snapped a little better salute this time and replied with a simple, "Sir." He then ran over to Travis and took the telescope that Travis had been using and ran back down into the compound, while all the time yelling for someone.

Shortly, Mitchell could see a young man riding into town. He went straight to the church and soon he could see him in the bell tower. With his binoculars, he could see he was intently scanning the horizon, looking for signs. When Mitchell finally stopped looking and turned, he found Travis had already started walking back to the compound. Crockett stayed on the wall with him. As they just stood there watching the activity in the town, Mitchell said to him, "Today should be the day we see the Mexican Army."

Crockett just continued to lean on his rifle and calmly replied, "By the looks of all the activity in town, I could have told you that, even without knowing the future." After he finished his comment, they both had a little laugh and headed down into the compound. Mitchell guess the word had already spread about what was happening. He could see the mood of the men had changed from the day before.

In the days leading up to today, most of the men were on work details or just sitting around talking. Most of them didn't even carry their rifles around. Today, however, every man was carrying his rifle or had it slung across his back. No one was just sitting around talking, but there were little groups that would stop for a moment to chat while continuing to look all around.

Crockett and Mitchell headed over to Bowie's quarters and found him out of bed and just sitting on a chair. He had his foot up on a stool and had a bottle of something on the table next to him. When they walked in, he was in a good mood. Mitchell made an immediate guess that the doc, or someone else, must have given him some really good stuff in that bottle.

Crockett and he went over their plans with Bowie again and told him about the activity in the town. He agreed with their assessment that Santa Anna was probably nearby. He took another sip from the bottle and attempted to stand. Someone had made a crutch for him to use, but in his doped-up condition, he wasn't very good at using it. Crocket and Mitchell gave him a hand to stand. He then announced he wanted to go sit up on the wall to watch the town.

They got him outside and headed for the wall. While they were walking, Bowie yelled to one of his men to find a chair for him. By the time they could get him up the ramp to the gun platform, the chair was already there waiting for him. He sat down and put his broken foot up on the wall and just watched all the activity.

Crockett and Mitchell just left him there and headed back to the compound. Mitchell went to check on his people and Crockett headed off to take care of whatever it was he needed to be doing. As Mitchell got into their little camp, he called Jose over. When he came up running, Mitchell said, "I want you to get the drone ready. Don't bring it out yet, but just check the batteries are good and everything is working."

"You got it, Boss. You think they are going to show up today?" Rodrigues replied.

He simply nodded to him and said, "Today is the day, according to our time line schedule."

Jose looked around the area and without saying anything, he went over to the hummer and grabbed the case with the drone, and took it over to his tent.

Next, he called for Wilson, but she wasn't nearby. He stood up and started walking around. After a while, he found her in the church. She was leading a class for the ladies in self-defense. He just stood by the door and watched for a while.

Wilson was trying to teach them some basic moves. Nothing fancy, but she was having a hard time getting around the dresses the ladies were wearing. Every little move became a lot more complicated because the dresses would get in the way.

Finally, as the class was breaking up, and he called Anna over. "How long have you been doing this?" He asked her.

She gave him a look as if he had caught her in the middle of stealing a couple of cookies out of the jar. Sheepishly she looked down and said, "Some ladies started talking to me about this after the fight with Bowie. I agreed to teach them a little, but I had to promise to keep it a secret."

The ladies were all watching him as he talked to Wilson. He put his hand on her shoulder and said, "I think this is a great idea. I can understand the secrecy, giving the men-women relationships of this time."

Anna relaxed a little, and about this time, he heard footsteps behind him. He turned and found Kat was right behind him. "Are you taking this class with Anna?" He asked Kat.

She was a little embarrassed and started to say something, but Anna spoke up first. "It was Kat who came up with the idea of me teaching them."

Kat gave an angry look at Wilson, but before she could say anything, Mitchell said, "That's great. I think this was a wonderful idea, but why didn't you tell me?"

Now Kat spoke, saying, "I wanted to, but the other ladies didn't want any of the men to know, not even you. They made us promise not to tell anyone."

He thought for a quick moment. As he did, he noticed the other ladies had come a little closer. When he looked at them, he could see some concern on their faces. Mitchell just smiled and said, "Well, I think it is a great idea and I can certainly understand why you want to keep it a secret and I will certainly honor your wishes. Your secret is safe with me. However, I believe we have run out of time. I believe the Mexican Army will be here today."

This brought a couple of deep breaths from the ladies, and they all gathered closer to him, Anna, and Kat. "More than likely, the actual fighting won't start for a day or two, and even then, it will be mostly light as Santa Anna tries to get an idea of our strong and weak points. You can still get your classes in, but with the walls all being maned, it may be more difficult." He turned to Anna and asked, "Have you talked with the Chief about this?"

Anna just shook her head, so he said, "Maybe it is time you consulted with him to get the best ideas of what to train in the short time you have."

Anna said to the ladies, "He's probably right. If the fight is this close, we need to step up the training above what I can teach you."

Mitchell then said to the ladies, "I will speak to Redcloud. He is a good and honorable man. I know he will also keep your secret."

The ladies all looked around and nodded to each other, and soon they looked back at him. He then made a little laugh and said, "I notice you have had some difficulty with the dresses you are wearing. I seriously doubt there is much he can do about that, but I do have an idea that might help." He told Anna to get some para-chord from the hummer. When she returned, he used Kat as a model to teach them how to tie a Spanish Bowline knot. With a little modification to hold the center up around their waist, it pulled the hem of their dress up and almost made the dresses into pant like clothing. Each of them tried it and while it was not the best answer to the problem, it appeared to help a little with their movement.

While they practiced getting this setup with each other, Mitchell pulled Anna off to the side. He gave her the instructions for the day. "I want you to make sure everyone has two fully loaded mags from now on. Also, give each person, but not August or Kat, one hand grenade. From now on, we are going to have half our crew on watch at night. They can do half night watches."

Wilson was taking this all in, and he could see her already making plans in her mind. He continued, "Like I told the ladies, I don't believe there will be any real fighting for a while, but I want all our people ready. I'm not one hundred percent sure that I remembered all the facts correctly or that the battle will fall the same as it did in our timeline. You know the adage; a battle plan is only good until the first bullet is fired. I just want us to be ready. You sleep in the hummer next to the sixty and be ready."

"Got it, Boss." Anna said, but before she turned to walk away, she turned and asked, "What do you want to do about Kat?"

Mitchell really had intended for her to say near him, but that looks to be impossible. He figured he was going to be all over the place. He thought a moment and then, kind of thinking out loud, he said, "Put her with her father on top of the church. She can keep an eye on him, and he can protect her better than anyone else." After a moment, he added, "Also, it's not too far from our rally point, if things go bad."

"Rally point?" Wilson asked.

"Yeah, I figure our rally point is going to be the hummer. I figure, other than the cannons, they got nothing that will penetrate it and it would move too fast for them to hit. It will be the safest place around. If things go bad, then we all climb in and get the hell out of here."

Wilson nodded and said, "Makes sense to me." She then turned and headed off to the group of her ladies before she went to gather the others.

After checking the positions around the Alamo, Mitchell went back to their camp. Most of the people had already had lunch and were just sitting around. He found a MRE pouch and got ready to eat. He didn't even pay any attention to what he had grabbed. The water was still hot, so he was ready to mix it up and start eating. However, just as he got it mixed up in the pouch, he heard the bell from the town. He threw down his food and, like everyone else, he ran to the wall. As he ran up the ramp to the southeast gun platform, Bowie was pointing out to Crockett that things were happening in the town.

He and Travis got there at just about the same time. Just as Bowie was saying, "Just as soon as the bell started ringing, there was a large group of people that headed out of town, mostly to the east."

Mitchell scanned the horizon to the east and could still see many people and a large dust cloud in that direction. He then pulled out the binoculars and started scanning to the south. Now and then he thought he caught a little motion, but when he settled on that area, there was nothing moving.

Shortly after the bell stopped, a rider came in at a run from the town. He came in through the south gate at immediately reported to Bowie. Bowie just sat there and pointed to Travis. The man then turned to Travis and said he had seen what looked to be a cavalry unit to the southwest.

Just as he finished his report, everyone on the wall shouted and point to the town center. A small cavalry unit came into the center. They were quite the sight. Uniforms were bright colors with a lot of shiny metal. The men lined up in formal ranks and just sat there. A larger unit shortly followed them. They, too, got into formation. The officers in charge came around to the front and everyone could see they were talking.

After a short time, one officer and a soldier carrying a white flag began a slow ride to the Alamo. When the two of them got to the wall, they halted. The officer saluted and pulled a paper out of his belt. He read it in extremely good English. As Mitchell expected, it was a demand for surrender. The officer had not finished when Travis tuned to the nearest cannon and ordered them to fire. That resounding boom of the cannon cut the reading short. The officer simply folded up the paper, saluted, and began a slow ride back to town. He was obviously showing his contempt for the Alamo defenders.

Everyone just watched as the officer rode back. No one said anything. Finally, Travis spoke up, "I think that is probably going to be all for today. This cavalry unit is not big enough to take us on and it will be awhile before the actual fighting forces get here." He again looked through his glass for a moment, then turned to his three officers and said, "From now on, keep half the men on the wall while the other half eats and gets some rest. I want to be notified as soon as the primary force gets here. Captain Dickenson," he said, looking directly at the captain, "Make a list of the units as they arrive and their strength."

"Yes Sir." Came the standard reply from Dickenson.

Travis then turned and walked back to his quarters. The men could see he was not excited about what happened, and this action allowed them to relax a little. Slowly, some men came down from the wall and went to relieve themselves, maybe. Mitchell knew it was high on his list of things to do.

He then headed back to his area and slowly all his group formed up around the fire. He grabbed another MRE and, while the water was still hot, he fixed himself something to eat. Mitchell also announced, "I suggest you also eat, if you haven't yet. Travis has ordered to keep half of us on the wall at all times. The time off the wall is for eating and sleeping, if you can." After he finished talking, everyone just stood there for a moment before they moved.

Kat came over to him and sat down. He offered her a bite of his food, but she turned away. He put his arm around her back and pulled her closer to him. Whispering, he said, "Don't worry. I believe Travis is right. There won't be any fighting today. Santa Anna needs to get his main force here before anything will start. Maybe tomorrow, but that will depend on when the big boss man gets here to see what the situation is."

Kat relaxed a little, but still didn't smile. She just looked at the ground and slowly said, "Where do you want me to be?"

He just now realized Wilson hadn't given out the assignments yet. "I think you and your father will be assigned to the chapel gun platform." He could see the concern in her eyes, but before she could say anything, he continued and added, "I know you would like to be with me, but I am going to be running from place to place as the fighting needs. Also, your father is not a young man. You are the only one that he will listen to. I need you to watch him. Plus, he is the only one that I trust to do whatever is needed to protect you."

She looked down at the ground for a little while, then slowly said, "I'm scared." He pulled her close to him and held her tight. She continued to say, "I not scared of the fighting. My father and I have been doing that since my mother died and we moved north." She then looked up into his eyes and as a tear formed in her eyes, she continued, "I'm so scared of losing you." She then put her head on his shoulder and started to cry softly.

He just held on to her until the crying softened some. Then he softly said, "I will not do anything that might spoil our life together further down the road."

She pulled away and looked him in the eye and with an almost angry voice said, 'You can't control what is going to happen. There could be a stray bullet that hits you or a cannon ball comes closed enough to you. These are things you can't control." She then turned away a little.

He moved closer to her and again put his arm around her. He didn't know how to answer her. For a little while, he didn't say anything but had to say something to help her understand. Softly he said, "Yes, these things you say are true. All this and more. But, you forget, I know something about what is going to happen. I know that in the first days, while some minor injuries happened, no one is killed. We have a very good chance that some may get wounded, but we could come through this thing with no one dying. "

"Your plan is that good?" she asked.

Now that he had her attention, he had to make sure that she would feel comfortable after this talk. "Yes, I think our plan is very good." He told her as he sat back and tried to show her how relaxed he was. "Crockett has a keen sense for things like this and together we have come up with an excellent plan."

She thought for a moment, then said, looking at the ground, "Crockett is a very famous fighter, as is Jim Bowie." She sat there thinking a little while longer than asked, "Where are you going to be?"

He explained to her, "I will be on the wall in the south-west corner. This is where I believe the action will be in the first couple of days. The other place where there will be a lot of action will be the north wall. Redcloud and a couple others of our team with be there, but that won't be until the last days. By then Santa Anna will have his full force here and we will have led him to believe this will be an easy win. We will not show our full abilities until the last, so we can draw him into a trap and destroy his army."

"It sounds good, I guess." She said as she thought about it, but then added, "The problem is you're going to be in the worst parts of the battle. That is what I am afraid of." And then she cried again.

He reached out to hold her, but she pulled away and got up. "Please don't leave." He said to her.

"I must." She said as she ran away.

Mitchell just sat there. He didn't know what to do or say. He just continued to sit there, looking at the food he no longer had any desire to eat.

"Women are like that." Came a familiar voice from behind him. It was August. He sat down and just watch as his daughter ran away. "I don't know what was said, but I can guess. She is now more worried about you than me." He said with a little laugh.

"Something like that." Mitchell replied without looking up at him.

"And now you are worried about her. You must keep your head in the fight that is to come tomorrow, or whenever. She will come to understand what is at stake here and do her part. You must concentrate on doing your part." August said with authority that he had never heard in him before.

"You sound like you have been through this before." Mitchell said, more than a question than a statement.

August sat back and was chewing on a twig as he spoke. "Ah yes, I was in the army for a short time before we came to America. Once we got here, it's been one fight after another. If not with the Indians, then a fight with mother nature or some other foe who is out to destroy us. Yes, I have been through this before. I will talk to her after she calms down. I had this same talk with her mother several times."

He would never have guessed this of August. He did, however, feel much better now that her father was going to talk to Kat. This was new. He'd never had this kind of problem going into battle before. It was always just him and his soldiers.

August stood up and patted him on the shoulder as he left to follow Kat. Then he remembered he didn't give him his assignment yet. "August, wait. I want you and Kat to stand to on the chapel gun platform. From there you can cover the entire east and south sided. If there is a problem and we need to get out quickly, you two get to the hummer as fast as you can. They can't shoot us in there and we'll get out fast."

August turned slightly and gave him an off-the-cuff salute and said, "We'll be there, Boss." He then smiled and continued on.

Mitchell now felt a little better and finished his meal. After, he made the rounds of the wall. He headed first to the north wall to check in with Redcloud. He found him, like most of the other men on the wall, just sitting with their backs up against the wall and trying to catch a few zzzs.

As he walked up, Redcloud looked up at him and he asked, "Well, anything to report?"

One of the local defenders looked over at them and laughed a little. Redcloud then said, "Only that this is a waste of time. We know Santa Anna will do nothing today and probably not much for a few days."

"Yeah, I know." He said, looking around and then added, "This is more just a show of force. This is something that was done in these days. The forces line up and look at each other, trying to intimidate the other side a little."

Redcloud just grunted a little and put his head back down and mumbled, "Stupid."

"I hear ya," Mitchell said as he turned and walked away to check on the others.

Next, he checked on Johnson. He, too, was sitting with his back against the wall. The only difference was he sat by himself. The closest person to Stretch was a good twenty feet away. Too much open space on the wall.

"How's it going?" he asked as he walked up.

Johnson laughed a little and said, "Me, Myself, and I are all doing just great, here by ourselves."

"Yeah, I see that. I'm going to have a word with Travis about this and it either stops or you're out of here and they can defend it by themselves."

Again, Johnson laughed a little more this time and said, "Yeah, let me know how that goes over. I'd love to see it." But then with a serious tone he added, "The problem with that is, I don't know that I trust these white boys not to kill me and say it was the enemy that did it."

"I have a plan for that." He told him, "But it won't happen for a few days. I plan to have Travis assign Juan Seguín and his men to this part of the wall. The Mexican people are not treated any better than the blacks at this time, so you shouldn't have any problem with them. Mexico does not allow slavery, now. Then when this battle is over and you'll have shown what you can do, then things might change, a little at least."

"Ok Boss, whatever you say, but just to let you know, if any of these boys start something, I'm not going down without a fight." He said to Mitchell with a serious a look as he'd ever seen on a man.

"I wouldn't expect any less." Mitchell said to him as he reached up and grabbed him by the shoulder and pulled him in to put his arm around his neck. "I know I've said this before to other people, but this time I'm dead serious. Watch your back."

Johnson just nodded and as Mitchell walked away, then said over his shoulder, "I'll have the Chief check in on you now and then until the reinforcements arrive."

Johnson just waved at him and turned back to the wall.

Now Mitchell headed over to the northeast corner to check on Blake. He was the one Mitchell was most worried about for the actual fight. He is so new, and they never had much of a chance to train him. As he walked up the ramp to his position, he saw a young kid who couldn't wait to get into the fight. He was on the wall in a shooting position and intently watching everything outside the wall.

As Mitchell got to his position, Blake came to attention and almost saluted him. "Sorry, Boss, I can't help it. Everything is happening so fast."

Mitchell held up his hand to stop him. "Relax kid," he said in a calm voice, to calm him down, "Things will not happen for a day or two. Santa Anna has to get here, his forces have to get here, and only then can he think about doing something. We have a couple days before well see any real action."

Johnny seamed to calm down a little, but was still intent on watching the town. From this point on the wall, he could see all the action in San Antonio. Now, Mitchell was second thinking about putting him here.

One man, he thought belonged to Bowie, said, "Don't worry, Captain. Your boy here going to defeat the entire Mexican Army by himself."

The men standing around all laughed a little, but they, too, were a little concerned. Even Johnny smiled at that, but Mitchell could see it was a scared smile, not a laugh. He walked over to look down the outside of the wall and to get a little away from the other men. Johnny followed him and when he stopped, Blake came to attention again, but then quickly relaxed. "Don't worry about those other men," he told him in a low voice. "They are also scared. All men will try to cover how scared they are. Some with jokes and some with bravado, but when the time comes, they will fight." He stopped to let Blake think about that and when he looked back and smiled, Mitchell added, "And so will you."

He now just looked around and focused on the town. Not too much happening there. People were still trying to leave. He turned back to Johnny and said, "Just try to relax and get some rest. You're going to need it in a couple of days."

Mitchell patted him on the shoulder and started back down the ramp. About halfway down, he turned to look back. The wall in this area was short and now Blake was sitting on the ground like the other men, however he did position himself where he could still see the town and all its goings on.

He just smiled a little and continued on his rounds. Next was Rodrigues. He had some time in a combat area in the middle east, so Mitchell was not so concerned about him. He was sitting and relaxing when he walked up.

Before I could say anything, he looked up and asked, "What's up, Boss?"

Mitchell just smiled at him and said, "That's my line."

Jose smiled and looked over his shoulder at the town. Then he looked back and simply said "Not-a."

Mitchell squatted down in front of him, and he leaned a little closer. In a low voice he said, "I don't think we will need the drone today or tonight, however tomorrow night I want to send it up to see what we can see."

"Got it, Boss," he said back and added, "I checked it out this morning and the thing is fully charged and everything appears to be working fine."

"Good deal," He said and looked into the town and added, "Just stay loose for now. I believe nothing is going to happen before tomorrow night. Just keep your eyes and ears open in case this timeline doesn't cooperate with us."

"Got it, Boss," was the only reply, and he appeared to just want to go back to sleep.

Mitchell left him and headed for the hummer. He found Wilson resting in the driver's seat, but he could see a belt in the gun and a few more hanging up around the inside of the hummer. As he walked up, she smiled at him. He knew he could count on her to be calm in this situation. The windows were down, of course, so as he walked up, she asked, "When do you think they'll start?

"I don't think there be anything before tomorrow night. I know from our timeline they tried to move into those building close to the wall, but I don't remember when. I don't believe it will happen before tomorrow night." He just shook his head and added, "It doesn't matter. These buildings are all wired to go up whenever we're ready."

Anna just nodded and moved her head to show him to look up at the chapel. When he did, he saw Kat standing there, looking down at him. He turned back to Anna and said, "Thanks. Stay loose for now."

Anna simply replied, "I always am."

He waved as he walked over to the chapel, and Kat waved back. That was a good sign. When he reached the gun platform on top, she came over to him and gave be a big kiss and an even bigger hug. "I'm sorry about the way I acted before." She whispered in his ear as they hugged.

He held on to her for a short time, then stepped back and, looking into her eyes, he said, "I totally understand what was bothering you. I take it your father has talked to you."

She nodded and said, "Yes, we talked. I understand what going to happen, but I am still scared for you."

He reached up and grabbed her by the shoulders and looked into her eyes. "Just as I am worried about you. However, when the fighting starts, we must focus on our duties. That is the way it must be, or things can go bad quickly." He said to her.

"I understand, and I will try my best, but I don't think it will be as easy as you say." She replied, looking down at the ground.

Mitchell dropped his head down to where she was looking and again looked into those beautiful eyes and simply said, "I never said it would be easy. All I said is, it must be this way."

She smiled a little, and he felt her shoulders relax a little. Now he pulled her close to him and wrapped his arms around her. They just stood there for a long time while he held her close.

After a while He let her go, as much as he hated to do it, and stepped back. Looking around, he saw her father on the other side of the platform. He was intently watching them. Mitchell dropped his arms and said, "I need to go talk to your father."

As he turned, she went with him. He quickly held up his hand and said, "Young lady, you are on watch here. You need to stand your post."

But then he smiled at her, and she smiled back. She turned away and went back to her side of the platform.

He watched her go and then turned to head over to August. As he walked up, he could see him smiling. He turned back to watching outside the wall as Mitchell approached. His rifle was leaning against the wall, and he looked to be very relaxed.

"How is it going August?" He said as he stepped next to him.

He calmly replied, "As I expected. Nothing is happening."

Mitchell didn't reply to him, so he continued, "I really expected to see some of the cavalry ride around the outside of the walls to check us out, but there was nothing. They must not be too worried about us."

Smiling, Mitchell said, "Yes, that is what I'm hoping for. I want them to think this will be easy. That will give us even more of an advantage. "

August thought a moment, then said, "Or they are just not worried about us at all."

He sighed and said, "This is possible, but I don't think so. Either way, they will get a lesson in humility when they finally decide to attack."

"We'll see." He simply said back to Mitchell.

They stood there in silence for a short time, but then he finally got the nerve to talk to him about the other matter that had been on his mind all day. "August," He started out, and he turned to him, "I need to talk to you about Katherine."

He turned and sat on the wall. Looking up at Mitchell took on a serious face and said, "I figured you might."

Mitchell looked down at the dirt and shuffled his feet a little, but then he looked up at him and said, "I would like to marry your daughter Katherine. I have asked her, and she has said yes."

August brought his hands up and put them on his legs and threw his elbows forward. He looked down at the ground and in an almost angry voice he replied, "I don't know what it is like where you come from, but now it is customary to come and talk to the father, before you ask his daughter to marry you."

Mitchell didn't know what to say. This is not the response he had expected. He looked around, trying to think of what to say. He stammered out, "I….I'm sorry. I don't know the way to do these things now. I…ah, this is all new to me." He continued on, but August laughed out loud.

Mitchell just stood there in complete shock. August had seen the look on his face and quickly stood up. "Katherine and I already talked about this." He said as he grabbed him by my shoulders. He then added, "I couldn't be happier. I would be proud to have you as my son-in-law."

Mitchell was a little slow on the uptake and again he stammered, "You…You already talked?"

"Yes, my son. When I talked to her about the fight, she told me about it and I could see how happy she was. I haven't seen her this happy since before her mother passed."

"Then why the big show?" He said, still in shock.

He sat back down but continued to laugh. "I couldn't resist putting you through that. It is my right as her father to make you work for it." Then, after a pause, he added in a more serious tone, "Also, I thought I knew you, but I wanted to see what kind of man my daughter would be marrying. You turned out to be a man of honor and a man who will protect her."

Mitchell sheepishly put his head down and shuffled his feet some more. When he looked up, August was signaling for Kat to come over to him. When she got to him, he gently grabbed her hand and placed it in Mitchell's and said, "I approve of this marriage, and I give you both my blessings."

Kat didn't wait. She threw her arms around her new fiancé's neck and planned a huge kiss on his lips. When after a while she didn't let go, August cleared his throat, picked up his rifle and began walking his post as if nothing had happened.

Mitchell broke away from the kiss and politely said, "Thank you, Dad."

August turned slightly and had a giant smile on his face.

Now he turned back to Kat and gave her a kiss of his own. After a little while, they turned and headed back to the other side of the platform, where she was supposed to be standing watch.

He gave her another kiss and explained he needed to continue his rounds. He slowly walked away. It was a strange feeling in his gut. He was so relieved and so happy, but yet still anxious, all at the same time. He continued to think as he walked down the ramp. Thinking about this feeling. He wasn't sure how to deal with it.

As he came up to the hummer, Wilson was up in the turret, watching outside. As he passed, she simply said, "Congratulations, Boss."

Stunned, he stopped and said, "What?"

She turned and leaned on the back of the turret and said again, "Congratulations on your engagement."

Again, he was taken back, "How did you know? I just asked her father."

Anna smiled and stood back up as she said, "The Chief told all of us this morning, before you got up. But he said not to say anything until it was completed. From what I could see about what was going on up there and I figured it was now official."

Mitchell just stood there. He didn't know what to say to her. His mind was totally numb by now. So many unexpected things happening so quickly. Finally, he looked up at her and said, "Thank you. Redcloud and I are going to have to have some words."

Anna laughed and turned back to her watch as he walked away.

Redcloud, he thought to himself almost angrily, but then considered it a moment and almost smiled, but stopped as he looked around. Something was happening. He took off running to the southeast platform where Bowie had made his camp. When he got there, Bowie looked at him and pointed to the town. As he was getting his binoculars out, both Travis and Crockett came running up.

He scanned the town and in the center courtyard, he could see a man on his horse out in front of the others. There was much activity behind him, but he just sat there looking the fort over with his own glass. As he watched, he heard Bowie tell Travis, "Santa Anna, El Presidente."

Mitchell continued to watch him. He talked with the officers behind him and pointed to different areas. He assumed he was giving orders to start the siege. Mitchell turned to Travis and said, "OK, it appears the big boss man is here now. Soon we can expect the artillery to fire at us. I would suggest that if people are not on watch, they keep under cover. They have a lot of shot for their cannons and we have a limited supply. Best we just save it."

Travis thought about it for a moment as he looked over the town to take it all in. Slowly he said, "I'm afraid that if we do nothing, the men will lose morale and it will hurt us later when we need them."

"That," He said back, looking him straight in the eyes, "I'm afraid this is a decision you're gonna have to make. I can only make suggestions."

Travis tuned to the wall and walked a little closer to the edge. After what seemed to be a long while, he finally turned around and asked Bowie his recommendation.

Bowie first tried to sand, but then dropped back into his chair. He was not looking good, but his mind appeared to be still sharp. He also looked at the town before speaking. Then, looking up at Travis, he said, "I must agree with you. These men are here to fight. I say let them fight but tell them to conserve as much as they can."

Travis nodded and looked at Crockett. "Colonel Crockett, what do you think?"

Crockett was the only one who didn't look at the town first. He spoke right up, "Oh, I agree with you, but for different reasons."

After a pause Travis said, "Please continue."

Crockett now leaned on his rifle and slowly spoke, "Santa Anna, no matter what we think, is no fool. If we just sit here and do nothing, he will suspect something is up and may change his plans. That would throw everything we set up for into the fire."

This time, Mitchell nodded. This not so simple-minded man, as he appears to be. He had a different way of seeing things and putting it into simple forms that so anyone could understand."

Travis turned back to the wall and continued to take in everything that was happening. Finally, he turned and said, "Tell your men to keep a close watch. Don't take any shots unless they can ensure a hit. If there is a scout close enough, then kill him, but don't waste ammunition on useless shooting. We'll have enough of that in the days to come." He turned back to the wall and continued, "I want an hourly report on the progress they are making, especially with their artillery. As more troops show up, they will probably deploy them to surround us. Keep watches on all walls. I want an NCO or an officer to supply these hourly reports from each wall."

Mitchell heard some "Yes Sirs." From the other officers that had gathered and some men, who he was guessing were the NCOs. It was hard to tell with most of the men because they were not in any kind of uniform.

Travis's orders appeared to be reasonable and probably the best compromise between Mitchell's recommendations and those of the others.

Finally, Mitchell turned away from the wall and found Redcloud standing just behind him. He should have known. They turned and walked down into their camp area and sat by the fire. It must be near dinner time as someone had put some water on the get hot. Only Blake was still on the wall. The rest had moved to see what was happening and then followed him to the camp. They all took a seat near him, waiting for him to say something.

He looked around into each face. He'd seen these faces before. Every time he was about to go into battle or on some kind of combat patrol. The men were not so much scared of the fight, but unsure about what to expect.

After sitting there looking at them, he figured he must say something. "I've seen the looks on your faces before. Some of you have been in combat and know what to expect. You newer guys don't yet know. I can tell you. You're gonna see the same as we have done countless times in training. You, except Blake, have been around long enough that I know you are ready. Your training, while not preparing you for this exact situation," that got a little laugh out of them, "has prepared you to fight. A fight is a fight. This is going to be a little different, though. We have them out gunned by ourselves. Our problem is ammo. These other men can just grab some lead and melt it down and make more balls. We can't do that. This is going to be our limitation. We must conserve ammo. Therefore, I have put limits on what we can do during these first days of the battle. Plus, the fact, I want to lead Santa Anna to think this will be the push over it was in our timeline. If we go full auto on him, he'll run and make the job of taking him down all that harder and wear down our resources in the process."

He paused and got a drink from his canteen while he looked at them. They had their faces glued to him, even the more experience ones like Wilson. Continuing, he said, "We must lure Santa Anna in where we can then use our firepower to destroy his army."

Now there were nods of agreement. Little smiles were replacing those blank stares. But, he hadn't finished, "Now comes the bad side. This is a battle above all other things. People in battle get hurt and some will die. I don't think any of you have really faced that yet, except The Chief and I, maybe Anna." He took a quick look at her, and she nodded. "There is a strong possibility that the man right next to you is going to get shot. Remember, your first concern is to defend this place and try to protect the others that are not wounded. If this happens, all of you have had some combat medical training. Do what you can when you can, quickly, but don't let up on our defenses."

Mitchell let them think about this little while and then asked, "Any questions?"

Everyone looked at each other a little, but it was Jose who broke the silence. "Yea Boss, I got a concern."

Mitchell jokingly said, "I'm pretty sure I asked for questions, not concerns." Jose stopped, not knowing what to say. He then smiled at him and said, "Go ahead Jose, I'm just kidding."

Jose smiled and looked at the others. "Boss," he started, but then acted like he wasn't sure how to bring it up or if he even wanted to. After stammering around a little, he finally spit it out, "What happens if it is one of us that gets shot? I've read books and seen movies about what they call medical procedures here."

He had a good point. Mitchell hadn't really given much thought, but his concern was valid. "I don't know what to tell you. If it's a simple wound, then we might take care of it with the supplies we have. If it's a bad one, then we're all going to let the Doc make the call. He's all we got. Unfortunately, I didn't get a medic in this detail." He didn't want to dwell on this point. He had just got them going, and this was going to take away all that he was trying to say.

Jose looked at him and in as serious a voice as he'd ever heard from him, he said, "Just promise me you won't let him cut anything off."

Mitchell could say little, but he had to tell him straight, "I can't make you any promises about things that are out of my control." Mitchell knew his was not the answer he wanted to hear, however he accepted what the Boss said.

After a little, no one else had anything else to say. He turned to Wilson, "Anna, get them fed and start our half and half watch schedule tonight after dinner. I'll take a watch at midnight."

"You got it Boss," Anna replied to him and then to the others she said, "You guys heard him. You know the schedule, so those of you on watch grab some chow and get back at it and the rest try to get some sleep. Sleep may be scarce for the next week or so. Get all you can now."

Mitchell got up and walked to where August and Kat were standing. As he walked up, August said, "Your young lady Sergeant has me on the late shift and Kathrine on the early shift. I'm going to switch with her so you two can have some time together."

He nodded and said, "Thanks August. Just make sure you let her know. You don't want to get on her bad side by not keeping her informed."

He thought a moment, and laughed, "I understand. I saw what happened when the colonel got on her bad side."

He jumped up and, as best he could, he ran over to talk to Anna.

He looked at Kat and they both laughed out loud together. It took a little while to stop laughing and he had to wipe a tear out of his eyes. Kat was a little more reserved about her laugh. He thought it was not polite for ladies to laugh out loud like that at this time. She covered her mouth and turned her head, but he could still see she was laughing almost as hard as he was.

While they were recovering from their laugh, Redcloud came over and just stood there while Mitchell tried to regain his composure. Finally, he tired of waiting and spoke up, "We might have a problem."

This got his attention, and he snapped right out of it. "What's up?" Mitchell asked and as he did, he just caught Kat looking up out of the corner of his eye.

He was not sure if Redcloud saw it. It was so difficult to read him, even after all these years together. He leaned a little closer and almost whispered, "I heard a little chatter on the wind that some men were talking about 'Giving that 'Boy' a lesson tonight'."

Mitchell thought about it, and he knew something had to be done about it. He looked around a saw Stretch looking for an MRE. "Stretch, come over here a minute." He yelled over to him, just loud enough for him to hear.

He dropped what he was doing and grabbed his weapon, and trotted over. "What's up, Boss?"

"The Chief just informed me of a situation concerning you." He said kind of low. "It would appear that some men around here might be planning a little blanket party for you tonight. Most probably while you're on watch."

He just stepped back and nodded. "You know, I kind of got a bad feeling something was up. I noticed that even the people who didn't really care one way or the other were steering clear of me. Also, I heard some comments that just didn't seem right. Now it's all fitting together."

"Well, what do you want to do about it?" Mitchell asked.

He smiled and said, "You know, boss, I'm not really fond of the idea of getting the shit beat out of me or getting all cut up. What can I do?"

He thought about it for a minute. "This might be just your time. I don't know you well enough to know if you're up to it, but would you like to take them on?"

Stretch laughed a little and said, "I don't think I'm up to taking them all on. I did some boxing in high school and college. I could handle myself in a fight. Plus, I've been learning from the Chief since I joined this unit. However, I'm not good enough to take on a whole gang of them."

"Don't worry about that." Mitchell said as he stood up. Putting his hand on Johnson's shoulder, he continued, "That is my job. The Chief and I will be close by and insure this is going to be a fair fight."

Johnson looked at the Chief, who nodded, but when he looked back at Mitchell, and he could see a worried look in his eyes. After thinking a little, he said, "I don't really like this idea. It's not that I'm scared of fighting one or even two of them. What if there is a whole gang that comes for me?"

"Like I said," Mitchell smiled back at him, "the Chief and I will make sure this is fair. You might end up fighting more than one, but never will we let it be more than one at a time."

Stretch straighten up a little and looked around at the group. He was slowly nodding. When he got to Redcloud, he got a thumbs-up and replied with the same.

As Johnson turned back to Mitchell, he added, "If you want to earn their respect, it is probably going to hurt a little and it certainly won't be easy, but his is your chance to prove to them who you are."

He thought about that a moment and said, "I know you're probably right, but it doesn't make me feel any better about it."

Mitchell simply patted him on the shoulder and turned away. Johnson sat back down, and he could see he was contemplating what was to come. Redcloud moved his seat over next to Johnson and began giving him a pep talk and trying to explain some moves that might work well for him here. The boxing would help him in what was to come, but Mitchell truly thought it will take more than that. He is going to have much to prove himself to get the approval of, at least, some of these men.

The rest of the day and evening went by with little excitement. About midnight, Mitchell moved to his spot in the southwest corner to monitor the town. Redcloud and Johnson moved to their positions on the north wall.

After a short time, he got a double tap on the radio. This was from Redcloud that something was going down. He slowly and quietly removed himself from his position and made his way to the north wall, where Johnson was stationed. Within a few minutes, Redcloud found him and together they moved to where they had a view of Johnson, and they wouldn't be seen.

It took about a half hour for Redcloud to nudge him and pointed to the left of Johnson. He dropped his night vision down and could easily see a group of about five men slowly making their way towards Johnson.

Redcloud and he waited until they were in position and ready to move. They slowly stood up and moved towards the group. The advantage was theirs's as they had the night vision, and that group of men were mostly blind to them. They could get close to them, but because there was about half a moon, there was enough light to keep them from getting too close.

Just as they neared them, they made their move. Two of them slipped up behind Johnson and pulled him down and put a gag in his mouth. While those two held him, the rest came up and formed a half circle around Johnson.

The first man walked up to Johnson and said, "Nigger, we're gonna teach you your place." This man was, Mitchell assumed, the leader. As he pulled his arm back for a punch, Mitchell coughed.

Every one of them jumped and looked back at the sound. The two men released Johnson when they saw Mitchell with his rifle up to his shoulder and aimed at them. Redcloud had moved off to the right and at that moment, he also coughed. In unison, they all swung to their left to see him in the same position.

Johnson grabbed his rifle from the man that had picked it up and gave him a little tap in the face with the butt. "Enough!" Mitchell sternly said to Johnson. Johnson then moved over next to him. He nodded to Johnson and lowered his rifle, however Redcloud kept his up and aimed at them.

So far, it was only Mitchell that had said anything. Now he wanted to hear what they were up to. "You fellas having a little party, are you?" He took a couple of steps closer and continued, "It appears you didn't invite the rest of the camp."

They all looked at each other, not knowing what to say. The leader then took a step forward and boldly said, "They were invited, but no one else wanted to have some fun."

"Fun, ah." He said sarcastically.

"Yeah, fun. We wasn't gonna hurt the nigger." He said, looking around at the other men. They all nodded in agreement.

Mitchell took another step closer, pivoted on his foot to swing around to add extra force, and drove the butt of his rifle into the leader's belly. Looking at the rest he said, "The next man that calls him a nigger, or any other name other that the one given him, is gonna die."

He had paid little attention to the man he butted, but when he tuned back, that big man was picking himself up off his knees. Mitchell could see even in this light he had lost whatever it was he had recently eaten.

Now he turned back to him and moved closer. He took a half step backwards but almost tripped and came close to falling on his ass. Mitchell waited until he recovered and took another step towards him.

This time he didn't move, but Mitchell could see he wasn't as steady as he was before.

Slowly he walked around behind the big man, who turned slightly to follow him but didn't turn completely around. Once behind him he stared to talk, "It would appear to me you five men were going to inflict some injury on one of my men." Mitchell had emphasized 'my'. Continuing, he added, "Did you think you had enough men to beat up one man?" After pausing, he added, "Not what I would call an honest and fair fight."

Mitchell continued to walk through and around the rest of the men. They were all nervous as he came near each of them. As he went back to his position in front of the leader, he asked, "Does it really take all five of you for one man?"

The leader shuffled a little, but said nothing as he looked down at the ground.

Mitchell turned and looked at the rest of them. They too had suddenly turned to mute. "Johnson, what do you think about all this?"

Johnson cradled his rifle in his arms and said, "It sure sounds like the thinking of a bunch of lowlife backstabbers."

This brought most all the heads back up and one man that had been holding Johnson took a step forward and started by saying, "Now wait a minute, you can't…"

As fast as He could Mitchell shouldered his rifle and aimed it right at him saying, "The hell I can't. And from what I saw, it was a fair and accurate description of what was going on."

The man threw up his hands and froze. Mitchell then swung the rifle around to the rest of them. They all put their hands up, even the leader. He motioned them to move closer together. As they did, Redcloud moved around behind them. This, Mitchell could see, was very unnerving to them.

Now he lowered his rifle to his side and stood there acting like he was thinking. Shortly, he looked up at them and said, "I got an idea." Smiling at them. He stepped back and stood next to Johnson and said, "How about I let you fight them, one at a time?"

Johnson looked at them and thought about it for a moment, then slowly said, "I don't know, boss. There are five of them and only one of me. I could probably beat two, maybe three, but those last two might be a little tough."

"Hmmm…," Mitchell though and then said, "how about you just take on two of them? Two of their own choosing."

Johnson thought about it for a moment, then said, rather confidently, "Yeah, boss. I think that would be just fine."

He turned back to the group of men and asked, "Would that be acceptable to you?"

Of course, the leader stepped forward and proudly said, "Oh yean, that would be just fine with me."

Again, Mitchell wanted to put him in his place and said, "What about the rest of you? Who is going to be the second one?"

The effect was what he wanted. The rest of the men looked at him with the look that they really didn't want to be any part of this. Turning, the leader moved towards them and shouted, "Bill, you join me in this and we'll wop the ni…, that boy and call it done."

It was easy to see who Bill was. He was the one who took a step back and raised his hands up.

The leader then looked at each of the rest of them. Finally, he shouted, "Alright you cowards, I'll take care of this myself."

"This is the way you want it?" Mitchell said, looking at the group. All except the leader raised their hands up and stepped back. The leader looked back at his men and made a grunt of disapproval. He then turned and stepped forward. Mitchell motioned for Redcloud to come up and cover him. He moved forward and removed the big knife from him and check for any others. He found a second smaller knife in his boot.

Now he showed for Johnson to remove the knife from his belt and ground the rest of his gear.

The leader made stepped forward and said, "That ain't right, you search me like a criminal and you're gonna take his word for it?"

Mitchell simply turned toward him and said in a loud and clear voice, "Certainly, I know him to be an honorable man, and likewise, I know you to be a lowlife backstabber."

Oh, that had the effect he had expected. The big man came at Mitchell, but Redcloud was right there and gave him a light butt to the back of the head. The leader went down, but not hard. Just enough to make him even madder.

Mitchell walked over to Johnson now. He got close to him a whispered, "OK, I think he is ready now. He is angry and will make stupid mistakes. Just be ready and watch for the right time to strike." He patted him on the shoulder as he walked by. Johnson stepped in to begin the fight. As he went by, Mitchell added, "You got him."

Johnson moved to within a couple of feet of the leader. They later found out his name was Will. The two stood there a moment, sizing each other up.

Johnson was tall and thin, and probably had a longer reach than Will did. After giving them a couple minute to size each other up, he yelled out, "Fight!"

Will took a giant step towards Stretch and tried a huge hay maker. Stretch easily ducked it, which threw Will off balance. Stretch side stepped and threw three quick jabs into Will's side. Mitchell could see that Will was still felling the effect of the rifle butt he got at the start of this. He was obviously still tender there. Stretch didn't miss that point. He danced around and threw little but solid jabs into Will's belly. Mitchell couldn't tell, but from watching, he thought Stretch might have been a little high and might have cracked a rib on Will. He was wincing in pain more than Mitchell would have expected from each of Stretch's punches.

The others had cheered for Will, but as it became obvious that Will was hurt, the cheering weakened. They could see things were not looking good.

Now Stretch stopped dancing around. So far, Will had not laid much of a punch. He deflected most, or they were too weak to do much harm. Stretch now looked him face to face and bobbed and weaved right in front of Will and landing a lot of solid punches, both in his gut and in his face. Will was slowly showing he was going down. His guard was dropping, and Stretch was getting more and more punches in where it counted. Finally, Will could no longer put up a defense and Stretch turned his back, took one step and turned around with a round house hay maker and Will went down hard.

Stretch was dancing a little around the body of Will. As Mitchell walked up, he grabbed his hand and held it up over his head, while he continued to dance around. He came around towards the other men. Looking at them, I asked, "Does this end it?"

They all knew what he meant and looked at each other and began to vigorously nod agreement.

He said, "then I suggest you congratulate the winner and get Will, here, down to wherever it is he sleeps and patch him up."

The other men made a kind of line and shook Stretch's hand as they went by and some said, great fight, while the others said congratulations. They then grabbed an arm or leg and took Will back down somewhere in the compound. Mitchell grabbed up Will's knife and handed it to Stretch. He told him, "You and keep it as the prize or give it back. Up to you"

Stretch took the knife and looked at it. He then stuck it in his belt and picked up his gear and headed back to his watch. He motioned Redcloud to take off and follow Stretch to his post. "You OK?" Mitchell asked as he walked by.

Sadly, he said, "Yeah, Boss, but it still doesn't feel right."

He turned and leaned up against the wall. "What do you mean?"

Slowly, he said as he finished putting his gear back on, "It was a hollow win. When I won, it felt like it was pointless because I didn't want to fight anyone. I don't know that I really won anything or just prolonged the problem."

"I see," he said to him. "I suppose only time will tell. The secret is not to rub it in or let it slide, but to just stand up for what happened and play it by ear. Let the word get around and see how it all falls."

As he left, Mitchell was worried that it might not be over. He found Redcloud on his way back to his post and told him to keep an eye on Johnson for the rest of the night. Redcloud assured Mitchell that he fully intended to do so anyway. Not just to look out for trouble, but to make sure it wasn't weighing too heavy on him.

Mitchell finally strolled across the compound and took up his post. He scanned the town with his binoculars, but because it was so dark, he saw little. He then put on his night vision and could see soldier working to build the placements for their big guns. Right now, he didn't think they could do much damage at that range. He was sure they will get moved closer after a little while and then they'll have to do something about them.

The rest of the night, he just sat back and watched the town and occasionally looked through the night vision or got up and walked around. It was a long night.

CHAPTER 11

Well, his first night of watch was over and Mitchell was looking forward to heading off to bed. This was not to be, at least not right away. He had no sooner got to his tent when Redcloud came to get him. He opened the flap and stuck his head in, saying, "Good morning, boss. The Colonel would like to see you right away."

He pulled his head back out while Mitchell gathered himself and waited for him. As he came out of the tent, Redcloud handed him a coffee, and they walked towards Travis' office. As they approached, he could see Johnson sitting outside, under guard. He walked up to one guard and demanded, "What is this?"

He said nothing back, but motioned with his rifle to go inside. Opening the door, he found Travis at his desk and Bowie sitting next to him in a chair. He didn't look very well. Crockett was also there, standing along the wall.

Mitchell walked up to Travis and said, "What's going on here? Why is my man under guard outside?"

Travis just stared at him a little and then slowly spoke, "It would appear from reports that you, your Indian and your nigger held one of my men at gunpoint and beat him so badly that the doctor says he will be useless for the battle to come."

Mitchell looked down at the floor to stifle a laugh. Looking back up at Travis, he could see anger on his face. "Well, Colonel Travis," He started with, "That is not exactly the correct story. My man was standing at his post. Redcloud had heard some talk about a sneak attack on my man. This turned out to be the situation. Sargent Redcloud," he said, putting great emphasis on the Chief's name. After a short pause to let it sink in, he continued, "When we got there, we found five men ready to attack my man. We let them sneak up on him to make sure there was no misunderstanding and when they grabbed him away from his post, My Sargent and I stepped forward to confront them. The leader of the group was just preparing to swing at my man with two others holding him."

He looked at the others in the room, but nobody gave any signs that they believed him. He, however, continued with his account of the situation. "After disarming those men, I gave them the option of fighting my man, one on one. The only one to accept the challenge was the leader of the group. The others were too afraid to confront him in a fair one-on-one fight. Sargent Redcloud and I were there to insure this was a fair fight, and it was."

After he finished, Travis stood to look at him, saying, "Well, that is your story and I have five men that are telling me a different story. Not knowing you, I am inclined to believe my, ah Colonel Bowie's men, that you held them at gunpoint when the Indian and the nigger went after a single man."

Luckily, Mitchell had expected something like this might happen. Looking at Travis, he said, "I can prove my story. Can your men prove what they are saying?"

Travis leaned over his desk. Not in anger as much as curiosity. He looked at him and then at Bowie. Turning back, he said, "How do you intend to prove it?"

Slowly Mitchell took a half step back and said, "It would be almost impossible for me to explain it so that you could understand. It would be best to show you. Could you please send one of your men to find my man, Rodrigues?"

Travis stood up and thought for a moment and then yelled. Almost immediately, a man, he didn't know, came in. Travis instructed him the find Rodrigues and to bring him here. Before the man left, Mitchell yelled, "Tell Rodrigues to bring the controller with him. He'll know what that means."

The man left, and Mitchell turned back to Travis. Slowly, he told him about the drone and how it could take pictures in the dark. Mitchell was pretty sure none of them understood what he was saying, even though he tried to keep it very basic and simple. He could see the only one that he might have a chance with was Crockett. He at least looked like he understood some. The other just had blank looks on their faces.

After he set up the idea of the drone and night vision, he explained, "Before I went on watch last night, I put Rodrigues on alert to be ready. When Sargent Redcloud signaled me that this was starting, I woke up Rodrigues and had him use the drone to record the entire fight."

After a brief wait, Rodrigues came in carrying a small case. Mitchell took it from him and set it on Travis' desk and opened it. Pulling out the small controller with the screen, he motioned for Travis and the others to gather around Bowie, since he could not move. He loaded up the video of the fight. As it started up, he explained they were looking from above and that the bodies would appear as all white because they were seeing only the body heat.

It was a small screen, and the men gathered close to look. First, it showed the group of 5 men hiding near a single figure. Mitchell pointed out that these were Bowie's men. The video zoomed out a little, and they could see Johnson standing next to the wall. The picture then opened up a little more, and they could then see Redcloud and Mitchell. Slowly, the men snuck up behind Johnson. They saw where two of them went forward and grabbed Johnson, and a third man grabbed his rifle. Slowly Redcloud and he worked their way up to them and you could see the leader ready to swing and then jump when Mitchell had made a noise. All the time the video was playing, he was giving them a running narration.

Travis and the others watched the entire fight and how everything actually went down. When it had finished, Mitchell put the controller back in the case and handed it to Rodrigues, who simply smiled at him.

Then, turning back to Travis, he waited for everything he had just seen set in. Suddenly, he sat down at his desk and looked up at Mitchell. Rather contritely, he said, "Captain, that will be all. On your way out, please tell the guards I said to release your man and ask Captain Baugh to come in here."

He snapped too and gave Travis a sharp salute, which he returned. As he turned away, he nodded to Bowie and Crockett. The three of them quickly left Travis' office and the guards release Johnson to them even though it was obvious they didn't like it.

Mitchell told the others to take off, and he hung around a little while. Shortly, Captain Baugh came out of the office and spoke to the two guards, and they took off towards the area that was set up as the doctor's office. Soon after going in, they came out with the man that was the leader in tow. The two guards were helping to carry him. They all went into Travis' office and soon the captain and the guards came back out and hurried over to the long barracks and came back with four other Mitchell recognized as the rest of the group. He slowly started heading back to his tent for a much-needed sleep. Before he got there, though, he heard some shouting and as he turned around; he saw the group of five men, all with their hands bound, being taken away. They went to the other side of the compound, where he was guessing they were being placed under arrest. He just nodded to himself that justice was quick and right and went off to get some sleep.

Hearing some noise, Mitchell too soon woke up. Looking outside, he saw the men running over to the west wall. He grabbed his gear and headed over there as well. He found Travis and Crockett on the south-west gun platform and came up to stand with them. Using his binoculars, He could see what the focus was. The Mexicans were placing their artillery. Turning to Travis, Mitchell said, "Now it will begin. He is going to try to weaken the wall and our morale. If I remember right, he will continue to use his artillery to pound us while only pausing while trying some attacks to feel out our defenses."

Travis just nodded and simply said, "I agree."

Turning to one of the gun platforms, he yelled, "Capitan Dickenson!"

Standing next to one of the bigger guns, a man turned and yelled back, "Sir!"

Travis yelled back, "Are you loaded?"

Dickenson replied, "We are loaded and ready, standing by."

Travis took another look through his glass and without looking away, he yelled out, "Fire when ready."

The men on the gun moved. First, they turned the gun and once in position; the Capitan got behind the gun and adjusted the elevation. Shortly they were ready as Capitan Dickenson called out the commands. They all took their positions and quickly the cannon fired. It surprised Mitchell at how quickly they could aim and fire the gun. The Capitan had a well-trained crew. Mitchell still had time to turn and watch the impact. The shot hit just a little short, but it was aimed well enough to take out one gun on a bounce and probably several of the men.

Immediately, there was a cheer from the men on the wall. Using his binoculars, he watched as what appeared to be Santa Anna, and a group of other officers ride up. There was a lot of saluting and what he guessed was shouting. The soldiers were now moving much faster and in short time had a couple of guns in position. They didn't have any protection built yet, but they were ready to fire. There was the normal ritual of loading and aiming, and soon those guns returned fire.

Some men ducked behind the wall, but most men just stood there and watched. One round hit the wall a little further down from them and the other went into the dirt and then bounced into the wall. Neither one did much damage. He looked over at Captain Dickenson. His gun crew was just finishing up the loading of the gun that had fired the first time. Soon he was standing ready. Dickenson looked over at Travis, who was just standing there.

While they watched, Santa Anna turned and rode off with his entourage. The soldiers returned to their work to complete the placement of the guns.

Travis turned to Mitchell and asked, "Is that it for today?"

He just shrugged his shoulders and told him flat out, "I don't have an hour-by-hour breakdown of what is going to happen. First, our records of the actual battle are mostly from the Mexican side. Second, I just don't have the knowledge in that much detail."

Travis walked away, but he called to him and added, "I know that there was not too much action right away. The next major thing I remember is that Santa Anna will try to occupy those little building to the southwest."

Travis turned to look at the row of buildings and then asked, "Are we ready for that?"

"Yes, sir, the explosives are in place. When we are ready, I'll connect the detonator, and those buildings will no longer exist. Should only take a few seconds once I get there."

Travis looked him up and down and nodded, but said nothing as he turned and walked away.

Mitchell watched as the Colonel walked away and just slightly shook his head. Over his shoulder, he heard a familiar voice of Crockett. "You'll get used to it. That's just the way he is."

He turned back to Crockett, and they both just smiled. Walking back to the wall to watch, Crocket asked, "Are you sure this will work?"

"It doesn't really matter." He said as he checked out the progress of the Mexicans. "I have a couple of backup plans, just in case there is a SNAFU."

"SNAFU?" Crockett asked.

Mitchell just started laughing out loud. Shortly he could answer him, "Sorry, it is a term we use in the Army where I come from. It stands for 'Situation Normal, All Fucked Up'"

Crockett smiled and then laughed a little. He looked around the entire compound and simply said, "True enough."

With that, he slapped Mitchell on the shoulder and they both headed down into the compound. He split off to his people while Crockett headed off to take care of some other business. As he got to his area, the team gather around. Once they were all there, he stated to talk, "OK guys, the battle has officially started. We…"

Blake interrupted me, "Officially!"

"Yeah Johnny," Mitchell answered him, "Officially. Both sides have fired at each other." Blake just looked down while most of the rest of the group caught the humor. Mitchell continued, "We need to keep watch on the walls, more now than before. Anna, make sure we have half the group on the wall at all times." She simply nodded to him. He normally had more to say about going into combat for the first time, but thinking back, they have already killed, so he forwent that speech, "Remember to watch your assigned area close and still watching each other's back. Also, no automatic fire. You must not fire in rapid fire either. Just take your time and make sure every shot counts. The idea here, people, is to let Santa Anna think this will be easy until he commits his main army. Then we'll unload on him."

He finished up with the standard, "Any questions?"

There was a lot of looking around at each other, but nobody asked anything.

After a moment He turned towards Anna, "Make sure they have their assignments." Then he turned back to the group. "I suggest that if you're not on guard, you catch some zzzs. The next few days will probably be a couple minutes of insane activity followed by long periods of waiting. If I remember right, though, the waiting time will be filled by artillery fire. Try to sleep if you can." They all just stood there looking at him for something more. He put his hands on his hips and slightly yelled, "Get to it, people!"

Everyone jumped. Most went to Anna to get their assignment. She had everything ready and in short order, those on duty were off. Before Redcloud went to his station, he came over to Mitchell and asked, "Boss, you want me to take out those other cannons now or wait?"

Mitchell sat down and made a cup of coffee. This distraction gave him a moment to think. After he finished, he turned back to him and slowly said, "No, not now. I think they will try to move closer because at the range they started at it'll be ineffective. Let them waste time and effort. Remember, as I recall, there were no deaths in the initial days of the battle. I think we will be safe for now. Besides, I know you're an excellent shot, but letting them get closer will help to insure we get good hits and not waste any of our precious ammo."

What he said sunk in quickly and after a moment, Redcloud just slapped off a quick salute and turn to walk away. As he left, Mitchell yelled to him, "Make sure you keep a watch on everything over there."

He knew Redcloud knew what he was talking about. He wasn't sure how the rest of the locals will take the incident with Johnson.

Redcloud swung around and as he walked backwards, he gave him a thumb up sign.

Smiling, Mitchell just sat there and enjoyed his coffee, as best he could for what was passing as coffee, anyway.

The rest of the day went by with nothing happening. A couple of times, he checked on the progress of the Mexican artillery. Slowly, they were getting things set up. He figured that probably by dark, they will start the barrage. When he checked the north wall, He could see they were also setting up the artillery there.

While he was standing there, Redcloud stepped up and stood behind him. He felt him more than he heard him. He was quiet, but before he turned, Mitchell said, "I just know you're there." As he turned to face him, he could see the smile on his face. Mitchell simply continued, "They're making good progress with their emplacements on this side now. Let them sit out there and fire away for now. Even if they hit something, at that range there'll be little actual damage."

Redcloud didn't say anything, but made a grunt that Mitchel was going to take as an agreement. As he started walking away, there began a ruckus on the west wall. Mitchell made his way over to that gate when a band of men came in. It was obvious they were Mexican, but it was also obvious they were friends with some men. As he approached, Travis also came up and shook hands with the man Mitchell assumed to be the leader of the group.

As he came closer, Travis saw him and said, "Captain Seguin, I'd like you to meet Captain Mitchell."

Mitchell took his hand and as he shook it, he still got that tingle from meeting such a famous figure for this time. "A pleasure and honor to meet you, sir." He said to him.

He nodded and in and heavily accented speech he replied, "For me, as well."

Travis gave a little bow and turned, saying, "Gentlemen." He then motioned that they should follow him. He led the way back to his office, and they all went inside, including Crockett.

When they were all inside, Seguin looked around and then turned to Travis and asked, "Is Colonel Bowie no longer with you?"

Travis took a quick glance in Mitchell's direction and then answered him, "Colonel Bowie is indeed still with us, but he was injured. I have sent men to bring him here. He should be with us soon."

"I hope it is not too serious." Seguin responded with genuine care.

Mitchell spoke up and told him, "No, no. There was a misunderstanding, and he ended up with a broken foot."

Seguin nodded and then noted Mitchell's rifle. Mitchell had it on his back when they met, so it was not until now that he could see it. He said nothing but took obvious note of it. Turning back to Travis, Seguin formally said, "Señor Colonel, my men and I are here at your disposal."

Travis stood up and shook his hand, saying, "This is splendid news. How many men do you bring with you?"

"I have thirty-seven men, but not all are here at this moment. The rest will soon be here." He replied to Travis.

Travis didn't appear to be overly thrilled by this number, but he hid it well and just continued, "Juan," he said as he sat back down at his desk, "We have had some interesting developments here." He said, nodding in Mitchell's direction. He then turned back to the rest of the group that had gathered in his office, saying, "Gentlemen, please clear the room, except for Colonel Crockett and Captain Mitchell."

Just as he finished saying that, the door opened and a couple of men helped Bowie in. Travis added, "Colonel Bowie, I am happy you are here. Please have a seat," pointing to the chair next to his desk.

The men helped Bowie into the seat and quickly left the room. The rest of the men who were there also left. Travis then returned his attention to Captain Seguin and motioned to another chair for him to sit in. "You had better sit down for this." He added.

Travis then went through an explanation about who and from where and when Mitchell came. Captain Seguin kept looking back and forth between Travis and Mitchell. When Travis had finished, Mitchell cleared his rifle and walked up and put it out for the captain to take it.

Captain Seguin slowly reached out and took the rifle out of his hands. He looked very surprised as he picked it up. He exclaimed, "So light!"

Mitchell smiled down at him and shrugged his shoulders as he nodded.

Seguin continued to look over the rifle and shortly Travis continued, "Captain Mitchell, please explain your plan for the good Captain?" using his hand to point to Captain Seguin.

He reached out to recover his rifle and Captain Seguin gave it another quick look over and handed it back to him. Quickly, he slapped a mag in and charged it. Closing the dust cover, he said, "This rifle is now ready to fire thirty rounds faster than you can take in a breath."

He got the reaction that he expected from a person who has never even dreamed of something that could fire over one round at a time. After a quick pause, Mitchell outlined the battle plan that Crockett and he had come up with. When he finished, he turned to Travis, saying, "Sir, I have a simple request."

Travis didn't hesitate and said, "Yes, what is it?"

Stepping up to his desk between Seguin and him, he said, "I would like to request that some of Captain Seguin's men get assigned to positions of two of my people, Rodrigues and Johnson." When there was no immediate response, he added, "I would like to head off any further problems like last night."

Travis looked at Bowie and Crockett, and then at Captain Seguin. Slowly, he stood and leaned on his desk and said, "Given the tension we have right now, this might be a good idea." Then to Seguin he said, "Please coordinate the placement of your men with Captain Mitchell. He will explain."

Captain Seguin simply responded, "As you wish." However, the look on his face made it clear he did not understand this request.

After leaving Travis' office, Crockett, Juan, and Mitchell went over to the wall to check on the status of the Mexican Army setup. Looking through the binoculars, Mitchell found a small group of officers that were looking at the building just outside the wall. He handed the glasses to Crockett and, after finding the group he was talking about, Crockett handed them to Captain Seguin. He took the binoculars and looked it over. Finally, Mitchell showed him how to use them.

When he first looked through them, he kept taking them down and looking with his own eyes and the back through the binoculars. Mitchell looked over at Crockett, who was watching Juan. He slightly laughed and asked, "Did I look like that when I first used that thing?"

Mitchell smiled back and, tilting his head slightly, he nodded and said, "Just about the same as everyone."

Crockett looked down, and while shaking his head, he let out another little laugh.

After a while, the captain handed the binoculars back to him and said, "I think that is the finest eye piece I have ever used. It is fantastic."

Mitchell just nodded at him and said, "Oh, you ain't seen nothing yet."

Turning back to the wall, he asked of both of them, "What do you think is up with those officers?"

Crockett spoke right up, saying, "I think those buildings will not be there in the morning."

"Yeah, I think you're right." He said back as he watched the officers through the binoculars. When they turned to leave. Mitchell turned back to Crockett and said, "Should we tell the good captain here about our surprise?"

Crockett couldn't wait. He laid out the plans for Captain Seguin, who was very intent on every little detail. When Crockett had finished, Mitchell said, "Gentlemen, if you will both meet me back here just after dark we will see about our surprise, and David, I believe I will let you have the honors."

Crockett stood up straight and smiled. He turned to him and said, "How will we know when all the men are in there?"

"I have just the thing for that. It will allow you to see into the night." He said and then looking back out across the field to the town, he added, "Just as if it was daytime."

Crockett rubbed his hands together, saying, "This I must see."

Seguin was just listening, but they had defiantly caught his attention, as well. As Mitchell turned to walk away, he simply said, "I'll see y'all this evening."

He went back to the group area, but there was no one around. After thinking a moment, he went into the chapel and found Wilson leading her class of ladies. He wasn't one hundred percent sure, but it appeared the class had grown since he first discovered it the other day. As he walked up to Anna, the ladies started walking away. She could see his smile and gave a little huff as he got near. "I just looking for Rodrigues. Have you seen him?" He asked even before he got there.

Anna thought for a moment and then simply replied, "He should be on duty now."

Mitchell tipped off a quick salute to her and turned and quickly left. As he started out the door, he looked back to see the ladies had again formed into a circle and had taken a defensive stand. They were looking very good for such a short time doing this. He nodded his approval to Anna as he walked out, but he didn't know if she even saw him.

He found Rodrigues in just about the same position he found him the first time he looked for him. When he came up to him, he stood up and stretched, like he had just woken up from a nap. "I hope I didn't wake you." Mitchell said rather sarcastically.

He smiled and shrugged his shoulders, saying, "Don't give it a second thought, boss. We've all been taking turns, and it's now my turn to watch for a while, anyway."

He sat on the wall and asked, "Have we fixed the battery issue for the night vision yet?"

"Yeah," he said, "I told the Chief a little while ago. Didn't he tell you?"

Mitchell didn't show his anger, but just went on like it was nothing. "OK, suppose you tell me now?"

He turned away from the town and looked at him and explained, "I checked it out and found the charger that came with the drone can charge many types of batteries, even the ones for the NOD's." he thought a second, quickly continued, "The issue now is the actual charging. We can charge directly off the battery in the hummer, but then we could drain the battery enough we can't start the hummer. If we run the hummer to charge the batteries, then we will run out of fuel quickly. It takes about an hour to fully charge the batteries for the goggles, but I don't know how much it is really draining the battery. Also, we can only charge two at a time."

Mitchell just sat there while he explained everything and then looked out at the town as he thought it all over. He then asked, "What is the status of all batteries right now?"

Jose smiled and said, "We haven't used them for much of anything since we got here. Once I figured it out, I got them all fully charged and made sure the spares were also fully charged." He thought for a moment, then added, "Also, both batteries for the drone are fully charged."

Mitchell nodded to this and said, "I want you to get me three goggles."

He just looked up at me and asked, "Right now?"

"Yes, right now." He said and added, "I'll take your watch while you get them."

He smiled and said as he turned, "You got it, boss. Be back shortly."

Jose was taking his time as he strolled away. Mitchell thought he was no fool and was going to milk his time away from the watch for all it was worth. He just turned back to watch the town. He could still see the units arriving at regular intervals. Looking over, he could see Captain Dickinson watching the Mexican units as they arrived and taking notes. Other than the normal placing of the units and watching them setting up their camps, there was little out of the ordinary that he could see.

After waiting a while, he could see why Jose and the men here were taking turns. Just sitting here watching the Mexicans arrive was putting him to sleep. The only note of any actual interest was the establishment of the artillery. These soldiers were very efficient at setting up a battery. He would say they looked almost finished, and that means they could soon see the bombardments start. With any luck, they will wait until morning to start. He didn't recall from history when the actual artillery barrage started, but his best guess would be as soon as they were all set.

After about an hour, Jose returned with three sets of goggles. Mitchell greeted him with a fake scolding. "Did you enjoy your time off? It sure took you long enough."

He just looked up at the captain and smiled, and then as he handed Mitchell the goggles he added, "Sure did, boss. When I got to the camp, the water was still warm, so I grabbed some chow first."

He just took the goggles and as he walked away, he said, over his shoulder, "I'm so glad you are so well fed on my time."

While he walked down the ramp, he heard Jose laugh, and that caused him to smile. He was feeling good about the morale here. While everyone was nervous, he thought they were all in surprisingly good sprite.

As he left the west wall, he headed over to check on Johnson. When he found him, he was setting with his back against the wall and appeared to be sound asleep. As he got close to him, he could see the effects of the fight last night. When Mitchell got next to him, he woke up and tried to jump up, but Mitchell could see he was a little stiff. "Hurting a little?" He asked sympathetically.

Johnson just stretched out a little and nodded to him. Mitchell looked around, but there was no one that was really close to him. He then asked, "I thought you were supposed to get some of the Mexicans over here? I'm still feeling a little lonesome here." Then he added, rather sarcastically, "I don't think anyone wants to be near this nigger."

"Hey," Mitchell said with as much seriousness as he could muster, "enough of that shit. You are better than any of these turds and you proved that last night. You stood up to that group and all of them, but one backed down." He stopped to let him think about that a moment, then he continued, "Then when you had to fight, you proved yourself, and then some. You had him and showed what you are made of when you let him go."

Stretch just look down at the ground and nodded. "Yeah, Boss, but I still don't enjoy being here with no backup."

Mitchell tried to get him to relax, "Don't worry. Nothing is going to happen here today. They may start the bombardment, but that is more phycological than anything. Captain Seguin is getting his men settled and should have some people on the wall with you soon. Most of the Mexicans of this time were treated only a little better than the blacks. So, you shouldn't have any problems with these men, other than maybe a little language issue."

Johnson smiled a little, saying, "Well, I picked up a little Spanish in school and a little TexMex from being stationed down here."

Mitchell just smiled and told him, "We'll have to see how far the TexMex will take you in this timeline. I have no idea if it has had time to even develop here, yet."

They both got a little laugh at that. He thought Stretch was relaxing a little, so he changed the subject to help get his mind off things. "How's it going over on this side? Have they made much progress setting up a battery over here yet?"

Stretch turned to look out over the grounds on this side. Slowly, because of his stiffness, he pointed to the northwest. "There's was a couple of men on horses milling around in that area. I think they may have been officers. With all the shiny stuff they all have on their uniforms, it's hard to tell who is an officer until you get close to them. I don't have binoculars over here, so I'm just guessing." He stopped and looked a little closer before he continued saying, "Now it looks like there are some men doing something out there."

Mitchell looked to where he was pointing while he talked and pulled out his binoculars to scan that area. After he got a good look around, he handed him the glasses so he could look. While Stretch was looking, he said, "Yeah, that is the area where they set up an artillery battery in our timeline. If I remember right, they will start way out there, but the fire wasn't effective. They later moved in closer. We'll probably wait until they get closer before we do anything about them."

He stayed there with Johnson for a little while just to give him a little company. However, just before he left, a couple of Mexican men showed up. He didn't pretend to understand Spanish, but he could usually pick out enough words to get an idea. This, however, wasn't even close to anything he could understand. When they got close, they switched to a broken English to say hello. Mitchell stayed around to see how things started out. Johnson and the two Mexicans hit it off just fine. They were very curious about him and especially his rifle. Johnson was trying to explain things to them, so he just left him and headed over to check in with the Chief.

Redcloud was just sitting on the wall and taking in the activity. He didn't really say much until Mitchell pressed it and he said the same thing that Johnson had about the Mexicans checking out that area and some men working.

After some small talk, he asked Redcloud when he thought they should set up the Claymores.

He didn't even think about it and just flat out said, "Not until we need them."

Mitchell just stood there looking at him a little and Redcloud finally gave up the rest of his thinking. "We should be able to hold off until the main attack. That's how it went down in our time, so we should be able to do at least that. History tells us they held out until the thirteenth day. I would probably put the Claymores out the night before the thirteenth day."

It made sense to Mitchell, so he just nodded back to him, even though he wasn't even looking in his direction. Then he brought up a question Mitchell hadn't even thought about yet. "What do we do then?"

"What do you mean?" He shot back at him.

This time Redcloud turned to face him before he started talking. "OK, say we defeat him and his army right here. You know from history that he was a coward, and he is probably going to run again. In our timeline, it was pure luck that someone caught him trying to sneak away for the battle and that person didn't even know who he had captured until later. We can't rely on that kind of luck this time. We need a plan to capture him before he can sneak away in this time."

Mitchell had to admit it. Redcloud was right. He hadn't even given the after battle much though. He looked straight into his eyes and said with a seriously straight face, "You know, for a person who tries to pass himself off as a dumb Indian, you really have a keen eye for the here and now."

Redcloud sat up straight and tipped his nose up a little and gave me a little snort before he smiled.

"You and me are going to have to sit down this evening and come up with some kind of plan. You're right, we can't let him slip away. This must be a decisive blow, just as it was when Sam Houston took him down at San Jacinto. But more, we need to make sure he stays alive until Houston and the Texas government can deal with him." He let it drop there. They both had some thinking to do before they sat down tonight.

On another subject, He almost forgot to tell Redcloud about the ambush tonight, "Oh," He started out, "After you get off watch, you should grab a few Z's. We're probably gonna blow the huts outside the wall tonight. You might want to be there to watch. I told Crockett he could have the honors of blowing them."

Redcloud gave a little laugh, saying, "That might just be worth watching, thanks."

Mitchell then simply waved at him as he turned and walked away. Heading back down the ramp, he stopped to take a quick look around. The atmosphere had certainly changed, but it was not a bad change. Now, just about every man was carrying his rifle with him while he did whatever work he was doing. The level of alertness was also much higher, he thought. No one appeared nervous or scared, at least on the outside. These men were all acting like professionals who, even though they probably all knew what was coming, went about their business much as they had in the days before. He guessed the history books had it right about these men. It really made him feel quite proud to be here with them, no matter the outcome.

When he got back to their camp, Mitchell put some water on to boil because he felt he needed to get some food in him and being it was close to lunchtime; he felt he should help by putting enough water on for everyone. He went into his tent to lie down for a moment while he waited for the water to boil.

Mitchell suddenly woke up. He didn't know how long he had been sleeping, but it was already getting dark. Crawling out of his tent, he saw some of the group had already gathered around the fire. His watch said it was near 6:30. He figured he must have needed some sack time, but it just came up and hit him. He started looking around for the night vision goggles. They weren't where he left them. Anna was by the fire, and he first asked her, "Have you seen the three sets of NODs I left here?"

"No Boss, haven't seen them. I only sat down a little while ago and they weren't here then." Was her reply.

Now he was getting worried. He went looking in the wagon and all around their campsite. Nothing. Just as he was about to lose it, he heard a soft voice behind him say, "Are you looking for something?"

It was Kat. He hadn't seen her all day. He was so busy he didn't even have time to think about her, and then he fell asleep. Now Mitchell felt so bad. He wanted to run over and hug her and tell her how sorry he was, but all he could think about was the lost equipment. "Yes, my Darling. I set some equipment down right here and now it is gone. This is a very important thing, and I need to find them before tonight." He said to her as he continued to look around.

She just stood there, kind if swaying, and softly said, "And just how important are these things you lost?"

It wasn't so much the question, but the way she asked it that caught his attention. She was saying it playfully. The way two little kids might say something when they are playing a game. That made him stop and turn to her. She was just standing there, swaying back and forth. He walked up to her, but before he got there, she brought her hands from behind her. She was holding the goggles.

Stopping, Mitchell put his hands on his hips and stood there staring at her. She shook them a little, saying, "Are these the little things you're looking for?"

He took another step toward her, and she quickly put them behind her back again. This time she said in a firm, but still joking voice, "How important are these things and what is it worth for me to give them back?"

He walked up to her and with his hands behind his back; he played along with her. "These are very important. They could be the difference between life and death for many people in here."

She thought about that for a moment, but still didn't give up the game she was playing. "Well then, I suppose they are of very great value to you. What would you be willing to give for them?"

He put his head down and slowly took a couple more steps until he was face to face with her. Softly he whispered to her, "I would give you my whole life for them." Then he slowly leaned forward and gave her a gently but passionate kiss.

As he put his arms around her, she brought her arms out and wrapped them around his neck. They were only a fraction of an inch apart and just stood there, swaying together.

As Mitchell slowly reach up and took the goggle from her hand. She said, "I found them just laying over there. I went to look for you, but you were asleep in your tent. I didn't want to wake you, but I also didn't think I should leave these out."

"You were right, my darling. These shouldn't be left lying around. I didn't intend to go to sleep, but I was so tired I must have just passed out. I forgot all about them. Thank you for covering for me."

She smiled and gave him a little kiss and said, "That is what a wife does for her husband. She should always be there to help him."

Mitchell nodded his head and put his forehead on hers and simply said, "Thank you, my dear."

When they finally separated, and he turned back to the fire, everyone, including Redcloud, was just standing there watching them. He could feel his face turning a deep shade of red. Mitchell lowered his head and headed towards his tent to gather the rest of his gear. As he walked by the fire, there were whistles and applause, and shouting.

When he got to his tent, he crawled inside and gathered the other things he would need tonight. When he finally crawled back out, the gang was still gathered around the fire. Even Kat was there. They were all laughing, and Mitchell was pretty sure it was at his expense. He didn't let this bother him now. This time he walked up to Kat. put his arm around her and said, "Tonight we are going to hurt Santa Anna. There will be a couple of very large explosions and maybe some rifle fire. Don't worry, we are going to be the ones attacking this time." He then gave her another kiss and turned to leave. Looking at Redcloud with his big shit-eating grin, he said, "You going to join me or just stand there looking stupid?"

Redcloud quickly turned and grabbed his gear and trotted to catch up with him. As he came alongside, he said, "You know I'm gonna be with you. Someone has to cover your ass. You sure don't know how to protect it."

Mitchell looked over at him and replied as sarcastically as I could, "Yeah, right. You're gonna cover my ass?"

When they got to the meeting place, it was almost dark. Crockett and Seguin were already there. Bowie had also stayed to join in, but he was sitting in his chair a little away from them. Before it got too dark, he showed Crockett and Seguin how to use the goggles. He explained it will take a little while to get used to seeing through these things, but they would just have to learn as they go.

As it was now really getting dark, Travis came over to where they were. He just stood off to the side and said, 'I heard you might be planning a little surprise for our guests out there."

"Yes Sir," Mitchell softly said to him. "We have quite a surprise party planned for them."

"Boss," He heard Redcloud call to him, "They are moving out over there. I caught a small group of men head out to the left a little and then hide behind some bushes."

"OK gentlemen," He said, "We are about to throw a party. Please put the night vision goggle on and turn them on like I showed you. It will take a moment for them to warm up and for your eyes to get used to the light. Just be patient and keep watching the entire area."

He then turned to Travis, "I'm sorry Sir, I didn't know you would be here, and I didn't bring enough night vision goggle for you. If you would like, I could send for another set."

"I would like that very much. I would like to see some of this magic you claim to have." Travis said, but Mitchell couldn't tell if he was being sarcastic or not.

He turned to Redcloud, "Chief, would you be so kind as to run back and get another set of NODs for the Colonel?"

Redcloud jumped right up and as he turned to leave, he said, "Sure think, Cap. I'll be right back."

Mitchell knew he would not let this captain thing go. He just turned back to the task at hand. He could clearly see several small groups of men as they slowly made their way to the old huts. They didn't appear to be in any hurry, so his guess was they would not make any aggressive moves until morning.

"Colonel Travis," He said after lifting the goggles away, "I'm going to guess, buy the way they are moving, that they are planning to attack in the morning. If it were me, I would coordinate this with a cannon barrage at first light. Now, if I am right, we have two options. We can blow the buildings tonight and just disrupt their entire plan, or we can time it with a counterattack just prior to the start of theirs."

"What are you saying, Captain?" he asked.

"Well, we can simply blow up the building and end the whole attack right now. However, if we wait and just before they start their attack, we open up with an attack of our own. Either way, those building will be destroyed, and we won't have to worry about them anymore. Then, we open up with our own artillery barrage. We cut loose with all the cannons we have on this side and a few well-placed shots from Sergeant Redcloud. We can accomplish several things. First, we will have broken up their plans as we take the offensive. Second, we can destroy much of their artillery while keeping our secret weapons a secret. Last, we'll show them what we are made of and that they are going to have a hard time to take this fort. All his men will see this and hurt the morale in his camp."

Travis just stood there for a short time. He turned and shouted for the Sergeant-major.

While they waited for the Sergeant-major to show up, he said, "I like your plan. This could be a tremendous blow to Santa Anna and take him down a notch or two."

When the Sergeant-major showed up, he slapped a very nice salute and simply said, "Sir."

Travis turned to him and started giving orders. "I want you to get every man we can spare and put them on the west wall. Don't take any from the walls where they are now, just the extra men off watch. However, Hiram, this must, above all else, be done quietly. Also, inform Captain Dickenson that he is to have all his available guns aimed at the Mexican battery just on the other side of the river. The signal for him to open fire with be the blowing up of these buildings." Travis waited while all his orders sunk in.

"Sir, we'll be ready." Was the only reply from the Sergeant-major.

With that, he snapped another salute to Travis and turned to leave before Travis could return it.

Travis just turned back to watch what was going on. Just then Redcloud returned with another set of night vision goggle and handed them to Mitchell. He quickly went over the operation with Travis, who then put them on and in no time was watching the action outside the walls.

Behind them, they could hear the men moving into their positions. Redcloud turned and was watching what was happening in the fort. Just then, Anna came up to Mitchell and kneeled down. "Boss, we were to report over to this wall. What's going on?"

Before he could tell her, Redcloud also came over and asked the same thing.

"OK guys," He started out, "There's been a slight change in plans. We are still going to blow those building, but we are also going to open a counterattack on Santa Anna's artillery at the same time."

Redcloud took a long look around and then looked back at him. "Was this your idea, or did someone from this time come up with this?"

"It was my idea." Mitchell admitted. "What's the problem? It's a sound tactic."

"Well," Redcloud said with some concern, "we were counting on the timelines being similar. Everything we have done so far has been minor and in the support of what we knew. This is the first major change to this timeline and could affect things in ways we can't even imagine right now.'

This was true. Mitchell hadn't considered that when he proposed this plan to Travis. He looked around at Redcloud and Anna and, lowering his head, he mumbled, "You are right. I had not thought this through. I was only thinking of the tactical situation at hand. As the leader of this group, I should have thought this through." As he spoke, he became angrier at himself. "Against the rules of our group, I made a decision that will affect the future and all of us. I should have brought this before the group and voted on it. I was wrong, but I don't know what I can do to correct this mistake."

Anna just looked at him, like he should have all the answers. Redcloud just hung his head down and started playing in the dirt with his finger. He didn't have an answer for them.

After a long pause, he finally spoke up, "OK guys, I can't think of anything we can do about this situation right now. I suggest we get the entire group together later and discuss this."

Both Anna and the Chief slowly nodded their agreement. He looked each of them in the eye and continued, "I would ask one thing right now. Keep this to yourself. I will bring this to the entire group later. Right now, we need to focus on what is happening here and now, not on our mistakes, uh, my mistake."

Redcloud simply said, "Agreed."

Anna said nothing, but nodded her agreement.

Turning to Anna, "I don't expect that we will see much action on the wall tonight. Tomorrow I am pretty sure Santa Anna had planned an attack in combination with the artillery barrage at dawn. Now that I have stuck my foot in my mouth on this, I can only guess. I think our counterattack will break up his plans. At least for the first thing in the morning. He may plan some minor attacks during the days to feel out our defenses, at least at first. Go around to each of our guys and tell them our rules of engagement have not changed. Two mags each during an attack and no automatic fire."

"Got it, Boss," she said and turned, but then spun back. She said, "I just want to say right now that any of us could have made that mistake. We will probably still make mistakes in the future. We just need to minimize it as much as we can and support each other."

This touched Mitchell. From her initial concerns about his actions, this was not what he expected to hear from her. He looked down and quietly told her, "Thank you, but for now, save it for the group."

She just nodded and turned away. Quickly, she was off to find the rest of their group. This left him alone with Redcloud, who just sat there with a look on his face, telling Mitchell that he screwed up. "I know, I know. We'll try to fix it later. Right now, let's just get through this mess." He said to him.

They both slowly turned back to the activity outside.

Mitchell just sat there for a little while, cursing himself for being so stupid. He probably screwed up any chance they had of coming out of this unharmed. Now he had put his entire team in danger. Also, these men in the Alamo that know about them were counting on him and he might have just let them down. He knew he'd have to come up with a recovery plan, and quickly, even though he knew there was probably no turning back from this plan, he laid out for Travis.

After knocking his head against the wall for a little while, he finally decided the only thing he could do is to take it directly to Travis and tell him about his mistake and hope that he will resend the order he gave.

Mitchell stood up and walk over to Travis, who was still using the night vision. "Colonel," he said to him and waited until he turned and removed the goggles and then he continued. "I need to have a word with you. I may have not thought this through, and the counterattack may be a mistake."

"I don't understand," Travis said as he took a step back. "Your plan is good for all the right reasons. How could this be a mistake?"

He had to be careful about how he answered him. "Sir, this counterattack will probably work great, however, we are going to lose one of our greatest assists."

That had him. He was now curious what that could be. Slightly turning, he leaned in closer to Mitchell and whispered, "And just what would that be?"

He simply said, "Knowledge, Sir."

Travis stood back up straight and with just a little anger he demanded, "You had better explain yourself, Mister."

"Sir, we based all of our plans on using the knowledge I bring from the future." He had to whisper this part, as there were just too many ears around. Before he continued, he took a few more steps away from the group of men nearby. "This counterattack is going to change everything I know about what is going to happen. This did not happen at all in my timeline. If we go ahead with the counterattack, then everything from that moment forward will be new. Sir, for our plans we need to keep everything as close as we could to what I knew happened until the last day. Hell, Santa Anna could turn around and send in all his soldiers tomorrow morning and overwhelm us because we are simply not ready for it."

Travis just stood there for a moment and then turned to take a few steps away. There, he paused for what seemed like forever. Slowly, he turned around and asked, "If he changes from what he would have done, do you really think he could take this fortification?"

"Sir, I can't say for sure, but if he does, he will take a much greater toll in lost men than he did from my time. To be honest, Sir, I think we could get hurt bad, but there is still a fair chance we could still defeat him, but we can no longer rely on future knowledge."

Travis again turned away from him and stood for a long time. It would appear that commanders at this point in time had much a longer time to decide. Finally, Travis stood up to full height and turned back to him. Mitchell thought he knew what his decision was before he even spoke. "I understand your concern, and they are valid. What you pointed out in your original plan, however, is a powerful argument." He started walking back towards Mitchell as he continued to speak. "I believe that the show of a strong force now will do more to harm to Santa Anna than anything your prior knowledge could do for us."

As he got back next to him, Travis took off his hat and leaned towards Mitchell, saying, "We will continue with the planned counterattack. Do I still have your support?"

Mitchell didn't expect his last question. However, he quickly answered. "Yes Sir. We are here with you, whatever comes."

Travis stood back up and put his hat back on. He just simply nodded as an acknowledgement of the answer and walked back up to the wall.

Mitchell just stood there for a moment, then walked over to Redcloud. He sat down and said nothing.

Redcloud spoke up first, "Well?"

He just shrugged his shoulders and told him, "I tried to talk him out of this plan, but he believes that the short-term benefits will outweigh the loss of the future knowledge."

"Shit!" was all that the Chief could reply with.

After a while Mitchell put on his goggles and returned to looking out over the wall. He could see that some men had made it to the buildings, but there were more still maneuvering to get there. His best guess is they will still take a couple more hours before they get all their men in place.

He turned back around and sat with his back against the wall. There was nothing he could do now except go through with his plan and hope that they can recover from this during the rest of the battle.

Soon August and Kat found him and took up positions on the wall right next to Redcloud. There they all pass the time with a little small talk as Redcloud explained what was happening and the plans for the morning. August seemed please that something was about to happen. Mitchell believed the old soldier in him had awoken and he was now back in his youth, ready for a good fight.

Kat, however, had a completely different emotion. She was scared. Mitchell could see the nervousness in her, even in the dark. He didn't say anything to her right now. There was still a long wait until morning. If he tried to calm her now, the wait would only bring the nervousness back again. He just kept watching her and every time she would turn his way, he would simply give her a reassuring smile. This needed to be a surprise for everything to work and everyone knew it, so there just wasn't much talking going on.

He must have dozed off, because the next thing Mitchell knew was Redcloud was shaking his shoulder. He held up his hand to signal to him he was awake. Slipping the goggles back on, Mitchell looked over the wall. Occasionally, he could see some bodies moving inside the building and there were a lot of rifles barrels sticking out all over the place. He leaned closer to Redcloud and, without taking his eyes off the buildings, he asked in a whisper, "Best guess. How many?"

Redcloud didn't even look away, he just simply replied, "Best guess, upwards of one hundred, maybe a little less."

Mitchell stood and walked over to the other wall and began scanning the town. There we no lights, but there was still enough moonlight that he could clearly see the men around the artillery battery we up to something.

He looked up and down the wall. He suddenly wished he had a radio with him. The battle was going to begin soon, and he wanted to check on his people. He wanted to send one or two of them to the gate on the south wall. If it were him planning the attack, that was the place he would have the men in the building trying to take. The sun would come up soon, so soon the action will begin. So many last-minute thoughts it was driving him crazy.

He finally decided it was time for him to take control and begin. He went over to Travis and explained to him he needed to go outside the wall to the corner, where they hid the detonator wires. Taking 4 of the firing devices, he found Crockett and waved for him to follow. They went down to the south gate and slowly crawled out to the firing point that had been set up. They had already made all the circuit checks when they set up everything. However, he double checked again. All the claymores checked out. He connected the firing devices and made sure they had a suitable cover in the pit they dug. Now came the most hard part… the waiting.

He had told Travis to keep watch on the artillery. Mitchell was pretty sure they would start off the attack and that would give them just a few moments to blow the building between the first shot of their artillery and when the soldiers in the building started their attack. He whispered to Crockett, "OK David, to fire these mines, you need to squeeze each of these devices three times quickly. As soon as you do that to one, move to the next until you have fired off all four." He had saved the last detonator with the shorting attachment still in it, so he could give Crockett the feel of them. As he spoke, he showed him how to move the safety out of the way and he simulated how to squeeze them. Crockett then took the last one and went through the steps like Mitchell had showed him. He was an excellent student, and everything went fine. When he finished, he handed it back and Mitchell, who then connected it to the last wire. He then motioned for Crockett to be ready and whispered, "The moment you hear the first cannon fire, quickly hit all four."

All this time, Crockett didn't say a word. He was used to this type of close quarters fighting and knew how to be silent. He picked up the first detonator and held it at the ready. They both still had their night vision on and could see the activity. Mitchell could see the batteries on the other side of the river and the activity over there, as well as the men in the building, getting ready.

They laid there for about fifteen minutes or so before they heard the first cannon fire. Even without Mitchell telling him, Crockett began hitting the detonators. In quick succession, the closest building went up first and then the others, one right after another. The men on the wall and around the fortification at the south gate opened fire. Those Mexicans that had survived the blast still charged the south gate, but quickly cut down. Mitchell could hear the cannons of the Alamo open fire at the same time. He couldn't see the effect because of the dust and smoke in the air, but in between the cannon fire, he could hear the unmistakable sound of Redcloud's grenade launcher firing. He heard three shots, but he was sure he fired more.

Within five minutes, Mitchell heard a shout from Travis up on the wall to cease fire. Slowly, all the shooting stopped. Crockett and he made a run for the south gate and made their way back to the gun platform. Travis was standing there looking through his glass at the town. Mitchell pulled out the binoculars and scanned the town.

As he looked over the artillery battery, he could also see a lot of activity all over that side of the river. Units were being moved into place. He couldn't tell if this was part of Santa Anna's plan or if this was a reaction to their counterattack.

As He checked it out, Redcloud came up beside him. Mitchell noted he was there and simply said, "Report."

Redcloud began his report. "I fired five rounds and believe I destroyed three of their cannons with direct hits. I am sure that the remaining two shots took out the crew on two more cannons."

As he gave his report, Mitchell shifted his scan to their artillery. There appeared to be a little more damage than Redcloud was reporting. He noted this to him. "Chief, I see a little more damage than you are describing."

As he lowered his binoculars and looked at him, Redcloud simply replied, "Then I would guess that Captain Dickenson was more effective than you gave him credit for."

He was probably right. Mitchell wasn't considering the damage by the Alamo's guns. This was better than he could have hoped for. He would say more than half the cannons on this side had been destroyed. The effect will depend on how good Santa Anna's men were at repairs.

He only had a few minutes to take in the amount of damage. His attention was now on the Mexican Army forming up outside the town. He turned to Redcloud and told him, "Quickly, as you can, run back and grab a couple of radios. Bring one to me and take the other to the high point of the chapel. I need to know what's happening around the rest of the area."

No sooner than he said it, Redcloud was off. Within a few minutes, Redcloud returned with a radio and tossed it to him, and then turned and headed off to the chapel. He waked over to Travis, who was still checking out the activity in the town.

"Sir," he said as he came up to him. Lowering his glass, Mitchell explained, "I have sent Sargant Redcloud to the high point of the chapel. He will report on the surrounding activity."

As he was talking to him, the radio came alive. Travis took a little jump back and pointed to it. "What is that?" he asked.

"This, Sir, is a radio." He explained. "If you remember when I first got here, I could contact the rest of my group with this while there were still miles away."

"Yes, I remember." Travis said as he looked at it.

Mitchell held up the radio and keyed it, saying, "Go ahead, report."

Redcloud's voice came back, "The north side is quiet and the east." There was a pause before he continued, "The south side, however, is showing a sizable bit of activity."

Mitchell replied, "What size?"

After a moment Redcloud replied, "Probably a couple of companies .. uh regiments, at least."

All this time, Travis was standing there listening. He turned towards the town for a long moment, but then spun back to Mitchell and asked, "This plan was set up before we did our counterattack. Is this what happened in your time?"

Mitchell had to think a little. He looked around to give himself a moment to think. After he took that moment, he was ready. "I believe this happened, however like I told you, we only have the reports from the Mexican side of the battle. During the early days of that battle, Santa Anna made several attacks at different point to test out the defenses. So, this sounds right."

Travis was a little disturbed by that answer. He took Mitchell by the arm and lead his away from the rest of the group. Suddenly, he stopped and turned to him. "Is this the best information you can give me?" he said rather angrily. Before he could answer, Travis turned away and continued, "What you are telling me now, I could see for myself, so your future information is not that important."

Mitchell didn't even look away, but kept his eyes on Travis, "Sir, I told you from the start I don't have a minute-by-minute breakdown of the battle and to complicate things more, the information we have only comes from one side. So yes, the information I have is limited, but it told you of the attack this morning and this information allowed you to make a plan to counter it." He was talking with a little more anger than he should, but what he had to say to Travis was important. Continuing, "Because you continued with the counterattack, everything I knew is probably gone. Yes, this attack was planned before our action, but if he continues or breaks, it off is all new and now I can't tell you. And, to add to the problem, I can no longer advise you about what I know.

I can only supply you with an advantage with the equipment and weapons I have."

Travis did not look happy, however, he remained calm and slowly asked, "What can you do right now?"

"Well, first off," He started, "We have instant communication just about anywhere in the fort. This is one reason I placed my people all around.". He then walked back over to the wall and looked out to the south. He could see the forces beginning their approach from the south. Glancing over to the west, he could also see those troops now moving. He continued, "From the looks of things, today is going to be the first assault on the Alamo, much as it did in my time. My guess is even though we changed things, it will take a little while for the changes to occur. Today, I think we are safe. You have the men in place on the east wall, now you just need to reinforce the south wall."

Travis asked, "Can you have your people move by telling them on this thing?" pointing to the radio.

Unfortunately," Mitchell said, "I had not planned for this action and do not have the radios passed out to my people. Only Sergeant Redcloud currently has one."

Travis quickly turned and shouted for the Sergeant-major. Mitchell didn't know how he was always close by, but he guessed that was the job for him. He came running over and again with a simple. "Sir" he stood waiting for the orders.

Travis turned and said, "Hiram, take every fourth man and fortify the south wall."

"Yes, Sir." The Sergeant-Major said and turned.

Before he could run off, Mitchell shouted to him, "Sergeant-Major, a moment, please."

Turning to Travis, he said, "Sir, I would like to get half my people along the palisade with Crockett's men. The other half should stay along this side," indicating the west wall, "or staying at their assigned post."

Travis said to the Sergeant-major, "Hiram, do as he asks."

Before the Sergeant-major could do anything, Mitchell turned and told him, "Please have Sergeant Wilson report to me."

"Who?" he asked.

"The woman." was the only reply he could think of quickly to get him to move.

"Oh," he said with a little laugh, and then said, "Sir." And ran off.

When Anna reported, he asked her, "Who is not on post right now?"

She thought for a moment and said, "Jose and Stretch. Also, Kat." Even though he didn't ask, she continued, "Blake is near the north-east corner, and I believe Kat and her father are here with you."

He thought for just a second. "Have Jose and Stretch stay on this wall with Blake, but spread them out down the wall. Keep Stretch near me at this end." He added the last as an after though. Continuing, "Have Kat and her father report to their post at the chapel. Tell the Chief to grab everyone's radios and pass them out so we can all talk, then report back to me."

Without a second thought, she simply said, "You got it. Boss." and was off at a run.

Mitchell walked over to the wall and gathered Kat and August together. "I need you two to report to you posts. It looks like we are going to come under attack, and we need everyone at their posts."

They both just nodded and before she turned to leave, she leaned forward and gave him a kiss. Quickly turning, both she and her father left to take up their positions. He watched as they hurried off. Of course, August could not run, but he was doing about the best he could, and Kat stayed right with him.

He watched them until they were near the chapel and then turned back to the battle. Now he had to shake off any other stray thoughts and focus on the fight. Santa Anna's men were closing in. They formed the typical battle lines of the day, and with more of a march than a charge, slowly approached the walls.

Santa Anna got a couple of his cannons back in action and they fired, but most of the shots were high and not doing anything in the way of affecting the fight in front of them. Travis moved a little further down the wall towards the artillery command post. This left him alone with Captain Dickenson and his crew in the southwest corner.

Shortly, Redcloud brought him his squad radio, and he put it on. Then he made a check with everyone. Redcloud said he left the hand-held radio with Kat so they could stay in touch with her. Mitchell then sent him to take a position in the fortifications around the south gate and then quickly he made a radio check with Kat and after a little trouble, she got that hang of talking on it again. Both she and August were ready.

No sooner than they had everyone in place the Mexicans charged. They were still more than a hundred yards out when they started their charge, but still the men on the wall fired.

A couple of Mexican soldiers fell, but only a couple at first. It wasn't until they were within about fifty yards that the actual damage showed. The Mexicans were dropping right and left. Mitchell could distinctly hear the difference between the nuzzle loaders shooting and his men's weapons. Now he raised his rifle and began firing. It didn't make him feel good to see the men go down he was shooting at, but it was necessary. He made a note to himself to talk to the rest of the people about this feeling tonight after this day's battle. Most of them are new and never really killed anyone before, so he had to make sure they understand the thoughts they were having were normal and that they needed to control them.

The Mexicans almost made it to the wall before the fire power had driven them back. It was a similar sight to the south, as that side also retreated. Slowly, the firing died down and today's battle ended.

Mitchell left his position and walked over to where Travis was. As he did, Crockett came up to join him. Together, they climbed up to where Travis was and took up a position behind him. Travis was scanning the battlefield with his glass and slowly lowered it and turned back to them. Looking right at Mitchell, he asked, "Is this what happened in your time and what do you believe is going to happen next?"

"Well Sir," He started, "Like I said before, things are probably going to change. How much I have no way a knowing. My best guess," and he placed a lot of emphasis on "guess,", "is that he will continue with the way things went. I can only advise you when I think things are changing. In my time, he planned several half-hearted attacks trying to feel out the defenses." Mitchell stopped to think a little while Travis waited. "I think he will try this a little longer. Also, he does not yet have his full force here. There were some reports of heavy artillery that were late getting to this battle, but I don't know how accurate that information is."

Travis turned back to watch the Mexicans retreat and then turned to the Sergeant-major. He ordered, "Have the men stand down. Those on watch stay at their posts. Those that are off have then grab some rest and reload. Have the men staying on the wall reloaded first, just in case Santa Anna changes his plans." The last bit, he said as he looked over at Mitchell.

Mitchell didn't let that affect him in the least. He knew that they still have quite an advantage over Santa Anna, things these people haven't even seen yet. Speaking of which, he needed to discuss the placement of the claymores with Redcloud, since he screwed up and they couldn't depend on thirteen days anymore.

CHAPTER 12

Things finally quitted down a little. Mitchell guessed Santa Anna's plans must have changed some because the artillery barraged did not start today. However, he can't really tell if this is a change or not because he didn't actually know when it started. Things are now getting fuzzy. He didn't think he could really tell what his old history was and what is now new. He can only focus on any major changes that are obvious to him or the others. Oh yeah, the others. He needed to sit down and have words with them about his stupid mistake. He motioned for Anna to come over to him. When she came near, he asked her, "Who is on watch right now?"

She thought for a moment and looked around. After doing a quick head count, she said, "Stretch and Blake or on the wall and August and Kat are up on the Chapel."

This is something he had to do, like it or not. However, taking people from their posts for this was important. Looking up at her, he told her, "I need to have a family meeting to discuss what happened today. Send someone to get the guys off the wall. I'll go get Kat and August."

Before he could even stand, Anna had already dispatched Jose to bring in the others on the wall. Slowly, he walked up the ramp and found August and Kat on opposite sides of the Chapel platform, keeping watch. When he got up top, both of them turned to look at him. He just motioned for them to follow him and turned and went back to the camp.

It wasn't long before the group was all together. It was Stretch who spoke up first. "What's up, Boss?"

"I wanted to get everyone together this evening to discuss what happened today." He laid out for them.

Stretch again spoke up, "We kicked ass, is what happened." Then after a moment he added, "And tomorrow we'll do it again."

This got a positive reaction from most of the rest of the group. They were all thrilled with themselves and their performance today. Mitchell thought this was much the feeling of everyone in the fort, as best he could tell from the noise he was hearing.

He just hung his head down and slowly spoke, "Yeah, we kicked ass, but there is a problem."

It was the college boy, Blake, that caught the problem. He quickly spoke up and said, "Yeah, I'll say. This is not the way it happened in our time." He waited for everyone to calm down before he continued, "The Alamo never had a preemptive attack in our time. They were always on the defense."

Now every head turned back towards Mitchell. There was no easy way to do this, so he decided to just spit it out. "Our new guy, Johnny, is right. In our timeline, the results of the attack were just about the same. The problem is now we struck first, and this never happened in our time."

This time it was Jose that spoke up, "What happened, Boss? Has there been a change in the timeline?"

Now comes the hard part. "Yeah, it appears there is now a change, and it was me that caused it."

Quickly, there was a rush of questions. There was no way he could answer, so he just held up his hands until everyone had quieted down. He had practiced this little speech in his head, but now everything was coming out as a mess. "I screwed up. I didn't think this through when I gave Travis the idea that hitting Santa Anna first would be a significant advantage. The Chief quickly pointed out my mistake, and I tried to talk Travis out of this course of action. He would have nothing to do with it. I told him that doing this would probably change everything we knew about what was going to happen, but he felt that showing our resolve and how hard it will be to take this place would be a greater advantage against Santa Anna and his men than the loss of the future knowledge."

Mitchell let it rest with that because he knew in his heart what was coming. And it didn't take long before it started. Blake was the first to hit at him. "Boss, you had no right to take these matters into your own hands like that." He was angry, and Mitchell couldn't blame him.

Then Jose, with a little less anger, added, "Yeah Boss, I know you are in charge, but in the beginning we all decided we would vote on such thing and the majority had to rule."

He just kept nodding his head in agreement with everyone. Quickly, the meeting broke down into twos and threes talking to each other while he just sat there, waiting for the impeachment.

After about ten minutes of letting them talk, Mitchell stood up. This got everyone's attention, and they all quieted down. Standing there as humble as he could be, he said, "Everything you have said is right. I made a stupid mistake and then I couldn't take it back. I got caught up in the moment and was only thinking about the battle we were about to have and not past that to our new future. My thinking was wrong and may have totally screwed things up." Now he just stood there for a moment, shuffling his feet around. Then he continued, "We have a situation now that is because of me. Still, we must decide on how to handle it."

He heard a couple of cursing and other remarks under their breaths, but no one really spoke up. Mitchell sat back down and carefully tried to outline their new future possibilities. "OK, I think the first thing we need to do is watch for what anyone thinks is changing from what happened in our time. Today, the results of the first attack on the Alamo were just about the same as the first attack in our time." Looking over at Blake, I asked, "Would you agree, Johnny?"

After a moment of thought, he said, "I guess, but this is still not how it happened."

Mitchell held up his hand to keep him from going off on another tangent again, then continuing, "OK then. This is what I think, so listen carefully and give it a minute or two of thought before you answer back." He looked around and everyone was, more or less, nodding. Continuing he said, "Because there were actions already in play before I put my foot in my mouth, today's battle came off, more or less, the same, however, without accurate records it is hard to say how close we were to our history." He let that sink in before I continued, "In the end, the day ended just about the same."

Mitchell really didn't have an idea where he was trying to go with this line of thought, but he needed to get to the point soon.

It was Redcloud that spoke up. Because he seldom ever said anything, they all shifted the gaze from him to Redcloud. He stepped into the middle to begin. "I think there are a few things we need to be watchful of and make a few plans."

There were nodes around the group, so he continued, "First we need to keep a watch for changes of what we know happened. Since we got here and started breathing the air and killing things, we have made changes. So far, these changes have not interacted with each other and this timeline in our local area has continued pretty much as before. However, we don't have the internet to log on to check the history database, so we are just guessing."

He walked around the fire while he was talking. Mitchell thought this was the most he had ever heard from him. Continuing, "Let's go over a few things so far. First there was the meeting with the Schmidt here that never happened before." Everyone nodded. "Next there was the killing of that band of Indians and the herd of horses." He paused because everyone had a big question mark on their faces.

Redcloud looked around before he continued, "Yes, the horses. It is a small thing, however, taking something away that might in some small way change things can have a profound effect on our new future."

Now Wilson spoke up, "Then there were those men that got hung because of Kat and me."

Redcloud jumped back in, "Exactly. On the trip to get here, we inter-reacted with some people on the way and maybe change what would have happened to them had we not warned them about the dangers."

Wilson again jumped in. "There was my fight with Bowie."

Johnson now said something before Mitchell could speak up, "And my little interaction with the people here that never happened before."

This got an unexpected laugh from most everyone. It was more the way he said it that lightened up the mode a little.

Now Mitchell came in with a thought, "As Anna said, her fight with Bowie. However, in the original battle, Bowie got hurt and laid up through the entire battle. I believe that history may try to correct itself, no matter what we do."

Redcloud then look directly at him and walked out of the center of the circle. Mitchell took the hint and stood up and came to the center of the group. Looking around, he could see he had everyone's attention. "Correct. As the Chief is pointing out, we have already made a few profound changes to this timeline. Even though I made a grievous mistake by not bringing it before the council." He almost stopped and laughed, thinking about the Star Wars movies, but continued on, "We do not know what these minor changes will bring down the road for us. Oh, I am sure we will see some effects of what we have done somewhere later in time, but that is later. I can't say for sure how much affect my error will have on what happens now, but I really don't think it will be a significant change. The battle today still turned out just about the same."

Redcloud chimed in one more time. "However, we still need to watch for changes. Some may mean nothing, but some may have a significant effect on our near future. For sure, everything we do will influence the distant future."

"Anyone else want to add anything before we move on?" Mitchell asked.

Anna stepped forward and spoke her mind now. "I agree with everything that's been said, especially that part about making a stupid mistake." Blake and Johnson both made a grunt of agreement, but Anna ignored them and continued, "This is a problem, and it will always be a problem for us. Every little thing we do will change things. Something as simple as saying hello to a person who delays them enough from what would have been a tragic accident. Because of the domino effect, we can't even imagine what will happen just by killing a bug. I believe that the near future will have little change, but as time goes on, there is a thing that is called the ripple effect. The further from the center point, the greater the change. We are all going to make mistakes like what happened today. The best we can hope for is the effect will be small, at least for now."

After saying her piece, she just simply tuned around and returned to her place. Mitchell gave it a moment before he asked again, "Anyone else?"

After a little while of silence, he continued, "Ok, next we have another problem that is again going to change history significantly."

Blake just threw his hands up in the air and started shaking his head and then blurted out, "How much can we change things before we screw up the entire future?"

"That is something we can never tell and are going to have to have a huge discussion on in the future. Us just being here will have a huge effect on the distant future. We have already decided that this is what we wanted to do and then guide the future to be better." Mitchell said to settle him down. He didn't think it was working very well, though. He just waited a moment before he continued, "The Chief had brought up another issued that we are going to have to deal with soon. To take you back to school. In our time, the Alamo fell, and Santa Anna caused a lot more death and destruction before they cornered him, and Sam Houston defeated his army." This little recount of history wasn't holding the attention of some, however he just continued, "In the battle of San Jacinto, Houston defeated Santa Anna's Army, but Santa Anna escapees. they only caught him by accident when one of

Houston's soldiers captures a Mexican private running away. Santa Anna tried to slip away as a private, however Santa Anna's own men gave it away later and they forced him to sign a surrender. Now, the problem is if we defeat him here, he is going to run away again, and we may not be lucky enough to catch him. Houston only caught him by accident. We need to come up with a plan to not only capture him, but to keep him alive until Houston and or the government of Texas gets here to work out a surrender. Otherwise, he'll just come back."

Now Mitchell thought that most of his people couldn't care less about what happens to Santa Anna, past the Alamo. They are only thinking of their old time where they catch him and that ends the problem. To his surprise, it is August who spoke out, "We just need to hang him and end the whole thing."

Mitchell had to think in his time to answer him. "Let me ask you something. In Germany, where you came from, what would happen if during a battle they killed the king? Do you think his army would just go back home and forget about it? No, his next in line would take the throne and his army would have a greater reason to go after the enemy and destroy them."

August took a step back and lowered his head. However, to his surprise, it was Blake that stepped up to support him. "The Captain is right. We must capture Santa Anna alive and force him to sign a surrender document, or this war will just go on for years instead of the couple of months it did last for us in our old timeline."

Mitchell corrected him. "We must capture him and kept him alive. Given the feeling about him, it may be harder to keep him alive than to capture him."

No one disagreed with his assessment on this point now. He thought they all had a clear picture in their minds about what could happen.

With no further discussion on this matter, Mitchell brought up the third concern he had. "Last, and this is only an idea. We need to think about what we are going to do after this is over. We need to think about how we are going to get out of here, where we are going to go, and what we will do." Before anyone could speak up, he held up his hands. "This is not the time or place for this discussion. This is something that we will need to deal with in the future. I just want everyone to have this in the back of their minds, so when we finish here, we will have a plan. We will meet like this again soon, so have some good thoughts and we'll discuss it."

Wilson spoke out again, but this time a bit sarcastically added, "And vote on it."

This was a good point, and everyone laughed. Mitchell wasn't sure if they were laughing at her comment or laughing at him and his mistake, or both.

"OK, those on watch get back to your posts and the rest of you should probably catch some sleep, while you can." He shouted as they all broke up.

As everyone left the meeting, Kat came up to him. "Will you walk me back to my watch?" she politely asked.

He didn't even need to think about it. He simply offered her his arm and as she placed her arm on his, they walked back into the chapel and up the ramp.

Once she was back at her post, he let go of her and they both turned to sit on the edge. The look on her face was just a little concerning, but he couldn't figure out what was bothering her. Softly, he asked, "You look worried. What is the matter?"

Not answering right away worried him, but she finally found the words saying, "I didn't understand what that gathering was all about. I could follow only a little."

A little embarrassed, Mitchell now had to explain the mistake he made. "Oh, my dear, the problem is that I set the rules for how our group would do things, but then I broke the rules because I didn't think about it. Now I have put the whole reason we are here in danger."

"This is what I don't understand," she said. "How are we in any more danger than we were before?"

"Dear," He started out as slowly as he could, "I come from the future, and I have some knowledge of what was to happen here. This part you know." She just nodded, so he continued, "In my time, Santa Anna won this battle and killed just about everyone in here. There were only a few survivors, and all of them were people who didn't fight, like the women and children and slaves."

So far, he believed she understood what he was saying, but he thought she was not following the implications of what he did. Now, he had to explain the meat of the problem. "We based our entire battle plan on what I knew happened before. In my time, the battle today did not happen this way. Today, because we already knew what was going to happen, we attacked him first, before his attack could start. This never happened in my time."

Now he let her think for a moment, then I asked, "Do you understand?"

"Yes, I understand what you are saying." She answered me, "The fight today went very well, and Santa Anna's soldiers did not get close to us."

"Yes, and that is the problem." He told her.

"I don't understand. Why is a victory like this a problem?" She asked with some frustration in her voice.

Now he needed to slow down and carefully explain it so she could understand. "It is a problem because this did not happen before. Now, all the plans we made to fight him may be no good. Because we changed what happened today, we may have also changed what he will do tomorrow."

Mitchell thought he saw a little light come on. Kat just sat there for what seemed to be a long time, thinking about what he had said. He thought maybe she was beginning to understand the actions that happened and the implications of these actions. He just sat there and let her sort it out.

After a little while, Kat slowly tried to form her thoughts into a question. He didn't know if it was a language issue or an understanding of the situation that was giving her such a problem. Finally, she asked, "What will we do now?"

"That, my dear," He tried to answer her, "is the big question. I just explained what happened to everyone, and we discussed my mistake and now everyone needs to think about what we will do now."

He let that thought just set a little and then added, "This is going to be a big problem as everyone will have their own ideas for our plans. There will be a lot of discussions and probably many arguments about this. Hopefully, in the end, we will work out something that everyone can agree on while still keeping our little family together."

Kat nodded, as though she understood all the issues. Mitchell couldn't really tell how much she really understood, but she was an unusual person for this time. She is smart and clever and a strong woman. He hoped she will understand most of the issues as time goes on.

After a moment, he just leaned forward and gave her a little kiss and stood up. She didn't move, but just watched him. Smiling, she said, "I think I understand some, but I will continue to think about all you have said and maybe later we can sit in a quiet place and discuss this in private."

"That sounds like a good idea." He replied, looking into her eyes, however he still wasn't sure what she was suggesting was or that he was on the same line she was thinking about. There was just something in her eyes and her smile that was nagging at him, and he was thinking there may be something else going on in her mind.

He just shrugged it off and bent down to give her another little kiss before going back down to the camp. She surprised him with the forcefulness of her response to the kiss. She stood and put her arms around his neck and held the kiss for a long time.

Slowly, she let him go and even pushed him away a little. Again, there was that look in her smile. She just bent over and picked up her rifle and turned away to look out over the wall. There was not another word. Mitchell just took a couple of steps backwards and slowly turned to leave. Before he went down the ramp, he looked back and she was just watching him over her shoulder. It was difficult to tell for sure if she had the same little smile on her face or if he was just imagining things. Either way, he thought he might have something to look forward to soon.

As Mitchell walked back into the camp, Redcloud was sitting near the fire. It wasn't really that late, but he was extremely tired and didn't want to have any great discussion with him right now. Redcloud, however, had a different idea about that. As Mitchell walked up, he stood and saluted, saying, "A word, if you would, Captain."

He stopped and shot Redcloud an angry look. "Enough of that shit. When are you going to give it up?"

He just sat back down and turned towards the fire and replied, "Oh, I don't know. Maybe never."

Mitchell knew he really could do nothing, so he simply shrugged and shook his head. He sat down next to him and said, "OK private, what's on your mind?"

He retorted, "That's Sergeant."

Mitchell looked him in the eye and simply said, "Not if you keep it up with the bullshit."

Redcloud looked down into the fire and laughed. "OK, I'll just leave it at Boss, like the others."

He also laughed and said, "That works for me. What's up?"

He got a little serious now and while stirring the fire with a stick he said, "Things have changed now, and we can no longer count on thing going the way they did before. We are going to have to change our plans." He paused a moment to stir the fire a little more and then continued, "Before, I wanted to wait until the last moment before we put out the claymores. I think now that we need to get them out tonight, or at least soon. Not only that, but we also need to put out more and spread them around to the other areas that might be potential weak areas."

It took little thinking about this. Mitchell knew right away that he was right. As Redcloud was talking, he was nodding. Now, there is the question, do they need to bring this up to the group as this changes the way things happened, or does he need to decide right now? Slowly, he responded to the Chief, "Yes, I see and agree with you. However,

I don't want to make another mistake. So, let's get everyone together in the morning to talk about it. As for tonight, let's hold off until tomorrow night. Tonight, you come up with a plan for the placement. I also agree that we need more coverage, however I don't want to use our entire sock on this. Give us the best coverage with the least amount, so we will have some in reserve."

Redcloud didn't really say anything, but just grunted. Mitchell took this as an agreement with him, but it was hard to tell for sure. After a little while of silence, he stood and as he walked away, he told him, "I'm going to go grab some sack time. I would recommend you do the same. Either tonight or early tomorrow morning, I think Santa Anna is going to bombard us. Sleep will soon become a luxury."

He didn't wait for a response from Redcloud, but continued on to his tent. As he crawled in, he suddenly felt exhausted, and it took every bit of energy he still had to just remove his boots. He just laid on top of his fart sack and was, what seemed like, instantly asleep.

As Mitchell's eyes opened, he still felt tired. He couldn't tell what time it was, but things outside were quiet. After laying there for a little while and deciding he couldn't go back to sleep, he grabbed his boots and crawled out of his tent. It was now dark, and some had gathered around the fire. As he walked up, Stretch got up and showed for him to take his seat. It just so happened that he was sitting next to Kat. After nodding to him a thank you, Mitchell pulled the stump closer to her and sat down. Kat got up and went to the wagon and grabbed an MRE for him. She fixed him a plate and a pretty decent cup of coffee.

After taking the plate from her, he smiled at her and said, "A person could sure get used to living like this." Oops, big mistake. She quickly stood back up and almost threw the coffee at him, spilling some on his leg. Good thing it wasn't too hot. She turned and instead of sitting next to her man, she went to the other side of the fire and sat next to her father.

Everyone that was sitting around the fire had a hard time trying to stifle a laugh. Some of them were less than successful at it and the laugh quickly spread around the fire. Kat now turned around so that her back was towards the fire.

A stern look from Mitchell to each person cut the laughter short. It didn't take long before Kat and he were alone at the fire. Even her father left after giving him a stern look and shaking his head. He already knew he was in trouble, but was not sure how far into the pit he was. Slowly, he got up and went over to the crate her father had been sitting on and sat down, looking at her. Quickly, she turned so that her back was to him. He got up and walked around her and sat so that they were now face to face. As she tried to turn again, he reached out and gently took her with both hands. She didn't resist, but she didn't raise her eyes from the ground to look at him. He slowly ducked his head down until he could see that he caught her eyes. As she finally looked at him, he made a face that he hoped would express how sorry he really was for the comment he had made.

Mitchell couldn't be sure, but he thought he saw her hardness soften a little. Now, he spoke, "My Love, I was not trying to embarrass you. It is just a saying from my time that people say to someone who is taking wonderful care of a person who they love."

"But everyone one was laughing," she cried.

He smiled a kind smile back at her, saying, "They were not laughing at you. They were laughing at me." Now she looked up at him and he continued, "They were laughing because they knew, before me, that I had said the wrong thing to you because you would not understand and that I was in trouble."

She slowly put her head down again. He wasn't sure how he could explain to her, but he had to try. "Sometimes a person says something they think is normal or perfectly innocent. Others who hear it can see faster than that person who said it. That happened here. I said something that in my time would be a compliment, but here you took as an insult. For this, I am truly sorry. I did not mean to hurt you or to say anything bad about you. I truly love you, and I am hoping you still love me."

After a long time, Kat finally raised her head and looked at him. He couldn't tell if she understood and was ready to forgive him or to get up and walk away. Finally, she talked in such a low voice he almost couldn't hear her. "I think I understand, and yes, I still love you. There is much I need to learn about you and your time, but in the same way, there is still much you need to learn about my time. The time that you are now living in."

My God, this simple woman from a very simple time had a better understanding of reality than I he did. She is truly a treasure in a simple wrapping. He moved closer to her and was on his knees in front of her as he slowly put his arms around her and pulled her towards him. She did not pull away or resist. When her head was on his shoulders, he felt her arms around him, and they both pulled each other into a long hug.

Mitchell felt they could have remained there forever had it not been for the sound of a cannon, followed by the explosion just outside the wall. They both jumped. He went over to where he was originally sitting and grabbed his rifle. Then he spun back to Kat, but she was running up the ramp with her rifle in hand. The thought of such a woman brought a smile to his face, but only for a second as he heard the fire from another cannon.

Quickly, he ran to the southeast corner and stood next to the big gun that was located there. Shortly Crockett and then Travis joined him. As they watched, there were several more cannon shots fired. The effect, mostly, was minimal. However, Mitchell thought Santa Anna was only doing this to bring down the morale of the men inside.

After a little while, Travis turned to Mitchell and asked, "Are things still happing as they did before for you?"

He had to be very careful about how he answered him. Thinking for a moment and then looking at him eye to eye before he spoke, "It is difficult to say. I don't have an exact schedule of things to go by. However, as best I can remember from my history, yes, things are going just about the same. Santa Anna started the bombardment in the first few days and kept it up. Soon, he should have the rest of his artillery here. He will set up the gun emplacements to the northeast.

I can't say if the exact moment the first shot fired was the same, but overall, I think we are still on schedule."

Travis didn't respond to him. He simply turned back to watch as more cannons fired. Some shots were good hits, but Mitchell would guess that most of the firing caused minor damage, other than to the morale.

Soon Travis turned towards Mitchell and with little concern told him, "Please inform me if there is any change in the future." He then turned a walked back towards his office or quarters or whatever they were.

Crockett watched him walk away and then looked at Mitchell, like he might have something to say. Truthfully, Mitchell could think of anything to say so he just said, "I'm going to go check on my people and I need to discuss something with Sergeant Redcloud."

"Come back later and we'll also have a sit-down chat." Crocket replied to him.

He just looked at Crockett strangely and turned to walk away. He wasn't sure what that last comment was about, but he couldn't worry about that right now.

Mitchell went around to each position and checked in with his people. Everyone was good, except Kat. She was quite nervous, but he really expected that. He didn't have time to sit and baby her and he knew how strong she can be when she needs to be, so he drew on that strength. Once he had her calm enough to talk to, he told her, "Dear, listen to me. This is nothing right now. They are closing their eyes and shooting rounds at us just to make us nervous. This is something we can't let happen. We need to be stronger than anything they can throw at us." All this time she was looking around but nodding her head. He could tell he wasn't getting through to her because he didn't have her attention. He decided it was time to get her attention first. Reaching out, he grabbed her by both shoulders and in a swift, powerful move, he turned her to look right at him. When he finally caught her eyes, he gently shouted, "Calm down!"

This appeared to work. Now he had her looking at him so he could talk to her. "You need to calm down. There is nothing going to happen today. They are just shooting to make everyone nervous. This is a common tactic, and we cannot let it work. Where you are right now, you should be safe. Just stay low so that if any debris comes your way, it won't hurt you. They will not attack today. We hurt them badly enough that it will take them a day or two before they get another plan together."

She was still nodding at everything he was saying, but this time he could tell she was listening. She was becoming calmer now and focusing again on where she was and what she should be doing. Mitchel then said, "My Dear, I know you don't have any training for what is going to be coming. Right now, your only job is to keep watch so Santa Anna can't sneak up on us." Mitchell continued to whisper to her and keep her calm. Continuing he said, "Once the fighting really starts, you can go down to be with Anna and support her, or just go across to the other side and be with your father. I will be with you when I can, but I have to cover a lot of different areas and running all around."

Kat now had a little smile, as she was relaxing. "You will come see me later?" she asked.

He gave her a soft smile and leaned in closer to her before he softly said, "I will be with you all that I can. However, when I can't be with you, stay close to your father."

This was key, He thought. She now realized she was not alone. He would be here, and when he couldn't, she still had Anna and her father very close to her. She slowly stood up and picked up her rifle. She moved close and held him. He could feel that her shaking was over, and things were coming back into focus for her. He slowly let her go and took a step back, but still held onto her, trying to keep things calm as he told her. "I have to go right now and check in with the rest of our team, our family. Then I need to meet with Redcloud to discuss some plans." He could see she got tense, and he pulled her close to him and held her as he continued, "I'll be back just as soon as I can. Your father is right over there." He turned her so she could see him and waved at him. He waved back, and she then raised her hand in a wave.

He then let her go and this time she stepped back and gave him a weak, but nervous, smile. With a little shaky voice, she said, "I'll be fine."

He smiled back at her and said, "I know you will. You are probably the strongest woman here, after Anna."

This brought a shy little smile to her face, and she looked down. Mitchell reached over and put his finger under her chin and gently lifted her head back up and whispered, "Stay strong." And as he turned, he said, "I'll be back soon. Just stay low."

As he walked backwards away from her, she waved to him. Now tuning he went over to her father. "August, how are things with you?" He said as he walked up to him.

August looked past him to Kat and said, "Better than my daughter is doing, I'll wager."

Mitchell looked back and agreed with him, "She is quite scared, but I think I have calmed her down for you, but you'll need to watch her for a while."

He replied with a laugh, "Oh, I will keep a very close eye on her."

"I'll come back to her as much as I can, but if things get bad here, send her down to be with Anna. She will be safe inside the hummer." He said and then turned away.

"You will not stay here?" He asked.

Mitchell stopped and turned to him. "You know better." He said, "I am in command of my people, and I need to check in with all of them. After I talk with Redcloud, I'll be back to check on her again."

He just nodded in a way that said he knew his son-in-law to be was right.

Mitchell walked back down the ramp and into their area. He went over to the hummer where Anna was. Relaxed, she was just watching out over the stockade. He almost startled her when he spoke. "How's it going down here?'

Once she regained her composure, she replied, "We're good here. Nothing happening." Just then, another shell burst up against the wall and Anna corrected herself, "Well, nothing of any great importance."

He didn't need to worry about her. She had at least been under fire in the middle east before. He wouldn't actually call her combat hardened yet, but other than the Chief and him, she was the next closest thing.

He waved and turned to continue his tour. Next, he went along the south wall and found Rodrigues. Just like before, he was sitting with his back against the wall and looked to be sleeping again. As the Boss walked up, he raised up his head and shouted, "What's up, boss?"

The cannon fire was a little less often now, but they were still shooting. Mitchell thought some rounds had hit near him and that was why he was yelling. "You OK?" He asked,

Jose just gave him a thumbs up and looked back over the wall as another cannon fired. This time, the round fell a little short and further down the wall.

Mitchell just shouted back to him, "Fine, you can go back to sleep."

He just smiled again and gave the Boss another thumbs up sign.

Mitchell left him and continued down to where Blake was. He was intently watching over the wall. He just watched for a moment and as the next cannon fired and Blake ducked down a little. As he walked close, Blake stood up. He shouted at him, "Stay down. Don't get up from cover, just because someone walks up."

He quickly squatted back down and continued to look at the town. He appeared to be just a little nervous, but not too bad. Mitchell figured he'll be alright. They did just appear to be chatting, and he felt comfortable with him. As Mitchell turned to leave, he called out, "Stay loose."

He immediately appeared to relax some and shouted back, "You too, Boss."

Blake may be new, but he appeared to have a good head on his shoulders. His next stop was with Stretch.

When he came up to the top, he found the Mexicans all gathered around a little fire and he thought they were cooking something. Stretch was right in there with then and was even smiling. Something he really hadn't seen him do for as long as he could remember.

As Mitchell walked up, Stretch stood and with a simple greeting that told him he was going to be fine, "Hey Boss, these guys are alright." Looking back down at the group, he added, "I don't know what they're cooking up, but it smells pretty good. Gotta be better than MREs."

Mitchell had to admit it smelled good. He took a quick look around and everything appeared to be quiet on this side. "Anything happening on this side?" He asked.

"Nah, there were a couple of riders before dark that looked like they were riding around the entire Alamo." He said and then turned before he continued, "They stayed well out of range for these guys, so no one really paid attention to them."

Walking over to the edge, Mitchell looked around. "Yeah, probably a recon. I think the next attack will be a little more spread out." He said while he was thinking. "It is what I would do. Check for weak points."

Turning back to Stretch, he noted he was already eating something. Now it was time to quit worrying about him. "Stay loose and don't start liking this food too much." He said to him as he walked away.

Stretch had his mouth full, so he just shot the Boss a thumbs up and a big smile.

Mitchell finished up his rounds by going over to Redcloud. He found him just sitting on the edge of the wall, looking out into the dark. He didn't even turn as Mitchell walked up but spoke first. "What's up, Boss?" Then he turned to him with a little laugh. He added, "You know, if you're going to be a ninja, you're going to need to be a lot quieter."

"Ninja, right!" Mitchell said back to him with a snort. "If I wanted to do something to you, I would sit on the other side of the compound and just shoot your ass."

They both laughed a little at that. Then he turned serious. "What do you have in mind for the claymores?"

"Well, I was thinking," Redcloud started out and then after a brief pause, "We don't really have that many claymores to mount a real defense. However, if we use what we have properly, we might just hurt them badly."

"What do you mean?" Mitchell asked.

"Well, before someone stuck his foot in his mouth, I was planning on placing three claymores across this wall and in front of the palisade." He stopped to let the comment about his mistake set in hard. "That is where we are the weakest. Now I am thinking a little differently. How many claymores do we still have with us?" He asked.

Mitchell didn't even think about it, he just spit out, "Eight."

He thought about his plan for a moment and said, "That should be enough."

Redcloud now stood up to emphasize his point. "Yes, but then if we use all of them, then we have nothing in reserve, for just in cases."

Redcloud was the planner, and Mitchell knew he had a valid point. Mitchell could tell by the way he was talking, "OK, so you got a plan ready?"

He sat back with a big smile on his face, "You hurt me, of course I have a plan."

He just sat there looking at Mitchell with that big smile on his face. Mitchell waited as long as he could before he broke. "Well, you gonna keep it to yourself or you gonna let the rest of us in on it?"

"It's so simple, I can't believe even you didn't think of it." He said as he leaned towards the Boss and brushed the back of his hand off his shoulder. When Mitchell didn't reply, he felt Redcloud was finally catching on that this game was getting old.

"OK," he said, but when Mitchell didn't respond again, he gave up his game. "OK," he shouted out. "Man, you're no fun anymore. Anyway, like I said, it is simple. We place only two claymores out in each position. We place them a little further apart but angle them in about forty-five degrees, so they will cross in the middle."

After thinking about this for a moment, Mitchell got the picture in his mind and there was one concern. "What about the side blast?

Some pellets will come out the side and send them towards the wall, won't they?" He asked Redcloud.

He knew Redcloud must have also considered this problem, because his answer was way too quick. "Yes, this is a concern, but if we dig out a pit to put the claymores in, that will help to make it more directional. Grant it, the side blast might still spit some at the wall, but I think with the plan and a warning when we are going to fire will make any danger to the Alamo very negligible."

Mitchell had to admit it was an interesting use of the claymores, but he had to think about this a little more.

Redcloud continued, "This will allow us to make the best use of what we have while also letting us cover a greater spread."

"What about the wire? Will there be enough to come back to a fire point?" He asked.

Redcloud now lost a little of his confidence in his plan. "No," he said, "this is the only drawback to my plan that I can think of. We are going to have to run the detonator to the closest person from our group and we may have to move a couple of people to make sure we get a good placement."

Yes, now Mitchell could get this together in his mind. It will take careful placement of the mines, but it should work. Now the last question, "How long will it take you to place all the mines?"

Redcloud, again, didn't even take a second to think about it. "It shouldn't take more than two nights if I can get some help, both from our group and a few of the locals."

Mitchell nodded while he thought about it, then finally he looked at him, "OK, I'll clear it with Travis, and I know Crockett will be happy to send us a couple of men. I'll have him send his men to you in one hour. Meanwhile, you get our guys together. Tonight, you should be able to dig the pits, but wait until tomorrow night before you plant the mines. I want all the placements to be invisible to anyone approaching them, though."

"Great, tonight I'll teach them what I need. We'll start on the north wall and then move down near the chapel. The west wall will have to be the last as that is the most dangerous right now." Redcloud said as he pointed to the different areas.

"Yeah, that sounds about right." He said back at him without really looking at him. He started walking away, but over his shoulder he said, "You grab our guys and I'll have Crockett's men meet you right here."

Redcloud didn't bother to answer him while Mitchell went looking for Crockett. He found him sitting near a fire with a few of his men.

As he approached, Crockett didn't bother getting up but just motioned to come and join him, saying, "Have a seat."

Mitchell held up his hand and said, "Sorry to disturb you, but I need to have a few words with you."

As Crockett got up, Mitchell turned and took a few steps away, so they could talk privately. After a few words with his men, Crockett finally came up next to him and said, "What can I do for you?"

Mitchell laid out the new plans. "I just talked with Redcloud. We have changed our defense plans a little. Because I made a mistake by changing the battle this morning, we can't depend on what we knew."

Crockett just stood there nodding and made a couple of grunts in agreement. He was a clever man, so Mitchell was fairly certain that he's following what he was saying. "We are going to put out some explosives starting tonight."

Crockett interrupted him, saying, "And I believe you have come to me for some help?" It was more a question than a statement.

He kind of shuffled his feet and replied, "Yeah, to make this work the way we planned, we need people to help dig shallow pits to place the mines."

Crockett shuffled his feet a little and said, "Well, I've got good men with strong backs that can dig a hole as deep as you want. I also have some men who have a little smarts to understand, what I don't have very many men with both qualities."

When Mitchell looked at him, Crockett was smiling, so he couldn't tell if he was serious or joking with him. He decided that either way it didn't matter, so he played his game, "I guess a few of each would probably work best."

Now, Mitchell just stood there smiling back at him and he believe now Crockett couldn't tell if he was serious or not, this time. After a little thought, he reached out with one arm and took him by the shoulder, saying, "I like your style, sir." And then turned back to his group. He called out some names and five men came up to stand next to him.

"I thought we needed half and half." Mitchell said, noting there were only five men.

Crockett took a step forward and, with a thumb to his chest, said, "Six. I am number six."

He grabbed Crockett by the arm and gently took him a couple of steps to the side. Once they were away from his men, he asked, "And which group are you with? The smart group or the strong and dumb?" But before he could answer, Mitchell continued, "You are a commandeer here and we can't afford to lose you this early in the battle. This will not be a safe job, especially when we do the side where they are launching cannon balls at us all the time."

Crockett just smiled at him and said, "If you're going to put it like that, then I guess I'll just let you decide which group I'm in."

With that remark, he turned back to his group and said over his shoulder to Mitchell, "Where do you want us?"

Shaking his head, Mitchell quickly realized there was no use arguing with him about this. He looked at the group and said, "Grab something to dig with and report to Sergeant Redcloud on the north wall. He will instruct you in what he needs."

The men went back and grabbed their rifles and some other gear and walked off together. As they walked away, Mitchell yelled to Crockett, "He may not be there right now, but he'll be right back with the people from my team."

Crockett did a walking about face and saluted to him, and then quickly turned back around.

He just stood there for a moment as they walked away. Slowly, he turned around to go inform Travis about the new plans. This should take much because he didn't seem to be too interested in the details of the plans, anyway.

After filling in Travis Mitchell went to sit with Kat for a little while. Other than the cannon fire, it was really a beautiful night. Kat and had calmed down from earlier.

"Are you feeling a little better now?" he asked as they got comfortable.

"A little." She replied, "I still jump a little every time they shoot that cannon."

He smiled a gentle smile at her while he tried to explain things. "Yes, this is normal for everyone." He paused a moment while he thought about Blake, but then he continued to make her feel better. "Even one of my men, Blake… uh, Johnny. He is scared shi…uh, scared to death, too. "

He needed to be careful about how he talked to her. The way he used to talk won't fly here and now. When she didn't respond to what he said, he continued, "This happens to just about everyone the first time they come under fire like this. Just look around."

She slowly looked around the Alamo. She then looked back at him, saying, "Everyone else looks like they always do."

"Exactly," He said, "that is because just about everyone else has been under fire before. Everyone except Johnny. He was just assigned to me right out of training. This is the first time someone has actually shot him, just like you." He smiled at her and this time it brought out a smile on her.

Sitting there smiling at each other, it soon turned into a laugh. After a little, the laugh got a little louder. Loud enough to get August's attention and he turned to look at them. Mitchell just waved at him and continued to laugh. Until a shell landed pretty close to them and Kat jumped into his arms. He knew it wasn't close enough to hurt them, probably. However, she had no way of knowing these things.

She was shaking as he held her, and the longer he held her, the shaking slowly went away. After a short time, he loosened his hold a little, and she sat back. Again, he gently smiled at her and gave her a kiss. She kissed him back, and they both smiled again.

"That one was a little closer this time. However, I think that was probably an accident. They are trying to weaken the wall and our courage. They just missed, and it went by the wall. I really don't think they will waste shot on this side of the compound. Their interest will still be on the north, west and south walls."

As she was weighing what he said, she looked around the compound and then outside the wall. Suddenly, she jumped up and grabbed her rifle. "There is someone down there!" she shouted at him.

He put his hand on the rifle and gently applied pressure to lower it. Gently, so as not to startle her into doing something. He gently said, "That should be Redcloud and his gang of men putting out some mines to stop any attacks that come from this direction."

"What are mines?" she asked, while tilting her head to one side.

"What are mines?" He repeated the question back while he tried to think of a simple way to explain this to her. He began slowly to explain, "A mine is something you hide that will explode and hurt or kill anyone near them. We usually hide them on the ground. We can set them to go off if someone is near or can be set off by someone who is watching so the damage will be greater."

"Why would you want to do that? We could be hurt as well. If the explosion is big enough to hurt many of them, can't it hurt us?"

Now things were getting complicated. He didn't want to have to explain how a claymore mine worked, but he couldn't think of a way around it. He will need to keep this as simple as possible. "These mines I have are special. They will explode, but they are built in such a way we can make most of the damage go in a certain direction. When, probably Anna, is ready to explode the mine, she will yell, Fire in the Hole. This will mean she is going to set it off quickly. When you hear this, you need to drop behind the edge of the wall. There is a possibility some parts of the mine may be thrown back this way. However, if the mines are set right and exploded at the right time, one of these mines could kill or hurt one hundred men or more."

She sat there for a little while, thinking and watching what the men below were doing. Finally, she said in a surprised voice, "I think that is Anna down there now. She is telling those men what to do."

Mitchell really had paid little attention to the workers, but now he looked more carefully. He had to smile at now quickly she could pick up on things. He replied to her, "Yes, I think you are right. And this makes sense. Redcloud would have assigned her to do this area because this is the area she will fight in and needs to know exactly where these are."

"She knows about such things?" Kat asked.

"Oh yes, she is quite good at this. At one time she was fighting in a war in our time. Other than Redcloud and me, she is the only other one in my group with any fighting experience."

Kat said nothing. She just continued to watch as the men dug the pits to place the mines. Kat watch Anna, and he watched Kat. She was focusing on everything Anna was doing. Finally, she turned to him and asked, "Will this be loud?"

He smiled back when he answered her, "Yes, it will be very loud. I would guess much louder than these artillery shells they are throwing at us now. Also, the ground will probably shake a bit."

She quickly turned to him. "Shake?" she said, but he couldn't tell if she was asking him or just repeating his statement, so he took it as a question.

"Yes, the ground will shake for a second when it goes off." Mitchell said in a way so as not to frighten her. "I'll tell you what. We are only digging the pits tonight. Tomorrow night, we will actually set out the mines and set them up for use. I will need to go out and check each one to make sure we set them up correctly." He looked her in the eyes because he wanted to see her response. "Would you like to go out with me while I check them?"

She quickly got a big smile on her face, however it just about as quickly faded. She got a serious look in her eyes and asked, "Will this be dangerous?"

He got just as serious when he replied, "Yes, in some areas we will be right where they are trying to weaken the wall. They will shoot the cannons into this area."

She sat down on the edge of the wall and thought a moment and then asked, "Can I stay next to you?"

He remained serious when he answered her, "Yes, you can stay near me, but we can't be too close. If there is a problem, I may need to react and fight. I may not have time to break holding hands or take my arm from around you to respond. This will not be a walk like we used to take. We will need to be ready to fight at any moment."

Again, she thought about it a little. Suddenly, he could see she had decided. "I think I would like to go with you. I want to see these things, and I also want to know what it is like when we will have to fight."

She had a good point. This might be the safest way, if there is one, to get her some experience under fire. He needed to make a note to take Blake and get him some true-life experience.

"OK, it's settled. However, you can't wear that dress. Tomorrow night, I need to have you in the uniform that Anna gave you. But don't get dressed too early. Wait until dark."

She gave him a look that he knew all too well was a question. So, before she could ask, he answered her, "These men around here are not used to women doing things like this. It will complicate things if they have too much time to think about it."

She nodded in understanding. She then got that excited smile on her face like the first time she drove the hummer. He'll see if she is still smiling after she comes under fire.

They must have been sitting here together, talking for more than an hour. Slowly, Mitchell stood up and picked up his rifle. Looking down at her, he said, "I need to go make my rounds to make sure everyone is still good."

"Will you be coming back?" She asked.

He reached out to take her hand as she held it up for him. "Of course, I'll be back. I just don't know how long until I'll be back."

"Hurry back," she said and added as he turned, "I'll be missing you."

Mitchell did a walking turnaround and blew her a kiss, and turned back to head down the ramp. He was now having second thoughts about inviting her to this little outing tomorrow night.

He just headed for the south gate and went around to where Anna was working. Things were quiet except for the digging noise and a few words of direction from Anna. As he walked up, everyone dropped what they were doing and grabbed their weapons. Mitchell used his little flashlight to shine a notice to Anna.

Quickly he heard, "Hold your fire, friendlies." from Anna and then she walked over to meet him with her rifle cradled in her arm.

"How's it going? You having any problems with these guys?" Mitchell asked her.

Before she could answer, he heard a voice from the dark that he recognized as Crockett say, "She better not." And then a quick laugh as he added, "I need both my feet."

Mitchell couldn't help but laugh. It was very dark, but he was close enough that he could even see a smile on Anna's face.

She turned and walked back to the dig with him. As he looked over the ground, he could see how things were going. The pit was deeper than he expected, but well-shaped to direct the blast to cross the land in front of the palisade. It almost had the look of a giant dustpan dug into the dirt. "Have you started the other pit yet?" He asked her.

She began walking to the wall near Kat and said, "This one's finished," pointing it out as they got closer. "We plan to cover the hole with some hay and straw or something. In the dark it should make a good enough camouflage."

Mitchell looked it over and could see that the aim point probably crossed about fifty to seventy-five yards out in front of the center of the wall. It was just about the perfect, effective range for the claymore. As he stood up, he looked around. The ground was a bit on the dark side. "Anna," He said as he pointed to the ground around the pits, "this ground is dark. If you set a patch of light colored straw out, it will stand right out. You're gonna have to come up with a way to darken it or use something darker to hide these things."

She shrugged her shoulder, "Yeah, I was thinking the same thing. What I told you was the plan. I intend to talk to the Chief about this when we get back." She said as she was looking around the ground.

He told her, "Take Crockett with you. He's pretty sharp and such things and can probably add a lot of good advice."

"Aye, aye, boss," she replied with a smile.

"My, my, aren't we getting into the time of things here?" He said back to her as they turned to walk back to the dig. Then he continued, "I'm going to take a walk around the outside here to see how the others are doing. You come find me when you're finished here."

Again, she replied, "Aye, aye, Boss" and even though it was just a little too dark, he was pretty sure she had a great big smile on her face.

As Mitchell turned, Crockett spoke, "Mind if I join you Jim? I'd like to see how the others are doing."

"Sure, I could use the company." He replied.

He turned to one of his men to say, "PJ, you take over and listen to the lady. I mean the Sergeant here and come find me when she's done with you."

Mitchell just heard an "OK Davy" from the dark. It was a young sounding voice, but he couldn't see the man.

Crockett and he made their way around to the west wall. Just before they got to the corner, they heard another cannon fire. Mitchell was pretty sure he heard it hit the ground far enough away from them that there was no danger, and then it hit the wall. However, there was no explosion. He turned to Crockett and said, "OK, I guess we can go now. Their rate of fire has not been too quick. We should be alright for a little while."

They turned the corner together and took only a dozen steps when there was another cannon shot. This time it exploded short of the wall, but much closer to them. They both squatted down and Mitchell turned to Crockett and said, "You know, I could be wrong about that, though."

Crockett quickly stood up and slapped him on the shoulder and jogged, but tuned back over his shoulder saying, "I guess we should move a little more quickly, then."

Mitchell had no choice but to follow him. Luck for them. They fired only one more shot while they were moving, and it landed about halfway down the wall. It only took them a few seconds of running to get to the first pit, which wasn't too far from where that last shell landed. He found Jose digging a pit there. When Crockett and he got near them, they all stopped the digging and grabbed their rifles. They both stopped, and Mitchell quickly yelled out, "Hold your fire. We are friendlies"

Jose and his men quickly lowered their rifles and Jose yelled back, "Of course you're friendlies. Who else would be crazy enough to be out here for a stroll?" There was a pause, and he finished by yelling, "Come on in!"

Jose's brief comment brought a chuckle from Crockett, who said, "I like this man. He is steady under fire."

Mitchell just looked at him and replied, "Yeah, but he is right. Who else would be crazy enough?"

They both just grunted an agreement and made the last quick dash to the dig. He found Jose with a couple of Crockett's men. They looked just about finished. "How's it going" He asked Jose.

"Pretty good, Boss. We're almost finished here. The other pit is already for the claymore about fifty yards down there." He said, turning and pointing further down the wall.

There was another shot fired. They all crouched down and this time the round was a little closer. He told Jose, "You guys need to hurry. They're zeroing in on you." He didn't know if Jose could see the smile on his face, but he thought he understood the sarcasm.

Jose replied right back, "Christ, Boss, these guys would have to have a direct hit with these little bombs they got."

Just about then, one of Crockett's men stood up and asked, "Jose, is this good enough?"

Jose turned around and pulled out his flashlight. He got down near the hole and turned on the light. Jose had fitted it with a red lens, so it was not bright. He took a quick look at the hole and then sized it up for position with the other hole. After using the entrenching tool, he had to clean it out a little. He stood and announced, "Yeah, it looks really good. Head back in and I'll show these guys to the other hole."

The two men that were working with him quickly grabbed up their tools and rifles and ran back to the little gate on the wall. Then, turning to Crockett and Mitchell, he said, "Gentlemen, if you'll follow me." He then quickly turned and ran down the wall towards the other hole. The two of them just looked at each other and followed him.

It only took a couple seconds to get to the other hole and it look to be just about right. Then Mitchell looked around. This hole, and he was guessing the other hole, was standing out like sore thumbs. Something needed to be done about this. "Jose…ah David," He called to both of them, "These pits kind of stand out. If I can see them in the night, then they will be no problem for Santa Anna's men to see in the daylight. What would be the quickest way to cover them quickly?"

Jose began looking at the holes, and Mitchell could see he quickly saw what he meant. Crockett got down low and looked over the entire area. It didn't take him long to figure out a quick way to cover the holes up. He stood up and now looked around the area before he turned back to me. "I recon the answer it pretty simple." He said, looking around.

Mitchell looked around but couldn't figure out what he was seeing. "Alright, what's so simple?" He asked, giving in.

He got a big smile on his face before he started, "You fellas from the future sure ain't very smart about such things." He let that set in on Mitchell and then continued, "It's simple. The holes are already dug. All we gotta do is fill em' back in until tomorrow night. Then we just scoop out what's already dug."

Both Mitchell and Jose could see it now. The dirt was all the same color. All they had to do was fill it back in a little and it would all look the same again. Mitchell had to hand it to him. He could quickly look over a situation and then come up with an answer to the problem. He just shook his head and chuckled a little. Then, looking over to Jose, he said, "You need help, or can you handle this?"

Jose looked down like he was shamed and said, "I guess I can handle this, Boss." He then turned his back and mumbled as he spread the dirt back into the holes, "being that it's so simple."

Just then, there was another shot from the cannon. Crocket and Mitchell hit the dirt, but again the round fell short and bounced into the wall further down. He looked over at Crockett, and they both stood up and trotted down to the north end of the wall. Before the next shot fired, they were well around the corner and he could see Redcloud and his crew.

He didn't even stop as they came up. In fact, he didn't even look up and yelled out before the men with him even knew they were there, "For a man of your reputation, Colonel, you sure make a lot of noise."

Mitchell looked over to Crockett and even in the little moonlight there was he could see his face. Mitchell believed there was concern in his look. He thought the Chief was getting under Crockett's skin a little. He just hope it was not in a bad way.

"Noise?" Crocket said as they got close enough to see well.

Redcloud got up from the digging and simply said, "Yeah, I heard you two as soon as you came around the corner."

Mitchell turned to look and from where they must be, it was around one hundred yards back. Now he was wondering if Redcloud was being truthful or if he was trying to play one of his head games on Crockett. He figured at this point it wasn't really important, so he just let it drop.

Redcloud had everything set up with his gang. They were already covering the holes with a bunch of sticks and brush. It really looked good. He turned to the men with him and quietly said, "You guys head back. We'll be in shortly."

As the two men who were with Redcloud headed back to the gate, Redcloud motioned for Crockett and Mitchell to follow him. He walked a little way from the wall going towards the northeast. Crockett and he followed and just a little way out, Redcloud stopped and got low. Crockett and he follow the lead and got down. It didn't take long for both of them to pick up on what Redcloud was doing. They could hear the noise of men working and now and then they heard voices, very low, talking in Spanish. There wasn't enough light to see, but Mitchell already knew what was going on. Santa Anna was setting up the second artillery battery.

They didn't stay long because there wasn't really much they could do about it right now. He tapped Redcloud on the shoulder and grabbed Crockett's arm. They both knew what he meant, and they all got up and quietly moved back towards the gate. As they got closer to the wall, Mitchell turned to Redcloud and asked, "How long have they been working?"

Redcloud looked back in the direction they had just come from and, without even a pause, he stated, "I believe they started right after sundown. About the same time we went out to dig the pits."

Crockett was pretty quiet the whole time they were at this end of the Alamo. Now he spoke, "Do you think they will be ready by morning?"

Now Redcloud stopped and looked back to think before he answered, "Probably, but if not by first light, I think they will start shortly after sunup."

When they were standing just outside the gate, Redcloud stopped Crockett and said, "You're probably going to hear a few things from your men." He paused a moment before he went on, "And, whatever they say is probably going to be true."

Crockett just stopped and leaned on his rifle and took a relaxed stance before he said anything. "Let me guess. It's gonna be about your negro soldier?"

"Yes," Redcloud immediately replied, "I put him in charge of setting up a place where we could set off the mines, and I assigned a couple of your men to work with him. There were some… ah, complaints, and I might have threatened some severe bodily damage if there was a problem."

Crockett chuckled a little and responded in a way neither Mitchell nor Redcloud hadn't expected, "Yeah, I believe it. All my men are southern born and bred. I can understand that for them to work for a negro would cause a bit of a problem." He stopped and then turned to Mitchell and asked, "Earlier you became furious when Travis called your man a nigger, but yet you say nothing about me calling him a negro. What do you call him?"

This took Mitchell aback a little. This was not a question Mitchell expected right now. After thinking a moment, he answered him, "In our time we call his people 'black' or African Americans." After a moment to think, he explained, "I...ah we, understand that in this time they call his people negroes. However, the term nigger was always used to insult and put down his people in both times."

Crockett thought about this for a moment before he asked, "And this is really important to him? To you?"

How could he explain a couple hundred years of cultural change in just a few minutes? He had found that Crockett was a very curious man, so he needed to respond so he could understand and that will satisfy his curiosity. He decided he needed to give a quick history lesson. "In our history, we freed his people from slavery. The institution of slavery ended about thirty years from now. This did not end the treatment of his people, though. Slowly, his people became accepted into society as equals. Their rights protected under the law." Mitchell stopped for this to set in his mind, but he seemed to accept was Mitchell was saying and continued to listen. Continuing, he went on, "In this time in history his people were called niggers to put his people down and to treat them as a lesser people. This continued to even my time." He now had to gather his thoughts, because this is important. "Throughout all this time, we had different ways to refer to his people. For a long while we called them 'Coloreds', but this was only to describe his race and still meant to keep them down. It was just another way to still kept them as being treated as different."

All this time Crockett continued to lean on his rifle and listen, with an occasional nod. Mitchell decided he needed to cut this short and get to the point, "The point is, through all this time and use of different words to describe his people the use of the word 'nigger' was always used to hurt and put his people down." He stopped and looked Crockett right in the eye and said, "It was always a hateful word used in a hateful way."

When he stopped talking, he thought Crockett would try to continue this conversation, but Mitchell really didn't want to go into this more right now. This was not the time or place to have this discussion. However, to his surprised Crocket just grunted and then picked up his rifle and headed through the gate.

Looking over at Redcloud, he just shrugged his shoulders, and they both followed him in. Mitchell guessed he had answered his question for now, but he still had a feeling this conversation was not over.

As soon as they got inside, Mitchell found Stretch working to fill some sandbags and set up a safe place where Redcloud could control the detonators, but very little actual work was done. The other men that were supposed to be working were all just standing around. One of them was the big guy that had the fight with Stretch. Crockett came to a stop just short of the place where Stretch was filling the sandbags. There was one man helping him, but Mitchell thought he was one of Seguin's men.

Crockett turned and handed his rifle to Redcloud. and went to Stretch and asked him, "What's your name?"

Stretch looked a little worried and glanced over at the Boss, who just nodded towards Crockett. He then replied, with a little shaky voice, "Private Johnson, Sir."

Crockett just stood there and said, "No, what is your name?"

Stretch took a moment to realize what Crockett was asking before he answered him, "Sir, my name is Milton Johnson, but they call me Stretch."

Crockett just nodded and said, "Yes, I can see that." Probably because Johnson stood a few inches taller than Crockett. He then extended his hand and said, "Give me that shovel."

As he handed the shovel to Crockett, Stretch looked over at Mitchell and again he just nodded to reassure him it was all Okay.

Crockett took the shovel and walked over to where his men were standing and threw it and the nearest one. The man tried to catch it but ended up letting it fall to the ground. Crocket just pointed at it and the man bent over and picked it up. Crocked then got right up in the face of the big guy that had the fight with Stretch. Mitchell couldn't hear everything he said, but when he stepped back, he spoke to the entire group. "I'm going to be back in one hour. If those sacks ain't filled and where Stretch says to put them, you're going to answer to me. He is in charge of this work, and you had better listen to him."

The big guy wanted to say something, but Crockett took two steps and was again face to face with the man. He quickly shut his mouth and thought again about saying anything.

After a moment, Crockett came back and took his rifle and walked away. While trying to cover a smile, Mitchell turned to Redcloud and said, "Make sure Jose has a couple of places set up for the detonators on his side. I'll check on Anna's area."

Redcloud smiled and leaned in close to say, "Yeah, I figured as much."

He wasn't sure what he was saying, and Mitchell guessed that the look on his face showed that. Redcloud continued, "Isn't that where your girlfriend is standing watch?"

Mitchell said nothing. He just turned around and as he walked away, he waved a dismissal at what his old friend said. However, he could hear Redcloud laughing as he walked off.

As he strolled back to check on Anna, he took time to relax a little. Mitchell figured he couldn't have been up for very long and it was already a long night. Other than the occasional firing of the cannons from the Mexican Army, it was really a quiet night when you take a moment to notice. As he walked, he was checking out everything.

He noticed one of Crockett's men still talking to Anna as he came up to her hummer. He thought it must be one man who was working with her to prepare the pits for the claymores. As he got closer, the man noticed him and immediately became very nervous.

Keeping his eyes on him, he asked Anna, "Is everything good?"

She looked at the young man and smiled, then said, 'Yeah Boss, everything is fine."

"Who are you?" Mitchell asked the young man,

He stood up straight before he answered, "I'm Peter Bailey."

"Aren't you one of Crockett's men?" He continued.

"Yes, Sir" He replied with a bit of pride.

"What are you doing here? Where are you supposed to be?" Mitchell demanded.

Now he could see Peter was a little nervous. The young man took a little sidestep and stuttered out, "Uh, I was just talking to Anna, Sir. I didn't mean no harm." He then took another sidestep and continued talking, "Uh, I'm assigned to the west wall, sir."

Mitchell didn't know if the young man could tell that he was trying to stifle a laugh, but Mitchell just continued to play the part. "Then don't you think you should get back to your watch?"

"Yes Sir." He said with a scared voice, then quickly turned and trotted off.

Anna leaned out the door and said, "Come on, boss, did you have to scare the shit out of him that way?"

He could tell in her voice that she thought it was a little funny as well. He couldn't hold it any longer and laughed. When he could talk again, he said to her, "We got a little puppy love going here."

This time it was Anna's turn to have a little fun poked at her. She jumped out of the seat in the hummer and walked around the back to watch young Peter leaving. "I don't know, Boss. He started following me around yesterday, but he never tried to talk to me until we put together this detail." She turned to continue watching him go while she kept talking, "He seam really nice and he has a college education, which in this time says quite a bit about him, I think."

This time it was Mitchell's turn for a little shock. He thought this might be the first person he'd met since he got here that really had some kind of education. Now he watched as the young man continued across the compound.

She continued to talk. "I think he might have volunteered to get on my crew. And then, once we got outside the wall, he stayed pretty close to me. It was really cute because I think he thinks he was protecting me."

Mitchell looked down and shuffled a little and then laugh again before he could say, "That boy's got a lot to learn."

This time Anna laughed a little too, saying, "Don't worry Boss, I'll teach him everything he needs to know."

Now he looked at her and couldn't help but to think this puppy love thing might be a two-way street.

He had to bring himself back to the business at hand. "You need to set up a spot to run the detonators."

Anna quickly turned back to him and was serious now. "I would love to, Boss, but the others are using all the sandbags we brought. I intend to run the wire into the hummer. I can't think of a safer place to put them."

He walked over to the wall. This part was so low he could see pretty good, just looking over it. Judging from the positions, he felt the wires should be long enough. Turning back to her, he said, "Sounds good, but if the wires aren't long enough, let me know and we'll see about repositioning the hummer."

"OK, Boss." She said and then looked up at the chapel area and said with a smile, "Looks like you got your own puppy lover to worry about."

He quickly turned and in the dim light he could barely see, but he could tell that Kat was leaning over and looking down at him. He waved, and she waved back. Turning back to Anna, she was just smiling at him. He quickly smiled at her and said, "I think mine has already gone past puppy love."

Turning away from Anna before she could make a comment, he headed off to the chapel. He climbed up the ramp and went over to Kat. She greeted him with a wonderful hug and a kiss. They then walked over to the wall where she was standing watch. Mitchell simply sat down in the dirt and leaned up against the wall while she sat on the edge. She was still a little jumpy each time there was a cannon shot, but she was handling it a lot better that when they first started. They didn't talk too much, and it wasn't long before he dozed off.

CHAPTER 13

Mitchell woke up to Kat shaking his shoulder. "Dear, please wake up." She whispered, but her voice showed an urgency to him.

He glanced around to get his bearings. Jumping up, Kate grabbed his arm and pointed out over the wall. It was still quite dark, but he thought it would not be long before the skies brightened. He couldn't see anything, but he could sure hear a lot. Troops were on the move. He grabbed her by the shoulder and quick said, "Go tell your father and keep a good watch on things."

As she did, he ran down the ramp and headed towards the west wall. Travis was already there, and he could also see Crockett heading to the same place. Coming up the ramp, Travis turned to him and asked, "Well Sir, is this an expected action?"

He tried to see what was happening, but it was still too dark. He listened carefully to see if he could determine what the Mexicans were doing. After a moment, he told Travis, "Yes Sir, as I recall Santa Anna made two or three attacks before the last attack. Our historians believe he is trying to feel out the defenses more than actually trying to take the Alamo down right now. Also, I recall he doesn't have his entire army here yet."

Travis said little for a while, but continued to listen, just as the rest of them did. However, after about a half hour, the sky was lightening, and Mitchell could make out some forms in the dark. By now, Travis had the entire crew there. Also, Mitchell had the Chief and Anna with him. He turned to both of them and asked, "Do either of you know much about what happens next?"

There was no actual answer, just the shaking of heads. Quickly he said, "Go get Blake. He had some education. Maybe he can remember what's going to happen."

As the Chief ran off, it occurred to him how funny that really sounded. To remember what is going to happen in the future. This brought a little smile out, but not for long.

"Mister Mitchell," Travis called without turning, "What do you think is going to happen?"

He started out with his standard disclaimer, "Like I said before, Colonel,"

However, before he could continue, Travis quoted his words back to him, "Yes, I know. You don't recall specific things. You do, however, have a general idea."

"Santa Anna," He started out, "will first try to hit us at a few points around the wall. We need to strengthen the wall where his forces attack without taking too much away from the defenses at other parts of the wall."

Travis never turned, and now he didn't even reply to what Mitchell said. Instead, he scanned the Mexican forces on the moved around the fort. They had helped Bowie to get up on the gun platform with them. After Mitchell's report, Bowie kept watching Travis. It looked like he was expecting orders to be given. However, when Travis just stood there watching the Mexican Army move, Mitchell thought Bowie got angry. After a little while, Bowie addressed Travis. "Are you going to do something or just stand here watching?"

Travis just kept scanning the Mexican Army as it moved to positions around the Alamo. Shorty, he lowered his looking glass and turned to Bowie. In a slow and sure voice, he said, "I will issue orders when we see what Santa Anna's plans are. It does not do us any good to run around guessing where he plans to attack.

Bowie said nothing, but they all looked up when cannon fire started from the northeast. It sounded like there must have been five or six shots fired in quick succession. Over his squad radio he heard Redcloud say, "Jim, I think they have the northern battery up and running."

Mitchell replied, "How bad?"

There was a brief pause before Redcloud responded, "Light damage. I think they are too far away right now."

He turned to Travis to relay that report. "I just heard from Sergeant Redcloud. I believe that northern battery is too far away and there is minor damage. However, I recall they will move this battery closer and become more effective on the north wall later."

Travis just nodded and as he turned back to watch the Mexicans move, he said, "Good. We will worry about that later, then."

Bowie looked at Crockett and Mitchell and just shrugged his shoulders while shaking his head. He, too, turned his attention back to the Mexicans.

Now that there was enough light, Mitchell brought out his binoculars. He, too, scanned the movement of the Mexican units. Mitchell could see what he thought were senior officers along the south wall and around the northwest corner. He took this as an indicator that this is where the focus of their attack was going to be. They were, however, spread around the entire compound, but there was a larger concentration at these two points. Over the radio, he said, "Chief, it looks like the northwest corner will be under attack. Blake and Jose, stay put to support that area." Continuing, "Stretch, I want you to move over and support Anna on the palisade. Anna, stay off the MG for now. Only use rifle fire. I want to keep that in reserve."

No one talked. He just got little static bursts as he called out the assignments. This was all he needed to know that they received and understood his orders. He continued to watch as the Mexicans continued to get their battle formations into place. After about half an hour, he approached Travis. "Sir," Mitchell said, "I am going to be on the palisades for this battle. I've got my men spread between the north wall and the south around the palisades. Sergeant Redcloud can direct the north wall group." When he didn't respond to him, Mitchell asked, "Is this satisfactory for you?"

Travis now turned around to say to him, "Captain, I am the commander here. I will direct the way this post is to be defended. Before you assign the people who came in with you, you will check with me first." This scolding took Mitchell aback, but then Travis drove his point home. "Is this understood, Mister?"

He tried to take it in stride. He took a step back and came to attention and rendered a proper salute, saying, "Yes Sir, understood."

Travis did not return his salute, but just tuned back to look out over the battlefield. Mitchell dropped his salute, not really expecting him to return the salute. As he recalled, Travis was not a real, trained officer. He looked around and found Bowie sitting on his chair nearby, shaking his head. Crockett had a look on his face that said he didn't agree with Travis, as he tilted his head to one side as he shrugged his shoulders.

Mitchell just slung his rifle over his shoulder and headed off to the camp area. He found Anna up on the hummer, but she had tuned the machine gun to the side, and she had her rifle ready for action. Looking up, he didn't see Kat, but he knew she was there. There were also more men, both up on the chapel roof with Kat and down on the palisades with Anna.

Before he to turn to head up on the Chapel, he noticed that young man had joined the group and had taken up a position near Anna. Walking over to the hummer, he motioned for Anna to lean over. When she did, he showed the young man and asked, "Is this your private protection?"

She just stood up with a smile and shrugged her shoulder. He thought she was enjoying the attention of the young man. He may have to deal with this, but he decided that this was going to have to wait until later. Now, he turned back to his original plan and headed up the ramp to the chapel.

Kat didn't see him when he came up. Her attention was on the Mexicans that were forming up right in front of her. There were several men around her, but none of them were really paying any attention to her. As he walked up to her, she finally saw him, and he could see her almost immediately relax.

When he got to her, he put his arm around her waist and gave her a brief hug. He thought that more than that might disrupt the men who had come up here to fight. However, none of them paid any attention to them at all.

The view of the battlefield was much better up here, and he could clearly see how Santa Anna had deployed his forces. Mitchell gave himself a nod because he believed his assessment was correct. Thinking back a few moments, he realized Travis must have thought so also, because after his dressing down, he didn't change a thing he had done. This thought brought a smile to his face. Kat saw it and tilted her head, almost ready to ask him about it, but he stopped her. "I'm going over to check in with your father." He said, "I'll be right back."

She dropped her arm from around him and leaned over and planted a kiss on his cheek. He quickly stiffened and looked around. He must have turned a little red because she just giggled a little. Again, no one seemed to notice at all.

He turned away and hurried the short distance to August. Most of the men that came up here were on the other side with Kat. There were some Mexicans on this side, but it was only a token force. Even if they got over the wall, there wasn't much they could do. As He walked up to August he said, "How are you doing over here, old man?"

Immediately, August became flustered. He yelled back at him, "What, old man? I've still got a lot of fight in me." And then he added, "And lots of experience."

Mitchell had reached him by the time he finished, and he placed his hand on August's shoulder and laughed a little. "Of this, I have no doubt." He said and patted his shoulder.

He quickly realized Mitchell was only teasing him, and he also laughed. Turning away, he looked out over the battlefield on this side. Raising his arm in a sweeping gesture, he said, "It doesn't look like there is going to be much of a fight on this side."

Mitchell didn't speak right away, but just nodded his agreement with him. Then, looking back over at Kat, he said, "Yeah, I think the fight is going to be over there." August turned to where he was looking, but Mitchell continued, "And on the north wall. These troops on this side are just to keep part of our men busy here."

August just nodded, but he kept looking over at his daughter. Mitchell now followed his gaze and again put his hand on August's shoulder to reassure him, "Don't worry. I'm going to be on the wall right next to her."

Looking back, right into his eyes, August slowly said, "Thank you."

Mitchell gave him a good slap on the shoulder and turned to walk away. As he walked back, he heard the bugles sound from the Mexicans. First it sounded in the town and then at different points around the Alamo. He picked up his pace and ran to the wall next to Kat.

Quickly, the command by the Mexican commanders and echoed down, just as with most all armies. The foot soldiers then moved forward. The men all around him were already aiming their rifles and getting ready to fight. He yelled out, "Hold your fire." As some of the head turned to look at him, I again yelled, "Let them get a little closer where we can hit them hard."

There were nods and yells of agreement as the men again prepared to fire, but they held off firing, for now.

Up on the wall, they had a clear view of the Mexicans as they moved forward. For Mitchell, he couldn't imagine men fighting in rows like this. Of course, he had read about this in all his schoolbooks, and he'd seen it in movies, but this was not the same. It was real now. The Mexican lines had reached about halfway to the palisades. It was clear this was the focus of their attack on this side. Already he heard shooting on the north and west walls. Slowly, he raised his rifle and took aim. No sooner than when he pulled the trigger, there was a barrage of fire from around him up on the chapel platform and from Anna's group down below.

The Mexicans continued to move forward, but with each step, more of their force fell. From here, he could see clearly as the men fell.

Most of them continued to move, but now they are wriggling in pain. Mitchell continued to shoot, and it suddenly became clear he could hear the difference between the sound of his rifle and the other men around him. He stopped for a moment to listen. He could tell all over the compound when his guys were firing. There was more difference, and to him, it sounded a little strange.

Intermixed with the rifle shots was cannon fire. All the while, the ground pounders in front of them continued to move forward. The attack went on a while longer, but the Mexican lines never really got too close. There was an occasional shot fired up at this part of the wall, however it didn't hit anyone. Looking over at Kat, she focused on the battle. She continued to load and fire. He couldn't tell if she hit anything, but knowing how good a shot she was, he assumed she had connected with some of those men.

It was a brief attack, from his point of view. The Mexican advance slowed and suddenly they were turning back. First, it was only a couple of those that were the closest, but then it turned into a mass retreat. Slowly, the firing stopped. There continued to be shots fired now and then but, mostly, the attack was over. Mitchell thought the surrounding men were all watching him. As he finally lowered his rifle, they too stopped firing. Quickly he sat down on the wall and spoke into the radio, "Report," was all he said.

The first to report back was Redcloud. "All is well here. They never got close."

Then, one by one, everyone checked in. Once the report was over, Blake came back on the radio. "Boss, is that it for today? Are they going to attack again?"

Mitchell keyed up his radio to say, "That's probably it for today. However, stay at your post for now and keep watch."

Blake responded, "Roger, Boss."

A thought just occurred to me him and Mitchell quickly added, "The Mexicans will probably come out to recover the dead and wounded. Hold your fire. Do not shoot at them. This is a more civilized time than we are used to."

Again, the only response was the static click on the radio that they all heard.

Now, he got off the wall and sat in the dirt and leaned his back against the wall. Kat didn't sit in the dirt, but kind of squatted down while leaning on her rifle. She had a curious look on her face when she asked, "You had to tell you men not to shoot at them as they took care of those who are hurt. Are thing that much different where you come from?"

It really hadn't occurred to him how much different things in battle were now. He didn't really know how to tell her this. He had to think a little before he tried to answer that. Slowly he said, "Yes, in my time, things have become less civilized in battle. Because sometimes the enemy would try to use times like this to get an advantage. Slowly, we stopped trusting the enemy to use this time to help their people."

She stood up and then sat on the edge of the wall and quietly said, "That is sad."

Mitchell had to agree with her. Slowly, he also stood up and told her, "I need to go check in with Travis and the others. You should be alright up here now."

She stood up next to him and took his hand. Raising it up, she gave it a kiss and then let him go. Reluctantly, he slowly turned and walked away. When he reached the top of the ramp, he tuned back and waved to her. She waved back as he went down, out of sight.

Mitchell found Travis near the north wall. He was talking with some men, so he just waited and listened. They were discussing the damage to the walls and there was more disagreement about how well they will hold up.

Travis mostly just listened and finally said to them, "Alright, do what you can to repair and reinforce the walls where needed."

The men all took a step backwards and turned and left. Travis turned around and saw Mitchell now. As Travis walked up, he saluted. This time, Travis returned it. He got very close before he spoke, "Is this all he has to offer. I think we can hold out for quite some time, if that is it."

"I don't believe so," Mitchell said in response, "If I recall correctly, Santa Anna doesn't have all his men here yet. Also," He continued before Travis could speak, "I believe he will have more artillery show up soon."

It was clear this reply was not what Travis wanted to hear. Shortly he asked, "What should we expect next?"

Just as he asked, the Mexican artillery, again, fired. This time from both the west and the northeast. Mitchell put a thumb up over his shoulder, indicating the cannon fire and said, "More of this."

Travis looked up and around, but he continued, "I think it will become more intense and continuous, day and night."

Travis said, "Yes, I see." More to himself than to anyone in particular.

Suddenly, there was a call from further down the wall, "Colonel Travis." Someone yelled.

Travis at the man that had called, and Mitchell followed his eyes. The man pointed towards the town. It took a moment to figure out what he was pointing at, but quickly Mitchell saw it. The famous red flag was now flying over a church in the town.

Mitchell figured Travis was not aware of the meaning of that flag. He asked the man who called him, "What does it mean?"

The man was obviously not from around here and said, "I have no idea, Colonel."

Then a Mexican man who was nearby spoke up and in broken English he said, "It means they will take no prisoners."

Travis just looked at the man and then back at the flag. He didn't say a word, but walked back down the ramp and looked to be headed back to his office. Now, Mitchell stepped up to the wall and looked out over the battlefield towards the town. He could see a group of Mexican officers gathered to watch the Alamo as the men of the Alamo watched them. Mitchell pulled out his binoculars to get a good close look at them. There was one officer in the middle and the other arrayed around him. He guessed the man in the middle was Santa Anna, because the other were talking to him.

He watched Santa Anna for a little while, but then their leader turned his horse and rode back into town, out of sight. Now Mitchell looked down on the battlefield again. He could see a bunch of soldiers out there. They were all holding their rifle down in a carry position. They slowly weaved back and forth around the bodies out there. Occasionally, one would bend over to check a body. Once in a while, they would stop and try to help a wounded man. A couple of them would get together and carry the wounded off the field.

What really surprised him, and he didn't know why, because he had always heard and read about it, but all the women and a couple of children were also going around looking at the dead. When they found their loved one, they would fall upon the body and hold it. Sometimes, he could see, they would find their loved one was just wounded and would get water and try to help him. It was a sad scene to watch. Mitchell dropped his glasses and looked up and down the wall. Many of the men here were also watching and he could already see deep sadness in their faces.

Mitchell didn't stay too long. Walking back down into the courtyard, he headed over to find the Chief. It didn't take long. He found Redcloud right where he should be. He was just sitting there, looking out at the same sad scene Mitchell had just left on the other wall. As they watched, a couple of carts showed up to take away the dead and wounded. Mostly it was women and children, but now and then a soldier would find a buddy and take care of his friend.

He and Redcloud just stood there in silence for a long time, watching. Finally, he had seen enough and came down off the wall. Redcloud followed him down and they found a quiet place to sit and talk.

Mitchell took a long drink from his canteen and passed it over to Redcloud, but he just waved it away. "How did the new guy do?" He asked.

Redcloud looked over that way and thought for just a moment before he answered me, "He did OK, I guess. I was a little busy myself, but he was right there, firing away. Can't say he hit anything, but he sure burned up some ammo."

Mitchell chuckled a little and said, "I suppose we all did our first time out. I'll go have a word or two with him."

Redcloud just looked at him and smiled before he said, "Speak for yourself. I never had any problems, even on my cherry fight."

Mitchell smiled back at him and as sarcastically as he could he said, "Oh yeah, I forgot. You're the perfect warrior."

Redcloud said nothing back to his comment. He just shot him a thumbs up and they both giggled a little. Then he asked, "How did August and Kat do?"

Proudly, he announced, "Kat was great. She stood her ground and continued to fight just as good as any of the men that were over there." Then he thought back for a moment before he continued, "I can't say about August. I didn't check on him before I left, however, his side shouldn't have had too much action."

Redcloud just grunted and nodded a little. He then laid back and closed his eyes. Mitchell was pretty sure he would not sleep, but just trying to recover and let the adrenaline level to come down. He stood up and announced, "I'm going to check in on Blake and Jose, then head back to the camp."

Again, Redcloud said nothing. All Mitchell got was a grunt to recognize he had said something. So, he just left him there and headed over to Blake's position.

He found Blake still down behind the wall, still in a firing position. As he approached, Johnny turned his head and waved his trigger hand, but never got out of the shooting position. Mitchell supposed he was still feeling the adrenaline rush, so he tried to act as calm as he could, because he also was still feeling it a little.

"Hey," Mitchell called out to him, "you can relax now. The battle is over for today. In this time, they have an unwritten rule that they can come and clear the field of their dead and wounded."

The soft tone that he used with Blake seamed to relax him a little. He fell back away from the wall into a sitting position and hung his head down. Mitchell couldn't tell for sure, but he thought he might even be crying a little.

Mitchell sat down with his back against the wall and facing Blake. Quietly he asked, "Are you OK.?"

Again, he didn't speak, but look at him and nodded.

After waiting for a reply, he just continued to talk quietly, "It's a little different from what you thought it would be, isn't it?"

Blake raised his head and looked around to see if anyone was watching them before he said, "Yeah, boss. I think I came really close to pissing my pants."

At first, he wanted to laugh, but Mitchell could see he was serious, so he continued to get him to talk. "We all have had that problem the first time out, but the next time you should be good."

Now Johnny looked right at him and asked, "Did you have this problem the first time you got into a fight?"

Mitchell had to dig back a little to remember his first combat action. Slowly, he recalled that time. "It was not quite the same as this." When Johnny didn't interrupt him, he continued to tell his story. "I was on a recon patrol. We were searching a group of buildings, trying to find the Taliban. My team got pinned inside a home and surrounded. We called in an air strike for support. Within a few seconds, the fighting stopped all around us. The exploding rounds from the Warthog just tore them up. The sound of the air assault was beyond belief. I crouched in the corner and tried to hide my face. When it was over, we came out to find bodies and parts of bodies all over the place."

He stopped and took a drink before he went on. "The smell was already something else. I immediately fell to my knees and puked my guts out." Mitchell said with a little chuckle. Then seriously, he said, "The guys I was with had no mercy. They started laughing at me and making fun. It took me a long time to live that down, but it helped to fortify me for future battles."

Blake just sat there looking at him as he told his story. Mitchell thought he saw a little smile when he told him about the puking. He leaned in a little and as seriously as he could, he told him, "Now, if you tell anyone about this, you'll never live long enough to regret it."

From the look on Mitchell's face, Blake couldn't tell if he was serious or pulling his leg. So, Mitchell just let it sit like that. He had more important thing to talk over with him anyway, "I need to talk to you about control. The Chief says you were going through a lot of ammo. How many mags you got left?" He asked.

He looked down at his gear before he realized he was out. Blake said, "I'm on my last mag."

Mitchell looked down at his vest to show him he still had two full mags, plus he had most of the one that was still in the rifle. Mitchell let him think a moment before he went on, "I only use a little over one mag and I was up on the south wall where the other side of the attack was. You gotta keep control, even when you're scared. Remember, I told you, you're only supposed to use two mags in each battle. You wasted a lot of ammo today." After letting that set in for a moment, he told him, "Don't worry. You'll be fine from now on. Your cherry was busted today so you're now a veteran, just like the rest of us."

He sat up straight now and focused again. Then Mitchell quickly said, "Now, police up your mags and brass."

"Brass?" he said questionably.

"Yeah, the brass. We don't have an unlimited supply of ammo. In the future, we may have to figure out how to reload them."

He looked down at his position. The mags were all there and easy to spot. His brass, however, was something else. The mags were important, but the brass, not so much. Mitchell was using this, hoping that keeping him busy like this will help him relax a little.

As he got up to leave, Blake was already picking up. Mitchell gave him a wave as he turned and said, "Just relax for now. I'll check in with you again later."

Blake looked up, smiling, and Mitchell could see he was already relaxing. He said, "OK Boss. I'm good."

He left Blake behind, and he couldn't find Jose right now, so he headed back towards their camp. As he approached, he found Anna, again talking with that kid that was part of Crockett's crew. This time, he didn't go right over to her. He went into their camp area. Someone had a pot of something that smelled pretty good cooking over the fire. He grabbed his kit out of his tent and scooped some kind of goo out and sat down to eat. Whatever it was, didn't look very appetizing, but it smelled good. He scooped up a spoon full and tasted it. It was a bit like tasting vanilla. It smells great but tastes really awful. He was, however, starving, so he ate it.

After Mitchell finished, he looked back over at Anna. She was still talking with that young man. He thought to himself that it is a shame he'd have to break up this little lover's encounter, but he needed his sergeant back and focused on business. He cleaned up his kit and put it back in his tent before he went over to talk to Anna. To keep it on a professional level, he called out as he approached, "Sergeant Wilson, report."

She had had her back to Mitchell and spun around. He saw a little red in her face. It was at this moment that he was pretty sure that the puppy love was a two-way street. She quickly straightened up and was a little shaky when she spoke. "Uh Boss," she had to pause a moment to get her thought together before she continued, "We are all ok here. There were no injuries and PFC Johnson did great."

Just to point out he had noticed the little thing going on here, he asked, "I see you got some support. Was it enough?"

She turned to her new friend and then back to him before she answered, "Yeah, we were able to keep them away from us. There was no real danger."

"I see." He said, nodding towards her friend.

Again, she got beet red and looked down. As they talked, her friend had turned away and was pretending to keep watch out over the wall. Mitchell took it down a notch to tell her, "I think this is probably it for today, Anna. Santa Anna was just trying to feel out our defenses. They will take a day or two to recover the dead and wounded and make new plans before they try it again."

Now she visibly relaxed a little and her friend had turned to watch what they were doing and talking about. He took a step towards them and asked, "Captain, do you really think we have a chance against all those Mexicans?"

"Son," He started out to keep it relaxed, "I know we have an excellent chance to even win this war right here."

He took a couple more steps to get closer and in a low voice, "Anna…uh Sergeant Wilson," he kind of shuddered a little not wanting to show his familiarity with her, "tells me you might know what is going to happen, and that it is not good."

Oh boy, how does he explain how things work. He tried to explain things to Crockett, and he acted like he understood, but Mitchell wasn't really sure he understood all the little things that go along with it. Mitchell remembered Anna said this boy has some education. Even as educated as he was, comparatively, he's not even sure about things. He thought right now is time to avoid the question, "Is this your normal watch?"

He kind of stiffened up like he thought he should stand at attention as he replied, "Yes Sir, I swapped my watch, so Anna and I could have time together."

Mitchell was seeing how serious this was. He needs to talk to Anna in private before this goes too far. He ducked the question for now and get rid of the young man. "Well, you can take the rest of the men and report back to your assigned station." After a momentary pause, he added, "We'll have time later to sit down and talk about things. It's way too complicated to explain right now."

At first, he slumped when Mitchell told him to leave, but then when he told him they'd talk later, he was all excited again.

He called to the other men and motioned them it was time to go, but as he walked past Anna, he paused and after a quick glance at Mitchell he said to her, "I'll come back after our watch is over to see you, if that is ok."

Anna smiled at him and answered, "That would be great."

He then hurried past him and headed off to wherever he should be. Mitchell watched him go and then turned back to her. He came up close to her and leaned up against the hummer before he asked, "How serious is this thing with him?" pointing in the direction the young man had just run off to.

Anna looked down and shrugged her shoulders as she answered, "I'm not sure, boss. He is really cute and very nice. He also has some education, so he's easy to talk to."

Mitchell realized he really hadn't thought about this much. Given their situation, he supposed this was about to happen, eventually. "How much have you told him about us?" He asked her.

"Not really too much," she answered. "Oh, he has figured out something is different about us." She said as she motioned to the hummer, "But I didn't explain about the time travel stuff. Shit, I wouldn't know where to begin."

He thought for a moment and then asked, "How does he know I can tell the future?"

She laughed slightly, saying, "It's not so much you can tell the future, but that you understand the situation and can read a battlefield better than anyone else."

"Oh," He smiled back, "it's a good thing that I didn't explain things to him then."

They both laugh at that thought, but then he asked her, "Is this going to develop into something I need to worry about, and do I have to polish up my explaining skill for later on?"

She put her head down. Again, and then looked up at him with her eyes, "It's possible. Hell, you've got Kat and I'm still much younger. I am thinking I might need someone like that, and he can at least talk to me almost at my level."

He had to agree with her logic. He hadn't considered the side effects when he started his relationship with Kat, but they were turning out alright. The other good point she was making is, they are all stuck here and are going to have to live out the rest of their lives here. No one wants to be alone.

He leaned forward and pride himself up off the hummer. Then turning he gave her a nod and a smile, "Ok, but don't tell him too much until we see how far this is going to go." he then walked away, but turn back to add, "I don't know about the much younger." Putting the emphasis on 'much'.

She put her fists on her waist and gave him an evil stare. However, he just smiled and continued to walk away.

Heading up the ramp, he saw Kat over in her area. She looked up to see him as he waved, but he showed he was heading over to talk to her father. She waved back at him, and they continued to look at each other as he walked.

When he got close to August, there was a lump in the dirt, and he tripped and stumbled a little. August had apparently been watching him and laughed out loud. When Mitchell recovered, he must have been a little red in the face because this caused him to laugh even more.

"You need to watch where you're going, boy," He said and quickly added, "not watching those pretty girls."

Trying to recover a little dignity, he replied, "But she is so beautiful, it is almost impossible to do that."

He stopped laughing and looked over at his daughter with a fatherly smile and just said, "This is true, very true."

Now it was Mitchell's turn to take a little dig at him. He stepped up near him and with just enough volume so the surrounding men could hear, he said, "I see for an old man, you did well today."

All flustered, he yelled back, "What do you mean, old man?"

Now it was his turn to laugh. This time, he wasn't the only one laughing. A few of the surrounding men laughed a little, too. August quickly turned and gave them a furious look. They all quickly stopped laughing and turned back to their watches.

August then turned his angry look back to Mitchell, but he just stood there smiling. He was quite the actor. He quickly dropped the angry look and, after a quick glance at each side, he smiled back at him and gave him a wink.

Now Mitchell stepped up to the wall and looked out. Because these soldiers were on the opposite side of the Alamo, there were only a couple of live soldiers walking around to check on the downed men. Luckily, there were only a few down. This side didn't have the rich target environment that they had on his side, so there were fewer casualties. Still, dead men are dead men.

August's first thought was of Kat. "How did Katherine do?" he asked as his gaze turned toward her.

Mitchell followed his gaze and while they were both watching her, he told him, "She was great, Sir. She stayed and fought, just like all the men on the wall. She never once flinched."

August's chest came out, and he immediately swelled up with pride.

Mitchell added, as he turned back to him, "You did an excellent job of raising her. She is quite the lady."

He wasn't sure, but he could swear he saw a tear in August's eye. He quickly brought his hands up and rubbed his eyes, like he would if he were trying to get a speck of dirt out of it.

Mitchell didn't know what to say, so he just smiled and turn his attention back to watching Kat.

"Excuse me, Captain." someone said from right beside him. Mitchell jumped because he hadn't realized there was anyone there. When he turned, the man continued to say, "Uh, sorry Sir. Should we expect another attack today?"

Mitchell stood and placed his hand on the man's shoulder and turn to look back out onto the battlefield. "No," He said, "I think not. He will need to recover his wounded and dead and make new plans."

The man gave a quick half nod, half bow and turned back to relay what Mitchell had said to the others that had been watching.

It didn't take long for the compound to get back to what was pretty much normal. Mitchell stayed with August for a little while and after most of the men put up there for the attack left, he moved over to sit with Kat.

They didn't really talk for a while. Just watched as the Mexicans came out with carts and wagons to clear the field in front of them. It was a grim sight, indeed. What was worse, to Mitchell at least, was the sound of the wounded men as they moved them to put in a wagon. It was not what he would call a gentle move. They would just grab the wounded man at each end and lift him and, not so gently, swing him up onto the wagon. The closer ones, he could even hear the thump as hit the wagon. Another wagon just piled the dead men into it at the same time. It would slowly move along as they piled more and more of the dead men in. Once the wagon was full, it headed off into town. After that, he couldn't see what was happening, nor did he want to.

After a while of watching this gruesome sight, Mitchel just turned his back to it and slid down the wall to sit in the dirt. This time, Kat joined him and put her arm through his and laid her head on his shoulder.

After a long time of just sitting there in silence, Mitchell finally spoke. "You know, I think as soon as this battle is over, we should get married as soon as possible."

She didn't move, except to tighten her grip on his arm. Soon her breathing slowed into a smooth rhythm that told him she was sleeping. He didn't move and just let her sleep.

Shortly, a man came up to Mitchell saying, "Beg your pardon, Sir,"

He stopped, waiting for Mitchell to acknowledge he was speaking to him. Quietly, in a whisper, he replied, "Go ahead."

Now the man bent lower and copied the whisper like speech, saying, "Colonel Travis would like to see you, at your earliest convenience."

"Very well." He replied, and the man quickly turned and left. Mitchell wasn't really sure about the niceties of this time, but he was guessing because that man was sent to fetch him, it meant for him to get his butt over there ASAP.

Mitchell looked down at Kat and her head had slumped down onto his chest. Slowly, he raised her head. This brought her back, and she finished lifting her head to look into his eyes. Bending his head down, he gave her a gently kiss and said, "Travis has sent for me. I need to leave for a while."

Quickly she sat up as it just occurred to her where she was. She immediately turned a bright red, and picking up her rifle, she stood up. "Yes, of course." She said in a formal business manner, as she looked around at the others on the wall.

Mitchell looked around also, but no one was paying any attention to them. Mostly, they were still watching the activity outside on the battlefield. Turning away as he stood, so he could smile without her seeing him, He also stood up, although, a little more slowly.

"I don't know how long I'll be, but they might relieve you from your watch before I get back."

She didn't really answer him directly. She just nodded and smiled while she continued to look at the other men around them.

Stepping forward, Mitchell put his arm around her waist and pulled her to him. He looked down into her eyes and said, "Don't worry about those other men. They will say nothing. If they were to say anything, it would be how jealous they are of me, because of how beautiful you are."

Again, she turned red, and shyly she put her head down turned slightly back and forth. She didn't say anything back, however, when she finally looked up at him, he kissed her. This time, it was a deep, passionate kiss. When it was finished, she stepped back and took a deep breath. Quickly, she looked around, as did he. Now a few of the men were watching them. As the two of them looked, the men's faces all broke into smiles and they quickly turned away.

Mitchell didn't really know what he expected, but what he got was not it. Quickly, she pushed him back and picked up her rifle. As she turned back to look out, she sternly said, "You had better go before you are late."

He just picked up his rifle and just before turning to leave, Mitchell said, "Yea Ma'am." Then turned and, hurrying away, almost at a run, he left. However, just before going down the ramp, he turned back and waved to her. He figured he wasn't in too much trouble because she waved back, just before he went out of sight.

Mitchell found Travis up on the same gun platform he usually found him on. Both Bowie and Crockett were also there. This time he was sitting on the wall with his back to the town. He could hear them talking as he came up the ramp, but he could not make out anything they were saying. As he stepped closer, Mitchell could see a little drawing in the dirt. There was no mistaking it, the drawing was of the Alamo.

As he stepped up, Mitchell announced himself by saying to Travis, "You wished to see me, Sir."

He hadn't bothered to salute this time, and he didn't believe Travis even realized this little slip. He just continued on and pointed to the drawing asked, "What is going to happen next?"

Mitchell looked at the other who were also there. They, too, waited for him to answer. He decided it was time. Time to fill them in on what he knew. He looked around and there were quite a few men gathered to hear them. He looked at Travis and asked' "Sir, could we have a bit if privacy?"

Travis was taken aback at first, then looking around, Mitchell believed he understood the necessity for the other men not to be there when he continued. He called out, "Sergeant-major."

From just behind him came the reply, "Sir."

Travis then ordered, "Kindly post this area."

"Sir," the sergeant-major replied and immediately started yelling at the men to clear the area. Once all the men were out, he took up a spot a little way down the ramp.

Mitchell noticed he was still close enough to hear, but he guessed at this point it really didn't matter if he knew what was coming. "OK gentlemen," Mitchell started out, "I believe the time has come to tell you what I know happened." Watching he saw Crockett move in closer and although Bowie couldn't move his chair, he also leaned in as far as he could. Travis, however, moved a little and only leaned slightly closer. "Right now, there are men up on the Brazos River trying to put together a government for Texas. I don't know about now, but in the future, it will be known as 'Washington, on the Brazos.' Houston is trying to raise an army to fight Santa Anna. The men here at the Alamo are giving these men the chance they need to give Texas a proper start by holding up Santa Anna. In my day, from the day Santa Anna arrived until the day the Alamo fell, was thirteen days. It was reported that someone said that was thirteen days in the life of Texas." He stopped at this point to let that positive side set in before he gave them the bad side.

Looking around, Mitchell saw in their faces what he expected to see. A bit of pride and agreement on what they were doing here. However, no one spoke. Now he had to give them the other side. "I don't remember exactly, but there were some attacks before the thirteen days were up. Maybe three or four attacks. None of them could breach the walls here. There were mostly trying to find the weak spots to set up the final attack. The final attack came early in the morning on the thirteenth day. I think the battle lasted less than an hour and, in the end, they killed all the defenders of the Alamo, either in battle or by firing squad after the battle was over. There was only a hand full of survivors. In the Alamo, Captain Dickinson's wife and children, I think some other women and the slaves. All others perished here."

Again, he stopped and again, what he saw on their faces was exactly what he expected. Their pride in being here was now mixed with the realization that they would die. Now looking up at Travis Mitchell said, "Sir, because of what happened the first day with our counterattack, I am afraid we have lost one of our best weapons, knowledge. From that point on, I could no longer tell you what was going to happen. All I can do is give you my best guess from what I know and my battle experience."

Travis sat back now but said nothing more than, "Continue."

Mitchell looked around at Bowie and Crocket before he continued. Their look of worry quickly changed to a look of curiosity. It was Bowie that actually spoke up, "What is it now that you think you can do for us?"

Looking over at him first, he said, "Well Jim, we still have knowledge of what he plans to do, even though how he plans it may change some. We also have superior weapons, some that you haven't even seek in action, yet." This got Travis leaning back into the discussion again. "As for what is going to happen. I believe that Santa Anna will still follow his basic plan. As I recall, he doesn't yet have all his forces here. He will work to surround the Alamo. He will still have minor attacks, and" just to emphasize what he was going to say next, the Mexican artillery just then fired again, "he will keep up with the bombardments, day and night."

When Mitchell stopped, Travis sat back to think for a moment, then he asked, "And what do you recommend we do?"

He didn't want to sound like they were giving up, but all he could say was, "Basically, nothing." However, before they could jump up and kill him, he held up his hands to stop them and then clarified what he meant. "I believe our original plan is still sound. We defend the same way we did today. We take out his artillery. And, we, I mean I, watch for changes that would show he is going to attack before day thirteen."

They all seemed to think a little, but Mitchell continued, "We basically follow the plan we had. The only change is we need to be a little more alert than before." Then, looking at Travis, he added, "And I need to have full command of my people to deploy them as I see fit. That is what we agreed on when I first came to you."

He could see in Travis' face that this did not sit well with him. However, it was Bowie that spoke up first, "I have to agree with Jim here. We do not know how to use him and his people. They got stuff we've never even dreamed of and couldn't possibly understand how to best use them in such a short time." After he finished, Bowie sat back and added with a smile, "Besides with such a noble name like Jim, how could he be wrong?"

Crockett immediately chuckled; however, Mitchell was afraid the humor was lost on Travis. He stood and reluctantly said, "Agreed, however, I would appreciate you keeping me informed about what you are doing."

"Agreed." He replied to him. Travis then walked away.

Now Mitchell got up from his squat and went over and sat on the wall. He looked at the two of them and it was so obvious. He had to say, "OK, ask me."

It was Bowie who spoke first. He leaned forward in his chair and flat out asked it, "How did I die?"

He thought about it a little. He figured it didn't really matter now. Things are going to change, hell they're already changing. He decided it wouldn't really hurt to let them in a little. "Jim," He said, emphasizing his name, "you are going to die in bed. In my time, it was not clear if you were injured or fell sick before Santa Anna got here, but you weren't able to get out of bed. It was reported that the Mexicans broke into your room and killed you, however, you took a few of them with you. You didn't give up without a fight."

He sat back and after a moment he said, "Strange. Even though you weren't here in your time, in both times I was injured and laid up."

Mitchell thought about that for a moment. He knew was right. Hearing him say it, Mitchell now had a stronger belief that time has a way of correcting things, or at least trying to correct things they messed up. Then Crockett brought him back by asking, "And what about me?"

"Your story is a bit more complicated." He started out, "No one is really sure what happened to you. Some say you died fighting and were one of the last to be killed. Some believe you were captured and killed in a firing squad. There was a report by one of Santa Anna's junior officers that says you were taken alive and sent back to Mexico, where you were paraded in front of the Mexican people and eventually tortured to death."

He stood up, saying, "That sounds frightful."

Bowie then asked, "What about Travis?"

Mitchell had to think for a moment to remember exactly what he heard about Travis. "It was reported he died. I believe, he was shot in the head. He was on the north or west wall and died within a few minutes of the start of the battle on the thirteenth day."

Bowie then sat back and gave a quick laugh before saying, "Well, what do you know? I would have bet the prissy little colonel would have run off and pissed his pants."

They all laughed a little at Bowie's comment, however when he turned to look around, Mitchell found the sergeant-major was staring at them with a stern look on his face. He quickly stifled his laugh and then made a little cough and showed to Crockett and Bowie that he was listening.

Crockett just turned and looked, but didn't say anything. Bowie made a dismissing wave with his hand and grunted.

Mitchell figured it was now a good time for him to leave. Trying to be gracious about it, he said, "Gentlemen, if you will excuse me, I need to go have words with my Sergeant to see what he thinks about the situation." However, before they could say anything, he pivoted and walked past the Sergeant-major.

He couldn't tell for sure, but Mitchell thought there was a bit of a scowl on his face as he walked by. However, he just kept on walking and acted like he noticed nothing. Walking over to the north wall, he looked for the Chief, but he didn't see him anywhere. Looking around, he saw Blake still sitting in a fighting position, but Redcloud was nowhere to be found.

Walking up to one local on the wall, he asked, "Have you seen my sergeant lately?"

When the man turned and saw it was him, and quickly stood up to answer, "Yes Sir, He was just over there a little while ago. I didn't see where he went off to."

Answering with a quick, "Thank you." He turned to walk away. Figuring Redcloud must have headed back to their camp, so he started back that way. When he was well into the compound area, he heard a voice yelling, "You lookin' for me?"

Turning around, he saw it was Redcloud, so he stopped and walked back towards him. When he was close enough to talk without yelling, he asked, "Where you been?"

"Well, if it is any of your business," Redcloud paused and took a quick glance around before he finished, "I had to go take a shit."

"Oh." was the only thing Mitchell could think to say.

After what seemed like a long, awkward pause, he continued, "I think we need to talk about the plans. Grab your stuff and meet me back at the camp."

Redcloud looked down at his rifle and, picking it up, said, "I got everything. Let's go."

When he reached Mitchell, they both headed back to camp in silence.

When they got to their area, Mitchell stowed his gear and sat near the fire. It was mostly out by now, so he threw a couple of small logs on the fire and fanned it back to life. He had been in Texas for many years, on and off, during his career, but he still had a hard time thinking that it can still get cold here.

Redcloud joined him and, after warming his hands in the fire, he asked, "Did you speak to Blake about burning through the ammo?"

"Yeah," Mitchell said, "but I really don't know if it will do any good. He's young and inexperienced. We are too thinly spread out to sit someone next to him. I think that if this is still a problem, the next time I'll cut down the number of mags we give him. That might teach him to control his fire better."

Redcloud only grunted his agreement.

Leaning back, Mitchell felt it was time to discuss their plans. "Do you still think we should set up the claymores this early?"

"Difficult to make that call." Redcloud responded. "I still think we need to wait to use them for the main attack later."

"Agree," He replied, "but when do we set them up? If wait, we can't be positive when the main attack with come. If we set them up now and don't use them for these little attacks, they may get damage and we are very limited, especially with the wires."

Redcloud sat there for quite a while. Mitchell could see he was running through everything in his head, so he didn't interrupt his thoughts. Finally, Redcloud said, "If were up to me, I think I would wait until after at least one more attack. After the attack, we wait until they clear their dead and wounded and then go out at night." He paused there, but then continued before Mitchell could say anything, "I also think the key thing to watch will be the cannons at my end. Once they move closer to where they will have a more effective shot at the wall, it will tell us when he is getting ready for the main attack."

Mitchell considered everything he said. "OK, then we watch the cannons to the northeast," He cautiously said, but then added, "and hope the timeline hasn't changed too much."

Redcloud had taken out his canteen and as he took a sip, and grunted an agreement. After they settled that business, they both just sat there in silence and Mitchell allowed his brain to rest a little, as best he could, between the Mexican artillery fire, anyway.

CHAPTER 14

Over the next few days, Santa Anna continued to move his men to surround the Alamo as they arrived. Travis also followed the history that Mitchell remembered and sent out dispatches. The men of the Alamo continued the work to reinforce the defenses here. There were a couple of small engagements, but nothing substantial. However, more importantly, there were no real casualties. So far, history was remaining as true as Mitchell could remember it.

On the twenty-eighth, Santa Anna sent a messenger to Travis saying that he would allow women and children to leave and be escorted to the nearest town. Mitchell remembered that many took advantage of this and evacuated the Alamo. This was a major change. Now, only a couple of women left and agreed to take all the children with them. All the other women refused to leave. Some had even taken up arms to fight beside their men. Mitchel truly believed this was a direct result of Anna's fight with Bowie and her training with them. The rest took over the cooking and set up a hospital area in the chapel. He couldn't say for sure if this was a positive move or not. For some, it added a stronger resolve to protect the women, while others found it distracting to having them here and became more focused them than the battle.

The next day, a group of men got through Santa Anna's lines and rode into the Alamo. They were not the expected relief from Fannin, but men from another nearby town. With them came that bad news that Fannin would not be coming.

Once the word spread about Fannin, Travis came looking for Mitchell. "Is this what happened in your time?" he asked.

Mitchell nodded and said, "Yes Sir, Fannin could not even get a mile from his post when weather and equipment failures force him to turn around."

Travis took a couple of steps to get face to face with him and asked, "And you still think we can survive this?"

Without a moment of hesitation, he looked Travis right back in his eyes and simply answered, "Yes Sir, I do."

They stood there a moment, looking eye to eye. Mitchell guessed he saw what he was looking for because Travis simply turned and walked back to his office.

Now, he needed to find Redcloud. He felt the time was getting near, and he need to hear his assessment of the situation. He found him in camp. Redcloud was eating whatever it was in the pot. Mitchell had become a little more careful about digging unknown food out of that pot.

He sat down next to Redcloud and, leaning in, he kind of whispered, "I believe the time is getting near."

"Agreed," he said once he swallowed a mouth full of food, "but the cannons at my end haven't moved yet."

"Yeah," He said while still thinking, "but how can we be sure they will move?"

Redcloud set his plate down and leaned closer so it was only Mitchell that could hear him. "I guess we will never be sure about anything. I think you and me, and even Blake, need to keep a very careful watch on things from now on."

Mitchell had to agree with him. They can't be certain about anything. Even if things happen the same, the number of days may have changed, or Santa Anna's battle plan may have changed. There was the idea that he got from Bowie's status. The timeline will try to correct anything they do. It then hit him full force as he whispered to his best friend, "You're right. Everything we are doing here might change the battle, but the end results would try to stay the same."

Now Redcloud spoke up. "I don't believe that. We must still follow our plan and do everything we can to make the changes we want to happen." He said and then, calming a little, he added, "Or we just pack our things and get the hell out of here now, to save our asses."

When he added his final thought, Mitchell looked up at him and thought how running away didn't set will with him. He felt running or fighting didn't matter. Things were going to happen no matter what they do. Their best hope was that they could make enough of a change to give their future world a better chance of survival.

"I guess we're stuck between the proverbial rock and a hard place." He said while looking back down at the ground.

"Dammed if we do and dammed if we don't situation." Redcloud said and then chuckled but continued, "You want to see who can figure out the most old saying from our time that applies?"

At first, Mitchell just smiled, but when he looked up at him and he had this silly child like look on his face, Now Mitchell just had to laugh, and laugh he did. It was a good laugh. It helped to relieve the pressure of the negative things he was thinking and brought him back to the here and now. "Let's just continue to march with our plan and see what happens."

"You got it, Boss." was all the Chief said back. This gave Mitchell a little reassurance about their plan.

A couple days later, the Chief woke Mitchell up to tell him, "Santa Anna has moved his artillery closer."

Crawling out of his sack, he could see it was still early in the morning. Mitchell went over to the water barrel and splashed some cool water on his face to wake up. Looking around, it didn't appear that this made much difference to the locals. Only Redcloud, himself, and maybe Blake knew what this meant.

He quickly told Redcloud to grab his rifle and several rounds for the grenade launcher and to meet him on the gun platform where

Travis always took up his position. "While you're getting ready, I'm going to inform Travis about this and what it means."

Redcloud just nodded and headed over to the wagon, where they kept their ammo. Mitchell grabbed his gear and took off for Travis' office.

When he entered the outer room, the adjutant stopped him. Some captain, but he couldn't remember the man's name. "I need to speak to Colonel Travis." He said, but when the captain didn't move fast enough, I added, "It's urgent."

Mitchell guessed this got his attention, and he ducked into Travis' office and quickly came back out. "Go on in." The captain said to him.

He found Travis was just finishing shaving, so he stood back, trying to remember about the niceties of this time. I said, "Beg your pardon, Sir. There have been some important developments."

Travis tuned to look at him as he wiped his face and motioned for Mitchell to sit in the chair opposite his desk. He quickly moved to sit as Travis came over to his chair and sat. "What is it?"

"Well Sir," He started, "Santa Anna has moved his artillery closer on the northeast side."

Travis set down the towel and simply said, "Yes, I know."

Mitchell looked down into his lap before he spoke again. Looking up at him, he adding to his report, "This signifies the start of the final battle."

Now he had Travis' attention. "Go on."

Mitchell had to pause to best think how to inform him of what was… is to happen. "He will pound the north wall in attempting to weaken it." He started out, "Then through the night, he will quietly move his men into position around us. They will slowly sneak up and before light, they will attack."

Now he had the full attention of Travis. "What are your plans, then?"

Now Mitchell stood up and leaned over his desk where there was a map. Pointing out his plan as he spoke it and went into more detail,

"First, using the cover of our artillery, Sergeant Redcloud will take out a few cannons, both in the town and those to the northeast."

He stopped at this point to see if Travis wanted to ask anything. But, when he said nothing, Mitchell just continued, "We will do a little throughout the day to not alert Santa Anna. Then,"

Now he interrupted with a question, "What do you mean alert Santa Anna?"

"Sir," He said to keep this a formal matter, "the sound of this weapon firing will sound a lot different from the cannons of this time, and if we destroy all his artillery with just a few rounds, he will become suspicious. We need Santa Anna to think we are destroying his cannons with our cannons." He paused, and Travis just nodded to continue. "Second, I need him to think that Captain Dickenson is a much better shot than his men. This will demoralize his men, I hope."

Travis was developing a little smile as he realized the simple plan he was laying out. "Please continue."

"We will fire our cannon at the same time Redcloud shoots his grenade launcher."

"His what?" Travis asked.

"It is a weapon that fires a small but deadly round. It is deadlier than one of your smaller canons, but with a great deal more accuracy. Once zeroed in, he should be able to take out as many cannons as we want."

"I see," Travis replied, and motioned for him to go on.

"We will switch back and forth between his two batteries and take out a couple canon on each." He said, but then to emphasize the plan, he added, "Just to weaken him." Before he could question him, Mitchell quickly went on. "Tonight, as soon as it is dark, we will go outside the walls and set up those mines I told you about. That shouldn't take over fifteen minutes to maybe a half hour. So even if he doesn't attack tomorrow morning, we will still be ready for him."

Travis just sat there and lit up a cigar. Then he offered one to Mitchell, who nodded a thanks but showed a no. He then stood up and leaning on his desk, looking down at the map he said, "I believe I remember you saying it was thirteen days before the final attack." He then took a long drag on his cigar and asked, "it has only been eleven days. When will the attack be, tomorrow or two days from tomorrow?"

As Mitchell sat back down, he quickly had to reassure him, without committing to ether day. "Sir, if you will remember, I can't be positive about anything, because we changed things. To the best of my reading of the situation, I say he is going to attack before morning, tomorrow. Maybe the next day,"

Travis took a few more puffs from his cigar while he thought about things. Mitchell could see in his face he had come to a decision. Standing, he called, "Captain Baugh, come in here, if you please."

The captain came right in. Mitchell thought he may have been listening right outside the door, he was so quick. He snapped to and simply said, "Sir."

Travis ordered, "Have Colonel Bowie and Crockett come in here as well as Captain Dickenson."

Another, "Sir" and the Captain was off.

While they waited, he said to Travis, "Sir, when I went out on this detail, my captain had me pick up his weapon to hold for him. I don't think he will need it now, so for the rest of this battle, I would like for you to use it. It will be a bit more effective than the pistols you are used to. Later this afternoon, I will bring it by and show you how it works."

Now he had his full attention. "What is this weapon?" he asked.

"It, like yours, is a pistol." He started saying, "However, this one will shoot eighteen times before it must be reloaded. You carry it with one round in the chamber and an additional seventeen rounds in the magazine."

Mitchell pulled his out to show him and quickly went through how the action worked and how to drop out the mag and put in a new one. Then he said, "With this, you'll have three magazines."

He let Travis hold it after he cleared it. His only comment was the same when he picked up the modern rifle when they first met, "It's so light."

Mitchell then reached over and inserted a fully loaded mag. "It's a little different when it's loaded."

Travis hefted it a couple time and got a little smile saying, "Yes, once you load it there is quite a bit of difference." He then picked up his pistol and compared the two, side by side. "Very nice he said." He then handed the pistol back to him and Mitchell prepared it by loading a round into the chamber.

When he put the safety on and put it back in the holster, Travis asked, "That's it. All you do is pull back on the top and it's loaded and ready to fire."

"Pretty much it." He said, just as the door opened and Crockett and Captain Dickenson came in.

Travis sat back down at his desk and after a puff or two he said, "Please have a seat, gentleman, while we wait for Bowie."

Mitchell just sat back down where he was. The other two grabbed some chairs from around the room and sat down beside him. Travis then said, "We'll wait for Colonel Bowie before we start."

There was a long, uncomfortable wait in silence. Travis indicated for the others to take a cigar. Crockett politely refused, but Captain Dickenson took one and lit it up.

After about ten minutes, his men helped Bowie into the office and placed him in a chair. The two men who were helping couldn't get out of that office fast enough. After Travis offered a cigar to Bowie, who took it and lit his, Travis turned to Mitchell, saying, "Captain Mitchell here has informed me there is a possibility that Santa Anna will attack us before morning with all his forces."

Now everyone turned to look at Mitchell. He just sat there, waiting to see what Travis wanted to do. It didn't take long. Travis sat in his chair on the other side of the desk and said, "Captain, please tell these men what you told me."

Other than the first day they met, Mitchell didn't think he had much dealings with Captain Dickenson. He didn't know how much he knew about him and his team. He needed to get this straight before he went into other details. "Captain Dickenson, how much do you know about me and my people?"

He looked around and then focused on Travis. Travis just nodded to him. It was OK to speak. "I've heard you came down here from northern Texas and that you have some very fancy weapons." He paused then.

Travis spoke up, "It's alright Dick, speak your mind. This is now just between this group of men."

The Captain then continued, "It is said, you come from a time in the future."

"Yes Dick, may I call you Dick?" After he answered him with a nod, Mitchell went on, "We come from roughly two hundred years in your future. Don't ask how we got here, simply because I don't understand it myself. All I know is that because of something that happened in my time, it threw me and my team back in time to now."

After watching for some sign from him, he finally just blurted out, "That is quite a tail to take in, if you don't mind me saying."

Mitchell laughed a little, saying, "No, I don't mind at all, because it is just as hard for me to believe this is happening." This got a little stir from both Bowie and Crockett. "What I can tell you is what I remember from what happened in my time in this battle."

Looking at Travis, Mitchell wasn't sure how much he wanted him to tell him. After another puff, he told him, "Go ahead, tell him the entire story."

Mitchell nodded to Travis and turned back to Dick. "In my time, this battle here went badly for the men of the Alamo. They killed all defenders. There was only a hand full of survivor, your wife and children, being among them. They allowed them to walk out of here." He paused a moment as a look of relief came over the Captain, then he told him, "Everyone was killed in battle or executed as soon as the battle was over."

He watched the Captain for a moment as everything he dumped on him set in. He was obviously in shock and disoriented, but there was nothing Mitchell could do to help him, so he turned back to the map on Travis' desk.

As he pointed out a few things, the other stood and gathered around the desk. Even Bowie hobbled over to the desk and leaned on it. "Gentlemen, in my time, shortly after moving the artillery battery in the northeast closer to the north wall, Santa Anna made this last attack on the Alamo. His main force will be centered on the north and west wall, with a significant attack against the palisades area."

As he talked, he pointed out these areas on the maps. After waiting a moment and no one speaking, he continued on, "Now, my people have set up areas outside the wall that we will place mines in. These mines are deadly and can take out one hundred or more men for each one. You all know what a shotgun is?" There were nods all around the desk, but still no one spoke. "This mine is like a shotgun you have never seen before. I will shoot out over seven hundred pellets out to anywhere between fifty to one hundred yards. In an arch about so." He showed about a sixty-degree span with his hands.

This got quite a reaction from the group. Even Crockett reacted. Mitchell now realized that Crockett never fully understood what he had been telling him before. He just continued, "We have set up areas to place these mines tonight. My team will go out after dark and get them set up. There will be two each at the north, south and west walls."

Captain Dickenson then asked, "What about the east wall?"

"Good question," Mitchell said directly to him, then to the others. "I don't recall there was a great deal of activity from that direction. Yes, they will attack from there, but I don't think it was a major threat. I believe the men we have there will handle it."

"Now for today, and why we have the good Captain with us," He said, indicating Dickenson, "We need to reduce his formidable artillery, but we have to do it in a way that he doesn't know what we are using. My Sergeant Redcloud has a rifle that has what we call a grenade launcher attached to it. It will fire a forty millimeter, about a one and a half inch round, with more explosive power than your smaller cannons and with a great deal more accuracy."

While he let that set in Bowie spoke up asking, "Well, if that is the case, why don't we just simply take out all his artillery and be done with it?"

"Ah, another good question from the good Colonel," he said as Bowie gave him an angry look. "We could, but then Santa Anna will probably not attack into our trap. We need him to attack with all of his forces so we can destroy them right here and now."

This started a flurry of question from everyone. After a moment, Mitchell raised his hands and then pointed to Travis, who asked, "What makes you think we can destroy his entire army right here?"

Mitchell had to correct some of their thinking, "For one thing, this is not his entire Army. He has also sent an army to attack at, I believe it was, Goliad."

Travis said, "Where?"

He forgot Goliad was not a town until later. "From the fort where Fannin was supposed to come from."

Travis didn't speak, but nodded, which told him he now understood where he was talking about. So, continuing, "The other thing is I still have weapons you don't know about that I can use."

"What other weapons?" asked Crockett. Mitchell thought he might have felt hurt that with all the time they spent together, he didn't tell him everything.

Mitchell grabbed one hand-grenades off his harness and held it out, flat in his hand. Then, holding up the ring on the pin, he told them, "This is a hand-grenade. If I pull this pin and throw it, it will explode seven second later. If I were to throw it anywhere in this room, we would all be dead or severely wounded."

Again, Bowie spoke, "You mean to tell me that, that little thing is going to kill all of us?"

"No," Mitchell said, "this is not a directed weapon. It is an area weapon, much like the mines. What I am saying is that it has the potential to kill, or wound, everyone within about fifteen to fifty feet."

No one commented on the grenade, so he added, "Each of my men will have four."

"Is there anymore?" asked Travis.

"Yes Sir," He responded, "However, I don't want to go into those things at this time. I don't believe they will be needed. However, we do have some really nice things that are not so much weapons."

There was a questioning look on everyone's face though, "I have a machine that can fly and see in the dark, much like those night vision things you used when we destroyed the out buildings. It can show us pictures from high in the sky. Tonight, we will use it to track Santa Anna's men as they sneak up on us and get into their positions. This will allow us to know how to best deploy our people."

Captain Dickenson spoke now. "This is all very interesting, but what am I doing here? What do you need from me?"

"Dick," He said as he put the grenade back and place a hand on his shoulder, "You are key to this. We can't let Santa Anna know or even think we have such weapons. Because the weapon we have differs from anything they have seen. If we just start shooting it, Santa Anna will suspect something and may call off the attack."

"That is a good thing, isn't it?" he asked.

"Not really. We need him to attack so we can destroy this part of his army."

Dick thought about it for a moment then said, "Alright, what is his reload time for this thing?"

Being able to watch his face change when Mitchell told him, "Oh, not too long, about five seconds." Was just great.

He took a shaky step back and sat down in his chair. He finally looked up at him and said, "I think I understand what you want to do, and I think we can do this. When you are ready, I will meet with your man, and we'll set this up."

"Great," Mitchell said with a clap of his hands. "Now, there is one more extremely important detail we must discuss."

Travis moved back behind his desk and sat down. Mitchell thought this made him feel he was in command. "Go ahead."

"This deals with Santa Anna, directly." Now Bowie and Crockett sat down again, and he continued, "In my time when Santa Anna was defeated, he ran. They caught him running away wearing a private's uniform. It was not until they brought him into camp and the other prisoners gave away who he was that they knew they had the great 'El Presidente'. Once they knew who they had, Houston could force him to sign an agreement that ultimately release all the land known as Texas to be a free country."

This took a moment to register, but it was the shrewd mind of Crockett to understand first. "This means we can't kill him."

Bowie spoke, or more like yelled, first, "We can't let him live!"

Now Mitchell spoke. Softly, as to calm the conversation down, he said, "Jim, we can't kill him. If he escapes our trap and returns to Mexico, he will be right back with a bigger army and we will have to fight him all over again, and this time we may lose. If we capture him and kill him, then whoever takes over will be right back with a bigger army. However, if we make him sign documents to release the lands north of the Rio Grande river, then let him go. He will have no reason to return and take over these lands again. We will have won."

Crockett sat there nodding, and Mitchell believed Travis understood how important this was, as well. However, Bowie was still sitting there, boiling mad. He wanted the man dead, and this can't happen. He walked over to where Bowie was sitting and said, "Jim, I think I know how you feel, but this is the only way that Texas will survive as a country. The worst part is that you will need to ensure he is kept safe until Houston or the new government of the Republic of Texas gets down here to secure the documents."

Bowie looked up at him and Mitchell could swear he saw tears forming in his eyes, but he could also see that Bowie understood how important this was to Texas.

After a long quiet time, Bowie yelled for his men. It took a moment for his men to come in and help him out. No one said anything. Mitchell believed that because, even though they understood what was said, they all wanted Santa Anna dead.

This, he was afraid, is something they may need to deal with in the future, after the battle is over.

Before leaving the office, Captain Dickenson came over and asked, "When do you want to start this?"

"Immediately," Mitchell replied, "My man is up on the platform that we have been using to watch things. You gather your crew and I'll meet you there momentarily."

Captain Dickenson reached out his hand, and Mitchell grasped it. As he left, Mitchell turned to Travis and said, "I'll get together with you later about what we were discussing." Then to both Crockett and Travis he said, "You two gonna come watch?"

He knew Crockett would go. He just squeezed Mitchell's shoulder and headed out the door. Travis, however, wasn't in his full dress. He pulled the cigar out of his mouth to say, "I'll be there as soon as I get dressed."

Mitchell waved and told him, "We're in no great hurry, we'll wait for you." And then he, too, was out the door.

Crockett came up next to him and they took the short walk over to the gun platform together.

Redcloud was already there and had his weapon and ammo ready. Mitchell took up a space right behind him to watch. "What's the plan?" He asked as Mitchell took out his binoculars.

The Chief leisurely rolled up on his side and calmly said, "The plan is to destroy a couple cannons."

He shot Redcloud a quick dirty look, at which point he got serious. "Captain Dickenson is going to use two cannons."

"Two?" He questionably asked.

"Yeah, when the captain got here, we discussed what was the goal. He suggested that if only one cannon fires and there are two explosions, someone will get suspicious." He paused for a moment while Mitchell thought about it, then he continued, "He is going to fire the first shot and then, about two seconds later, a second cannon will fire only a powder load. That is when I'll fire."

"Not too shabby." Mitchell said, looking down at him with a smile.

Redcloud looked up at him as if he was all eaten up with himself and said, "I have my moments."

Mitchell let it slide and just scanned with the binoculars. He thought it pissed him off a little that he didn't respond to Redcloud's last comment. He knew it would because he was sure Redcloud had another cute comment to come back with, no matter what he said, and now he didn't get to use it.

After a moment, he rolled back down into his shooting position and mumbled, "If the first shot hits something, then we'll get a two-for."

Mitchell just made a sound as if he was ignoring him, "Um-hum." He said, just to piss him off ever more.

Shortly, Travis showed up and, after looking through his scope, he asked, "Are we ready?"

"Yes, Sir." Came the reply from behind then as Captain Dickenson came up to stand next to Travis.

Travis looked over at him and simply said, "Fire."

With that, Dick turned slightly to the left and raised his arm. A second later, he quickly brought it back down. Half a moment later, the cannon on the left fired. The shot landed a little short, but this time it didn't get the bounce and just stuck in the dirt in front of the battery. Dick then turned to the cannon on the right and went through the same ritual. This time there was a distinct sound when the cannon fired, and a split second later there was the quieter pop from Redcloud's shot.

His shot hit the battery, and several men fell, but the cannon itself was not hit.

"You're gonna have to do better than that." Mitchell told him as he was already loading the second round.

Captain Dickenson's men were already going through their reloading process, so all they could do was wait. While they waited, Redcloud adjusted his position slightly. When everything was ready, the process started all over again. This time the Chief made a direct hit and fully destroyed the artillery piece he was aiming for. This brought a cheer from everyone in the Alamo.

Mitchell simply squatted down next to Redcloud and patted him on the shoulder and said, "Good shooting."

All he could hear was some mumbling from him as he picked up his gear, so he asked, "What was that?"

He angrily replied, "The wind, I forgot to check the wind." Mitchell knew Redcloud was directing the anger more at himself than anything else.

When Redcloud finally stood up, Mitchell told him, "As with any other thing, you need two things." When the Chief only looked at him, he finished, "Practice and luck. But, with you, I don't need luck. You, my friend, are just out of practice."

He couldn't tell by looking at Redcloud if this helped or not. He just turned and walked down the ramp, heading for their camp. Mitchell returned to looking at the damage done through the binoculars.

When he finished, Crockett came up and asked, "If you don't mind, may I look."

"Certainly." He said, and with a smile he handed them over to him.

Crockett remembered how to adjust them and quickly had them set for his eyes. He took a long look, but he wasn't too interested in the cannon that was destroyed. Judging from where he was looking, Mitchell thought his focus was on Santa Anna.

Crockett handed the binoculars back to Mitchell and, as he put them away, Crockett said, "I think you got his attention. He looks a bit riled up over there."

Mitchell quickly stopped putting them away and, after a quick change back to him, he zeroed in on Santa Anna's little group. It appeared there was a lot of yelling going on, but it was all one sided. He could almost make out Santa Anna's red face. There was one officer with a lot less shiny stuff on his uniform that was taking the brunt of it. He figured this must be the artillery officer. Poor guy, he thought to himself with a smile.

He turned to Travis and said, "In an hour, we'll run the same drill from the north wall."

This was the first time he thought he saw a genuine smile from Travis, who simply nodded, turned, and walked away.

As he did, Mitchell looked over at Dick. He had a very proud smile on his face. Looking back at Mitchell, he said, "Oh, we'll be ready."

Mitchell grasped him by the shoulder as he walked by and smiled. He then hurried over to find his man. He found him standing at the back of the wagon, preparing the clean his rifle.

As Mitchell walked up, he said, "I should have had that on the first shot." He could hear the frustration in his voice. This was a highly unusual tone coming from him.

Mitchell decided not to give into his self-pity. He flat out told him, "Yep, it should have been, but it wasn't. Deal with it and do better the next time."

He put both hands on the tailgate of the wagon and leaned over and put his head down. He muttered, "It was a rooky mistake. I should have done better."

Mitchell still would not let him draw him into the hole he was digging. He had to pull him out of it. "You know, not everyone is perfect, even you. Shit happens, and sometimes the only thing we can do is move on and try not to let it happen again."

Redcloud nodded his head, saying, "Yeah, I know. But I don't like it."

"Like I said," He started out, then leaned in real close and added, "Deal with it, before it deals with you."

Redcloud turned only his head to look back at him. He thought that he might have gotten through to him because he got a disgusted look on his face and nodded.

Mitchell patted him on the shoulder and as he walked away saying, "We'll do it again on the north wall, in about an hour.". Looking around for Kat, He found her still up on the chapel. She waved at her and headed straight up there.

When he got there, the first thing on his mind was why she was still on watch. "Why are you still on watch? Weren't your relieved?"

She laughed a little, saying, "Of course they relieved me. But being up here so long, I knew this was the best place to watch things. When I saw the Chief and you going over to the west wall, I knew something was about to happen. I just wanted to watch."

Smart girl, he thought as he looked into her eyes and smiled. He reached down to hold her hand, and she eagerly reached out to take his. Together, they walked over to look out at the battery to the northeast. He could clearly see it now that they moved it in closer. The men were busy loading the cannons, while the others were standing next to what he assumed was their assigned cannon. He could have pulled out the binoculars to get a closer look, but they were so close now he didn't need them to see what he wanted to see.

Kat and he both just sat in the dirt. He leaned back against the wall and Kat laid her head on his arm. He only closed his eyes when, suddenly, someone was kicking his boot. "Get up Boss, it's time for the next round of fun" He heard Redcloud saying before he could open his eyes.

"What?" Mitchell said as he tried to focus and figure out what Redcloud was talking about. "What time is it?"

Redcloud stopped kicking him and said with a laugh, "Time to go blow things up."

Suddenly, everything came back. Mitchell jumped up, realizing where and when he was, and he took one step to follow him. Then he remembered he wasn't alone. He turned back and took Kat by the hand, and quickly pulled her to stand with him. He gave her a quick hug, saying, "This won't take long. You just stay here and watch, and I'll be right back."

He then turned to Redcloud, who had just continued to walk away, and by running a little, he caught up with him. "Man, I must have been more tired than I thought. I only sat for a moment." He said when he caught up to Redcloud.

"Yeah, right, Boss." He replied with so much sarcasm it was a wonder he didn't slip and fall in it.

Mitchell said nothing, partly because he knew his friend was right and partly because he would only come back with something else to upset him. He'd known him long enough to know his games.

It didn't take long to get to the north wall. This time they were the ones who were late. Travis, Crockett, and even Bowie were already waiting for them. Redcloud steered a little off to the side to have a word with Captain Dickenson while Mitchell went right up to Travis.

As he walked up, Travis simply turned his head and nodded to him. He assumed he was not too late and to continue with the exercise. A moment later, Redcloud came back and set up against the wall and loaded a round into the launcher. After a couple of positioning adjustments, he waved his hand at Captain Dickenson. The good captain went through the same rituals, and this time Redcloud scored a direct hit with the first round. Even the round that their artillery fired made a good hit. I don't think it damaged the cannon itself much, but Mitchell believed it was good enough to take out some of the men on that gun crew.

There were a couple of follow-up explosions as the gun carriage for the canon Redcloud had hit was too close and it set off some rounds in it, resulting in a short chain of explosions.

Redcloud then turned to lean his back against the wall and look at Mitchell with a deep look of satisfaction. This time, with his honor restored, some of the surrounding men started shouting their praise to him. Travis even walked over to Redcloud, who quickly stood up for the Colonel, and came to a more or less attention position.

Travis reached out with his left hand and put it on Redcloud's shoulder while handing him one of those fine cigars.

Redcloud just looked over at his friend with a smile.

After the crowd that had gathered, broke up, Mitchell finally got over to talk to Redcloud. He was just sitting on the wall and enjoying the cigar. Thoughtfully looking at it, he turned his head and asked, "How is it you never, ever rewarded me with something like this?"

Mitchell didn't really have to think about the answer, "Because I never, ever thought you deserved it." Then he smiled and before Redcloud could say anything, he just turned and walked away.

He went back to find Kat. Now she had come down from the chapel roof and was busy in the camp area. He thought she was getting some food for her father. Mitchell hadn't seen August around all day and wondered if he got to see the excitement. She was bent over getting something when he walked by and only put his hand on her back as he went by to find a place to set down.

While Kat was busy with her father, Anna strolled into camp with her new boyfriend in tow. They were talking about the excitement today and he was asking about Redcloud's rifle. Mitchell could see Anna was trying to avoid the subject, but he was being just a little persistent as they both sat down on a log near him. As their discussion continued, Mitchell stood up and walked over to their wagon. He found a smoke round for the grenade launcher and walked back. Stopping a little way away from them, he just stood there. When they noticed him standing there and stopped talking, he tossed the round to the kid.

"That is a forty-millimeter round like the one we shot today." He flat out told him.

Mitchell thought he was going to drop it right on the spot. The kid started handling it like it would blow up if he even breathed on it. Both Anna and he laughed at him, but she didn't let it go too far. Slowly, she reached over and took it from him. Holding it to where he could still clearly see it, she explained how it worked. She also let it slip that the round her boss had tossed him would only throw out smoke and not explode.

As she told him, the kid just looked over at Mitchell, who could see he didn't see the humor in it, so he just smiled and shrugged his shoulders and went back to his seat.

In a little while, Anna got up to get them both some food and as she came near Mitchell, she tossed the smoke grenade back to him. He just let it drop to the ground, just to show the kid it wouldn't go off. Looking at Anna, he only smiled. However, her boyfriend loon back at him and nodded his head as if he would get back at Mitchell. Mitchell was starting to like this kid.

After a little while, Redcloud came strolling into the camp area, still puffing on that cigar. He was putting on quite the show. He sat down next to Mitchell, making sure he was upwind so the smoke from the cigar would blow over to him. "You're just pretty ate up with yourself, aren't you?" Mitchell said.

Redcloud didn't say a word. He just held his head up and took a long drag off the cigar and then turned to blow it right into his friend's face.

Mitchell picked up the smoke round and tossed it at him. When he caught it, he turned it over in his hand and looked back at him with a questioning look on his face. Mitchell just put his thumb over his shoulder, pointing at the kid that was talking to Anna.

Redcloud picked right up on it and laid the weapon down, so it was in complete view of the kid. It didn't take long before the kid came over and squatted down to look at it. Mitchell could see there wasn't a mag in it, and he was pretty sure the Chief didn't leave a round in the chamber. After a moment Redcloud said, "Go ahead, check it out."

The kid looked at him with surprise and asked, "Are you sure it is OK." Then he turned to look at Mitchell.

Redcloud chuckled a little and proudly answered him, "I am the Sergeant, and this is my weapon. If I say it's OK, then it's OK."

After another quick glance at Mitchell, he slowly reached out and picked up the rifle. He didn't say it, but the way he was bouncing it in his hand he sure the kid, as everyone else, was as surprised about the weight of it. He put it up to his shoulder a couple of times and inspected it from end to end. Redcloud then leaned forward and explained a little of the working of it. As Redcloud told him about certain things, he would go through the action of that part of the rifle. It didn't take too long before the kid was working it like any of the others on the team.

Watching him go through it, Mitchell began thinking about if this was a good idea or not. Letting these people know too much about the future might not be a good idea. He wasn't really second guessing about them taking action here, but only about them teaching the people of this time too much. He decided that after dinner tonight he was going to have to have a little sit-down with everyone and discuss this issue.

They just sat around the camp. Mitchell had a little to eat. The whatever it was in the pot was a little better this time, but not by much. After eating and washing up, he gathered Redcloud, and they headed back to the west wall to start this show all over again.

Redcloud was able to knock off another two cannons, this time around on the first shot for each. Captain Dickenson's crew got a piece of one also, but before dark, that one was back in action.

As darkness fell, the cannon fire slowed and then stopped. Now, Mitchell remembered. Santa Anna ordered the cannon fire to stop, to lull the defenders into a long needed sleep so his men could sneak up on the Alamo early in the morning.

Once he realized what was happening, he found Crockett, and they both went to Travis. After explaining to him what he had remembered, Travis ordered everyone to the walls. Mitchell then went back to their camp and gathered the team together. They had some work to do.

Once everyone was there, he had to prioritize what needed to be done. They needed to start with the claymores. "Okay guys, this is it. I believe this is the night that Santa Anna will begin his final assault on the Alamo." Looking over at Blake, he could see him nodding. "The first thing we need to do is get the claymores set up. It's dark enough for us to sneak out to get them set up. Anna, I want you and Stretch to set up the ones in your area. Jose, you and Blake take the two outside your side. The Chief and I will set up the ones on the north wall."

Everyone was nodding, even August and Kat. "Next, we need to get everyone armed and ready for the battle." Turning to Anna, "I want you to distribute the ammo and grenades after we get back in." She nodded at her assignment. Now he just noticed that her new boyfriend was hanging around and listening. This is something he'd have to deal with later.

Next, he turned to Jose, "You get the drone ready. I want to set it up on the chapel roof."

Jose quickly glance up at the rooftop and replied, "You got it Boss."

Then he turned to Redcloud. "Anything else I forgot?"

He just simply said, "Rules of engagement."

"Ah yes, the rules of engagement." He hadn't really considered what they might be. Yeah, there were some ideas floating around in his head, but he hadn't given it much thought until now. Slowly, he laid out some ideas. "First, I don't want any automatic fire unless we are in a Broken Arrow position." Everyone started nodding their understanding. "Next, we are not to fire first. Our weapons have a distinct sound. After the battle begins, then we'll just mix right in." Another round of nods. "Last, hold the grenades until they are right up against the wall. Make sure you throw them far enough not to damage the wall, but not too far that they will lose their effectiveness." Another round of nodes, but then he added. "Try to keep them in reserve."

Looking back at the Chief again, he asked. "Anything I missed?"

Redcloud shook his head, but then asked, "Where are you going to be?"

This he had given much thought to. "I plan to float. I'll start out on the chapel with the drone to get a good picture of how things are shaping up. After that I'll be on the move to wherever I think I can do the most good. We have the squad talkers, so try to keep me informed of important changes or problem, but don't hog up the air with useless chatter."

The last part he tried to add a little touch of hummer to relax everyone. It worked, kind of. Most of the group gave a little laugh, but it didn't last long. This was the first actual battle for most of them. "Guys, the most important thing is to say loose. Pay attention to everything that is going on around you. Don't just stay focused on one area. And last, keep your asses down. These rifles the Mexicans have aren't particularly accurate, but the sheer volume of fire will be quite enough to make up for it."

After a moment, he quickly added, "One last thing. If things go south and bad enough that it looks like this place is going to fall, I'll give the order to rally. The rally point will be the hummer. We'll pack in it and drive out of here. They got nothing that can penetrate its armor."

He quickly glanced at Redcloud and who gave him a single node. "Okay guys, take off and get things set up. Remember, they are probably going to be watching the walls closely, so keep low and quiet."

Everyone quickly broke up and headed to the ammo wagon. Each group picked up two claymores and headed off to their respective assignments. Redcloud quickly came over and tossed Mitchell one claymore, and they both headed to the north wall.

Once outside, they crawled to the first location they already prepared. Mitchell let the Chief set it up while he kept watch. Once he had this claymore set up, they moved onto the next. It only took a few minutes to make sure everything was good. Redcloud then took both the bags and headed back in. Mitchell waited at the bottom of the wall with the wires. When I heard Redcloud call him, he took a few steps away and tossed the spool up to him. He quickly set it up in his area and then Mitchell tossed the second spool up. This time Redcloud missed, but on the second try he caught it and in the dim light Mitchell could see a thumbs up from him. On the radio, he briefly told him he was going to check on the others.

Staying low, I made my way around the corner and found Jose and Blake. They were just setting up the second one when he came up. Blake was aiming the claymore and as Mitchell squatted down next to him, he motioned for him to angle it a little more out. He did, and things looked good. In a whisper, he told them how to run the wires. They both nodded, that they understood, and finished up their work.

Now he made my way around to where Anna was working. By the time he got there, they were already making their way back in. They squatted in a group and whispered. "Have you run the wires already?" I asked.

Anna quietly said, "We ran them up to the wall and just laid them over the top. I'll hook them up and check them when we get back."

Feeling a little foolish, he was thinking of a tall wall, and they needed someone to toss up the spools. He forgot to consider the palisade on this side was barely taller than a person. He didn't think they could see him smile about it, and just said, "Good." As they all headed back in.

Again, they all met at the ammo wagon and Anna began handing out the mags. They each filled up their pouches and everyone took four grenades. Redcloud also took several rounds for his launcher.

After they finished passing out all the ammo, they all gathered in a huddle. He noticed Anna's boyfriend was still hanging out nearby. "Is he going to follow you all night?" He asked her.

She looked around and quickly saw him. "Can't say Boss. This is his assigned area, after all."

Mitchell took this as a yes and continued. "Stay alert, but I don't think anything will happen until just before dawn. As I get status updates from the drone, I'll pass it along." He looked around at the group, where he could see a mix of emotions. There was fear in some faces and confidence in the ones that had been through this before. However, He thought he could see the most important thing, determination. He couldn't really explain it. Maybe from knowing they had much superior weapons. Maybe that they already knew what was going to happen that was giving them this emotion, but it was good to see. It was then that he knew they would be alright and each of them would do their job.

"Okay then, let's get to our positions. Hook up your claymores and hunker down for the night." Just as they all got up, Mitchell added. "And Blake, ah Johnny, remember to slow down and make every round count."

Again, he had said it in such a sarcastic way to poke a little fun. Johnny took it as it was meant and even laughed as everyone poked a little fun at him as they walked away. This ragged group had now become a team. They were ready.

As Mitchell grabbed his gear, Kat came over to him. Her father was already heading up the ramp to the roof. She had her rifle tucked in her left arm and hooked her right are into his. When they got to the top, He found a place that was quiet, but still let him see the compound and most of the outside pretty clearly. Kat just stood by him and didn't say a word. He could see she was nervous, but he believed that once things start she will focus on the battle and will be alright.

A few minutes later, Jose came up with the drone. It was all still packed in the case. He just set it down, gave Mitchell a quick two-fingered salute, and took off running. He watched as Jose trotted over to his area. It didn't take long before he lost him among the real defenders of the Alamo.

Opening the case, he found everything was in order. He took out the drone and got it ready to fly. However, he thought it was way too early to send it up. He waited until after midnight before taking a look.

He closed the case and set the drone on top, so everything was set for when he needed it. Then he stood and reached out a hand to Kat. She took it and they strolled the few steps to her place. Tuning his back to the wall, Mitchell sat and leaned against it. Looking around, he could see this part of the fort was well manned. A few were sitting like him, and he thought some of them might have been trying to get a little sleep. Some were standing in groups, and he could hear talking. It was too low for him to make out what they were saying, but having been in situations like this before, he could guess what their talk was like.

Kat didn't sit right away. She just stood there, looking out over the wall. He had a moment to relax and think. Just then, Mitchell realized he hadn't taken the captain's pistol to Travis. When he jumped up, he scared Kat and some of the surrounding men. Quickly, he held up his hand as he said. "It's alright. I just remembered something."

He took Kat's arm and said, "I'll be right back. I need to go see Travis for a few minutes, and then I'll be right back. Don't worry. Nothing is going to happen until morning." Then, as he picked up his rifle to leave, he turned back to her and added. "Please keep an eye on the gear over there until I get back." pointing to the drone.

She looked over at the thing and said, "Don't worry, dear. I'll watch it for you."

He quickly gave her a kiss on the cheek and turned and ran off. Back in their camp, he went to the hummer and grabbed the pistol and then stopped by the ammo wagon and grabbed three mags for it. He also picked up a box of 9mm ammo, just in case.

Now he headed to see Travis. As he came in, Captain Dickenson was leaving. He stopped and reached out a hand. Mitchell shifted his load and took his hand. The captain solemnly said. "Good luck."

Mitchell shook his hand and replied, "The same to you, sir." And then added. "I'll see you after this is all over." And then smiled.

Dick then looked him in the eye, and he almost saw a half smile coming back, but he didn't say anything. He just turned and walked away.

The door to Travis' office was still open, so he went in. Travis was standing over his desk, looking at the map and puffing on one of those cigars. When he looked up, Mitchell asked. "Do you have a few minutes, Sir?"

Travis said nothing, however, with his cigar in hand, he pointed for Mitchell to sit in a chair, which he did. Quickly, he pulled the holster with a belt around it out and set it on his desk. "This is the pistol I was telling you about earlier."

Travis just stood there, looking at it for a moment. Mitchell then picked it up and unwrapped the belt and laid it out on top of the map.

Now Travis set down the cigar and reached to pick up the pistol. Mitchell, however, stopped him and picked it up. Walking around behind him, he put the belt around Travis and hooked the latch. Once the belt was in place, he took it by each side and adjusted it until he felt comfortable with it.

Now Mitchell came back around to the other side of his desk and pulled his pistol out. When he didn't move, he motioned for Travis to pull out the pistol on his belt.

It only took a second for him to figure out the latch on the flap, and he grabbed it and smoothly pulled it out. After a moment or two of looking it all over, Travis looked back at him.

"Right now, this pistol isn't loaded. The first thing I am going to show you is how to open the slide. On the side," He leaned over the desk and showed him. "This is the slide catch. With the pistol like so, you grab the back end of the slide and push it open. As you are doing this up push up on the slide lock."

Mitchell dropped the mag out of his and showed him as he explained.

The first attempt didn't work, but after repositioning the pistol in his hand, he got it on the second try. He then handed Travis an empty mag and showed him how to put it in. This he did without a problem.

"Sir, you notice the magazine is empty. When you fire your last round, the slide will automatically stay open in this position. You'll then take a full magazine and load it into the pistol." Which he did to his pistol. "Next, you'll grab the slide on the back and pull it just a little. This will unlock the slide and let it go forward again." As he told him, he showed it on his.

"Sir, remember the slide lock?" He looked down at the pistol and quickly found what he was talking about. "Now I want you to push down on the lock with your thumb. When you do this, the slide with jump forward into position."

He did exactly as Mitchell told him. When the slide jumped forward, so did Travis. Shyly, Travis looked up at him and he could see a hint of red in his face. Mitchell pretended he didn't see it and continued on. "Now I want you to just pull the slide straight back and let it go."

He did just as he was told, and the slide locked back. "This is going to happen when you empty the magazine." He reached into his pouch and pulled out a loaded mag and put it down on the desk in front of him. "Now Sir, see this button on the side here." As he told him, he showed him the button on his.

Quickly, Travis found the button and pushed it. When he did, the mag fell out on the desk. He picked it up and put it back in and tried it again. Mitchell could see he was trying to figure out how it all worked.

Before Travis could do it again, he told him, "Now pick up the full mag and put it in."

He did, but it took him a couple tried to get it lined up right. Eventually he got it in, then on his he slapped the butt with his hand and said, "Hit it like this to make sure the mag is all the way in."

Travis immediately did.

Holding his with his trigger finger laying along the side, he explained to him, "Now we are going to load the pistol. Hold the pistol like me. Make sure your finger is not on the trigger." After he did as Mitchell said, he continued. "Grab the slide like you did before. Pull it back and little and let it go."

This time, when the slide went forward, he didn't jump. "Now, you loaded the pistol with seventeen rounds and are ready to fire." As Mitchell explained, he turned it back and forth in his hand. "On the side, near your thumb, is a little switch." Again, he pointed it out, and Travis quickly found it. "Push this switch up."

He pushed the safety up and looked back up at Mitchell. "Now, the pistol is loaded, but on safe. It can't be fired." Using his, he showed him by trying to pull the trigger. "All you need to do when you're ready to shoot is push the safety down and pull the trigger."

After He finished showing him, Mitchell stayed a while to watch him and answer any question he might have.

It took a little longer than he wanted it to because he still had to show him how to load a magazine. However, by the time he left, Travis was fairly proficient with the operation. Now, if he can just shoot, there shouldn't be any problems.

Mitchell left Travis still practicing, and he warned him it wouldn't be a good idea to practice with a loaded gun. He agreed he will probably get enough practice tomorrow. As he left, Mitchell stopped and reminded him. "This is just on loan until the battle is over. I will need to have it back."

Travis looked up with a smile like a kid with a new toy on Christmas and said, "Certainly, of course." And then his attention was right back on the gun.

Leaving Travis to play with his new toy, he went back to his spot and found Kat standing guard over the drone, more so than on watch over the wall. As he topped the ramp to the roof, he couldn't help but to smile. As he approached her, Mitchell said, "You are relieved, soldier."

She smiled back and tried to give him what he thought was supposed to be a salute. However, it wasn't really close and with the wrong hand. He thought they were going to have to work on that. Maybe later, when they had some private time.

It was now dark enough, but he still wanted to wait awhile to use the drone so Santa Anna would have a chance to move his troops. So, he sat back down in his usual position, but this time, Kat sat next to him.

Mitchell felt sitting here with her like this was so comfortable he could go right to sleep. But, remembering what happened earlier, when Redcloud had to wake him, he sat up a little to make sure he didn't get too comfortable.

After a little, he stood up and said, "I'm going to go over and check on your father and see if they can see anything on their side."

Before she could get up or say anything, he turned and walked away. It took him a moment to find August with all the men over there now. However, he figured by looking for the fattest one, it would get him right to him. And he was right.

August was sitting with a group of men near a small fire. As he walked up, one man put a small jug behind him. Mitchell should have known that August would find something to drink if it were around.

"Anybody hear anything over this way?" He asked as he walked up.

"Not a thing, Captain." said one man. "We give it a listen now and then, but as near as we can tell, there ain't nothing out there on this side, anyway."

"Yeah, but you might wanna lay off the drinking, anyway. Might not be much shooting on this side, but you still need to shoot back straight."

This got a little giggle out of a couple of them. They all knew that he had caught them, but Mitchell let it go at that and walked closer to the wall to look around. He just wanted to get away from the light of that fire before he lost all his night vision.

"Boss." He heard just behind him from a familiar voice. Then August came to stand right next to him. Mitchell said nothing, so he continued. "You really think the whole group of them is going to attack tomorrow?"

He asked in a very low voice. Mitchell didn't think it was because he thought the others might think he was afraid, but because he didn't want them to hear the rest of the conversation.

"I heard you talking to some officers. You said everyone here is gonna die."

He could hear it in August's voice. He wasn't worried about himself, but about his daughter. "Well, my friend, you only heard part of it."

Looking over at him, Mitchell could see the strange look on his face, saying he didn't understand. "You remember we talked about not only where I come from but when?"

August nodded.

"Well, when I was talking about everyone dying, I was talking about the time I came from. It is hard to explain and understand, but you need to trust me that this time things are different. I not only believe we will survive this battle, but we may even win the war."

August looked down and shuffled his feet, not from the cold, but because Mitchell felt he didn't understand. "I am a simple man and do not understand these things."

He gave a little laugh and, leaning closer to August so no one else could hear, he said, "Trust me, August, I am not a simple man. I am quite educated and have traveled to many places in the world, and I am still having a difficult time understanding what I think is happening.

That still doesn't mean I don't understand the dynamics of a battle. I am confident we have the upper hand and can win this thing." The last part he spoke a little louder so the other could hear and then added. "As long as they can still shoot straight come morning."

Out of the corner of his eye, he could see the men at the fire stir a little and there was a low talk over there, but he wasn't able to understand what they were saying.

He hoped this helped August a little. He seemed to stand a little straighter, with a little more cockiness in him, as he said. "You can damn sure count on me shooting straight tomorrow."

"I know I can," Mitchell said as he stepped up beside him and put his hand on August's shoulder. "You have the added incentive that you are also protecting your daughter."

He quickly turned so Mitchell's hand came off his shoulder. There was a fire in his eyes, directed at Mexicans. Mitchell knew he had hit a cord that he hadn't realized yet.

He looked Mitchell in the eye for a little, then turned his attention to outside the walls. His focus was now where it should be. Mitchell just hoped his resolve will be a strong throughout the night.

Nothing more needed to be said. He just walked back to Kat and sat down. Mitchell knew she wanted to ask, but she didn't, and he thought it best not to tell her that her father had been drinking because he felt sure that her father had finished his drinking for tonight.

It was getting late now, and everyone was so quiet. Now and then, he thought he could hear something in the distance. He looked at his watch, and according to it, it was now past midnight.

He got up and walked over to the drone. Kat followed him, so he put her to use. He stood her a little out into the small open area where they had set up. He took her rifle and laid it down near the case. When he came back, he had the drone. It was small and very light. Mitchell lifted her arm out and put her hand flat with the palm up. Carefully, he placed the done on her hand and slowly let go. She didn't move. He walked away, but then remembered he forgot to turn it on. He quickly took it back and flipped the tiny switch and placed it back on her hand. "Don't move until it lifts off your hand, Okay?" he said.

With a nervous voice, she answered, "Yes."

Mitchell smiled and went back to get the controller. Turning it on, the screen lit up immediately. This got the attention of the men that were standing watch on this side. Many of them moved closer. It had been a while since he had flown one of these things and some controls were a little different, but like riding a bike. He hit the lever for the motor and the thing jumped up into the air. Some men jumped back a step, but curiosity kept them close. Kat quickly lowered her hand and ran back to his side.

"That thing scared me."

When he looked over at her and smiled, she surprised him with a hit on his shoulder. When he lowered his shoulder and grabbed it with his free hand, she smiled back at him.

It didn't take long for the drone to get high enough to see. He had it set on FLIR so they could see the heat of the bodies. There was not much light out tonight to help the night vision, so he thought this might work better. As the drone got higher, there were more and more little white dots on the screen. "Each of these little white dots is one of us. This thing can see the heat your body gives off."

One man laughed and said, "But it's cold as hell out here."

Not trying to go into any detail, he simply said. "This makes the heat of your body stand out even more." He pointed to one man and said, "Move over to the other side."

As he walked away, one dot on the screen moved further away from the others. "See, this dot is him." He said as he pointed to it.

There was a lot of low muttering, so to shut them up, Mitchell said. "Let's go look for Santa Anna's Army."

As he moved the controls a little, the group of dots got smaller as the drone moved higher. According to the compass, it was moving to the east. Soon he could see several long lines of dots. Some were moving, other were stationary. Talking mostly to Kat, he said. "These are the men to the east. There are some, but not many."

Changing the direction, he moved south. Now we could clearly see a large concentration of white. There were too many for the drone to show them as individual dots. With his free hand, he pointed to the south and said, "This is the group to the south. This is the group attacking along this side."

Now Mitchell could hear a lot of muttering from the men standing around. He didn't linger too long on this and mover to the west wall. He had to move a little higher to get the entire group in over there.

By now, he thought some men were understanding what the picture meant. Even Kat took in a sharp breath when the size of the group along the west came up on the screen.

He moved on and someone from the side said. "That's to the west?"

"Yes," was all he said.

Now looking at the north side, he couldn't say if it was a larger group than on the west or not, but either way, it was a force to deal with.

Clicking his radio twice told the group to check in. He got a single click in return. Then a double click. After a second or two, there was a triple click. This went on until he got a reply from everyone in the group. Now he keyed up, saying. "Things are happening just as we expected. Each group is approximately five hundred yards off the wall. I suspect they will try to move in close before light. Stay frosty."

No one responded an acknowledgment. There was no need. This was simply a SITREP.

He moved the drone back. As it got closer, he said. "I need a brave man to help me."

He didn't notice, but Anna's boyfriend was in the group. He stepped up and said, "I'll help."

Mitchell looked at Kat and smiled. He thought she might guess what he was planning. To the kid, he said. "Alright, what was your name again?"

"Peter Bailey, Sir."

"Alright Peter Bailey, go about twenty feet over there." he said, pointing to the area where Kat had been standing.

As he walked over there, Kat gave her boyfriend a discrete elbow in the side. He turned and smiled at her. She had to cover her mouth so no one would see her laughing.

Peter got to the area Mitchell had showed and turned around. He said, "Now, put one arm straight out in front of you with your palm up."

He did, with just a brief hesitation.

Then Mitchell said, "Now the most important thing. No matter what, Don't Move!" The last part had a great deal of emphasis on it.

Turning back to the screen, he could clearly see their area. As the drone got closer and closer, it came lower and lower. Soon he could only see the white dot that was Peter. Now they could also hear the buzzing of the drone. It was not loud, but there were no other sounds, so it stood out and sounded louder than it actually was.

As it closed in to where he could see it, Mitchell no longer needed to look at the screen. He watched as it came down. Peter turned his head away and lean away from the drone. Mitchell yelled out, "Don't move! That is most important."

He stopped moving instantly.

Slowly, he moved the drone until it was just over Peter's hand. Ever so gently, he set the thing down right in the palm of his hand. When he cut the power to the motors, it was quiet again. He thought he heard a few people take deep breaths. He casually walked over and carefully picked it up and turned it off. Then, looking at him, he said. "Good thing you didn't move. These things almost never blow up when you land them right. The problem comes when someone moves. Then it's not a pretty sight." Mitchell kind of shuddered as he turned to walk away.

As he went back to the case to put everything away, only Kat came with him. Furiously she said. "You mean that thing could have blown up in my hand?"

He took her hand and pulled her close to him. Trying to stifle a laugh, he said. "Of course not. There is nothing explosive about it. But Peter doesn't know that."

It took a second for it to register and again she covered her mouth and looked back at the group of men around Peter. "Anna will not be happy with you."

"Why not?" He asked. "Look at him now. Before, he was just a kid. Now he stands out as the bravest one in that group."

Kat thought about it for a little and she thoughtfully said. "This is true, but I still think Anna may not be happy."

"Oh, well." He said and finished packing up the drone. "I need to put this away and tell Travis what we saw. I'll be back shortly." He then gave her a quick kiss and turned and walked away.

On the way to speak with Travis, he ran into Crockett. Mitchell waved for him to come along. As he got to the door, Crockett caught up with him. As Mitchell held the door, he motioned for him to go on in. After knocking on the inner door, Travis yelled to come on in.

They both came in. Travis was just finishing up with a young man. Travis gave him an envelope and said, "Good luck and safe passage."

The young man quickly went by Crockett and him, almost without even a sign that they were there. In a second, he was gone.

"What is it, gentlemen?" Travis asked as he sat back behind his desk.

As they walked over to the desk. Travis motioned for them to sit.

"It would appear that I was correct." Mitchell started out. "I sent my drone up." When he got blank stares from both of them, he backed up. "The flying machine that lets me see in the dark. You'll remember what we saw of the fight."

Both of them nodded, now.

"From what I can see, the battle is shaping up just as I expected it to. There is little to the east. From the spacing, I would guess maybe cavalry. To the south there is a medium size force. The bulk of his army is to the west and the north. Just what we planned for."

Travis said little. Slowly, he stood and turned away from the desk and took a few steps. Turning back, he said, "I have just sent a message to the government explaining that without reinforcements, I don't see hope of defending this post any longer."

Crockett spoke up before Mitchell could say anything. "Jim here thinks we can hold this place and even defeat Santa Anna."

Travis looked at Mitchell, and sadly he said. "I have seen the things he has and while they are quite wondrous, I do not believe they will be enough to defeat Santa Anna."

"What are your plans?" Crockett asked.

"Captain Baugh is out quietly assembling the men. I will go out and speak to them and see how many want to leave and try to make arrangements for them to slip out."

Thinking to himself, this must be the famous line in the dirt speech. His people will stay out of this and stand to the side.

Just then Captain Baugh came in and said in a sad voice, "The men are assembled."

"Gentlemen, if you will excuse me. I need a moment to prepare."

Crockett and Mitchell simply stood and walked out without a word.

He told Crockett, "I'm going to go find my people. We are going to stay out of whatever happens here. I'll meet up with you after."

Crockett just nodded and waved his hand. Mitchell felt he too knew what was coming. However, his group was the only ones that really knew what was going to happen, or what happened. He hoped that it only starts the same way in this timeline.

Finding his group all together, he pulled them off to the side where they could watch, but not get involved.

Kat asked, "What is happening now?"

Turning to the group, "Some of you may know this. It was a famous and pivotal moment in the defense of the Alamo. Travis is going to tell them the truth of the situation here and how desperate they are. He will famously draw a line in the dirt and ask those who cross will stay to defend the Alamo. The other my go with no shame placed on them." He stopped the story there.

August spoke up, rather excitedly asking, "Well, what happens… happened?"

Just then, Travis came out to speak. Mitchell quietly said, "Listen and you will see."

Travis laid it all out for the men of the Alamo. He didn't say a word about Mitchell and his group. It was mostly about the purpose of what they were doing and the need for this post to defend until the last. Just as in some of the history books, he took his saber and drew the famous line in the sand and then stood back. At first, there were only a couple of men. Quickly it grew until it was a flood of all the men.

Mitchell could see from where they were standing, the pride that swelled up in Travis. Putting his sword away, he simply said, "Return to your posts."

When he turned around, Mitchell saw Blake with his cell phone out. He looked at him and said, "I couldn't resist recording such an important moment in history."

Jose responded before he could and said, "Yeah, but by the time they will view it, no one will believe they had the technology to record it. They will deem it a fake."

At first, Blake kind of seemed down with that thought, but then he proudly responded, "Yeah, but I'll always have it to give me strength when I need it."

Mitchell walked up to Blake and place his hand on his shoulder, "Bold move my friend. Nice."

Everyone, even Jose, went by Blake and patted him on the shoulder, some expressing their feeling about it.

They now broke up and everyone headed back to their spot. Mitchell walked along with Kat back to her spot where they sat down and just held on to each other. The mood was quiet. So quiet now that he could actually hear the Mexican Army from time to time.

They were definitely moving closer.

CHAPTER 15

Looking at his watch, which may or may not be right, Mitchell could see that dawn was quickly approaching, however it was still extremely dark out. The clouds were too thick to allow much moon light through. However, his people have their night vision and could see.

From where he was standing on top of the chapel, he could see just about everything. The Mexican Army was mostly in place. In his mind, he had to give compliments to the order and discipline in which they moved. Had it not been for the night vision and the FLIR on the drone, we would never have known they were going to attack.

He needed to get to the north wall, in the opposite corner of the Alamo, before the attack starts. This is where the firepower is going to be needed.

He stood up and gave Kat a giant kiss goodbye. "You stay safe. Remember, if things go bad, run to Anna and get inside the Hummer. Drop your rifle. The Mexican's probably will not shoot a defenseless woman."

She nodded at everything he said. However, as he turned to go, she threw her arms around him and cried. "Be strong." He whispered. "It will help to keep you alive. If you are not thinking about the fight in front of you, you may not survive."

She stepped back and used the end of her sleeve to wipe her eyes. They both smiled at each other, and he turned and ran off.

As he ran down the ramp, he called to Anna, "Anna, please keep an eye out for Kat. I must go to the north wall."

A calm reply came back from Anna. "You got it, Boss. I got her back."

Thank you, he said, but into the squad radio he said, "Chief, heading your way. I'll take up a position between you and Blake."

Redcloud just said, "Copy."

He was taking the comment about cutting down on the chatter seriously.

Running at a trot, it didn't take him long to get to the gun platform near the northwest corner.

When he got into position, he could make out the lines of Mexicans out in the field in front of him. It would appear there might be more than he could remember being reported. It was still too dark for the regulars to see anything.

He believed it would start soon, and he wanted to make one last check before all hell broke loose. "Status check. Everyone report in."

Redcloud was the first to check in. "Chief here. All set claymores armed and ready."

Anna came next. "Anna here. Claymores set, MG ready."

Jose spoke up, "Jose, check in. All set. Claymores ready."

Johnson came up next. "Stretch checking in. I'm ready."

Last came Blake. "Ah, Jimmy here. I'm ready."

Blake sounded a little nervous, but Mitchell really expected that. He knew he'd be alright once things got underway.

"Stretch," Mitchell called out

"Copy." Mitchell recognized his voice.

"Your primary area is to the east. However, if the action is slow, swing your fire around to support the north."

"Copy. Secondary target to the north wall."

He is a young kid, but a good soldier. If they were still back at Hood, Mitchell thought he would probably be a Corporal by now and on his way to Sergeant.

That was it. All they could do now was wait, the worst part of any battle.

After a while of just sitting there and looking out from time to time, Mitchell detected a slight movement of Santa Anna's army. Some units in the front ranks were creeping up. From where he was located now, he didn't have a good view of the entire area. He could clearly see the force to the north move in. Standing up, he looked over to the west and at first there was no movement, but while he watched, they also moved. It is surprising how quietly such a large group could move.

"They are on the move." He said on the radio. "Quietly, make sure everyone in your areas is awake."

He got copies from every. Then he remembered Kat didn't have a radio. "Anna, send a runner-up to the chapel roof and make sure they know."

Anna came right back, saying, "Copy. Already sent Peter up there."

He should have known. She was right on top of the situation.

He continued to watch as the Mexicans made their way to the wall. They were now only a couple hundred yards from the north wall. He couldn't see that well to the west, but he was getting a little nervous waiting for Travis to give the open fire command.

He didn't have to wait too much longer. Captain Dickenson opened fire with the big gun on the west wall. As soon as he did, the cannons from all around the Alamo opened fire. As soon as the Alamo cannons fired, Santa Anna's batteries opened up. Now he was thinking He should have taken out more of his firepower yesterday.

It had started. All the men around the wall came up in position, but held their fire and waited for the Mexicans to get closer. This didn't take too long. As soon as the cannons opened up, the Mexicans began their charge.

When the lines got within about one hundred yards, the men on the wall began firing. It started first in the area around Travis, so Mitchell guessed he gave the command. Right away, there was a massive volley from the defenders. It amazed him how few Mexican soldiers actually fell from that amount of fire. Before he started firing,

Mitchell got on the radio with a last second thought. "Don't aim for the officers right now. Let them continue to lead the attack. When they get to the wall, then take out the leaders."

There was no response, but he could clearly hear their rifles intermixed with the muzzle loaders of the time. Mitchell didn't wait any longer. Leaning on the wall, he began firing. He started at one end of the front rank and just started working his way down the line. He had already given orders to hold the claymores until the first rank was right on top of them. The first one went off down the west wall. Then quickly, the second one on that side went off.

Jose came on the radio. "Status report. Both claymores used. Effect was very good, but the attack continues."

"Copy." Mitchell replied and looked over at Redcloud. He wasn't able to see him right away. He then stood up, but wasn't holding his rifle. However, while he waited, he heard both claymores go off at the other end of the compound.

Now Anna came up on the radio. "Same here on this end. The attack paused but has resumed."

Before he could respond, Mitchell heard Redcloud yell, "Fire in the hole!"

A second later, the Claymore nearest him went off and a second later, the second one went off. At first, he had ducked down to avoid and back blast, but quickly came up for a look.

It was still dark, but he could clearly see a large area in the center of the attack that was all bodies. Some were still moving and trying to crawl back, but the second wave was right behind and walked right over the dead and wounded. Mitchell now fired in earnest. He changed his tactics now and started with the soldier closest to the wall and worked his way back. Even with his advanced rifle, he wasn't able to hold back the tide of the attack for long. There were simply too many of them.

He believed it was the same on at least three sides of the Alamo. Mitchel then heard what sounded like a grenade going off in the area around Jose. he looked over to the area near Redcloud and saw they had reached the wall.

The light was getting better, and he could see Redcloud toss a grenade over the wall. It was a good throw. He placed it right in the middle of a group that was trying to get some ladders up to the wall. A good part of them went down, but others grabbed the ladders and continued up to the wall. Now it was his turn. The Mexicans were at the base of the wall, just in front of him. He pulled out a grenade and gave it a short toss over the wall. After it went off, he braved a quick look and got up to lean over and check the area in front of him. As he did, a ladder came up right next to him. He took out the first three that tried to climb it before their fire made him duck back down. One man fighting next to him used the butt of his rifle to push the ladder back. When it passed the point of no return, the soldiers on it jumped and it went crashing back down on top of others.

There was no actual damage there and the men all recovered and grabbed the ladder and quickly put it back up on the wall. This time, the other soldiers around the ladder took up positions to lay down some cover fire while their buddies climbed up.

While Mitchell was taking cover, he looked up and down the wall and saw much of the same thing happening at several places along the wall. Mostly, they kept the Mexicans from getting on top. However, there we a few spots where they made it over the top and quickly cut down by the surrounding men.

Mitchell didn't have time to worry about the others right now. The force of the attack was surprising to him. They had wave after wave coming against them. He thought that even with the fire power his group could put down, it would not be enough.

This line of thought strengthened his resolve, and he came up firing. He emptied the mag in no time, and he was sure he took out at least one soldier pre-bullet, but they still kept coming at them. Just down from him, the Mexicans appeared to have made a beachhead on the top of the wall. The men there were falling back as more soldiers poured over the top.

Mitchell got on the radio and called, "Blake, they are breaching the wall between us. Take 'em out."

Before he could bring his rifle back up, he could see the soldiers drop. When he began firing into them, the beach head quickly collapsed, and the Alamo men began moving back up. He didn't have time to think about that, however.

The Mexicans were breaching the wall in more places. Mitchell started taking them out but had to turn his attention back to the wall right in front of him. He used a second grenade and just barely got it over the wall. When it went off, he could feel the force of the blast. This put a pause in the attack for him and he move back up to the wall and looked over to lay down more fire.

There was a pile of dead and wounded at the base of the wall in front of him. Mitchell just continued to add to the pile. When he stopped to reload, he took stock of his situation. He had already gone through about half his ammo and could only assume the others were in about the same situation. He didn't have time right now to call for SITREP.

All up and down the wall, Mitchell could see more breaches. In many of those places, it was hand to hand and usually the Mexicans were outnumbering the defenders. In the northeast corner, he could see the wall had partially collapsed. He could see Redcloud was having a hard time holding the area he was defending right in front of him.

He called Stretch on the radio, "Stretch, you need to move and cover that opening in the wall. Can you see it?"

"Roger." Came the reply after a few moments. "Already working it, but I don't know that we can hold it. The whole Mexican Army is moving to come through there."

Just then, there was an explosion in the opening. Redcloud had put a grenade round right in the middle of it. It helped, but not enough. Mitchell got back on the radio. "I'm moving."

He didn't expect anyone to respond. He was too busy running to pay any attention to it if they did. When he got down into the courtyard, he could see some of the Mexican soldiers were already fighting hand to hand there. He saw a lot of the men on the ground among the soldiers. They were losing men faster than they could afford to. He took up a sheltered position and started taking them out, one by one.

It wasn't helping a lot. Santa Anna's men were pouring through the hole in the wall like water. He thought for a moment and then decided. On the radio he announced, "Broken Arrow. Northeast corner only. Set for only three-round bursts."

Right away, he heard Redcloud open up. From his position, Mitchell also had a good line on the hole. The problem was this is eating up ammo like crazy.

"Chief, report on ammo." He called out.

He only said, "Running low. Also, low on grenade rounds."

He didn't hear from Stretch, but he figured he was probably about the same.

After a few more rounds into the breach, he called out. "Making an ammo run. Be back in a flash."

With that, Mitchell took off at a dead run. Lucky for him, they had plenty of mags and Anna made sure they were all fully loaded. He filled his pouches up and then found a bag and threw a bunch into it. Looking around, he found the grenade rounds and threw in as many as he could carry.

Quickly, he ran back to the hole in the wall. Now there were quite a few Mexican soldiers in the compound. They were also making their way along the top of the wall. Stopping short, Mitchell took a spot and started picking them off. First along the wall and then focusing on those in the compound. He could hear Redcloud firing, but nothing from Stretch.

No time. He quickly cleared out the compound and ran to Redcloud's position. He was like a madman. No automatic fire, but quick deadly shots. Mitchell threw that bag at his feet and turned to lay down more fire into the hole.

The Mexicans had spread along the top of the wall down the east side toward Stretch. Mitchell started picking them off while also trying to maintain some fire in the hole.

He thought they might hold for the moment, and then he heard Anna come over the radio. "My end is secure. They are retreating. Waiting orders."

Mitchell keyed up and yelled, "Get your ass over here and help me plug this hole!"

"Copy, on my way."

He continued to try keeping them off the wall and stopping the flow through the hole. In no time, he saw Anna come running up. Dropping into a prone position, she opened fire. The Chief was throwing grenades into the hole and still laying down fire outside the wall. All this time, the west, while being hit hard, appeared to be holding. The four of them continued to lay down fire in the hole. Slowly, the flow lessened and eventually stopped.

This, however, was not the end of the battle. Jose radioed, "There is a breach on the south-west corner."

Mitchell quickly turned and saw a small force of Mexican soldiers forming a circle around that opening. Taking the situation at both ends into account, he called out, "Anna, maintain fire on the north wall. Chief, put too HE round on the group to the south, then back to the hole." Taking off, he headed towards that end and took cover at the corner of a building along the west wall. By the time he got there, Redcloud had already put one round on target and, as Mitchell watched, the second round found its way home.

He now stepped out from cover and began firing into that group. These soldiers weren't organized like the force against the north wall and while they kept bringing in reinforcements; they could not expand their beachhead. It wasn't long before they tried to get back out, but most of them got cut down before they got out.

Running Mitchell made his way to that corner gun platform he had used so many times before to watch. Taking up a position there, he saw Bowie sitting in his chair and firing away.

The entire army, while holding, had ceased to advance with any strength. Mitchell swept across the front line and just taking out as many of Santa Anna's men as he could. Now, though, he was specifically looking for the officers. They are going down by the hundreds, maybe thousands, by now. Mitchell couldn't believe they could hold out this long, but they were obedient soldiers and continued to push until there was nothing left to push with.

Slowly, the advance stopped entirely. Some continued to fight, but slowly, a few at a time, they retreated. The firing was slowing. Mostly it was coming from the defenders, and they continued to fire at the retreating Mexicans.

Mitchell stopped shooting and inspected the surrounding area. Keying up his radio, he called, "Cease fire. Hold your fire. Let them go. We'll see what happens next. Stay put."

He got a few clicks of acknowledgement, but it didn't sink in that there were some missing right now. His first concern was Kat. He ran to the chapel and up the ramp. Looking to the right, he couldn't find her. He ran to where she should have been, but then he caught sight of her, kneeling by a body.

"God, no." He thought to himself as he ran to be with her. As he got there, Mitchell kneeled down beside her. It was August. He was not dead, but the wound was probably going to be mortal. He threw his arms around her and held her tight. There was nothing he could do except hold her.

August look at him and a managed a smile. "Take good care of my Katherine." He said through blood-soaked lips. He then closed his eyes and put his head back down.

Mitchell put his hand on August's chest and told him, "Yes, don't worry. I will take wonderful care of her."

He then coughed out some blood and said something in German Mitchell didn't understand. This cause Kat to cry even more and she buried her head in his arm. He then smiled and went limp.

Everyone standing around him fell quiet. The only sound was coming from his daughter as she cried.

Someone found a blanket or something and covered him. Slowly, Mitchell lifted Kat up and walked her back to their camp. Anna was there and right away she knew what was happening. She ran over to hug Kat and help her find a place to sit.

Redcloud came into camp next, but he didn't say a word. He just remained off to the side a little and watched. Everyone was silent. Only Kat continued to cry.

A few minutes later, the man who had the fight with Stretch came into their camp carrying a limp body. Everyone could see right away it was Stretch. The man walked right up to Mitchell with a strange look on his face. One of the other men that was involved in the fight was carrying Stretch's rifle. Redcloud came over and gently took it away from him.

Without being asked, the man carrying Stretch started talking, "He saved my life. While I was fighting, a Mexican to my side was aiming at me. Your man jumped in between us and took the bullet. He saved me."

He gently laid Stretch on the ground and continued to kneel by his side. Looking up at the entire group, he said, "Before he died, I asked him, 'After all that we did to you, why did you do that?' His reply was." And before he could say it, he got all choked up. "In battle, there is no color."

That big man then hung his head down and began to quietly weep.

Mitchell stepped up beside him and placed a hand on his shoulder. When he looked up at him, Mitchell said, "Now you know this man and where he came from. Remember this."

The man just nodded and hung his head down again.

Mitchell went back over and sat next to Kat, and continued to hold her tightly. Looking around, he said, "I was always confident that we could win this, but I was not prepared for the price it would cost. My group has lost two of its members. My family." He corrected himself. "However, there are many families today that will have lost members on both sides."

Other than his group, the people drifted away. Slowly, it was just Mitchell's group left around the fire. Blake and Jose had come into camp and just stood off to the side. Jose had a field dressing on his left arm.

"Are you Okay?" Mitchell asked.

He smiled a little and said, "Yeah, boss. Just a minor scratch."

Looking around, he found Anna. She was being comforted by her new boyfriend. Mitchell was now sure he like this kid. "Anna." He softly called out to her. When she looked up at him, he told her, "Take the guys and help take care of any wounded. Then try to collect up the used mags and reload. I don't know if this is over now or not."

She only nodded and got up. Grabbing her gear, she moved off. Everyone except the Chief, followed her without a single word.

"What's it look like out there?" Mitchell asked Redcloud as he moved over near him.

He sat down and looked in the town's direction. "It would appear that we defeated Santa Anna today, but he still has quite an Army. My guess is he may have lost half his force today, but that leave quite a powerful army to fight with."

Mitchell followed his gaze and thought about it for a moment. "What do you think he will do next?"

Redcloud didn't even think about it. He quickly said, "If it were me, I would send word to my other general to get back here and fortify my position here. Then attack again with a stronger force."

He had to admit it sounded logical. With the renowned arrogance of Santa Anna, a defeat like this will not set well. If the books and movies had it right, he will have to redeem himself.

"I think you may be right."

"Of course, I'm right." Came the smart-ass retort back.

Looking down at Kat, Mitchell gently lifted her head. Even though she had stopped crying, he could still see the sorrow in her red eyes. Softly, he said to her, "I need to go speak with Travis. This is not yet over, and we need to make plans."

She sat up and wiped her eyes and nose. Mitchell had a handkerchief in his pocket and handed it to her. She took it and continued to wipe her face. Leaning closer to her, he asked, "Will you be alright for a little while?"

She gave him a weak smile with her answer. "I'll go find Anna and help with the wounded."

He asked, "Are you sure? This will be very difficult."

Standing with assurance, she replied with something he didn't expect. "It will not be any more difficult that sitting her with an empty head thinking about things." Then, looking at him, she added, "Without you."

Mitchell just stood up and took her in his arms and held her as tight as he could. She wrapped her arms around him and hugged him back. He looked over at Redcloud. This time, there was no shit-eating grin on his face. He kept a straight face and nodded his approval. Knowing him, he did not easily give this to just anyone.

Mitchell released her and picked up his rifle and he and Redcloud both headed into the compound. There was a place near the gate where they placed the dead, both Mexican and Americans.

As they walked through all the horrors of the battle, the big man that brought Stretch back came over to Mitchell and asked, "Would you like me to take care of your man? It would be my honor."

"His name was Milton, but he asked to be called Stretch, because of how tall he was."

"Did he have a last name?"

"No last name. Just Milton will do." Mitchell didn't want to complicate things in the future when the experts look back at this with detail.

He looked at Kat, and she nodded. "Would you also, please, take care of her father? He is on top of the chapel. His name is Au…."

"August," the big man responded before he could finish, "yes, I know him. I would be honored to care for him, too."

He spun to his friends and wave for them to follow. They headed off to take care of the men. Redcloud gave a little chuckle and said, "I never expected that."

Mitchell looked at him and said, "I did, and I told Stretch as much. Like he said, there is no color in battle and that thought will linger in the mind of that man long after this battle is forgotten."

Redcloud just looked at him and nodded, then they turned to head off to find Travis. Mitchell took Kat's arm and pointed to where Anna was. She smiled to started walking that way. After a few steps, she turned and waved with a small smile.

He waved back and continued with Redcloud. They found Travis on the wall where he had been fighting. As they walked over there, Crockett came up. "How bad?" Mitchell asked.

"Bad enough." He answered. "Last I heard, there were thirty-one dead, and I don't know how many wounded."

Just about what he was figuring from just looking around. He pointed up the ramp to Travis, and Crockett followed him up. There were a lot of dead bodies around Travis, both on the wall and down below. He guessed Travis figured out how to shoot that pistol and used it well.

As they walked up, Mitchell found a mag in the dirt. He picked it up, and after brushing it off, he handed it back to Travis. "We don't have any extras for this. You need to hang on to them."

Travis took the mag without a word. A man nearby heard him and found the second mag and handed it to Travis. He just took the mag and nodded to the man.

Travis turned back to the town and began looking through his glass. Without turning and even lowering the glass, he asked, "What do you think will happen now?"

Mitchell took a step forward and calmly talked. "There are at least two reasonable scenarios that could happen. First, Santa Anna sends for the rest of his army, fortifies himself until they get here and then attacks again with a stronger fresh force."

Travis brought his glass down and turned to him. Looking right into his eyes, he asked, "And second?"

"Second, we take the fight to him." Mitchell stopped to let that set in a minute.

He watched Travis as he pondered over what Mitchell had just said. He looked around the compound and then back at him. "Surly you don't think we have enough men to take on what he has left of his army?"

He wasn't sure if that was a question and a statement. It didn't matter. "No Sir, we are not strong enough to take him on. However, we have thrown his plans into the wind. He must now make new plans and wait until the rest of his army can get here. How long do you think it will take him to bring all his forces to bear on us?"

Travis quickly thought about it. "At least a week, depending exactly where they are."

"That is what I was thinking, as well." Mitchell stepped away from the men that had gathered. Travis looked around and followed him. They walked down the ramp with Redcloud following, but staying between them and the men. Of course, Crockett followed them. "We need to take the fight to him, but we don't have the men, so we need to be sneaky."

Travis stepped back onto one leg and crossed his arms. "Go on."

"I suggest we take a small group, mostly my people. Sneak into town and grab El Presidente. Then bring him back here. They will not dare attack if we have him and we can hold him until he agrees to our terms."

Travis looked over at Crockett, who just gave a thoughtful nod.

"When would you do this?" he asked.

"Tonight, Sir. We need to hit him hard before he has time to regroup what forces he has. Right now, his army doesn't know what to do. He hasn't had time to plan and send out orders." Mitchell thought for a moment, then continued. "Also, we took out a lot of his junior officers and leaders. He will need to take time and replace them before he can even think about another attack."

"Once you have him, how do you plan to get him out of their camp and back here?"

Mitchell only pointed at the hummer.

Travis said nothing right away. He just started walking towards the hummer. "That thing will bring him out of his headquarters and past his entire army?" he asked as they walked over to it.

"Oh, yes." Mitchell said, "It has a special metal that his bullets cannot penetrate. If it got hit by one of his cannons, there might be some damage, but it will still be able to run. It could get in and back out faster than you think."

Travis stopped at the small wall next to the hummer and continued to look at it. Mitchell continued, "With our night vision, we can sneak in and have him before they even know we are there."

With help, Bowie had joined our group next to the hummer. Travis didn't see him come up and was taken aback a little when he finally turned back to them, but he didn't show it too much. "I approve of your plan. Who will you take with you?"

"I'll take two of my men and a couple of Crockett's." He said and then turned to Crockett, "If he thinks his men are up to it."

Crockett smiled, saying, "Wouldn't miss this for anything."

Bowie spoke up. "What about me?"

Travis frowned. "You can barely walk. How are going to go along?"

Bowie got furious, but Mitchell spoke up before anything bad could be said, "Bowie can go in the hummer. They will need someone with them that knows the town well. I'm going to have a diver, my sergeant." Then turning to Bowie, "you remember her." Before he could reply, Mitchell turned back to Travis, "I also have a gunner, up top. However, we need someone to guard Santa Anna while we get him back."

Travis was well aware of the situation between Anna and Bowie. He looked at Bowie and asked, "Will this be acceptable to you, Colonel?"

"Yeah, if it gets Santa Anna back here to answer for all this," Then, looking at Mitchell, he added, "I can live with it."

Travis thought for a moment, then finally said, "I suggest your men get some rest. It would appear you are going to have a long night ahead of you." He then just walked away.

Bowie hobbled over to be face to face with Mitchell. "Why are you putting me with that woman?"

"You mean, my Sergeant? She's the best driver I have."

Redcloud coughed a little, but he ignored him.

"Yeah, you know she doesn't like me."

Mitchell smiled at him, saying, "I hate to break it to you, but I don't think she cares one way or the other about you. It was a friendly fight. You took it one step too far, and she stomped your ass."

God, he'd been waiting a long time and for just the right place to say it. Now said he almost wished he hadn't. Both Mitchell and Crockett could see the anger on his face.

Crockett spoke now and in his gentle and diplomatic way, he tried to calm things down. "You know, Jim, he has a good point."

Bowie looked at Crockett and then back down and he calmed down a little, saying, "Yeah, I know, but she still doesn't like me. Are you sure she won't try to kill me in that thing of yours?"

Crockett spoke up, saying, "If it makes you feel any safer, I can send one of my men along with you to protect you from the young lady."

Now Bowie was furious. He just turned and tried to hobble away. When the men that were helping him came up, he just pushed them away."

"Oops, did I say something wrong?" Crockett said, just loud enough for Bowie to hear.

Now Bowie took a swing, with his crutch, at one man trying to help him. The helpers both stayed back from him.

Mitchell couldn't help but to laugh. He tried to hold it in, but that was impossible. Quickly, he told Redcloud to find everyone and get them back to camp as soon as they are able.

After Redcloud left, Crockett and he headed over to the camp.

When they finally sat down, just to sit down, for the first time today, Mitchell immediately felt totally exhausted. The adrenaline of the morning battle was gone, and the drive of the after-battle thoughts was all gone. Nothing more to push him along. He was wiped out, and it hit him like a train.

Looking over at Crockett, it looked he felt the same way. Getting up, Mitchell went over to the wagon and, after rooting around a little, he found where August had kept his little jug. It was still about half full. Bringing it back, he found a couple of cups and poured them a drink. When he sat down, he raised his cup, saying, "To the fallen." That was all. Simple and to the point.

Crockett held his cup up and repeated, "To the fallen."

They both downed the drink. Mitchell didn't offer another, but Crockett went ahead and poured another, but when he offered to fill his, Mitchell declined. One was enough. He still had too much to think about.

It didn't take long for the group to gather. They came in, in ones and two, but it was such a small group it didn't take long. And, as expected, Peter was right beside Anna.

Some grabbed an MRE, while the others just flopped down. They were all showing the same signs as Crockett and him. Mitchell showed the jug, but most everyone was too tired to even respond.

Kat came in with Anna and sat down next to him. She looked over at her father's jug and then back at him. Mitchell smiled and told her, "David and I just had a drink to honor your father and the others who fell today."

She smiled back and nodded, but he thought having the jug just sitting there was too much for her to endure. He got up and took it back to the wagon and then came back to stand near the center of the group. "People," He called to get their attention. Once the little chatter that was there stopped, he went on, "You did well this morning. It was a hard-fought battle and a costly one, for us." He looked directly at Kat when he said that last part. Continuing, he said, "However, this battle is not over. We have a mission."

It took a second for that to set in on them. Some sat up to listen while others rolled away and didn't want to hear. "We are going after Santa Anna."

Now he had everyone's attention. "Until he we get him, we can't win this war. Right now, his entire army is disorganized and weakened. We plan to take advantage of that, along with our special skills."

He then realized that while Crockett knew what he was talking about. This new kid, Peter, only had a vague idea of what they had. He looked over at him and said, "Anna will fill you in on everything later."

He turned to look at her, but Mitchell continued with the briefing, "Tonight we are going to send a team into his camp, find him, and take him. Once we have him, Anna will bring in the hummer and we'll get him out of there while the rest of the team evades and makes their own way back to camp."

He stopped there and sat down. He was just too tired to stand anymore. More tired than he realized. Mitchell looked at his watch and, according to it, it wasn't even nine o'clock yet. If he was this tired, then everyone's brain was probably mush as well. He cut it there for now. "Right now, everyone is too tired to even think about this. I want you all to grab some sack time and we'll get together this afternoon and finish planning out the mission."

Mitchell heard Peter ask Anna what sack time meant. She laughed a little and told him. "It means to get some rest, sleep."

He just watched as those two went off together. Everyone else dispersed, and it was just Kat and him left alone. He stood and took both of her hands and helped her to stand. Slowly, he walked her over to her tent and then he headed for his. It took about two seconds to crawl in and get comfortable. A couple minutes later, he was just about asleep when he saw the flap open, and Kat crawled in and laid next to him. Not a word was said. She just laid there, and he put his arm around her. Even before he could fall asleep, he could feel her breathing in a slow rhythm that was telling him she was already sleeping. Mitchel was right behind her.

He wasn't sure what time it was. Mitchell woke up and Kat was gone. Somehow, she could move away from him without waking him. Either she was very good, or he was exhausted. Sitting up, he found his boots and pulled them on. He just quickly wrapped the laces around to a quick knot. Crawling out into the sunlight hurt his eyes. Even though the clouds blocked most of the sun, it was still bright enough to hurt for a little. Now looking at his watch, it was telling him that half the afternoon had already gone by. He must have slept five or six hours. He hadn't realized how tired he must have been, but now he was feeling much better.

Mitchell found the water barrel and splashed some water on his face. Even in the afternoon, the water was still quite cool and woke him up better than that instant coffee shit they had. While he was still shaking the water off, Kat came up and put her arm around his waist. At first, it startled him, but only for a second. He realized it was her quickly and turned to give her a kiss. She, however, would have nothing to do with that. She pulled away and walked away. This left him with a lot of questions in his head. Had he done something wrong in his sleep? Maybe she was still upset about losing her father.

He couldn't figure it out, but before he could go after her, Redcloud came up behind him and said, "Glad to see you finally crawled out of bed."

"You know us officers need our sleep." Mitchell shot back at him with a smile. Then, looking around, he asked, "Anyone else up and about yet?"

Redcloud walked by him and only turned his head long enough to poke at his friend. "Only everybody. You're that last to get up." As he walked away.

Now he felt bad. Mitchell felt he should have set the alarm and gotten up a while ago. Following Redcloud to the fire, he said, "I guess we should get everyone together and make plans for the night."

"I take it you're telling me to get them all here while you wake up?"

He didn't smile, so Mitchell couldn't tell if he was being sarcastic or if he was angry. He was not sure what was going on. Kat seamed angry and now Redcloud. What happened while he was sleeping?

The water in the pot was no longer hot or even warm at that point. Mitchell settled for a cup of cool water and a couple of crackers from an MRE. This would have to do for now. He just sat down at the fire and soon the people gathered. There was a little chatter between some of them while others just sat quietly. He thought maybe Anna and Peter got little rest as well. They were both hanging off each other. Kat came out of her tent and came close to him, but didn't sit next to him. He made a mental plan to speak to her as soon as they finish here.

Last, Crockett and Redcloud came strolling into the group. Now Mitchell had to figure out a plan. He had a vague idea what he wanted to do, but he didn't have time yet to plan the details. They were all going to need to get together to plan this on the fly.

"Alright people, we are going out tonight to find and capture Santa Anna." Mitchell spoke in a low voice. He didn't want this news to get out to the rest of the people in the compound. Not that he didn't trust them, it was more he didn't know them and didn't want anyone to accidentally giving the plan away. He also didn't want anyone outside this group to know they would come back with Santa Anna. "I haven't had time to come up with a solid plan, but"

He said, but then off to the side he heard Redcloud mumble, "Yeah, because you were sleeping all day."

This got a giggle out of some of the group. He shut it down civilly. Looking towards Redcloud, he said out loud, "Yes, and thank you for letting me get a good sleep in."

Now, he had put the blame on them for letting him sleep too long, but he had done it in such a way they couldn't even be mad about it.

Continuing with the plan, "I want to break into two groups. First, I would like to put together a raiding team to go in and find El Jefe and subdue him. Once we have him, the second team will come in with the hummer and we'll load him up and get him out of there before they have too much time to react. That is the basic plan, so let's start from there."

Redcloud was the first to speak up and all he said was "Fuel."

All eyes turned toward Anna. Looking at her, Mitchell asked, "How are we set for fuel right now?"

She jumped up and ran over to the hummer and a couple second later she came back, "We have a little over half a tank. That's plenty for tonight, but depending on idling time we do and how much trouble we'll have getting in and out, we probably won't have much after we finish this."

While he had to agree with her assessment, he hoped she may have been a little pessimistic in her estimate of how much we'll have after. "We'll see what we can do after. Maybe we'll drain all the booze out of here to keep her running."

"Any other issues you can think of?" He asked while looking around at everyone. He could see they were all thinking, but it was Crockett that spoke up next.

"It is near full moon, but if the clouds are still there tonight, we won't have much light to find our way through their camp."

"We're going to have the night vision that we use the other day. Also, before we head out, I'll send up the drone and see if we can pinpoint where he is, so we don't have to take too long to find him."

Crockett thought for just a moment, then added, "He won't be all by himself."

From behind Crockett, they heard another voice saying, "No, he won't be. If he doesn't have a woman with him, he will probably have his staff there. Either way, there will be plenty of guards all around him."

"Colonel Bowie," Mitchell said, "Good of you to join us." He wanted to put the blame on him for not being here instead of himself acknowledging the fact that he forgot about him. "Jim, do you have any idea where he might hold up?" I asked.

"I have a couple of ideas, but without having strolled through the town since he got here, I couldn't really say for sure." His reply was so sarcastic Mitchell thought Bowie knew he forgot about him and trying to make up for it.

"Good," Mitchell said. "We'll meet just after dark and use my flying machine to find him."

Mitchell didn't know about Bowie, but that surely caught the interest of Crockett. All this time, Anna was whispering things into Peter's ear. He appeared to be quite interested in all she was saying.

Now was the time for the bad news for those two. "Anna, I want you to drive the hummer. You'll have Jose in the turret and Colonel Bowie siting shotgun to give you directions and stand guard on the boss man when we have him."

"Can I take Peter to help me?" She asked.

"No, sorry. He will go out with us on the raiding team." She looked a little down, but Peter seemed to be all for it. "I'll let you two have a kiss when you get there to pick up Santa Anna."

Now both of them were embarrassed. Everyone had a little laugh about that, but when Anna turned and planted a big kiss on him in front of everyone, the laughing got much stronger. Mitchell wished he had the video going to record the look on Peter's face. It was priceless.

Continuing on, "That leaves the raiding team. The rest of my group, plus Colonel Crockett and young mister Peter, will go out." Then, turning to Crockett, he added, "Anything you would like to add?"

"I got a couple other good men that are good at night fighting. I could bring them along."

Mitchell thought about that for a moment then said, "We don't have enough night vision for that many men."

Crockett just proudly said, "I told you they was good. They won't need your machines."

Trying not to insult him, but Mitchell had reasons, "That's fine, but young Peter here goes."

He thought Crockett understood what he was doing and said with a smile, "He's going to have to learn someday. This is as good and any other day."

"I want everyone to have a knife. We are going to go in as quietly as we can. No shooting unless it is absolutely necessary." He added.

Looking around, he could see it was all still setting into their brains. There was little time and a lot of things that needed to be set up. Looking over at Anna, he said to her, "After the Mexicans clear their people off the battlefield and have gone, I want you to move the hummer over to the east gate. We need to do it nice and quiet like. We'll get enough men to push it over to stay quiet and save fuel."

Looking around at the group, he was quite pleased with them. "Just after dark, we will head out the south gate and make our way towards the bridge." Everyone's eyes were on him. "Chief, I want you to take the point. Take Crockett with you and remove any guards they may have put there."

Crockett and Redcloud both turned to look at each other. A simple nod was all that they needed. They both had enough experience to know what to do and nothing more needed to be said.

"Peter," Mitchell called, looking at him, "I want you to stay near me. You are both new to the equipment and new at night raiding. The rest of the group will spread out. Once we cross the bridge, we'll make our way to wherever he is hiding."

He began drawing it out on the dirt, and everyone gathered closer. Colonel Bowie believed Santa Anna has his headquarters just on the other side of the plaza to the north. Just before they head out, he will have Jose send up the drone and they'll try to see if this is the spot.

Blake asked, "What happens if he is not there?"

It was a valid question. "We'll split up into twos and search the entire area until one group finds him. We'll then converge on his tent or building and take him. Crockett, you'll have to stay with Redcloud because he has the radio."

"The what?" Crockett shot back at him.

Mitchell snickered a little and pulling the head piece off and held it out. "It is another tool that allows us to talk to each other for up to a couple of miles."

Both Crockett and the kid let out a whistle while looking at each other. "Each of my people will have one, so I need both of you to team up with one of my people."

Peter started to say something, but Mitchell cut him off. Looking straight at him, he said, "No, you're teaming up with me."

He looked at Anna and shrugged.

"Kat," he said, turning to her, "I want you on the wall. I'm going to leave you my binoculars and you'll so you can keep a watch. If anything looks strange, you'll have the spare radio from Stretch. You'll also have one of the night vision sets to use."

She didn't say anything but nodded and smiled. He returned a nod back with his own smile.

"Any questions or concerns, before we break up?" He asked, standing back up.

For right now, there were none. He was pretty sure his people had a good grasp on the mission, but he couldn't say for locals. They were all excellent soldiers, and while he was sure they would be fine in their own environment, now it was a new environment with a new set of rules. Mitchell was just going to trust that they'll be able to work together. After all, fighting is fighting, when it comes right down to it.

There were no questions. He took a deep breath to prepare for a pep talk, but it was Crockett that spoke first. "I suggest we all get some more rest for now. It is going to be a long night."

Mitchell had to chuckle a little, because that was just about what he was going to say. So, he just added, "We'll gather back here about an hour before dark to get ready and take a peek with the drone." He also added, looking at Anna and Peter, "That means getting some rest alone."

Anna just shot him a dirty look and turned away. Peter wanted to say something, but she grabbed his arm and pulled him to her and whispered something they couldn't hear.

Crockett and Redcloud stepped away from the group and began talking. Mitchell's guess would go over the two-man tactics they would use. Blake and Jose just went over to their tents.

This left Kat and him alone. Now, he moved close to her, but she still wouldn't look at him. Leaning over, he gently asked, "Is there something wrong?"

Slowly, he could see tears forming in her eyes. She turned away to hide them, but he moved to still be in front of her. Kat then buried her face in her hands and started crying uncontrollably. Moving forward, he put his arms around her shoulders and held her close to him. She continued to cry for a long time, while not a word was said.

After a long time, she gently pulled away and began wiping her face with his handkerchief he had given her earlier.

"What's the matter, my Love?" He gently asked her.

She could hardly speak and some of her German broke up the English, but he could gather what she was saying, "I am so ashamed of coming and laying with you before we are married."

It took him aback a little. This he had not expected, although, for this time and place, he could understand. She slowly continued, "My father, god bless his soul, would be so ashamed of me, too."

Mitchell just let it be for just a little while. Finally, reaching out, he put a single finger under her chin and lifted her face to see him. "You were lonely and had just fought a fierce battle and lost your father. I don't think anyone here will think badly about it."

He could see in her eyes, this was of little help. Moving a little closer, so his face was just inches away from hers, he whispered, "And it really doesn't matter. You and I know that nothing improper went on this morning. We just wanted to be together in our sorrow and fatigue."

"But the others will talk about this." She blurted out.

"So, what? It is only what you and I think that matters about such things." He said rather sternly. He wanted it to sound almost as if it was coming from her father. "The others don't matter."

Now the worry really came out, "You mean, you will not be ashamed to still marry me?"

Mitchell reached out and pulled her to him and held on. "Of course not. You are my love and my wife to be. Even if things had progressed to something that was inappropriate, it would still not matter to me. I love you and will always be there for you. In my time, a young woman, such as you, would be with anyone she wanted. However, I am respecting the customs of this time and waiting for you."

She hugged back with an even stronger grasp. The crying began again, but it was different this time. Mitchell had a feeling she was crying tears of joy now. He couldn't tell because she wouldn't let go long enough for him to see.

After a long while, she slowly let go and leaned back. Then she asked something he didn't expect and was unsure how to answer. "Would you like to sleep with me now?"

This again took Mitchell by surprise so much that he fell back on his butt. Looking up into her eyes, he could see she was serious about this. Quickly thinking, he said, "I would love to; however, this is not a good time or the right time for this." Leaning back, she just looked at him while he continued, "For you and regarding your father, I would like to wait. I want our first time to be a pleasant and happy time for you. Not something we rushed to do in the middle of a battle."

She nodded as he talked. "You said a woman has a right to choose."

Smiling a little, he answered her, "Yes, you may choose when, where, and with who. However, that man has the same rights. They must both agree for it to be a beautiful thing."

She thought about it for a moment, then smiled. "I understand. We will wait for the proper time and place." Then she leaned forward to give him a kiss and a big hug.

After releasing him, she just got up and headed for her tent. After disappearing into it, Mitchell got up and turned to go back to his tent and think about tonight. As he did, he found Redcloud, again standing over next to the wall, watching. Mitchell just flipped him the bird and went into his tent. As he went in, he could see that big ass grin on Redcloud's face again.

Mitchell just laid in his tent, trying to go over the plans for tonight. Batteries. I forgot to have Jose get all the batteries charged up for tonight. I know that drone had a good charge, but we used the night vision and radios today. He thought the night vision should be fine. They didn't use them that long. However, the radios were his biggest worry now. Leaving his tent, he headed for Jose's tent and went to wake him up. Unfortunately, he grabbed Blake's foot first. "Sorry," He said, "I need to speak to Jose."

Jose spoke up, "What is it, boss?"

"How are we set for batteries? We are going to need just about everything tonight."

It took a moment for the fog to clear from his head, but he agreed with his assessment, "The night vision should be OK. We have enough spares for the radios, but I don't know that we will need them."

"OK," He told him, "After you get up, I want the spares put in the radios, so we have a fresh supply. Give the others to Anna to charge while she has the hummer running."

He quickly shot back, "She won't have time to charge all those batteries."

"Yeah, I know, but she can get a little charge on some of them while she is running around."

"I guess, Boss," he said back, "I'll take care of it."

"Good man, now get some rest."

"That's what we were trying to do." Mumbled Blake.

He just closed the flap on their tent without saying any more.

About an hour before dark, everyone gathered again. Mitchell went back and recovered the pistol from Travis. After showing Crockett how to use it, he felt fairly sure he could make excellent use of it. Unfortunately, they didn't have a radio or night vision for him. The only spare went to Kat to keep watch. Crockett's men got paired up with one of his guys, and each team began going over tactics while he got with Jose to send up the drone.

Going over to their spot on the southwest gun platform, Jose and he deployed the drone. Even though it was a little dark, they still drew a bit of a crowd. Crockett and Bowie also joined them. They needed Bowie here because he knew the town better and could guide them to find Santa Anna quicker. He took Crockett off to the side to get him to help with crowd control and move the lookers back a bit. With no words from the men that had gathered, Crockett quickly had them moved back. Bowie had his chair brought up and sat where he could see the screen and look out to San Antonio.

As soon as Jose had the drone ready, they sent it up. Even though Crockett had moved the crowd back, they could see well enough to let out a collective gasp as the drone shot up into the air. Glancing over, Mitchell saw Travis watched and was standing at the front of the crowd. Raising his hand, Mitchell waved at him to come closers. He came to the top of the gun platform but didn't seem interested in watching the screen. Turning his attention back to the task at hand, Mitchell softly told Jose, "Move it over towards the bridge and let's see what they have waiting for us there."

Jose nodded and played with the controls and quickly he was a couple hundred feet above the bridge, looking down. There were two men at the bridge. One at each end. The one closest to the Alamo side appeared to be sitting and asleep. The other guard looked to be standing and just leaning on his rifle. Neither one appeared to be too interested in taking their guard duty seriously.

Putting his hand on Jose's shoulder, he leaned down and told him, "Great, now get a little higher and move over the center of the town."

Again, Jose played with the controls and the view they were looking at spread out. In no time, he was over the central plaza and hovered. They could see the hot spots of many people and the campfires from this height. Moving closer to the screen to see better Mitchell motioned for Bowie to get a better look. After a moment, he pointed to the corner of the screen and said, "Can you move it this way some more?"

After a second, the image on the screen moved and they could see many more people now. Some appeared to be moving in and out of a building, while others had a less brightness to them. Mitchell's guess was they were probably in a tent. They could make out the people and what looked like lanterns or candles on the inside. "OK, hold it there. I think we may have found his headquarters." There were several grunts of agreement from the small group around the screen. He added, "Let's try to figure out which one is the boss man and track him a little."

As they watched, it appeared there was a table in the middle of the tent and most of the people gathered there took seats around the table. There were a few that stayed on the outside edges. He guessed these were the servants or the guards. There was one figure that continued to move at one end of the table and occasionally would circle the table. That had to be him, Santa Anna.

Reaching out, Mitchell pointed to that white spot on the screen and asked, "Watch this one and tell me what you think."

Jose narrowed down the view and everyone around leaned in to look. Now, even Travis had come closer to see. They stood there watching for a long time. Bowie commented, "I look like El Presidente is not happy."

Mitchell added, "I'll bet they are all getting a good ass chewing for their failure this morning."

From the looks on some faces, they had not heard that said before, but no one said anything, so Mitchell figured they quickly got the idea."

Looking over at Crockett, who was being silent, He asked, "What do you think?"

He looked over at Bowie before answering him, "I think you are right, but by the time we get there, I don't think he is going to still be in the tent."

Now Bowie spoke up. "He will probably have a nice, comfortable room in that building right next to his tent. Right now, he has too many men around him. We need to wait until he goes into the building. He will probably have a woman with him and won't be paying much attention to us."

Looking around, Mitchell said, "I agree."

Bowie again spoke, "He is arrogant and will probably think we are hurt too bad to do anything to him. He won't be expecting us to attack his headquarters."

This got another round of approving grunts from the small group.

Crockett now threw his two cents into the planning. "How are we going to know when he's going into the other building and which room he will end up in?"

"How much flying time do we still have?" Mitchell asked Jose.

Hitting a key brought up the control panel. Looking up at it, he said, "Probably around forty-five minutes, less if we keep the camera going."

Quickly thinking a moment, he said, "Find a place on top of a nearby building and land. Turn off everything, but keep it on standby."

Now, standing up, Mitchell stretched his back. The others did the same thing. Next time, they'll need to bring a table up here to save their backs.

Slowly, he moved over to the big gun on the platform and leaned up against it. The others followed him and gathered around. After a moment to consider all the things that were going into the operation tonight, Mitchell looked at each of the men around him, then asked, "Does anyone have any thoughts?"

Bowie spoke up, "We're gonna have a hard time finding exactly where he is, and he will not leave himself open. He'll have plenty of guards around him."

"That will not be a problem." Mitchell said and before Bowie could start an argument with him, he continued, "I left the drone, the flying machine, in town. When we all get set, Jose will locate our man and give us details about what we are up against. We still have a few things up our sleeves you haven't seen yet."

Jose had joined the group and added, "I parked the drone on top of the building we think he is using. We'll have about twenty minutes of flying time, but I am going to need a couple of minutes of that to recover the drone when we're done."

Turning to listen to him, Mitchell nodded to show he understood. Again, he looked at the gathered men. No one said anything. "Let's do it, then." Mitchell said as he stood up. Each man picked up their rifles, and they all turned to leave.

As they walked back to the group area, Mitchell turned to speak to Crockett. "You and Redcloud are going out first. I want you in position for the start, but just get into position and wait for the rest of us to get into position."

"We'll be ready." He replied with a smile.

When they got back to the camp, Mitchell could see that Redcloud and Anna had been busy. They had broken out the cammo sticks and everyone was painted up, even Crockett's men. When Crockett saw them, he laughed, but with a stern look from Redcloud, the laugh quickly died out. Redcloud then handed a cammo stick to Crockett and said, "I assume you know what this is and how it works. You and the Captain can pair up to get ready."

Crockett took the cammo stick from Redcloud and held it up in a gesture of thanks, then turned towards Mitchell. He also grabbed a stick and headed towards the hummer. Looking in the mirror, Mitchell showed Crockett how to apply it and explained about how to blend the colors. He was pretty sure he had used dirt and other stuff to camouflage himself before, but this thing was new. He was quick to pick up on it and soon they both looked like the others.

Going to Redcloud, Mitchell said, "I think it's about time for you two to head out. Signal me when you're both in position. We'll be ready and shouldn't take much time to get to you. As we start out, you'll execute and join this group when we cross the bridge."

"Got it." Was the only thing Redcloud said to him, then he turned to Crockett and asked him, "You ready to go?"

Crockett picked up his rifle, saying, "You lead off and I'll be right behind you."

Redcloud picked up his rifle and headed for the gate in the southern wall, with Crockett about a half step behind him.

Before they even got to the gate, Mitchell turned to the rest of the crew. "I want to push the hummer to the other gate and get it just outside the walls before we leave." He said and turned towards the hummer.

Anna got in behind the wheel. He went to the passenger side and opened the door. Turning to Bowie, He motioned for him to get in the back. With a little difficulty, he climbed in. The uncomfortable look on his face was almost too much. Mitchell had to work hard to stifle a laugh, but after a look around Bowie nodded back at him and he shut the door. The rest of them got behind the thing and pushed.

Getting through the hole in the little wall wasn't too hard, mostly because they had knocked part of it down before getting in there. As they pushed it across the compound, a bunch of the men gathered around to watch. When they got to the other gate, it took a couple of tries before they had it lined up well enough to get through the tight opening. Jose had gotten in and was standing up in the gun turret to help guide. His wound wasn't bad enough to prevent him from manning the gun, but Mitchell didn't want to take a chance with him on the capture team.

Quickly, they were outside the compound. During the push, Mitchell was checking out the group. Blake had something that was still making noise. When he checked him out, he quickly determined his dog tags didn't have the plastic case to help keep them quiet. He took the set from around Blake's neck, saying, "You don't really need these anymore. Just leave them in your tent."

He was a little nervous and Mitchell singling him out didn't help. As he moved to head back to the camp, Mitchell patted him on the shoulder, and he turned and gave him a weak smile. Crockett's man assigned to him stayed with him as he walked away. "Meet us at the south gate." Mitchell said before they had gotten more than a couple of steps away.

Blake said nothing but gave a thumbs up as he walked away.

Turning back to the group, he yelled, "Let's move out!" Then to Anna he said, "We'll give you a shout when we've got him. You be quick about it."

"You got it, boss." She happily said. He thought she was finally happy to show some of these men what she could really do, especially Bowie.

At the gate, they did a quick weapons check. He made sure everyone had a good knife. The two men who Crockett brought into this also had very impressive tomahawks tucked in their belts. Anna's Peter didn't have a tomahawk but had a very nice knife.

After everyone was ready, they moved just outside the gate, but still inside the berm. It wasn't long before he heard the static clicks from Redcloud telling him he and Crockett were in position. Slowly, Mitchell raised his hand and then signaled for everyone to follow him out. Staying low, they went over the top of the berm and began making their way towards the bridge.

It didn't take too long to get there, and he signaled a stop just short of the bridge. Whispering into the radio, I said a single word: "Execute."

After a short while, only a couple minutes, he heard Redcloud's voice come up in a whisper, "Clear."

Mitchell signaled everyone to move out. They gathered on this end of the bridge, and, after a careful scan of the town, Mitchell motioned for the first pair to go across. Working like this, they got across in no time, with Redcloud being the last to cross.

Mitchell really wanted to get closer to the town before he called Jose to send the drone back up to confirm Santa Anna's location, but there were still several men in the plaza and he didn't dare try to move up and talk. He signaled Redcloud to come to him. I told him, "Take the group to the edge of the town and wait while I work with Jose to find Santa Anna."

Redcloud didn't say a word. He just went to the head of their group and signaled for everyone to spread out and stay low.

Peter stayed with Mitchell, which was good. Keying up his radio, Mitchell called, saying, "Send up the drone and find our man."

He got a click back, indicating Jose had heard him. It didn't take long, and Jose's voice came over the air. "He is still in the tent, but only has a couple of men still with him, plus what looks like two guards on the outside and two on the inside with him."

"Roger, keep watching." He said and waved for Peter to follow him to join up with the rest of the group.

Before he got to the group, Jose came back up. "He is on the move. Looks to be going in the building. The two guards outside the tent are staying in place. The two that were in the tent have taken up positions at the door to the building."

With a quick answer, him with, "Copy." They continued to meet up with the group.

Just as he arrived, Jose came back again. "He appears to be on the second floor in the south-west corner. There appears to be someone with him. Colonel Bowie says it is probably his woman for the night."

"Copy," Mitchell said and added, "Good work. Bring the drone home."

He replied, "Copy, good hunting."

Calling the group together, he quickly and quietly explained to them their assignments. He had Blake take his two men and move up the south side of the plaza and past the tent and take up positions there. Crockett's other man paired up with him and Redcloud. Mitchell had them go up the next street north of the plaza and cut back to be near the building. He took Peter, and they moved up the north side of the plaza and took up positions in front of the tent.

Before he let them all go, he gave Kat a call on the radio. "Kat, is everything still good from where you sit?"

He didn't know if he surprised her and she just was taking time to check, but it took a little before she answered. After what seemed like forever, she answered back, "I don't think there is anything happening. Everything still looks the same."

Her voice was a little shaky in her reply. He thought she was both nervous and worried. Trying to make her feel better, he quickly said, "Thank you and good work."

She replied, "Thank you."

Mitchell had to hold in a smile, thinking they were going to have to practice on her radio procedures later. He looked up at the group and gave them the signal to move out. It took some time for each group to get into position. Santa Anna's men were still moving around the town. He didn't think they were guards, though. For the most part, they were unarmed and talking. He didn't speak Spanish, but from the tone it was more talk about the day, and maybe about the future. It then dawned on him he should have brought someone who could talk to the boss man when they caught him.

It took a little while longer for the others to get into position, but soon they were already. Mitchell pulled out the silencer and screwed it into the barrel of his pistol. Using the side of the building to steady his hand, he quickly took out the two guards in front of the tent. They fell, almost without a sound. He motioned Peter to follow and after pulling the two guards inside, out of sight, they moved into the tent. Just inside he whispered into the radio, "Two, move up" After what seemed like a long time, he got a double tap on the radio from Redcloud telling me he was in position.

Moving to the side of the tent next to the building, Het pushed the barrel of his pistol through the flap and again took out the two guards at the door. Before he could do anything else, Mitchell heard a thump. Quickly turning and ready to fire, he saw Peter running to the side door they had just came in. Bending down, he quickly pulled his knife out of the body that was laying there. He then pulled the body to the side and out of the way. Making his way back to him, Mitchell nodded to him, however being so dark he didn't know if he actually saw it. He then turned and double tapped his radio.

Within seconds, Redcloud, Crockett, and the third man made their way to the door. The third man took up a position just inside the door and after a quick wave to him, Peter and Mitchell moved back to the front of the tent where they came in.

Now came the waiting. Mitchell wished they had more life in the drone. It would have been nice to have a play-by-play from Jose about what was happening. They saw a couple of men come their way, however they turned off before they got there. He got a feeling these soldiers didn't want to be anywhere near this tent.

What seemed like forever finally passed and Redcloud announce over the radio, "Jackpot."

Mitchell then keyed up his radio and whispered, "Execute."

A quick double tap on the radio told him that Anna got the word and was moving out. It was hard to say at this distance, but he thought he could hear the hummer as it started up. He quickly called out, "Kat" on the radio.

She quickly answered back. "Some men are moving to the center area. They started moving as soon as Anna started the, uh… hummer."

Mitchell could hear her voice stammer a little as she tried to remember what they called that thing.

He called out to Blake, "Johnny, you two move up to this side of the plaza." Then to Redcloud, "A minor change in plans. We are going to pass the boss man off to Anna in the central plaza. The hummer is just too noisy."

"Copy. You two move out. We'll be right behind you."

Mitchell replied with a simple, "Copy.'

He signaled Peter to follow him. They moved out of the tent and crossed the road and made their way back to the central plaza. They stopped at the corner and took up a good position behind a couple of barrels. In a moment, he saw Blake come up to the edge of the plaza. He stopped and looked around. Mitchell motioned him to move to the other side of the plaza so they would have a good crossfire.

Blake gave him a double tap to say he understood, then he and his partner moved down the road to the other side. Now they all could clearly hear the hummer as it moved towards the town. Best guess is they just crossed the bridge. Just then, a sound behind him made Mitchell jump. He raised his gun as he turned, only to see Crockett coming around the corner. Redcloud and the third man were right behind him, and they were dragging a limp body.

Turning his attention back to the hummer, he called to Anna, "We are in the northwest corner of the plaza. Large welcoming party in the plaza. Be ready."

He heard her say, "Copy." However, the noise of the hummer was drawing a bigger crowd. More men were running into the plaza. A few men came around the corner and surprised when they saw Mitchell's group there. Redcloud was quick to respond and quickly took out two men. Crockett was now slouch either. Using his tomahawk, he gutted the next man and then planted the tomahawk in the man's skull. The two of them then took up a position at the corner and stood ready in case any more surprises came around. The third man stayed with Santa Anna, who was still unconscious.

Shortly, Mitchell heard a couple of shots come from the direction of Blake. They didn't sound like his weapons. From what he could see, Blake was taking fire from further back in the town.

Now some men in the plaza were turning to the gunfire, but just then Anna turned on the headlights and hit the horn. This was nothing like Mitchell had ever seen before. Some men dropped their rifles and ran, while others just hit their knees appeared to be crying. Only a few returned fire in the hummer's direction. Jose was quick to lay down some fire from the Machinegun. It only took a little fire from Jose to change the minds of those men that wanted to fight. They quickly turned and ran.

Blake was still taking fire from further back in the town. The volume of fire was slowly increasing as more of Santa Anna's men moved up. Anna came right to them and quickly loaded the limp body of El Presidente into the back of the hummer. Bowie was there with a pistol and his knife. After seeing the boss man was out cold, he turned back to looking out the window at the fight.

Mitchell yelled at Bowie to get his attention above all the noise of the firefight, "Colonel, he is your responsibility. Remember what we talked about earlier?"

Bowie looked down at Santa Anna with a disgusted look on his face and flatly said, "Yeah, I remember. I don't agree, but I'll make sure he gets back."

He then reminded him, "Not only back, but keep him safe from everyone else."

Again, he gave Mitchell an angry look and yelled, "Yeah, yeah, yeah,"

Mitchell then yelled at Anna, "Take off!" And slammed the door shut.

She quickly spun around and headed right back the way she came.

Now, the rest of them had to fight their way out of town. Jose and Anna had cleared most of the plaza with the hummer. This looked to be the best way out of here. He got on the radio and yelled, "Keep fighting and fall back to the bridge!"

Crockett, Redcloud, and the third man had moved a little closer to Blake while he loaded up their prisoner and got him out of there. Peter and he fell back on the north side of the plaza. Some more men were coming around the corner on this side, and the fighting picked up a bit. Blake and his men had fallen back a little, but it was slow moving. Redcloud's group was keeping up fire in the middle area on both sides, but now it was time for them to fall back. On the radio Mitchell yelled, "Chief, fall back, we'll cover you."

He saw Redcloud pass the word along and the third man moved to run. When he had made it to cover, Crockett was next. Mitchell saw him run, but then he went down. His heart came up in his throat. A second later, Crockett was up and running again. Quickly, he turned his attention came back to the fight on his side.

They slowly made their way back out of town, however, before they got clear, He heard a sharp yell. Turning, he saw Peter holding his left arm and blood pouring out. Mitchell took his knife and cut away the sleeve and pulled out a bandage from his kit. He wrapped the wound tightly. Young Peter, however, could no longer shoot his rifle, so Mitchell slung it over his shoulder and handed him his pistol. The silencer had to be removed, and then it was ready to fire. He showed Peter the safety and said, "Just point and shoot until it is empty."

He looked the thing over and soon was firing. It didn't take him long to figure it out and was soon dropping the soldiers coming at them. By now, the others had cleared the town line and taking cover while they tried to get out. He helped Peter to his feet as he emptied the gun into a group of soldiers coming their way. Mitchell grabbed the pistol and dropped out the mag and quickly put another in. Cycling the pistol, he handed it back, saying, "You got another seventeen rounds. Take it easy and make them count."

Again, he looked it over, just like the first time. This time he looked up at Mitchell and with a big smile said, "I like this thing." He then went back to shooting, as did Mitchell.

As they moved out of the town, the others covered them. The soldiers didn't move beyond the edge of the town and slowly the fire died out. Keeping low, they made their way back to the bridge and in no time; the group was back safely behind the walls.

When they came into the compound, there was a lot of cheering and slaps on the back. However, Mitchell had more important things on his mind. He grabbed Crockett and headed towards the crowd outside the room Travis called his office. These men were also happy to see them, but the mood was less festive over here.

Approaching the door, they found a couple of guards and Captain Dickenson standing outside. As they approached, Dick said, "Colonel Travis wants you two to go right in."

They opened the door, and Captain Blugh motioned for them to go into the back room. Coming in, they found Travis sitting behind his desk and Bowie was sitting behind Santa Anna, still with his pistol and knife at the ready.

Shortly, Captain Seguin joined the group and Travis talked, while Juan translated for him. It didn't take Santa Anna long to understand his position and that he would remain safe, as long as his men did not attack.

Santa Anna then stood and, in Spanish, asked for paper and a pen. He wrote out a couple of pages. The writing, although is Spanish and Mitchell couldn't understand it, was very elegant. When he finished, he handed it to Captain Seguin, who read it in English to Travis. They were orders to his commanders stand down. Also, to allow free passage to anyone coming or going from this fort.

When Juan had finished, he handed the papers to Travis, who politely smiled and reached out his hand. Santa Anna just stood there and did not shake his hand. Travis quickly dropped his hand and sat down. Turning to them, he asked Crockett, "What is it like outside right now?"

Crockett put the butt of his rifle on the floor and leaned on the barrel. Something Mitchell would consider very unsafe, however, it was something he could picture him doing. Slowly, he said, "Most of the men are thrilled and already celebrating. However, there is a not too small group of men just outside your door, that are waiting. They appear to be much less happy."

Travis just sat there for a moment. Mitchell was not sure if he was trying to decide what to do, or trying to decipher what Crockett was trying to say. Shortly, he stood and lead the way out of the office. In the outer room, there were a couple of men waiting. These men were in uniform and must have been soldiers in his command. Turning to them, he said, "Keep an eye on him. Don't let anyone near him other than these men with me."

One man snapped a salute, and they both headed into his inner office.

Travis then led the way outside. Mitchell had a feeling this was going to be one of those long drawn-out speeches. Taking the center, the rest of them spread out behind him. He began, "Men, it is over. We have won."

A couple of men gave a quick cheer, and they all mumbled some chatter between them. One man took a step forward and asked Travis, "What's going to happen to him now?"

Another man yelled from the back, "We should hang him!"

This comment got a lot of positive reaction from the crowd.

Travis took a step forward, and the men quickly quieted. Softly he said, "Gentlemen, if he dies now, everything we have fought and died for will be for nothing." He paused while the men looked back and forth at each other. Continuing, he said, "He must be kept alive to sign papers with the new government of Texas and agree to our terms."

Mitchell could see a lot of those men were now nodding at this. They hadn't thought past the anger of the moment to consider what was best for the future. Now they were seeing the action here and how it will have a profound effect on the future of Texas.

Travis said, "What we have done here is to breathe life into Texas and keeping Santa Anna alive to fulfill our destiny is the only way Texas will remain a free republic where the tyranny of men like Santa Anna will never again have power over our people."

It was not a long-drawn-out speech, but very short, and it hit the spot. The men that were out front were not all pleased, but the way Travis put it, they now understood. Now, all the men were at least nodding in agreement and some of them even let out a cheer. More people had joined the crowd and the excitement of the moment quickly grew. The crowd slowly broke up and Mitchell thought they all headed off to find a bottle that some may have hidden away.

After watching the crowd leave, he stepped out in front of Travis and said, "Sir, with your permission, I would like to prepare to move out tomorrow with my group."

Travis said nothing. He just stood there looking at him for a long time. He then took a step forward and extended his hand. This is probably the single biggest honor of Mitchell's life. He firmly took his hand and then grabbed Travis' arm with his other hand. He shook it. When he finished, Mitchell stepped back and rendered a proper salute. For the first time, Travis returned a proper salute.

Mitchell did a fine military about-face and walked away. It wasn't long before Crockett caught up to him and walked along beside him. Slowly, he handed back the pistol Mitchell had loaned Bowie. Checking the safety, he put it back in his holster, but then he thought about it and needed to make sure he got his pistol back from Peter before they leave.

Crockett began talking. "What will you do now?"

"I don't know." Mitchell answered him. "My people will need to sit down and decide together what we will do. Even though I am the leader, we run our group as a democracy. These decisions will need to be agreed upon."

"It sounds like the people I wouldn't mind being with." Crockett said as he stopped walking.

Mitchell stopped and turned toward him. "David," he said and then smiled, "Davy, is what the history books will call you, even though I now know you don't like it." He kind of rolled his eyes, but Mitchell didn't let him say anything. He just continued to speak, "The history books have you dying here at the Alamo. I can't tell you what your future will bring. You have seen and learned a great deal more than I had intended. You are also a man of significant influence on others when you want to be."

Crockett looked down to say something, but Mitchell stopped him. "I believe your future may lie on a different path than ours. Not that we may cross paths again, but I will tell you this country is headed for a very terrible future soon. You have seen and heard what my future will be like. Some things will be good, others will be a horror. Men, with your integrity, are needed to lead this country in the future."

Mitchell thought since the first time he'd met him; this great man was speechless. He just stood there, looking at the ground for a long time. Finally, he looked him in the eye and said, "Jim, it has been an honor to fight by your side. I surely do hope we will cross paths again in the future. Not to fight together, but to sit and have a drink or two and swap stories. I'll wager you have a few whoppers."

Putting out his hand, Mitchell was again honored today and shook it. He pulled Crockett to him and put his arm around his shoulder and patted it. "I think I will miss you more than anyone else around here."

"Except that pretty little thing you have waiting back in your group." Crockett said back to him.

Mitchell laughed and nodded an agreement, saying, "I don't think I will miss her. I intend for her to go with me." he continued to shake his hand. Then he said, "If you want to have a drink with me again, then keep an ear open for strange stories about an injustice to some people."

He nodded back, like he understood, but Mitchell realized he should correct that statement. "Let me correct that. There is a great injustice that will come to this country that will cost the lives of hundreds of thousands of men. Our group will stay out of this. Before you ask, I will simply tell you that there is too much of a chance that we could mess it up and all the good that came from it in my time will be for not. The people of this time will need to decide what they feel is right on their own."

"You're talking about slavery?" he said, more a question than a statement.

Mitchell didn't answer him, he just turned and continued to walk to his area. This time Crockett didn't follow.

CHAPTER 16

Coming back into camp, Mitchell found Anna doctoring their poor Mr. Peter. He had forgotten that this young man got hit. Coming up behind her, he looked over her shoulder. It didn't look too bad. He would guess it was just a scratch or at worst a through and through. Standing back up, Mitchell asked, "How is he?"

She smiled up at him and said, "It's going to hurt for a while, but I think he'll be OK. The Chief bandaged him up real good. In a little while, I'll take him over to the doctor here and get it looked at."

Mitchell just grunted an agreement with her plan and walked away. Peter then called to him, "Sir."

When he turned around, Peter held out his pistol and the empty mag. He had forgotten he had given it to him during the fight, again.

Mitchell reached out and took it again, making sure it was on safe and tucked it into his pants. "Thank you." He said and then turned to go find Redcloud.

Redcloud was standing against the wall near the fire pit, just watching. When Mitchell walked up to talk, he just held up a single finger to stop him, then used the finger to point toward Mitchell's tent.

Mitchell did a couple of double takes with him and then headed over to his tent. As he got close, he heard soft crying. Mitchell got down and opened the flap. Kat was sitting in there with her face in her hands. As he opened the door and crawled in, she flew to him and wrapped her arm around him and held him so tight he thought he would stop breathing. She didn't let go of him for a long time. Finally, as she eased up the grip and he asked, "What is all this? Everything is fine now."

She poured it all out and between her German and broken English; he got the gist of what was going on. She could hear the fighting in the plaza and could hear everything over the radio. He gathered the fight was a lot stronger than he remembered it or seemed stronger just to her. Either way, it scared her terribly. When he came back, he went straight to check on Santa Anna instead of checking in with her first. She was scared and upset, but then she saw Peter, who she knew had stayed with him during the operation, and she lost it.

"I am so sorry I didn't come to see you when I first came back." He softly whispered to her. "It was very important that I make sure Santa Anna was safe. Otherwise, we would still have to finish fighting this battle. Now everything is fine. We will leave here in the morning."

"Leave!" she shot back. "So soon. I thought we were going to be married?"

He chuckled a little, saying, "We are still going to be married. I talked to your father about it a few days ago and he suggested we go north from here and find the little town that you came from. There is a preacher there that he said will marry us. If we do it here, the church will insist we convert to be Catholics."

She sat back for a moment and then laughed a little with him. Mitchell finally realized the problem was that she thought she would lose him before they married. He reached out this time and pulled her to him, holding her in a long hug.

After a little, they kissed, and he pulled her out of the tent.

Although it was still dark out, even though it was almost morning, the fire was going well. He didn't think anyone was really in the mood to sleep right now. Kat and he walked over to the fire pit and pulled up a log to sit on together. Most of the group was there already. As they sat down, he could hear they were all swapping lies about the fight.

As Kat laid her head on his shoulder, Mitchell just looked at his team. They had come a long way since that moment they first met in the dayroom for this detail. Nothing could have prepared them for what was going to happen, but they all pulled together as a team. Right at that moment, Mitchell found he was quite proud of all of them.

Finally, he stood up. After clearing his throat a few times, they all quieted down. "I was just thinking about how far we have come in just a short time. Only the Chief and I really knew each other before all this, but all of you have worked to pull together as a team that I would be proud to go anywhere and do anything with."

There were a couple of shouts of agreement from the group. He then added, "Even some of the newer members of this group put it all in." As he spoke, he indicated Kat, Peter, and one of Crockett's men that was still hanging around. As he pointed to each one, there was a short round of applause.

Then, as much as it hurt, Mitchell knew he had to add those that they had lost. "While all of us pulled through this, we must remember those that came with us but won't be leaving with us. Private Milton, Stretch, Johnson, who gave his life to save a man that just days before tried to fight with him and maybe kill him. What he did here might just be one of the most important things to come out of this battle. Time will tell." He let it sink in about how important Stretch's act was.

"Last," He said as he turned to Kat, "We will have to say goodbye to the father of our group. August Schmidt. Although he was not with us from the beginning of this journey, we could not have come this far without his wisdom and guidance. He was a loyal soldier and a loving father. We will all miss him greatly."

Kat just looked at the ground while he spoke about her father. She didn't cry this time. He believed remembering him with pride was stronger than her grief.

After a moment of silence to let everyone contemplate the losses, Mitchell brought the new business to the table. "I think it is time for us to leave. The sooner the better. I believe things are in place here and we are no longer needed. Tomorrow morning, we will begin our preparations to pull out of here."

There was a brief discussion going on that he hadn't expected. Anna was the first to speak up. "I thought we were going to vote on these things."

Mitchell became a little defensive at first. "Yes, of course we will vote on our plans, but we had already voted to leave as soon as this battle was over."

Anna continued, "We have wounded. Jose is hurt." She turned toward Peter to say how badly he was wounded but stopped short.

Ah, now he understood her issue. "I just want to get us away from here so we could openly discuss our future. There are many things we will need to talk about that should not be discussed in this environment."

Mitchell hoped Anna saw the truth in what he was saying and, although he knew she wanted to say more, she sat down in a huff.

Now Jose spoke up, "Boss, we are nowhere near ready to pull out of here. We don't have enough food, water, or fuel. The only thing we still have plenty of is bullets, and that won't get us very far."

Mitchell had to admit he was right. He was now thinking he may have underestimated what they still need to do. He needed to look to his man of plans to help him. "Chief, what do you think?"

Redcloud stepped into the center, beside the fire pit, "I agree with both of you. Boss, we need to get out of here quickly, before the politicians and others show up. However, I also agree with Jose. We are not near ready. We need to recover as much of our supplies as we can. Brass and missing mags and such. We need to scrub ourselves out of history as much as possible. Mostly we need horses and food. We can't just get these things at the local store now." He paused and looked at Mitchell. "I suggest we plan to leave here in at least two days, maybe more."

Mitchell watched as he went back to the sidelines out of the light of the fire before he spoke again, "Anyone else want to speak out before we vote?"

Kat now spoke up, "Do I get to say anything?"

Mitchell looked down into her eyes and he could see she was hurting about something. "Of course, you are a member of this group and have a say."

She stood to talk, but she spoke so softly, Jose asked her to speak louder. "I would like to say I don't want to leave here until we have taken care of our dead."

There were a couple of grunts of agreement, and even Mitchell had to admit she was right. She then sat down, and he looked around and asked again, "Anyone else want to speak?"

No one else showed they wished to speak, so he called for the vote. "Anyone thinks we should wait a couple of days before we pull out, or at least until we bury our departed family, raise your hands."

He only needed a quick look around to see every hand was up. He also slowly raised his hand to agree. "The vote passes, unanimously." He heard a couple of remarks about that.

He looked around but was already sure what was coming, but he opened the door, anyway. "Is there anything else we need to discuss?" As he asked, he looked right at Anna.

Anna stood up to say, "I don't know that I will go with you when you leave."

This was not what he expected to hear from her, and it took him by surprise. "What's the problem?" Mitchell asked, as if he didn't already know.

She shuffled her feet a little and slowly said what was on her mind, "Boss, you've found your love and it would appear that you will live happily ever after. What about the rest of us? I want to have a life and maybe even a family of my own, and I believe I have found it. I want to stay with Peter."

Mitchell was not sure if it was pleasure at the idea of staying with her, he saw on Peter's face or shock. He didn't believe Mr. Peter was expecting this.

He knew he had to think of something quickly. He knew he didn't want to lose any more of the group. Suddenly, an idea formed, "You know you don't have to leave the group to have that life."

"What do you mean, he can come with us?"

She seemed excited about the idea of him joining our group. Mitchell put his hand up to stop her before they went too far with this. "Hold on a minute. First, you need to explain things to him. How we work and vote together, what happens if you decide to leave the group, and a lot more. All these things you have to explain to him before we can agree to anything."

She now shot up and quickly said, "I understand and will explain everything to him."

Mitchell then added, "We will all need to talk to him, privately, before we vote."

This brought her back down a little, but she nodded her head.

Looking around at the group, he said, "Ok, we'll table this vote until Anna is ready. I would suggest all of you talk to young Peter here before you vote." There were nods all around the group, even Peter was nodding with a big ass smile.

"Anything else?" He asked and after a moment of quiet, finally said, "Great, now go get some sleep."

Soon it was just Kat and Mitchell left at the fire. The entire area had quieted down. There were still a lot more men on the walls than were normally there, but mostly, they were quiet as well. He just sat by Kat and enjoyed the peace and quiet while it lasted. She seemed to be content to just sit with him by the fire, too.

After a while, the excitement was gone from the night, and Mitchell suddenly felt exhausted. He thought Kat was just about to fall asleep in his arms. Softly, he nudged her and whispered, "I think we should get some sleep."

He didn't hear her say anything; however, he felt her head move in a nod. Slowly, he stood and help her stand. They walked the short distance to her tent and stopped. Turning to him, she was very close. She looked up into his eyes and asked, "Are you sure this is where you want me to sleep?"

"No," He said, "I am sure I would rather have you sleeping with me." With that said she put her arms around him and hugged, but then he added, "But, I am also sure I would rather wait until we are properly married, for your sake and peace of mind and out of respect for your father."

Again, she said nothing, but continued to hug him for what seemed like a long time. She then slowly pulled away and with a smile she planted a big kiss on him and then quickly turned to go into her tent, but before she got inside, she turned back and said, "That was only a kiss and a promise of things to come."

Mitchell just stood there like a young schoolboy who just got his first kiss, as she quickly ducked inside the tent and closed the flap. He couldn't move. For the first time in his life, he didn't know what to do. Shaking it off, he glanced around and expected to see the Chief leaning up against the wall with the stupid grin on his face. This time, however, Redcloud wasn't there. Even the powerful warrior must have needed sleep. He slowly turned and walked past the fire to his tent. It felt like he fell asleep on the walk to his tent because he didn't even remember going in.

It couldn't have been long before Mitchell heard a lot of noise outside. He still had his boots on, so he quickly went outside and saw that Travis was on the wall and the men there were all looking outside. A runner came to him and said, "The Colonel would like to see you, sir."

Mitchell grabbed his rifle and ran over to the wall. Bowie was being helped up the ramp, but Crockett was already there when he ran up. Looking in the direction that everyone else was looking, he saw a small force, maybe a couple dozen men, standing behind several men on horses. He assumed the men on the horses were officers. He could see the sunlight glinting off all the shiny stuff they had on their uniform. The important thing was, they had another man out in front with a white flag.

The Mexicans had stopped just outside of rifle range and waited. Travis turned and yelled for the Sergeant-major to hoist up a white flag on the Alamo. As soon as they put up the white flag, the Mexicans on horses slowly moved toward them, but the small force of soldiers remained where they were.

When they arrived at the wall, one man began to speak. Mitchell assumed he was Santa Anna's second in command. He moved his horse a few steps out in front of the others and then gave Travis a demand, "You will release General Santa Anna, or we will destroy this fort."

Travis, and Mitchell thought some others smiled at this silly demand. Travis walked over to the edge and put one foot on the wall, then leaned forward to say, "You do not make the demands here. We have the General and he is safe and being well taken care of. However, should you decide to take any action against my people here," he paused a second, but then continued, "This will all change, and I cannot guarantee the safety of your President."

Travis then turned and yelled down for a runner to take the papers that Santa Anna signed out to that officer. Even here Mitchell could see his face turning red as he read the orders. The officer rolled the papers up and held them out for one of the other men to take. As soon as the other man got the papers, the officer who was speaking spurred his horse in a sharp turn and rode back to town, with the others trying hard to catch up with him. The man with the white flag stayed until all those officers were safely out of range and then slowly turned and followed them. The small force that was still standing there stayed for a while longer, but eventually they were marched back into the town.

Travis turned to them when the entire spectacle was over and with a smile said, "I believe that went very well."

All the men that were in earshot of him laughed. Travis just walked down the ramp and back to his office.

As he walked away, Bowie, Crockett, and Mitchell gather. Bowie spoke first. "Rumor has it your group is pulling out today."

Mitchell had to smile. Even without mass communications at this time, the word still spreads at the speed of light. "Well, it isn't a rumor, but it also isn't correct." He answered him. Then, looking at both, he continued, "We figured we don't have the supplies to leave so quickly, so we postponed it for a day or two."

The mood, now, was lighter than just a day before. Bowie smiled back, saying, "That's too bad. I was hoping you'd stick around long enough for me to get another try with your young lady."

Before He could say anything, Crockett jumped in saying, "I don't know that this would be a good idea. Something tells me you might not be so lucky the second time."

Bowie stood up straight instead of leaning on the crutch. He looked at both of them and then gave a huff and turned to walk, or hobble, away. Crockett and Mitchell looked at each other and began to softly laugh. Mitchell then said, "I don't think he liked the thought of that."

Crockett quickly shot back, "That's not the problem. The problem is, he knows I might just be right."

Now they both laughed a little harder. Mitchell couldn't say anything, so he just shook his head and headed off to speak to Travis. He needed to see what supplies they could get from him. They needed mostly horses and some food. At his best guess, he figured they only needed to go a few days to get to Kat's hometown, where they should be able to pick up some more supplies. He was hoping Travis will be in a generous mood this morning.

There was a lot of activity around Travis' office when he got there, however he could go right in. Travis was busy writing at his desk. However, when Mitchell walked in, he looked up and saw him and stopped whatever he was doing.

"Ah, good." He said as he stood up. Walking around from behind the desk, he came up to him with his hand out, "I was hoping to talk with you before you left."

Mitchell took his hand and shook it, but Travis pulled it back when he said, "That is what I came to talk to you about. We are going to need to delay our departure until we can get a few supplies and bury our dead."

Travis quickly returned to the spot behind the desk. Sitting down, he asked, "And what supplies are you looking for?"

He didn't really have a detailed list, so Mitchell just said, "Mostly horses and a little food." but then quickly added, "And water. I know water is not a problem, but barrels to carry it in is."

Travis only thought about it for a minute before saying, "The food and water shouldn't be a problem; however, horses are a highly valued commodity right now."

"We came in with several horses that I will take when we leave, but my machine is low on the fuel that makes it run. I will need a team of horses to pull it until I can figure out something else."

"Would two horses be enough?"

Mitchell had to think about that. Two horses might pull the hummer, be we also had the trailer for it, and there was more weight in the two together. "I don't think two will be enough. We will need at least four." But then he quickly added, "Six would be better."

Travis sat back in his chair as he thought about it. Thoughtfully, he slowly informed him, "I could spare two horses easily enough. However, six is out of the question."

Mitchell didn't really think it would come down to haggling over a couple of horses, but he needed them badly. "There are enough dead that will no longer be needing their horses."

Travis now stood and with a little more force said, "These horses belong to the Texas Army, and I can't just let you have them. They are needed."

It then occurred to him; Travis was only counting the horses from the men in his command. "Is it alright if I talk to Colonel Bowie and Crockett about getting some horses from them?"

He sternly replied, "What Bowie and Crockett do is up to them. They are militia and not really under my command, outside this post."

That was great. Mitchell shouldn't have too much trouble getting a few animals from them. He then offered his hand over the desk, but as he did, he looked down at the paper Travis had been writing on. It appeared to be a report of activity to the Texas government. Travis quickly picked up the paper, so Mitchell couldn't read it, but it was a little late. He saw there was a mention of him and his people.

He stood back up and dropped his hand. "Sir, might I remind you, you agreed that for my help there would be no mention of me or my people in your report."

He shot back with, "You want me to falsify an official report?"

Mitchell stood his ground. "I want you to fulfill our agreement."

"How do you expect me to explain what happened here without mentioning you?" he complained.

"This is not my problem, but I will hold you to your word." But then added a "Sir." Just to emphasize the fact that, as an officer, his word should mean something.

Travis slowly sat back down in his chair. Mitchell could see he was trying to think of a way to avoid them in his report. Then he looked back at him and said, "The men here will talk about you and your machine."

This he was ready for, "Yes, and stories will spread, but who, that wasn't here, is going to believe them?" After that set in for a moment, He continued, "The stories will be told for some time, but soon they will die out, as most stories do and then just become legends that no one will really believe," but now he leaned on Travis' desk to drive his point home, "As long as there are no official reports to say otherwise."

Travis thought about this and slowly nodded. Standing, he offered his hand again, saying, "I will rewrite this report and disregard any mention of you."

This time, Mitchell quickly took his hand and shook it. "This is not yet goodbye. My people have a lot to do before we pull out. I guess the next issue, what are you going to do with the dead?"

Travis sat back down and confidently said, "I have sent for the Priest from the town. He will make all the arrangements. Bowie and Crockett are on their own for their dead, just as you are. However, I would suggest you also talk to the Priest to make the arrangements."

Thinking about this, Mitchell decided he would talk to the group about it. He then stepped back from the desk and gave Travis a proper salute. While not a good salute, he returned it and Mitchell felt he did it with genuine respect.

Leaving Travis' office, he headed straight for Crockett's group. He found him sitting and talking with his men. As he walked up, Crockett stood and came to him. "How did things go with Travis?"

"Pretty good. I got just about everything I'll need, except horses." He replied.

Crockett didn't really respond to his statement, so he added, "He said the horses belonged to the Texas Army and he didn't have the authority to just give them to me."

As he expected, Crockett immediately became defensive. "I'll be dammed if our horses belong to him."

Now that he had him where he wanted him. Mitchell acted his part out, "Ah, you don't understand. He was referring to the horses from his command. Travis doesn't consider your horses, or Jim's, under his command. I was told to talk to you about any spare horses.

He thought Crockett knew what he had just done, but said nothing. But then he asked, "How many horses are you talking about?"

"I think four more would do us just fine. However, I can also try to get a couple from Bowie." And then he stopped to give him time.

"I lost five men in this fight." He said, then looking at his men, he said, "I believe we could give you two."

"That would be great. I don't know how many men Bowie lost, but there were a few. I should be able to get two more from him."

Crockett then offered, "Be careful with Jim. He likes the deal."

Mitchell said nothing, but he understood exactly what he was saying. Just nodding, he turned to head over to Bowie's quarters.

He found Jim taking a drink of something he was pretty sure wasn't water. Before he even said anything, Bowie offered a drink. Reluctantly, Mitchell took the cup, and Bowie poured something in it. Mitchell almost choked from just taking a whiff of the stuff. "My God, Jim. You actually drink this stuff?" he said as I he held the cup away from his face.

Bowie laughed at him, saying, "It may not smell too good, but goes down real smooth."

With that, Bowie held his cup up in a toast. Mitchell reluctantly held up his, and they both took a sip. Smooth, my ass. He thought he had just drunk a cup of fire.

As he was coughing and trying to hide how badly he thought this stuff was, Bowie was just laughing at him more.

Once he had recovered, Mitchell just politely set the cup down. With the pleasantries of this time done, it was time to get down to business. "I need to ask for something from you."

He leaned back in his chair and just before he took another sip and said, "I've been watching you. You went to Travis and then to Crockett. I figured that is why you now came to me."

He couldn't argue with his logic, as he just stood there shuffling his feet. Finally, Mitchell worked up enough to spit it out. "I need a couple of horses from you to get my group going."

Bowie looked down into his cup, like there were some kind of magic tea leaves or something in it that would give him the answer. He swirled the cup a little and then took another drink. Finally, looking up at him, he asked the same question the others had. "How many?"

"Any number will do, but I need at least two."

"Two, is that all. Hell, I lost eight men yesterday who won't be needing their horses anymore. I can let you have half of them."

Now Mitchell was understanding Crockett's warning, "That's great, but what's the price?"

He now sat up straight. "I want another shot at the woman." Looking Mitchell right in the eye, he continued, "She might as well have gutted me when she beat me in that fight. I lost a lot of respect from my men and my reputation. I want it back."

He said the last part with a bit of anger. Mitchell understood what Bowie was saying and why he was asking for a rematch, but after the ass chewing he got for volunteering her the first time, he just couldn't do it again. "I'll have to check with her, but I really don't think you're in any condition to have a fair fight right now, and I don't intend to stay here long enough for you to heal."

Bowie got a smile on his face. Mitchell could now see he had been thinking about this for more than just a few minutes. He put his elbow on his knees and then looked up at him. "I will not fight her again. This time it is going to be an even match. Just like you did with Crockett when you first got here, we are going to have a shooting match, but this time," he paused a moment to look and see how Mitchell was taking it, but then continued when he showed nothing, "We are going to be even. She won't be shooting one of those fancy rifles of yours. We're gonna shoot two rifles from my time, and not just to break jugs. We're gonna have bona fide targets to measure the shots."

Mitchell knew Anna was a great shot, but he didn't know if she knows squat about a flintlock. "I'll pass your request on to her and let you know what she says."

Bowie leaned back in his chair again, and before he took another sip, he said, "That's fine, and I'll let you know if I find any horses for you."

His point was not subtle at all. If Mitchell wanted horses from him, then she would have to shoot.

He left Bowie to ponder the answers in his cup of whatever that stuff was and went back to the camp.

It didn't take long to find Anna. When he walked up, she just continued to talk to Peter. She was still laying out the entire story of how they got here. He didn't know if she had gotten to the stuff about the future and what our general plans were, but he needed to interrupt. "Anna." He said as he approached. She stopped and turned to look at him.

"I have a problem that only you can fix." He said to lead her into it.

"Sure Boss, anything I can." She said eagerly.

No easy way to say it, so he just had to lay it all out and hope she works with him. "I have most of the horses we need, except." Looking down at the ground so he didn't have to see her eyes, Ge continued, "Colonel Bowie is holding off giving us some horses. He will only give them to us if he gets a rematch with you."

"Hell no!" she shouted as she jumped up.

Holding his hands up to stop her, he continued, "Just wait. He thinks the fight was a little unfair because he was unprepared. This time, he doesn't want to fight. He wants a shooting match, just like I did with Crockett when I first got here."

He knew she was a great shot, and she also knew it, and now she was considering it when he threw in the last part. "You cannot use your rifle. He wants it to be fair, so you'll both be using flintlock from this period."

"I've never shot a flintlock before." She said, but before he could offer anything, she added, "I've shot a couple of caplocks with my father when I was a kid. A flintlock shouldn't be that much different."

Now Peter was standing behind her. He offered, "I can help teach you. I ain't as good as Davy, but I ain't too bad neither."

Anna turned to look at her boyfriend. Mitchell couldn't tell if he was helping or not. She thought about it and then asked, "What are we going to be shooting at?"

He told her, "He said it would be some kind of target, so the shots could be actually measured."

She turned to Peter and asked, "Are you really going to help me?"

He looked her right in the eye. With what Mitchell could only describe as true love, he said, "I would do anything for you."

Good boy. Mitchell knew he liked this kid.

She turned back to him and said, "Tell him it's on. And also tell him I really don't mind kicking his ass a second time."

What could He say? Mitchell just turned and headed back to Bowie. When he told Bowie what she said, Mitchell couldn't remember having ever seen anyone turn as red or as fast as he did. The cup of piss he was drinking went flying and as he struggled to stand as Mitchell said, "You say when and where, but she will need a little time to learn how to load and shoot one of these things. You set things up with Travis and make it for later this afternoon. Send a runner to give us the time when you're ready."

That red face just looked at Mitchell a moment and then Bowie was off to see Travis, without a word.

A couple of men nearby started talking, and he could tell right away that bets were already being made.

As Bowie was heading to Travis, he was having a little trouble. Mitchell couldn't tell, but he thought he had maybe drank too much of whatever that God awful stuff was. A couple of his men came over to help, but Bowie just swung the stick he was using as a crutch, and they backed off. When he was steady again, he continued in as straight a line as he could to see Travis.

The straight line he was taking was more like a series of curves. As Mitchell watched, the men were already talking about it. Mitchell waved his hand for them to go with him and he yelled, "Keep an eye on him!" The two men that originally tried to help him started following him, but Mitchell could see they were staying out of swinging range of his stick.

After leaving Bowie, Mitchell found Peter and Anna out beyond the chapel wall. As he stood there watching, Peter was very intent on showing her how to shoot the flintlock. As he watched, off to the left, he found Redcloud was also watching it. Walking over to stand with him in the shade, Redcloud only barely acknowledged that he was there, as he was fully engrossed with what those two were doing. After leaning against the wall for a moment, Mitchell asked, "What do you think about young Mr. Peter there joining our group?"

Redcloud didn't answer right away. Mitchell couldn't tell if he was thinking about the question or just watching them. Finally, he answered, "The boy appears to be competent enough and, from what I hear, he is probably one of the most educated men in the entire Alamo." After a short pause to watch a particular thing Peter was showing Anna, he continued, "But Anna is right. You found yours and she has the same right to the rest of her life. We need to face this. Sooner or later, we're all going to go through this. We must make sure that whoever we bring into this group keeps our secrets and obeys our rules."

Mitchell really hadn't given too much thought to the future, at least not to their immediate future. He had to admit Redcloud was right. Everyone is going to eventually fall in love and want to have a family. He felt this might be a good thing.

After watching them practice, Anna finally loaded the rifle for real. She took a shot and although she wasn't quite on target; He thought it was very close. He had to put a stop to this before the Mexicans get worried about the shooting and start another battle.

"Anna." He called out and waved both of them over. They quickly came over. When they stopped, he asked, "What do you think? Can you beat him?"

She looked at the rifle that she was still holding and confidently replied, "Shit, yeah." Then she spun to see the strange look on Peter's face. Mitchell could see she already knew, but he was going to have to remind her that ladies in this time don't talk like that.

"Great, I think Bowie is going to set it up for midafternoon. He is off talking to Travis right now."

She only looked over at Peter. Right then, he could tell this was not just a one-sided puppy love. They both had it and they both had it real bad.

She then told Peter, "We better get back to our practice."

Before he could answer, Mitchell spoke up, "About that. We just finished a sizable battle and people on both sides are still edgy. I don't think it's a good idea to be doing a lot of actual shooting right now. You can do a little dry fire with only powder in the pan for now."

"Shit!" she replied, but then glanced over at her boyfriend and reworded it. "How do you expect me to do anything against him if I can't practice?"

Before he could try to answer her, Redcloud spoke up, "A rifle is a rifle. You've had years to practice. Just because it is a different weapon, the same things apply to shooting this as it does to shooting any weapon. You are an excellent shot and you had plenty of practice yesterday. You only really need training on the loading procedures. This is an important step because with these rifles it can mean the difference between an accurate shot, or a miss."

Anna took that all in but, it was Peter that replied, "He's right. I need to work on your loading more than anything right now. I already saw how good you can shoot." As he finished, he gave her a huge smile.

Anna nodded, and they both turned to go back to where they were before.

This kid was really growing on him. He had a good head on his shoulders and could handle himself in close quarters.

Before leaving, Mitchell asked Redcloud, "Do you know if anyone has talked with him yet?"

He never turned away from watching the two practice when he said, "I saw Rodrigues and Blake talking with him, but I don't know what they were talking about. Anna was with him when they were talking."

Mitchell saw he should have told her to let the others talk in private, but he guessed it didn't really matter that much. He left this area and went back to their camp. When he got there, he saw little had been done to get ready. Jose and Blake were both there and not really doing anything. He called to both of them.

"What's up, boss?" said Jose when they were close.

Mitchell looked around at the camp. "We have stuff scattered all around and the wagon was a mess. You guys need to start packing. I want all our stuff gathered up and packed away in the wagon. Make sure the wagon is packed in an organized way. Make sure somethings, like full mags, food and other stuff we'll need on the trail, is easy to grab when we need them."

They both just stood there, looking around at everything and then at each other. The standard looks of, "What me again." was on each of their faces. Finally, Jose shrugged, saying, "You got it, boss."

But then it was Blake that asked, "Is it going to be just us two doing all the work, boss?"

The last boss part dripped with sarcasm. "No, but right now everyone else is working on something and you two were just sitting around and jerking off." He replied with his own bit of sarcasm.

He thought Blake realized he had just stepped in it and before he could continue to walk through it, Jose took his arm and turned him to work.

Mitchell smiled as they both walked away and shook his head a little. He headed over towards Bowie's area to see if he had talked Travis into this little shooting match. As he cleared their area and crossed to where Bowie was bunked, he saw him coming out of the command building. He was heading towards his area, but seeing Mitchell, he changed course.

Before he could say anything, Mitchell asked first, "Did Travis agree to your little shootout?"

He leaned on his stick. Mitchell thought he was trying to catch his breath and his balance. After a moment he said, "Yeah, but he said tensions were too high to try it today. He wants to wait until tomorrow."

Throwing a little gas on the fire, Mitchell laughed and told him, "That's too bad. She was looking forward to whipping up on you today."

Mitchell figured he sobered up a little. He didn't get near as mad as he thought he would. Bowie just looked a little sideway at him and smiled. Then he got around to why he was smiling. "I already heard you got your little girl out there practicing with one of Crockett's men."

Surprised the word had already gotten to him, He must have someone watching them. Mitchell simply told him, "Aw, they ain't practicing. He is just making sure she knows how to load one of those old things. We ain't had to shove a bullet down the barrel like that in a hundred years."

Bowie didn't say anything, he just grunted and continued on his way back to his quarters. As he left, Mitchell shouted, "What time?"

Bowie just slightly turned his head as he continued to walk and yelled back, "Just after the noon meal."

Sounded good. He watched Bowie hobble his way back over to his room for a bit and then turned to go give Anna the good news.

They all had a quiet night and Mitchell thought everyone finally got a good night's sleep. The morning went without any issues. He got the horses picked out from Travis and Crockett. They put them together in a separate area with their original horses, so there wouldn't be any problem tomorrow. Before he knew it, the morning was gone, and it was time for lunch. Getting back to camp, the group had gathered. Everyone was talking about the upcoming match-up. Anna appeared to be calm, and Peter was still right by her side. He believed she would use Peter's rifle for the match. He didn't think about what she was going to shoot, but he guessed things got worked out.

Soon enough, it was time. The entire post had gathered, and this time there was a proper shooting area set up. There were two tables at one end of the compound and a couple of stands at the other end. On each stand was a paper with a V notch cut in each. Mitchell walked up with Anna, as well as Peter.

As they approached Bowie said in a loud voice, "You can turn around, boy. She is on her own now."

This brought a couple of laughs from the men that had gathered to watch. Mitchell continued to walk up with Anna. As they got there, Bowie showed Anna to the other table for her to set up her stuff. Anna walked over and place the rifle on the table, and she even had a pouch with all the things she needed. Mitchell guessed that Peter also supplied this.

Now Crockett came over and stood in front of the tables. He laid out the rules, "Lady and gentlemen. This is the way this is going to work. Each of you will take a single shot. I will be down at the targets and look to see who has the closed shot. There will be a total of five shots each. The one shot closest to the notch wins." He then paused to take any question. Where there was none, so he continued, "Is this agreeable to each of you?"

Mitchell thought Anna was going to say something about not having time to sight in Peter's rifle, but she kept quiet and just nodded.

"Colonel Bowie, you are the challenger and therefore you shoot second." Continued Crockett.

Bowie also said nothing, but simply nodded.

Anna already had her rifle loaded, so all she needed to do was put some powder in the pan. Taking her time, she fired. Bowie also took his time to fire his shot. However, while he was firing a little voice in Mitchell's radio told him, "About three inches left and low." This was Redcloud. He was up on the wall where he could see the targets by using the binoculars. He was letting Mitchell know where her shots hit. Mitchell then used little hand singles to tell Anna where her shot went. Three fingers for three inches and a thumb pointing to show left and low. Just about the time he got his message to her, Bowie fired.

Now Crockett moved in to check the targets. It didn't take long for him to signal that Bowie was closer to center, for the first shot. After he walked back to the side, Anna went through the loading process. Peter had taught her well. She loaded it like she might have been doing this all her life. She took aim and fired her second shot. While Bowie was loading his rifle, the Chief radioed Anna's shot was still to the left about an inch left and the shot was even with the notch in the paper. While Bowie prepared to fire, he passed this on to Anna.

After both had fired their second shot, Crockett again checked. This time he took a little longer, but showed the Bowie was still closer. The third round of fire went off just like the others, but this time Crockett indicated Anna was closer. Redcloud informed Mitchell she was indeed closer, but not by much. The fourth round again went to Bowie. However, Redcloud said it was too close for him to call from where he was.

Everything came down to the last shot. Bowie was looking very confident while he waited for Anna to load and shoot. After the shot, Redcloud informed him she had cut the notch on the target. Mitchell simply gave her a thumbs up signal and waited for Bowie to shoot. After it was all done, Crockett took his time. Redcloud radioed it was so close. He couldn't call it. Crockett even called Captain Dickenson over, and the two of them actually used something to measure with.

When they had finished, Crockett walked back to the tables. After a delay to build the tension, he finally spoke. "This has been one of the closest matches I have ever witnessed. There wasn't much more than a hair's difference between those last shots, but Colonel Bowie's shot was closer than hers."

Bowie raised his rifle over his head, and most of the men around cheered. After it had calmed a little and Bowie had taken a few bows, Anna walked over and put out her hand. Bowie stopped the showboating and faced her. He first looked down at her hand and then back into her eyes. Finally, he reached out and grabbed her hand hard and gave it a good shake. He then leaned in and whispered something in her ear. Everyone was still cheering, so Mitchell couldn't hear what he said. When he finished, Anna's head snapped back, and she smiled, and Mitchell could see it was her that gave him a good shake.

After a moment of looking at each other, Anna grabbed his wrist and held his hand up and again everyone one started cheering more. Bowie's men came over and took him away and Anna turned back to her group, who had gathered at her table. Gathering her things, she came over and handed Peter back his rifle and bag. Mitchell couldn't stand it anymore. He had to know what Bowie had said to her. He took her by the arm and lead her to the side where they could hear each other. Once they were away from the crowd, he stopped and when she turned to face him; she didn't say anything. Finally, he shouted at her, "Well, what did he say?"

Until now, she had kept a straight face, but she couldn't hide it any longer. With a huge smile she said, "He said that I had him scared in the last round, and that he couldn't remember a closer match." She then stopped for a moment and, now looking at Peter, she added, "He then said good shooting."

It really wasn't so much to make a big deal about, but then Mitchell realized that, for him, it was. In his time, women were doing just about everything a man was and most of them doing it just as good or better. However, for this time in history, that was quite a compliment, especially coming from a man like Bowie. She deserved it. He reached out and put his arms around her and gave her a big hug, and then as he let her go, her kind of gave her a push towards Peter. She didn't need a second hint. She gave him a big hug, but he also got a wet kiss to go along with it. Mitchell turned and left those two to celebrate and walk over to Crockett.

He was just leaning against the table while watching Bowie celebrate. "You'd think he had just whipped Santa Anna all by himself, the way they are going on." Mitchell said as he also leaned against the table.

"Don't tell anyone else, but it really was a tie on the last shot." Crockett leaned in to whisper to him.

"What the hell? Why didn't you call it that way?"

Crockett didn't answer him right away. He just pointed to Bowie and slowly said, "Because he needed it. I like your lady very much, but he is in command of men and when she beat him in the fight, he lost all respect. He needed to get that back."

They both just stood there watching Bowie celebrate with his men. Mitchell could understand what Crockett was saying, but shit, it hurt.

Finally, Crockett added, "Besides, the last shot was closer than any I had ever seen. Captain Dickenson and I both couldn't say who was closer, so we decided to give it to Bowie because all his shots were on target. Your girl didn't even come close the first two shots."

"That's not fair." Mitchell protested, "She never even had time to fire the rifle until just now."

Crockett shrugged his shoulders, saying, "Maybe so, but the call's been made and if you protest it, I think Jim's men might just hang ya."

Just that way he said it, Mitchell had to hang his head down to stifle a laugh. "Alright," he said. "But you're gonna owe me one."

Crockett got off the table and, before turning to leave, he said, "That's fine. You know where I'm at to collect."

He watched Crockett walk away. But now he had a decision to make. Should he tell Anna or just let it go?" He decided to think about it later and that right now he wanted to go find Kat.

He made a wide circle around the celebration to get back to camp. His group was mostly there, but the only one that really mattered to him was Kat. She was sitting around the fire pit, and it looked like she had put a pot of water on to boil.

He pulled another log over to sit next to her, but before he sat down, he gave her a big hug and kiss. He felt she could tell that things were good and a little more relaxed. After a moment, she turned to him and whispered, "I talked to the priest, and he says we can have the funeral tomorrow if we want."

With all the excitement of the shoot-out, he had forgotten all about the funeral arrangements. He knew the others would be interested. This is the last thing that needs to be taken care of before they can leave. He smiled at her and whispered back, "I'll talk to the others to see what they want to do."

She simply smiled and turned back to watching the pot of water. Mitchell just sat there watching the same pot for a while. He didn't really think about anything in particular. He was more or less daydreaming. For what seemed like a very short time, he didn't need to worry about anything.

Unfortunately, it didn't last long. Suddenly, he was brought back to this reality when a young man came by saying, "Sir, Colonel Travis would like to see you."

He nodded to him, and the man turned to walk back, when Mitchell added, "Thank you."

He turned back, a little surprised that he actually said something, but then just continued on his way. Mitchell looked over at Kat and leaned over to give her a kiss. All he could say was, "I'll be back as soon as I can."

She replied with a smile, "I'll have dinner ready whenever you get back."

He guessed she was getting used to the MRE's they were eating a lot. As long as you've got hot water, you can eat anytime. However, she took to mixing other things in them and turned out some delicious meals. He smiled back at her and left her to continue watching the pot. As he walked to see Travis, the celebration for Bowie had kind of died out, but he could still hear them celebrating a little in his room. He was thinking Crockett was right. He needed this. As he continued to walk, he couldn't help but notice the change in the men. Over the last couple of weeks, the men had become quiet and melancholy. It was slow, so he didn't really notice. But now they were back in high spirits. There was loud talking and laughing. It was as if there was a whole new garrison here. When he got to Travis' office, he stopped to take one good look around the compound before he went in. Thinking about how amazing the change was in a single day, he shook his head and went in.

Captain Baugh was sitting behind a desk doing some paper shuffling. He didn't even get up now. He only motioned Mitchell to go in. Mitchell simply nodded and went into the back office. Travis was also sitting behind his desk and again writing something.

Taking a stand in front of the desk, he rendered a salute. As he continued to write and ignore Mitchell, he held his salute until Travis finally looked up and, with a little huff, returned it.

He started talking as he stood up. "I just received word that a delegation from the new Texas government will be here tomorrow or the next day." However, before Mitchell could say anything, he continued, "I have made arrangements to give you the horses you required, and a couple extra we were able to find. They might be Mexican horses, but that will be your problem. Also, the priest tells me they will begin having the burials this afternoon. Please check with him to find out when your people will be buried."

Stopping, he just stood there, looking at him. Mitchell wasn't sure what he should say. "Thank you, Sir" was all he could quickly come up with, and immediately it sounded so empty.

Travis smiled, knowing he had him flustered, but continued, "Then I would suggest, Major, that you get your business done and get out of here quickly."

"Major?" Mitchell finally stammered.

Travis' smile got even bigger. "Yes, Major."

"I don't understand, Sir."

Travis scooped up a few papers and came around to face him in front of his desk. As he handed the papers to Mitchell and laughed, saying, "Even though you wished to stay anonymous, I have drafted up papers for each of your people to say thanks for pledging their life to the life of Texas. I have also given you paper making you a Major in the Army of the Republic of Texas for your service."

As he took the papers, Travis continued to hold out his hand. Mitchell was at a loss for words. First looking down and the bundle of papers he had just handed him and then at his hand, he quickly reached out and took the hand. As he did, he leaned closer and whispered, "Per your request, all mention of you and your people has been eliminated from all reports, but if you are still here when the delegation shows up, there will be some explaining to do."

Mitchell nodded to him while he continued to shake Travis' hand, and while he didn't whisper, he did quietly say, "I'll try to get our people buried today and we'll be leaving in the morning. And I thank you very much, on behalf of all my people."

Travis now dropped his hand and with a last word he said, "I have even included papers for your two dead men. Just in case there is a family that would need to know."

Again, Mitchell looked at the papers and then, taking a step back, he came to attention and rendered a proper salute and said, "Thank you, Sir."

This time, Travis was very formal. He, also came to attention and returned a somewhat proper salute. When he dropped his, Mitchell dropped his and did an about face and headed for the door. When he reached for the doorknob, Travis finally said, "Take care, by friend."

He paused with his hand still on the doorknob and looked back, but no words came to mind, so I just smiled and nodded, then opened the door and left.

Once he was out in the compound again, he stopped and looked over the papers. Everyone had papers with at least their first names on it. The one for Stretch had his full name, and it took him a moment to remember that he had told it to those men when they brought his body into camp. Travis must have talked to them at some point. This made him realize it was not a last-minute gesture by Travis and that gave it meaning.

Before he returned to the camp, he found the priest and made the arrangements for August and Stretch to be buried later in the afternoon. It appears the burial place will be just outside the wall and there were men already digging the graves. He got the word passed around to his group that they would meet here this afternoon and go over together. He also passed the word that they needed to pull out at sunrise tomorrow.

There was mixed reaction to the news, but most seemed to be happy to be going. He put the papers away for now. He figured this would be something better for when they get out on the road. Then it just dawned on him that Peter would come with them. He quickly looked through the little stack of paper and found one with his name on it. That explained a little something. Not many people knew about him leaving with Mitchell's group. Crockett was one of them. Travis must have talked to Crockett to get all this information. He just couldn't imagine Travis talking about personal things to a regular soldier.

After lunch, Mitchell and the entire group went outside the walls to the new cemetery. There was many graves dug already. A couple had already been filled, and there were people standing around them. When he and his group came around the corner, Crockett was already there with a few of his men. He signaled to Mitchell that this was where his men were to be buried and they all gathered around the two graves. Kat stayed right next to him at the front of the line as they all lined up. Even Peter was with them and holding Anna. Crockett stood off to the side with his men. The men that were with him were mostly the men that had tried to attack Stretch that night. The big man was right in front, standing next to Crockett with his head down.

Both the women were softly crying as the two bodies were brought out and placed in the graves. There wasn't enough time or wood to build enough coffins, so both men were simply but nicely wrapped in white cloth. The priest stood at the other end of the graves and as both of the men were lowered; he prayed. Most of the prayers were in Latin which none of them understood, but when it came time, the priest said more personal things about the two lost comrades and the sacrifices they made during the battle. This he spoke in Spanish and Jose translated as best he could.

After all the talking was done, each of them took a hand full of dirt and gently tossed it into each of the graves. Kat cried hard when she did this to her father. Mitchell held her close as he followed her, and they slowly went back to their area.

Soon, the group had gathered again. The mood was very somber as they all just sat around looking into the little fire that was still going. No one spoke for the longest time. The only real sound anyone made was a soft cry, mostly from Kat and an occasional sniffle from the others as they remembered their lost family.

Mitchell could feel the mood had changed in the whole compound. Most of the men were silent as they too remembered the friends they had lost during the battle. Yes, there were still a few that wanted to party and get drunk, but they did most of the drinking to honor the lost.

Mitchell decided this was enough. He quietly got up and went to the wagon to find August's jug. Bringing it back, he stood in the center and asked, "Will anyone like to join me in a drink to honor the members of our family we lost? Maybe even say a word or two about them. Some of you people were closer to them than I was, and I think it would be fitting and proper to say something."

Surprisingly, Kat spoke first. She stood up next to Mitchell and began by talking about her father before he came to America and finally settled in Texas. The others had retrieved their cup and Mitchell poured each of them a drink. As Kat told of August, someone would raise their cup when she said something good about him. It was mostly good. They all got to toast him a lot. Mitchell felt this helped her deal with her loss.

When she had finished, she sat down and then held her cup up to drink to her father. Mitchell couldn't remember ever seeing her drink before and after choking on the first sip, he could see she hadn't drunk before. Now Rodrigues stood up and moved to the center and spoke a little about Stretch. He didn't speak long because he admitted he didn't know him that well. They played a little company sports together but didn't hang around together. However, in the end he said, "I wished I had known him better because now I can clearly see the kind of man he was, and I would have liked to know that man." With that said, he raised his cup with everyone else and they drank a toast to Stretch.

No one else wanted to say anything, so Mitchell again stood up in the center. At first, he didn't speak, but only slowly looked around at the group. As he stopped and looked at each one, they looked back at him for a moment, then put their heads down. He didn't know what to say, but Mitchell knew it was up to him to bring this team back to life.

Finally, he raised his cup and made a toast. "To the fallen, all of them."

Everyone raised their cups and repeated back the toast.

When that toast was done, Mitchell again raised his cup and made another toast. "To the survivors, all of us."

Nobody raised their cups, but only stared at him. Mitchell took a drink. He then spun around, pointing to each of them and finally said, "All of you are the survivors, because of these two men and all the others that fell here, as well as all the others that survived like yourselves. In our time right now, everyone you see here would be dead. You and they have made a difference to everyone else that you can see. Including yourselves." He stopped and again held up his cup and turn around. This time, as he looked at them, they raised their cups. When he had completed the circle, he took a drink, and everyone drank with him.

He felt that this was a little better, but he hadn't finished yet. "August would not want us sitting around and crying in his drink." He started and slowly turning around again. "As for Stretch, I also never really knew him that well until he came to this detail. However, I found that even when things were wrong, he didn't mope around. He just went with the group and stepped in when needed. I don't believe he would appreciate us crying about him, either. Both men died proudly for what they believed in, and I truly think they would do it again, even knowing the outcome." Mitchell had to stop. His throat was getting a little dry, so he took another sip, but then continued, "Like they do in New Orleans, we need to celebrate the lives of these men, not morn at their passing."

This got a nod of approval from most of the group as he looked around. Kat, however, was still thinking about her father. However, even she came out of her dark place as people remembered the good things they all did. When Anna told the story of August's first try at driving the hummer, she even smiled and tried to hide a little giggle.

Mitchell looked over to Redcloud, who just showed him a thumbs up sign and he knew the group was going to be OK.

By dark, they had finished the last of August's stash and some had a little trouble trying to prepare an evening meal. In the end, everyone got fed somehow and everyone crashed early. They all knew they would move out in the morning and that Redcloud would start waking them early again.

CHAPTER 17

Just as before, it was happening again. Before light, Redcloud was rousting everyone out of bed. Mitchell moaned as Redcloud came by his tent and he slowly crawled out to see only the stars. Redcloud had moved on to wake the others and it was the same sounds that came out of each tent. He swore Redcloud enjoyed this part of the day way too much.

As he sat on the ground trying to get his boots on and nursing a hangover, Redcloud came by and gave Mitchell a little kick in the butt and said, "Come on, Major. We gotta get this show on the road." He then dashed away.

Mitchell mumbled something when it finally hit him, "Major, where did you hear about that?" He shouted to the back of Redcloud as he continued to walk away. Mitchell just stood up, looking at him. Redcloud never turned or made any sign that he had even heard him.

Mitchell slowly turned back to getting his boots on. He figured if anyone knew, it would be Redcloud. He also figured it was probably Crockett who let it slip. Also, knew that if he hadn't done it already, it won't take long for Redcloud to get the word out to the rest of the team.

The group had not had to break camp for a while, and it showed. The sun was already coming up, and they were still not ready. Both Mitchell and Redcloud were running around and yelling at everyone to get it done. The biggest problem was with the hummer. They hadn't really thought it through about hitching the horses to it. With August gone, they didn't have a clear idea of how to do it. August was the only one in the group who had experience with putting together a horse team.

Anna had driven the hummer out of the compound, and they were all standing around trying to figure out the best way to pull it using the horses and what they had. Finally, it was Peter who came to the rescue. He went back to Crockett and got enough leather straps to put together a harness. They ran it back to the gun turret. This gave them control of the horses. While someone would still need to steer the hummer, they could get it moving. The last thing was to put together a makeshift yoke to get the horses to pull it. Once they had it all together, they could finally move out.

Mitchell calmed down now and took time to check everything out. Redcloud was also looking over the contraption they had put together. While they were still checking, Crockett came up and confirmed that while it will probably work, it was not the best setup. However, Mitchell felt they could fine tune it while they were on the road and get the needed materials from stops along the way.

The group gathered to shake hands and say their goodbyes to everyone. The hummer and wagon were ready. They could also get the extra saddles and other necessities from the owners of the horses, who no longer needed them.

Most of the group had already gotten on their horses. Only Mitchell and Redcloud remained. Mitchell walked over to say goodbye to Crockett. As he did, Bowie hobbled over as well. The three of them just looked at each other for a moment and then the hands all went out. There was a lot of handshaking and slaps on the back.

After the goodbyes, Mitchell went over and got up on his horse. He still felt uncomfortable in the saddle, and Redcloud just laughed as he rode off. Crockett come over to him and with one last handshake said, "Don't be surprised if I decide to come look you up in a few years. You and I still need to sit down so you can tell me about those stories over a couple of drinks or more."

Mitchell just smiled down at him, saying, "I couldn't even come close to the stories you could probably tell." He then added, "Besides, I do not know where we will be past the end of the day."

Crockett let go of his hand and stepped back and laughed as he said, "I don't think that is going to be a problem. I'll just keep an ear open for a group of strange travelers. Who else could that be?"

Mitchell laughed and spurred his horse as he waved to Crockett. Before he went out of sight, he stopped and turned to wave again. He now noticed that just about every place on that side of the compound had people watching, and most of them returned his wave.

Mitchell finally caught up with the group, and while it was slow going, they were making headway. They took a lunch break at the first real river crossing, which wasn't too complicated. Then later in the day, they came upon a hill that was just too much for the horses to handle. Unhitching the hummer, they took the horses up the hill. Anna fired it up and just drove up. Once there, they had just a little trouble getting the horses hitched back up and after about an hour; they had it figured out and on the road again.

By the end of the day, they had really only gone a few miles before they made camp for the night. Mitchell didn't like the speed at which they were moving, but there was nothing he could really do about it.

They hid the hummer in some bushes, and Jose was pretty good at driving the wagon. He found a nice flat spot and unloaded the gear. Now setting up the camp went a lot smoother than it did breaking it up this morning. They had gained a small table and set it up for the food prep. Kat had been riding in the hummer with Anna and was now busy getting something ready for their dinner.

Mitchell unsaddled and hobbled his horse, just as Redcloud had taught them. He then went over to see if Kat needed any help. As he walked up, she smiled as she asked, "Oh, you finally remember me?"

He was trying to figure if he should just turn around and walk away or stay and face her wrath. He could only stand there while she just starred him down. Finally, he got the nerve to say, "I am awfully sorry, my dear. It has been a very busy day, and I have been so tied up taking care of getting this group moving. I never really had time to spend some time with you today."

She just put her hands on her hips and turned away from him. She couldn't continue looking at him because she could no longer hold in her smile.

Mitchell came up behind her and put his hands on her shoulders, saying, "Now that we are moving, and things organized, it will be different from now on."

She just jerked her shoulders out of his hands and took another step. With her back still to him, she continued to play her part and came back at him with, "It better be different. I will not allow my husband to ignore me in such a way."

Now he was worried, and she could hear it in his voice, "But dear," He started out but then stammered, trying to find the right thing to say.

Kat could not hold it in any longer and laughed out loud. However, that wasn't the worst part of it. The entire group had been standing around and watching. When she finally gave it up, everyone started laughing, too.

It only took Mitchell a couple second before he realized she was just playing with him. Then he grabbed her by her shoulders again, but this time, he spun her around to look at him. This started her to laughing so hard that tears began running down her face. Mitchel looked around the camp and everyone was laughing harder now. He held up a single finger and started shaking it at her, but he couldn't say anything, as even he laughed.

When everybody got it out of their system and thing settle back down, Mitchell looked around and the entire group was still happily doing the things needed to finish getting the camp set up. Kat went back to work preparing the meal. Redcloud and Jose were tending to the horses while Anna and Peter got the fire going. Blake was sorting out the tents and setting up his. Mitchell appeared to be the only one with nothing to do. So, he turned back to Kat to ask, "Now that all of you have finished playing with me, is there anything I can do to help?"

"Get some water boiling and set up a place for us to gather." Was all she said without even looking at him.

Mitchell guessed it was her way of letting him know she was now too busy to deal with him. He went over to the wagon and got the water pot out and put a couple full buckets of water in and set it up over the flame. Then he turned to see about an eating place. There were few possibilities at this site. He just let everyone find their own spots. Now it was his turn to find his gear and set his tent up. He then took Stretch's tent and set it up right next to his for Kat. Next, he took their sleeping bags and made a place for them to sit and eat near the fire.

Anna and Peter had chosen a site for their tent a little further away from the rest. Mitchell thought this was expected, but he might have a hard time explaining it to Kat.

It was now getting dark, and the food was ready. The others had taken the example from Mitchell and pulled up their sleeping bags and a blanket for Peter. They gathered close together to eat, and the talk was mostly about the trip so far. There were a couple of discussions about the horse team for the hummer and better ways of doing this or that. But it was just a pleasant evening, so far.

After dinner, Mitchell got up to stretch, and everyone stopped talking to look at him. He froze and looked around with a simple, "What?"

Redcloud spoke up now. "I think they are all expecting you to plan our next move."

He just looked around at the nodding heads. With no actual plans, he wasn't ready to start this discussion right now. He thought for a moment, then said, "Or future is to find August's village north of here and pick up some supplies and other things and get married."

The way he added the getting married at the end made a couple of them laugh. He was pleased to see they were still in a good mood.

Anna now said what he was afraid of, "No Boss, the Chief is talking about after. Where are we going to go and what are we going to do?"

Again, Mitchell didn't want to deal with this right now. He suggested, "Well, I think the first thing we need to do is head back north and find August's old place and dig up the duce. We salvage what we can and destroy it as best we can."

Redcloud stepped in to save his friend. "I'll second that."

Mitchell got the hint. "Any discussion on that?" He asked.

No one spoke up, but he could see in Anna's face this was not what she wanted to talk about. After giving it a minute, Mitchell called for a vote, "All in favor of this, raise your hand."

Slowly, every hand went up. He looked around and said, "It's unanimous."

Finally, Anna couldn't stand it anymore. "Boss, you know what I'm talking about. We need to decide what is going to happen to us from now on."

He could hear the anger in her voice and figured he could not put this off until later. "Yes, I know what you want to talk about," He started out, "And we will get to that, but first things first. We still have some unfinished business to discuss."

She looked at him and he could see it finally dawn on her what he was talking about. She quietly asked, "Peter?"

Mitchell smiled, saying, "Yes, Mister Peter. We still need to vote on him." He didn't continue for a moment while everyone thought about it. He then added, "I think everyone has had time to talk to him, except me. Yes, I know what you're going to say. I have talked with him, but not about this."

He couldn't decide if the look he saw in her eyes was anger or fear. However, he continued, "Tomorrow I want Peter to ride next to me and we will talk. Tomorrow night, we will take the final vote."

Now he was certain it was disappointment he saw in her eyes.

Although Mitchell had already decided about this young man, he still wanted to talk about joining this group and what that means. But, to keep Anna happy, he will address her other concern. "Anna," He called her out by name, "Before we can vote on our future, we first need to settle this matter. However, while we do, I want each of you to think about what we should do. I'm talking about realistic plans and a timeline of some sort that we should follow. After we make our next stop for supplies, we will have a long and slow trip to August's house. I think this would be a fitting place to take the vote. After all, this is the place where we set up this group and these rules. In the meantime, we can meet each night and discuss these plans after dinner, so when it is time to vote, we will be ready."

He looked around but couldn't get a feel from the group. This time it was Johnny that seconded this idea. Mitchell asked the standard question, "Any discussion?"

He looked at each of them and no one showed they wanted to speak. So, he added, "All in favor, raise your hand."

All hands eventually went up. Anna was the last hand, but even she knew it was the right way to go.

The next day, they broke camp and headed north, as usual. This time, however, Mitchell hung near the back of the group with Peter. They talked most of the morning and after the lunch break; he let the poor boy join his wife-to-be for the rest of the day.

It was now clear to Mitchell about two things. First, Peter was a smart young man and had an open mind. The second thing was that he was truly in love with Anna.

That night after dinner, they had the vote, and it was unanimous. Peter was now a member of the group. The rest of the trip to find August's old village wasn't too eventful. They had a couple of difficult river crossings where it took a while to find a place to cross, but they eventually made it. The village wasn't too difficult to find, and most of the people remembered August and Kat. They couldn't believe how she had grown since she moved away. They were also sad to hear about what happened to her father, but excited about the news of Santa Anna's defeat. Much of the time Anna needed to do some translating, because most of the people only spoke German with a few English or Spanish words thrown in.

The first night there was a little party that was quickly thrown together, and everyone had a great time. Mitchell met with the Pastor of this town who agreed to marry him and Kat, out of respect for her father. Anna and Peter were a different issue. They did not belong to this community, and he didn't feel it was right for him to marry them. Kat finally stepped in and explained that this group was now a family and that they had already voted to accept Peter in as part of her family. There was much discussion between her and the Pastor, mostly in German, and Kat was very forceful. The Pastor finally gave in and agreed to marry all of them.

They set it for two days from then. It was going to be a double ceremony. Redcloud would stand with Mitchell and Johnny agreed to be the best man for Peter. Since Anna was already busy with this ceremony, Kat asked an old friend of hers from the village to be with her. They also found another friend to stand with Anna.

There were a couple of days before the wedding and the team picked up some supplies they needed, including a proper harness for the hummer. With a few modifications, it was fitted and attached to the hummer and was much better than the makeshift one they had been using. They traded two of the extra horses they had to pay for everything and by the time the wedding day came around; they settled everything.

The wedding was simple, but nice. The pastor even spoke it in broken English so they could all understand. Some ladies from the village found a couple of exquisite dresses for the ladies. Mitchell and Peter got cleaned up as best they could.

The genuine excitement came after the wedding, when it seemed like the whole town gathered for a dinner party. There was some music and dancing, and like magic, a rather large keg of beer appeared. It wasn't a particularly good beer, but it was the best around.

Mitchell had taken his tent and set it up far away from their camp and the town. He found a very nice clearing and also set up a little fire pit and had everything all ready for their first night together as husband and wife. He assumed Peter and Anna had some similar arrangement, because they weren't at the party long before those two disappeared.

Just before dark, Mitchell and Kat thanked everyone and said good night. There was the usual poking of fun at the newlyweds as they went off together, but it was Redcloud who surprised him the most. They had just left on the trail to where Mitchell had set up the camp when Redcloud stepped out in front of them and it startled Kat.

Redcloud apologized and looking at both of them as he said, "Katherine and Jim, I can't imagine the life ahead of you, but I am sure it will be interesting for both of you and that the love I can see between you will carry you through the days and years ahead."

Mitchell was shocked. Redcloud was so serious and respectful that he couldn't remember hearing it before. He stepped up and gave Kat an enormous hug and then turned to his best friend. He added, "I wish the best for the both of you, no matter what comes." He then pulled Mitchell to him for another big hug.

As Redcloud let him go and started heading back into town, Mitchell swore there were tears in his eyes. He and Kat just watched as the big man left. Mitchell had known him for many years and Kat had also come to know him pretty well, but neither of them had words for this moment. Quietly, they turned and continued on to his camp. When they got there, Mitchell was shocked again. Even though he had taken some effort to keep this place a secret, Redcloud had found it. This was not the part that surprised him. Redcloud had cleaned the place up. He cleared all the brush from around the camp and stacked up a pile of wood for a fire. He had found some lovely plants and placed them around the tent to make it look nice.

As they approached, Kat turned to him and whispered, "It is beautiful."

Mitchell chuckled a little, saying, "This is not me. Redcloud was here and did all this."

Kat smiled as she told him, "You truly have a good friend in him."

He just looked at her and when he pulled her to him, he said, "We truly have a good friend in him."

She quickly nodded, and they kissed and long and passionate kiss.

The next morning, there was no Redcloud to wake them up. Mitchell and Kat could finally sleep past sunrise. They didn't come out of the tent for a long time, but when they did, they both held on to the other. Neither of them wanted to let go. However, it was cold, so they had to part while Mitchell stirred the fire back to life. They then sat down together to get warm. Mitchell now realized he forgot something. He had brought no food for the morning.

Neither of them really cared much about it, and they laughed and joked about needing some food after the long night. Quickly, they broke down the tent and headed back to the camp. When they arrived, Anna and Peter were already there. They were all smiles, as well.

As he sat down by the fire and Kat went to get some MREs for breakfast, Redcloud came and sat down next to him. Mitchell quietly leaned over to him and said, "Thank you, that was very nice."

Redcloud just leaned back and, with a smile, replied, "I have no idea what you're talking about."

He should have guessed. Redcloud was now back in character and Mitchell just let it ride.

Redcloud asked while they were still alone, "What's the plan? When do we pull out?"

Mitchell figured they were in no real great hurry now. He thoughtfully said, "Let's just rest for the day and leave tomorrow morning, unless someone wants to stay, for some reason."

Redcloud just stood and laughed as he said, "The rest of the group is fine, but I guess you four might need a little rest." He then just walked away.

Mitchell knew he was not one to stick around for a reply to his smart-ass remarks. He just watched him go as Kat brought over some food. She asked about Redcloud, but he only told her, "He just wanted to see what the plans were for leaving."

She smiled and before she took a bite of the food, she asked, "Did you thank him for what he did for us yesterday?"

Mitchell had some food in his mouth and almost choked when she asked. He had to swallow before he replied, "Yes, but he said he didn't know what I was talking about."

"But he..." she started to say

He just stopped her, telling her, "That is his way. You'll need to get used to him. He is not one to show deep emotions, even though he has them."

She just looked at Redcloud as he headed to the horses. She had a sweet smile on her face as she nodded, saying, "I understand. He is much like my father, only he doesn't talk as much as he did."

This was the first time he had seen her talk about her father since his death and didn't get all choked up and cry.

Shortly, everyone gathered. Mitchell told them, "Today we rest and tomorrow morning we will begin our journey."

"Journey to where?" Anna asked.

"We'll decide that while we are on the journey." He said back to her, rather sarcastically, but then added, "I suggest that each night one person will stand up and give us his or her plan. That person will need to lay out all the good and bad parts of this plan. We then discuss that plan. At the end, when we get to August's old place, we will make the final decision. In fact, we will not move any further until we decide."

"How does that sound for a plan?" He added when no one spoke up.

There was a lot of mumbling, but no one really wanted to second the idea, so after a while Mitchell continued, "Okay, does anyone have a better plan? Let's hear it."

Again, no one spoke up, so he tried to close it out. "Okay, if there is no discussion and no one has a better plan, then we move on with what I suggested."

Anna finally spoke, "Why can't we just simply throw out ideas and vote on them now?"

Now Mitchell thought he had them. They were ready to think. "Well Anna, this is probably one of the most important decisions, not only in our lives, but in the lives of everyone in the United States, both now and in the future. In fact, probably in the entire world. Everything we do from now on is going to affect the world. We need to be responsible about it and not just jump into any idea without thinking it through as best we can. One person can't think of everything. We will need all the minds that are sitting here each night."

Mitchell then sat down to see if anyone else would step in. He could see a lot of thinking was going on and some heads nodding. It wasn't long before Johnny stood up to say, "I'd like to second that plan. It sounds like a reasonable course of action."

Again, Mitchell called for a vote, and they all agreed to the plan. Now Mitchell sat back down and looked at the team and told them, "I would suggest you get some rest today. Tomorrow we will pull out and heading back north and you all know what that means."

Jose said something in Spanish, but the only word they all recognized was when he said, "Redcloud."

Anna then agreed, "I don't know what you said, but I agree, Redcloud. Means no more sleeping late."

Everyone started laughing. Redcloud stood up with a hurt expression on his face and then smiled, saying, "Just for that, I'm getting ya'll up extra early tomorrow." Now it was his turn to laugh as everyone groaned because they knew he meant it.

The next morning, Redcloud was true to his word. It was still a couple of hours until sunrise. There was a lot of complaining and Redcloud was just eating it up. When they headed out on the road, he took off and rode point with one of the handheld radios in case there was a problem. The rest of the group stuck together and just made the best time they could.

This time, Mitchell was not remiss in his duty to pay attention to Kat. She had the window down and he rode next to it and they talk on and off as the day went by. Anna poked some fun at those two and they had fun teasing her back.

Redcloud called on the radio, "Hey, tell the big boss man there is a crossing up here. I think we may cross, but I'm going to look around to see if there is a better place. If you get here before I get back, just wait."

Kat just looked up at her new husband and asked, "Did you hear?"

Mitchell was looking ahead to see if he could see the crossing, so he just nodded to her and she keyed the radio to tell Redcloud, "He heard you."

"Good." Redcloud said, but continuing, "tell him to send Jose up here to look upstream. I'll go down and meet you back here."

Mitchell leaned over to tell her, "Tell him I got it, but I'll look up stream. I think Jose stopped to take care of some personal business."

Kat passed that on to Redcloud as she watched her husband ride away.

Mitchell got to the river and found the spot Redcloud had called from. There were enough tracks that even he could follow. He turned to ride upstream and rode maybe a mile. However, he didn't find anything that looked better than the crossing where he started. Making his way back, he now thought he should have taken the radio from Kat to talk to Redcloud. He decided this was something to remember the next time.

When he returned, he found Redcloud sitting on the bank of the stream. As Mitchell rode up, he got up and walked out to meet him. Before Mitchell could say anything, Redcloud said, "I found a place maybe half a mile down. I crossed, and it looks ok, but the water is still a little on the deep side. I didn't try this place yet." He then jumped up on his horse and headed for the water. When the water got up to the horse's belly, he turned to say, "This one is a little deeper and softer bottom. I say we go downriver."

Mitchell looked down the river and he was pretty sure the hummer could makeup, but it looked too rough for the wagon. Especially since Jose and Johnny were rather new to driving it. "You think they can get the wagon down there? It ain't looking too good." He asked.

Redcloud turned and looked, saying, "These rocks and junk clear away just on the other side of the hill. They should be able to handle it if we go slow enough."

Mitchell decided, "Okay then. We go downstream. I'll go tell them. Maybe they'll find a path that will lead that way before we get here."

Redcloud just waved, and turning his horse around, he headed back downstream. Mitchell didn't wait for him, but kicked his horse to head back to the group.

The team wasn't far away and as soon as he got there; he filled them in. Blake said he noticed a small game trail that headed off that way and was just a little way back. Mitchell quickly rode back and found it. From the limited trail he could see, it looked to be better than the rocks by the stream. He rode down it a little, and it continued to be a small but good trail.

After making his way back, he found the group just waiting for him. He filled them in he watched Anna swing the hummer around, but she had to wait for Jose to get the wagon turned. He did alright, but it took him a little while to get it figured out how to turn them that sharply.

Now Jose was in the lead, and they quickly made it back to the trail. Mitchell turned to lead them up the trail and everyone made good time. When they found Redcloud, it surprised him they were coming from a different direction than he expected. As the group pulled up, Redcloud walked up to meet them and, laughing, he said, "My, aren't you guys becoming quite the trailblazers?"

Mitchell just ignored him and called for lunch before they crossed. For those on horses, it felt good to get down and walk. For Jose and Johnny, it was quite a different story. When they got down off the wagon, they both had stiff backs and sore butts. Of course, the ladies in the hummer didn't have any problems or complaints. Mitchell decided they were going to have to have some kind of rotation to get everyone a chance at the good life in the hummer.

After crossing the stream, the group continued on until before dark. They found a nice place to camp for the night. This time they were in a small clearing and there was plenty of wood for the fire and they drug up a couple of logs to sit on. They had rabbit for dinner this time, compliments of Redcloud. He caught a couple and Kat cooked them up in a stew. They still had some bread from the village. This made a pleasant change from the MREs.

After dinner, Mitchell called for a volunteer to be the first to come up with a plan. No one volunteer, so Mitchell said he would go first. Stepping out to the center of the group, he announced, "I am doing this one for Stretch. I know what he wanted to do. He and I talked about it before he died."

Jose and Johnny liked this idea and gave a couple of fist bumps to show it. Mitchell continued, "I know he wanted us to go east and support the Union in the Civil War. We could end this thing years earlier and save many lives. One problem is this may not end slavery."

Anna jumped up to say, "Of course, if the north wins, then slavery we be through."

"Not necessarily, Anna." Mitchell corrected her. "The Civil War did not begin with the idea of ending slavery. The setting of the blacks free did not become a goal of the war until after the Battle at Gettysburg."

Now Johnny threw in with Mitchell. "This is true. If we get involved and end the war too soon, the freeing of the slaves might not happen for years or even decades after."

Mitchell just stood there watching the reactions of everyone. When he looked at Peter, it was clear he did not know what they were talking about. He decided he would teach him a little tonight. Just enough to understand the discussion, but it would ultimately be up to Anna to teach him about these things. He looked over at Peter and said as he pointed to him, "One of our group is totally lost. Pour Mr. Peter hasn't the foggiest what we are talking about."

Anna just turned to look at him while the other laughed a little when they realized they had forgotten all about him.

Mitchell then pointed to Kat. She had heard them talk about the Civil War before, but really didn't know what was going on. He looked back and forth between the two of them as he started his history lesson. "For the new people in our group who don't have the knowledge of the future, I am going to give you a brief history lesson. This is going to be quick and without great detail. Anna, you'll have to bring Peter up to speed later, and I'll take care of Kat. For right now, though, so you understand what we are talking about. In about twenty-five years, there will be a war fought between the states. It will be mostly the northern states fighting the southern states. There will be many reasons we fought this war, but one of the biggest and the most important one will be slavery. The war will go on for over four years and over six hundred thousand people will die. The question of us taking our knowledge and weapons and getting involved is what we are discussing."

He saw Peter nodding that he understood this much. However, Kat had a blank stare in her eyes. Mitchell thought he might have lost her when he said the unbelievable number of dead from the war. She could not imagine so much death. He continued, "As a result, the north won the war and slavery ended. It also resolved several other important issues about our government, but slavery is the key that we are concerned about. Now, if we get involved, we could easily help the north win the war and save many lives, but as we were just talking about, we could mess up the whole thing and slavery would continue. Oh, I am certain that, in this future, slavery would still end. However, it might go on a much longer time."

He had to stop and get some water. And while he was away, there were a couple of small discussion going on. When he returned, Anna suggested, "We could slowly feed information to the north and ensure that the war doesn't end too soon."

"This is true," Mitchell responded to her, "however, this is a quick action and extremely complicated. We know how it will end and what the results are, but if we go messing thing up with the complexities involved, we could just as easily let the south win. Prior to Gettysburg, the south had won most, if not all, the battles and many in the north wanted to end the war and let the south have it their way."

Anna sat back down. Mitchell needed them to see his point on this one major plan. "I believe Stretch could have possibly left the group over this issue. It is not something I would take lightly. The good from this war will come, even though we have changed some things. I think the war will go pretty much as it did. Yes, it will be bad again, but the alternative is, we may change things the other way."

Jose and Johnny were nodding their heads. Mitchell couldn't read Anna or Peter. He knows Redcloud will stand by him on this, and he will just have to explain it to Kat, so she will follow him.

He ended this for the night. "I have thrown this out for Stretch, and I believe some of you might also think about this. I, for one, do not want to take the chance of messing up the good that comes out of it in the end, and I think we should stay out of this."

Johnny stood up to say, "I second this…."

Mitchell stopped him before he could finish. "We voted to just hear the plans right now. When we get to August's place, then we'll have a final discussion or two and vote."

He sat back down but continued to say, "That's it for tonight. Everyone, continue to think about your plans and we'll continue to discuss them. Also, before the next plan, we'll see if there are any new ideas about this plan tonight and continue this discussion if needed."

Everyone seemed happy with this, and the rest of the night was mostly quiet. Anna and Peter walked off so she could give him more details about the Civil War. Kat was content to just sit with her new husband in quiet and watch the fire. Redcloud made a last check of the horses and walk around the camp. When he was satisfied, he headed for his tent. The evening slowly broke up as the rest went to turn in.

Over the next week or two, the group continued to make slow headway to the north. Each night after dinner, they sat around discussing plans. Sometimes they would re-discuss a plan that was already brought up or simply just listen as another plan was thrown out there.

Jose's plan was to head to California. They knew where the gold was going to be discovered and they could move in and make a fortune before anyone really knew about it. This plan had some merit and Mitchell believed some might go for this idea. Johnny wanted to go back east and dominate the business world. With their knowledge of the future, they could dominate all the businesses and own Wall Street. Again, Mitchell thought this was also well planned, but he didn't think too many of the group liked the idea of going back east. Anna and

Peter kind of joined together for their plan and that was to go back to claim the property they had received for their part in winning Texas' freedom. Combined, it would be one of the largest spreads anywhere in Texas for quite some time. Mitchell knew he was going to have to shoot this one down because that would put them back into the middle of the paradox they had just run away from.

Mitchell, Redcloud, and Kat still hadn't thrown out their ideas yet. With any luck, he could stall them until they got to their final voting place. As luck would have it, Mitchell soon figured he had none. The ideas had run out, and the discussion finished, and now it was their turn. The next night Anna spoke up after dinner, "Hey Boss," she started out in a joking way, "We've all heard our plans. Why is it we haven't heard from you or Redcloud?"

Redcloud spoke up before Mitchell could respond, "We haven't heard from Kat yet." He reminded Anna.

She shot back, now getting a little more seriously, "I figured she would join the Boss like Peter and I did."

Now Mitchell stepped in, "You know as well as anyone that we believe women should have their own mind. I will not force her to take my idea as her own. She may say what she wants to do, just as much and anyone else here."

Now Anna was on the defensive. "Gee Boss, I didn't mean that she couldn't say what she wanted. I just figure that you two would join forces like we did." Then, looking at Kat, she added, "Please Kat, say what you want. I would really like to hear about your ideas."

Until now, Mitchell's plan was working like a charm. He had steered the discussion away from his plans for the night, but now he had put Kat on the spot and this he didn't want to do. However, before he could say anything to defend her, she stood up and moved toward the fire. At first, she said nothing, but everyone remained quiet while they waited for her to begin.

Kat continued to stand there for a long time. Mitchell couldn't tell if she was just afraid to talk or if she was trying to think of a plan. The two of them had never really discussed this idea, so he did not know what she might be thinking.

After what seemed like a long time, Kat slowly began talking, "I think I would just like to stay at the home my father started and build a life from there. I don't understand all the things you have been talking about. I don't understand the need to change the future. From all the wonderful things you have already told me, I believe the future will be a beautiful place to live."

She didn't stay by the fire for the discussion part of it, like the other had. She just quickly returned to where she had been sitting and sat down.

Nobody said a word. They just sat there looking into the fire, but Mitchell could see they were all thinking. Slowly, he stood up and walked to the fire. Looking around, he only saw blank stares back at him. It took him a while before he thought of something to say, but he needed this discussion to go on so he wouldn't have to bring up his ideas. He thoughtfully said, "She has a point we never really discussed before."

Jose asked, "What point, boss? She said we do nothing."

"Exactly," Mitchell quickly replied to him. "We do nothing. We haven't considered that idea yet. Why do we have to do anything? Yes, there are many things we could do to change the future for the good, but also, we might change it for the worse. We don't know what happened in our time after the bomb went off. It could ignite a war that would destroy the entire world, but it might just as likely unite the entire world to work together to eliminate these types of threats and propel humankind into a peace like unlike anything before."

He stopped and looked around. People were now considering her idea. He added one last thing before he also turned and sat back down, "The point is we don't know if we are helping destroy the future or making it better. We just simply don't know."

This brought about one of the better and certainly the liveliest of the discussions they have had on the entire trip. It went long into the night. By the time people got tired and break it up, Mitchell felt confident that Kat's idea, although good, would not fly. All the future people felt that what was going to happen in their old timeline was no longer their concern. What they tried to make of this timeline was, and he believed the consensus was to try everything they could to make it better.

Because the discussion went late last night, Redcloud let them sleep a little longer the next morning, however he didn't let it go on for long. The sun was already up when he woke them in the morning, but just barely. They broke camp and started on again. However, by late in the afternoon, the weather had turned bad, and they made camp early and because of the rain, they canceled the discussion group for the night.

Pushing on the next day, Mitchell's luck had changed. They found August's old place. There was a little damage since the time they had left. It looked like there had been some visitors as well. Redcloud thought it might have been people from the tribe of Indians they had killed, come looking for their warriors. The visit appeared to have been quite a while ago, so they felt certain the danger had passed. Mitchel rode by the spot where they had buried the duce, and everything looked good there.

All things considered, they looked to be in good shape right now. If they needed supplies before leaving, they could take a couple of days and head over to the trading post they used when they left and get what they needed. They had the coral built so they could catch some more horses to trade with. Also, spring was coming. If they stayed long enough, they could plant some vegies in the garden.

After they set up camp, Mitchell decided he would let them take the rest of the day to rest. Jose went straight to bed while the others repaired the dinner table and cleaned up a little. Mostly, though, they were talking. It was now time to consider the plans and take a vote. Mitchell had been working on his plan and now that they were here, he was going to have to present it, but not tonight. Everyone had agreed that this was a day of rest and relaxation.

After dinner, they gathered around the newly repaired fire pit and Mitchell brought out a keg that he had hidden away for just this occasion. The party got going and everyone was having a good time. Before it got too dark, there was a little wrestling match. In the end, it came down to Mitchell and Redcloud. As the two faced off, everyone was cheering the two on. Unfortunately, it was short-lived. Redcloud had his buddy pinned in only a few second and a great cheer went up. It looked like the only support for Mitchell was his wife, Kat, and maybe Peter. The others all knew he had little a chance against Redcloud right from the beginning.

After the fighting, everything settled down to good natured talk, but mostly a quiet night. Soon, everyone headed off to bed. This time Mitchell walked Kat to her cabin, but he didn't go back to his own tent. They shared the cabin and an actual bed together for the first time.

The next morning, Redcloud didn't wake anyone. He got up as usual but went off hunting. Eventually, the others gradually woke up and started moving around. They got the fire going again and made breakfast and sat around, discussing what to do today.

After a little while, Kat and Mitchell came out of the cabin. He was ready for the jokes and poking fun of them, but nothing. It made him feel like they didn't even notice them. He fixed his regular cup of coffee and joined the group. As they were talking about things to do, he suggested the first thing they do was dig out the duce. They could then syphon out the rest of the fuel and get the hummer up and running and see what else they still had.

The group wasn't happy about the idea, but they all agreed that this was probably the best thing to get working on today. They spent the rest of the day digging. By late afternoon, Jose climbed in, and the thing actually started. A spontaneous cheer went up from everyone. Jose drove it out of the place they had put it months ago and ran a circle around the rest of the group while blowing the horn. He finally parked the duce near the well, and they went through the things they had left behind. Mitchell called Johnny over and told him, "Get a complete inventory of everything there, including amounts and a guess of how much fuel it still has. You're in charge, so use whoever you need."

Blake stepped back with a little surprise. He couldn't believe that the Boss had put him in charge of this detail. "You got it Boss." He shouted back. He then quickly turned to Jose and Peter, telling them, "You guys give me a hand with this. The Boss wants a complete inventory, right away."

Before he could walk away, Mitchell called him back to say, "You don't need to rush this. We're gonna be here a while. Take your time and do it right."

Blake now looked down with a sheepish smile and nodded as he went off to get started.

Redcloud now came up with a smile. He had been standing off to the side, watching. He turned his back to the group as he leaned in to say, "Did we ever act like that the first time they gave us command?"

Mitchell said nothing for a moment. He was afraid that all that would come out was a laugh. Finally, he got control of himself and nodded while just saying, "Probably."

They both stood there a little, watching as Johnny took over and got things organized by sorting everything out before they went to counting. Mitchell thought that he would have gone a long way in the Army they had come from.

Soon it was dinnertime. Redcloud had gotten a couple of rabbits, and Kat made up her stew that was pretty good. After dinner, they all gathered around the fire pit just like they had months ago. Now it was time for Mitchell to lay out his plan.

"Okay, I guess it is my turn to lay it on you." Mitchell started out. A couple of them had a little laugh, but he just continued, "Stretch wanted us to get involved in the Civil War because of the injustice done to his people for so many years. However, I believe if we just let time run its course, it will again free his people. Maybe not exactly as it had happened before, but I believe the results will be the same."

Anna interrupted him now, "Boss, I thought you were going to give us your plan. It is not time yet to rehash the other plans and start voting."

Mitchell just stared at her for a moment. He then sarcastically said, "Well, if some people would quit interrupting me, I will get to my plan. This is just my way of leading into it."

She hung her head down and softly said, "Sorry, boss. Won't happen again." And then she looked up at him with a smile.

Now most everyone laughed. Mitchell walked around the pit as he talked so he could watch everyone's face as he laid it out, "As I was saying before I was so rudely interrupted," a short pause and then, "The Civil War will work its own way out. However, it was a good idea for us to use our special knowledge to right some wrongs from our past, and one of the greatest wrongs that was never fully righted in our time. Our old time, that is. We have the chance to fix that in our new time."

He just continued to walk around and watching the faces. In their faces, he saw he was sure that he had everyone's attention, but none of them really understood what he was talking about. Finally, he stopped walking and as he made a slow turn he announced his idea, "My plan is to unite the Indian tribes and guide them so they will have the power, both financially and politically to right the wrong done to this point and bring their culture into the white man's culture. Their culture never truly integrated into the whites man's culture the way other culture had been throughout the history of America. I feel this was a significant loss in our time."

Now he slowly took a long drink. After he put down his cup, he again started walking around the fire and continued his talk. "I say we head north and find Redcloud's tribe and connect with them. After we convince them of our plan, we make connections to all the other tribes and set up some type of tribal government to unite the tribes. Something like a Native American UN. We start them looking for gold and other precious items. Then we can get high-quality teachers to come in a teach the children. Then send them to college to become, among other things, lawyers. With a united front that will overwhelm the US Army. We can negotiate proper ratified treaties to ensure the Native Americans will have a proper place at the table in the future."

He stayed at the fire pit to get this discussion going. It took a while before anyone could think it through enough to ask a question. It was Peter who asked, "I don't know if you have ever dealt with the Indians or not, but from my limited knowledge, they have a very hard time getting along with each other. What makes you think you can get them to work together?"

"That, my friend, is an excellent question." Mitchell responded as he pointed a finger at Peter. "I don't know that we can. I know there are some tribes that are friendly with each other and some that are mortal enemies. If we do this, we will have our work cut out for us. All we can do is try. The first thing we must do is convince them of who we are. If you thought that was difficult down here in Texas, wait until you try it with them. We must then get some of them to work together and try to tell them what will happen if they continue the way they have. Then try to get the word out to the rest and try to get them to join us." Mitchell had to pause for another drink. "I never, ever said it would be easy, and they could just as easily turn on and kill us. However, if we could pull this off, we would right a wrong that was never corrected in our time."

Now was the time for his trump card. "The only real thing we have going for us is our own Native American, Redcloud." Everyone's head turned at the same time to look at Redcloud, but Mitchell just continued, "Do you think we call him the Chief for fun? His father is the chief of his tribe in the future. He would have become the next chief if his tribe. Of course, this knowledge will not help us in this time, but his father raised him from a baby and taught the ways and history of his people that most of the rest don't know. He is our way in. We'll just have to hope it is enough."

Still looking at Redcloud, Anna asked, "Is this true, Chief? Are you a real chief?"

Redcloud smiled in his own way and replied, "Not yet. My father was still alive when we left our time, but I would have been upon his death."

Johnny was the next one with a question. "Do you really think you can get us in and out if necessary?"

Redcloud now stepped up to the fire pit while Mitchell sat down. Looking at the group, he explained, "There are things a chief will pass down to his son. Things that only chiefs will know. Things about medicine and spirits and such. My father started training me when I was still a baby. Yes, I think they will listen to me. I cannot guarantee they will listen to you, though. However, I am pretty sure they will respect that you are my friends and you come in peace, and they will let you go in peace."

He stayed in the pit a little longer, but no one had any more questions at the moment, so he returned to his place outside the circle.

Mitchell stood up again. This time, he didn't walk around. He started out by telling them, "That is it. Anna, you called it the other day, only it wasn't Kat and me that joined, it was Redcloud and me. This is our joint idea. So, this makes all the plans heard now. Tomorrow, we will discuss them together or separately. However, we decide to do it. We need to understand each plan and chose the one that will do the most good and one that we all agree on. So tonight, and tomorrow, start getting your ideas together and your questions so we can hash this out."

Everyone nodded and then started a lot of mumbling as they broke into groups and started talking. Mitchell wondered over to Redcloud, with Kat on his arm, and asked, "How do you think it went?"

Redcloud didn't even take a second to think, "I don't know, boss. There weren't as many questions as I thought there might be, but that could be a good thing or a bad thing. Hard to say. Although, I think you laid out a convincing argument."

Mitchell nodded his agreement with Redcloud and added, "But the questions they asked were right on target. That tells me they were listening and actually considering it."

Redcloud got up and patted Mitchell on the shoulder as he turned to leave. Neither of them said another word. Mitchell just watched him go until he was out of the light. He and Kat returned to the fire pit and just sat there quietly, watching the fire.

Mitchell, however, was also listening to the talk. There was a lot of discussion in the background about the plans. Mostly, they were each lobbying to put each of their plans in the spotlight. Occasionally, he heard a comment or two about his plan, however he couldn't get a good feel on the mood toward it.

People drifted from one little group to another. However, soon the little groups broke up and everyone headed off to their respective beds. He and Kat were the last to leave. They walked back to the cabin and turned in for the night as well.

The next day, the weather had again turned bad. This stopped most of the work and also force the group discussion to be canceled for the night.

The next day after wasn't a lot better, but also on the cold side. It threatened to rain all day, but the rain never came, so they could get a small fire going and the group met to discuss the plans. Mitchell was the first to speak. "I am sorry, Anna," He said, looking at her, "But, I am going to have to disagree with yours and Peter's plan."

Anna stood up. "What's the problem, Boss? It's a perfectly good plan."

"It is a good plan, except it is going to put us right back into the mess we just got ourselves out of. We have already created a paradox, if you will, and this is just going to throw us right back into it."

She just stood there for a moment but said nothing. After a little, she just sat back down and started talking to Peter, who just kept nodding to her.

Jose stood up next to put his idea back out there. "What about my plan, boss? We would be out of the way, and we could become very rich."

Mitchell also agreed with him. "This is very true." He said, but added, "Both you and Johnny have some excellent plans for making us rich, however the problem for me is, what good are we doing for the future of this world? I thought our goal was to make things better for the world, not just our pockets."

Jose just sat back down. He knew right away that it now sounded like a very selfish plan.

Johnny didn't even try to defend his plan. Mitchell had already shot it down.

Anna stood up to say, "So you're basically telling us you don't support our plans because they don't provide a goal for the future of the world?"

"I am telling you what I think. Isn't this what we are supposed to do in a discussion?" He said rather sternly back to her.

Anna said nothing, but she also didn't sit down right away. When she did, it was in a huff. Mitchell realized this was not a good night to discuss things. The fire was going out because the wood was still wet from the rain they had. Mitchell stood up and put a suggestion out, "How about we table the discussion for the night? It's getting cold and that fire ain't gonna last much longer."

There was a lot of mumbling and comments about the cold. Johnny spoke up, "I am gonna second that. It's just too cold for us to talk tonight."

Before he could even finish the question about who agreed, they all yelled it out and got up to leave. When Mitchell helped Kat to stand. She was shivering. He pulled her to him, and they hurry back to the cabin. Once inside, they sat down for a cup of coffee and Kat asked, "Why was Anna so angry?"

Mitchell had to admit that Anna was angry. He just nodded his agreement to her and added, "I'm not really sure what her problem is. I could be as simple as she thought hers was best and thinks everyone should support it, or there could be something else between the two of them we just don't know about. Hard to say. I guess we will need to get her to say during further discussions."

Kat just sat there for a moment, looking at her coffee. She then looked up at her husband to say in a whisper, "Or I could just ask her in private, woman to woman."

It wasn't so much what she said, but the way she had to say it in a whisper, like anyone could hear her, anyway. Mitchell had to smile, "Yes, you and only you could do that."

Kat just leaned back in her chair and smiled as she sipped her coffee.

The next morning was still cold, but the weather had cleared. By the time everyone was up and moving around, the sun was already up, and things were warming, just a little. Some of them gathered around the table to eat, but most took their kits over and got a little fire going. The fire wasn't big enough to warm them, but they sat there to eat none the less.

Mitchell and Kat sat at the table and shared an MRE. Neither one of them was hungry, but the coffee was hot and that was all that mattered to them.

After a while, Johnny came over and sat near them. Pulling a piece of paper out of his pocket, he handed it to Mitchell, saying, "Here is that list you wanted. We got lots of ammo left and the list includes everything we brought back with us. We are short on fuel, explosives, and some types of ammo." He sat back but then shot straight up and added, "Also, the MREs are down to lest than half."

Mitchell first asked, "How much fuel do we still have?"

"If we drain the tanks on the duce, we could probably fill the hummer twice, maybe three times. The problem is, how do we carry it?"

Mitchell thought about that for a moment. It was a good question. This was something they were going to have to bring up for discussion at the meeting tonight.

Before he could ask any more questions, Johnny brought up another issued, guessing what was on the Boss's mind, "There is another thing, Boss. The batteries. We have enough for everything, however if we lose the hummer, we lose a way to charge them."

Mitchell just stared at Johnny for a moment. This kid was good. Not only did he follow directions to a "T," he also was thinking ahead. He finally looked at this young soldier and told him, "Thanks, Johnny. That was very helpful. I'll look this over after I've had my coffee and we'll discuss these things at the meeting tonight. Tell the other about this and tell them to think about the future, other than the plans, and see if they can come up with anything else we might need to think about."

Johnny got up when Mitchell threw in, "Good job, Johnny."

Johnny stood straight up and got a great big smile on his face. The recognition from Mitchell really hit home with him.

After he walked away, Mitchell spotted Redcloud walking by and waved for him to come over. When he got there, Mitchell handed him the paper and Redcloud took a moment to go over it. He looked at Mitchell to say, "Don't look too bad, except for the fuel."

"Yeah, I agree, we are going to have to decide what to do about the hummer."

Redcloud simply shot back, "Leave it."

"Not that simple, Chief." Mitchell started, "According to Johnny, who already figured this out. If we lose the hummer, we lose the radios and everything else that runs on batteries."

Redcloud now sat down. "Good point."

Mitchell smiled to realize Redcloud was now changing his mind about the new guy. He was seeing him as a very useful part of the team. "I sent him back to get the others to think about this and anything else they can think of that might be a problem in the future."

A short "Hm." Was the only reply from the Chief. He then stood and walked over to the fire pit area and started watching the new guy.

When Mitchell turned back to look at Kat, she was hiding a smile. Mitchell knew just how she felt. Redcloud put up a lot of fronts, but when you got to know him well enough, it was pretty easy to see through them. She was learning to see through them. He leaned closer to her and whispered, "The trick is to not let him catch you smiling.

Just let him think you can't see the man he really is. Then it is easy to read him."

Kat immediately covered her mouth with her hand at turned away from him.

The day turned out to be rather normal. The only thing different was the actual work they were doing. After Mitchell suggested they all take a walk up and look over the corral, the entire group moved together. They found it in relatively good shape. A few of the cross logs came loose, and the branches used to camouflage it had shed their leaves, but otherwise it was ready to be used today. They set to cleaning it and making the repairs. They tied the branches together from the camouflage and dragged them down to the fire pit with the horses. After they checked and repaired cross logs, they gathered more branches to line the sides.

It took the rest of the day, and still they hadn't finished. They had about a quarter of the branches needed. One more day, if the weather holds and Mitchell figured they should be able to catch some more horses.

While he was working, Mitchell noticed that Kat and Anna were working together as they drug the branches in. He could only see that they were talking and occasionally they would stop and talk for a while. Sometimes the talk became very animated, especially with Anna. Then Kat would talk a little and they would begin work again. Unfortunately, he was too far away to hear the conversation, however; he was pretty sure what they were talking about.

After dinner was over, most everyone was too tired to have a meeting that night, so they took a vote, and everybody voted for bed instead.

Once they had reached the cabin, Mitchell asked Kat, "I noticed you and Anna doing a lot of talking while you were working. It looked very serious. Do I need to guess what you were talking about?"

Kat put down the thing she was working on and came over to lie next to him on the bed. After cuddling up close to him and laying her head on his shoulder, she softly said, "No, not really. We were just discussing the plans. She thinks your plan is the right one for what you set out and do, but now she is married and wants to start a family, but she doesn't want to do is as an Indian. That is all." Kat then paused for a moment, but continued, "That is why she wants to stay here in Texas, where there are already people."

Now Mitchell understood her reasons. She is ready for motherhood and thinking of her children. He didn't reply to Kat. He just thought about ways that he could make this work for everyone. Unfortunately, his brain didn't agree with his efforts and soon quit working as he drifted off to sleep.

The next morning, the weather had cleared. It was still a little cold, but not like it had been for the past week or two. The sun was out, and Mitchell could see the change in the people. They were talking and joking some, even though they were tired from the unusual amount of heavy work they had been doing."

After a rather pleasant breakfast, they all headed back to the corral. By noon, they were so close to completing it that no one said anything about lunch. By midafternoon, it was finished. There was a lot of congratulations and thanks to each other on a job well done. Jose brought up food by saying how hungry he was. That was all it took. They all now realized how hungry they were, and it was almost a run back to camp to get the food ready. Everyone just grabbed MRE packs and even though the water was just barely warm, no one waited to heat it up again. Mitchell swore that if anyone reached up towards someone else's food, they would probably only drawback a nub. There was no talk, only animal like sounds to show how the food was making them feel more like people again.

In no time, the meal was over and just about everyone laid back on the ground or put their head down on the table. Mitchell stood up and grabbed Kat's arm. Turning back to the group, he said, "I don't know about the rest of you, but we are going to take a well-deserved nap."

There were sounds of agreement from the rest of the group, and everyone headed back to their own beds.

When Mitchell got up and headed outside, he found Redcloud, and young Mr. Blake were already up and had the fire going. It wasn't quite dark yet, but close. There was hot water in the pot, and everything was ready for dinner and the meeting.

Mitchell called Redcloud over to talk in private. He explained the situation about Anna's concerns. As he did, Redcloud just nodded. Finally, he replied, "I was afraid that this was what the problem was. I have also been thinking about what to do."

Mitchell just stood there waiting, but when Redcloud wasn't forthcoming with his thought, Mitchell said out loud, louder than he should have, "Well, what did you come up with?"

Redcloud smiled, and Mitchell understood just then that he had been playing with him. Redcloud started laying out his idea. "We are going to be up in the wild, so to say, away from most all white men for some time before they get there."

Mitchell just nodded.

"However, this plan requires us to connect with the white man."

Mitchell nodded again, saying, "That's right."

"What we need is a midway point." Redcloud said with a shrug, "We need to establish some kind of village or trading post that can work as neutral ground for all sides. This would be a place for young Natives go lean white man's ways before going off to schools in the east. It can be a connection for the white man to deal with the Indians. It would also be a place where the Indians can learn to live with each other."

Mitchel was thinking as Redcloud talked and, after considering everything, he said, "Not bad, not bad at all."

He continued to think about the idea and running different things through his head as fast as he could. He stood up and walked around a little and then added, "Anna and Peter would be the perfect people to run this thing."

"Yep." Came the only reply from Redcloud.

Mitchell finally decided, "Okay, we'll bring this up tonight at the meeting and see how it floats."

"Hold on there a moment. It will not be we who will bring this up. If she doesn't like it, I don't want her mad at me. You can take the blame. If she does like it, then you can also have the glory. I want nothing to do with it."

Mitchell laughed out loud, "You coward." He said jokingly. "Are you afraid of her?"

Redcloud stood up and leaned in to say, "Remember the warning from our time about a woman scorned? Well, I've been down that road before and it is not a road I want to take again." He then quickly turned and walked away.

A stunned Mitchell didn't know what to say. He couldn't remember a time when the Chief had ever been close enough to a woman to scorn her.

After dinner that night, they all gathered around the fire for the meeting. Mitchell took the floor first. He looked around the fire pit at everyone. It was difficult to read the mood. He slowly started talking. "Is there any discussion anyone wants to start out with?"

Johnny raised his hand, but didn't get up to say anything. He just sat there as he said, "Yeah Boss, I want to withdraw my idea."

"I see." Replied Mitchell.

Jose raised his hand next and without waiting to be recognized, he simply said, "Me too, Boss."

"So be it." Mitchell said and turned to Anna and Peter, who just sat there.

Kat spoke up and Mitchell turned to look at her and she started talking, "I'm not sure why, but I think I want to take back my idea as well."

Jose spoke up to say, "I can tell you why. We have all felt that each of our plans only serviced ourselves. What is this whole thing about if we don't use it to do good for others?"

Mitchell again looked at Anna. He could see she was near ready to cry. He took a couple of steps towards her and softly said, "I understand your concerns. Kat and I have talked about it."

Anna shot a look at Kat, but Mitchell held up his hand. "She did this because she loves you and was very concerned that you might leave the group, the family."

Now Anna hung her head down and started crying. Peter took her in his arms and held her close as he looked to Mitchell. "What can we do, Boss?"

Mitchell reached out and took her hand. "I have a plan. It will require you and Peter to work together, but away from us."

This got her attention, and after wiping her eyes, she sat back up.

Now to everyone, he said, "We will need a midway point between us with the Indians and the white man. We can choose a place along the frontier to set up a trading post. This could become a place where the white people we need to work with can come to live and grow into a village or town. It will also be the point where young Indians come to learn white man's ways before going east to school. I would also be a place where Indians and white men can learn to live together."

Mitchell stopped and looked at Anna. He wasn't sure if she understood the idea he was suggesting, nor the importance of this bridge between the two peoples. Finally, he saw the corner of her mouth go up a little as she realized some of what he was suggesting.

She looked at her husband and softly said, "What do you think, dear?"

Peter smile back at her and nodded.

Anna smiled and grabbed young Peter and gave him an enormous hug. She then turned to look at Mitchell and said, "I would also like to withdraw my idea and I propose to second your idea."

Mitchell smiled back at her and stood up. Looking around the group, he said, "There is a motion that has been seconded. Is there any discussion?"

He took a quick look around the camp and each person shook their head as he looked at them. He then said, "All in favor or going north and working with the Indians, raise your hands."

Mitchell quickly turned as he watched each hand go up. When his eyes came to Anna, she sat there a moment and then, with a laugh, she jumped up with both hands high and yelled. "Yes."

The rest of the night turned into a party. Mitchell brought out the last of the hidden booze and it didn't take long for it to disappear.

As Mitchell and Kat left the party later, he passed by Redcloud. He leaned in close to him to ask, "You sure you don't want some of this glory? It sure does make you feel good inside."

Redcloud just smiled and whispered back, "My insides feel really good, anyway. This is my way. You should know that."

Mitchell just stood straight and nodded and offered a hand.

Redcloud took the hand and instead of a shake, he pulled Mitchell in and they both had a good man hug.

Back in the cabin, Mitchell and Kat laid there and listened to the party that went on for a while longer, however, their attention soon went to somewhere else.